I0721627

Where There's a Witch There is a Way

Heather L. Butler

Published in Australia by Sid Harta Books & Print Pty Ltd,

ABN: 34632585293

23 Stirling Crescent, Glen Waverley, Victoria 3150 Australia

Telephone: +61 3 9560 9920, Facsimile: +61 3 9545 1742

E-mail: author@sidharta.com.au

First published in Australia 2023

This edition published 2023

Copyright © Heather L. Butler 2023

Cover design, typesetting: WorkingType (www.workingtype.com.au)

This book is a work of fiction. Names, characters, places and incidents are either a product of the author's imagination or are used fictitiously. Any resemblance to actual people living or dead, events or locales is entirely coincidental.

The right of Heather L. Butler to be identified as the Author of the Work has been asserted in accordance with the Copyright, Designs and Patents Act 1988.

All rights reserved. No part of this publication may be reproduced, stored in a retrieval system, or transmitted, in any form or by any means without the prior written permission of the publisher, nor be otherwise circulated in any form of binding or cover other than that in which it is published and without a similar condition being imposed on the subsequent purchaser.

Heather L. Butler

Where There's a Witch, There is a Way

ISBN: 978-1-922958-27-3

p656

Heather Butler has enjoyed writing pieces of poetry, some of which she has won awards for including a Henry Lawson award in 2015. She has penned several short stories covering a range of topics, although these have never been formally published. Heather also assisted in the publication of a cookery book by a First Aid team encouraging CPR. Heather is also quite artistic and has delved into painting, drawing, china painting and she been known to make teddy bears and other critters in the past. She so enjoys drawing, some of her sketches are on these pages.

Heather ran a local school canteen for many years while her children were at the school and enjoyed penning little snippets to one of the teachers there who also enjoyed writing poetry. Not only did Heather enjoy this repertoire with poetry, but she also became intrigued with mystery solving, mysteries being something she has always enjoyed reading about or trying to solve; one of her greatest joys was to solve the mystery before the end of the book she was reading, so after a while Heather came up with this plot which had begun to develop into a book.

After several years she gathered the courage to have the book published. It has been a real experience to get this book to the publishing stage and we hope you all enjoy the book as we do.

*I apologise for my constant ramblings involving
the characters and plot.*

*To all my family in particular and friends who have listened to my
enquiries on how they think that the plot is going …
is it making any sense?*

*To the publishing company for the hours that they have
put in to ensure that the book is correct and makes sense,
that I have got the right characters with the rights words,
I did miss some, whoops.*

To Jane, Paul and in loving memory of John.

It was much later when the last lingering visitors had been ushered quietly but firmly from the museum as the bored and weary security personnel began to make their rounds of the exhibits that the horrible truth emerged.

Passing by the case that held the scrolls, the guard gave it more than a passing glance. Where one of the scrolls had been, there was now only an empty space … and the case was still locked!

How could such a precious manuscript just go missing … in broad daylight … and with a security guard only metres away? It was quite impossible to comprehend; how could a thief get anywhere near it to open the case without being seen? It had obviously been opened with a key as the case was undamaged but by whom and where did they get the key?

Contents

Part One

Chapter 1

A Case of Grand Theft

The small group of tourists listened attentively as the voice of the museum guide droned on, his somnolent expressionless tone like a long-playing record, painting a faded picture of ancient history. Long forgotten illuminated manuscripts lay open under thick glass cases. Stained and cracked with age; ancient scrolls, some partly opened, lay carefully positioned beneath the shatterproof glass, exposing the puzzling cuneiform hieroglyphics.

Others still lay tightly rolled around the decaying wooden spools that had held them since their discovery in ancient and secret hidden places.

Several of the group lingered to examine the scrolls more closely, among them an ageing Grey Friar; the cowl of his coarsely woven habit still covering his head such that nothing showed beneath. He moved as one suffering the pangs of arthritis and the disability of old age — his step slow and shuffling as if every movement was an effort. As the group moved languidly on to further concentrate on ancient treasures being revealed to them by their impassive guide, the Friar remained standing at the case containing the scrolls, peering at them closely, as if attempting to decipher the strange symbols. He gazed at them for a few moments more, before reaching into his voluminous robes to produce a spectacle case.

Fumbling with seemingly stiff fingers, he finally extracted the glasses and adjusted them carefully on his face before resuming his stooped examination of the contents on display.

The remainder of the small knot of visitors had begun to move away to another room where their lacklustre guide led them to a group of Egyptian antiquities, his monotone vocal documentary preceding their progress. The well-rehearsed narration of the many archaeological wonders of the period holding his listeners spellbound as they eagerly absorbed these ancient wonders they could otherwise only read about.

At a point between the two rooms a smartly uniformed security guard watched the little group from behind tired eyes. Barely stifling a yawn, he glanced briefly down at his watch, noting with some relief that he was nearing the end of his shift. It had been a long day but then it always was in this sort of job. The only thing that broke the boredom was finding the parents of a distraught screaming child, who had been left behind when the parents had moved on assuming the child had dutifully followed, which they never did. Small children, he decided, should never be brought to places like this, they couldn't see above the glass cabinets and generally took to trying to dismantle smaller objects nearer the floor to see what they were made of and if they were suitable to play with.

The Grey Friar had put his glasses carefully back into their case and looked around as if he had suddenly realised the group had moved on and that he should hurry to catch up to them. In his haste to replace the glasses case back into his robes he clumsily dropped them, in bending down to pick them up he stumbled heavily against the display case.

Putting out a hand to steady himself, he gradually gathered himself clutching his loose robes about himself as he did so. Like the aged and rheumatic person he portrayed, he managed to shuffle to his feet and hurried as best he could after the departing tourists.

It was much later when the last lingering visitors had been ushered quietly but firmly from the museum as the bored and weary security personnel began to make their rounds of the exhibits that the horrible truth emerged.

Passing by the case that held the scrolls, the guard gave it more than a passing glance. Where one of the scrolls had been, there was now only an empty space … and the case was still locked!

How could such a precious manuscript just go missing … in broad daylight … and with a security guard only metres away? It was quite impossible to comprehend; how could a thief get anywhere near it to open the case without being seen? It had obviously been opened with a key as the case was undamaged but by whom and where did they get the key?

Questions, questions, but no answers! The precious scroll was gone and no amount of reprisal was going to lead to its recovery. Chaos reigned … who could remember the last group of tourists that had passed through, as they usually came in organised assemblies complete with a recognised guide? The now wide-awake and justifiably nervous guard tried to remember.

He had heard them talking as they discussed the exhibits. Several English visitors, a couple of Germans, or were they Austrians — they sound so much the same. Who else now, yes, there was a small group of French schoolgirls he had noticed; they did tend to lean a bit over the cases as they excitedly pointed something out and … well, yes, their skirts were a bit short. Who else? Wait, yes, he recalled hearing an Australian accent or two, they were with an American couple. He remembered the American man, very loud and didn't seem to stop talking but then they were always the same, you always knew when the Americans were in the building. No, no one else … yes there was, he'd almost forgotten the aged monk who'd almost got left behind as the group moved on. Really no one could possibly remember everyone who came through the museum each day, they were just tourists!

*   *   *

No trace of the precious scroll was found, it had disappeared entirely. The stolen parchment proving to be yet another link in an intangible chain of somewhat similar thefts of a highly professional nature that had occurred over a period of time. It had however not been dismissed by a small detachment supported by the local police department who visited the museum a short while after the whole area had been screened off. A close examination of the locked case, extensive questioning of the Curator and security guards revealed little; but one tiny factor was evident — a minute trace of wax still clung to the Curator's key that opened the exhibit, yet all the keys were housed inside a securely locked cupboard in the Curator's office! The main investigative puzzle being how and when, could this key have been taken long enough to make an impression and who, among the dozens that had passed through the museum that day, had been able to open the case unseen?

When questioning the Director and checking through the personnel records, it was discovered that one of the security guards employed some time previously, had to leave his place of employment, his sudden departure attributed to a death in the family. The employee had come to the museum with excellent references and on recollection, his name rang a tiny bell in a few of the investigator's minds, who duly added it to a growing list of suspects.

Experience had informed the investigative team that, as is often expected, some precious objects occasionally reappear but only to those with large enough pockets to afford a rare item of interest, but as luck would have it, the ancient scroll did not, leaving not a whisper. Moreover, its theft and the ensuing lack of clues was not a good fit with the general pattern that had been emerging — frustratingly, it had simply vanished from the face of the earth. It was, of course, an irreplaceable antiquity and the museum, doubled its guard. The guards remained nervously at their posts, ever mindful, tending to regard each group of visitors with grave suspicion from then on.

*   *   *

At another place and at another time, a restoration was taking place, but not everybody was happy with the proceedings. Monsieur Renuado clasped his long and elegant fingertips together under his long beaked nose and frowned. To say he felt a trifle nervous was an understatement. As Curator of the gallery, the priceless works of art that blithely stared down at him from the walls of the Old Masters Room were his responsibility, a responsibility he took very seriously.

The Directors ... ah the Directors! What did they know about responsibility and security? Perhaps the gallery did need refurbishing and the simultaneous cleaning of the priceless paintings was perhaps an opportune move. Fresh paint on the walls, new seating and nice clean works of art in nice clean frames; this was what the Directors wanted. Their only concern was the influx of summer visitors streaming in to view the magnificent, ageless masterpieces and of course, to purchase the carefully crafted and presented copies in the renovated tearoom, strategically positioned just off the foyer.

But the security! He paced nervously about tugging at his short and oh-so fashionable Vandyke beard, cracking his knuckles, as he often did when he was stressed. He moved from room to room issuing many instructions as the precious paintings were carefully removed from their coveted positions on the walls.

The larger paintings in their massive, gilded frames were placed carefully onto special rubber wheeled trolleys and moved to the vast storerooms at the rear of the building, where they would remain under lock and key with tight security while the renovations were in progress. Several painters and plasterers were already laying large sheets of paint-spattered canvas over the floors. Others in equally paint-stained overalls were moving to and fro with hand carts, carrying cans of paint, plaster, with an assortment of brushes and trowels. Ladders were carried in and propped up against walls. It was suddenly a hive of activity — the Directors explicit, stating that the gallery should have its makeover done as quickly and efficiently as possible.

Monsieur Renuado watched the painters arranging the canvases over the floor for a brief moment, then cracking his knuckles again, he began to walk toward the gallery where the staff were still removing the smaller paintings– the Rubens, the Goya, and the little Cezanne he loved so much. He would be glad when all this work was over, he hated all this confusion of workmen doing things around him. He just wanted the pictures back in their proper places on the walls where they should be, arrayed in silent splendour, where they could be admired and appreciated by lovers of fine art. After all, people came to see the paintings, not the colour of the walls around them. He had almost reached the next gallery when an angry shout behind him made him stop and turn around.

'*Gauche imbecile! Vou avoir op-cette le coleur, regarder, regarder le pantaloons!*'

'*Je-regretta—casuel, le be'vue!*'

'*Imbecile!*'

'*Je-regretta … contretemps!*'

"*Etourdi I'dieute!*'

Renuado and the security guard, who had been standing at the entrance to the gallery, turned to stare at the confusion that was taking place. A large can of cream paint was emptying its contents onto the canvas-covered floor. It had also spattered heavily onto one of the painter's overalls and was dripping from his knees, adding to the ever-widening pool on the gallery floor. A torrent of abuse broke out between the two men as they argued loudly and gesticulated wildly with each other, the clamour of their angry voices echoing and rebounding through the empty chambers. Spilled paint … that was all Renuado needed to further upset his day. He hurried to the scene to sort the matter out accompanied by the concerned security guard.

It was quite a few moments before Renuado could restore peace, having sent the guard back to his post. He sighed heavily, he liked his job and he loved being surrounded by the beauty of the paintings entrusted to his care. However, he did not like any disruptions to the orderliness of his daily passion, he silently cursed the Directors for their folly in insisting on this rushed 'make over' for the gallery.

It was not until the painters and decorators had finished their task, that the dire truth was laid bare — bare patches on the walls! The small Van Dyck and a Quentin Matsys masterpiece should be hanging there! A frantic search was mounted, perhaps they had been overlooked when the paintings were being returned and after all, they were only small pieces. The storerooms where all the paintings had been housed were searched thoroughly, the restorers questioned extensively but as everything had been done in the same security-enclosed building, there seemed no possible way the paintings could have been removed without anybody knowing. Other rooms in the gallery were searched, but to no avail … the paintings had vanished.

The tempest that followed the complete and utter disappearance of such valuable works of art was almost too much for Monsieur Renuado. He was questioned closely by the police, the Directors and a small detachment of personnel who followed later to probe his every movement on that day. He cracked his knuckles constantly as he tried to remember every incident and detail that had diverted his attention from the task of overseeing the removal of the paintings from the walls.

In the end, a totally distraught Monsieur Renuado was led quietly away, to spend a sequestered three-month 'holiday' in a secure, secluded sanatorium until he regained some of his former responsiveness and had ceased to subject his knuckles to more disjointed damage.

To the small detachment of personnel who had shown much interest in these audacious thefts, it was to add another link in the endless chain that they hoped would ultimately lead them to the mastermind responsible. The trouble was, many of the minions who provided the dramatic background scenarios to these highly organised thefts, were often found floating in canals or rivers or had suffered a fatal accident or just simply disappeared. It made the extraction of vital information for these specialised agents almost impossible; they needed names, places. Calculated suspicion was fine, but they needed something solid to base those suspicions on.

In the aftermath of the gallery theft however, this time; fate offered a helping hand in the form of a survivor … if only just.

*   *   *

Above a colourful Mediterranean tourist destination, basking in its hospitable aura of whitewashed villas and narrow twisted streets, crammed with purveyors of local souvenirs and massed produced mementos of a 'once in a lifetime' visit, a narrow road led the traveller to further savour the delights of tiny modest villages hidden amongst the olive-clad hills. Here the traveller could motor the twisting, turning tortuous high-country roads, offering vistas of breathtaking beauty and glimpses of brilliant blue sea blending seamlessly into an equally blue sky.

The only disadvantage to the tourist motorist were the serpentine bends in the highway that required one's full attention, though there were plenty of sightseeing points where one could pull into and admire the scenery from the safety of a designated spot. To those who knew the road however, there was no such thing as concern for the many twists and turns the road presented. They drove as if the roads were theirs alone, regardless of other traffic as well as the impossibly steep ravines and cliffs that fell sharply away to almost infinity. They drove with the confidence and recklessness that came from local knowledge and repetition.

However, not all negotiated this hazardous route unscathed and accidents did occur, most often with devastating and usually fatal results. Reports had been received by the local constabulary that a car had run off the road at one of the high mountain passes. A dangerous bend that had seen many close calls, with signage adequately posted to remind motorists of this fact. The vehicle had plunged down the steep cliff face, seemingly showing no signs on the road of applying the car's brakes and coming to rest against a stout young tree on a ledge, preventing the vehicle from tumbling further into the ravine below.

Though it had become an immediate death scene for the driver of the car, his passenger was found to be barely alive when rescued. It was, however, to the medical team who attended the unfortunate victim, reasonably obvious that he should not make any plans for the future.

An astute young police officer — Gerard Bouchere — who was a little more alert than his colleagues, when searching the wreckage of the vehicle for possible clues as to the identity of the occupants, found two pairs of overalls. One pair was heavily stained on the legs with cream paint, while the other bore spatters of the same paint. The overalls had been stuffed deep inside the car's boot, as if deliberately hidden there.

By some other good fortune, Gerard and the museum's security guard were old friends and often met for drinks at a local bar when their respective shifts were over. The saga of the paint spill, with the intense hysteria and commotion that followed was forever etched in the security guard's mind. He was lucky to still have his job! It certainly broke the boredom and he related the affair in some detail to his companion over a glass or two of ale.

Of course, this aroused the interest of the young officer. Why would two so-called 'professional' painters be so clumsy? Clearly, he surmised, the same paint-splattered overalls involved in the gallery's incident had been hidden in a vehicle that had fortuitously tumbled over a cliff. Something didn't add up. Eager to rise in the ranks and make his mark in the force, Gerard at once notified his superior officers of his suspicions, therefore setting in motion a hurried investigation.

As the members from Special Branch were still in the vicinity gathering their information, this was good news indeed. Not so for the unfortunate victim perhaps, but here at last was the break they had been waiting for, much haste would be necessary to interview the survivor before their only witness succumbed to his injuries.

The men from Special Branch were now only too well aware that the 'accident' with the paint was a deliberate decoy to distract the Curator and the guard's attention for a few vital moments. Long enough for an accomplice to secrete the small masterpieces elsewhere other than the storeroom and now fate had provided them with a living suspect … if only just!

*   *   *

The survivor of the car crash had suffered severe internal injuries and had surprised the doctor in attendance by clinging to life as long as he had. There was no doubt the damage would be fatal; it was only a matter of time.

'Could he answer some questions?' asked an officer from Special Branch.

'He has moments of consciousness,' frowned the doctor, 'but we cannot leave him without the oxygen mask for too long, we must stay and observe.'

'We just need a few moments; it is vital we speak with him.'

'As you wish, but I warn you, he may not be conscious enough to fully understand you.'

'Oh, he will understand alright,' said the other, 'we are aware of the seriousness of his condition and you can be assured we will not alarm him.'

The two Special Branch men were led to a room at the far end of a long corridor, where a languid uniformed police officer sat innocuously on a hard wooden chair outside the door. Inside the room, the victim lay surrounded by tubes, monitors and other medical paraphernalia, he indeed looked more dead than alive. After a quick examination, the doctor was able to assure the visitors that the patient was conscious enough and could hear what was being said but warned them to linger no longer than absolutely necessary.

One of the two agents stood a little apart beside the window of the small room. The other drew a chair very close to the bed and looked into the dying man's eyes, he spoke softly and directly to the stricken man, never taking his eyes from those of the victim. 'I want you to answer my questions as best you can and we will not tire you any more than necessary. We have reason to believe that you and your companion were very much a part in the thefts of valuable paintings from the city Art Gallery. No doubt you are now aware that you and your deceased friend were disposable pawns in the thefts from the Gallery?'

The man in the bed blinked and there was the faintest nod of the head. The inquisitor went on, 'However, you were probably not fully aware that this gang of thieves use people such as you and your friend to create diversions such as you did, then disposes of them permanently. You, so far, have been the only survivor. Once you had performed your task, you were no longer of use to them and would pose a danger to their identity, so must be disposed of. So, it would seem that any money paid to do your little dramatic piece is no longer of any use to you, is it? Do you understand what I am saying to you?'

The man in the bed looked at him, closed his eyes for a second and nodded slowly and then made an effort to speak, putting his hand slowly up to his face. The doctor who was standing by stepped forward and removed the mask. The voice when it came was husky and whisper quiet. 'The brakes—the brakes were—gone.'

'Yes, we do know the brake lines were severed, it's a wonder you got as far as you did, but it was a calculated sabotage.' The man from Special Branch continued, 'There are just two questions I want you to answer now, the name of the man who hired you, was it Casini?'

The man nodded again and said in the husky voice that was difficult to hear, 'It was Vin—Vinnie Casini—he—we knew each other—long time ago—said we could make big money—if we followed his—his orders.'

'Did you hear him mention anything else in your conversation with him, a location?

An address? Is there anything you may have heard that would help us find him and his brother Victor? Please think carefully, this is *very* important.'

The man in the bed coughed and his breathing became a little shallower. The doctor stepped forward again, but the patient waved him weakly aside. When he spoke, it was with a little more strength, his eyes were held firmly in the other's gaze.

'Phone rang while—we—were talking, think he forgot—I was—was there. Spoke to someone—think it was Vic—his brother.' The man swallowed hard, but found his voice again, 'They argued—about Leo. He was making trouble, said—why did they still have to— to be holed up in some ancient old—ab— abbey—on some godforsaken—mountain top?'

There was a pause, then he went on. 'Vic was—not happy— with him, said—' Here his voice began to trail off, 'though he rallied again and tried to speak, his voice had grown weaker.

'I'm listening, please continue if you can.' The inquisitor laid his hand gently on that of the victim.

There was a long moment of silence, as if the patient were gathering more strength, but even though that strength was waning, he waved the doctor's hand away again as if determined to finish what he had to tell. 'He said—it was best place, no one knew and—well aware—the monks do this—sort of work all the time, so—so they, they were—experts and— and—' The man in the bed began to cough, his body shook as he struggled for breath, the doctor again stepped forward, this time placing the mask efficiently over the patient's face.

He glanced at the monitors and said in a brisk voice, 'I must ask you to leave now, you'll get no more out of him tonight, in any case, I doubt that he'll even see the morning.' He added in a whisper, 'His injuries are *very* serious, we're amazed he managed to get this far.' He shook his head. 'I'm surprised he was able to talk to you at all.'

The agent from Special Branch pushed back his chair and stood up. His companion closed the notebook he had been writing in, sighed and turned to face the window, staring out almost unseeing at the bustle of the city below. 'You can't help but feel sorry for them, it might be easy money to begin with, but it comes at a hell of a price!'

'That we know,' said the former, 'but this one hasn't all been in vain.' He stood a while longer at the man's bedside watching the uneven rise and fall of the man's chest and the indications on the monitors. 'I rather think the diagnosis is correct, he won't see the morning, but at least we do know now for certain that it is the Casini brothers we are dealing with.' He pocketed the small tape recorder he had been holding and moved toward the door.

'Well, we have suspected them all along, haven't we?' Responded the other — a short thickset man with close-cropped iron-grey hair. 'All we've needed is the actual proof.'

'Now, I guess our next move is to find this Abbey.' The agent opened the door then stood aside as a nurse bustled through in answer to the doctor's call. He watched for a moment as nurse and doctor administered to the patient, then said sadly, 'I just wish he could have given us more information on the whereabouts of this abbey.'

'Perhaps he didn't know, from what I gathered Leo didn't know himself. It's always Victor who organises what they do.'

'I guess you're right.' The man from Special Branch shook his head and followed his companion out of the room. A tall slightly built man with keen grey eyes under a thatch of dark hair, his lean face set in a purposeful frown. 'Now, the difficulty is knowing which abbey and where?'

They walked a few paces down the long corridor in silence. 'I wonder what he meant by "monks do this sort of work all the time", what sort of monks?'

'Restoration work,' the grey-headed man spoke after a pause. 'Seen it done.' He cleared his throat and said gruffly,

'Some Orders of monks are artisans, they spend their time restoring books and rare pieces of art and manuscripts, that sort of thing. Should have realised that Casini would resort to them to do his dirty work.'

'Franciscan monks, of course!' replied the other. 'Well, that might narrow down our search area a bit.'

'That's still going to be easier said than done,' replied the gruff voice, 'do you realise how many abbeys there are?'

'Quite a few I expect.'

'I know and just where are we going to start looking for this place?'

'Well, for a start it's on top of a mountain.'

'And how many mountains do you think there are?'

'I don't know, but I guess we're going to find out.'

'Well … I just wish we could have narrowed it down a bit more than we have.'

'Where's your sense of adventure?'

'My sense of adventure's getting too old to climb mountains.'

'Ah, come on old man, I'll buy you lunch to keep your strength up.'

Their voices and their footsteps echoed down the long corridor, while behind them another hapless victim of insatiable greed struggled against the inevitable.

Chapter 2

Witches Abroad

At a much later time and in another part of the world, a strange happening was taking place. Of course, what could be considered strange to the observer would not be so to the participants directly involved in *this* happening.

To them, it was a perfectly normal procedure and if it excited curiosity, then they were not immediately aware of it. So, anyone irrational enough to wish to stand outside in a torrential downpour and gaze skyward at just the opportune moment, may have seen something quite peculiar indeed. Peculiar enough to send them scurrying indoors to clean their eyeglasses or take a glass of a different sort and fill it with a good splash of Scotch.

While it is not widely known that most modern-day witches often remain unobtrusive and reject the traditional mode of transport for a more up-to-date means — and in doing so, also save scaring the neighbours out of their wits and their sense of sanity, plus a few awkward questions — there are still unfortunately those few in that sibyl category who haven't yet caught on.

On this particular occasion, a curious cavalcade was making haphazard progress through a turbulent and darkened sky, with just a hint of a languid struggling moon here and there to light the stormy heavens. To the average eye, if slightly imaginative, it appeared as a pair of large ragged black birds, rather like pterodactyls, with another large indistinguishable black object trailing behind. However, to the more intellectual and astute observer, it was what it was — two black-robed witches astride broomsticks. The third object was a heavily laden broom trailer following obediently behind, despite the extreme buffeting it was being subjected to, but which was following closely as if held by an invisible cord.

One might well wonder when this phenomenal vision was correctly identified, why even witches would be abroad in such foul weather. One was, of course, not aware that a hasty departure from previous lodgings amid a mysterious fire had been catalyst enough for an urgent exit. By sheer good fortune of course, it had been apparent that two sisters had barely escaped the ravages of the flames that unfortunately burnt out a small residential area inhabited by ordinary folk and witches alike.

In some respects, one could say, it was a fortuitous fiery end to an overcrowded and far from adequate tenement the sisters had shared with one or two others of their ilk.

The remaining residents were made up of an odd assortment of proletarian classes of humanity — street Arabs, drunks, thieves, and those just content to have a roof over their heads, even if it did leak a little … kindred humanity, who would vehemently deny they ever saw anything unusual about their immediate neighbours and in most cases if anything unusual did happen it was either too much or not enough for the generally drink-sodden ones. As for the rest of the inhabitants, they simply didn't want to know; lodgings were hard enough to get at the best of times.

*   *   *

In a small room at the very top of a flight of stairs in the rundown building that housed this motley assortment of human flotsam, two young women were busy packing the few belongings they possessed into what appeared to be a large black cauldron which sat in the middle of the confusion littering the floor.

Marilla, the elder of these two sisters had been kneeling beside the cauldron pushing in the smaller packages. She now straightened her long legs, sat on the floor and looked about her, vigorously massaging her thighs and ankles to ease the stiffness. 'Only a few more things left to sort out now,' she said as she brushed aside a stray lock of her long reddish hair.

'You know, Bella every time we move there seems to be more stuff to pack, and do you think we really need all those books? Don't forget we have to make some room for Lucifer as well.' Her unusual shade of green eyes rested for a moment on a black cat curled up on the still unmade bed, and who, at the mention of his name opened one yellow eye, blinked and went back to sleep again.

Isabella, the younger and so very different from her sister in many ways had sat her ample figure in one corner and was busy carefully wrapping paper around the books in question. Snatching quickly at a ball of string that threatened to roll away from her outstretched fingers, she replied to Marilla's question in her quiet voice, 'You know we have to keep Grandmother's books safe and take good care of them; what do you think would happen if they fell into the wrong hands, there are too many important secrets and spells in them to just leave behind?

Marilla looked up at her sister and the corner of her mouth twitched a distinct 'Yes, I know'. Just the sort of things someone like Grizelda Henwick would like to get her hands on no doubt, she thought wryly.

Isabella just nodded and reached for the last book.

Marilla was silent for a long moment, then said, 'It's time we moved on anyway, this was never going to be a permanent place for us, and besides which, there's too much competition here. Grizelda thinks she is so clever and I really don't think I can listen to too much more of her pompous bragging about where she's been and who she's been with.'

The competition in question, Marilla's rival was fortunately away at a convention at the time. A notable witch and quite proficient in her spells, she was achieving recognition in the covens and was not one to be trifled with, but the closeness in which the sisters found themselves with her was too explosive to be tolerated for too long.

Marilla and Grizelda had never seen eye to eye about anything and the sparks flew literally whenever their paths crossed which in the confined quarters they were obliged to share was much too often — something had to give.

To the other residents, this was unknowingly a mild source of annoyance who, when conscious enough, would suspect a faulty electrical supply. Fuses would blow, lights would flicker constantly and the few electrical appliances they did possess had a habit of turning themselves on and off without warning.

Additionally, both sisters had never once been invited to any of the coven gatherings Grizelda attended. Not that they really would have gone to one being still so unsure of their own magical capabilities and whether they felt that they could stand up to the close scrutiny they received from their peers.

Marilla was too proud to let Grizelda be privy to that, so it was left as a kind of unresolved tension between them. Thus, it was now or never that Marilla and Isabella prepared to vacate the premises while the moment was in their favour with no antagonist to look on with displeasure.

So, the sisters were quietly packing the few possessions they had with them when they had started out on their travels, which now seemed such a long time ago, but so far much of their time had been in transit as everywhere they went trouble seemed to hang over them like a persistent dark cloud. Ordinary people just didn't understand them and more often than not it was only by the quickest of moves that they eluded getting themselves locked up by the local constabulary.

Escaping without undue notice would be simple enough as their room was the top floor and an access to the roof was easily obtained through an angled skylight, which, with a little encouragement could be made larger. Already waiting on the floor were two heavy duty broomsticks equipped with the latest in travelling comfort and accurate compasses, together with a sturdy trailer broom.

It seemed the only drawback to this departure was an approaching storm that was a bit unexpected as they had hoped the skies would remain clear.

Marilla glanced at where Isabella sat in her corner, but her fingers were no longer busy with the balls of string, her hands were held over her plump face and her shoulders were shaking slightly.

'What's wrong, Bella?'

'Nothing,' was the muffled reply.

'Well, it must be something!' Her sister replied rather gruffly.

Isabella shook her more than ample head of bushy brown hair and looked up at her sister, the beginning of tears brimming in her large brown eyes. 'I've never liked this place Marilla,' she said her voice choking a little, 'nor any of the other places we've stayed in. I am tired of all this moving about and there's always these weird people who are not like us at all! I do wish we had never left Harewood, it was always so peaceful there. You had said that it was only 'till we found our own place, but where is our own place, Marilla?'

Marilla looked quickly away, not wanting her sibling to see the same look of concern and doubt on her face. This grand adventure that she had planned to live and explore the world beyond the confines of the coven was proving to be more difficult and dangerous than she had first thought. Her dreams of emulating the skills and mastery of magic in a real world was fast becoming a nightmare instead.

Not wanting to convey her innermost thoughts and fears to her sister at this point, Marilla spoke quietly with what she hoped was assurance. 'This time, Isabella, it will be different, very different, I promise. We are to head more to the North this time where it will be more rural and a lot quieter and I'm sure you'll be a lot happier there, in fact, I'm sure you will be.' Hoping to divert this small crisis with her sister, Marilla turned her attention to the last of the packing. 'Now there's only Grandmother's scrying mirror to go. I've found a piece of old blanket and if I wrap it in that we can put it between the books where it will be perfectly safe, don't you think?' She added quickly, 'There's just enough room now for Lucifer to squeeze in and I'm sure he won't mind being a little bit cramped.'

Isabella did not answer her sister, she had risen from the floor and was peering through the tattered lace curtains that were pretending to cover the only window in the room.

'It looks awfully stormy out there,' she said in a worried voice. 'I don't think this weather was expected, are you sure we should be leaving tonight?'

'Absolutely, no better time,' said Marilla lightly.

'Well, I suppose so,' said Isabella turning to face Marilla. 'At least we won't have Grizelda to worry about, did you know she's leaving here as soon as she gets back?'

'Is she?' Marilla turned to her sister in surprise, 'Where did you hear that?'

'I heard her talking to one of the residents here on the stairs and very adamant about it she was too, said she was fed up with living here in this derelict building and was going to pack up and leave as soon as she got back from the convention.'

'Oh! She said that did she? Well we just might surprise her by vacating this derelict place before she does!' Marilla fired back vehemently. 'So, Bella, let's get that broomstick trailer over here and tie everything down, then we'll tackle that skylight on the roof. One good point in having a room at the top of this place, it makes an easy exit to get out of with no one noticing, that skylight won't be too much of a problem to dispense with and then it should be clear sailing for us.'

'Except for the storm that's coming,' muttered Isabella.

Together the sisters began loading the last few packages into the precious cauldron, which they took great care of, as it had belonged to their grandmother and still held the aura of her many spells. 'There now, there's just these few odd things left with enough room for Lucifer.' They then placed the cauldron very carefully onto the broom trailer, which looked like any other heavy weight broomstick in front but fanned out to several stout branches at the other end. Lucifer, now use to this mode of travel was to be tucked into a soft padded corner where he mostly slept during these unorthodox flights; now it remained only to tie the cauldron and its contents safely down.

'Come on, Bella, let's start getting these things tied down.'

Isabella, although she wouldn't dare say so, sometimes found her older sister's ideas a bit unfathomable and impulsive, which so far had not produced the new and exciting life she had been promised when they had set out on this enterprise. It would be 'a wonderful adventure', her elder sister had said. All the wonderful places they could visit and things they could do. They might even drop in on their mother … wherever she was. Isabella shook her head and cast another apprehensive glance at the wind-swept sky.

The first few drops of rain spattered against the windowpane and with some foreboding she watched as they made trails down the glass. There was never any point in disagreeing with her sister — and in truth she hated their dank, overcrowded surroundings, often wishing they had never come here. She sighed and shrugged her ample shoulders. Still, one could have at least hoped for a moonlit sky; a proper time for witches to be abroad.

Marilla took up the rope lying ready on the floor and proceeded to tie everything down firmly in her special impossible-to-undo-unless-you-know-the-right-words knots. 'There!' She said as she stood up, 'that should keep things in place; we're ready to go.' She stood for a moment with her hands on her hips, then walked to the door of their room, opening it a crack. 'There doesn't seem to be anyone about out there, it's very quiet.'

She hesitated a moment, then turned back to face Isabella and said in a quiet voice, 'I wonder if Grizelda has remembered that she left some of her big candles at the top of the stairs outside her room?'

'I don't know, she might have.'

'Silly place to leave them, she's usually so fussy with her things.'

'Yes, usually.'

Isabella nodded in agreement.

It was, as Marilla had suggested, time to move on.

Chapter 3

Grandma Hackett

arilla did have a place in mind as she set her broomstick compass for a point many miles distant. An old forest where Grandma Hackett once lived, hopefully the tiny cottage would still be there. Isabella, on the other hand, thinking that leaving on such a stormy night was still a bad idea, cast a glance behind her. The brilliant red and orange glow below them with the distant shouts and wailing sirens indicated that, considering the circumstances in which they had departed, it did seem the best option after all. Secretly, Isabella was looking forward to the seclusion of the forest and the cottage that would be there. She had been enormously pleased when Marilla had finally agreed to her proffered suggestion of going there. Marilla did not often agree with any of Isabella's ideas; but if the truth be known, it was now about the only place they could go without getting into more trouble.

However, Marilla reasoned, it would be acceptable accommodation, 'till something better came up. There were still plenty of places to go, they were really getting better at fitting in with ordinary folk now; it just took time to understand how they think.

*   *   *

Their mother had been born in the pretty little cottage set deep
in the woods. A grey slate roof iced with mosses and lichen
hung protectively over mullioned windows that looked out
onto an overgrown garden, heavily perfumed with flowers and
herbs. The tiny front porch entwined with a rather vigorous ivy,
sheltering a simple wooden front door that welcomed the odd
visitor; but above all, it was a peaceful tranquil retreat. It stood
quite alone in a small open glade in the cool forest, guarded by
great oaks and beeches that stood sentinel beside the only road
that ran close by. Very few travelled it, however there was one
that passed by who was to change their mother's life forever
when she had opened the door to a stranger ...

A smooth talker with straight slicked-back hair and a small
waxed toothbrush moustache, he had introduced himself as
Monsieur Claude Duperie and was in the market of broomsticks,
among other things.

He had noticed the pretty and isolated little cottage several
times when he had been passing that way, noting its lonely
setting, he felt the impulse to knock on the door and find out
who lived there. As business was quite slack at this time, he had
hoped to also make a sale.

To his delight, when the door was opened, he beheld a young
and delightfully pretty damsel, all alone. Smoothing back his
hair in a nonchalant manoeuvre, his inherent Gallic charm
slipped into overdrive. In answer to his question, no, her mother
was out. Miriam supressed a yawn of boredom, having been in
the house all day, she wished her mother would return soon
from the urgent problem that had arisen at the coven.

Claude Duperie was enraptured with such a beautiful

creature; all alone too. Perhaps this was destiny he thought, a decree of fate that had come his way. He decided that he would need to amplify his charm to the utmost, also knowing he would eventually claim his prize.

Monsieur Duperie had no trouble convincing their naïve mother that rewards and riches lay just waiting, beyond her simple forest habitat. The smooth silkiness of his voice bewitched her, as she dreamily listened.

Such a waste, said he, for a beautiful flower such as she to wither away in that isolated wilderness, when there were so many things that were new and exciting happening in the world outside. There was so much to see and do and he regaled her with exciting glimpses of Paris, Rome, the things he had done there and the important people he was on first-name terms with. She had leant against the door feeling his words wash over her like the ending of a fairy tale. She was the Princess, he her Prince and they would live happily ever after.

He himself was making his rapid rise in the sphere of development and was, at that very time, negotiating for his own company, with which he would achieve great fame. Already he had extensive plans afoot to produce faster and ultimately more versatile broomsticks; everything was updating and it was good business sense to keep ahead of the competition.

He had kept smoothing back his hair and straightening the slightly askew collar of the chequered suit he wore. It did seem a size too big for him as the shoulder pads kept slipping out of place slightly. But a meaningful shrug of his shoulders as a positive business gesture kept it intact and the toothy smile beneath the toothbrush moustache held her captivated.

Of course, had Grandma Hackett been there, she would have sent him on his way in a cloud of blue smoke. Unfortunately, she had been called away to an urgent convention, assuming her daughter would heed her warning about opening the door to strangers and most of all to keep her witch's wit about her. Witches and wizards are supposed to be able to see through the most elaborate of disguises, but mother, being the dreamy 'castles in the air' type of person was very naïve and vulnerable. She was soon enraptured, captured and fell for his charms. Forgetting all of Grandma Hackett's warnings, at the ripe old age of seventeen, she had run off with a broomstick salesman, who turned out to be a wheezy wizard, well past his prime.

Several years and two daughters later, the spell wore off, as did the slicked-down hair and even the moustache began to look like a very well-worn toothbrush, eventually he disappeared altogether. However, mother now had too much a taste for the alternative lifestyle to want to return to the loneliness of the little cottage in the forest. Plus, there would be the overtures of: 'I told you this would happen, you wouldn't listen to me' saga. So, their mother did the only worthwhile thing she could do, in the circumstances — she joined a travelling circus troupe.

Her natural Bohemian demeanour befitted her new role in life perfectly. She became a fortune teller and mystic, she was very good at it too. Mother became the exalted Zena, she surrounded herself with exotic drapes, misty smoke-filled glass balls and festooned her elaborate tent with stars and crescent moons that changed colour every few minutes.

Her clothes were voluminous layers of multi-coloured skirts or dark mysterious cloaks, depending on her mood at the time. Every movement was an inharmonious jangle of sound from the many bangles on her arms and from the yards of beads and icons hung about her neck. With an adopted dreamy aura, which wasn't hard to do, she soon became quite a success. The only drawback to this exotic and ambrosial lifestyle was the disadvantage of two growing girls that did not quite fit into the present scheme and they could even encroach on her new-found fame.

So it was that Grandma Hackett, unable to induce her daughter to return to the simple life and not wanting her granddaughters to become too influenced by the bright lights of a travelling sideshow spectacle, found herself raising the girls as her own. Her dear friend, Edwina Grimsby, whom she had known since her own girlhood, had just returned from somewhere in the backwoods of a Scandinavian country where she had been for some years; with a small dark-haired orphan boy in tow. She persuaded Hilda Hackett to leave her forest home, it was not a place to bring up two young girls she argued and they needed to be with others of their own kind.

Harewood was not that far distant and Hilda would have the company of other witches. It would be better for the children too … so much more secure and the children would learn the crafts that were the intrinsic element of their bloodline.

It did not take too much persuasion for Hilda to agree and while mildly disappointed with her own daughter's lack of perception, it did seem a wise move not to allow her granddaughters to succumb to the same grandiose fantasies their mother had fallen victim to.

So, she packed up her cauldron, her grimoires and spell books with her other precious belongings and set off for a new life with Edwina and the now, three children.

Of the young boy in her charge Edwina said nothing, at least she didn't when the girls were present. He was her grandson they were told and needed to be treated kindly as he had suffered a great loss as he was no longer able to see his parents.

He was a very quiet withdrawn boy with a pale face and a shock of dark hair, but very pleasing grey eyes. He only answered when spoken to, kept to himself and did not make friends too easily. When he did speak it was with an odd accent that made it difficult for the girls to understand him, but in time his speech became the same as theirs and the accent had all but disappeared.

The witch's commune was known as Harewood it had been known to those of the following for many years, centuries perhaps, but few people knew it was there, or even bothered to visit. It consisted now of a half dozen or so neat little cottages clustered around a gently flowing stream that flowed through a pleasant, but secluded wood. Some little distance upstream the pleasant woods merged into a dark forest that seemed as old as time itself. Huge trees festooned with dark mosses and lichen crowded close together, their pendulous branches groaning and creaking as they rubbed together as if in deep conversation that only they could understand. The air within these dark walls of green was moist and cool, a haven for the many forest creatures who made their home within its undisturbed hollows.

Further in, the forest gave way to steep mountain ridges and the now restless stream reduced to a frenzied series of roaring cataracts that plunged savagely and unceasingly down craggy rock faces from deep fissures carved into the face of the mountain. Legend had it that a great and powerful witch once dwelt in caves behind the falls of swiftly flowing water and had placed a curse on the forest, allowing only those of the blood to enter. Of course, not everybody believed it, but nobody was going to tempt fate that far, so it did have the desired effect of keeping the odd wanderer out.

Here then was the ideal place for the young witches to grow and develop without undue interference, able to stay safely in the company of other young witches and wizards, although it did not exactly equip them for life on the 'outside', it was still a pleasant childhood. They were schooled in the general way, they read their books and learnt the same things children all over are taught, not just witchcraft alone. There was time a plenty for them to hone their skills in their play and become what their heritage decreed they should…even if there were a scant few who didn't quite get it all together.

It was a happy childhood and the sisters rarely gave their mother a thought, although she did visit them once in a while. She would arrive amid a flurry of skirts and a jangle of beads and bangles to regale them with tales of where she had been and whom she had seen. Her quick and constant chatter, punctuated with a glorious cacophonous accompaniment was almost deafening as she waved her arms expressively about as she talked. An animated whirling dervish, grandmother would later describe to Edwina.

Mother would pat the girls on the head, remark on how much they had grown since she had last seen them. She would fuss a little as she bestowed a small gift upon them, all under the disapproving eye of Grandma Hackett. The visit ended; she would disappear again with a final inharmonious jangle as she waved goodbye. Happily, from Grandma's point of view, these cloudbursts of maternal obligation did not seem to influence the girls at all. They accepted the gifts graciously but were quick to forget their mother once she had made her dramatic exit.

All things come to an end and as childhood gave way to womanhood, Marilla, in particular grew more and more restless. Time passed on and so too Grandma Hackett, who in her later years became one of the wisest, most respected witches in the Commune. Her books and treasured cauldron in which so many magnificent spells had been created became the sole responsibility of the sisters and so too some of the old grimoires, but Hilda Hackett was wise enough to cleverly conceal most of her more difficult and dangerous spells.

She knew her granddaughters well enough to know that Marilla, for all her pretentious and audacious behaviour would never be able to control them, until she learned to control herself. Isabella perhaps, though, not as impulsive as her sister was more inclined to deep thinking. She was quieter and kept to herself a lot, she was an avid reader; even when very young Isabella was more interested in plants and their properties than performing magic tricks. Given time and wisdom of years it would be Isabella who might unlock those secrets, but when Grandma Hackett faded away like an old piece of parchment, so did the visible key to a 'Pandora's Box of mystical murmurings and enigmatic mysteries.

Sadly, it would seem the art of pure witchcraft was dying out, the world was changing. Technology and scientific development were another thing altogether … but witchcraft was as old as time, an inherent gift that had to be nurtured and coaxed into being. Regardless of the scientific advantages, somewhere in the rush and confusion of an ideological world it would still be possible to find someone with the knowledge and skills in the mixing of potions, and the casting of spells, but mostly they remained hidden to a knowing few.

Marilla was determined she would remain first and foremost a witch, not just any witch, but one equal, if not better than her grandmother. However, though she would never admit it, even to herself, she despaired of ever really reaching that status. In fact, for all her outward pretentiousness Marilla harboured a deep sense of insecurity and seldom followed through with her ambitious ideas; though to all intent and purposes she always gave the impression that she was in control of any situation, regardless of how inadequate she really felt.

Isabella, on the other hand was simply content to follow along behind her sister, stopping occasionally to smell the flowers and touch the herbs, savouring the aroma as she rubbed the leaves between her fingers. Books were her passion and she devoured every word, hungering for more. Once her head was immersed in her reading she would be lost in another world. There was no hurry or rush of ambition for Isabella, for her, time was meaningless.

Chapter 4

A Series of Events

'Not sure I remembers 'em old monks now, too long ago.'

'But you *do* remember them?'

'Oh yeah 'course, bu' I were only young-un then, use t' go huntin' rabbits tup there past pine forest, but we's never went too nears Abbey … never knew what 'em monks might do. Ya' knows what lads 'r like, makin' tup all sorts o' stories.'

'What sort of stories?'

'Well, ya' knows, creepy things like — if they's caught ya trappin' rabbits too near their place, they'd chuck ya in one o' 'em dungeon-like rooms they got there below 'em walls, an' ya never see light of day agin.'

'A bit drastic a sort of punishment one would think.'

A conversation was taking place in the front garden of an old ivy-covered inn, the focal point of the little village that sat contentedly beside clear calm waters of an expansive lake. Several wooden tables and benches that had seen the ravages of too many seasons stood about in the dappled shade of a magnificent elm tree.

Seated at one of these, in a corner where the warming rays of the early afternoon sun was taking the edge off a crisp Autumn day, an elderly man regarded the full glass of brown ale that sat on the weather-worn table in front of him.

'Yeah, well, 'at's kids fur ya, they's got wild imagin'ins.' Old Tom picked up the glass and took a long swallow, returning it to the table before wiping the froth off his full white beard with the back of his sleeve. 'Good drop that, locally brewed ya know.'

Like most of his kind, born and bred to country life in isolated rural communities, Tom wore the badge of his heritage proudly — the calloused hands, and the ruddy weather- beaten face of a lifetime in the fields.

'Are there monks up there now?' The question was asked by his companion, a stranger who had recently taken lodgings at the inn.

'Perhaps there is … well, not sorts we's knew when we wus young-uns. No-un sees t' much o' lot 'at's tup there now, they just seem t' have disappeared; haven't bin 'round o' late.' Tom scratched his bearded chin and continued thoughtfully, 'Maybe they's havin' spiritual confinement or summat, 'ard t' tell 'ow these religious people thinks sometimes. Knows they don' talks too much, vow o' silence or summat … only speaks when they's 'ave ta.' He hesitated and stared absently at the sky. 'Pretty long confinement though, it bin mighty quiet with 'em for 'while.'

'But they've always been there haven't they?'

'Long's I cun remember I's guess.' Tom picked up his glass, and drained it, looking at the other keenly from under his bushy white eyebrows. 'What's your interest then? Thinkin' o' joinin' 'em are ya?' He set the now-empty glass back on the table and looked hard at the young man seated in front of him. 'You's askin' lots o' questions aint ya, what business ya' got there then eh? You's aint bin 'ere long have ya?'

He squinted a rheumy eye at the young man seated across

from him at the weather scoured table. 'We's 'aven't seen you's 'round these parts afore, you's a city bloke aint ya? Can always pick 'em, but most o' 'em don' stay 'ere long, too quiet they's reckons, but we's likes it that way.'

The stranger regarded the old man for a moment. Tall and lean, his finely chiselled features hidden somewhat by a few days' beard growth, he hesitated before replying, meeting the old man's rheumy-eyed gaze with his own clear grey one.

'I'm a journalist, a writer if you like, I'm working on the theory and beliefs of different religious sects and the Franciscan Grey Friars have an interesting and diverse history. Not a lot has been written about them, I thought you may have been able to shed some light on this present group … if they are still there.' He paused for a moment again, then continued in a quiet voice, 'I guess I'm just looking for a bit of solitude myself … in a way.' He passed a hand slowly over the stubble on his chin and looked down at his own glass.

Tom leaned back on the bench and seemed to stare thoughtfully into his empty glass, and after a long silence put one gnarled hand into the pocket of his old jacket and pulled out a smoke-stained pipe. Fumbling in another pocket he produced a crumpled leather pouch full of sweet-smelling tobacco.

'Well, there aint much t' tell,' he said as he put a full pinch of the tobacco into the bowl of the pipe and proceeded to tamp it down with a dirty thumb. 'This lot's bit different t' 'em ones what used t' be 'ere when I were a bit o' lad, more unfriendly like, I s'pose.'

'How can you know that?'

'Well nows, folks 'round here keep well 'way from that old Abbey, reckons it's cursed or 'aunted … can't say I blames them for thinkin' so, especially when Eddie never came back alive, an' fire burnin' 'alf place down.' Tom shook his head sadly.

'Eddie — what happened to him?' interest sparked in the other man's eyes, but he waited patiently for Tom to get the ancient pipe alight. The old man puffed silently away for a few minutes, the now-burning tobacco glowing in the bowl of the pipe.

At last he spoke. 'I's aint much fur talkin' with empty mug in front o' me,' he drawled and belched out a great cloud of tobacco smoke that drifted slowly across the table.

The glasses were gathered up and the young man hurried back into the inn, returning with the brimming glasses full of frothy brown ale. During those moments, Tom had leaned back on the bench, thoughtfully blowing smoke rings that drifted in ever widening circles until they vanished in the thin mountain air.

'So, what did happen to Eddie, what do you mean he never came back alive … from where … from the Abbey?' The question was repeated as the young man sat down again.

Old Tom shifted his pipe to the other side of his mouth and folded his arms across his chest. 'You's got a name?' he asked abruptly, 'I likes t' know who's I's talkin' t' these days.'

'Jack,' said the other, meeting Tom's steady gaze with his own. 'Who knows, I might be able to find out what happened to him, there's always a reason behind things that happen. People don't just die without a reason. What about your local authority here, did they investigate his death — how did he die?'

Tom removed his pipe and said slowly, 'Aint no reason as t' why he were drowned. We's found him wash tup on shore o' lake down by 'em reed beds, nears bridge. It were some time after 'e went tup Abbey as I recalls.' He paused before continuing. 'Police come an' poked 'bout bit an' ask few question but couldna find reasons why 'e drowned an' Eddie bein' … well, sort o' bloke 'e were, I guess we's wasn't tall surprised. In end, blokes from city police an' our local copper 'ere figure 'e'd got 'isself drunk an' fell in lake — 'e'd bin locked up afore fur bein' drunk an' disorderly, as they's puts it.' The old man sighed and stared thoughtfully at nothing in particular, taking another deep puff.

Jack looked keenly at the older man and said softly, 'Was it you who found him, Tom?'

Tom nodded slowly before picking his glass up off the table. He took a long draught, set the glass down again and replaced the pipe in his mouth.

'Do you want to tell me about Eddie?' Jack said after a while.

Tom sighed again and leaned his swarthy arms on the table, removing his pipe as he did so. 'Eddie were born 'round these parts, 'is parents owned land ways cross bridge bit. 'E always were wild-un, 'e an' his brother was always gettin' in t' trouble. Then he lost 'is Pa an' 'is brother in accident at farm, didna find out 'ow happened, but there were rumour that 'is brother shot 'is Pa when 'e were drunk, then turned gun on 'isself. They was wild bunch likes I said, an' Eddie just took off after that. "Is Mam went 'way t' live with 'er sister, an' Eddie just become bit o' loner after that 'appened, an' didna really fits in I s'pose, 'e just drift from place t' place. Did stint in army once when 'e were young, they got trainin' place not far from 'ere, but 'e didna last long there … weren't type t' be regimented. Sometime 'e'd do few job t' earn crust, but never settle anywhere proper like … but one thin' was for sure, 'e always come back t' village, cause 'e sorta belong 'ere.'

'So, Eddie did go up to the Abbey?'

'Yeah, he did,' said Tom solemnly, and took another large swallow of ale and continued. 'Somewheres 'e'd heard that 'em Fran…— whatever ya call 'em monks, have policy that they 'ave t' take in travellers, an' feed 'em——'

'Yes and give them shelter for as long as is needed,' finished Jack. 'It's an unwritten commandment of their order.'

'Well, 'e wouldna 'ave stuck it long, all that prayin' an' chantin' an' stuff woulda got is goat an' 'e would bin outa' there in coupla week or less. What with winter comin' on though I's guess 'e thought better than 'avin' t' shift for 'isself with a feed an' bed.' Tom paused, then went on. 'Not long after, we's saw Eddie headin' tup road that go up Abbey. Then later some o'local lads, just like we's did then we was young-uns, went tup t' top stream that runs past pine forest on northern side an' quite near's Abbey. They's went tup there t' go fishin' and come back with weird stories about hearin' screams an' what sound like someone firin' gun. Or maybe they was lettin' off firecrackers, whatever it were, there was somethin' goin' on at Abbey, cause that stream run fairly close t' back of it, see. Then one of them said 'e'd seen what look like someone hangin' from bell tower an' that bell was ringin' like mad. Ya can just see top o' tower if you stan' on very top o' them big rocks above where we fished, if we wasna goin' after rabbits. Mind you, we bin told dozens of time not t' go there when we was kids, but young-uns still don' listen do they?'

'No, you're right, Tom, I guess it's all part of being young and reckless, they all do the same thing regardless of how many generations apart. Kids don't change much no matter how many years go by. Was there really someone hanging at the tower there, Tom, or did the boy just imagine he saw something?'

'Dunno,' said Tom. 'Don't think anyone here 'bouts want t' believe what kid was sayin' an' this lad was always bit of troublemaker, fur tellin' truth was, so no-one were sure. Folks considered it best t' stay 'way from place an' keep their mouth shut, aint no business o' ours what they's dos tup there. Anyways, folk still reckon place is 'aunted. Them monks bury their dead tup there y' know an' some say's 'ow they walks aroun' some nights still wearin' them grey cloaks.' Tom shook his head and sighed, then emptied his glass of ale, wiping his mouth on his sleeve as he put down the empty glass.

'When was this fire you spoke about, Tom, was that about the same time as Eddie disappeared?'

'Yeah, t'was, then them young'uns come runnin' back all excited like an' talkin' 'bout 'earin' explosions an' that there must be fire tup there, 'cause they could see smoke, one of them said he could see flames as well. When we look' that ways, we could see bit of smoke driftin' way over tops of them pine tree. So, bein' neighbourly like, some of men from 'ere went tup hill t' see if we's could help put out, besides, far as we's knew Eddie was tup there anyways. Only got about harf way up afore we saw couple of monks comin' down t' meet us. Pretty gruff they's was too an' told us they's didna need help an' t'wus all under control, t' go back t' village. As I said afore, real unfriendly like,' said Tom, shaking his head.

'So, you didn't get the chance to ask them about Eddie?'

'Nope, they's run us off that hill afore we's could ask 'em anythin'.' Tom knocked the remains of his pipe out against the leg of the bench and drew out the little pouch once more, silently refilling it, nodding toward his empty glass as he did so. Jack got the message and gathered up the glasses again. Returning with the brimming glasses, he seated himself across the ancient table and waited until Tom had the pipe going again. He puffed contentedly for a few more minutes with a full pipe and a full glass to contemplate.

However, there was one more question Jack wanted an answer to. 'Do you want to tell me if anything happened after that?'

Slowly the story came out and Jack could see through Tom's eyes what these simple, honest country folk had experienced in trying to comprehend the unfamiliar.

*   *   *

They had considered that after a fire and what appeared to be a whole lot of mayhem within the Abbey, Eddie would return to the village, disillusioned. However, knowing what an unpredictable recluse he was, maybe he had moved on; but then they reasoned, his path would have brought him back through the village. Nobody had seen him, so perhaps he was still there … perhaps there was some good reason why he had not left.

A niggling picture had been placed in their receptive minds of 'someone hanging near the bell tower' by an overzealous youngster much prone to tampering with the truth. However much as they dismissed the thought, it kept surfacing to the forefront of the rational portion of their collective minds. Why was Eddie still there?

Finally, after a day of discussion on the matter and over several pints of ale to bolster the decision making, a small delegation of village stalwarts, together with a revered elder, made the decision to boldly go up to the Abbey to see for themselves if Eddie was there. The elder and unfortunate candidate Ned Bagely, being of reasonably sound mind and with a coveted position on the town council to his credit, would confront the monks and politely ask if their comrade were still there and if would it be possible to speak with him. They were only interested, they would say, in his welfare and they only wanted to see him. If he wanted to stay … then that was his business. It all sounded easy enough.

On their approach to the Abbey, the small detachment of searchers were surprised and momentarily pleased to find their advancement into the sacred hermitage was unchallenged. They were also close enough to see the amount of damage that had been inflicted. The outer wall of the nearest building adjacent to the church had suffered considerable damage, in fact it was little more than a pile of rubble. Other walls nearby had suffered some damage as well, some of the great stones from atop the walls had fallen adding to the confusion. Indeed, it almost looked like a war zone. However, they had come this far, there was to be no turning back now, so with Ned being gently nudged to the forefront of the core of the sortie, they advanced.

The small band of hopefuls began to pick their way through the rubble, glancing fearfully about them as they did so. Charred timbers from the roof structure lay about and they could see that the great iron-gate was mangled, even part of the church wall bore black scorch marks on its sacred pristine surface. They had actually hoped to have been met by one of the senior monks to whom they could state their business and leave but there was no one about; it was as silent as a grave and they shivered a little as they moved slowly onward.

'Probably got sick o' bein' alone tup here with this lot an' went somewhere's else, could've cut through forest tup further an' we's just didna see him,' was one gruff remark. A thought to which they all nodded their heads in agreement, though it did seem highly unlikely — the forest was very thick and in places almost impenetrable and Eddie wouldn't make things too hard for himself, most surmised. If he had left the Abbey at all, it would have been by the lake road. The only sign of life visible to them were a group of coal black ravens perched side by side atop a wall that still stood around the outer court. Like small black robed priests, they sat silently, staring fixedly down at the nervous muster of intruders, their beady little black eyes watching every move.

'Perhaps he just tup 'n died an' them their ravens picked him clean,' said one of the group with a perverted attempt at humour.

This remark was greeted with horrified sidelong glances and the quick intake of breath, as if half expecting to stumble over Eddie's mangled body, the group quickly admonished the author of such a dire statement. The elder, who was a small wizened little man lagging a few steps behind the others, now curiously poked his head into a darkened alcove of fallen stone. He was about to withdraw it, when in the half darkness, a huge pair of eyes appeared out of the gloom. They disappeared again for a split second and were there again, even larger than before.

Two simultaneous screeches rent the air. One from an owl, rudely disturbed from her sleep and the other from the small, terrified man, who had felt the thud and the flurry of feathers full in his face, as the startled owl hurriedly left her perch on a ledge inside the alcove.

Screaming and flapping his arms wildly, the little man turned and fled across the court, coming to a stop only when he tripped then fell headlong over a large block of stone that had fallen from the battlements above. He lay stunned for a moment, his cheek resting on the cold hard stone. Then slowly raising himself on his elbow from his prone position, he found himself staring into the grinning face of one of the gargoyles that had once adorned the parapet. The grotesque face of this leering demon so close to his own sent him into new paroxysms of terror and he fled into the arms of his companions, who half dragged, half carried him across the rubble to the remaining stone wall, where he was propped up, still breathing heavily and clutching his chest.

The others stood close together and gazed nervously about them. These were hardened country folk who knew how to handle the tragedies and triumphs that comes from wrestling a living from the good earth but when it came to understanding what they took to be supernatural and alien to the general order of things, they were completely confused and out of their depth.

Poor Ned trembled violently as he tried to cover his face with his hands, while his companions stood nervously by wondering what to do next. They were awed by the eerie stillness of the place, not even the ravens grouped on the wall had made a sound. There appeared to be no sign whatsoever of another living thing. They did not even dare to break the silence and call Eddie's name in case something appeared that they did not want to see. What they could see was the looming bulk of the Abbey itself now in front of them; but no one felt inclined to go any further. The dark imposing structure seemed to weave a malevolent air about itself, almost daring them to venture further.

The heavy silence was suddenly broken by the strangled gasp of Ned who was still leaning against the rock wall. The others turned toward him fearing that the old fellow was having the heart attack that, according to him, should have carried him off long ago. However, his agonised gaze was fixed firmly at the gap between his feet, his face contorted with horror and his lips moving as if he were trying to say something, but his voice had failed him completely. Following his gaze, they saw, half hidden amongst the grass at the base of the rock, a cleft that almost split the stone in two. At its entrance waved the head of a snake, its forked tongue flicking rapidly in and out.

A second louder screech issued from Ned, when he had

found his missing voice and in an instant had leapt up onto the top of the rock. For a man of his years and riddled with rheumatism, it was a surprising feat of agility that surprised his companions as well as himself. The equally startled snake, feeling the loud thump on the roof of his home, shot out of the hole, quickly vanishing among the rocks and tall grasses bordering the wall.

Half fainting with fear and shock, old Ned fell into the arms of his equally terrified companions, who, without any further thoughts of exploration decided that discretion in this case was definitely the better part of valour, if Eddie wanted to live within these unearthly ruins, then he was welcome to it. This was not at all what they had envisaged, if this was an Abbey … where were the monks? They had expected to be met with frankness or even a brusque reception in their quest for Eddie's welfare but the carefully prepared speeches were lost in the sudden breeze that stirred the grasses and ruffled the black feathers of the watchers on the wall.

From their vantage perch atop the high wall, the ravens watched the now somewhat erratic progress of the search party return swiftly down the hill, the little man struggling to keep his feet as the group of men dragged him along between them. He was still waving his arms about and screaming words like *Devils! — Demons! — we's all be cursed! — killed!* These words came drifting back up the hill and to where the birds sat, their heads to one side, as if listening and watching curiously as the small group dropped beyond the belt of trees at the bottom of the valley. They ruffled their feathers up and went back to the business of preening themselves and searching the ground for a likely lunch, quite unperturbed by the drama that had unfolded before them.

High up in the bell tower, not all was deserted, someone else was watching the departure of the search party as well.

Ned's experience, so he claimed later had been proof enough that the Abbey was indeed haunted, dark forces were at work there, he had always known that and was regretting his decision to lead the foray into such a place; he would never be the same again. One of the more elderly residents scratched through the remnants of his ancient mind and added his thoughts on the matter. He recalled that his father … or was it his father's father had told a relative of his that the Abbey was built in the wrong place. It was sacred Druid ground, or was it Devil's ground, he wasn't sure which but whatever, it boded ill for any structure that was placed there and anyone who did go there would be cursed. At least, that's what he remembered being said. He had overheard it, he claimed when he was a young boy.

Little matter that the Abbey had been standing for a considerably longer period than any of the ancients could ever remember, but it did have the desired effect on the village folk and they kept a respectable distance, only speaking about it in whispers. Even the village children were further issued dire warnings not to venture too close.

They feared it even more when Eddie's body washed up a few days later trapped in the reeds that grew thickly on the shores of the lake close to the village.

*   *   *

Old Tom finished his narrative of events and gave a deep sigh. 'We was bit stunned when Eddie got washed tup like that, but he was odd sorta bloke an' I guess we's all knew he might come t' bad end sometime.'

'Yes, I can understand how you must have felt. It's not something that you want to experience, but these things unfortunately do happen,' said the young man gently. 'It must have been quite traumatic for all of you, has anyone apart from that first group been up there since?'

'Nope … well, not from here anyways.' Tom paused, then spoke again, 'but we's had bin hearin' some delivery type vans 'n trucks goin' through but then most a'night. Maybe they was carryin' stuff t' do repairs tup there.'

'Yes, possibly,' said the other who rubbed his chin thoughtfully. 'It certainly sounds as if there were extensive repairs needed from what you've told me.' He thought for a moment. 'Did anyone in the village have anything to do with the monks, Tom?'

'They use t' do bit of business at Post Office from time t' time but canna say I's know of anyone else. Anyways I aint bin interest' enough t' find out, did see them walkin' 'round sometime', but most folk don' take no notice.'

After a moment of silence, Jack stood up, obviously there was little else Tom could tell him. 'It's been an interesting morning, Tom, thank you for talking to me. I'm sure it wasn't easy for you finding Eddie like that, it's always hard to talk about something as unpleasant as that afterwards.'

Tom nodded and put his head on one side as he shifted the position of the pipe again and regarded the young man with a curious expression. 'Ya still plannin' goin' tup there?'

'I might take a look at it sometime, it does sound interesting enough to do a bit of a story on and a little bit of drama thrown in as well, it could be worth more than a passing glance.'

Jack picked up his backpack, then leaned across the table and laid a hand on the old man's shoulder, 'Look after yourself, Tom, I've enjoyed your company this morning, you've given me something to think about, thank you.' Shouldering his backpack, he walked away from the inn.

*   *   *

The village main street was much like any other rural town. Small, neat houses fronting the main thoroughfare; white picket fences standing proudly beyond borders of bright flower beds and carefully tended patches of lawn here and there. A small dog, becoming aware of unfamiliar footsteps approaching, roused itself from its slumber on the front step of a house and yapped its way along the boundary of the property 'till Jack was beyond the guarded territory. Satisfied that the stranger was no longer a threat, it gave one final warning yap before returning to the warmed place on the step.

Jack smiled to himself, even the smallest can muster bravado when necessary.

The morning was bright and sunny, the air smelled fresh and clean and he could almost forget his purpose in visiting this tiny township and revel in its unsophisticated plethora of the simpler things of life. Here there was no sense of urgency, it was as if time stalled in its headlong rush and had become stuck in a groove, leaving this tiny corner to spin on its own, undefaced and unpolluted. Shops displaying their wares spilled over onto the narrow footpath and Jack found himself picking his way between open boxes of potatoes, melons and sun-ripened fruit. The rich appetising smell of newly baked bread drifted across the road from a bakery on the corner, reminding him that it had been some time since he had last eaten. However, it was the austere façade of the building on the opposite corner that drew Jack's attention — the local Post Office.

He climbed the few wide steps, taking a letter out of his pocket as he did so and pushed open the heavy glass door, the faded lettering proclaiming it as an establishment of regional importance.

A small bell had tinkled somewhere above his head and the close air was filled with the musty smells of inks and old papers. There were shelves of paper goods, racks of postcards and souvenirs. Here and there in the crowded interior were cartons of goods on display not normally associated with Her Majesty's mail system but so much a part of unified country living.

Jack found his way to a broad high countertop and looked about him. A kettle on the boil was issuing its shrill impatient whistle from somewhere beyond in an inner recess. Then its dying discordance was silenced as the contents were poured into a waiting mug he could just see on the end of a bench in the back room. He coughed politely, a voice called out in reply.

'Coming, just making a cuppa.'

A tall thin-boned woman with a gaunt angular face and an inquiring expression appeared, carrying the steaming mug which she deftly cleared a space for somewhere below the counter. She looked to be somewhere in her sixties, Jack thought, greyish hair piled on top of her head made her face look even more angular, her eyes were bright and piercing behind rimless spectacles perched near the end of her nose. Her manner was brisk and business-like as she appraised Jack over her glasses.

'Sorry to keep you waiting but the kettle was just on the boil,' then noticing Jack's letter, 'stamps, you'll be wanting stamps … now where did I put them, had them out a little while ago.' She began to turn over piles of letters and papers on the crowded countertop, pursing her thin lips and glancing up at the man in front of her every now and then. The stamps located, she went on, 'You'd be new in town I expect … just passing through or staying a while?' She looked at him intrusively over the top of her glasses as she carefully detached the required stamp from the sheet.

Jack answered her question, but sensed he'd have to choose his words carefully. 'Well, yes and no … actually, I've been here a couple of days. I'm a writer you see, I travel around a bit, just looking for interesting or unusual stories about people or places.' Quick to notice the spark of attentiveness in her eyes, he turned on the charm. He had found the town quaint, sort of old world-ish, he remarked enthusiastically and so interesting but all the more so because of an old Franciscan Abbey close by on a mountain top. How utterly fascinating to have such an ancient monastery within a short distance of this charming village, surely there was a lot of history to be found here as regards the Abbey.

Edna, as the Postmistress introduced herself, drew herself up even taller and adopted a particularly important air. Yes, the village did have a most interesting history and not just because of a Monastery on a mountain top. Her father, who had held the position of Mayor for eight years running — eight years mind you — had been the Postmaster here for almost thirty years! When he died Edna had taken over and this Post Office provided the vital link between their small village and the outside world … and of course the Abbey. 'Though not so much these days.' She added flatly.

'Your father must have led a busy and industrious life then,' ventured Jack carefully. 'Indeed, he did; *his* grandfather was one of the founding fathers of this town, if you must know. There's a very good portrait of him hanging in pride of place in the Town Hall in the Council chambers. A very popular man he was, and there's been none in this town to equal him since,' she declared as she rummaged around beneath the counter looking for the stamp pad.

'And probably never will be, if my thoughts are correct,' Jack murmured, half to himself. 'The monks, from the Abbey, did they come down into the village often, Edna?' he asked politely as her head emerged from beneath the counter, stamp pad in hand. 'Did they come in here too?' He added as his clear grey eyes met hers, 'What were they like?'

Thoughts of her esteemed father now pushed from her mind; she began. 'Oh, hard to say really, they all looked the same in their long grey habits, like grey ghosts you know,' she whispered dramatically, 'all covered up and gliding along, their faces always hidden under the folds of cloth that covered their heads, but they had to come down from their retreat sometimes.' She shrugged her shoulders meaningfully and added in a business-like tone, 'Any business they had in the village was always done reasonably quickly and quietly, general transactions always kept to a bare minimum, then they would leave.'

'Did they ever say anything?'

'Not much, they weren't great talkers … didn't say anything unless it was necessary, and then only used the least words possible or just pass a note across, they seemed rather peculiar in my opinion — not normal.' Edna was warming to her subject now. 'Of course,' she said, as she deftly stamped Jack's letter, 'I know it was *always* the same one who did all the monastery business at the Post Office.'

'How could you be so sure of that if you never saw their faces?'

'Well, you couldn't help but notice it,' Edna replied, leaning over the counter as if providing a confidential secret, 'he always wore a heavy gold ring on the little finger of his right hand; you *couldn't* miss it!'

Jack's interest quickened and he began to probe Edna's mind for additional information. It wasn't hard to persuade her to reveal more; gossip was her subsistence and the Post Office the melting pot of all that entered the web of local intrigue. She soon appeared almost anxious to tell him that she had even asked the said monk a personal question. 'Whatever do you gentlemen do up there all day to pass the time?' she had asked, indicating the general direction of the Abbey with a jerk of her head, as she expertly thumped the stamp and applied the required imprint on one of the packages the monk had placed on the counter. 'The answer had been a long time in coming, as if the hooded figure was thinking whether he should answer or not. "We write books," he said in a gruff voice.'

'Oh,' had been Edna's reply, 'then that probably explains why you do have a lot of this sort of mail; going to the publishers I suppose. My cousin Harriet's uncle used to be in the publishing business, said he used to get some dreadful things sent to him sometimes that he wouldn't dare put in print, but then yours would be different, wouldn't they?'

'Yes,' had been the quick reply and the robed one had put his finger to where his mouth would be under the hood as if to silence any more words, then turned on his heel and with a blur of grey cloth he was gone.

'Really,' said Jack, 'and he spoke no more than that?'

Edna shook her head 'No, yet I can remember when my father used to talk to them quite a bit in the old days, there was never any problem. If they wanted something, they'd ask for it. They were friendly and um,' she searched for the right word, 'humble, I would say … yes, humble, as if they didn't want to put you out. I know my father used to like them coming into the Post Office, because they were so … well educated. I remember he often used to say that it was a pleasure to have a decent conversation for a change. They were a pleasure to talk to instead of some of the more ignorant ones that come in from the farms. All they could talk about was the state of health of their livestock.' She sniffed scornfully, as she absently moved some papers. 'But then this is a rural community mostly, so one must expect that some of the customers would be, dare I say it — less educated in the ways of the world and the only reading material they pick up is the *Agricultural Monthly*, or the latest trends on the stock market and I'm not talking stocks and bonds money market mind you, I mean cows and pigs you see.'

Jack had been leaning against the other side of the ample and overcrowded counter a look of interest on his face and sympathised with a nod of his head. Yes, he agreed, in rural communities one had to put up with the inadequacies of education among the masses, but then one doesn't really need an Oxford degree to raise pigs, but none the less, they were still an essential part of the community.

Edna sniffed again in reply.

'So,' said Jack, returning her philosophical thoughts to the subject in mind, 'in other words the monks have become more … secretive?'

'Yes, yes, you could say that, and they don't use the services of the Post Office as much either.' She shook her head defiantly as she gave Jack a critical look over the top of her glasses. 'If you're looking for something to write about, there's just as much interesting and informative history in this town as there is in that old Abbey. My great grandfather was one of the founding members of the Council; one of the original inhabitants you know, when it was little more than a hamlet by the lake and he—'

Jack had taken a quick look at the watch on his wrist and now broke into her flow of genetic history. 'Oh, Edna, I'm sorry; but I have to go. I'd love to hear more about this charming village … and your grandfather, but I did promise to meet someone and I see that I'm already late.'

Edna forced a rueful smile. 'Well, don't forget now, if you *do* want some interesting facts about the village for your writing, I *do* know an awful lot about this town and the people here.'

'I'm sure you do, yes I'm sure you do,' replied Jack with a smile, as he pulled the heavy glass fronted door open. 'I'll try to call in again.'

He reached the safety of the footpath and drew a deep breath. 'The things one has to do to get significant information,' he muttered to himself, then turned his footsteps in the direction of the bakery, as his stomach was reminding him that breakfast was a long time ago.

Chapter 5

A Rendezvous With An Ally

Very early the following morning as the sun began to creep its infinite path above the craggy mountain tops, a slight figure carrying a backpack was making slow but steady progress along the road that wound its way beside the rushing waters of the mountain stream. He had left the placid waters of the lake behind him, with its waving reeds and rushes bordering its rippling edges. He had lingered on the little wooden bridge that crossed a wide creek emptying its small contribution to the vastness of the lake. A simple bridge made from stout timbers cut from the surrounding forest, wide enough and strong enough for the few vehicles that used it; but a boundary that separated the modest little village from that which loomed like a dark and forbidding stronghold on the mountain, misunderstood and maligned by the village folk.

He had stood there for some moments listening to the wind sighing in the tops of the fringe of pine trees that edged the creek and marked the beginning of a forest of dense green that followed the line of the creek that had its beginning hidden high near the mountain top; also marking the separation of the village from the surrounding forest.

It was a pleasant morning; a light breeze had sprung up and

the air was crisp and clean. There was no sense of urgency in the young man's ramble up the steepening path and he delighted in the subtle scents of autumn. The breeze that sang in the pine trees overhead, rustling its way through the feathery tops, whispered of many things and of colder winds to come. Old briar rose brambles had hung their colourful rose hip 'lanterns' out to view and the brilliant orange-red berries of hawthorn gathered in mosaic clusters against a canvas of bracken fern. Over it all, the symphonic tumble of the stream beside the path that fed into the great lake became louder and more forceful as it rushed and cascaded over wayward rocks that dared to impede its headlong rush into the valley below.

He paused as he reached a great tumble of rocks that marked the turn of the road before the last steep climb up the boulder and bracken strewn hillside. The road itself wound its way further along the mountain side, before climbing in serpentine curves to reach the citadel perched on its plateau, like the eyrie of some gigantic bird.

Here, where he had stopped it was cool and moist, the great stones carpeted in moss and lichens and grouped together, standing upright as if gathered there by some titans' hand. Overshadowed by a leafy canopy and fed by rivulets of water that seeped through the gaps in the stones, lush grasses and ferns grew thickly to spread a rich carpet of green by the roadside.

Easing the backpack off his shoulders and placing it on one of the smaller boulders that lay scattered at the foot of the monoliths, he unzipped a pocket and withdrew a flask of water from which he took a long drink. He stoppered the flask again and leaned back against the coolness of the rock and let his gaze wander over this deceptively peaceful scene. The river here was narrow and he could hear the roar of the tumbling waters as they poured over the last great obstacle to fall in a great cascading deluge, plunging into a deep pool below. Across the river, a sea of pines stretched like a verdant ribbon around the base of a formidable barrier of mountain peaks, their tops hiding demurely within veils of mist and cloud. The brilliant colours of the autumn however were much in evidence on this side of the river, the poplars and elms that dotted the riverbanks seemed reluctant to begin shedding their dress of red and gold leaves for the bare starkness of winter.

The young man sighed and glanced at his wristwatch. Picking up the flask he was about to stow it away again into his pack when a voice spoke almost at his side.

'Now don't put that away just yet, I could do with a drink, this is thirsty work.'

Jack looked around to see a shortish stockily built man emerge through a narrow opening between the great rocks. He was clothed head to toe in the rough robes of a Franciscan monk. Jack raised a hand in greeting.

'Amos, good to see you old friend, it's been quite a while. I hope the brothers have not completely converted you, otherwise our cause is lost. So, tell me — what's the present situation, what are we facing, and how many souls are we interested in saving?'

'At the moment fourteen, including myself and we have three minders,' came the deep-voiced reply, after he took a long drink from the flask Jack handed him.

'Everyone okay then?'

'Scared, confused, they don't know what to expect next, but okay otherwise, they just get on with what they're commissioned to do and try not to ask too many questions, although they are becoming restless, wouldn't be surprised if they start some sort of revolt themselves soon.'

Jack nodded his head and looked quizzically at his friend and grinned. 'So how was your transition into the inner sanctum, you've obviously been successful?' He looked him up and down as he spoke. 'I wish I'd been there to see your performance,' he grinned and quipped, 'You know those robes really suit you.'

Amos muttered something, fortunately mostly under his breath and replied tersely, 'It wasn't all that difficult and my "performance" as you put it must have been convincing enough, they took me at my word.'

Jack smiled as a mental picture formed in his mind of a portly, greying, middle-aged monk 'puffing' his way up the last few steps to the gate and breathlessly asking to see the Abbot. 'He's expecting me you know,' he'd puffed, placing his portmanteau on the ground beside him, waving a thick folder of papers to a guard at the gate, who would have eyed him suspiciously from the inner side of the barred gate. Amos, in return showing surprise on his round chubby face and innocent blue eyes at someone other than clergy answering his knock.

To all outside appearances, the bumbling demeanour of this ecclesiastical pilgrim, dutifully hurrying after the retreating guardian of the gate was that of a scholarly personage, only vaguely aware that perhaps he may be in the wrong monastery as he looked nervously about him. The keen blue eyes however were mentally absorbing all within their vision, while the sharp mind was concentrating on the next plan of action. Ruefully, he knew, as a little voice reminded him at the back of his mind that he was going to be there for some time.

'Any sign of Dan yet?' asked Jack after a short pause.

'No,' sighed his companion. 'I've poked around as much as I dare without raising too much suspicion and spoken to some of the other monks, but have to be careful to remain in character.

Most of them don't want to talk about it; too afraid it could be one of them next. One or two hinted that he may have fallen, or been dropped over the cliff, or else, as one did suggest, buried somewhere in one of the underground tombs. There's quite a lot of underground area under the Abbey, Jack. I haven't been able to explore much of it yet, as we are kept under close watch, but from what I hear, you could hide an army and a couple of Matilda tanks under there! Been trying to find out as much as I can from books in the library, but they don't give you much time to spend there; however I did get a clue as to where he might be, but can't get to it yet. They lock us up at night so there's no time to do any snooping and I don't want to give myself away by acting suspiciously in front of the others. So, everything is purely from observation and carefully worded conversations.' He paused and then said slowly, 'There is one thing that's been pretty obvious though. There's more going on up there than meets the eye, apart from Victor's usual business lines. I think our quarry is branching out into a much more lucrative enterprise, and the sooner we put a stop to that the better.'

Jack had another question. 'What about the Abbot himself, can you communicate with him, or is he completely under their control too?'

Amos frowned. 'Now there's a hard one, Jack — I can't quite work him out and I get the feeling he's not all he's supposed to be. He's scared yes, but there's something odd about him. I wouldn't be at all surprised to find out that there's a shady past there somewhere. People have all sorts of reasons to turn the other cheek as it were and seek a new vocation in such a place as this; it's happened before.'

Jack said nothing as he stowed the flask back into his pack, then putting his hand on to the stocky well-muscled shoulders of his friend he said, 'All understood, old friend, but perhaps we can loosen his tongue a little.'

'You know,' Amos said, rubbing his hands through his thatch of grey hair in an exasperated fashion. 'I could have taken the three of them out, at any time — I was *itching* to do it! It would have been so easy!'

'That's what I was afraid of!' Jack flung his backpack over his shoulders. 'Then it would have been impossible for them to talk to me once you've finished with them. At least this way they are not expecting anything … yet, but we need to have their leader — *he's* the Jackpot prize, *he's* the one we want.'

Amos muttered an oath and turned to retrieve a brace of freshly killed rabbits that had been placed on a nearby rock. 'We'd better move before my minder comes looking for me, he gets a bit edgy if I'm out of his sight for too long.'

'By the way,' said Jack as they began to push their way through the bracken and prickly gorse bushes behind the rock outcrop, ignoring the well-trodden path and keeping their voices little more than a whisper as they moved silently through the underbrush, guided by Amos. 'Forgive my curiosity, but how have you managed to evade 'protective custody'? I was afraid you wouldn't be here this morning and I was prepared to make my own way up and try to access from the back.'

'It's been relatively easy so far, since they found out I could cook, so the kitchen has become my responsibility,' Amos carefully parted the bushes in front of him, 'but I've had to make them think I'm as scared as hell of them and won't dare put a foot out of line, I've had to play the blubbering idiot for them.' He spat in disgust and continued, 'Of course I don't make it easy for them to ride shotgun on me when I check my traps. I've been able to get to know this part of the forest pretty well,

I've been leading them in and out of some pretty rough places particularly that patch of thorny brambles high up on the side of that hill there. That's where he thinks I am now. My "minder" got himself scratched up so many times in the thick bush that he doesn't bother to follow me now, so he gives me a half hour or so to get on with it, while he waits at the end of the back wall. He'll be getting real fidgety by now, so we'd better keep moving or else he'll come looking for me and I really don't want to take him out yet … as much as I'd like to.'

Jack laughed softly. 'I find it hard to imagine *you*, of all people being submissive, but if it gains their confidence and relaxes their vigil, then you can say your solo performance was worth the effort.'

'Not for much longer,' growled the other, 'this is not the sort of role I like playing, I've had to put up with a lot I normally wouldn't and it's been a devil of a job holding my temper. I don't know how much longer I can hold out without tearing him to pieces. I just want to get my hands around his scrawny neck and get this operation over and done with!'

Jack couldn't help smiling to himself as he watched the broad back of his companion leading him through the tangle of bracken fern and bushes. Amos … he always liked to shoot first and ask questions later, but he also knew his job and would not make a move without Jack's approval. They worked well together, Amos recognised the special talents that Jack possessed and in turn, Jack appreciated the loyalty and the uncanny ability that Amos had to blend into any situation he was thrown into, plus the fact that he had shown himself to be a dammed good actor!

This short grey headed man was his mentor and friend, they had been through a lot together since their early days in the Forces and now too in this Special Investigation Branch, where they were embarking on a two-fold mission. The immense strength and courage of Amos was beyond reproach, Jack reflected and had saved them from some perilous predicaments in their time together. He had seen him snap a man's neck with his bare hands, yet those same hands could pick up and cradle a baby as gently as any mother's.

'You heard about the fire then from the folk in the village?' said Amos, still keeping his voice low and soft as he led the way.

'Yes, I did and that whole episode could have jeopardised our strategy, having a vagrant turn up at the gates was something nobody, not even we had counted on. He chose the wrong place at the wrong time unfortunately, or perhaps fortunate in a way, as he was not able to blow the whistle on Casini, and stuff up his plans. He paid the price for it though; one of the villagers found his body washed up on the shores of the lake.'

'He certainly did cause a great deal more confusion and damage than they were prepared for; damn near blew the place apart trying to play the hero,' said Amos. 'Poor beggar got himself totally confused with the smoke and the noise and ran the wrong way. Before he had realised it, he was heading for the cliffs above the falls and was over it before anyone could get to him.'

They walked silently for a few moments.

'What's the word in the village, Jack, do they suspect anything? I was aware that a group came up the hill on the day of the fire, but they didn't get too far, I could have made a move that day with ease, as two of our minders sent them off home again. No point in taking over then though — I didn't have the back up to follow through with it and it's no good without the big fish.'

'I had a long conversation with one of the senior residents yesterday,' said Jack. 'They're convinced the Abbey is haunted and did make that half-hearted attempt to search for the bloke, Eddie, but it apparently went horribly wrong for them and they haven't been game to go near the place since.'

'Yes, I know, they were watched and they wouldn't have been allowed to get too far, so perhaps it's a good thing they do believe it's haunted. The 'boys' have tightened their security up now — part of the front wall is gone and they're not happy I can tell you; they don't like it much themselves … reckon it's a spooky place, even the monks think it's bad Karma. One thing is pretty obvious though, their boss is not going to be too happy when he sees what a loose nut can do with a couple of big firecrackers!'

Amos continued, 'I'm actually surprised I was permitted to check my traps today, after the furore that occurred, I thought they might get a bit more trigger-happy. I rather think they've taken a liking to my special rabbit stew,' he added with a grin, 'but I don't think it will change their boss' mind — he's got plans for that place, Jack and they're *big* plans. The only trouble was that poor idiot, Eddie, found explosives stored rather carelessly up there in one of the rooms and that's what he was throwing about. What he hoped to gain by it, I'm dammed if I know. Now, the big question is — what are they wanting explosives for? That's what we have to find out.'

They had reached a small clearing where the gorse and bracken was less prolific, and Amos stopped. He pointed to a place a short way ahead and slightly East of where they stood.

'Now, Jack, see that clump of firs up there by that big rock outcrop? There's a hollow up there big enough to rest up in 'till dusk. From there you can sight off the end of the wall at the back of the Abbey, and it's a fairly easy passage through. There's a break, part way along the wall there where a big old elm tree has leaned a bit too heavily on it, the gap should be wide enough for you to get through. You'll probably see old kitchen gardens away to your left and part of an old orchard, but there are gaps in the wall there where part of it has fallen years ago, so you shouldn't have too much trouble finding a way through. The orchard will give you plenty of cover and the building that will be directly in front of you is the back of the kitchen. There is a heavy door there, usually kept shut, keep your eye on that. I will be making a bit of a disturbance around there at the time we agree on, is that okay so far?'

'Sounds good,' said Jack, 'now, are you still wired for sound?'

'Yes, they haven't bothered to search me, took me at my word. I made such a nervous fuss about having to be locked up; just a little touch of hysterics as it were, that they're convinced I'm for real. Now then, they lock us up in our cells at eight pm; but I'll be making an excuse to go back to the kitchens at about that time, so watch for my signal. From what I surmise at this time, we've got about fifty or so hours up our sleeves before Casini Senior and the rest of this entourage turn up, so we'll have to make the most of it.' He looked skyward as he spoke, 'It looks as if we've got a storm coming up too, which could work in our favour.' He put a hand on his friend's arm. 'Have you got everything you need, Jack?'

'Yes, I have thanks. Now you'd better get back or that minder of yours will come looking for you and it wouldn't do to see me here; we would have to dispose of him a little earlier than expected and that would spoil the surprise.'

'Now wouldn't that be a pity?' Amos gave a grim smile. He turned and in a few moments, his stocky figure was lost in the thick growth of the surrounding pine forest.

Jack stood watching and listening for quite a few more minutes, before turning away to make for the rocky outcrop that Amos had indicated. He had heard a loud voice shouting in the distance that sounded angry and assumed Amos' minder had been getting a trifle anxious about the long absence, but at least they had not been seen … not yet anyway.

It wasn't long before Jack found the hidden spot — a deep depression among the rocks protected by an overhang of tangled gorse and stunted trees, entangled with a curtain of bracken fern. Though not far away from the cluster of outbuildings that made up part of the complete Abbey complex, he could see, as Amos had said, a rough track that would lead him to the outer wall. He had already decided he would make his move before it got too dark, but the position in the hollow for the moment was safe from prying eyes.

Jack climbed down into the sheltering hollow and taking off his backpack he leant it up against a flat rock. Shading his eyes, he scanned the sky. Amos was right, clouds were beginning to build up and the wind now had a keen edge to it. However, here it was quiet and sheltered, apart from evidence that forest animals had also found it a sheltered haven too. No matter, he would share it, for the moment.

He settled himself into this small cavern, leaning against his backpack and closed his eyes. He too would be glad when this operation was over. It had been a long time, an extensive search, but they were closing in on their quarry, it wouldn't do to act too quickly now and give a chance of escape.

He sighed, then removed the backpack from behind him and drew out a small transmitter and busied himself with it for a few minutes, running up a slim antenna. Quickly and quietly, he spoke to someone for a moment or two, then packed it all back into the pack and put it behind him once again.

The trap was set, all that was needed now was for the

mastermind of these illegal enterprises to enter the net then Jack and Amos would close the loop.

Jack's superior officer Steve and his band of merry men were waiting not far off. The nearby army base had been their headquarters for a few months now, with transport choppers at the ready, were just waiting for Jack's signal before moving in to make the arrest. This covert operation had taken much time and planning and they needed to take their quarry by surprise.

However, it was not the capture of the Cassini's that was occupying much of his mind at the moment. It was something else … something that had lurked in the corner of his mind for a very long time, for as long as he could remember in fact. There was something he had to find, something precious that had been instilled into him that he must recover and possess, before it fell into the hands of the enemy.

The enemy — was that who it was — the enemy? He had found it hard to think of it like that and why did it have to be a hostile adversary, when it could have easily been so different, but deep in his heart, Jack knew it was true. The enemy — someone who would stop at nothing in their quest, someone Jack was almost afraid to confront, but he knew also that it would be inevitable and soon.

Was it just incidental that the Casini trail had led him here, to this place? He had heard the whisperings. The breezes that stirred the ferns above his head, the same voices he had been hearing whispering through the pines earlier, when he had trodden the path beside the river. He listened and a deep longing stirred within him, flashes of memory, things he had almost forgotten came bubbling to the surface of his conscious mind. Faces, voices, the essence of one loved and lost so long ago, it was guiding him now … guiding him to this place … this

Abbey. Here was the answer, here was the key. Daniel had found something to guide him, he felt sure of that now. Other forces were leading him here, that he knew and he had also guessed who was behind the drama that might be played out here … in this place.

The clouds had moved swiftly now and the sky was full of the looming grey masses, but a shaft of late morning sun suddenly flooded the hollow with light and warmth. Jack turned his face gratefully toward it, his eyes dreamily watching the tumbling clouds as they raced to obscure the comforting warmth.

His preoccupied mind totally unaware that those same storm clouds and racing winds would be the harbinger of two more elements of his distant past.

Chapter 6

On Friars and ...

The task before Jack and Amos had been well planned. It had taken many months of painstaking fact finding and research to finally pin down this dot on the map ... with the help of an old friend. To install Amos as a confederate within was a coup, but the risk was great. Recognition by any of the criminals in question and Amos would be swiftly dealt with, as they held no qualms about wasting human life. It was a risk that Amos, who was well suited to the role, would take. Having spent a few years of his checkered life amid the high walls of a monastery, he had known what to expect when entering those hallowed grounds, so he had drawn the 'short straw' as he ruefully remarked.

Though Jack and Amos were aware that the remainder of their Special Forces group were not far away, the last thing they wanted now was for the Interpol cavalry to come charging in with all guns blazing. There would be time enough for that once they had the key figure. To show their hand too soon meant Casini could slip through their fingers again. He had shown before that he was indeed a slippery customer and could vanish into oblivion only to resurface in a different place. Worse still, now he had the convenience of an Abbey full of hostages

— Franciscan Friars held within their own monastery against their will. The safety of the monks of the Brotherhood was essential, even though the isolation of this spot would keep them somewhat contained, there were still the lives of those within that had to be carefully considered in the process. Stealth and caution were indeed the watchwords, along with the element of surprise.

Victor Casini was the supreme mastermind behind some of the cleverest of forgeries that the European world had seen. He was ruthless in his pursuit of rare books, manuscripts and fine works of art. Fervent collectors were happy to pay thousands for a rare item considered to be the only one of its kind in existence and Casini, as noted dealer in fine arts was only too happy to provide … no questions asked. He had the contacts; he had the means; he could deliver.

In catering to the assertively compulsive collector, who, providing he had the money would generally stop at nothing to obtain the object of his desire, Casini had found a profitable market. Procuring a rare item, which was in itself an infinite risk, required some liberal 'palm greasing', or more often than not some convenient blackmail in an effort to gain access to some of these treasures. Any unlawful dealings regarding thefts or mishandling of a treasured piece could not possibly be proclaimed, so many lips were sealed, sometimes permanently …

However, the eventual buyer, aware of course that to openly display such a rare piece would arouse incriminating and very awkward questions, could only covet his prize in secret and inwardly gloat over its acquisition … as would several other collectors in various parts of the world.

Therefore, to openly confess to owning a rare piece would be to invite suspicion and attract attention from the long arm of the law. Wealthy connoisseurs could then, on no account, risk open scandal and likely financial ruin were their 'only one of its kind in existence' prove to be either genuine *ob-jet d'art*, or an *ob-jet trou-ve* — a commonplace object presented as a genuine work of art. True, there were genuine artefacts, but Casini was clever enough to research his buyers and would hold certain genuine articles up for private auction at secret locations. This was a very lucrative enterprise, but also entailed a higher risk factor in obtaining it initially, so with the stakes lifted, it became a very delicate balance of power.

Somehow, Casini discovered that a monk from the Franciscan Order was himself an avid collector and the cause of several thefts of highly prized religious artefacts for which the blame had been falsely laid on his own shoulders. Not altogether happy about this accusation being allocated in this un-business-like manner, he set out to find this sacrilegious thief and eventually discovered him secreted away in an ancient Abbey perched on a remote mountain top.

Victor Casini had presented himself at the monastery as a traveller and found to his delight that not only had the said monk been recently relegated to the temporary position of Abbot for an indeterminate period, but this worthy personage also had a permanent 'staff' of artisans in residence at his disposal … so wonderfully convenient!

Historic pieces of literature, in books or parchments from various institutions, came into the Abbey for repair or rebinding or other detailed finishing. The reverend brothers in the Abbey were renowned masters in the arts of illuminating manuscripts, lithography and book binding done in the old ways using, where possible, the same materials as of centuries ago. The desire to equip his own library with some of these exquisite works of art were too much a temptation for the temporary Abbot in residence and so, over a period of time, many that left the Abbey after restoration were not as original as one would have expected them to be.

After obtaining a personal and private audience with the Abbot, it didn't take Mr Casini long to convince the good Friar that a semi-partnership in the 'business' would be of benefit to all and really, to him, there would be no point or gain in making the full truth known to the ecclesiastical hierarchy … unless there was a need. Things could continue as normal, but under new management.

The Abbot, now thoroughly backed into a murky little corner, had no choice but agree to the new arrangements.

So it was that Victor Casini, his younger brother Vinnie and two henchmen of doubtful parentage, soon took up residence within the Abbey. However, the semi-spartan subsistence that had suited the brothers of the Order, was not so readily accepted by these new arrivals. Their tastes were much more cosmopolitan and they preferred the pleasures and little luxuries that life could and had, until now, afforded them.

Changes began to take place much to the chagrin of the Abbot and his disciples, who, though not minding some of the influx of modern living conditions that infiltrated into the hallowed halls, were still resentful, mainly at having the well-ordered regime of their lives changed.

A wave of unrest had begun simmering among the few, which at times threatened to spread into a minor revolt spurred on by one or two of the younger lay brothers, as they all too soon realised that they had become prisoners within their own walls. They suffered the indignity of being locked in their quarters at night and accompanied during the day by a 'minder' with a

45-calibre pistol being waved under their noses, should they even consider an objection.

What was worse, their leader — the Abbot — was doing nothing to stop these unorthodox individuals and indeed appeared quite frightened of them. Perhaps there was truth in the rumours that the Abbot had something to hide and perhaps he was more deeply involved in the unlawful activities that had been taking place under their noses that they didn't like to talk about, at least openly.

Victor had once again left the Abbey, 'on business' and once again Vinnie had been left in charge. His mood was not improved when a delegation of the brothers announced that they would no longer be treated like slaves in an enterprise that was severely compromising the very roots of their reputations in the work of fine art. It was time to speak out and voice their opinions, which were taken none too kindly by the three equally despondent desperados, who immediately decided to act. So, to further frighten them into submission, the monks were herded into a restless group in the main courtyard. Vinnie's intention was to let off a few rounds of gunfire accompanied by some harsh words and threats and hoped it would return them to a submissive state before Victor returned.

All this however was very much to the bewilderment of one scraggy visitor, who had presented himself at the gate that very day in search of shelter and free food, firmly believing it was a place of refuge and that he would be treated kindly. Instead, he found himself embroiled in some sort of civil war, not at all what he had expected! True, he had hesitated about going to the Abbey, but he was getting too old now to be fossicking around himself for food and shelter as there were not too many people in the village willing to employ him. He had figured he'd do a winter up here then maybe head north again. Now, it seemed he had walked into complete chaos — there were men with guns here … in the Abbey?

The Casini group had come well prepared and were not about to let anyone, even a ragged tramp at the door — loudly proclaiming it was nothing to do with him — interfere with the plans afoot. So, Eddie, along with the rest of the resident clergy, were hustled at gunpoint into the courtyard, where barked commands and several volleys of gunfire over their heads seemed to have the desired effect of quietening the now terrified monks.

The Abbot, his nerves now thoroughly shattered, stood close to the wall of the bell tower, trembling and wringing his hands in disbelief … how could it all have come to this? What had he done? Surely this now must be divine retribution for the many secret transfers to his own library of many valuable manuscripts … not to mention other small treasures gathered up along the way. They were all being punished … and it was his fault!

Then, in a desperate attempt of some measure of atonement for his sins, the Abbot gathered his robes about him and fled as fast as his legs could carry him up the steep winding staircase to the bell tower high above the courtyard. Slamming the small door shut, he pulled off his corded girdle, desperate thoughts running amok through his head. He hoped to elude his pursuers long enough to attempt a suicide bid by hanging himself from one of the huge support beams of the tower roof, also hoping that his God would help him, or at the very least forgive …

Having no idea at all about how to fulfil such a dire demise, he stood for a brief moment with the cord in his hand. It was now he realised that he would have to clamber up on to the small parapet that ran around the edge of the tower floor, in order to even reach any of the heavy beams that crisscrossed the vaulted ceiling. Would the cord be long enough? How was he to throw it over the beam? Was it strong enough? One clear thought did emerge from his befuddled mind at this point — he should have chosen a less complicated way to do away with himself … if that was what he really wanted to do.

Gingerly he climbed onto the bordering parapet, hugging one of the huge stone pillars as he did so. He clung to the pillar and looked down to a sea of faces staring up at him, faces and figures that looked so small beneath him and only then did he become aware of his fear of heights. Hearing the shouts from below and the heavy pounding of footsteps on the winding stair behind him, only caused his hands to tremble more violently and his feeble efforts to throw the cord up only allowed it to drop from his fumbling fingers and spiral down to the courtyard below.

In an effort to grab at the falling cord, the now hopelessly disorientated Abbot found himself teetering precariously on the very edge of the narrow parapet and in trying to keep his balance he threw his hands instinctively upward. Fortunately, his frantically grasping and scrabbling fingers closed over a thick rope; the bell pull, which immediately came away from its mooring, a great hook on the supporting pillar. A terrified scream issued from his open mouth as he felt himself falling and he instinctively tightened his grip on the rope as his body was swung into space; he became a living and extremely vocal pendulum.

The added weight of the terrified Abbot on the end of the bell rope carried the unfortunate man out and over the edge of the parapet, at the same time the great bell began its upward roll, the huge clapper resounding with a tremendous clamour. The Abbot's mouth opened and emitted another shrill scream that became a mute pantomime in the deafening peal of the bell and of the sheer terror that was overtaking him. The same abysmal drop to the ground below far outweighed his conscience-stricken mind of any thoughts of self- destruction, the need for self-preservation was now the uppermost thought in his tortured mind. He tightened his grip on the rope as his pendulum swing now took him rapidly back to the tower, he closed his eyes and waited for his body to slam into the buttressed stonework.

He was, however, to be saved from his perilous position by a swift turn of events. His ardent pursuers in the form of Vinnie, with one of the younger, fitter monks, had raced up the stairway after the fleeing Abbot and arrived panting and breathless from their exertion onto the tower floor. They had only a moment to witness the venerable brother, clinging tightly to the bell rope making his pendulous swing back to the tower, his mouth still opened wide and his voluminous grey habit flapping about his unclothed legs like a half-open umbrella.

As the Abbot's legs passed over their heads, the young monk made a quick grab for them and was successful in grasping one bony ankle, the momentum of the Abbot's swing dragging him across the rough floor of the tower for a short distance, before the startled Vinnie recovered enough to throw himself on top as an added weight. The bell was beginning its downward roll and the slackness in the rope had the desired effect in allowing the now hysterical Abbot to release his hold as he came to a relatively soft landing on top of his rescuers.

Amid a confusion of arms and legs and grey cloth, three bodies managed to untangle themselves into separate identities. Vinnie was the first to recover and he began dragging the unhappy Abbot to his feet. To admonish the now thoroughly dejected Abbot was not going to achieve anything Vinnie decided, as he stood glaring at the man swaying unsteadily before him, his unbelted habit falling about him like an untidy tent. Instead, he promptly frogmarched both clergy back down the stairway, making sure the Abbot was between the younger monk and himself as they retraced their steps to re-join the subdued remainder of the residents waiting in the courtyard.

Vinnie's problems with the rebellious inmates however, was not yet over. The ragged individual who had been swept up in this minor revolt was not about to let himself be incarcerated with the rest of the grey-robed Friars, he had noted that the heavy iron-gates to the Priory were securely locked — there had to be a way of escape.

To the irrational mind of Eddie, this was not what he imagined a monastic existence to be. The cloaked and hooded figures should be chanting their prayers, or otherwise going about the business that monks do … but here was complete anarchy! Unnoticed by the others during the daring rescue of the Abbot, Eddie had stepped into a narrow passageway at the side of the courtyard.

Looking fearfully behind him in case he was being followed, he hurried along it only to find his way blocked by a room, the door of which was slightly ajar. With nowhere else to go, he pushed the door open and stepping inside, closed the door carefully behind him.

As his eyes became accustomed to the gloomy interior, he realised with a stab of fear that he must be in a room that had been occupied by these men with the guns, at least that was what it looked like. Apart from two beds on the far side of the room and several suitcases spilling their contents onto them, the only other object was a large wooden box in the middle of the floor.

Chapter 7

... Fireworks

Curiously, Eddie approached the box. The lid was half off and a familiar smell greeted his nostrils, something that stirred his memory. He reached inside and his groping fingers closed over what felt like short greasy sticks of something. He drew one out and looked at it. Yes, it was. It was a stick of dynamite — T.N.T.! What were they doing with that sort of stuff here, he wondered? Cautiously he felt around further in the box and his hand closed over a heavy round object, he knew from the feel of it as he drew it out carefully just what it was — a hand grenade. He had hated his short stint in the army and apart from the endless marching, he had been given the task, with several others, of moving explosives and other armoury from one place to another and he had become familiar with these things. He thought he knew immediately where this stuff had come from, but why would they want it here ... in a monastery?

He didn't have much time to ponder the subject further as a slight noise outside the door alerted him and he quickly took refuge in the dark corner behind the door. Peeping from around the door, he saw a grey robed, hooded figure glided into the room and a thin direct beam of light from a small powerful torch swept the room, it then settled on the open crate. Eddie heard the figure give a soft grunt as the beam of the torch washed over the contents, then the torch was switched off as the man turned to exit the room, then stopped.

Eddie held his breath; sure he had been seen. There was a moment of electrifying tension as he waited for a hand to reach out and grab him. He had the impression the face beneath the hood was looking directly at him, but suddenly the cloaked figure strode from the room and was gone.

Fully realising the danger now of lingering in the room, Eddie made a hasty decision. Darting back to the crate, his probing hands closed over one of the grenades and what felt like a very small bundle of dynamite sticks. He shoved them as quickly and as carefully as he could into his old hessian bag that he carried his meagre possessions in and quickly slipped out of the room.

He'd blow his way out if he had to, there was something going on here that he didn't understand, but whatever it was; these men with their guns meant business and he, for one didn't want to be involved in it. Perhaps a boring life in the village wasn't so boring anymore, the sooner he got back there and alerted the authorities the better, he might even be hailed as a hero!

Clutching the bag gingerly to his chest, Eddie began to make his way quickly back down the passageway reaching the courtyard again in time to see the Abbot being escorted from the bell tower to re-join the now mostly silent group of monks. The other two men had been engrossed in watching the drama unfolding above their heads, but now turned back to the shuffling group of monks. Nobody seemed to notice Eddie moving surreptitiously behind a couple of the robed figures at the back of the courtyard in an effort of concealment. Eddie also wondered which of these grey robes covered the one who had followed him into the room.

Circling the restless group, Eddie made his way slowly and carefully back to where the great iron-gates stood adjacent to the church. The Abbot, he noticed, was seated on one of the stone benches, his head in his hands and he appeared to be muttering to himself. The big black bearded one, the one they called Bruno was standing next to him, one foot up on the bench, his gun cradled on his arm and berating the distressed Abbot for employing such a rash action. The third member of the group, he knew as Leo, hovered anxiously nearby. A lean sallow-skinned entity, his gaunt features were highlighted by deep-set dark eyes that seemed to constantly flicker. A thin wisp of straggly beard clung to his retreating chin and his nervous hands tugged at it now and then.

Eddie fingered the hessian bag, feeling the shape of the explosives hidden inside, while he groped in his pocket for the cigarette lighter he always carried. He realised he'd have to act quickly now while they were otherwise occupied. He was standing fairly close to the church now and wondering what to do next. A diversion … yes, he'd create a diversion, then while they were busy with that, he could blow the gate away. Once down the hill and safe in the village, he could prove his worth. He would explain what was happening here to the proper authorities and they would come and arrest these men for whatever it was that they were doing here. He was sure it was for evil purposes, but, whatever … he would be a hero and prove his worth in the community.

Slipping behind one of the stone pillars that supported the cloisters, he opened his bag and grasped one of the dynamite sticks. His shaking fingers flicked the lighter into flame and he applied it to the short fuse, which, at first refused to light. Peering around the pillar he could see that the three men were beginning to get the monks organised to move them on and some were coming toward the church. Frantically he tried again and this time the wick sputtered into life. Without any more hesitation Eddie flung the stick as hard as he could into the church, where it rolled to the centre of the nave. His half-crazed idea to draw attention away from the gate was soon realised, as a massive explosion rocked the sacred citadel, the crash of breaking glass and the smell of acrid smoke filling the air.

The group in the courtyard threw themselves on the ground shrieking and covering their heads with their hands. Eddie stood transfixed for a moment horrified at what he had just done. A shout from the other side of the courtyard brought him back to his senses and he looked up to see Vinnie and Bruno beginning to run toward him. Eddie turned, eyes wide with fear now, dashed into the large, long refectory building, fumbling with his bag as he ran, dropping the lighter in his haste.

Thoroughly confused, Eddie had run straight past the gate he had meant to blow apart and it was not until he was inside that he realised his mistake, but he could hear the angry voices shouting outside with the bellowing voice of Bruno almost upon him.

Frantically he scrabbled in the bag, his fingers closing over the hard metal lump that was the hand grenade. Holding it tightly in his hand within the bag, he looked briefly about him, but could see no other exit, just a long building filled with beds, cupboards and some partitioned areas — no other way out!

Thinking this escape out in his mind had been easy, but the real undertaking of such an act was a lot more daunting, his dramatic escape to freedom had turned into a disaster. Eddie was now feeling only mad, blind panic as the shouts became nearer — he *had* to get out!

Eddie closed his eyes and pulled the pin, throwing the bag as far as he could toward the outer wall of the refectory.

The multiple explosions when they came lifted him off his feet, flinging him backward into a sprawling, stunned heap. He lay motionless for some moments, his ears ringing, deafened by the blast in the close confines, even though the building had been relatively large. Bricks and dust were still falling about him, the air heavy and choking. He could not see any light, it was black above where he lay and he felt he was suffocating. Eddie tried to push himself to his feet, only to discover that a heavy cupboard had fallen partway across him, its bulk partially supported on an iron bed frame. This had saved him from being crushed completely; it was with some difficulty that he managed to wriggle out from under it and crawled out onto piles of rubble.

He thrust his fists into his eyes and tried to clear them to see just what had happened. His mouth was dry and full of dust, it felt like someone was hitting him on the head with a hammer, the air was hot and choking … but at least now he could see a little.

Swirling clouds of smoke and crackling flames mingling with the acridity of the detonation took his breath away, holding him spellbound as he clutched the bed frame for support. Eddie could feel blood trickling down his forehead and he touched it gingerly with his finger.

Across the wreckage of the building, he could see wavering figures silhouetted against a background of sunlight streaked with black smoke. That same acrid smoke caught in his throat and burned his lungs as he tried to breathe, but sheer terror had overtaken him, amid paroxysms of coughing he managed to hoist himself properly to his feet.

Eddie stood there swaying, trying to see through the blinding billows of smoke, he could see that there was now light streaming through what was left of the outer wall of the building. Where there had been a solid wall, there was now an enormous gap and a great pile of rubble. Above his head he could see the roof beams ablaze, with burning pieces dropping into the debris below, adding more fuel to the fire rapidly spreading there.

Figures … he could see figures gesticulating and hear muffled shouting, though he could barely hear anything for the ringing noises within his head, but the great gap in the outer wall beckoned him and Eddie began to stagger toward it, stumbling over the broken furniture. He reached the open space and gulped in a great lungful of fresh air, then began to run.

Looking back over his shoulder as he staggered and stumbled over the blocks of fallen masonry, he could see several figures trying to follow. They were obviously shouting at him, but the roaring in his ears made it impossible to hear properly and in his deafened state he could make out nothing. One cloaked figure was pointing away from the direction he was heading, but by now Eddie was completely disorientated, blood was pouring into his eyes from the gash on his head, but he felt he was running for his life down the hill and home.

Suddenly a large rock loomed up in front of him and he scrambled to the top of it, only to find to his horror that the roaring noise in his ears was not still from the explosion, but from the tumbling torrent of water cascading below him! He stood poised, unbalanced on the rock for a split second before his overwhelming momentum carried him forward, to fall headlong into the seething fast-moving water.

Chapter 8

A Surprise Attack

The sound of the wind stirring through the pine trees became a restless and melancholy sigh that portentously echoed down through to the brackens and ferns, their long fronds tossing restlessly when a fitful breeze caught them in a turbulent embrace. The approaching storm was still a little distance off yet, but the preceding probing gusts were already gathering the dry leaves from the trees and whirling them in a merry sporadic dance through the surrounding forest, until they would eventually fall, exhausted, to pile up into deep drifts and heaped against the boles of the great trees.

Lingering rays of a setting sun flickered through the tops of the pines, throwing a glittering array of light, like golden candles on a Christmas tree. Streaks of pink and gold outlined rolling clouds, constantly changing their shape from a kaleidoscope of colour to the deep greys and purples of the gathering night.

It was under this cloud of sound and shadows that a man stood waiting under a large elm tree that overhung a stone wall. After finding the breach in the outer wall, although narrow and partially obstructed, he had little difficulty in pushing his lean body through the space. A tiny red dot on his wristwatch alerted him now, as he made his careful way through the broken crumble of bricks. There was still just enough light to see that he was standing in what was a small orchard, beyond which was what presumably had once been kitchen gardens. The corner of a substantial stone structured building was only a few yards in front of him and it was from there he could now hear the voices clearly. The tiny transceiver he wore strapped to his body brought the voices into such close proximity, they could have been standing beside him.

'But, but … I really should get them in, if I don't do it now, they'll be soaked, as I'm sure it's going to rain tonight.' The deep voice was plaintive and tremulant, 'it will only take a minute to collect them.'

'Bloody great *oaf*, why couldn't you think of this earlier? It's cold out there and my feet are freezing! So just make it snappy and don't try anything funny, I'm not in the mood for playing hide and seek!'

The voice that spoke was thin and reedy, a vacuous pitch that seemed to suit the individual from whom it issued. Jack, watching from the shadows saw them emerge from the building through a heavy wooden door that creaked open on its great iron hinges. In the light of the open doorway, a short thick set grey robed figure appeared, closely followed by a man of medium to thin build, the glowing cigarette that he held to his lips highlighting a wispy straggle of beard.

*   *   *

Leo stayed in the doorway, leaning up against the framework, the hand that held a thick coat closed over his body to protect from the chill air, also held an automatic pistol. He watched the monk move away into the gloom before taking another draw on the cigarette, but his eyes were flickering this way and that as he smoked nervously. He had glanced up at the lowering sky and drew his coat closer to his lean body. It did look as if it was going to be a cold wet night … and he hated the cold.

He disliked this place, disliked having to be a watchdog over these stupid monks. It was like being on another goddamn planet! It was at the end of the world as far as he was concerned. He'd be glad when the boss came back, only another day or so and they could get on with what they had come to do then he could get back to a place where it was warmer with real people to talk to. He disliked the cold winds that seemed to come through the very walls, the stone floors and every conceivable crack in this medieval monstrosity of a place. How could these monks live here in a place like this year after year! He shook his head; it was totally beyond his comprehension.

He shivered slightly as the wind picked up, the cold breezes howling around these old buildings and rattling at the windows, seeped into his bones. More than once he'd felt regret that he hadn't stayed in the little coastal village he had come from, where the balmy Mediterranean climate was now only a comforting memory. He could wait, it would not be long before he would be a very rich man and living in a large sumptuous villa on a sun drenched mountainside overlooking the sea. It would no longer be a dream but a reality … he would live like a king! He smiled as he pictured his life.

His smile vanished quickly as something caught his eye, for a brief moment, he though he saw a tiny pinpoint of light appear from somewhere beyond him in the darkness. Damn! This place was spooky…that was it! He was about to call out to the monk to get him back to where he could see him, when there was a sudden cry and a groan from a point away to the left where the monk had gone. Leo dropped the cigarette butt and stepped from the light of the doorway, one hand groping in his coat pocket for his torch and the other firmly grasping the gun now held forward in front of him.

He had only moved a few tentative steps, when he felt a hand close over his wrist holding the gun, a hand that held his wrist in a vice like grip. At the same time, any cry that may have issued from his lips was choked from him by a powerful arm that was encircling his throat, crushing the very breath from him. A deep menacing voice was whispering very close to his ear. 'Bloody great oaf are we?' The arm drew tighter on his throat, 'I need a bloody good reason not to break your skinny neck right now.'

A soft voice nearby spoke, 'Not yet, Amos, maybe later … if he doesn't cooperate.'

Leo felt the presence of another person close beside him and the gun extracted from his now nerveless fingers.

*   *   *

Vinnie was restless, he had been pacing up and down a well-worn carpet in front of a glowing fire in a room on one side of the Chapter House. A well-appointed room, usually reserved for senior clergy and filled with bookshelves with comfortable overstuffed chairs, one of them occupied now by a man playing Solitaire with a pack of cards. A well-built heavy faced man with a full black beard and an equally thick thatch of black hair.

'Aagh!' Bruno threw the cards down onto the table drawn up in front of him, 'I'm bored with this.' He picked up a fine crystal goblet from the table, the heavy gold ring on the little finger of his right hand clunked on the stem of the glass as he raised it to his lips. Taking a mouthful of the deep red wine, he savoured it around his palate, then looked critically at the remainder, holding it up against the light, then swirling it around the side of the glass.

'You know, Vinnie, this stuff is not too bad once you get a taste for it — could do with a bit more refining though.' He leaned back in the armchair and put one foot up on the corner of the table. 'Maybe we could do a little marketing with this too, just needs a bit more finishing.' He tilted the glass so that the few visible dregs had now settled on the bottom.

Vinnie stopped pacing and stared at Bruno incredulously, then spoke harshly. 'Obviously it hasn't registered in that thick skull of yours Bruno; that we are in big trouble here!' He stared at Bruno angrily awhile before resuming his pacing, then said testily, 'Vic and Moody are due back anytime now with the engineers, how the hell are we going to explain why we've got a bloody great hole in the front wall!' He kicked savagely at the end of a piece of wood that threatened to dislodge itself from the fire, sending a shower of sparks everywhere.

'Who the hell let that village idiot get in here anyway? No one was supposed to be let in through that gate at all, someone's stuffed up and I can't keep an eye on every goddamn thing. Vic is not going to be happy about this, I can tell you!'

'Yeah.' Bruno shifted his foot off the table and stood up. 'I know it's going to take some explaining, but how were we to know the village idiot was going to get his hands on that stuff and chuck it around like that!' He threw the dregs from the glass into the fire and set the glass on the mantelpiece. 'Shouldn't have been able to get anywhere near it in the first place anyway!' He threw a scornful glance at Vinnie, 'you were supposed to keep that door locked, that box was your responsibility.'

The anger was visibly rising in Vinnie's face. 'If you had kept a closer watch on that dumb Abbot like you were supposed to and not expect me to go after him instead of doing something about it yourself, I wouldn't have left it unlocked, would I!' He turned back to Bruno and shook his fist at him, 'you like always, are just too damn slow to react, but you can always find good reasons later!'

They stared at each other in hostile silence for a while before Vinnie spoke again. 'Someone let that idiot through the gate, I don't know who did, but we weren't to let anyone else in after that monk came through that time to see the Abbot. Vic gave strict instructions to keep everyone else out, the less people who come up here the better, so ... who let him in?'

Bruno spread his hands, 'I don't know, maybe one of the monks did, maybe Leo did, he was the one keeping an eye on the gate!' He snorted scornfully, 'Leo can't be trusted to follow simple orders anyway.'

'It must have been one of the people from the village, though why he'd want to come here beats me,' said Vinnie, 'looked like a tramp anyway.' He sat down heavily into one of the other armchairs and was lost in thought for a while, then said, 'Probably one of the monks talked Leo into letting him in because of the wayfarer policy these monks have, I'm just damn glad that lot that came up the hill that day and must have been looking for him turned tail and ran ... something must have scared them.'

Bruno grinned. 'Yeah, they think this place is haunted, can't say I blame 'em either, it is a bit creepy what with all those tombs down below,' he laughed, 'You know Leo is shit scared of the whole place, can't wait to get this all over with and go home.' He kicked at the fire, then bent to put another piece of wood onto the glowing coals and stood in front of it rubbing his backside.

'Anyway, from what I saw when that guy went over the falls, I very much doubt he would be alive to tell the tale.'

There was silence from them both for some moments, 'Where is Leo anyway?' said Vinnie, he's been gone a long time hasn't he?'

'Should be back any time now.' Bruno had resumed his seat and picked up the cards again, 'He's out the back. That monk that runs the kitchen suddenly remembered he'd left some things hanging outside and wanted to bring them in. Says it's going to rain tonight and by the look of those clouds that rolled up this afternoon, I reckon it will. I've checked on all the others and locked them in while Leo went out with him. He usually keeps close to that one anyway, says he's just a big pussy cat, all brawn and no brain, he's a good cook though.' He shuffled the cards expertly as he spoke, but Vinnie was silent and thoughtful.

'That monk,' said Vinnie after a long pause, 'isn't he the one we let in before Victor left?'

'Yeah,' said Bruno dealing the cards again, 'he was the one that turned up carrying all those papers, religious papers or whatever and said that the Abbot was expecting him, that they were to have some sort of discussion on them. Said he'd gone to a great deal of trouble to get whatever it was, but he was beginning to think he might have got the wrong monastery. It's way beyond me, all this religious stuff, too complicated.'

Vinnie was silent again, he was thinking. 'I remember when Leo brought him in, I was there with the Abbot at the time and he didn't seem to know who this guy was. I thought it was a bit strange at the time, but the Abbot is such a queer mixed up sort of nutter that I just figured he'd forgotten that he was bringing him these papers.'

'Well, from what we know of the Abbott's private little

collection, I guess he has a right to feel a bit edgy.'

This was all quite true of course.

*   *   *

When Amos, peering over the thick glasses he wore, had been ushered into the Abbot's presence, the clergyman had declared he did not know who he was, or why he had come. Amos would have preferred to have been left alone with the man, but instinctively realised that was not going to happen. These were dangerous waters, he fervently hoped his disguise of the grey habit and thick glasses plus a hesitant and faltering demeanour would be enough to convince the group that he was who he pretended to be, an unobtrusive, dedicated member of the Holy Order.

He was also becoming aware of a slightly disoriented state of mind in the Abbot, so became a little more insistent about his errand. Surely the Abbot must remember the papers and illustrations of the sacred frescoes by Pietro Cavellini of St. Francis in the monastery in Perugia that he had been most anxious to see? Why, he himself had gone to so much trouble to obtain the precious copies and had come at the express bidding of the Abbot.

The Abbot opened his mouth to speak, but Amos got in before him, 'Oh dear, oh dear,' he said in a disappointed tone as he began to gather up the folder from the table where he had placed it. 'Then you have not received my forwarding letter. I had hoped it arrived at the correct monastery.' He adjusted his glasses nervously and said hurriedly. 'I rather think I have arrived at a most inopportune time for you I see.' He cast a quick glance at Vinnie and Leo, who were standing close by. 'Perhaps I had better depart for the moment and leave you with your, er, colleagues and call another time. I can find lodgings in the village, I am sure.'

As he fully expected, he was ushered, not to the gate by which he had entered, but to another part of the Abbey and a large airy room, where he was eyed curiously by a group of grey robed Friars seated at various worktables. In odd contrast, a black-bearded hulk of a man was seated in an armchair turning the pages of a book, while on his knees rested an ominous looking pistol. It was, as Amos had surmised, a hostile environment with the monk's virtual prisoners within their own walls. He quickly became integrated with the other residents, not giving too much away, but quickly proving his worth and talents in the kitchen to where he was appointed. His culinary skills in that department soon made him an indispensable member of the society and to all there, he seemed genuinely of a rather nervous and timid nature, despite his obviously powerful build. 'A tame gorilla,' Leo had remarked to the others one day, when he had returned from shepherding Amos around the rabbit traps he often set in the surrounding bush, to help supplement the food supply.

However, something about Amos had always worried Vinnie. He felt sure he had known him, seen him … perhaps a photo, there seemed a vague hint of recognition there. He had brushed it aside, as perhaps, a coincidental thing, most people were supposed to have a double. Someone with much the same features somewhere in the world, but he couldn't see that this great bumbling fool of a monk, could have been anyone associated with his world. All the same he would have much preferred now that Leo dismissed this man's request, regardless how short the duration. It was difficult enough keeping watch over them during the day, but at night in this

'Rabbit Warren' of a place, it would be impossible. It only needed one to slip away and raise the alarm and the whole enterprise would be lost.

Victor had repeatedly told his younger brother that money speaks all languages and anyone can be 'bought', if enough incentive were dangled in front of them. Indications were already surfacing that one or two, particularly among the younger lay brothers, would perhaps only need a little more encouragement to bend the ecclesiastical rules of course, should a reasonable gratuity be offered. It just might take a little time to convince them.

The point was, the Casini's needed the skills these artisans possessed and they could not afford to lose any of them now it was better to have an agreeable working system than a coercive one. In any case, there were always ways to dispose of those that did not agree entirely with the proposals put before them.

Vinnie turned to Bruno, who with a grunt of triumph, had just succeeded in getting all the cards in the right sequence. 'Bruno, Leo has been gone too long. I don't like it. Go and get him and see he's locked that monk up in his room. I don't care what excuses he's making.'

'Yeah okay.' Bruno stood up and stretched, then walked over to the door. 'Wouldn't expect Leo to want to be outside for too long anyway, it's too cold out there.' He opened the door and was immediately encumbered with the securely bound and gagged body of Leo falling on top of him, eyes wide open with fear, as the first rumble of thunder sounded overhead.

Vinnie's face was a picture of surprise and anger, which deepened to a savage scowl as he sat back in his chair close to the fire on the orders of the two intruders. Bruno had rolled Leo's bound body from where it had fallen on top of him and was sitting staring stupidly up at the barrel of a revolver levelled at his head.

'Nice to meet you again, Vinnie, it's been quite a while hasn't it?' Jack said, as he stepped into the room, 'I think you already know my friend here — Mr McAllister?' A little incident in Milan I believe with a stolen painting that brought you to his attention, among a few other things. However, that was of course under different circumstances.'

Vinnie was glaring now at Amos who was directing a bewildered Bruno to a straight- backed chair nearby and deftly slipping a pair of handcuffs over his wrists held taut behind the back of the chair.

'I knew there was something about you that was familiar,' growled Vinnie, and made a move to rise from the chair.

'No, no, don't bother to get up, we can talk just as comfortably here,' Jack pulled the other armchair up closer to the fire opposite Vinnie and sat, cradling his gun in an almost careless manner in his fingers. Vinnie sat back in his chair tight lipped, a set and determined look on his face but a trace of his fear remained, his eyes moving from one to the other of these unexpected visitors.

'So, Vinnie, when is big brother coming back?'

'How the hell would I know,' snarled Vinnie, 'we might as well be in bloody Siberia for all the information we get here!'

'I really can't believe that,' said Jack softly. 'I'm sure you have excellent communication with the outside world.'

'Yeah, we send up bloody smoke signals!' said Vinnie with a sarcastic sneer as he turned his head to stare moodily into the fire. Vinnie was angry ... and afraid, this intrusion by two feared representatives of the law, was something none of them had counted on. He knew very well who they were, but neither he, nor Victor had expected to be tracked to this remote Abbey.

Victor had said that no one would even think of looking twice at such a place, but Vinnie had viewed it with scepticism. He would have preferred the anonymous protection of a busy city, where one could truly disappear at will. Here, he felt isolated and exposed, in spite of what his brother had insisted on.

Several moments of silence followed, broken only by a clock on a mantel over the fireplace ticking away. Vinnie, staring into the fire was worried at this turn of events. Vic was going to be as mad as hell when he returned and there was no way at the moment that he could warn him that he could be walking into a trap. He cursed silently, at least in the city there were generally scouts, early warning lookouts that foretold of any undue interest by the arm of the law ... but here!

Why hadn't he followed his instincts when he had first laid eyes on that monk? Of course, in Victor's eyes it would be all his fault ... it always was.

Vinnie had been staring fixedly into the fire as he tried to think of a way out of the present predicament. They'd had tense moments before, he'd just have to wait his chance. He knew these men, knew they'd try to get information out of him, but he was not going to divulge anything.

The fire seemed to be burning brighter now than it had when he had first looked at it. Great tongues of red and yellow flames were flickering this way and that, their curling tendrils of barbed crimson almost reaching out to where he sat transfixed by their writhing shapes. Strangely he felt as if he were being slowly drawn into the all-consuming fury of it as it burned brighter, as if fed by an invisible force. It was mesmerising and his face reflected the fiery glow as he leaned further forward, his eyes fixed on the dancing flames. He began to think of nothing else ... the flames were drawing him into the bottomless pit they were issuing from … he could feel himself falling …

Wrenching his eyes away with an effort he passed a hand over his forehead and felt it glowing hot with beads of sweat beginning to form. There was panic rising in his throat and it was difficult to swallow. Dimly, as if from a great distance he could hear Bruno trying to say something, but it was unintelligible, mainly because Amos' hand was clamped over his mouth.

Vinnie's head was reeling, the flames so close, he felt he had to tear himself away, as he lifted his head and looked up, his eyes came into contact with Jack's now dark grey ones fixed firmly on his. The flames were still there, but they were reflected in the steady unwavering gaze searching his and he could now no longer look away.

'When is Victor returning and who will be with him?' the question was asked again, the voice now cold and hard.

'The day after tomorrow as far as we know,' came the sullen reply after a pause. 'Moody will be with him, maybe one other. I don't know, he didn't tell me everything.'

'Anyone else we should know about?'

'A couple of engineers and some equipment they're bringing with them.'

'Hmm, this must be to do with the explosives you've got stored here isn't it, Vinnie, what do they plan to do with them, or do I have to guess?'

Vinnie was moving restlessly in his chair. 'They … they're going to open up some of those crypts under the Abbey and put in a permanent water supply, from the river and install some machinery.' He bit his lip and frowned, muttering almost indistinctly, 'We picked up the wrong stuff, which was Leo's fault, should never have trusted him to get it in the first place. I thought he knew what he was doing — *bloody* idiot!'

Vinnie's voice was hesitant now. 'This was all Victor's idea; he wants to expand the business!'

Jack was silent for a moment or two. 'Moody, hmm, that wouldn't be Moody Brahman now would it?' he said, turning to glance at Amos who was stepping over the prostrate body of Leo, who, in turn was glaring at Vinnie with hateful eyes. 'I think we know him don't we, Amos?'

'Certainly do, Jack.' Amos was busy untying Leo's feet and shoving him into another chair. 'If my memory serves me correctly, he was released from prison about three months ago. Forgery, supposed to be the best in the business, never met him, but I've read his dossier.'

'Expand the business eh, Vinnie? Well, I'm not sure it will be the brightest thing to do, I rather think he might be pushing his luck a bit. You should be aware that it's going to attract a lot more attention than the scheme he's got running at the moment. Greed will be his downfall and yours too Vinnie, big brother isn't always right you know,' said Jack, shaking his head at Vinnie.

A flash of lightning suddenly lit up the room, to be followed seconds later by the booming crash of thunder. The rumblings they had been hearing in the distance were now evident above them and echoes of the first clap of thunder had barely died away before another reverberated through the lightning slashed sky. It was immediately followed by the steady drumming of wind driven rain that hammered at the dark mullioned windows. The promised deluge had begun.

Jack cast a glance out at the stormy darkness lit occasionally by the lightning flashes and said, 'It's going to be a cold, wet night, Amos; however, after we've finished our little chat here, I'm sure you can find a cosy and private cell where we can accommodate these gentlemen for the next few days. I'll help to escort them to their new lodgings, then perhaps I'll have a quiet word with the Abbot.'

Vinnie snorted. 'You won't get much out of him,' he muttered when he was dragged to his feet and hustled over to join his confederates, Amos deftly tying his hands behind his back. 'He's a complete nutter, apart from being in the same business and up to his reverential neck in it, so it's no surprise he tried to make a messy splash in the courtyard below the bell tower.'

Jack chose to ignore the remark as he and Amos got their captives to their feet. Amos grasped the front of Leo's shirt and hauled him to his feet with one hand bringing his face very close to his own. The blue eyes locked onto Leo's and the gruff voice was cold and compelling, 'If I were you Leo, I would be very careful that you don't give any reason for this 'tame gorilla' to tear you apart with his bare hands.'

Leo opened and closed his eyes and glanced quickly across to Vinnie, then back to those intense blue eyes, now minus the thick glasses, so close to his own. His face screwed up as he tried to say something, but it came out as a muffled expletive through the gag in his mouth.

'I think he's trying to tell you something, Amos,' said Jack.

'And perhaps I don't want to hear it.'

After confiscating the huge bunch of keys that ensured all the other inmates were confined to their quarters, Jack and Amos deposited Vinnie, Bruno and Leo into an empty cell apartment comfortable enough to accommodate them and locked them in. They saw no immediate need to free the other monks at this time, things were better left as they were, any explanation could wait until morning.

It was some little while later that Jack returned from the Abbots private quarters and found Amos busy preparing a light supper in the huge old kitchen.

'Guess you didn't get very far with the Abbot, Jack,' Amos said as he set a plate of food and a mug of coffee down on the long bench table.

'No, I didn't, he's highly agitated and very unresponsive, I can't reach his mind right now and I'm a bit worried that he might consider the easy way out before we've had a chance to talk to him. He doesn't know me and he's very suspicious of my intentions, even though he is aware that there has been a change of power over Vinnie and his confederates, he seems very unsure of his own position.'

Jack took up the mug of coffee and said quietly, 'You know him better that I do, Amos, perhaps it might be a wise move for you to pay the Abbot a visit before it gets too late. Your little box of tricks just might keep him blissfully quiet for a time. To me he seems desperate, I think he's got a lot more he can tell me. Do what you think is necessary to make him comfortable and perhaps he'll be more responsive in the morning.'

Another loud crack of thunder rumbled overhead, its reverberating echoes bouncing off the not-too-distant mountains. 'Quite a storm we're having, but I also fear all this on top of what has happened might have an adverse effect on the Abbot's state of mind,' continued Jack. 'He could consider it the wrath of his God, as I get the impression that Vinnie may have been telling the truth when he suggested the Abbot's mind is hanging in a precarious balance, so I would make haste if I were you lad and calm him down. It's no good me going back there, he doesn't trust me. Perhaps after a good night's sleep he'll feel better about talking to us in the morning.'

Amos had been foraging in the back of the extensive pantry while Jack was talking, and soon returned carrying a small black leather case. He placed it on the table and opened it to reveal a small but very comprehensively compact medical kit. Under Jack's watchful eye, he selected a package containing some tiny white tablets, a phial of colourless liquid, and a small syringe that fitted neatly into a slender capsule. He filled the syringe carefully from the phial, tapping away the air bubble, and slid it into the capsule snapping it shut. He returned the medical kit to its hidden cache deep in the bowels of the pantry and selected a bottle of wine from the huge racks that lined the entrance to the pantry. Gathering up the package of tablets and the capsule, he slipped them into one of the deep pockets of his robes, and tucking the bottle under his arm, started for the door.

'I may be a while, Jack,' he said, 'a quiet discussion over a few glasses might take a little while to achieve the desired result, but he'll get a good night's sleep out of it if nothing else.'

Jack nodded as he held the mug of coffee to his lips, but it wasn't long before his mind was busy with other thoughts. How long had this Abbot been head of the monastery, somehow, he just didn't fit the mould of an ecclesiastical Superior … and was he right in guessing who had preceded him and did Daniel know them both? Other thoughts began to creep in from the corners of his mind too, becoming stronger as much as he had tried to push them away. He knew there was another reason to be here, he had been aware of that for some time. There was someone here that he had to see … and it was not this present Abbot, but someone else with the power to direct his path down a road that he had tried to avoid … a path that was apparently his destiny to fulfil.

He sighed and turned his attention to the plate of food that Amos had prepared for him.

Not thunder this time, another noise now aroused him. It came from outside and close by. Though the walls were thick, he had sensed rather than heard the noise. A thud, the sounds of scrabbling, then silence, but whatever made the sound he felt sure it was still there. There would not be anyone from the Abbey about at this time of night, only he and Amos. His first thought was that a curious villager may have been trespassing, but quickly swept that thought from his mind. No villager would come here now, not at night or in this weather. Besides which, to them the Abbey was haunted. Victor Casini and his entourage were not due for a day or so yet, Jack would hardly have expected him to arrive with a bump in the night and a stormy one at that. Victor Casini had too much prestige and smart showmanship, he expected his minions to pave the way for his eminent arrival and wouldn't get his hands dirty unless he had to. Besides which, there was no way he could have been forewarned with the surprise capture of his younger brother and his associates.

Perhaps a forest animal foraging for food, that could be the only answer … but no, it was something else, Jack suddenly felt as if part of his past life was at that moment very close to him. He quickly pocketed his gun and with torch in hand, but not turned on, opened the heavy outer door and crept out into the cold wetness of the night. The rain had ceased for a while, the pale beams from a straggling moon penetrating the scurrying clouds gave him just enough light to see by.

The noises had seemed to come from the other side of the wall adjacent to that of the building he had just left. It was here that some of the older walls had fallen, the rubble had been high enough to leave one of the walls partially supported. It was from behind this that he thought he could hear faint voices, but another rumble of thunder drowned out any further sounds. As Jack crept along the perimeter of the wall to where the falling stonework had left the rubble still piled high, he could see the flicker of a fire in the gaps between the stones.

Feeling his way in the semi darkness, Jack declined to turn on the torch for fear the extra light would startle whoever was there, so he crept forward cautiously.

The moon was still giving off the faintest glow now and then, he quietly and carefully picked his way over piles of broken stone, until he reached a point where he could almost see into the cavity. The voices began again amid sounds of more scuffling and as he listened, Jack realised with a shock that he knew those voices! His memory was stirred, he found himself thinking back to another time, another place, which was where those voices belonged.

He listened and watched for a few minutes longer, smiling to himself as the sound of heavy snoring reached his ears, then shook his head in total disbelief. Of all the people in the world to meet up with in such a faraway spot! He would not disturb them now, they were warm and dry enough where they were and he doubted they would appreciate his presence upon them at this time, it could wait. He would approach them in the morning and at least satisfy his curiosity as to why they had chosen this place to drop in to and for what purpose?

Something else was there too, something that had been aware of his presence and had been watching him. It was there … right above him in the semi-darkness. Eyes, large yellow eyes staring at him. Jack turned his head slowly and beheld them, shining, luminous eyes that glinted down at him in the darkness.

Chapter 9

Any Port In A Storm

The storm seemed to be getting worse as the two figures on their broomsticks attempted to make some headway through the tempest. The winds howled and rain beat at their faces as the two sisters attempted to ride above the storm, even though they were making some progress, it was difficult to stay on course. Several times Marilla had to wrench her broomstick around to the compass reading she had set, but it almost seemed to have a mind of its own. Eventually she calculated that they would have to be just about over the old forest, so she signalled to Isabella that she was dropping in altitude and turning slightly westward, which should drop them close to the clearing in which the little cottage stood. A pale moon struggling to wrest itself from the dark rain clouds had given Marilla the faintest glimpse of tall trees far below them.

However, there was to be no escaping the fury of the wind and the rain that intensified as they descended. It pushed and pulled them unmercifully, until they had no idea which way was up or down. Their usually reliable form of transport, weighed down with the heavily laden broom trailer, was proving no match for the blustering gale that was whirling them around like rag dolls that had been tossed into a washing machine.

There was no alternative but to try to set down somewhere and seek shelter until the storm abated. For a brief moment, the wind ceased to blow and the shrouded moon gave a momentary glimpse of a wall of green looming in front of them. Before they had a chance to turn away, they found themselves being rudely tumbled through the top branches of what could only be a pine forest. Though it did have the advantage of slowing the rapid descent, they were still dumped unceremoniously to the ground in a flurry of broomsticks, packages and curses.

Isabella, who as always, was behind Marilla and towing the trailer broom, had at least taken a little less buffeting, but still managed to canon into Marilla from the rear. They landed heavily and tumbled over into a tangled and confused heap. Isabella opened her eyes and pushing her broomstick aside, struggled to a semi-sitting position, carefully feeling her limbs to see if she had broken anything. Apart from some scratches and a few bruises, everything seemed intact, except for her hair. Blessed with an enormous mop of unruly reddish-brown hair, which always refused to be tamed, it was now entangled firmly in the stiff bristles of Marilla's broom.

As she began to untangle her hair, Isabella tried to look about her, but it was still too dark to see anything, she had the impression there was something large and blacker in front of them. The side of a mountain, a cliff perhaps — they would have to wait until morning to see just where they were, but at least they were safely on the ground.

She tugged at the last few strands of hair still entangled and was free … even if her hair did look more of a mess than usual, at least she could sit upright. She called out to Marilla, she was answered by a low groan and a curse. Well, at least her sister was alive, if still quite stunned.

The fury of the storm appeared to be lessening now, even though the wind was still blowing briskly, the sky was becoming a little lighter. Looking up, Isabella could see clouds scurrying before the wind with the pale moon trying to shine through the thinner patches. Perhaps now with a little extra light, she might be able to see where their wild ride had deposited them.

Somehow though, she had that feeling that they were not in the forest that she remembered, it felt different, it smelled different … this forest smelled of pine trees. She couldn't remember pine trees around the cottage. Where were they?

Peering through the gloom as the light of the moon grew stronger, Isabella could see that the cauldron had fallen free of its 'impossible-to-undo-unless-you-know-the-right-words bindings' with the force of the impact, it had rolled several yards away, coming to rest against a large boulder. Still pulling a few bristles of Marilla's broom from her hair and now able to sit upright, she looked about for their scattered belongings.

Presently, apart from Marilla's rumblings and curses as she attempted to come to her senses, Isabella detected a movement near the top of the cauldron, a low rumbling sound issuing from within its interior. In a moment a large black cat, just visible in the dim light, emerged from its bowels.

The bedraggled fur was jet black, save for a white tuft at the end of its tail, the eyes were huge and deep yellow, which now narrowed to glint as mere slits, as it glared back at the sisters. The cat was attempting to stand upright but swayed unsteadily on its feet as it tried to lift its paws one at a time to shake the water off. It toppled back against the side of the cauldron in the process, but after a few more unsteady tries it managed to stand upright again. Then with a curious stiff-legged gait, it staggered somewhat unsteadily into the blackness beyond them and began to disappear into the darkness.

'Wha–where are we?' Marilla was sitting up and rubbing the back of her head, which had connected with the cauldron as it went flying past, torn free from the ropes it had been so carefully secured with. She looked up in time to see the white tip of the cat's tail vanishing into the black void beyond them, 'Now, where's he going?'

She looked about her, still rubbing her head. 'What is this place?' Marilla stared after the disappearing tail of the cat as the moon attempted to throw a wan light upon the two figures still sprawled among their scattered belongings. 'Is that a cave, or what's left of a building … I think there's a wall there, can you see what it is, Isabella?'

'I'm not too sure where we are, Marilla, but this doesn't seem to be our forest … it doesn't even smell right, are you sure you had the compass set correctly?'

'Of *course* I did!' snapped Marilla, the bump on her head beginning to give her a headache, but she managed to struggle to her feet. 'If it's shelter of some sort, you can bet that's where Lucifer will be heading. Come on Isabella, help me get these things together and we'll see if we can find somewhere where it's drier; you can bet Lucifer has already.'

Stumbling around they managed to collect some of their packages and hurried to the spot where they had last seen the white tip of Lucifer's tail. As the moon gathered strength the sisters were able to see that it was not so much a cave, but more a shelter of fallen masonry. Turning their attention to the cauldron, they carefully rolled it into a corner of the shelter, where high above on a projecting ledge, Lucifer was licking his sodden fur and rumbling his displeasure to himself.

'Well at least its dry in here,' said Isabella, as she shook her head of wet hair, 'but we could do with a fire, we're both wet through. I'll see if I can find some tinder that's not too wet.'

While Marilla rummaged in the packs for some dry clothes, Isabella was able to gather up quite an armful of small branches, bits of bramble and some pinecones from near the entrance to the shelter. Pushing them together into a bundle and finding the driest bits, she flicked her fingers, a small spark appeared at the tip of her finger. Directing this into the heaped-up brush, it soon flared into a glowing fire. The fiery glow extended to the upper reaches of the shelter and reflected in the yellow eyes of the cat like a beckoning mirror. He watched the flames dancing merrily, 'till they enticed him to leap down from his perch and finish drying himself by the crackling warmth of the fire.

With their wet clothing draped over a couple of boulders, the sisters soon sat hunched around the fire, munching on a couple of biscuits from one of the packs.

'I can't understand why that storm was so fierce,' said Marilla, 'the weather bureau hadn't predicted it would be that bad. All it said was, a passing storm, with some rain — but that was a positive hurricane!'

'Do you think we were deliberately blown off course?' ventured Isabella.

'Now, why would anyone want to do that?'

Isabella shrugged her shoulders. 'Stranger things have happened.'

'Humph!' snorted Marilla. 'Unless of course Grizelda had something in mind; I wouldn't put it past her to poke a finger in where it's not wanted.'

'I don't see how,' yawned Isabella, 'she's not due back from the convention until next week.'

'Anyway, we might as well get some sleep,' mumbled Marilla

as she rubbed the back of her head again. 'I don't know where we are and at the moment I don't care. Let's get some sleep, we can investigate in the morning.' She pulled one of the long cloaks they wore up over her head and curled up on one side close by the fire.

Isabella looked about her for a few more minutes, peering into the darkness. She had the oddest feeling that it was more than just a strong wind that had brought them down here, however she gathered up some thicker pieces of wood lying close by and fed them to the glowing coals, sending up a shower of sparks that glittered in the darkness of the cavern. The fickle moon had disappeared again behind a bank of clouds, but at least it had stopped raining. Isabella rubbed at a few bruises before pulling one of the softer packs under her head for a pillow. She tucked her knees up under her long skirts, and very soon both sisters were asleep, snoring loudly.

Lucifer, on the other side of the fire, stopped licking his fur, sat with his ears twitching slightly, his head on one side as if listening. The sound of the sister's snores echoed in the cold darkness that enveloped the cavern beyond where the fire still glowed, but Lucifer was listening to something else. His eyes were wide, the flickering flames glinting deep within the yellow orbs as he turned his head this way and that, before lifting his nose and sniffing the air.

Silently, he got to his feet and padded off into the darkness.

Other ears had been listening and other eyes had been watching from a distance.

*   *   *

By morning, the storm had passed, and Marilla and Isabella were able to see just where their rapid and unexpected descent

111

had dropped them, which looked so different in the full clear light of morning. Their 'cave' was formed by a leaning wall of masonry that had been propped up by other debris, creating a large open cavern, quite waterproof and sheltered. They had indeed been fortunate in landing close to it during their dramatic exit from the forces of nature's fury.

Isabella stifled a deep yawn and stepped out into the morning's pale sunshine where she took in several breaths of the cool air, saturated with the powerful scent of pines. 'Marilla, come out here and see, just smell that fresh air. This makes a change from the stale tobacco smoke and cooking smells we've been putting up with!'

A grunt was the only reply she got at first, but slowly and grumpily Marilla emerged from the shelter, trying to straighten her skirts and unsuccessfully attempting to push unruly wisps of escaping hair back into the tight bun she usually wore. She aimed a kick at the dead coals of the fire and muttered something under her breath but followed her younger sister to stand in the coolness of the morning and take a deep breath.

'Hmm yes,' agreed Marilla, after a few moments, 'but then pine trees do give off a refreshing smell, particularly after rain.' She looked about her and said, 'I wonder where we are, this is certainly not our forest.'

'Let's find out,' said Isabella cheerily, stepping away from the shelter of the broken wall and onto the open patch of ground that fronted it.

Their shelter opened out onto a small area that they could only assume had once been cultivated gardens and the like. Orderly arranged garden beds close by had once contained vegetables and herbs with a bare few struggling to survive under the virulent competition of weeds. A compact orchard of untended, but still fruitful trees grew quite unrestrained to one side, giving a small element of privacy to the area, which was further strengthened by a glimpse of a stout stone wall just beyond. A thicket of bracken and thorny bush contained them on the other side of this patch, like a petticoat peeping beneath the skirts of the forest of tall pines.

Moving out from beyond the wall that had sheltered them, they found themselves to be, at first glance, in the grounds of some sort of castle. One large and forbidding structure towering close by had walls of solid stone, slotted here and there with narrow lancet windows — little more than slits — giving the whole structure a medieval look. More so too, as their eyes travelled to the very top, where they perceived a crenelated battlement high above.

Finding a rough path beside the crumbling remnants of an ancient outer wall they caught a glimpse of more buildings and further still, what looked like a church? With a steeply sloping roof, topped with a soaring spire and a tall square bell tower toward the rear of the building, it overlooked a large open area bounded by tall columns, like a palisade enclosing the fortress behind it.

The foremost large building behind this palisade was a peculiar mix of medieval Gothic and Norman architecture and though of considerable size, it seemed strangely devoid of any inhabitants. The sisters heard no sounds, apart from the chorus of birds that flitted in and out of the thickets of brambles.

'Let's not go any closer,' whispered Marilla, 'we don't know if there's anyone here.'

'Well, it does look a bit forbidding …' Isabella whispered back, 'perhaps we should keep close to this broken wall, there seems to be a bit of a path here anyway, it must lead somewhere.'

Keeping close to the crumbling wall, the sisters followed the faint path around, passing a couple of smaller cottage-like buildings, 'till they found themselves on a small promontory that overlooked a deep valley. They stopped and gazed down a long rock- cluttered slope bisected by a rough road, visible only here and there through the clumps of trees that clung to the boulder and bracken-strewn hillside.

Further around and behind them the pine forest rose up — a formidable green barrier — broken only by the tangled masses of brambles, ferns and large moss-covered rocks. As they stood in the clear coolness of the morning, another sound came to their ears, other than the twittering of the birds amongst the brambles. The sound of rushing water could be heard, somewhere away to their right and below them still. Scrambling around the edge of a huge flat rock overhung by a fallen pine tree, they reached a tiny plateau perched on the edge of the mountain side. Here they could only gaze in wonder at the vista now opened fully before them. A long deep valley, almost filled with the waters of a blue-green lake, its surface gleaming before them like some gigantic mirror, reflecting distant mountain peaks with more pine forests on its other side. Scrambling a little further around this tiny perch and still high on the mountain side, they were able to catch a glimpse of tumbling water from a chasm, which seemed to split the mountain in two. As the water fell and gushed its way over barricades and strictures of broken rock, the spray hung momentarily in the clear morning air. The droplets shimmered and sparkled like miniature rainbows, caught in a fleeting second of splendour in the rays of the morning sun before falling again into oblivion.

The cold waters of the swiftly flowing mountain stream had carved a tortuous path through ancient bedrock, to eventually spill itself out into the deep and placid spaciousness of the vast lake, to lap quietly and contentedly at the feet of a picturesque little village nestled at its edge. Red and grey slate roofs of the houses were barely discernible amid the profusion of pine trees that enshrouded them, with only the single white spire of the distant village church visible amongst the multitude of the towering green spires of the surrounding forest. Beyond this hamlet, the now quieter waters gathered in narrow confines again, to pass unhindered under the time-worn arches of a stone bridge, to further wend its way as a broad and swift benefactor of life to far distant pastures. The eyes of the sisters followed the river's course onward, through more stands of pines until all was invisible and seen only as a pale haze of colour in the infinite distance.

Isabella, the shortest of the two sisters and inclined to a slight pudginess, both attributes inherited from her paternal parentage, clasped her hands together in front of her pleasantly round plump-cheeked face. Her soft brown eyes shone with pleasure as they took in the beauty that lay before them. 'Oh, Marilla, what a *beautiful* place, I'm so glad we stopped here!'

'Don't be too sure about that,' retorted her sister, as she stood with one hand on a bony hip and pushed another stray lock of hair back into the loose knot of untidy bun at the back of her head with the other. 'We don't know where we are yet and pretty as this valley looks, it's the place behind us that is of more concern. Maybe there are people living here, maybe there's not, but we'll have to find out; I can't imagine a big place like this being deserted.' She swished her skirts about her and turned to look at the edifice rising above them, shading her green eyes against the brightness of the sun. Taller than Isabella with a willowy bony frame, Marilla held a rather different perception of life than her younger sibling. Of a naturally suspicious nature, she firmly believed the world was full of opportunities to be grasped and made use of before they escaped, possibly never to beckon again. Not that much in the way of opportune moments had ever come her way however, but it was an attribute her father would have been proud of.

Isabella, on the other hand, embraced the simpler and more predictably 'earthy' temperament so enamoured of her mother and was content to wallow in her books, to enfold herself in the wonders of the natural side of life. This, in some sense, was a source of annoyance to Marilla when some of her more challenging ideas were greeted with muted disinterest.

Two sisters, so less alike, but bound by mutual genetic forces.

'Come on, Isabella, let's see if there's any sign of life in this place, but we'll have to be careful we don't make ourselves too obvious.'

Isabella reluctantly turned her gaze away from the tranquillity open before her and dutifully followed her sister as they cautiously picked their way up the rock-strewn slope. Then with some furtiveness the two sisters crept across a large open space, the termination of which they had seen snaking its way down the valley in the direction of the village. Here the ruined remains of an outer building lay before them, some walls still standing, but the ground littered with huge blocks of fallen masonry. Beyond and to their left rose the church, behind it the high tower they had noticed earlier with what appeared to have once been the main entrance beside it. All that was left of that were two partly destroyed massive stone pillars and a ruined iron gate. However, it was the sign, almost obliterated on a bronze plate hammered into the stonework of the damaged entrance that caught Marilla's eye. 'Isabella … this is not a castle; it's a monastery!' And indeed, it was.

With some trepidation, the sisters peered at the bulk of the remaining buildings visible some distance beyond where they stood in the scant concealment of the gate pillars, but it was the one great building on the other side of that courtyard that held their immediate attention.

A citadel of vast proportions, Gothic in its basic structure, later additions offered a choice of what was discerned to be in tasteful architectural grace. High stone arches around its many mullioned windows gave the façade a surprised and inquiring look. Buttressed walls lent an aura of formidability, a fortress, complete with crenelated towers and battlements, a stronghold to keep intruders out, or protect those within. Who could tell, both sisters mused, but whatever architectural anomaly it possessed, it was an imposing structure and looked even less a lodge of scholastic endeavour, and the humbler aspects of its teachings. Along with the passages of time, the Abbey had seen many changes in the hosts that had dwelt, or otherwise sought refuge within its sheltered confines, each had left a mark.

To the folk who dwelt in the village below, it harboured too many secrets, it was a strange place that they chose to ignore, pretending it did not exist.

*   *   *

Little was known of its early history, save for the few tales handed down or that lingered in half-forgotten folklore. Even then, no one really believed the old stories and dismissed them as over imaginative figments from those who had little else to talk about. Simple farmers and country folk, they considered it none of their business if men wanted to shut themselves away behind stone walls in such a solitary place and not enjoy, at least, some of the pleasures of ordinary living. Each to his own, they'd say, shaking their rural heads in bewilderment, but the monks kept to themselves and the people in the district did likewise. As neither interfered with the other, what did it matter anyway?

Some of the more ancient ones in the village could remember the monks coming down to the village quite often, in little carts drawn by donkeys, but that was a very long time ago. Though, there were still occasions when the little donkey cart would appear trundling down the High Street and return laden with provisions for whatever livestock was kept up there. Many things had begun to change over the years, the monks now mostly came and went in more modern modes of transport. The quiet and generally unobtrusive passage of these reclusive shadowy grey figures through the village from time to time, drew little attention from the residents. They considered them to be much like the trees that surrounded them — always there, but only noticeable if you felt inclined to acknowledge them.

Way beyond the boundaries of the lush and well-ordered farming communities were large towns, with schools, universities, hospitals and all the business trappings of commercialism. Very few of the village populace had need to travel that far afield, quite comfortably self-sufficient in their own way, as were the Franciscans enclosed in their own piece of 'Utopia'.

It was as if an invisible line had been drawn in the roadside dirt to indicate a time warp of three dimensions, a division between antiquity, the rustic of yesteryear and the frenetic pace of a modern world.

Things were changing though — a balance of unhallowed power blended with a subtleness and depth of transition that even the most astute of the villagers could never have foreseen.

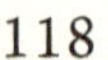

*   *   *

To Marilla and Isabella, any history behind this monastery was nothing to them. Their only concern was firstly to find some food and satisfy their curiosity as to whether they had landed in somebody's private back yard, if so, then what explanations were going to be necessary and how quickly they could dispatch themselves with their belongings to another place should a move become necessary.

Do you think there are still people living here?' asked Isabella, as she paused to examine more closely the grinning face of a carved stone gargoyle that had once adorned the upper walls.

'As we haven't seen any welcoming party as yet, I don't know,' remarked Marilla tartly. 'I'm sure that if there was anyone here, they would have seen us by now.'

'I guess so …' said Isabella slowly, 'so it looks like those ravens up there on that wall could be the only ones here.'

Marilla glanced upward to where about a dozen coal black ravens sat side by side on the broken top of the stone wall. Then, as if on cue, one of them cawed loudly and took flight, the others, followed after a moment's hesitation. Their raucous calls echoing above them as they wheeled in their flight, heading in the direction of the tower.

'That could be a bad omen,' said Marilla frowning. She stood still, looking carefully about her, then spoke in almost a whisper. 'There's something wrong here, these stones …' she sniffed the air suspiciously, 'this all looks like very recent damage … these ruins are not old, Bella!'

'What do you mean — not old?' Isabella set the stone gargoyle's head carefully back down again.

'Something has happened here only recently,' replied Marilla thoughtfully, 'these walls didn't just fall down by themselves, see — there's a lot of black marks on them. If they had just collapsed with age, they would be covered with moss and stuff.'

'Yes, I guess you're right, I never thought about that. I really didn't notice that before.' She stooped and looked at the stones again carefully, touching them with her finger, 'It looks like there's been a fire here; the stones are scorched.'

Marilla, peering from behind the gate pillar, was now staring at the centuries old stone monolith, which sat crouching like some great beast on the other side of the courtyard, watching them with lidless eyes. Its many turrets and towers concealing a multitude of secret places, where other eyes could be watching also.

She tugged at Isabella's sleeve, 'We should move from here, I feel somebody could be watching us. No, no. Not back *there!*' she insisted, quickly clutching Isabella's sleeve, as her sister turned to go back in the direction they had come from. 'We don't want to cross all that open space again; we need to find some cover. Quick, this way!'

Chapter 10

A Gruesome Discovery
and a Chance Meeting

Marilla pulled Isabella toward the church building, which was close by, where the stout columns of a flanking colonnade shielded them from prying eyes. It was here too that the sound of rushing water was loudest and they realised that the outer wall of the church was built almost on the edge of the great cliffs that bordered this plateau. It was almost as if church walls and rock wall were one. Creeping past the great iron-gate that had once been a magnificent and opposing entrance to the monastery, but now lay as a crumpled mass of steel, they found a broad set of steps that would lead them to the comparative concealment of the church.

They hoped to find a quiet spot to analyse their position and decide whether to explore further or try to get back to their meagre den. Surprisingly, once inside, the church was eerily quiet, the sound of the rushing water came only faintly to their ears. It wasn't until they were actually within the confines of that citadel that Marilla realised it might have been a bad idea. She was almost expecting to be confronted by monks, or whoever was here, but it was empty and their voices echoed in the vast stillness of its lofty ceilings.

'Oh dear,' whispered Isabella, 'I've never been in a church before … it's very big isn't it Marilla? And … ooh, look at the pretty coloured windows!'

'*Shh,*' hissed Marilla, 'there could be someone in here!'

Slowly the sisters made their way quietly down the centre nave of this reverential sanctuary, nervously waiting to hear a voice challenging their entry, but there was nothing. Four huge, pillared columns flanked by much slender ones ran down either side of this great hall and supported massive arches of timber beams that led to a central domed roof, many feet above their heads. Smaller arches travelled in sequence toward the back of the church and led to an ornate fretwork overhang, where slender intricately carved columns supported another dome, but of lesser proportion. In the centre below the dome they could see a series of wide shallow steps led up and onto a raised platform area, with some plain wooden seats arranged either side. A narrow aisle between the seating led to a high altar covered completely with a crisp white cloth embellished with what appeared to be symbolic embroidery.

It was, however, the huge arched windows along the outer wall that had caught Isabella's eye. A blaze of light and colour, they portrayed biblical scenes in brilliant, coloured glass, but for two of them, which now lay in shattered fragments amid broken tiles on the floor. As they looked about them, they could see evidence of some damage here also. Apart from the scattered jigsaw of broken glass, there were signs of a recent fire on the great arches. Some of the timbers and the great columns were blackened and scorched in places and the tiled floor beneath, agape with a large hole and was strewn with scattered tiles.

Marilla eyed the damage cautiously. 'There's something very strange here ... this damage looks very fresh, and I can smell something odd in the air. I don't think we should be here, Isabella, the sooner we get out of here the better.'

Isabella was looking up at the smoke-stained vault of the ceiling and said quietly, as if not listening to what her sister was saying, 'You know, even if there has been a fire here at some time, there doesn't seem to be all that much damage done, apart from those pretty windows of course. Don't you think it rather odd that nobody has cleaned it up and tried to do some repairs? Either that, or there's nobody here at all now.' She had picked up a broken piece of the coloured glass and was turning it this way and that, admiring the pattern of light and colour reflecting back onto the tessellated floor.

'Probably had good reason not to,' muttered Marilla. She was already forming suspicions in her own mind as she stooped to pick up a crushed cigarette packet. She had looked at it briefly and after a moment's hesitation, dropped it again.

'*Bella!*' said Marilla sharply, 'pretty as that might be to you, finding our way out of here and maybe some food when we do, holds more interest for me than bits of coloured glass. Let's get on with it, there has to be storerooms of some sort somewhere around. I don't want to have to persuade Lucifer to hunt down a rabbit or something, he doesn't like having to share what he catches. Come to think of it,' she said half to herself, 'we haven't seen him since last night ... I wonder where he's got to.'

'Oh, I do hope he hasn't become lost!' said Isabella. She slipped the piece of glass into the ample pocket of her skirt and hurried toward her sister.

'Hardly likely,' said Marilla pursing her lips, 'he's probably doing some exploring of his own.'

She stood motionless for a few more moments as if listening intently but all was quiet within the church itself, only the faint cawing of a bird from somewhere outside came to their ears.

'We'll try this way,' said Marilla and moved to where she thought the sound had come from. Rounding a corner of the shadow-filled columns and the soaring overhang of the inner sanctum, they followed a short passage and were soon greeted by a shaft of sunlight illuminating a set of steps that appeared beyond them.

'This could be a way out,' muttered Marilla, 'let's see where it leads.'

A broad set of pale stone steps lay before them as they emerged from the semi- darkness of the church's' interior. The morning sun reflected back from their whiteness, making the plumage of the large black bird, perched motionless on the pedestal column at the top of the flight of steps, all the more a sharp contrast. The bird ruffled its feathers and regarded them quizzically with one beady black eye, its head cocked to one side. Then suddenly, with a loud caw, it spread its glossy black wings and flew up to the nearby tower.

'Don't you think that's rather odd of that bird?' said Isabella as she watched the bird fly off.

'What's so odd about it?' replied Marilla as she descended the steps, looking carefully around her as she did so.

'Didn't you notice that it had two white feathers on its breast?' continued Isabella, as she followed her sister down the steps.

'So?'

'Well, black birds or ravens don't have any white feathers at all!'

They had reached the bottom of the steps and Marilla noted with satisfaction that they were closer to the far end of the courtyard now and almost out of sight of the front façade of the main building. A short distance in front of them was a blank stone wall, part of the end of the great building, behind this and flanking another courtyard were several more buildings surrounded by colonnaded walkways. Several ornamental trees and thick old vines enshrouded these walkways with stone benches set at intervals between them. However, it too looked deserted.

Marilla glanced quickly about her and drew her sister into the shadow of the near wall. 'Isabella,' she said, in her firm no-nonsense manner, 'I'm not in the mood for a nature lesson right now — we need to find food and a way out of here. I don't believe this place is abandoned, so we may have to move quickly. I think I saw a narrow corridor down there behind us and I thought I saw some doors. It's quite apart from the rest of those other buildings, it may possibly be storerooms of some kind. People who live so far from civilization have got to have supplies ... so we're going to have a look!'

'Oh, dear,' said Isabella nervously, 'do you really think we should? It really does look like private property and we are trespassing.'

Marilla didn't answer, already creeping stealthily down the narrow passageway. Isabella looked about her but shrugged her shoulders and dutifully followed her sister. They found that there were indeed rooms there, but from all outside appearances, they had not been used for some time. Dust and cobwebs and general decay hung about them like a shroud. Some of the heavy wooden doors swung half open on great hinges, discoloured with rust, showing the wear and tear of years of neglect.

'There's nothing here, they look as if they've been empty for ages,' whispered Isabella.

'Perhaps they have,' Marilla replied, 'but there's something very odd here all the same.' She poked her head around one of the doors that lined this small and obviously forgotten corridor. Pushing the door open a little further succeeded in disturbing a large hairy spider, which scuttled away to the opposite corner, where it sat with its legs huddled together.

Marilla sniffed the air, and muttered, 'Mischief has been done close by here — evil human mischief.'

They had walked the length of the corridor and were about to turn back when Marilla noticed the door at the end. It was set back slightly from the others, half hidden behind a thick column. Something about this door caused her to stop and examine it more closely. This one was firmly closed. A heavy iron hasp was across it and from this hung a large padlock ... minus the key.

'That's interesting,' murmured Marilla, peering more closely at the door, which was in much better condition than any of the others.

'Why, it's locked!' said Isabella who had been following a little way behind, but now came forward to peer around her sister at the locked door. 'Perhaps, you're right, Marilla and this is a storeroom; that's probably why it's got a lock on it. I wonder where the key might be.'

'Certainly not where we would find it, but it is the only one along here that is, so there must be a reason for that.'

Marilla scratched her head and stared at the lock on the door. Why would only one of these seemingly deserted and unkempt rooms have such a heavy lock on it? 'No key,' she muttered, 'however, a little gentle persuasion might shift it.'

'Marilla! You just can't break in!' exclaimed Isabella, a horrified look on her face. 'Perhaps the monks, or whoever is living here have a reason for locking it!'

'Well, there doesn't seem to be anybody here at the moment,

if there were, why haven't we seen any sign of life so far, it's not as if we've been entirely invisible. Besides which, I'm curious to see what's in there that has to be kept locked up, besides this door looks newer than the others along here, so there must be a reason.'

'But you said you didn't think this place was abandoned!'

'*Shh,*' hissed her sister again. 'I can't see anyone about, it just may be that it is abandoned, if these rooms are anything to go by, so stand back, Bella!' Drawing herself up to her full height and extending her forefinger, she pointed it at the lock and mumbled strange words under her breath. A flash of blue light and a crackling noise erupted from the end of her finger striking the lock, causing a black scorch mark to appear on the padlock and part of the surrounding door. The lock itself merely quivered slightly but remained firmly closed.

'Hmm, well, perhaps this time we'll get it, just needs another blast.'

'Marilla, you really shouldn't …' began Isabella with concern. 'What if …' her voice trailed away as Marilla drew herself up again and extended her finger once more. A brighter flash this time emerged from the fingertip causing the scorch mark on the timber door to get bigger, whilst several bits of wood splintered off the door with a loud crack. The lock only quivered a bit more this time, but still remained firmly closed.

'Would you like me to try?' said Isabella hopefully.

'No!' Marilla's voice was firm. 'I've nearly got it now, just a bit out of practice that's all.' Her face contorted with concentration, she rolled up her sleeve, steadied herself, took a deep breath and quite loudly this time, said '*Maxima brutum fulma!*' pointing her now shaking finger at the lock. More splinters of wood flew off the door and the lock began to spin wildly around.

Marilla, quite exhausted now from her efforts, pushed a few

strands of hair from her flushed face and peered at the door once the wood dust had settled she noted with satisfaction that the holding pin had now detached itself from the padlock.

Her powers, though she hated to admit it, even to herself, were somewhat erratic and inhibitive. Sometimes her spells worked, but there were many times they didn't, which to her, was indeed a source of much irritation.

'Perhaps if we both give it a push, it might give,' said Isabella in an anxious voice, as she hovered behind her sister. 'There's not much wood left around it to hold the lock anyhow.'

'Shh.' Marilla put a finger to her lips. 'I thought I heard something.' She looked quickly up and down the corridor, then pulled Isabella in close beside her as they squeezed in as much as they could behind the column, which didn't really hide too much of Isabella, as most of her body was still outside in the corridor. Isabella looked startled, but there was obviously nowhere for her to hide, so she just stood there, bewildered.

'I don't see anything,' she whispered tremulously, glancing fearfully around.

Marilla's face emerged from around the column, 'I've got this feeling there's someone else close by ... and then ... oh, I'm not sure. Isabella, go up to the end of the corridor and have a peep into that courtyard, see if you can see anyone coming,'

'Why me! Why can't you?' she whispered nervously.

'Bella, just *do it!*' hissed Marilla.

Isabella grimaced and tiptoed as silently as she could up to the end of the corridor and poked her head furtively around the corner. The courtyard was as deserted as it was when they had first entered it. She almost flew back to her sister's side. 'There's no one there at all, you've just imagined it, you're hearing things,' she said, pouting crossly at her elder sibling.

'Well, my inner feelings about being watched are usually never wrong,' retorted Marilla. 'Anyway, let's give this door a push now and see if we can get it open.'

It still took the combined efforts of both of them to finally push the door open, the hinges groaning in protest.

'I wonder what's in here that needs locking up like this,' panted Isabella, as she rubbed a slightly bruised shoulder, she being at the forefront of the push. 'It doesn't look like the sort of place people would use; it hasn't been opened for ages.' They cautiously edged past the scarred wooden door, now hanging oddly by one hinge.

A waft of chill and fetid air greeted them as they pushed the door open further, they wrinkled their noses at the odour that pervaded the room. As their eyes became adjusted to the gloom, they could see that the only passage of light and air came from a tiny window set high in a wall. A thin shaft of sunlight from the morning sun was filtering through the dust particles, partially illuminating the only piece of furniture in the room — an old iron bed.

Marilla approached the bed cautiously. 'I think that might be a good enough reason,' she said pointing at what appeared to be disarranged clothing on the bed.

'Oh *dear!*' gasped Isabella, her hand flying to her mouth. 'I–I wouldn't have expected to find something like this in here!'

'Perhaps not.' Marilla stepped closer to the bed and studied the tattered, still clothed decaying body that lay there. She could see that the hands were crossed over the chest, and the now loose strands of frayed rope lay across the withered wrists, while a similar piece of rope joined the feet together.

However, it was the skull that Marilla was peering closely at ... and the small round hole in the centre of the forehead.

Engrossed as they were in the discovery of this gruesome find, they did not at first become aware that someone else was also there.

'So that's where he got to, Amos was right!

The voice at the door was startling in the stillness that hung in the air of that ghoulish scene, made both sisters turn around quickly to stare unbelievably at the figure framed in the light of the doorway. A man, tallish and slightly built, clad in dark jeans, t-shirt with a black leather jacket with his gaze directed at the body on the bed.

Very little could be seen of his face, partly obscured as it was with a dark coloured woollen beanie pulled low over his head, there was a short beard concealing the lower part of his face. Only the eyes were bright as they focused on the bed with its grisly contents.

Marilla was the first to recover her composure and as if by instinct to protect herself from this intruder, raised her hand to point a finger at the man as he entered the room.

'Don't bother!' he almost snapped at her. 'I've grown up with that sort of stuff and it just bounces off. In any case,' he added carelessly, he gestured toward the cell door, 'if that's anything to go by, you could do with a bit more practice, your aim is way off.'

He had reached the side of the bed and looked down at the body for a few moments before carefully moving what was left of the clothing, as if searching for something.

In the meantime, while Marilla had regained some measure of control, Isabella remained staring open-mouthed at the stranger who was so openly defying their presence. If this was indeed a monastery as the sign on the gate had stated, then they may have expected to be confronted by a very surprised monk. If so, then they could have perhaps bluffed their way out of their trespass ... but this brash young man was an unexpected surprise and Marilla had finally found her voice.

'Who are you, where did you come from and what—' Marilla began, the words tumbling out, her green eyes flashing.

The man, still searching the tattered clothing had turned and raised his hand to silence her saying, 'Now, I could ask you the same question, couldn't I?'

Carefully replacing the clothing he had disturbed, he turned away from the bed and looked keenly at the two sisters. 'Look, I know who you are; it's Marilla isn't it?' He turned clear grey eyes on her, then they flickered toward Isabella. 'You must be Isabella, right? You can close your mouth now.'

Isabella's jaws snapped shut, but her eyes never left him.

'I've already made acquaintance with your cat, I wish you'd taught him some manners!' He pulled the sleeve of his jacket up to reveal a reasonably fresh scratch on his forearm.

'But, but!' Marilla was in full voice now and spoke angrily, 'Who are *you*, and how do you know who *we* are?'

The young man grinned at them, his white even teeth lighting up his otherwise grim featured face. 'My, my, how quickly one can be forgotten. The name's Jack, Jack Grimsby — we've met before, a very long time ago. It's been quite a few years now ... surely you haven't forgotten me that quickly?'

Marilla's mind was racing. Grimsby ... why was that name so familiar?

'I know who you are,' Isabella spoke, 'you used to sit with me sometimes when we were little.' Her voice was whisper quiet as she gazed up at the face turned toward her.

'Edwina Grimsby!' Marilla snapped her fingers, 'that's it! I remember now, Edwina and our grandmother were best friends!' She came closer to him now and stared up into his face, carefully studying it. 'You would be Edwina's grandson, am I right?'

'That's about it.' He laughed at the amazed expressions on the faces of the sisters, the sound echoing around the small chamber, an oddly discordant sound in such a macabre setting.

'Mind you,' he said, as he returned to his grim task of searching the unfortunate corpse, 'we were only kids then, so I wouldn't expect that you would remember me. I did not go down the path intended for me but I see you certainly did, however,' he turned his head and gave Marilla a wicked grin, 'I think Grandma Hackett would have been a mite disappointed with your efforts on that door.'

Marilla felt the colour rise to her cheeks and heard the barely audible snigger from Isabella, which quickly earned her a kick in the shin.

'You were watching—I knew it—spying on us! That was a heavy lock — how was I to know it wasn't—wasn't bewitched!' Marilla was waving her arms about in an agitated manner, furious in barely suppressed anger at the reference to Grandma Hackett's expertise in contrast to her own. Plus the fact that he must have been somewhere close, close enough to have watched her efforts with the door. 'Anyway,' she spat at him, her hands placed firmly on her bony hips, 'if you were watching, why didn't you open the damn door for us, or at least help?'

'I believe it's called breaking and entering.' Jack bent to the task of searching the dead man's clothes. 'Perhaps you've never heard the term before.'

Marilla opened her mouth to pour forth another tirade but stopped and stared curiously at him. 'Maybe we should ask you just what you are doing in a place like this.'

Jack glanced at her and Isabella and said just as curiously, 'Now that's a question I should be asking *you*. Isn't a place like this a bit out of the way for you both?'

'I asked you first!' she glared at him, green eyes blazing.

'Ah Marilla, Marilla,' he grinned, his grey eyes twinkling now, as he carefully moved one of the dead man's feet so he could sit down on the corner of the bed. 'Things haven't changed have they? It didn't take much to get you all riled up when we were kids, it still doesn't.' He shook his head and grinned widely at Isabella saying, 'I bet she's got you following along behind as usual, eh, Bella?'

*   *   *

Marilla continued to stare at the tall young man in front of her. She remembered now, he was a skinny dark-headed kid then, even though he was only about a year older than she was, he had the mischievous, natural ability to intercept and control her thoughts. To her, it was as if he had singled her out in particular and would often upset her concentration when performing little feats of magic. The results would be harrowing for her and she would have to begin the process again.

It didn't help her credibility and confidence at all, particularly when enthusiasm got the better of her, when trying to emulate her grandmother's skills and things did not develop the way they should have. Even simple transformations with frogs and mice ended up a disaster, with frogs hopping about with long mouse tails and ears ...

While she did have some success with incantations and spells, he was always around when something went wrong. She did remember seeing him around the village occasionally although he often went off by himself for days in the woods. At other times he would sit with Isabella on a nearby log by the stream, not talking, even to Isabella, just watching.

Orphaned as a small child, it was Edwina who had raised him as her own but he had never really fitted in with the other children. When they all gathered in their favourite playground, on the grassy banks of the meandering stream that ran past the cottages in the wood, it was Jack who sat to one side. Seated on the big hollow log with Isabella close by, he would just watch, as all the young ones played tricks on each other or chased and caught toads. These were tossed into the air with gestures and allowed to fall, only to be held suspended at the last minute, before dropping gently onto the grass. Marilla's toad would hover nicely 'till about three feet off the ground, then at the time when she should have been lowering it gently to the grass, it would suddenly drop with a splat and a plop and when she looked up, Jack would be staring at her.

Oddly enough, nobody ever played tricks on Jack, not that some of them hadn't tried. The steady gaze of those grey eyes seemed to capture their minds momentarily and they would suddenly forget what they were about to do. Jack was just content to sit and watch their games from a little distance anyway. To Marilla he was a strange mixture, hard to understand when they did speak as his accent was hard to follow, so they generally had little to do with each other.

Through her childhood, Marilla was so sure that she would follow in her grandmother's footsteps. After all she was born a witch and she would declare to anyone who would listen, that she would be the smartest and cleverest witch ever. Of course, Grandma Hackett had harboured other thoughts as she watched the children at play. The intrinsic skills were there right enough, there was no doubt about that. One thing was clear though, it was no good having the power to perform magic, if you did not have the power to control it.

Isabella would have been just a little over six years old and Marilla almost nine when her grandmother moved into the Harewood Commune. She could still recall some memories of the simple surroundings, particularly the woods where she often rambled, picking wildflowers for her grandmother. She too had vague memories of sitting on a big log near a stream that ran through the woods, watching her elder sister and the other children, playing there in the soft grass that bordered the gentle stream. She also had a memory of a slightly built dark headed boy who would sometimes come and sit beside her. Like Isabella, he would say nothing, just sit and watch.

His presence always seemed to make her sister nervous. She would get angry with him and tell him to go away, which after a while he would do and Isabella would be alone again.

Being the youngest member of the Commune, she, like Jack, just didn't seem to fit in anywhere. However, to her, there was always something reassuring about his company and when he left some years later, it was Isabella who missed him most. It was as if she had lost a brother, even though she really had very little to do with him at all ... perhaps it was more like a comforting shadow melting away.

Isabella had liked living in Harewood. Nobody from 'outside' ever ventured there, it was a peaceful childhood, with the woods and the stream a playground of delight and discovery. As she grew, so did her knowledge of what was about her. She could name all the birds that visited the wood also identify all the wildflowers and herbs that grew there.

Isabella looked at Jack now, sitting on the corner of the bed next to ... what was left of someone he had obviously known.

How handsome he looked, so sure of himself, as he bandied words with Marilla. He had always been a mystery to them, not really knowing just who he was. Nobody else seemed to care, he was just Edwina's grandson ... but was he really? There was never any mention of his parents and when he was discussed among the elders, it was with hushed tones.

Jack had spent much of his childhood wandering deeper into the woods than Isabella dared to go, sometimes not coming home for days. He would bring back interesting things for his grandmother that he gathered and kept in a small bag carried over his shoulder. Once he brought home a baby rabbit and gave it to Isabella. Its mother and the other young had been killed by a predator, he had found this one still alive. She kept it 'till it had grown enough to take care of itself, then, reluctantly let it go. She did not believe in keeping any creature of the woods locked up, Jack had approved when she had let it go and that had made her happy.

As Marilla had grown to adulthood, she became increasingly restless. To her, the Commune was stifling, she needed to 'find her own space' so she said. Jack had already gone some time before but nobody, except Isabella seemed to notice his absence. Edwina did not forward any details of his departure, except, he would not be back. There were other paths to follow and he had gone with her blessing.

Edwina herself had left Harewood several times while the girls were growing up. She would disappear for several months, then just as mysteriously appear back in the Commune again. Her travels were not discussed in front of the children ... away on business they would be told.

Then, with Grandma Hackett gone, Marilla had decided it was time to strike out on their own and with nothing else to hold her to Harewood now, Isabella was left with no choice but to follow her sister. She had hoped they would settle somewhere but so far nothing had met with Marilla's approval and any likely place had as yet eluded them.

*   *   *

It was Isabella who spoke now in a quiet voice, 'Do you know who that is?' as she pointed to the grim relic on the bed.

Jack turned his grey eyes onto her brown ones. 'Yes I do, as a matter of fact, I had hoped to find him in a better state of health. This cell was my next search area but you've beaten me to it.'

'Just what are you doing here anyway?' Marilla repeated the question, 'that sign on the front of this place says it's a monastery — what are you doing in a monastery?'

'That's a long and involved story,' sighed Jack, 'there's something I need that's here, I've just got to find it.' He looked down at the body of the man on the bed, and said softly, 'If only you could talk.'

Marilla's attitude was softening now towards Jack, the body on the bed was apparently someone to whom he had been attached. Finding a dead body was not a desirable thing to come across at any time but when it was a friend, well, that was another thing altogether and her heart went out to him. She spoke hesitantly now. 'Is he—was he, a friend of yours?' She pointed to the neat round hole in the forehead. 'Whoever it is, someone wanted him dead.'

'Yes and that's the pity of it,' said Jack with a hard edge to his voice, 'he was a good man.'

'I don't understand—' Marilla started to say, as Jack interrupted and began to move around to the other side of the bed to continue his search.

'I'll explain later. This is more important right now and I need to –' he broke off to touch a tightly laced boot still clinging to the wizened foot. 'Of course!' He tugged gently at the boot, which came away easily in his hand and began to untie the laces.

The sisters watched in mute silence as Jack carefully began to pull away the inner soles of the boot, until finally he said triumphantly, 'I knew you'd talk to me, Dan!' He had withdrawn a finely folded piece of parchment extracted from the toe of the dead man's boot.

Chapter 11

Some Questions Are Answered

'Is that what you were looking for?' said Isabella quizzically, 'a piece of paper?'

'Yes, however, I'll look at it more closely later, not here, not now.' Jack put the piece of parchment carefully into an inside pocket of his jacket. He looked down at the man on the bed and whispered softly. 'I'll come back for you, Daniel; I won't leave you here, not like this.'

Jack turned to where the sisters were still standing wide-eyed and wondering, as they watched the sad cloud pass from his handsome face. 'I know this must seem all very strange to you both and—' Marilla opened her mouth to say something, but Jack quickly silenced any outpour with an upthrust palm. 'Look, neither of you have any idea of what you have stumbled into and frankly you've chosen a damned awkward time to arrive!' He began to walk toward the door, passing very close to them, studying them both with his steady grey eyes. 'However, you're here now and I'll try to explain, but …' and his eyes suddenly looked darker and more menacing.

'Now that you are here, I'm going to have to trust you, as you must trust me and keep everything you see here to yourselves; also, you need to do as I ask. Who knows, when they come back, some old friends just might be useful.' He began to chuckle quietly to himself as he turned to stride out the door, but paused and said, 'Welcome to the Abbey of St Dominica, ladies!'

It was a few moments of breathless silence before Marilla and Isabella realised what he had said and after staring blankly at each other, they hurried out of the door, running to keep up with his long strides.

'What do you mean, when *who* comes back?' panted Marilla, as she caught up with him.

Jack did not answer immediately but kept walking toward what they assumed to be the rear of the Abbey. 'I guess you'll find out soon enough anyway.' He stopped short, Isabella almost ran into him as she hurried along. 'Why did you open that door anyway, what did you expect to find?'

'We—we thought it might be a storeroom—or something,' stammered Isabella, 'you know, for um—for food. We weren't expecting to find—find, what we did, you see.'

'Okay I understand, Bella,' he smiled, showing the pleasant smile again. 'Come with me I'll get Amos to find something for you two. He seems to be able to put his hands on most things. I expect he's got something on the go now anyway.'

They crossed the courtyard keeping close to Jack as he strode along, not caring now whether they were seen by other eyes or not but their eyes took in all that surrounded them. They were crossing the second large courtyard although the sisters could not see much beyond the cloistered colonnades shade as they were partially concealed by the vines that grew around them and the shrubs bordering the sheltered confines. Soon they were outside a substantial stone building which they found to actually be storerooms and kitchens. It was situated oddly enough, as they found later, very close to where they had landed the night before.

Jack pulled open a heavy iron-hinged door and ushered the girls inside. Entering hesitantly, they found themselves in a short but wide flag stoned entry, the sides of which were lined with various wicker baskets and casks along with rows of rubber boots. The walls were hung with a variety of cloaks and jackets and a huge pottery urn behind the door was filled with umbrellas.

The room beyond felt warm and a strange mixture of aromas assailed their nostrils as they walked through this entry. The damp, dank smell of wet clothing and boots, onions and old wine permeated this passage, they wondered who would use all these things, if there actually was no one else here. However, it was a smell of a different kind that interested them more, it was issuing from the kitchen beyond, the rich enticing smell of a stew. The room they entered was of huge proportions. A high, thick oak-beamed ceiling rose above them, heavily stained from the enormous fireplace that took up much of the opposite wall. Above, and around the huge old stove that filled the fireplace were blackened pots and pans of all sizes and shapes, together with various cooking utensils that also hung within easy reach.

A long trestle-like table of solid, heavily scarred timber dominated the centre of the room with bench seating of the same heavy timber ranged along both sides. In spite of the size and aptness of the room, it exuded a feeling of homeliness, but the sisters still felt decidedly nervous, they hung back a little, as Jack strode confidently into the room.

The sisters' attentions however were riveted on the grey cloaked figure, that stood at the stove with his back to them, stirring something in a large pot that was responsible for the delightful fragrance wafting from it, reminding them of just how hungry they were.

'Amos,' said Jack, removing his woollen cap and dropping it on to the end of the bench seat, 'I've found our two visitors who flew in last night. Old friends of mine from a long way back.' His voice hardened sharply as he added, 'Found him, Amos but we'll talk about that later.' Running a hand then through a mass of dark hair, he turned to the sisters who still stood hesitantly in the doorway, nervously eyeing what was obviously a private domain. He called out to them, 'Marilla, Isabella, come and meet Amos, right hand man, all round good guy as well as an excellent cook!'

The figure at the stove slowly turned to face them and they found themselves staring into the bluest eyes they had ever seen. They were framed in a clean shaven round cherubic face, which beamed at them, albeit a little nervously. The hood of the rough woven habit he wore hung loose over his broad back, revealing a close-cropped thatch of greyish hair.

Shortish in stature, his round head and thick neck seemed to melt as one into a barrel-chested large body and the arm that extruded from the rolled-up sleeve of his robe was muscular and almost apelike in appearance. He was holding a large metal spoon in his thick fingers and seemed unaware that it was dripping liquid onto the floor at his feet, as he stared back at the two women standing there.

The voice, when it came was gruff and deep, as if issuing from the bottom of a well, 'I hope you ladies like rabbit stew.'

Jack, who had disappeared into a room on one side, emerged carrying plates, knives and forks and balancing a loaf of bread in the crook of his elbow. He motioned with a nod of his head to the sisters. 'Sit down, girls and don't worry about Amos, he's quite harmless,' then added half under his breath, smirking slightly, as he shot a sidelong glance at the hulking figure by the stove, 'sometimes.'

Amos ignored the remark as he moved to take the plates from Jack, transferring them to the warmth of the broad hob at the side of the stove.

Somewhat nervously, Marilla and Isabella sat down at one end of the smoothly worn bench seat and watched as Amos ladled stew from the pot onto the waiting plates. For perhaps the first time in her life Marilla seemed at a loss for words, while Isabella's mind was transfixed on Amos' broad back as he bent to his task. Was he really a monk? She wasn't really sure what a monk should actually look like, though she had seen pictures of them. What was Jack doing in his company? If he really was a monk. What had Jack been doing in all the years since he had had left the Commune? He had an air of authority about him that she didn't understand, she guessed Marilla was thinking the same thing.

Isabella half turned to nudge Marilla and speak her thoughts, when a slight clatter of china on wood made her look up again, and she found herself looking into those intense blue eyes that held her gaze like a magnet.

'Oh, er, thank you,' she mumbled and lowered her eyes as he pushed the plate toward Jack, busy handing out cutlery, and cutting huge slices from the loaf before sitting down, spoke in a matter-of-fact voice, 'I've told Amos who you are and your–um– occupations, I think he's quite intrigued.'

Amos, who had seated himself next to Jack, muttered in his deep voice, 'I said that it was interesting, that's all.' Isabella noted that the tips of his ears began to redden slightly.

There was a sudden movement, and a large black cat with several white hairs on the tip of his tail, had jumped up onto the bench next to Amos and was rubbing its head against his arm. Marilla's mind snapped back to order. 'Lucifer! Where the *devil* have you been?'

Amos looked across at her as he playfully pulled the cat's ears, receiving a friendly bite on the arm in return. 'So that's his name, is it?' then chuckled softly. 'That name should stir up a few monastic ghosts around here.' He slid off the seat and went back to the stove with the cat padding quickly behind him. 'Well, now that we've been properly introduced, Lucifer, I guess you'd like your meal.' Reaching to the back of the hob, Amos picked up a warmed dish of stew and placed it on the floor in front of the waiting cat, who immediately began to greedily demolish the contents.

Marilla, whose mind had been struggling to come to terms with what was happening, voiced her astonishment. 'I don't understand! Lucifer never willingly goes to anybody! He barely tolerates us—he's a devil—he's—how did you, you must have put a spe—', she stopped awkwardly without continuing and she felt her face beginning to redden.

Amos was gathering his robes together and swept back onto the bench as he spoke, interrupting her awkward rush of words. 'Let's just say we reached a gentleman's agreement early this morning over hunting rights to the local rabbit population.'

Jack was grinning as he watched the changing expressions on Marilla's face. 'That would be right, one hunter to another eh, Amos?'

'Something like that I guess,' said Amos, as he looked around at Lucifer who had finished what was in the dish and was now licking up the drops of gravy that had fallen from the ladle. 'Damned fine animal though, seems to understand what you say to him too. Worked as a team this morning … eventually.'

'After you explained the rules of combat no doubt,' laughed Jack.

Isabella caught Amos' eye and smiled. 'He really is a lot smarter than the average cat, he is rather special.'

Marilla suddenly remembered something, and turned to face Jack, an incredulous look on her face. 'You knew we were here last night, didn't you?'

'As a matter of fact; yes I did,' he replied, 'you made enough noise to wake the dead. However, I didn't want to disturb your slumber and I figured anything else could wait until this morning. That was when Lucifer and I had a slight disagreement but I put that down as a hint not to approach any closer to where you were.' He grinned at them impishly. 'I would say that having Lucifer about is like have a miniature Rottweiler watching over you two. However, I do believe we have established a code of conduct now; we both know our place in the hierarchy of this establishment.'

Marilla opened her mouth to say something, caught the look on Amos' face and decided not to say anything. Instead, she concentrated on what was on the plate in front of her. There were many questions brimming over in her mind. Questions, lots of questions she wanted answers to.

Little more was said during the meal, which both sisters had to admit was better than anything they would have put together themselves. Jack was right, Amos' stew, fragrant with herbs and thick with meat and vegetables, was most satisfying.

Marilla who had been watching Jack closely, now asked the question that was still burning in her mind. 'Just what are you doing here, Jack? After all these years we run into you of all people, here, in a place like this, an obviously abandoned Abbey?'

'Ah, yes,' replied Jack as he pushed his plate away. 'I know you've been waiting for an answer, but before I answer your question; I want an answer to mine. Where were you headed before you got caught up in that storm? This was not your intended destination, was it?'

Marilla looked into the grey eyes for a moment and said, 'We were … we were trying to get to the old forest. Grandma Hackett has a cottage there and we thought we'd stay there for a while.' Marilla drew herself up and regained some of her flint-like composure, then said in a cool and almost arrogant voice, 'After all, it does belong to us now that Grandma has gone. We only intended it to be a short stopping place before we moved on.'

'If it's still there, which I very much doubt,' said Jack, in a voice just as cool.

There was suddenly a shocked look on Isabella's plump round face and her brown eyes looked even larger. 'It is! It must be there!' Isabella broke in. 'I know–I saw it–I looked and …' Here she cast a quick glance at Amos, who was following the conversation with a surprised expression on his face, his blue eyes fixed firmly on her.

Isabella twisted her hands together on the top of the table, her eyes darting anxiously at the three faces silently watching her, waiting for an answer.

'I–I used Grandmother's scrying mirror with one of her special spells from her book and I could see it … just as it was, there in the forest!' She clutched at her sister's arm, 'I know you've told me I was not to use any of Grandma's things but I knew I could do it; I knew! It wasn't hard at all and Marilla … I did want us to go back there!'

Marilla stiffened; it wasn't just the fact that Isabella had disobeyed her explicit order not to try any of Grandmother's special spells. She had considered her sister far too young and inexperienced to fully understand them, after all they were difficult. No. The fact was that Isabella had managed to not only understand Hilda Hackett's odd way of writing her spells but had actually mastered the scrying mirror! A thing Marilla herself had been unable to do, not for the want of trying!

'Well now.' Jack broke the awkward silence and Marilla's indignant thoughts, he addressed himself directly to Isabella. 'The mirror didn't give you the full picture, Bella. It didn't show the bulldozers that are clearing part of the forest near the cottage.'

'But how could you know that?' It was Isabella's turn to be indignant.

'I was given permission by your grandmother to use the cottage if I needed to when I left Harewood. I had stayed there several times over the years and when I came through there less than a couple of months ago, changes had already begun. Plans had been drawn up and there is work already under way to clear part of the Western fringe ... for some distance in that it has most certainly already violated the isolation of the cottage. As it is, the road that runs past has already been widened with some of the old oaks cut down ... you really don't want to see it, Bella, it's not a pretty picture.'

'Oh,' said Isabella, a look of disbelief and sadness furrowing her smooth brow, her large brown eyes began to fill with tears. 'Then there's no point in going back there now is there?' She turned to her sister. 'What are we going to do now, Marilla? We've nowhere else to go, I was so looking forward to going to Grandma's old cottage.'

Marilla had remained silent. She was, in reality, trying to think where she had gone wrong with the scrying mirror. Not that it mattered now, she would take that up again later, but Isabella was right — where would they go now? 'I really don't know,' she answered flatly. 'I'm sure there are plenty of other places, in any case there's still Harewood.'

'I thought you said that you would never go back there,' sniffed Isabella, wiping her eyes, 'that's why I suggested the cottage.'

'I don't really want to go back to *either* place!' retorted Marilla, 'there's more to life than just sitting around in a boring little cottage with no incentive, no excitement or any challenges to make life interesting. There's better things to do, Isabella, than just go wandering around picking wildflowers, talking to birds and trees, it might be what you might like to do, but I *don't*! We'll just find somewhere else!'

Jack had been sitting back with his arms folded over his chest, one hand absently rubbing his bearded chin, while Amos unnecessarily found something wrong with a fingernail. At last, Jack spoke. 'You know, Edwina taught me a lot of things when I was growing up, one was, that there is a reason for everything that happens. Even if you really don't fully understand the reasons, you can sometimes look behind the obvious and find the stimulus that brings something into effect. Perhaps it doesn't happen straight away but it's going to happen whether you're ready for it or not. I believe that you two were dropped here on purpose, the storm carried you so far and intervention did the rest. I don't know how it was done or why but my inner feelings are usually never wrong.'

He unfolded his arms and leaned across the table. 'In essence, ladies, I rather think that storm meant to drop you here but for what purpose I have no idea as yet or have any information. However, I am sure that this copious and certainly not entirely abandoned Abbey could handle two more. What do you say, Amos?'

Amos, who had been listening intently to the conversation while surreptitiously examining the said fingernail, looked up and cleared his throat before replying, 'Certainly, of course we can. There's plenty of room, it would be, er, interesting and a pleasure to have two ladies such as yourselves as extra company.'

There was silence from Marilla and Isabella as they considered this offer.

Isabella would have been happy enough to stay for a while. Meeting up with a childhood companion was reason enough for her and she sensed there was more to this ancient pile of buildings than they had first supposed, the urge to explore these strange new surroundings was a tantalising thought.

She also knew that Marilla would not go back to Harewood, mainly on principle. To go back would, to her, mean that she was a failure in making a life for themselves outside of the Commune, as she had pronounced to the company there so emphatically.

Her elder sister was too proud to admit that she was finding life a lot harder outside the protective circle of her kin. She wanted to make a name for herself in the skilfulness of her craft and return to take her place as a true granddaughter of a Grand Witch. So far though they had drifted from place to place like gypsies with no idea of where their path was to take them. Privately Isabella had thought that Marilla could have proved herself just as easily had she stayed at home, but she had felt it her duty to stay beside her sister at least until she tired of wandering; then perhaps they would settle, even if it was back at Harewood.

Another thought entered her mind, this was an Abbey. Jack said the Abbey was not entirely abandoned; were there still monks here? If there were, where were they? She wasn't sure they could live among a group of monks; she'd have to think a lot about that.

Marilla, however, had other ideas. She had listened to what

Jack had to say, pursing her lips and frowning at him. 'That was just a storm, like any other storm and I don't read anything else into it. My compass reading must have been thrown off by it, led us this way by accident and anyway,' she said almost haughtily, 'what if we don't want to stay, there are plenty of other places we can go to, it's just a matter of finding something that suits us, which of course we will.'

'Are there?' said Jack, raising an eyebrow, 'I really wouldn't be too sure of that, Marilla. I have to remind you both that you don't have a choice of where you'll go, because you cannot leave here … not now.'

'And why *not?*'

'Well, for one thing you're a long way from anywhere up here, not that it would bother you much I think but as I said before, I think your travel plans were deliberately diverted, you were meant to be dropped here, instead of near the cottage. As I said, for what purpose I have as yet, no idea,' he shrugged his shoulders meaningfully.

'That's ridiculous, who would want to do that?'

'I rather think it might be something that has been mapped out by somebody known to both of us, but until I learn more, I have to ask you not to attempt to leave here. I can assure you both, you will be made comfortable.'

'But you still can't keep us here if we don't want to stay, regardless of whose idea it was to force us down to this place.' Marilla was almost sulky.

'But I can,' said Jack, his grey eyes steady on her defiant green ones. 'Marilla, you know *who* and *where* I am; we would like that to remain secret for a short while longer. There are events that have happened and events that are going to happen right here in this, not quite abandoned Abbey that in the end, just might have need of your special skills. However, for the first part of proceedings, Amos and I would prefer that you were both safely out of the way.'

'Oh dear, that sounds all very mysterious,' piped up Isabella. 'It sounds like it could be the sort of excitement you've been looking for, Marilla.'

Marilla gave her younger sister a scathing look, before turning back to face Jack. 'I don't understand what you are getting at, Jack Grimsby, what possible help could we give you with whatever it is you are here for?'

Jack sighed. 'Frankly I don't fully understand it either but Amos and I have a very ticklish situation to address within the next twenty-four hours or so, I just can't let you wander off, not now, at least not until we have matters cleaned up here. Once we have accomplished our mission you will be free to go if you still want to. Things could occur here that are way beyond anything you could possibly imagine, the last thing I want is for anything to happen to either of you, so I just have to keep you tucked safely out of the way.'

'Just what is happening here that we should be so concerned about anyway?'

Jack stared at his hands clasped before him on the table for a moment, then lifted his gaze to hold theirs and replied. 'Well, let's start with some high-class forgery, a little blackmail, the ongoing hunt for a valuable lost treasure, oh and a few murders thrown in for good measure.'

Isabella's brown eyes opened wider as Jack ticked them off on his fingers and Marilla's mouth stayed open with no words coming out this time.

Amos sighed as he slid off the bench and muttered in his deep rumbling voice, 'I think I'll go and make some tea.'

"the ongoing hunt for a lost treasure, and a few murders for good measure"

Chapter 12

The Abbot Makes A Confession

Abbot Peter Gleeson sat with his head in his hands, his head and shoulders shaking slightly every now and then. Jack Grimsby sat with his arms folded, quietly watching him across the broad desk in the Abbot's private quarters. At last Jack spoke. 'Perhaps you don't feel like discussing this situation right now but I can assure you my dear sir that it is of the utmost importance that we do. Your life and that of your fellow brethren are at risk here, or hadn't you taken that into consideration before you became embroiled in this mess?'

Jack looked over to where Amos was leaning against a window frame and received a slight nod in return before continuing. 'You are also well aware, I am sure, that the second half of this mob will be walking back through that gate in a few hours from now, Mr Casini will not be in a happy frame of mind, in fact, he will be dangerously annoyed!'

There was silence for a while. Then the Abbot lifted his head and looked at Jack with tired eyes. 'I—I didn't know it would come to this, I had no power to stop Mr Casini, and I'm dreadfully afraid now of what might happen.'

He looked across to where Amos stood and looked at him for a long moment. 'I was right, I had never seen you before this.

I had no idea you were connected with … the law.' He drew his hands over his face again.

Amos unfolded his arms and sat on the substantial arm of an overstuffed sofa under the window and said in his gruff, but patient voice. 'We don't usually openly identify who we are, this is the way we work; no prior advertisements, otherwise we'd be out of business.'

'But I thought … everyone here thought that you really were one of us.' The Abbot spread his hands as he looked at Amos. 'I would never have known you were not of the Order.'

Jack laughed softly. 'It might interest you to know that brother Amos here was a Grey Friar once, of course that was a very long time ago.'

Amos shifted uneasily on the sofa and rumbled reproachfully. 'That was a very, very long time ago, Jack and doesn't fit this equation.'

Jack addressed the Abbot again. 'Peter — I may call you by that name, sir, it's easier that way I think? Peter, as we have told you, we now have the present three of this fraud gang locked away, we are also relying on you to give every assistance in securing the capture of Victor Casini and his other associates and any relevant evidence. It would be in your best interests to do so, things may not go as badly for you as you might think. Do we have your word on that?'

The Abbot was silent for a moment, looking down at his hands and twisting a ring around his finger. He had suddenly begun to look and feel very old and tired. He was a tall thin man, who looked much older than his years. His pale face was long and angular with a strong square jawline and when he looked up at Jack, it was with deep-socketed eyes below thinning grey hair. His hands were large, the fingers long and tapered as they twisted the ring nervously. At last he spoke, his voice trembling slightly. 'I suppose I will have to go to prison for my part in this, even though Mr Casini has been the prime perpetrator in this business.' He looked from Jack to Amos then back to Jack, his voice steadier now. 'You know he did threaten me, so I cannot be wholly responsible for my actions, we were being held here against our will.'

'I'm well aware of that,' replied Jack, 'and that will be taken into consideration. However, at this point I want to ask you some questions regarding another matter of which you may have some knowledge.'

Jack pulled his chair a little closer to the desk and leaned his arms on it, meeting the Abbot's hollowed, tormented eyes with his own steady grey ones. 'Does the name Zaharoff mean anything to you?'

A startled look crossed the gaunt features of the man seated before him and the little colour there was in his face paled. He opened his mouth, but no word came from it.

'So, you do recognise the name then?' said Jack casually again. 'Perhaps you can also tell me who held the position of Abbot before you and if there was any connection between that name and the head of the Abbey at that time.'

'That—that was Henri Du Pont. He was … rather odd.'

'Really, in what way was he odd?'

The Abbot put his large hands to the side of his head, resting his elbows on the table, while the long fingers rubbed his forehead. 'I can't think, I've got a dreadful headache.' He looked up as Amos walked over to him. 'You put something in that wine last night, didn't you?'

Amos had fished in his pocket and brought out a packet of aspirin putting the packet on the desk in front of the Abbot, he then walked to a side table and poured a glass of water from a carafe there placing that beside the aspirin. Pausing briefly, he said quietly, 'You had a good sleep, didn't you?'

'Well, I suppose I did, probably the best sleep I've had for weeks. I presume you drugged me with something didn't you?' The Abbot picked up the aspirin packet and looked at it closely.

'Don't worry,' said Amos, 'they are just aspirin and I expected you would be suffering from a hangover.'

'But was that really necessary?'

'Yes, it was,' interjected Jack. 'I could not get any sense out of you when I tried to talk to you last evening. Perhaps your mind is a little clearer today. I am assuming you were here during the time that Henri was in position as Head of the Abbey. There was a monk appointed as "keeper of the gate". I believe that may have been you at that time.'

The Abbot did not answer straight away, he was turning the aspirin packet over in his hands as if reluctant to open it and he looked suspiciously at Amos as he spoke with a deep sigh. 'Yes, I was as a matter of fact. I was a senior then; it was part of my duties.'

'Then the arrival of a woman at the gate to see the Abbot would have been a surprise to you, would it not?'

The Abbot looked up at Jack and caught his eye. 'Indeed yes, it was, but how did you know, she did not give a name? She said Abbot Du Pont was expecting her, so I escorted her to his apartments.'

'But you were curious as to why a woman would want audience with the Abbot, weren't you, Peter?'

'Yes—I mean—no! It was really none of my business. I left her there and went back to my own quarters!'

'Would I be right in suggesting that you may have lingered

long enough at the door to hear part of the conversation, would that be a correct assumption?'

Peter Gleeson ran a nervous hand through his sparse crop of hair and replied haltingly. 'I, well–ah, no–I don't recall doing so, it was nothing to do with me really, nothing at all. It was Henri's business, I assumed that she might have been a relative of his. I'm really not sure I remember now, it was so long ago, years–I'm not sure that I can remember that far back.'

'I think if you search your memory bank, you will remember,' said Jack, his grey eyes steady on the pale ones blinking before him.

The Abbot went back to twisting the ring on his finger as he answered. 'I didn't really understand what it all meant, I only heard snatches of the conversation and …' he paused.

'Go on.'

'Well, I heard him ask her if the boy was alright, and was he safe, then he said, "Have you got the book?" … at least I think that's what it was.'

'At which point you were almost discovered eavesdropping, weren't you?' said Jack. The pale eyes looked at Jack in amazement. 'How could you know that?'

'Never mind how I know. What I want to know now is, what happened to the book. Did you find it and tuck it away into your own private collection?'

'No, no,' he stuttered nervously. 'The Abbot just told me … if I was interested, that it was a Russian Bible, that had been given to him by a family friend for safe keeping and would be of no interest to anyone else. It was just a family Bible!'

'Did you see it again? Do you know where Henri put it?'

'No, I didn't, I didn't know where he put it at the time … but I do know that he was more peculiar than ever after the woman had gone.'

The deep voice of Amos cut in, 'Peculiar — in what way exactly?'

Peter glanced at Amos and said, 'As I mentioned before he was a strange person to begin with. Not that he did anything wrong as far as the church and the Abbey were concerned. He held a strong code of ethics and followed our code of conduct diligently, but his, er, private life was something else … it was weird. He would lock himself in his rooms for days and … and.'

'And what?' prompted Jack.

'And then he took to wandering around the church, through the nave, at night, particularly when there was a full moon. He would walk about muttering to himself, he would touch the floor, or the walls. We were all naturally concerned about his, um … health. He did not appear to be a–dare I say–a sane man, yet at other times he was perfectly normal.'

'You witnessed him doing this then,' interjected Amos.

'Yes.' The Abbot turned to face Amos. 'I was worried about him, so I followed him a couple of times, discreetly of course.'

'Of course,' said Amos gruffly.

'He also spent a lot of time in the old library and wandering through the lower rooms and cellars, though he did not entirely neglect his duties as Head of the Abbey, it did leave us with more responsibilities that he seemed unable to devote time to. I was by then his understudy, you might say. He had appointed Brother Clarence as his representative a little while before but Clarence unfortunately suffered a heart attack less than a year into his appointment, so I became acting Abbot in his place.'

'When did this happen, how long ago?'

Slowly the story emerged as Peter Gleeson had observed. Though Henri Du Pont had followed the doctrine of the Franciscan Order closely, his private life was something of a mystery. Very few of his monastic peers had occasion to enter his private apartments, indeed he discouraged such intrusions. All business relating to the running of the monastery was conducted in another ante-room adjacent to his quarters. However, the very few who did enter that inner sanctuary, could not help but notice a number of strange objects within, that one would perhaps never have associated with a man of such status. Of course, there was a simple answer for such a collection that closed the minds of the inquisitively curious visitor.

Peter Gleeson had, at one time, occasion to intrude on the Abbot in his private domain somewhat unexpectedly and in truth, his intense curiosity as to what really lay in that room drove him to knock at his door one late afternoon. He knocked and entered; he found the aura within the room almost eerie, which sent a slight tingle up his spine … yet it was an ordinary room. 'It was a large room', he related later to those who were interested, 'with a high domed ceiling that exuded a distinctive Gothic atmosphere upon entering. Dark oak panelled walls were relieved of their gloominess by a large, mullioned window on the Southern side that provided a view of the distant snow covered mountains and there was subdued lighting from several wall sconces that provided further illumination to a somewhat spectral chamber.'

A massive oaken desk dominated the room and the direct light from a heavy green shaded lamp that stood upon it highlighted several large volumes lying there, the pages open.

More books bound in the same dark burgundy leather filled a bookcase beside a smoke blackened fireplace, where brass dogs gleamed dully in the reflected light from the desk lamp. An old leather sofa beside the window and an armchair near the fireplace; provided some items of recognisable comfort among other objects that defied accurate description.

*   *   *

As Peter self-consciously entered the room, the Abbot rose from his chair behind the desk to greet him with reserved cordiality. He was a very tall thin man, with a long white beard and an untidy mane of long white hair that hung loosely around his shoulders, His gaunt face was dominated by penetrating dark blue-green eyes, his large, hooked nose was framed by high cheek bones. He moved with a smooth grace that belied his obvious aged appearance.

'Brother Peter,' he had said in a surprisingly deep voice. 'I had not expected you, there is something you wished to discuss with me no doubt?'

Peter had hesitated then, almost wishing he had given this entry second thought, but mumbled an apology. Yes, it was very remiss of him to burst in upon the Abbot like this, but … well, he was here now, but his excuse for an audience began to diminish lamely in his nervousness.

As the Abbot moved forward to steer him toward the armchair, Peter could see the open books on the desk. Large old parchment like pages, filled with spidery writing and strange symbols caught his eye. His curiosity was dampened however, as the Abbot carefully closed the books as he advanced around the edge of the desk. He tried to look about him as he turned to sit where he was directed, on the old armchair. His eye fell on an unusual intricately carved tripod that stood to one side and supported what looked like a mirror, but it was very dark, more like a pool of water sitting flat upon the tripod.

'It's amazing what one picks up in one's travels,' said the Abbot in his carefully controlled deep voice, at the same time throwing a dark cloth that lay nearby over the tripod. He then sat on the arm of the sofa in a position to tower over the other, who had now almost forgotten what his hurried errand had been about. Peter had been glad to escape from the room, its cloying mustiness and the hurried glimpses of other strange objects that seemed to glitter and move of their own accord unnerved him, as he stammered out his reason to intrude into this inner sanctum.

*   *   *

'Was the woman the only visitor the Abbot had from "outside" at the time?' said Jack as he stood up and began to pace the floor, his hands deep in his pockets.

'Yes, though she did return several times later and at one time she spoke at length to Daniel. When I asked him what she wanted, he just said that she wondered if he had been able to translate some of the Bible as she was interested in it, not being able to understand Russian herself.'

'What else did Daniel say?' probed Jack coming back to the table to sit down once more.

The Abbot shook his head. 'Nothing, he never mentioned it again.'

'You seem to have shown a lot of interest in what was going on as regards Abbot Du Pont's affairs,' said Amos accusingly, 'any good reason for that?'

'No, I—was,' he turned to face Amos again, 'as I said before I was concerned about his ah, shall we say, his mental health and his inattention to the running of the Abbey, that's all.'

'I see,' said Jack looking up at Amos quickly. 'Tell me, Peter, did Henri say why he was leaving the Abbey?'

Peter shrugged his shoulders, 'Just that he would have to leave for a while, but not that he would sever ties with the Abbey completely, he had other business he had to attend to elsewhere and would only be away for a while, he felt quite sure we could manage things without him; as I said before, he was a strange man. Nobody really knew too much about him, even though he seemed to have all the right credentials.'

'So, he appointed you as Abbot in his place, is that right?'

'Yes, but it was apparently only until he returned but he never gave any indication when that would be, it is really quite a confusing position to be in.' He rubbed at his forehead again with his hands and said in a very quiet voice. 'He did say something very strange to me before he left. I–I wish in a way I had listened more closely to what he meant, but we thought–I thought, he was, well–slightly mad and perhaps not what he assumed himself to be. I mean, all those strange books and the odd things he kept in his room.'

'Do you remember what he said to you?' asked Jack.

There was a pause before Peter spoke again, and his voice seemed far away and distant. 'He said to me and I quote, "*Two who bear the same name shall come here. One will be evil, bearing malice and hate, the other will seek only the truth and justice for a wrong that will be righted*". I remembered the words because though I didn't understand them, they stuck in my mind. He also turned to me as he was leaving and stared straight at me for a long moment, then he said–he said, my own fate rested in my own hands, hands that could let my life slip through them.'

The hapless monk laid his head on his arms on the desk and muttered to himself. 'He was right, he was right, I should never have let my love of the beautiful things become a selfish obsession.'

Jack had risen from his chair and moved toward the window, where he stood, his hands thrust deeply into the pockets of his jacket, his fingers closing over the folded piece of parchment secreted there. He gazed out of the window, his eyes taking in the magnificent view of white capped mountains above the sea of green pines. A few fleecy white clouds lingered like a protective blanket over the tops of the mountains, the straying mists like unravelling threads drifted down the dark forbidding slopes. He could see the gleam of the distant forest bosomed lake, glistening like a mirror in the morning sunshine, a peaceful vista, a world away from the dark clouds of destiny gathering about him.

Jack knew who Henri Du Pont was or had been. Wizards don't often get to become the Head of an Abbey but Peter Gleeson didn't need to know that. He also knew a bit more about Peter Gleeson than the man himself realised, thanks to Daniel but the Abbot didn't need to know that either. He cast a quick look at Amos still sitting on the arm of the couch, his arms folded across his massive chest, his cherubic face impassive, as he observed Peter straighten up and run a hand through his thinning hair.

Jack walked back to the desk and stood there looking at the unfortunate man for a long moment. Then placing both hands flat on the desk he leaned forward to look intently into the Abbot's face. Then he said in a quiet but firm voice. 'What can you tell us about the man, the very dead man we found locked up in one of the old cells behind the church?'

The Abbot's face went ashen and his hands shook as he covered his face with his hands again.

'Perhaps you had better take these aspirins now,' said Jack gently, pushing the packet toward him, together with the glass of water.

His hands still shaking, the Abbot took the two tablets that Jack broke from the foil wrapper but spilt most of the water before he got it to his mouth. 'It was terrible–terrible,' he choked. Then his head snapped up. 'Victor Casini did that. I saw him do it! He made me watch–told me that he could do the same to anyone here who–stepped out of line–he made us prisoners with that threat hanging over us–he is an evil man–an *evil* man!' he repeated, almost sobbing.

Jack caught the look on Amos' face, the hard line of his jaw and the deepening frown that furrowed his smooth brow. Turning back to the Abbot, Jack asked, 'Did this man come here as a member of the Brotherhood?'

'Yes, he did,' said the other shakily, as he took another sip of water. 'He had come here quite some time before as a lay brother, Bother Daniel. He seemed a nice man, intelligent, an artist, an interpreter of languages, he proved to be a very useful member of our community. French born I think, he spent quite a bit of his time with Henri–the Abbot, both being French, I suppose they had much the same interests.' He looked up at Jack and forced a weak smile. 'You know we did find that book, that Russian Bible. Daniel had found it very interesting, because of the language as it was Old Russian, he had translated some of it, Daniel understood the Russian language and he was very clever … such a pity he's …' His voice choked up again.

'You say the book was found. Where was it, who found it?' Jack endeavoured to keep the Abbot's mind on the subject.

'It was quite strange actually, but when Henri Du Pont left his rooms, there was just one thing remaining in the bookshelves — a package with Daniel's name on it. It was this Bible that the woman had brought here. I couldn't understand why Henri hadn't taken it with him, it seemed important somehow. Then I just … um happened to be … just by chance you understand, in Daniel's rooms and opened the book … it was just sitting there on his desk. The strange thing was, almost the whole inside of the book was cut away; like it was meant to hide something … it was very odd. It really was a beautifully bound book and such a shame to desecrate it like that. There was a piece of old parchment in the bottom of it with some writing on it that looked like Russian. Daniel came in and took the parchment and said he was going to translate it properly before the book was taken back to the library, but at first glance it appeared to be only names of a family history. He said that the Bible had probably only contained a small family keepsake put there so it would not get damaged, he assumed Henri had removed it and taken it with him, leaving the book for Daniel, as there were still some pages left of interest.

'I see,' said Jack, noting in his mind the brief cautionary note he had received from Daniel about being wary of Peter Gleeson and his inquiring habits. 'Is the book still here now?'

'Yes, but no … well; not as it was.' Here the Abbot gave a great shudder. 'That name you spoke of … Zaharoff, that name was in the book. He came here just after Henri left. A terrible man and he was very angry when he found Henri was not here and whatever was in the book not there either. Then he accused us of taking something from inside the book … something valuable that belonged to his family. He found the piece of parchment that Daniel had put back. He looked at it and read it several times before putting it in his pocket, but it still didn't stop him from throwing things around, there were these men that he had with him, big men, huge–like–like gorillas, one of them just picked up the Bible and tore it in half, as if it was just a piece of paper,' he spread his hands hopelessly, 'we couldn't stop them.'

'What happened then?'

'This Zaharoff person had these men of his search all through the Abbey, asking questions about Henri, but nobody knew where he had gone. As I said, Henri was very strange, he would often disappear without telling anyone where he was going. He'd be away for some weeks and then just turn up again, without saying anything about where he'd been.'

'Did Zaharoff say he was going to come back at all?'

'He said he was going to return when it was the proper time. I don't know what he meant by the proper time. Mr Zaharoff said he would find the thing he wanted, as he knew it was here somewhere or that Henri or someone else would show him where it was. I had no idea what he was talking about. Perhaps it was the thing that had been inside the book, but it was so long ago now.'

'So Daniel had put the parchment back in the book,' said Jack, 'do you know if he did translate it? Did he tell you what was written on it?'

'No, he didn't, except to say that it was not very interesting, just appeared to be names associated with the family who had owned the Bible originally, that he would put it back.'

Jack smiled ruefully to himself. He knew Dan would have taken a copy of the parchment and put the original back in the book, because that was what he had been instructed to do. Zaharoff was meant to find the original, Daniel couldn't falsify that, but there was still a lot that Jack had not been told and he knew he had to talk to Henri … when he could find him.

The copy already translated was safe in Jack's pocket, the copy he had found hidden in Dan's shoe but the Abbot didn't need to know about that either.

Amos rose from where he had been seated on the arm of the old chair and walked around to face the Abbot. 'I presume then, that it was about this time that you got caught up with Casini, right?'

Peter Gleeson seemed on the verge of breaking down again. 'Everything seemed to be happening at once. First this strange Zaharoff person and those huge men breaking up the place looking for something that wasn't here, then this gangster moves in with his henchmen … I suppose that's what they're called, and threatening us with guns.'

'Perhaps he had a reason for choosing this particular place,' said Amos dryly.

Peter swallowed and fumbled with his words. 'I don't know how he found out about my, um–private collection but he threatened to expose me to the Police and um–others in the hieratic ministry, which would have brought a great deal of shame upon the monastery itself; I couldn't let that happen.' He looked up at Amos and Jack with tired fearful eyes. 'I have felt remorse for some actions I have taken in the past, I have tried to repent and make good my somewhat selfish transgressions, but I fear it has all been too late. Mr Casini said that everything would be alright if I just kept quiet about what he was doing here and we … that is the Abbey, would both benefit from it.' His head sank down into his hands again. 'It's been like this for such a long time now, I have not been able to stop it.'

'Why did Victor kill Daniel?'

The Abbot was silent for a moment, then looked at Amos in something like bewilderment. 'I don't know, I'm not sure why but I got the impression that they knew each other. Perhaps he had a past life that had a criminal element, otherwise why would he recognise Daniel and persecute him as he did? Mr Casini was very quick to notice the transgressions of others … excluding himself,' the Abbot muttered ruefully. 'It's true some of the Brothers do have past lives they wish to forget and joining the Brotherhood to do something useful with their lives can have a healing virtue.'

'So Victor Casini just shot him and left his body in that cell,' said Amos in a low voice, trying to hide his anger and frustration.

'Yes,' replied the Abbot, his voice shaking. 'He said … he did it to prove what he meant about any one of us trying to escape or raise an alarm.'

Something occurred to the Abbot at that moment; he looked from Amos to Jack with his tired pale eyes. 'That cell was locked, one of Casini's men threw the key away, so we could not give Daniel a decent burial as he should have had. He was to remain there to be a reminder to us to keep quiet. It was not right or moral, how did you know he was in there, how did you get in?'

Jack and Amos exchanged glances.

'We have ways and means of knowing these things Peter,' said Jack, 'the locked door was no problem, we had, what you might call divine intervention.'

It was not the right time to tell the Abbot that there were two witches on the premises, he didn't need to know about that … yet.

It was some little while later that Jack and Amos returned to the warmth of the kitchen after assuring Peter Gleeson that if he stayed put for the next twenty-four hours, then they would try to sort his troubles out. However, the surprise capture of Victor Casini himself was their prime objective he was told and if the safety of the brothers was to be reassured, then he, like the others would have to remain locked in their quarters. Privately, they knew, of course, that there would have to be retribution for Gleeson for his part in high profile crime, but considering his nervous disposition at the moment, it was best to let him believe that all would be right in the end.

The two agents were silent for a moment as they contemplated the information given them by Gleeson. Both had their own private thoughts about their compatriot Daniel Montaigne, now a grim relic hidden away in a tiny cell.

A very private and intelligent member of the French Surete, Montaigne had been semi-retired but had been conducting his own investigations into stolen National treasures. A man who preferred to work alone and known by his confederates to live constantly 'on the edge,' his clues had led him to the isolated Abbey of St Dominica, where his linguistic talents soon won him a coveted place among the monks there. It was also there, that Daniel became a willing part of the plot devised by the Head of the Abbey with a certain witch to bring about the downfall and demise of a tyrant along with the eventual recovery of a precious icon to its rightful owner.

Daniel Montaigne and Amos McAllister were only two of a small handful of people who were aware of the mystery and intrigue that had plagued Jack's life. Only they were conscious of the shadows that dogged his footsteps, the jackals that followed from place to place, unobtrusively and persistently — the emissaries of a powerful antagonist. It was not so much his life that was threatened but something the enemy wanted, something that Jack would lead him to if he could contain his impatience long enough, but his patience was running out.

Now, it seemed that this two-dimensional quest had now centred into one target. Daniel had been able to filter through the channels certain information. The whereabouts of the Casinis, the enquiring habits of the present pseudo Abbot, but also the means to the location of an object very close to Jack's heart, and the desire of his contender, but he had to play the game according to the rules set out by the adjudicators. Judge and jury would see that justice was done. Once perpetrators in both scenarios were dutifully dealt with, Daniel would once more be a free agent. However, that was not to be.

It was unfortunate therefore, that Daniel had been confronted by an enemy who knew him well enough to ensure his silence permanently but it was a piece of parchment held by Daniel that would give Jack part of his answer, the rest he would have to find himself. It was to be here in this ancient Abbey that fate would decide the outcome.

Chapter 13

An Opportune Escape

'What are you thinking, Marilla?'

The sisters were seated on a large flat rock not far from the entrance to their shelter. Marilla was slowly breaking a twig into little pieces, her eyes staring without really seeing the beauty of the forest that lay before her. The recent storm had left the air clean and sharp, the stray playful tentacles of a passing breeze rustled the treetops who in turn played tag with the winds higher up that were busy pushing fluffy white clouds across the void of a blue sky.

Isabella had sat with her hands clasped in front of her, surveying the scene through wide open eyes, drinking in the tranquillity of the nearby forest. The dense tangle of brambles, adorned with colourful red and orange berries, a breakfast banquet for the tiny birds that squabbled incessantly over the choicest ones, became a delightful chorus to her ears. Every now and then she heard the soft scurrying of small forest dwellers scrabbling amongst the leaves and underbrush. To Isabella it was a symphony of nature in motion. The lush green of the pines, highlighting the yellowing leaves, looking like golden droplets, clinging tenaciously to the poplars further down the steep slope, provided a living backdrop to the symphonic interlude of nature's seasonal dramatisations.

A sense of wellbeing at being witness to this small portrait of creation washed over her; inwardly she could also feel a strange and determined magnetism that was to hold them to this place but she kept that thought to herself for the moment.

After what seemed an eternity, her sister spoke with a heavy sigh. 'To be honest, Bella, I don't know what I'm thinking.' It was peaceful enough, sitting on the sun-warmed rock outside their shelter, they both welcomed the fine morning with the warmth on their faces as the sun climbed higher in its arc through the now almost clear sky.

'Has it occurred to you, Bella that there is something more than a little strange about us landing just here, at this place?' said Marilla finally.

'I suppose it is, I'm sure Jack Grimsby was the last person we would have expected to see but I'm glad we have. It's nice to see him again after all these years, you have to admit that, Marilla.'

'Exactly!' Marilla threw her last piece of twig to the ground and turned to face her sister. 'That's just it, Bella! First that storm turned us unexpectedly in a different direction and then we run into Jack Grimsby, of all people — Jack Grimsby! Can't you see there's *got* to be a connection, somehow we were meant to be dropped here, but why?' She picked up a small stone near her feet and threw it at the nearest bush putting a startled bird to flight. 'There are forces at work here, Isabella, I can feel it … and it's beyond our control.'

She glanced up as a small flock of birds came wheeling close by to where they sat. 'That's it then!' Marilla firmly stated, 'I'm going to confront Jack right now and find out just what is going on here and I have no intention of staying here against my will!'

'What if I asked you to stay … as a friend,' said a voice behind them. 'I do believe you are right about that inner force that you feel, Marilla because I had felt the same way when I came to this place.'

Both sisters turned to find Jack standing behind them. He dropped down onto another boulder and regarded them both intently. 'I wasn't eavesdropping, I came to tell you that Amos is preparing some lunch for us and to inquire how you slept last night.'

Marilla more so than Isabella had refused Jack's offer to find them an empty cell or the use of the Hospice for the night, saying they would not feel comfortable there. They regarded the Abbey with awe and were conscious that although they had not seen any, the thought of grey shrouded figures gliding silently about unnerved them a trifle. That, coming from a pair of witches was rather odd, Jack thought but he didn't argue the point. Later in the evening he and Amos had taken armfuls of bedding with some provisions around to their meagre shelter to at least provide some comfort. Amos had eyed the cauldron in the corner of the cave with great curiosity, but felt no inclination to satisfy that curiosity, indeed, he pretended not to notice it at all.

It was Isabella who answered. 'Yes, we did, thank you, it was quite warm in there.' 'Yes, it was thoughtful of you,' conceded Marilla, 'but we are used to sleeping anywhere we can and usually make do. However, what I want to know right now, Jack is, why are you in a place like this and who did you mean when you said, "when *they* come back", and what—'

'Whoa!' Jack interrupted Marilla's rush of words. 'Too many questions too soon, Marilla. I can't answer all of them yet, except to explain briefly why Amos and I are here, why you must listen closely to what I say and do as I ask. I have to point out to you

that things could get a little heated and dangerous within the
next twenty-four hours or perhaps less now, so I must warn you
to keep out of the way so Amos and I can get on with our job.
Nobody knows you are here … yet. The monks that are living
here have been locked up in another part of the Abbey for their
own safety and are not aware that there are two ladies, such as
yourselves amongst us, I don't want to traumatise them any more
than they already are.'

'Then there *are* monks here!' Isabella's brown eyes widened.

Jack nodded. 'Yes, Isabella, but you needn't be concerned
about them, there are only a few and they're very quiet … quite
harmless,' he grinned at her.

'Amos and I have been interviewing the Abbot this morning,
we managed to gain a little more information as regards the
activities that are going on here and some more on another
matter that I will discuss with you both later. In the meantime,
we just need you to stay safely out of the way.'

'But who are *they* and *what* is going on here!' insisted Marilla,
'I think you could tell us something as well as how do you fit
into this?'

Jack drew a deep breath and said resignedly, 'I won't go into
it all now, Marilla, except to say that Amos and I are members
of Interpol, an International Law Enforcement Agency. We are
police officers and the Special Branch we are attached to, have
been following a particular group of criminals, some of whom
are now here, in this Abbey.'

Isabella's eyes remained wide, she looked at him with her
mouth open in shocked surprise, 'You mean there are criminals
here, as well as monks?'

'Don't be too concerned, Bella,' said Jack soothingly, 'Amos
and I were somewhat successful in capturing the small group of

baddies and they are safely locked up away from the monks, so you needn't worry your woolly little head about them … but, what I wanted you to understand is that the leader and head honcho of this group is the one we want, he's more dangerous than the other three. In other words, you've dropped in for a visit at a damn awkward time, even though I know it wasn't your intention.'

'Then this is what you were referring to last night,' stated Marilla.

'Exactly, Victor Casini is the man we're after, he's slipped through our fingers before and we're not about to let it happen again. That's why we can't let you both go wandering off again; at least not until he's safely caught in our little surprise net. He seems to have eyes and ears everywhere; he's as slippery as an eel and generally only concerned about saving his own skin, let alone his brothers or any other member of his little gang.'

'So, what are they doing here, in an Abbey … among monks?' queried Marilla.

'These men are art thieves, forgers and might I add — murderers, they will dispense with anyone who gets in their way. The monks in this Abbey are artisans who specialise in restoring and repairing manuscripts, books, valuable works of art, that sort of thing. This nasty little group are taking advantage of the talents these monks possess and are literally holding them to ransom, hostages if you like. They've picked the perfect place too as this Abbey is like a fortress, the only way we've been able to infiltrate this far is because of Amos; he's been among them for some time now and I might add he'll be glad when he can get back to normal civvies.'

'Then–then–Amos is not a monk at all!' exclaimed Isabella, 'you're both policemen!'

'Right,' Jack confirmed, 'but so far, only the Abbot knows

that and as he is locked up separately, I hope it will stay like that until we get the fly caught in our web. According to the information we have been given, Casini should be here sometime tomorrow and he won't be alone, so other than locking you both up somewhere, which I don't think you'd appreciate, I have to ask you to keep right out of the way in your little corner here. Nobody will notice you tucked away in there.'

Marilla gave a heavy sigh and was silent for a moment. 'That still does not explain why we are here does it? If we were deliberately blown off course and dropped down here; who was responsible? Nobody knew where we were going. If it was an intervention, as you say, then who would force us down here, surely it has nothing to do with this lot of crooks you're after?'

Jack suddenly looked very grim and spoke slowly. 'No, it isn't, it's something else that goes back a long way and somehow, I get the feeling that it isn't the only thing that this ancient pile of stone is going to give up, I rather suspect, Marilla that somehow it is the reason you are both here. There is a power here that I have felt since I arrived, you and Isabella are part of it, I'm sure of it now. There will be an explanation, I know but I guess we have to wait for the right time.'

'That man,' broke in Isabella, 'that man in the room we went into, was he something to do with whatever was on that piece of paper?'

'Yes, he was, he was investigating another matter, something that was important to me, as well as helping to track this gang down. Unfortunately, he ran into someone who knew him only too well … it's a risk we have to take in this business.'

'What are you going to do about him?' said Isabella pensively, 'you can't leave him there … like that.'

Jack put his hand on Isabella's shoulder, 'No, Bella, I won't;

unfortunately that will have to wait until we get this present situation under control.'

'This is all very strange,' said Marilla thoughtfully. 'The last time we set eyes on each other we were just kids, now suddenly, here, at what looks to be the end of the world, we find you. It can't be just coincidence … there's someone behind all this, the only person that is

known closely to both of us is Edwina Grimsby. Could this be something she has dreamed up?'

'I rather fancy it might be,' said Jack slowly. In fact, he knew that it was; however Marilla and Isabella fitted into her plan, he had, as yet no idea.

'Come on girls,' he said lightly, pulling Isabella to her feet. 'Let's get some breakfast or the cook will be getting cranky, he's not safe to be around when he's like that.'

As they made their way back to the kitchen, Isabella said thoughtfully, 'I never thought you'd turn out to be a policeman Jack and you know, Amos doesn't look like a policeman either.'

'Now, what do you think a policeman should look like?'

'I really don't know, maybe … he does look more like a monk after all.'

*   *   *

A thorough search of the rooms the Casinis had occupied revealed a radio telephone, a couple of handguns and a thick folder filled with rough drawings of what was to be Victor Casinis' latest enterprise concerning the Abbey, but the box of explosives was missing.

'I think I know where they might be,' said Amos, as they sat in the kitchen, the crumbs of lunch decorating otherwise empty plates. He reached for one of the steaming mugs of coffee that Isabella had put in front of them all. 'There are storerooms under where we are now, more than likely that's where it will be. As soon as we've finished here, we'll check on those rooms.'

'What about those monks that are here, Jack?' said Isabella cautiously, 'Where are they, are they in any danger when these other people you are expecting come here?'

'I checked them all this morning,' Amos spoke up, 'and explained the situation as it is to them and to sit tight. They are really quite comfortable where they are, the quarters they live in are reasonably self-contained, they just don't have access to the church at the moment, but they'll be alright.' His face clouded over, he frowned as he said, 'Although I am a bit concerned about one of them.' He sat silently for a moment. 'His name's Carlos,' he said finally, 'one of the engravers — I have the feeling he's about to turn the other cheek and go feral. I've been watching him on and off for a while now. I get the impression he doesn't want to be here. It's only a gut feeling, but, to me he's a shifty sort of character, he could stir up trouble amongst the others. He was very vocal earlier when we had that insane incident with Gleeson.'

'Hmm,' murmured Jack, 'that's just what we don't need right now; a rebel in the base camp.'

'I could isolate him from the rest on some excuse I suppose,' said Amos, 'put him in another cell where he can't influence the others.'

Jack grinned mischievously as he looked at Marilla. 'Perhaps we should leave him with a couple of female guards. With their reputations — it could be quite entertaining.'

Marilla drew herself up stiffly and was about to respond when Jack said quickly. 'You know I was only joking, Marilla.'

'And *you* haven't changed!' she retorted hotly.

*   *   *

After warning the sisters not to stray too far from their cave shelter, Amos and Jack explored what options they had in securing the capture of the remaining members of the gang, before calling in their re-enforcements to tidy up the rest. Taking Vinnie, Bruno and Leo by surprise was a coup they had hoped to achieve, leaving the way clear to set the trap for Victor. However, the now destroyed front wall of the monastery was a dead giveaway that something was wrong, he would have to be on his guard. In the meantime, the Special Forces duo would make a quick tour of the underground rooms to find the box of explosives and any other evidence of criminal activity.

Amos led Jack to a landing at the back of the scullery just beyond the pantry. 'There are two entrances here into the kitchen area,' he said. 'This is what you might call another back entrance, it's easily reached from the courtyard. One entry from the outside lead into the scullery and those,' indicating a flight of well-worn stone steps, 'lead down into the storerooms.'

The long and winding wide-flagged steps led down in a spiral of ancient stone, the curved treads a testimony to the passing feet of ancient and long forgotten humanity. Niches in the curve of the stone wall at intervals held small oil-filled lamps which lit their way to where the steps opened out to a sizeable landing, from there several rooms could be seen, their yawning cavities shrouded in the dim light. Beyond where the flitting shadows were deepest, the steps were vaguely seen ending at a dark forbidding door, heavily encrusted with metal bars and hinges.

'That door,' said Amos pointing down to it, 'leads directly

into some of the older crypts, it's an enormous space from the brief glimpse I was able to get one time I was down here and that's where I believe Victor is going to begin his new business venture.'

Amos directed his torch beam down onto the ancient door, the light reflecting dully off the huge hinges. 'Must be made of solid oak I think and damned thick, centuries old no doubt. From what I hear from the others, the crypt area is below the falls, which is just the other side of the rock that this monastery sits on. Nobody goes down there now but it was certainly used many years ago. There are burial chambers there and who knows what else, it's a vast underground complex so I've been led to believe. My guess is that these engineers Victor is bringing back with him are going to try to tap into the water's energy from here. It would be a tricky operation and full of risks.'

He laughed softly to himself. 'It would be interesting to sit on the sideline and watch. Either they'll have the Abbey on top of them or drown in the flood.'

'Perhaps it would,' Jack agreed, 'however, we have to prevent it happening at all, I am interested to know just what does lie below these walls but not right now my old friend. I want to see what is in those crates we saw in one of these rooms and find that box of explosives.'

Amos found a light switch, the amount of light was dim and they found the torches were still needed. Cautiously they began to explore the many rooms that ran off the landing. Barrels of wine and bottling equipment could be seen in the dim light of ventilation grates high up on the rough walls in one large room. Other rooms were filled with boxes and crates, almost incongruously, two huge refrigerators as well as a modern freezer, stood side by side, a modern-day addition to a medieval time warp. Nearby the solid hum of a generator broke the silence with its steady thumping beat. The air was musty and dank with the pervading smells of old wine and decaying vegetable matter filling their nostrils. The quick scurry of a rat alerted their senses as a small shape dashed in front of them to disappear behind a stack of crates in a dark corner. They continued their search, their flashlights piercing the dusty gloom of the cavernous rooms, then in the middle of one, Jack's torch beam swept over a large wooden box that sat in the middle of the floor.

'That's it!' cried Amos, 'they must have dragged it down here after the village idiot did his hero bit and damn near blew the whole place apart. I'll bet they haven't told Victor about that yet, keeping it as a little surprise for him no doubt.'

He pushed the lid off and flashed his torch inside it. Though the box was only half full, it revealed a conglomerate of what looked like engineering or army-issue explosives. The box smelled dirty and dangerous, the torchlight revealing several short sticks of greasy looking dynamite pushed to one side and other bits and pieces of old ammunition; scattered among them were a couple of hand grenades. A reasonably new assault rifle lay near the top and several rounds of ammunition for it close by.

'I bet they didn't pick this lot up at the local supermarket,' grunted Amos. 'These smell and look like ex-army disposal stuff. I can't believe they've been lugging this lot around like it was a bag of marbles.'

'We'll get Steve onto it when he comes to pick this bunch up,' said Jack. 'The sooner it's out from under here the better. I'd hate to think of the damage it would cause if it goes up. Now, I want to see what's in those crates we saw in that other room.'

They retraced their steps to one of the first rooms they had entered to examine more closely the large crates standing there. Amos looked about him for something to open them with and found a steel bar; a jemmy that somebody had previously used in an attempt to open one of the boxes. Amos attacked the nearest and soon managed to pry off one of the long timbers, the sound of splintering wood echoing in the subterranean stillness.

Jack shone his torch on the crate as its contents were partially revealed. 'I thought as much — a printing press, we can assume that these other crates contain more of the equipment necessary to produce their own personal brand of banknotes. You know I'm inclined to think our friend Victor Casini has really overstepped the mark this time, Amos.'

'They weren't keeping it much of a secret, it's about what I expected to find. These crates have been arriving on and off for weeks now, so it was pretty obvious Casini had big plans afoot.'

'We had better get back up top, Amos, I think we've seen enough down here, I want to have another word with Vinnie.'

They had barely reached the top of the winding staircase when they heard shouting and the sound of hurried footsteps on the sharp gravel of the courtyard. 'Come on, Amos, sounds like there's a problem up top!'

They ran quickly through the lower end of the scullery and out into the courtyard in time to see the hurrying figure of the Abbot followed by three or four of the grey clad monks making their way to the chapel.

'How the hell did he get out of his rooms?' muttered Amos. 'He was locked in the same as the others!'

'I don't know, but we have to stop them, you get the Abbot and I'll try to round up the others, we don't want them wandering around at this point in time.'

Marilla and Isabella on hearing the noise and the babble of

voices, crept quietly around the corner of the building in time to see the chaotic confusion. Other monks were now joining the few who had followed the Abbot and were standing in little confused groups, watching as Amos sprinted after the Abbot. Moving very fast for a big man, Amos soon caught up with him, grasping him by the shoulder and spun him around holding him firmly.

'Just where did you think you were going and how did you get out of those rooms?' Amos began to march him back toward the kitchen area. The Abbot squirmed in Amos' hands as he tried to break away but Amos held the quivering man up against the nearest wall. The Abbot's eyes were wide and he was clearly at his wits end as he struggled against Amos' vice-like grip. 'How did you get out? What's going on!' repeated Amos.

'It was Carlos–Carlos–he's going to free them, let them loose and warn Mr Casini!' He stuttered and swallowed hard. 'He has followed the evils of temptation–he–he has turned against us, we must pray for our salvation in the chapel.'

'How did he get the key; how did you get out?' demanded Amos.

The Abbot tried to wink at Amos but screwed up his face instead and gave a lop-sided grin, while flecks of saliva glistened at the corners of his mouth. 'Secret passage you know, I found it, behind the wardrobe, my hiding place, my secret place,' he laughed hysterically and his pale eyes rolled. 'I just wanted to say goodbye to my brothers–there are other keys you know,' he tried to wink again and laughed, an odd child-like giggle.

'Amos, Amos!' Jack was calling from the other end of the courtyard where he had attempted to gather the remaining monks in a group, who clearly were refusing to be made to go back to their quarters.

'Stay there and don't move!' growled Amos, and he released his grip on the front of Peter Gleeson's robe.

From their vantage point the sisters watched as the Abbot slowly slid down the wall into a crumpled sobbing heap as Amos let him go to hurry to Jack's aid. He remained crouched where he was however for only a brief moment, then to their surprise, he had sprung to his feet and casting a quick glance at the retreating back of Amos, began to move furtively toward the old orchard area. Keeping close to the wall they could hear him muttering to himself in short sobs as he rapidly made his way toward the old elm tree and the break in the wall through which Jack had crept two nights previously.

Jack looked up as Amos approached, apart from the two sisters standing and watching by the kitchen wall, he could also see the flash of grey cloth that was fast disappearing toward the gap in the outer wall.

As the sisters stood staring at the spot where the Abbot had disappeared, Jack called out to them. 'Marilla, *go*! Find a way of stopping him! Do *whatever* you have to and don't let him get too far! Isabella, I need you to come and keep an eye on this lot, we've got a serious problem on our hands, come *quickly*!'

Marilla threw her hands up in the air in a helpless gesture. 'How am I supposed to find a monk and hold him, let alone track him through that tangle of forest? What is Jack thinking of? I wouldn't know where to look for a start, you can't see through it, it would be hopeless to try and catch … however — yes!' she snapped her fingers, and a gleam came into her eye. 'Broomstick, of course, maybe I can't see through it but I could see over it!'

She turned and began to hurry back to their shelter calling out over her shoulder, 'You'd better do as Jack says, Bella. Keep an eye on those monks, whatever has gone wrong it must be pretty serious. I'm sure you can think of something to keep them there.'

Isabella stood still, trying to decide what to do. She would rather have gone with Marilla; however, Jack had asked her to do something and she could not let him down. The grey robed monks made her nervous, she looked at them now as they stood in quiet groups, some sitting on the stone benches in the early afternoon sunlight talking amongst themselves.

As she slowly approached them, they turned their heads to watch her with surprised looks on their faces. She could see that most of them were older men who looked just as nervous as she was, one or two of them had risen to their feet and begun to walk toward the church. At her approach they stopped and stared inquiringly at her.

'Hello,' stammered Isabella as she came closer. 'We've not met before, but I'm, er– that is to say, I'm er, um–'

Marilla had kicked her broom into gear and was soaring above the treetops searching for signs of the fleeing Abbot. She could see now how extensive the pine forest was and far beyond, the broad sweep of the lake below the tumbling rapids that effused from the narrow gorge that almost encircled the promontory on which the monastery stood. In the mist-shrouded distance the snow-clad peaks stood as silent sentinels, wreathing their own aura of mystery to an otherwise peaceful vista. She was surprised to note also how extensive this monastic edifice was when viewed from above, not far beyond the outer buildings she caught the glint of sun on water. Another smaller stream cascaded down from somewhere near the top of the craggy mountain and found its way down the valley some small distance from the rear of the Abbey complex. She could see it glisten as it tumbled over mossy boulders and plunging into deep iridescent pools to swirl around briefly, then tumble onward to course a more sedate passage well above and beyond the sleepy village.

A movement below near a clump of gorse caught her attention, she could see, emerging from the thicket, a grey-clad figure making its way toward the stream. Every now and then it paused looking back toward the Abbey but hurried relentlessly on.

Marilla hovered, unsure of just how she was going to stop him. However, Marilla, being Marilla, decided that the best approach was a direct one, so descended to come up behind the fleeing figure. She was about to call out to him when he turned his head once more and stared straight at her. A look of complete horror crossed his face and he dropped to his knees, clasping his hands in front of him.

Marilla dismounted slowly from her broomstick and began to walk toward the now totally terrified monk, her hand outstretched. 'You have to come with me, you—'

With a loud shriek, the Abbot sprang to his feet, pointed a shaking finger at her and screamed, 'No–no, you come from the devil, come to take me to your vile world–*no!*' He then turned and began running blindly, stumbling over rocks and shredding his robes as he blundered through the thorny bushes.

'Wait!' called Marilla. 'You don't understand, Jack sent me.' Her words were lost in his muffled screams as he fled, sure that Marilla was an emissary from the devil, his tortured mind completely devoid of any sane thought. Marilla darted forward in an attempt to block his path but he veered quickly around her plunging through the dense tangle of bushes and disappeared from sight.

'Damn!' Marilla cursed. 'How am I going to make him

understand that Jack wants to make sure he's safe.' Dropping her broomstick, she hurried on around the great clump of gorse expecting to see him a few yards ahead of her, but on picking her way around the bush she suddenly came to an abrupt stop. She was standing on the very edge of a steep embankment that dropped away suddenly to end in a great heap of moss-covered boulders some twenty feet below. Lying in a crumpled heap on top of the boulders was the Abbot and he was not moving.

'Now what am I going to tell Jack?' she muttered. A few yards further down the embankment Marilla found an easier path to scramble down and clambering back over the slippery boulders she finally reached the unfortunate man. One look was enough to tell her that the fall had broken his neck. 'Well, said Marilla to herself, 'I can't help him now, I don't think Jack is going to be too pleased about this. I can't understand why he should have been so frightened; it was almost as if he'd seen a ghost or something.'

She retraced her steps, mounting her broomstick and began to make her way back to the Abbey. From her vantage point she could see the road that led up from the village and along the shores of the lake to wind its serpentine way up to the Abbey gates. There had been nothing on that road when she had set out to follow the Abbot. Now, as she looked down upon it, she could see vehicles making a slow progress just out of the village, a large black car preceding two covered trucks.

Marilla drew in her breath sharply and hovered behind a tall pine as she watched the cavalcade begin to wind its way around the lake road. 'That must be that Victor person Jack was talking about; he's coming back and I don't think Jack was expecting him so soon, I *must* warn him!' She executed a sharp turn and sped back toward the Abbey.

Chapter 14

An Explosive Situation

The arguing, bickering and accusations had finally been exhausted. Vinnie and Bruno had now formed the positive opinion that the blame for the entire chain of events could be laid squarely on the narrow shoulders of Leo.

He was the one who had admitted the monk known as Amos through the gate in the first place. *He* was the one who let this same monk wander through the forest … alone … checking rabbit traps. *He* was the one who let him go outside after the usual lock-up time and come to think of it, noted Vinnie scornfully, it was Leo who had purloined that useless box of explosives. Victor had taken one look inside the box when Leo had brought it back and announced sarcastically that they were 'Not about to blow the monastery up completely, just a few well-placed detonations in the right places were all that would be needed'. He would bring the correct stuff, he had said, when he brought the engineers back with him.

'*Get rid of it!*' he had yelled at Leo and called him names that his mother would never have thought of. Little wonder then that Leo was well and truly peeved about this entire enterprise but his fear of Victor's reprisals buttoned his lip, though he seethed inwardly. Nor would it matter that Victor was his cousin, on his mother's side. Victor didn't hold too much about blood ties … except for when it suited him. Now more than ever he was wishing he had not agreed to join his cousins in this new venture of Victors but the promise of easy money and plenty of it, had been too tantalising to resist and once he'd paid off a few debts that kept him looking over his shoulder, he'd be rich.

The object of their recriminations was sitting dejectedly in a corner of the room they were at present captive in, throwing rolled up balls of paper into a wastebasket. Indeed, to say he was not happy with the turn of events regarding his miscalculation and humiliation at the hands of the man known as Amos, this irritated him beyond all endurance and was a huge understatement. How was he to know this Amos was not a real monk — they all looked the bloody same! Now he had run out of paper!

A slight noise at the door of their cell alerted their senses. Vinnie put a finger to his lips in a gesture of silence and moved carefully to stand behind the door. In the ensuing silence they could hear a key being inserted in the lock and with the click of the tumbler turning the sound was almost deafening in the quiet confines of the room. As they watched, the big brass doorknob began to slowly rotate.

Bruno was not waiting; he sprang to the door and he wrenched it open, as he did so there came a muffled cry as a grey-robed figure stumbled into the room. Bruno immediately fell on top of him pinning him to the floor, the robed one struggling feebly against Bruno's weight, the muffled voice trying to say something. Vinnie stepped from behind the door. 'Let him up, Bruno, let's see who we've got.'

Bruno rolled his victim over but the hood of the robe had fallen over the face. Leo was on his feet by now and reached down to lift the hood. If it had been Amos, he would have been ecstatic, but it wasn't.

True, their captive was short and plump, the eyes were pale and watery, but it was not Amos. Leo's face must have registered disappointment but he took another look at the face of the unfortunate man still trapped beneath Bruno's knee. 'I know who this one is,' he said decidedly, 'he's the one who does some of the engraving, his name's Carlos.' Grabbing a handful of the monk's robes, Leo lifted the man's head off the floor and stared him in the face saying, 'Are you for real — a monk that is, or just pretending to be?'

The voice when it came was a whining sort of a whisper. 'No, no! I mean yes–I am of the Brotherhood but I've come to let you out; you *must* hurry, or they'll be here soon.'

'Who?'

'Brother Amos, and that other man—'

Bruno hauled the monk to his feet none too gently holding him close and peered closely into his face. 'How do you know that?'

'The–the–Abbot–is not a well man, he must have escaped from his rooms. He–he had other keys, spare keys and I've still got them, see?' He jangled a huge bunch of keys in Bruno's face. 'He came to our quarters and unlocked the door. I–I pushed him aside and grabbed the keys from his hands and came here–to set you free.'

'Why?' it was Vinnie who spoke, Bruno punctuating with a harsh shake of the little man.

'Who *cares* why!' broke in Leo. 'The door's open and we've got a hostage, let's get out of here!'

'You must have a reason,' said Vinnie cautiously.

'I–I want to get out of here,' whined Carlos. 'This is not at all what I expected it to be, and–and I was hoping that if I let you out, you would help me leave here.'

Bruno and Vinnie looked at each other, both thinking the same thought — not likely, not now.

'Okay,' said Vinnie, winking at Bruno and grasped the monk roughly by the shoulders. 'Let's move out of here and see if we can find our guns for a start.'

*   *   *

'*Damn!*' said Jack. 'We're too late, they've gone!' He surveyed the empty room. 'I suppose they've taken Carlos with them.'

'My fault,' said Amos ruefully. 'I had no idea that the Abbot was in possession of any spare keys or that there was any other way out of that room.'

'Can't be helped, there's a lot we still don't know about Brother Gleeson, and I'm sure there's a lot more that he could tell us, that's if Marilla can get him back.'

'She wouldn't be in any danger from him, would she?' ventured Amos.

'More likely the other way around,' Jack said softly. 'Amos, where does this corridor lead to?'

'I don't think we've missed them by much, they can't be too far away,' said Amos, a now worried frown creasing his smooth forehead as he tried several of the doors along the corridor, all were locked. He pointed down the long corridor. 'The Infirmary is around that corner at the end of this passageway and there's another that branches off the end of it which takes you out to the Hospice. They might have taken cover in the Infirmary, there are a few herb gardens at the back of that but I don't believe there's any way out from there, other than over a high wall.'

'Do you think they would have made for the Hospice then?'

'Somehow I doubt it,' said Amos, 'plus we don't know how much start they've got on us, there's not much cover between here and the Hospice, I think we would have seen them from where we were. That's the trouble with this place, there's too many *damn* places to hide!'

'Let's start with the Infirmary, Amos and just so they don't slip past if they *are* in the Hospice, I'll get you to stay close to the door where you can see both ways, keep your gun handy, my lad and don't take any chances. I can do the search inside, just you keep your eyes open out here.'

The Infirmary at the end of the corridor sat at the junction of a covered colonnade where the enclosed path led to what appeared to be a cottage set among small shrubs and surrounded by a neat garden some little distance away. The other end of it wound its way further toward the other side of the courtyard keeping a boundary between the remainder of the building and the open yard.

Amos stayed close by in the shadows giving cover to Jack while he made a quick search of the Infirmary. He was angry with himself, he should have guessed there would be other keys, but it was too late now to dwell on it. *Damn* Carlos! If he had trusted his own inner doubts and put him apart from the others, this would not have happened but then, how were they to know the Abbot would make the rash move that he did? The man was definitely unhinged, Amos thought ruefully.

He glanced to where the covered walkway stretched out and away from under the arched portico where he kept sentinel. It was quite possible that Vinnie and co. had taken shelter in the Hospice, though they would have had to move very quickly to get that far without being seen. He and Jack would make a foray there next but they would have to move carefully; there was too much open ground to cover and he was not sure whether they had left weapons there, as Victor had at one stage used the cottage.

Carlos — there was a strange one too. He was a little younger than the rest of the fraternity and had always had a restless disposition he had been fidgety for a while. Amos had noticed it and had attributed it to nervousness at what was happening around them. As he tried to remind himself — you can't judge a man solely on just a vague suspicion. Frankly, Amos would never have believed Carlos would have had the courage to make such a bold move, his outward character showed a timid mouse-like aptitude, horrified at the thought of violence of any sort. So, why was he setting Vinnie and the others free? What could he hope to gain from it, unless it had all been an act and he was a 'sleeper'? Amos grimaced. That could be it, Carlos had been planted here earlier as extra precaution; mix in with the other monks and observe, unnoticed. Isn't that exactly what he had been doing himself? He allowed himself a little smile, if that were so, then Carlos had played his part as well as he had — the cuckoo in the opposition's nest was a role he had perfected, now he had met an equal.

A vague movement at the other end of the dimly lit corridor caught his attention and he stiffened, the darkness of the doorway hiding him from direct view. Somehow this emerging shadow did not look like what he was expecting as their quarry. It was a shapeless mass that seemed to float eerily in mid-air, stopping now and then as if to detach itself from the walls and then glide onward in his direction. His heartbeat quickened and he flattened himself against the doorway and waited.

Meanwhile, out in the courtyard Isabella had nervously been trying to strike up a conversation with the rest of the monastery fraternity, who were still looking a little aghast at this brightly dressed rather plump female, with the most enormous mass of bushy reddish- brown hair. A woman was a rare sight in the Abbey and this one would surely have made up for anything the old monks could ever have imagined. They just stared in astonishment. Comely, yes, some thought, but so very odd! Where had she come from?

She had begun by asking them what sort of work they did and after some initial periods of awkward silence, she seemed quite pleased to hear their honest reply that they repaired and sometimes copied rare and beautiful books, manuscripts, scrolls and other fragile objects brought to them. At the sound of 'books' Isabella's mutual interest quickened. Books were her delight, she began to warm to her subject. She loved books; old books, books with interesting old pictures in them and mysterious writings ... Her grandmother — she had rambled on to say — had some wonderful old books that she could show — no, perhaps not, she stopped herself in time, momentarily forgetting that these shrouded men were part of a religious order. Grandmother's books would have been startling to say the least, not at all what they would have expected.

Suddenly a swishing noise above them made them all look up and there was Marilla hovering above them, her flowing skirts billowing in the light breeze.

The now confused and terrified monks opened their collective mouths with an indrawn breath. Some sat weakly back onto the stone benches, while the ones nearest the church steps fled into its sanctity. Nobody took any notice of the tall grey-clad figure, who had been standing silently at the top of the steps, half hidden in the shadow of the enormous pillars, watching closely.

'Isabella,' Marilla's voice was brisk and business-like, 'where are Jack and Amos? I have to warn them that other one, that one called Victor something or other, is on his way up the hill.'

'They went through there,' said Isabella, pointing to the building through which Jack and Amos had disappeared in pursuit of the escapees.

'Where's the Abbot?' called out Isabella as Marilla wheeled her broomstick around to race off to catch up to Jack.

'Broke his neck,' answered Marilla in a matter-of-fact way over her shoulder as she sped away.

'Oh,' was all Isabella could say and turned back to face the monks who now looked in astonishment as they stared with mouths still agape. Before them was this visual phantasmal apparition hovering, announcing the stark and tragic news that the Abbot was dead, with little more lamentable fervour than the fact that he had just missed a bus.

Not knowing what to say to the still confused monks at this point, Isabella twisted her hands around in an embarrassed manner and said haltingly. 'That's my sister, she, we—um, well— we're witches you know.'

*   *   *

Amos didn't really believe in ghosts or rather, he kept reminding himself that there was always a radical explanation for everything supernatural. However, it still didn't slow his more than normal rapid heartbeat, as he waited for the floating apparition to come closer. Even though he had emerged from many sticky situations unscathed, being around a person like Jack had taught him that even the impossible was possible and to expect anything.

'Amos!' The apparition speaking his name almost completely took him off guard for a brief second and his hand shook slightly as it closed over the gun clenched firmly in his hand. It wasn't until Marilla landed lightly in front of him that the immediate thrill of terror subsided and Amos was able to get a grip on normality.

'Where's Jack?' Marilla dismounted and stood in front of him still clutching her broom handle, as if she had just stopped in the middle of housework to ask a question.

Before Amos could reply, Jack emerged from his search of the Infirmary and was quick to notice the look of incredibility on the face of his friend.

'Ah, Marilla, were you able to catch up with the Abbot, I was rather hoping he was not going to come to any harm as there are still a few questions I want to ask him?'

'Well, yes and no,' Marilla replied, leaning on her broomstick, then added hurriedly, 'Jack, I have to warn you. That other one you spoke about — Victor — you said his name was, well I'm not sure; it could be that he's on his way back here. They were on the lake road when I saw them. A big black car and a couple of trucks were just leaving the village.'

Jack frowned and muttered something under his breath. 'That gives us no time at all, Amos, I was hoping we'd be better prepared. I think we may have to call up the cavalry now. I'll get on the radio and warn Steve. We could have him here in about twenty minutes if he's got his men kitted up and ready to go. Where's Isabella?'

'She was in the courtyard talking with the monks just a few minutes ago.'

'And I bet you scared the hell out of them too, Marilla. I see

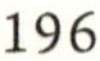

you've still got that old broomstick, I thought you might have traded it in by now.'

They were hurrying back along the colonnaded walk as they talked — or rather argued, thought Amos. Marilla was stating heatedly that there was *nothing* wrong with her broomstick, she had owned it for years and it had *never* given her any trouble. Jack was of the opinion that it was too old and antiquated and it was about time she went to a more modern form of transport. Amos sensed that Jack was just baiting her, he shook his head, still in disbelief. In his line of work, he had thought he had seen everything, even with the knowledge that Jack was a little, well … different from others in the business but this was scary … well, almost he told himself. It just didn't seem real, he'd never thought of witches existing, particularly those that still rode around on broomsticks. He was beginning to wonder where the 'once upon a time' story he was in was going to finish and would it end with *and they lived happily ever after*'. However, he had to remind himself, that when you worked with a person like Jack Grimsby, *anything* was possible!

'The Abbot?' enquired Jack, as Marilla paused for breath.

'Dead,' replied Marilla. 'He fell down a steep cliff up near that other stream and landed on some big rocks. He was dead; I think he broke his neck. There was nothing I could do for him, so I came back, that's when I saw the trucks.'

There was a moment of silence as they reached the courtyard again, only to find that it was deserted, except for a lone figure sitting on one of the stone benches. Isabella stood up and came to meet them. 'They all went in there,' she said indicating the chapel. 'They said they would be safer there than anywhere else and would be protected.'

'They're probably right,' sighed Jack. 'We've got to keep this lot contained somehow, and the sooner we can get Steve and his boys here to round them up the better.'

'Time to make a quick plan of action,' said Amos. 'If we can keep Vinnie and co. holed up in the Hospice — if that's where he is — we can still take Victor by surprise but we'll have to move fast. We need more fire power for persuasion, how much have you got, Jack?'

'Only one extra clip and the couple of guns we took from Vinnie but they're not going to be that much help if push comes to shove. Plus, we can't be sure if they've got more stashed in the Hospice, we hadn't really searched that thoroughly yet. What about that assault rifle in the crate and there's probably a few more ammunition clips there too?'

'I'll go and get it but I'm worried about the girls here, Jack,' and he glanced uneasily at Marilla and Isabella. 'Perhaps they could find better safety in the Library or the Monks' quarters.'

'I'll tell you now, they won't stay there, they're too inquisitive, look take Isabella with you, she could be more help than you think, I'll need Marilla and her old horse here for a 'spy in the sky' observer. Now I have to get to that radio, *get going*, Amos!'

Amos hurried off with Isabella close behind. How different Amos looked, Isabella thought, as he quickly shepherded her through the scullery and down the stone steps. He had discarded his monks' habit earlier and was dressed more comfortably in dark jeans, shirt and jacket. She felt more at ease now with him dressed like that; at least he didn't look like a monk any more.

Back in the courtyard Jack explained to Marilla what he needed her to do. An overall view was the only way to be able to see both the Abbey gate and any movement from the Hospice into the courtyard. She nodded understandably and for once did not stop to argue, but was gone in a flash and a few moments later he could just make out her shape atop one of the high walls.

Jack turned and walked briskly into the kitchen where the radio had been secreted in a spot deep in the pantry in the backpack. He knew Lieutenant Grayson would be waiting at the other end and previously laid plans would be swung into action.

Before he reached the pantry however, a cold voice behind him spoke. 'You can hold it right there, Grimsby, I won't need too much of an excuse to put a bullet through you now!'

*   *   *

Amos and Isabella had reached the underground room where the explosives had been stored, Amos gathered up the assault rifle and quickly checked it over to make sure it was in working condition. 'Hopefully this might keep Victor and company docile till Steve gets here.'

'What are these?' asked Isabella, looking at the small sticks of dynamite that Amos had put on the floor as he probed the box looking for ammunition.

Briefly Amos explained their use. 'Dangerous stuff, Isabella, looks too old to be any good, but would probably blow a hole in something, don't touch it, looks too greasy.'

Isabella looked curiously at the worn sticks and at the other objects in the box, but there was no more time to ask questions as Amos was on his feet, the rifle under his arm and clutching the ammunition belt over his shoulder. 'Come on now, let's get out of here' and he started toward the foot of the steps. Isabella, after a moment's hesitation following close behind him.

They had only climbed the first few steps of the winding staircase, when suddenly a bright light shone in their faces.

Before Amos could react, a heavy blow struck him on the side of the head and he reeled backward taking Isabella with him, falling heavily onto the floor below. As he lay there stunned, he could hear vaguely familiar voices and felt his clothes being searched, he knew that his gun was being removed from its shoulder holster. Meanwhile Isabella was struggling to extricate herself from where Amos had fallen partly on top of her.

'Who's the woman, how did she get in here?' The guttural voice of Bruno came faintly to Amos as he struggled to stay conscious.

'I don't know, but Vic won't like it when he finds out we've got extra company, he'll be mad enough as it is, so we'd better put them away somewhere. Vinnie's got the other one upstairs, he can deal with him.'

Amos could hear the thin reedy voice of Leo through the fog of half consciousness. 'This is the great hulk I'll be glad to see the last of!' Amos felt a very hard kick to his ribs that took his breath away and another to his head that closed the blackness over him completely.

Bruno was fumbling with the heavy barred door that led down into the crypt. 'Well, we 'ain't got much time before the boss gets back, so let's put whoever she is and your gorilla friend here, down below. Come on, Leo give us a hand, he's heavy, that'll keep them quiet, locked up down there for a while.'

Together they rolled the unconscious form of Amos roughly down the last few steps to the now open ancient crypt door and pushed him through.

Isabella was still sitting in a dazed heap on the floor where she had collapsed under the weight of Amos. Before she had a chance to raise a finger, she was grabbed roughly from behind and propelled down the steps, then pushed roughly through the doorway by Bruno.

'We don't know how you got in here, lady but you're sure as hell not getting out, you can join your boyfriend down there entertaining the ghosts.'

Isabella's faltering feet stumbled over a wide stone step, the momentum carrying her forward to a stone floor where she sat down hard. A heavy oppressive darkness filled with dank musty smells enveloped her, except for the dim slit of light from the still open door of the crypt. The bright beam of a torch suddenly shone through the doorway and with it, Leo's thin face with its wispy beard below a broken-toothed grin. His voice was a mocking taunt, he was holding something in his hand.

'Here's something to play with while you're down there,' he said as he threw the object he had been holding. It landed with a thud in front of her and rolled into the folds of her voluminous skirt. In that brief instant, she saw that it was a small round object that was making a hissing spluttering noise. Sure that her best skirt was going to catch fire, she grabbed at it and in the same movement, threw it away from her as far as she could.

The object had barely left her hand and rolled away into the blackness, when a terrific explosion shattered the stifling stillness of the crypt. The brilliant flash that came with it almost blinded her, she could hear and feel things falling around her and over her. She covered her ears and kept her eyes tight shut, after what seemed like an eternity, all was still again. She took her hands away from her ears, but the noise still rang loudly in her head.

The air was full of choking dust that was so dark and heavy that she felt she was enveloped in a heavy blanket. She tried to breathe but could only feel grit in her mouth, her eyes stung if she tried to open them. Grasping a portion of her skirt, she held it over her face for a few minutes to shut out the dirt, trapping a tiny pocket of air, she tried to breathe without choking in the thick dust and fumes that were enveloping her.

Amos! Where was Amos? They had killed him, she felt sure, a rising tide of panic began to sweep over her. Desperately she called his name and began to grope around her in the darkness trying to find his body. He had to be there somewhere. Her fingers scrabbled in dust and dirt and broken stone, but there was nothing. She was just about to burst into tears when, faintly, away to her left, she thought she heard a groan. 'Amos, Amos!' she kept calling his name and was relieved when she was answered by another groan, but where was he?

She reached out around her, the swirling black clouds of dirt were still thick in the acrid air that surrounded her making it difficult to see anything and then she could feel something under her groping fingers. Grasping it, she pulled … it felt like a hand. It *was* a hand, she could feel the fingers, but they were bone … and there was nothing on the other side of the bony wrist. She screamed and dropped it.

Shaking violently by this time, she managed, after several futile attempts, to conjure up her faint blue spark from her quivering fingertip. The pale blue light that issued from it picked up the grotesque whiteness of just a skeletal hand lying in her lap.

Now, there was silence; total and complete silence …

Chapter 15

An Unexpected Surprise

Jack turned slowly; his hands raised. Vinnie stood in the doorway, a gun clutched in his hand, and a vicious smile on his face.

'There's more than one way out of this rabbit warren, didn't think about the other rooms there, did you? It was easy enough to slip in and lock the door on one and let you walk right past. You were with somebody else besides McAllister — who was it?'

Jack smiled back and said calmly, 'Just some old friends who dropped in, you wouldn't know them,' he added dryly. 'By the way, what have you done with Carlos, he seems to have taken a liking to you? I hope he realises his mistake before he gets too entangled. It's not always a profitable lifestyle.'

'Very funny, Grimsby but you won't be so cocky soon.'

'Well, I do try to keep my sense of humour, even in the worst of company. I've also noticed you must have had another weapon stashed somewhere.'

Vinnie laughed, a hollow gloating laugh. 'You think you're so smart, didn't look in the right places, did you?'

Vinnies' opportunity to indulge in the self-satisfaction of Jack's capture however was to be very short lived. Heavy footsteps were echoing over the great flag stoned entrance floor.

A guttural raspy voice broke in and Vinnie's big brother, Victor was striding into the room.

'Vinnie you've got some explaining to do, that front wall—. He broke off as he saw who else was there in the room. 'Well, well, if it isn't Mr Jack Grimsby himself, now that's nice.'

He stood there and looked at Jack, a slow smile spreading over his pock-marked face. Slightly taller than Vinnie but with those same dark eyes and smooth black hair, the dark olive complexion suggestive of their Corsican heritage. He also looked the picture of sartorial elegance and every inch the businessman in a perfectly tailored faint pin stripe suit and very fashionable alligator skin shoes. A diamond stud glittered from his tie front but the dark eyes also glittered harshly as he turned from Jack's resolute face to that of his brothers.

'What the hell has been going on here Vinnie, what happened to the wall out the front, how did Grimsby get in here and for that matter, how many others of his kind?' At this last remark, the raspy voice was raised in anger, Victor reached inside his impeccably cut suit coat to withdraw a small handgun. Tiny, but still deadly, its ivory inserts in the butt gleamed in the half light of the vast kitchen.

He turned his attention now to Jack. 'Sit down, Mr Grimsby,' Victor changed his tone to an almost friendly purr and indicated the bench seating with a wave of the gun. 'It's been a while since our paths crossed, hasn't it?' Then without taking his eyes off Jack, he called out to his younger brother. 'Vinnie, where is Bruno and that idiot Leo?'

Before Vinnie could answer, there was the sound of a muffled explosion that seemed to come from somewhere under their feet, a rumble, almost like an earth tremor, which startled them all momentarily into silence.

'They er, they followed that monk down into the cellars,' said Vinnie hesitantly. 'We ah … had to move the explosives after the wall got blown up … accidentally and they—'

'*What* monk?' said Victor his raspy voice raised in anger. 'What the *hell* has been going on here while I've been away? Who's down there now, if that's where those explosives are, which *damn* monk are you talking about?' His face was livid with anger but Jack's was a worried frown. That was where Amos and Isabella were, that explosion was too small for what he had seen in the box. If it had all gone up, they wouldn't all still be sitting here.

Vinnie was pointing a finger now at Jack. 'McAllister — he's been impersonating a monk, been spying on us and must have arranged for Grimsby to get in. We've been tricked, he took us by surprise — but the tables are turned now, we've got Grimsby!' His face paled slightly as he went on. 'Bruno and Leo followed McAllister down to the cellars — I–I don't know what's happened down there.'

Jack stiffened. He had sent Amos and Isabella down there to get that rifle. Could Bruno and Leo have taken *them* by surprise, did some of the explosives detonate accidentally? The stuff was old and unreliable. He knew Amos could look after himself and had a sixth sense about trouble but with Isabella there too … no, he didn't want to think about that. They had obviously been followed by Bruno and Leo after they had been freed from the room they had been locked in and had made that move before he sent Marilla up to the roof. The bend in that corridor would have given them just enough cover to have slipped past without being seen as he, Amos and Marilla had gone back to the courtyard.

His thoughts were broken by the bellowing voice of Victor.

'Get down there, Vinnie, and find out what those *morons* are doing! I want to see Bruno and that dumb idiot Leo up here *right now*, that's if they haven't blown themselves up and tell those engineers to go back and wait in the trucks! See if you can do that without stuffing up!'

Vinnie pocketed his gun and walked to the door. It was no use arguing with Victor. He had always taken the upper hand and been the dominant force in all their exploits, it irritated him, even more so when he was made to look a fool in front of others, particularly someone like Jack Grimsby. There were times when Vinnie wanted to shout his defiance and assert himself but he could never quite pluck up the courage to do so. Victor was a hard man to please. So far, all he had done, Vinnie lamented, was to stuff up big time in this latest and most formidable venture that Victor was proposing. He had been left to perform an important task in his elder brother's eyes and it had all gone wrong; what's more, it had not even been his fault! Secretly he hoped that Leo *had* blown himself up, it would serve him right, he had caused enough trouble, they'd be better off without him.

He threw a hateful glance at Jack, who still sat motionless on the bench.

As Vinnie left the room, he passed by a small dark figure of a man standing close by. Pressed hard against the wall as he was in the half darkness of the short flag stoned corridor, only his eyes, sharp bright eyes, could be seen gleaming in the small brown face. After a moment, the little man stepped quietly into the room and stood with his back against the wall of the kitchen itself and remained there motionless.

Jack looked at the little man in surprise, he knew who he was, but had never, until now, seen him in the flesh, or what there was of it ... He was a little brown skinned man, stick thin, with a wizened little face that looked like a pickled walnut. His shoulders were stooped, making him look even smaller than he was but the eyes in that puckered little face were bright and alert. They took in the vaulted ceiling, the rough stone of the walls, the huge stove and long trestle table in the centre of the room. He walked quietly over to where Victor sat opposite Jack and laid a thin brown hand on his arm. When he spoke, the voice was like the sound of dry leaves rustling in a gust of wind.

'Vic, there … there are bats here?'

'Bats! *Bats?* How the hell would I know? Victor shook the small man's hand off his superbly tailored sleeve and instinctively brushed it down with his other hand, the tiny pistol waving about dangerously. He looked at the little man as if he were a bad smell. 'I suppose there is, somewhere. These old places usually do, why?'

'Well,' said the little man, his gaze still wandering around the room, particularly the high ceiling. 'I—I saw one, it huge! Well, I think it was bat.'

He sat down on the bench seat close to Victor and whispered, 'I not like bats, Victor, they creepy; not have come if bats here. No.'

Victor moved slightly away from the little man as if he were highly contagious, then said in a harsh voice. 'You're here now whether you like it or not Moody and bats or no bats, you're here to do some work, so you'd better get used to it. Anyway, bats only move around at night.'

Mahoud Brahman turned his wizened little face to look Victor in the eyes. In truth, the little man, with his leathery brown skin and puckered face looked much like a bat himself. Leaning closer to the pin stripe suit next to him he whispered, 'How, I saw bat, outside, now … it not dark yet?'

Jack couldn't help the smile that crept over his face and was glad of one thing. Marilla was not in the room at this moment to hear herself described as a bat. She would definitely not have been amused!

*   *   *

Marilla had followed Jack's instructions and had swept quickly up and out of sight, in a direction where she had hoped she would not be seen by Vinnie and his associates but to where she could get a clear overall view of the courtyard. She had just settled into her temporary observation point and looked down in time to see Vinnie step out from behind the buttressed portico of a nearby building and furtively follow Jack as he strode quickly across to the kitchen. At about the same time, in the shadows of the cloisters on the near side of the courtyard, two more figures were moving in much the same direction. They had not been in the Hospice after all!

For the moment Marilla did not know what to do. It was too late to warn Jack and she now had lost sight of the other two. She had almost made up her mind to fly down and somehow stop Vinnie, when a great confusion at the front of the Abbey turned her attention.

The vehicles she had seen along the lake road were now threading their way through what was left of the massive gateway, picking their way around the ruins and coming to a halt at the edge of the courtyard. The big black car had halted and two people emerged from it, a man, neatly dressed and a small dark figure that could have been a very small man or a child. Fearing she would be seen from that point, Marilla moved herself a little higher up the parapet and wedged in beside a particularly grotesque gargoyle.

The man in the suit, whom Marilla presumed to be Victor, had stood still for a moment gazing around in what must have been stunned silence. He had then raised his arms over his head and a tirade of words, quite foreign to her ears, poured forth as he walked around. He then turned to the ones who were following him and yelled something at them, after which he began walking quickly toward the kitchen area. Marilla hesitated, half rising from her position she felt she should follow him. Was Jack really in danger though? Amos had gone to get some guns or something from the cellars, he and Jack were experts in this sort of thing they would probably have the situation in hand anyway. Then there were the other people still near the trucks, maybe they had guns too; it would be better to stay where she was for the time being. The other two men who had been in the trucks now stood awkwardly where they were, but she could see no sign of the small brown man.

Marilla sat on the parapet gloomily trying to assess the situation. Isabella had gone with Amos; was she still with him? She was reasonably sure Isabella would be safe with Amos and she had to admit he certainly looked a formidable character and was apparently quite used to this sort of 'cloak and dagger' sort of life. To Marilla however, it seemed a dangerous way to make a living.

Oddly she had never thought of Jack doing this sort of thing. She had never given him any thought after he left Harewood. He was just Edwina's grandson, or was he? Nobody had ever said anything about his parents. Who were his parents, his real parents anyway?

There had always been that air of mystery about Jack Grimsby, Marilla reflected, as she sat rather uncomfortably atop the wall, with her elbow leaning on the shoulder of an extremely ugly gargoyle. She had to admit that his presence in the Commune was intriguing, if not just a little annoying to her, she had been glad when he had left Harewood altogether. Edwina would only say when asked, that he was an orphan and she his sole carer. Of his parents she would say nothing but her grandmother Hilda Hackett and Edwina often had discussions about him in low hushed voices, which ceased whenever either of the sisters were about. She did remember one time, just after Edwina had returned from one of her long absences, overhearing part of one of these conversations which left her wondering for a time but she soon pushed it to the back of her mind. She had more important things to think about.

She was thinking now. What was it she had overheard back then? Marilla tapped her fingers on the gargoyles head as she searched her memory. 'That's it!' she said out loud. 'For his own dear mother's sake, he must seek out the hiding place of the icon before 'he' does. He is evil and will stop at nothing to get it; but it will be hoped that my prediction will come to pass and he will destroy himself. There was something else too,' Marilla mused, talking quietly to herself. 'Something about a riddle that Jack was smart and would read the code correctly. I wonder what she meant by that? What was this icon thing this 'evil' person wanted?'

She shook her head impatiently and peered over the parapet. The courtyard was deserted except for the two trucks parked near the entrance and their drivers standing around, obviously waiting. Perhaps she should go and see where the others had gone. She wondered too whether the monks were still in the chapel. For a very brief moment she was almost beginning to envy the quiet unobtrusive way of life here, but for the present situation of course. For herself, she would wonder if the charisma would last. For Isabella, yes, she loved solitude and peace she would be happy to do just what I'm doing now, she realised with a start — sitting on top of a parapet talking to a gargoyle!

Marilla suddenly had an uneasy feeling made all the more manifest by a low rumble that seemed to issue from somewhere deep down under the buildings away to her left. Neither Jack nor Amos had emerged from where they had gone, and she began to realise with a start that something was indeed wrong. She *must* find her sister! Rising to her feet she was just about to mount her broomstick when a movement at the door to the kitchen stopped her. The heavy door opened and Vinnie came out. Even from where she sat in hiding, it was obvious he was not in a good humour as he was muttering to himself, he angrily kicked at a stone in his path.

She watched him walk toward the men from the truck and say something to them, then went back to the cloistered area where the other two had gone, it was only a few moments later before all three came out and started back toward the kitchen. They were having a fierce argument about something, and it appeared that most of the tirade was directed at the thin one, the one they called Leo.

Once they were out of sight, Marilla made up her mind that it was now time to fly down from her perch and try to find Isabella. She had completely forgotten about the two men in the trucks for the moment and rising from her hiding place next to the gargoyle, she mounted her broomstick and whirled down and across the remainder of the courtyard, she tried to immerse herself in the shadows of the cloisters where she had last seen Isabella and Amos.

She had barely time to squeeze in behind one of the large columns, when angry voices punctuated with the thin reedy whine of Leo came to her ears, the whole ensemble who had been in the kitchen came around the corner of the building and walked directly to where she stood in the meagre shade of the great building. Her body tensed and she hardly dared to breathe as she pressed closer to the massive column, realising they were going to pass her almost within touching distance.

Marilla could hear Jack's voice, he was saying something to the one named Victor, and he was speaking rather loudly she thought. Chancing a glance around the pillar she could see that Jack was looking almost directly at her, he was shaking his head slightly before he looked away. He had instinctively known she was there, even though she had remained perfectly still. Following closely behind him was Victor, holding a small gun pointed at Jack's back. He was followed by a sullen looking Vinnie, while the others trailed behind him. Even the little brown man did not see her, so absorbed was he was in scanning the roof tops, that he almost tripped over the low steps leading into the cellars.

It was clear that Jack's silent message was to deter Marilla from following, but Marilla was not going to be deterred, she followed silently a little distance behind, keeping her cloak tightly about her. She padded quietly down the stone steps following the sound of their voices, till she had reached the broad landing from which the many storerooms branched off. The others had already gone into the room where the explosives were, so she was able to edge into a room almost opposite without being seen. It smelt of cabbages and old wine, she wrinkled her nose in repugnance. She found a pile of empty crates close to the doorway that afforded a suitable hiding place, here she crouched down behind them, peering between their thin slats. Scurrying noises behind her was a reminder that the place would probably have a healthy rat population and indeed, one ran swiftly past her feet as she knelt down. Marilla ignored it, concentrating instead on what was going on in the room opposite.

A light had been switched on in the room, a single bulb that threw shadows over the stark walls. The throbbing pulsation of the nearby generator almost drowned out their voices, but Victor was holding court and his voice became louder as he became angrier. '*What* woman!' he was turning his attention to his brother for confirmation of another damaging fact. 'How the *hell* did a woman get in here, unless of course Mr Grimsby brought her in with him — did you?' he had now turned to Jack to ask the question.

'No, I didn't,' he replied truthfully, 'it was just a friend who drops in sometimes.' Leo mumbled something Marilla couldn't quite hear, but she heard Victor's reply.

'You did *what*! Have you any idea of the damage that could cause!'

Jack's heart sank and he just hoped Amos and Isabella had been able to avoid the force of Leo's delivery of a hand grenade into the catacombs beneath where they stood.

'Vic,' it was Bruno who spoke. 'we had no idea there was a woman here until we found her with McAllister breaking into the crates. We had to tackle him while we caught him off guard, he's no easy man to deal with as you know. Pushing them both into the crypt was the only option we had at the time. I had nothing to do with Leo's actions; that was his crazy idea, he'd done it before I could stop him.'

Victor sat down on the edge of the crate glaring at Leo, who stood defiantly against the far wall his arms crossed over his chest and glaring back. 'Well, the damage is done now, and I guess we may have to get rid of Grimsby the same way. I still don't see how a woman could get in here unnoticed and just *dropped in* as he says.' Victor scratched his head with the edge of the gun barrel. 'This could complicate things a bit, we don't know where she's come from, except maybe from the village. However, we have more pressing things to consider now. By the way, the monks — where are they or did you put them down there as well, Leo?'

'I think you'll find they are sheltering in the chapel.' It was Jack who provided the answer.

'Right,' said Victor, 'so with no one to watch them, how the *hell* do we know they are still there and not halfway down to the village by now!'

Jack spoke softly and evenly. 'You may be surprised to learn that they *are* actually still there.'

Victor gave Jack a long hard look, then, wrenching his eyes away from the compelling gaze of Jack, turned his attention to Leo, who was still sulking in the far corner. 'Leo, see if you can do something simple. Go and get those engineers and bring them here, I need to find out if your little act of idiocy has damaged anything under there and take Moody with you, he's giving me the creeps. He can keep the monks occupied, maybe trade monastic secrets or something.' He laughed harshly. 'It could make for an interesting cultural exchange.'

He turned back to face Jack, avoiding his direct gaze. 'In the meantime, we have to decide what to do with Mr secret agent Grimsby here.'

Leo muttered something under his breath and moved toward the steps with Mahoud following close behind. All the while he had been in the underground room, the little man's eyes had travelled to every corner and constantly raked the high ceilings in his search for the winged creatures he seemed to fear so much. Now he seemed almost pleased to be leaving the cellar and huddled close to Leo as they mounted the steps.

They had only gone less than halfway, when Leo thrust his head back around the curve of the wall and said in a pained but triumphant voice, 'I don't see that there's any complication, Vic, not when that hand grenade landed neatly in her lap, the only damage will be the mess on the walls. There won't be too much left to say a woman was there at all, the way I see it.'

Jack drew in his breath sharply and a thrill of horror ran through him. He suddenly felt weak, his head spun in mental turmoil. Victor opened his mouth to say something, but a sudden loud clattering noise in the room opposite turned their heads and four pairs of eyes and ears instantly focused on that room.

Chapter 16

Another Unexpected Surprise

Two large, covered trucks were parked nose to tail just inside the damaged gateway to the monastery. One was still occupied by the driver waiting patiently. He had turned the truck radio on and was whistling almost soundlessly to the music, tapping his fingers in time to the rhythm as it crackled forth. His eyes were scanning the valley, he was just thinking what a pleasant place it was, when something other than the tune from the radio caught his ears.

The other truck had its door wide open, the driver was not sitting in it. Instead, he was running about in small circles outside vigorously slapping at his clothing. His yells finally invoked the interest of the first driver, who eventually poked his head out of the cab to inquire what his friend was doing running around like that.

In reply the second man hopped from one foot to the other and began making frantic gestures in the direction of the Abbey buildings, all the while babbling incoherently as he slapped at his lower regions. Finally, finding his voice he yelled to his companion. *'Did you see it — did you see it?'*

It appeared he had been in the motions of lighting a cigarette when a movement at the top of one of the buildings across the wide courtyard had caught his eye. He had noticed a shadow there a little while earlier and some movement but assumed it was just another group of the black crows they had seen perched atop a wall on their way up to the gate.

Taking a pack out of his shirt pocket he had shaken a cigarette out and placed it between his lips. Groping around in another pocket produced a box of matches. He struck one and was in the process of drawing contentedly on the cigarette as he applied the flaming match, glancing idly at the rooftops nearby as he did so. His eyes caught movement on the high parapet, he stared in amazement as the shadow seemed to take form, the shadow rose into the air, a long cloak fluttering about what could have been a figure — on a broomstick!

His mouth fell agape and from it the glowing cigarette, to fall unhindered between his legs. It was only when he felt and smelt the odour of burning fabric and flesh, in that order, that he leapt from the cab of the truck and began his fiery dance of enlightenment, thrashing at his clothing furiously, making wild screeches of pain and panic.

His companion, shaken from his preoccupation of the view stretched out before him, took a few moments to register the other's dilemma and climbed down from his cab to calm the now hysterical burn victim, he seemed to have a great deal of difficulty understanding his friend's clumsy actions, let alone his babblings about witches, broomsticks, ghosts. He himself had not seen anything; couldn't he have imagined it? After all, the place did look a bit more medieval and spookier than they had first been led to believe. They were both beginning to wish that Mr Casini would hurry up and tell them where he wanted this plant they had been hired to put in, then they could get on with it and go. They didn't want to spend more time here than they had to.

The two drivers had eyed the damaged exterior of the monastery with some interest when they had driven up. The boss man who had hired them had said nothing about the place looking like a ruin. They were led to believe that it was a reasonably modern and entire edifice and of considerable historical interest. However, from their perspective now, it was appearing to be just the opposite, they had not imagined it to be as isolated as it was, here, on the top of a mountain far away from anywhere.

This job to transport and build this power plant was going to make them big money, very big money, an offer they could not refuse. Particularly, when as Mr Casini had explained, it was for a good cause, for the benefit of mankind in general.

Mr Victor Casini was a successful businessman, an entrepreneur, as he had introduced himself and had explained to the two engineers what the project was, how enthusiastic his associates also were in the enterprise about to take place. A 'fully equipped Convalescent Hospice for recovering mental patients', he had explained and for those just wanting some relief from the hustle and bustle of the modern world. A place where they could breathe pure mountain air, listen to tumbling waters and gaze across the placid lake to a verdant valley. Music to the soul, he had declared. A place where one could be at peace with nature.

The rather odd little brown man who was accompanying Mr Casini was an expert in architectural construction, it was explained, when the engineers had eyed him curiously as they set about on their journey.

Mr Casini had spoken highly of his brother and his two assistants who were already in residence at the Abbey, the enthusiasm they shared in retaining all of the ancient and unique architectural structure. Though in due course there would probably be a name change more fitting to its purpose, once the all-important power plant was installed, then work on reconstruction could begin. It would be lovingly refurbished with modern facilities but still retaining the ancient and fascinating appeal of its original purpose. It would be a wonderful project Mr Casini had carefully made them understand and would require their full cooperation in making sure that the power plant was properly and safely installed. Everything depended on the smooth running of the power plant, which would be the heart of the entire enterprise.

So it was with some great surprise that the demeanour of this impeccably groomed business tycoon suddenly changed, he had become a raving lunatic as he jumped from his expensive limousine and surveyed the wreckage in front of the Abbey. He had stood in the middle of the courtyard, looking about him, had raised his fists in the air and burst into a torrent of abuse. The brother that he had so fondly recalled earlier, was now subjected to a host of names that would curl the hair of the most battle-hardened navvy. So unlike the quiet positive businesslike manner they had been witness to a short time previously.

The two engineers had hesitantly followed Mr Casini into the courtyard though at a slower pace, gazing around them at what looked more like a medieval fortress. Their eyes taking in the ancient ambience of this isolated citadel, the heavily buttressed stone walls and the bell tower dominating the skyline above. Second thoughts about the job in hand for the engineers now seemed like a meal that would have served their nervous stomachs better had it been left on the plate, they became even more confused, when a completely irrational Mr Casini abruptly told them to go back to the trucks and stay there, while he walked quickly on, muttering to himself.

*   *   *

The singed engineer was still gently examining the front of his trousers and avidly attempting to convince his scornful friend that he had indeed seen something or someone, other than a large bird carrying a stick fly off the roof. The argument was becoming quite heated as to the extent the imagination would extend to cover a clumsy action, when a tap on the other's shoulder alerted him that someone was approaching.

A thin man with a straggly wisp of beard accompanied by the little brown man, they knew now as Moody was coming toward them. About halfway across the courtyard Moody turned away to enter the chapel but the thin man continued on to where the engineers waited by the trucks, he curtly told them that Mr Casini wanted them to look at something and to follow him immediately.

The engineers shrugged their shoulders and made to follow the sullen faced thin man across the courtyard. Something felt wrong and suddenly this job was beginning to lose its appeal. Looking fearfully about him, the man with the scorched trousers followed close behind his companion as they made their way across the courtyard … and to what?

Chapter 17

Leo Gets His Lumps

Isabella could feel something licking her hand, then her face. Its tongue was rough, it was making soft growling noises close to her ear. Then she felt the weight of something on her chest, the growling noises giving way to a deep rumbling purr. She opened her eyes and stared directly into two large yellow eyes shining in the semi darkness, only inches away from her face.

'Lucifer!'

Her face got another rough lick in answer. 'Lucifer!' Oh, I am glad to see you, but how did you get here and—and where are we?'

Lucifer removed himself from her chest and sat by her side, growling in his deep voice as she pulled herself to a sitting position. He allowed himself to be encased in an enormous hug before demanding to be put down.

'What is this place, Lucifer, those dreadful men pushed us down here and … Oh dear and where is Amos?' She struggled to her feet and looked fearfully about her, trying to see through the faint murky light that enveloped the crypt. The air was filled with dust and the strange smell of something that seared her nostrils, it burned her throat and then she remembered. That thin man with the horrible face had thrown something at her, something that spluttered and burnt, she had thrown it away; but it had exploded. Then she had found a hand, just a hand.

'Amos,' she called again, frantic now and trying to peer through the gloom. She could see Lucifer's white tail tip; he was digging into the soft dirt with his claws a short distance away. She heard a faint moan and giving a cry of relief, she fell to her knees beside Lucifer, and began pushing aside a pile of dirt and rubble and what looked like odd shaped white stones, to reveal a very bloodied and bruised Amos.

'Amos, oh Amos — I thought they'd *killed* you!' She knelt beside him and brushed the dirt from his face. His eyes opened, startlingly blue against the grime and blood on his face. 'Are you hurt?'

'I'm alright–I think,' he muttered as she helped him to a sitting position, brushing the dirt off him while he struggled to regain his senses.

'No, your head's bleeding badly!' There was a deep gash on the side of his head where he had been struck while on the stairs, the blood running down the side of his face and into his eyes. He lifted his arm to wipe it away with his sleeve and groaned again.

'Damn! He groaned. 'Feels like there's a rib broken ... or maybe just bruised. Whatever, it's not going to help, *damn* it!' He looked down as Lucifer brushed against his arm. 'Lucifer; you old devil, how did you get in here?' He rubbed the cat's ears and got a friendly bite on the wrist in return.

He turned his dirt and blood smeared face to Isabella. 'Are you alright, Isabella, nothing broken anywhere I hope?' he wiped his face again using his other arm. 'I could have sworn I heard an explosion but perhaps it was just in my head; it feels like World War Two is raging inside it.' He sat holding his head for a moment.

Isabella had rummaged in her capacious pockets drawing

forth the piece of coloured glass still there from where she had picked it up from the church floor. She was slashing at her bright multi coloured skirt near the hem, succeeding in cutting off a piece of the cloth. Holding it between her teeth, she was stripping it down to bandage-width pieces. 'Yes,' she said angrily, 'there was an explosion. That thin one with the straggly beard threw one of those bomb things in here and it landed in my lap, so I threw it over there.' She indicated a spot away to her right and behind them. 'There was an awful lot of dirt falling everywhere, my ears have been quite deafened by the noise, I still can't hear properly even now.'

Amos looked at her with a mixture of shock and surprise on his chubby face. 'A bomb! Isabella, that was a grenade, it could have gone off in your hands!' He continued to stare at her as she calmly stripped her last piece of cloth with unnecessary force. 'You must have been mighty quick getting rid of it, there's only seconds after the pin is pulled before it explodes!'

'Well,' said Isabella crossly as she began to wrap one of her strips about his head, after wiping away most of the blood and dirt as she could. 'It wasn't very nice of him to throw it down onto my skirt like that, I thought he was very rude, he said some very nasty things about you too.' She finished her bandaging and sat back on her heels, looking at him in the feeble light that crept into the gloom from somewhere, totally ignoring the still shocked look on his face. 'There, the bleeding's almost stopped now.' She put her head on one side and admired her handiwork, then broke into a giggle. 'You know you look a bit like a pirate.'

Amos regaining his composure tried to shake his head, it hurt too much. Isabella had been totally unaware of the extreme danger she had subjected herself to but if it had not been for her quick instinct in flinging the grenade away, they would both probably be dead.

'Yeah. Well, it feels like I've caught one of their cannon balls on my ribs.' Amos was running his hands expertly over his rib cage where he had received the vicious kick from Leo's boot.

'Is everything alright?' Isabella anxiously noticed the flashes of pain that crossed his face.

'I think so,' said Amos slowly. 'I can't feel anything broken, probably just bruised, maybe cracked a rib if anything … if you've got some more of those strips there, Isabella, perhaps you'll help me strap it, it would make it more comfortable until we can get ourselves out of here.'

Isabella helped Amos remove his shirt and with his instructions, she wrapped more of the brightly coloured fabric around his great barrel chest, keeping it firm where he needed it.

'Do you know where we are, Amos?' She tied a knot in the last piece.

'Yes,' he said with a grunt as he put his shirt back on. 'We're down in the old crypt.'

Isabella started to ask something about the crypt when a slight grating noise alerted them. The door through which they had been pushed was beginning to open slowly. The thin sliver of light was getting wider, and they could clearly hear Leo's whining voice.

'Why do I have to go down there, why can't Bruno?'

'Because *you're* the one who was so dammed smart in chucking it down there, *that's* why!'

The raspy angered voice of Victor came floating through, 'You've got a torch and your gun, what more do you want, besides, I'll need Bruno here to watch Grimsby — I can't trust you to do it. I don't know what you're worried about Leo, you've been down there before.'

'Yes, but I wasn't alone then,' he whined.

Victor said something that they didn't quite hear but it was enough to make Leo open the door a bit further. However, they did hear Victor say something about the engineers going to have a look at the outer wall of the crypt and he did not want any trouble while they were down there.

'We'll have to move,' Amos growled softly, 'their boss is back and his sense of humour hasn't been improved. It would appear they have Jack as well, just hope he's okay, but knowing him as I do, he can look after himself, by the sound of things, at least he's still alive.'

'Can you get up?' whispered Isabella.

'Yes,' answered Amos, as he rose rather painfully to his feet. 'Let's see if we can get behind this tomb here, it might give us enough cover, I want to get close to Leo. I've got that little runt in my sights, I promised him a broken neck.'

They moved quickly behind the broad sepulchre they had almost crashed into, a long rectangular granite tomb richly carved around its outer edge, just high enough to conceal them as they scrambled behind it. The dust had been settling and the faint light that seeped into this high vaulted catacomb gave them a clearer view of just where they were. Isabella could see what all the odd shaped white stones now were — they were bones, bones strewn everywhere — like the hand she had picked up, grey white in the ghostly light that filtered through this subterranean burial chamber.

'Amos,' she whispered close to his ear, 'it's full of bones down here, what is it?'

'I would say your not-so-carefully aimed grenade has neatly

blown up the last resting place of ancient ancestors of this place. This *was* their mausoleum, shh, quiet now!' he whispered back.

Peering around the lower edge of the tomb, Amos could see the slim figure of Leo framed in the dim light of the open doorway. He could not see his face but could well imagine the look of terror that must be on it. Leo still stood hesitantly by the open door. He was sweeping a powerful torch about and muttering to himself.

'Come on, Leo, *move* it!' Victor had stepped fully into the patch of light beside him. 'I want the engineers to look over the job right now and assess if there's any damage done to the foundations and I want to know, Leo, if McAllister *is dead*! I don't want him looking over my shoulder anymore, so get busy and find some proof.'

Leo stepped nervously down onto the wide stone step of the crypt and flashed the torch from side to side, clutching his gun so tight that the knuckles shone as white as the scattered remnants of the tomb's long-time residents. Two men followed behind, shepherded by Victor looking equally nervous, their heads swivelling as they viewed the high arched ceiling soaring above them and the enormous stone pillars supporting it. The shadowy niches in the walls had spilled some of their contents and they glistened ghostly white in the lights spilling from the torches. Vinnie trailed behind, carrying the substantially deadly rapid-fire weapon.

'What if he ain't dead?' There was no mistaking the tremor in Leo's voice.

'That's what the gun is for *stupid*!' Victor hissed irritatingly as he hustled the engineers out onto the step and down to the old flagstone floor. Victor paused a moment, then went back to where Vinnie had halted at the top of the step and spoke quietly to him. 'Vinnie stay close to here, that's a heavy door up there, I've blocked it open, I want to be sure we can get out quickly, if we have to. Keep your eyes open and shoot anything that moves.'

Leo nodded, of course that was what the gun was for. He didn't like this place anyway, particularly down here. He'd been down here only once before and couldn't wait to get out. He had felt as if the dead souls had been whispering things to him, he could have sworn that things were moving among the deep shadows. He shivered and held the gun tightly, his finger caressing the trigger. He hoped they wouldn't be down here long, he suddenly felt very cold, the sort of cold that made the skin prickle. Moving slightly, he looked back at the door and quietly estimated to himself just how quickly he could get back through it before the others. This was one place he did not want to finish up being trapped in.

From their hiding place, Amos watched the progress of Victor and the engineers until they vanished into the gloom. He could see Victor's torch beam raking across the vaulted ceiling every now and then and tracing down the pillars, he heard his gruff voice as it echoed in the vastness, explaining where cables could be strung and where extra lighting could be placed.

Amos smiled to himself in the half darkness. He couldn't compete with the weapon that Vinnie was holding, but if he could just get Leo to step a little closer to where he could reach him, they might have a chance at turning the tables in their favour. 'Come closer, Leo.' he muttered quietly to himself, and motioned to Isabella to remain very, *very* still and not utter a sound.

'Just where did you throw that grenade?' Vinnie had spoken to Leo who was teetering uncertainly on the edge of the lower step.

'Straight down there, almost in front of us, that's where

McAllister and the woman were,' said Leo. 'I'm positive it landed in her lap, I couldn't miss from here, so there won't be anything to look for now, so I don't see why I should have to go down there.' He was beginning to whine again.

Vinnie shone the beam of his powerful torch at the spot Leo indicated, some twenty or so feet from where they stood. 'I don't see anything down there, only a lot of broken stone and that old tombstone that's got a few chunks out of it. In any case you'd better go and make a positive check. Vic is mad enough already and he isn't going to be any happier if he knows you didn't do as he said. McAllister is a dangerous man to deal with, even if the grenade killed the woman, he just might have missed the blast, so we just don't know, do we?'

Leo sighed and took a firmer grip on his gun, then shining the torch directly in front of him, made his way down to the pile of rubble. He soon found himself at the foot of the great tombstone and kicked angrily at one of the pieces of stone that littered the floor there. Part of the ornate top had been broken away, for the amount of broken stone and the heaps of dirt at its base, it hadn't appeared to have suffered much damage at all. He was surprised, he would have thought that the blast from the grenade would have caused more carnage. There were certainly no bodies or evidence of bodies lying there either. Yet that was where he had thrown the grenade.

Puzzled, he swung his torch beam around to the left of the old tombstone and his heart gave a quick leap. Dozens of white bones and broken skulls lying half buried in piles of black dirt gleamed with a ghostly radiance in the light of his torch. His scattered mind soon realised that what he was looking at, were the remains of a tomb within a tomb — an ossuary, a separate chamber that had been erected for the remains of the dead, the bodies resting in regular niches built into the walls of the chamber.

This was not where he had thrown the grenade, yet here it was, destroyed! He shuddered and almost dropped the torch in fear as he stared at the remnants of grinning skulls and broken skeletons. His first impulse was to retrace his steps as fast as he could back to the step and comparative safety but his fear of Victor's anger at his actions up to date and his own desire to know that McAllister was dead, drove him to recover his nerve.

He shone his torch further into the blackness, into what was a narrow corridor that had apparently been filled with bodies of past clergy or whoever, from the Abbey. A burial ground! They must have been here for centuries; so many bones but not a recently dead or part thereof of one Amos McAllister. He had to be here somewhere.

He moved the beam of his torch around, then a flash of colour caught his eye. That woman had been wearing a brightly coloured skirt. He swung the beam of his torch back again to where he had seen it. There it was half buried under a clod of the black soil. He bent down to pick it up; as he straightened up again, he suddenly felt himself encircled by strong brawny arms, one across his throat stifling any sound and the other over the wrist holding the gun. Strong fingers were pressing into nerves, forcing the gun to fall from his fingers. A soft familiar voice was close to his ear.

'Don't drop the torch, Leo.'

He could feel the torch being taken from his hand by someone else.

'Keep it shining on the floor and moving about,' the soft deep voice said to someone, then came back to hiss in his ear, 'now, Leo, I promised you a broken neck and I keep my promises.'

There was a stifled gasp from Leo, a sickening crunch and Leo slid quietly to the ground at the feet of Amos McAllister.

'Oh dear ...' Isabella's voice wavered as she tried to keep the torch shining as Amos had instructed, though it shook considerably in her hands.

Amos drew her into part of the remaining portion of the tomb wall that would shield them from view from the step. He put his arm gently around her shoulders and whispered, 'Isabella, these men will kill, as they have done many times before. We are in a tricky situation here, even I have to admit our chances of getting out are pretty slim. Leo was expendable, he is one less we have to deal with; he had to go. Do you understand?' She nodded her head but even in the dim light he could see the tears forming in her fear filled brown eyes. He held her face for a moment in his strong hands and said, 'What you did with that grenade was very brave, I will respect you for ever for it and you saved both our lives. I don't think you realise just how bad it could have been, perhaps it would be better not to,' he added half to himself.

'What are we to do now?' whispered Isabella, 'I'm worried about Marilla and Jack — what if we can't get out of here at all?'

Amos looked down as a soft furry tail wrapped itself around his legs. 'Maybe Lucifer has the answer to that one, he came in from somewhere, so there must be another way out. Look, Isabella, I'm worried about Jack and Marilla too, just bear with me, if we work together, we'll find a way out of this mess. There's a lot more to being here at this Abbey for Jack than this scurvy mob but this is not the time or place for any further talk. Just hang on to that torch and keep it shining around as if you're looking for something. Don't forget that Vinnie is still keeping watch up there, he's probably trigger happy at the moment. I've got Leo's gun; that should even the odds up a little bit, but I need to move Leo a bit further away so they have to look for him. Perhaps we'll give him a burial they won't forget!'

Amos picked up Leo's body, even though there was little weight to the thin body, Amos found it an effort with his chest injury but he managed to push it into one of the ledges of the narrow burial corridor, now vacated by its original occupant and folded Leo's hands neatly over his chest.

'Just a minute,' whispered Isabella. She began to grope around in the dirt. 'There,' she said in a defiant voice, 'that should give them something to think about,' as she placed something on top of Leo's folded hands.

'Nice touch, Bella,' said Amos stifling a laugh, 'now let's get away from here, we can move further back around that other side and still be able to see the door from there. We'll have to move without the torch though, there's enough half-light to see by and this is the one time we don't want Vinnie to see where we are.'

*   *   *

Vinnie had been pacing up and down the broad step. He wished Victor would hurry up. He was beginning to dislike everything about this new enterprise of Vic's. Maybe Grimsby was right, maybe Victor was pushing their luck a bit far by wanting to set up this printing press here. They had been doing well for some years now, why take the extra risks? Now there were too many people involved, they had always worked as a close-knit family group. Anyone else was expendable, if necessary and the 'odd' disappearance didn't attract too much attention, providing there was nothing left to connect them. This was becoming a lot more complicated, especially now that Grimsby and McAllister were on the scene. Somebody would know they were here and would come looking … why was his brother being so blind about their presence here? Vinnie was becoming more convinced than ever that his elder brother was losing the plot; it was getting too dangerous. He had done a lot of thinking while Vic was away and maybe now was the time for him to split, leave Vic to it, he'd had enough.

'*Damn!*' Where was Leo?

Leo had been gone too long. He had seen his torch flash here and there, then for a few moments there was nothing, then it came on again. Vinnie wasn't too sure he could trust Leo either. The little weasel might be their cousin but he was proving to be a pain in the neck, he obviously couldn't be trusted in a tight spot. Vinnie was surprised he hadn't come running back before this, now his torch had gone out altogether. He stepped to the edge of the great step and was about to call out to him, when he could hear Victor coming back, his torch flashing on the huge grey flag stones of the crypt floor, but the light from Leo's torch had not been seen for some minutes now.

He shone his own torch carefully to where he had last seen Leo, then swept it back to the broken headstone. The bright light reflected back from two deep yellow eyes looking straight at him and he could hear a deep growl. He felt the hairs stand up on the back of his neck and he caught his breath, 'Wh–what is that?'

Victor and the two engineers, who had now reached the foot of the step, stood rooted to the spot as the eyes now turned in their direction. Vinnie lifted his gun and fired off a burst in the direction of the tomb, but the eyes had disappeared.

'*Wait!*' barked Victor, 'where's Leo?'

'I don't know,' Vinnie stuttered, 'he was over there, I've been watching his torch, now I don't see it at all. He went looking for McAllister or what might be left of him but he hasn't come back and now those eyes; what is it?' There was panic in his voice now.

'I don't know either,' said Victor, 'but we'll have to find Leo. He looked at his younger brother. 'I'll go, you stay here, If McAllister shows his face which I doubt that he can, shoot to kill, just remember where I am!'

Amos and Isabella meanwhile had cautiously made their way to the other side of the crypt and the great stone step and now stood sheltering behind one of the stone pillars. Amos had been weighing up the possibility of firing off a shot at Vinnie, but he knew it would bring answering fire from Victor. The gun he had taken from Leo was no match for the rapid-fire rifle, even if he did get a clear shot at Vinnie, plus it would also give away their position. He didn't know about the other two standing there either, were they carrying weapons? There were other factors to consider as well, he was aware his aim would have to be absolutely accurate if he did attempt to shoot and what of Isabella, she could get caught in the crossfire … no it wasn't worth the risk. The pain caught in his chest as he moved back behind the pillar. *Damn*, that was another reason for holding fire, his injury would hamper the swiftness and strength he would need.

From their vantage point they saw the flashes from Vinnie's gun and heard the staccato sound of the clattering weapon and the whine of bullets echoing loudly in the vaulted space of the crypt as Vinnie fired at the tombstone.

'He'll shoot Lucifer!' gasped Isabella. She had seen him jump up, onto the top of the broken tomb as they had hurried away.

'Don't worry, he's a smart cat, I'm sure he knows the danger,' whispered Amos. As the last of the echoes died away in that great vaulted ceiling, a gentle rub against Isabella's leg and a soft growl assured her that her fears for the owner of those two yellow eyes was indeed safe.

Dropping to her knees Isabella hugged the cat to her. 'Lucifer, you shouldn't have shown yourself like that,' she admonished him, 'you might have been killed!'

Amos rubbed the cat's ears. 'I think he might have wanted to give them something else to think about other than us. 'Now, Lucifer,' he whispered, stroking the broad black head, 'if you could just find us another way out of this, we would be eternally grateful.'

To his surprise, the cat turned, flicked his tail and began to walk sedately off through the great columns, to what they assumed to be the very back of the great emptiness of the crypt.

Vinnie had been closely watching the flicker of his brother's torch in the gloomy half- light. It seemed to set the shadows moving, as if the space was filled with spectral phantoms that glided and twisted into grotesque forms. The whole area seemed to be getting darker, except for the play of the torch giving life to the phantasmal shapes he thought he could see. The vision of those staring yellow eyes had completely unnerved him. The oppressiveness of this musty atmosphere was enveloping him in its closeness and he could hear Victor calling Leo's name but it seemed faint in the whispers that began to echo in his head. His mind was now set only on what horrors might be lurking among the huge shadowy columns that stretched out before him, like a stone forest full of unmentionable beings.

Where the atmosphere had been suffocating before, now he suddenly felt as if he couldn't breathe at all and voices were echoing inside his head. Even though the very air around him was icy cold, he had the irresistible urge to turn and run up those steps to where there was light and safety and warmth, real warmth. '*Vinnie!*' He realised with a start that his brother was calling his name.

'Vinnie, get down here *now!*'

Following the glow of his brother's torch, Vinnie ventured down into the gloom, past the broken tombstone and the scattered bones. He became acutely aware now of the shadows closing in around him, his heartbeat faster, but the urgency in his brother's voice had made him forget his fear for the time being. His own torch shone on broken skeletons that lay scattered about in the black earth, he shivered uncontrollably as he stepped around them. He could see Victor standing in the pool of light from his torch in front of what looked like a black tunnel.

'Did—did you find him?' he asked huskily, trying to hide the tremor in his voice. 'Yeah, I did, look …'

Victor led his brother a little way into the dank dark corridor that smelled as if the earth there was a million years old and shone his torch onto a ledge where a strip of brightly coloured fabric led their eyes up to where the still, white-faced body of Leo lay, as if in sleep, his hands crossed neatly over his chest. However, it was the skeletal hand shining ghostly white in the light of their torches that startled them. It too lay on Leo's chest, the bony fingers just touching Leo's broken neck and tucked beneath those bony fingers, the piece of coloured fabric hanging delicately, like a medieval banner.

Chapter 18

A Rat In A Trap

'There won't be too much left to say that a woman was there at all.'

Marilla froze behind the pile of crates as Leo's words sank in. A hand grenade? Isabella and Amos were imprisoned in a crypt and this, this person had thrown something at them, at Isabella! He said it landed in her lap and there wouldn't be anything left, wasn't that a sort of bomb thing? She tried to remember what Jack had said was in that crate.

Explosives, yes that was it! That Leo person had thrown an explosive at her sister and as far as he was concerned, they were both dead. She couldn't help but hear what he had said, he was only a few feet away from her as he climbed the steps, with that horrid looking little brown man following behind and his words had come as a complete shock. She was so startled by them, that she bumped the crates and the top one had fallen over with a loud clatter. Frantically, she looked about her, aware that her clumsiness had attracted the attention of the men opposite.

A few moments earlier, Marilla had seen a very large rat that had poked its nose out of a considerable gap at the bottom of a cupboard behind her. With whiskers twitching, it had then emerged fully and began to forage in an overturned vegetable basket. It now lifted its head on hearing the noise, prepared to make a dash for the safety of the cupboard.

Marilla saw her chance; she pointed her finger at the rat immobilising it. Now, if only her magic did not fail her! She was only too well aware that Jack would guess that she was hiding there and would be watching. She was also remembering his playful pranks with her magic when they were children, she hoped that now he would help her concentration, as she knew he could, when he wanted to. She had to be quick as the immobility spell only worked on small creatures and very soon wore off. She pointed her finger again at the rat, where not even a whisker was twitching, it was so still.

'*Mensa agitat molem fastina mero motic levator!*' she muttered in a half whisper. To her delight there was a slight popping noise and a rather bewildered looking rat was sitting inside the upturned crate that had fallen, making no attempt to run away.

Bruno cautiously ventured across the landing to investigate the noise, his gun drawn, with dark eyes in his black bearded face darting here and there as he stepped to the door of the room. Marilla had drawn herself further into the shadows and sat very still, holding her breath.

Then Bruno's eye fell on the open crate and the creature that looked back at him with the same black eyes. 'Aagh, it's a rat, I *hate* rats.' He spat in disgust and kicked at the crate. 'Go on *shoo*, or I'll use you for target practice.' The rat obliged, now that it had recovered its equilibrium and fled through the open doorway, disappearing into the gloom.

Marilla breathed a sigh of relief. She had been prepared to try her magic on Bruno himself had he come any closer but was afraid that in her haste to do so, the spell would fail, then she would be no use to Jack. She just had to wait her chance now.

Jack's hands had been tied behind his back and he was seated on the floor with his back against the box of explosives. Bruno had been left alone to guard him, while the two brothers with a reluctant Leo shepherded the two nervous engineers through the ancient wooden doorway to the crypts below. Victor, not taking any chances with the heavy oaken door closing prematurely, blocked the door open with a large piece of masonry lying nearby. Quite likely left there for that purpose.

Marilla would wait now until they had gone but still had no firm idea about how she was going to help Jack escape, wondering if her meagre magic skills could compete with a man with a gun in his hand.

Sitting hunched up in her dark corner Marilla pondered her situation. One part of her wanted to rush down into that underground crypt and search for her sister but she knew it was impossible at the moment and there was Jack to consider — she had to help him, come what may. If she could somehow disable the one man left to guard him, then he would know what to do, he was a policeman and dealt with people like this, didn't he?

She shifted her position slightly so she could peer out into the other room. Jack, seated on the floor where he was, had a clear view of the room opposite where Marilla crouched. Bruno was pacing backwards and forwards in front of him, although she could see that Jack's gaze was directed to where she sat. She had the intense feeling he was trying to tell her something. Then his eyes shifted and she noticed that he was actually looking at something behind her. She turned her head to see what had caught his attention and noticed a large rack holding dozens of bottles of the red wine that the monks had stored there. Puzzled she looked back at him and perceived a very slight nod of his head, as his eyes flickered from her to the wine rack.

What could he possibly want her to do? She frowned as she tried to think what sort of spell she could conjure up that would involve bottles of wine. The rat! She had made it move where she had wanted it to, why couldn't she do it again? She peered out at Jack again and nodded back at him, she saw the faint smile that played around his mouth as if he understood.

Bruno had stopped pacing. Jack had asked him a question and Bruno had answered curtly. Not satisfied with the answer, Jack repeated his question and added more, catching his eye as he did so. Bruno began to pace impatiently again, he suddenly stopped in front of where Jack sat and stood facing him, his hands on his hips and an argument ensued. Just what it was about Marilla didn't care much, she was too busy concentrating on the bottles of wine.

She repeated her spell over and over in her mind, then began to chant softly, '*Mensa agitat molem levator sine mora,*' and pointed a steady finger at the topmost bottle on the rack. She saw the bottle twitch in its niche in the rack and move slightly. Encouraged now and with intense concentration, she directed all her thoughts into what she was about to do, knowing Jack was keeping Bruno occupied and his back turned to the door of this room. Her pointing finger was emitting a faint blue haze and as she repeated her words, adding, '*Meo voto festina*' the bottle was slowly being fully drawn from its resting place and began to move of its own accord across the room, still high in the air.

From his place on the floor, Jack was able to see the bottle emerge from the room opposite and float silently toward where Bruno stood, it hovered uncertainly, high above his head. Bruno made a move to turn away and continue pacing, but a sharp comment by Jack changed his mind and he returned to facing Jack and shook his fist at him menacingly.

It was fortunate that Bruno was not looking upward. Had he done so he would have been most astonished to see a full bottle of wine hovering high above his head. Jack had been following the bottle's progress unbeknown to Bruno and now gave the almost invisible Marilla an unobtrusive but significant nod. She immediately snapped her fingers hard, the bottle came crashing down to land on Bruno's head, right on target. Bruno fell to the floor, the bottle smashing on impact, covering his head in the rich ruby red wine that ran freely down his face and dripped into a glistening pool on the floor about him.

'Marilla, *quickly!*' Jack called, 'he won't be out for long, help me get these ropes off.' She ran from her hiding place and began tugging at his bonds.

'No, Marilla, under my right boot against the heel, there's a blade there, held by a magnetic clasp. Press the sides of the hilt and it will spring open. It's small but deadly sharp, so be careful.'

Marilla found the little knife and careful not to cut Jack's wrists, she managed to slice through the cords lashing them together. It took them only a few minutes longer to tie the still unconscious Bruno up firmly and lean him up against the box in Jack's place. Jack rubbed at his wrists and glanced at his watch, noting that there was a tiny but faint red pulse of light emitting from it. It told him all he needed to know and he breathed a sigh of relief.

Marilla immediately declared she was going to go down into the crypt to search for her sister. There was deep concern in her eyes but there was anger there too. Jack grabbed her by the shoulders as she started off down the steps and looked into her green eyes.

'No,' he said gently, 'it's too dangerous for you or even me to go down there now, it's time to call in the cavalry. They would be here in twenty minutes, they have the fire power and the men to round this lot up. Marilla, your magic would be too unstable against the weapons they are carrying, believe me, I know what these men are like. You would be no match for them. What you did just now with that rat and the bottle of wine was brilliant, I couldn't be more proud of you but I don't want you risking your life. If there's a way out from down there and they are still alive, which I believe they are, then Amos will find it. Please believe me, Marilla.'

She looked at him for a moment and blinked away a little tear from those defiant green eyes, before she spoke. 'How can you be so sure of that, after what that man said?'

'Leo is a born loser, I doubt that he could even throw straight and right now, he'd say anything to stay in Victor's good books. He hasn't been too popular with his mates of late and I'd say he's about to draw the short straw on survival within the pack. Speaking of which, I'll have to block that door, we don't want the rats to escape do we?'

He ran lightly down the remaining steps and pulled the heavy door closed, then rolled the piece of masonry back across it. He leaned against the door for a moment and whispered to himself. 'Just hang in there, Amos, we'll get you out.' He cast a glance at Bruno as he bounded back to where Marilla stood waiting. He was just beginning to come around with the red wine still dripping slowly from his black hair down his face. What a waste, Jack thought briefly, I'm sure Bruno would have enjoyed it better had it been served in a glass.

He put a protective arm around Marilla and steered her toward the staircase. 'I don't know how long that will hold them there but it will have to do, come old girl, let's put that anger of yours to use.' He looked at her with a boyish grin, 'How do you feel about creating a bit of havoc and help me disable those vehicles out there but first, I've got to make that radio call, come on, we don't have a lot of time.'

Marilla bit her lip, yes, she was angry and thoughtful, as she fetched her broomstick. Isabella, she sometimes felt, was somewhat of a hindrance to her own advancement of ideas, and rarely wanted to try anything new but to lose her sister, her only sibling would be too much to bear. Regardless of Isabella's indifference, she was none the less a comfort to have near and without her, life would be unbearable. She suddenly realised then just how much she loved her sister and she fought to keep back the tears.

Jack seemed so sure that they would emerge from the depths of the crypt alright, she had no reason to doubt him. After all, this was his line of work, she and Isabella were aware of the risks. Perhaps there was nothing she could do to help her sister right now, perhaps she and Amos had managed to dodge whatever Leo said he had thrown down there. She felt a surge of anger again, yes, she would be happy to create a bit of havoc; quite a bit of havoc, her green eyes blazed in anticipation.

She grabbed her broomstick and together they raced up the stairs to the back of the scullery but not before Jack snatched up the gun that Bruno had dropped. It felt better to have something he was familiar with in his hand, at least it was a deterrent should there be more trouble.

Jack's first stop was to the huge pantry adjacent to the old kitchen to collect his backpack. Opening it on the long bench table, he revealed a small but powerful transmitter. Quickly he pulled out the telescopic antenna from the back of it, after leaving Marilla to keep a watch on the doorway, he began to transmit a coded signal. It was immediately answered by the

Lieutenant on duty at the Army camp just the other side of the mountain massif.

The voice that answered was bright and breezy but Jack was quick to notice the touch of anxiety that was there also. 'We were beginning to wonder if everything was alright, Jack,' said the voice lightly, 'you're a bit behind schedule.'

'I know Steve, there's been a few hiccups this end, we could do with that chopper right now and some back up. You'll have about seven to pick up, copy that?'

'Copy,' said Lieutenant Grayson. 'You were just about to get it anyway, we'd almost given up on getting the word and were going to drop in regardless, uninvited and take a chance. Are you and Amos okay?'

'For the moment, yes.'

'And the evidence?'

'As much as you'll need, Steve, just get that chopper moving, we need that back up now.'

Jack signed off, closed up the backpack and shoved it into a shelf of the pantry. Turning to where Marilla stood near the door, he took her elbow and shepherded her out into the courtyard. 'Now, Marilla, let's do some damage before that lot work their way out of that hole in the ground. I don't know how long that piece of rock will hold that door closed, so we just hope that it keeps them occupied for a while yet.'

The mid-afternoon sun was slanted across the open courtyard, mellowing the ancient stonework of the buildings in a soft glow, lighting the tops of the trees surrounding the Abbey in brilliant colour. As they hurried toward where the trucks were parked at the gates, several of the hooded monks emerged from the chapel and came toward them. One of whom apparently a spokesperson for the group, held up his hand and stopped Jack.

'We demand to know just what is going on here, we have been moved about enough.' The elderly monk, who looked tired and drawn went on, while he eyed Marilla nervously. 'We are all tired of this business and we would like to know what you have done with the Abbot, we want answers!' He glanced somewhat fearfully in Marilla's direction at this last remark.

'You're quite right and I do apologise for the discomfort you have all been put through but I don't have time to stop and explain it all right now.' Jack reached into his pocket and pulled out an identity card he put this into the monk's hand. 'This will explain who I am, now please, go back into the chapel for just a little while longer. I must ask you to find as secure a place as possible and urge you to stay there. A helicopter will be here in a few minutes from now, in this courtyard probably, I don't want any of you around when it does. There could be gunfire, so please stay put until we tell you that it's safe to come out. The man we want is Mr Casini, as you are in no doubt aware by now and the men that are with him.'

'Well,' said the elderly monk slowly as he looked at Jack's ID card. 'What is going to happen to us when you do put Mr Casini where you want him?'

'That's something I have no answer for; that will be up to other authorities.'

Suddenly Jack remembered Moody — he was supposed to be with the monks in the chapel, keeping them all together there. 'Where is the man who was with you — the little brown man?'

'Oh, he left some minutes ago,' said the elderly one, 'I didn't see where he went, he just slipped quietly out. Quite a strange man, but interesting to listen to. His views on Buddhist revelations were quite enlightening, he recounted his private visits to Tibet and of his many meetings with the Dalai Lama, discussing spiritual matters, indeed, a strange little man.'

No time to look for Moody now Jack thought, I've got to scuttle those vehicles before that mob break out and hopefully Steve's lot will be here before they do. He had picked up one of the hand grenades from the box before he and Marilla had left the cellars but was loathe to use it. There had been too much damage done around the Abbey already but at least it would be a viable deterrent should Victor and his cohorts break out of their prison before reinforcements arrived. He checked the cabs of both trucks and discovered that the keys had been left in the ignitions, so that was easy enough but there was no way he could open the backs of the trucks. They'd been heavily padlocked, no doubt Victor had the keys. He'd leave that to Steve's men. He had a fair idea of what was inside them anyway.

Marilla though, had other things on her mind and turned away, needing to be alone.

Victor's large black limousine stood a little apart from the trucks, Jack felt very tempted to toss the grenade under it but it was only a thought, remembering that more than likely the trucks would also be carrying quantities of plastic explosives and they were too close for comfort, even though they would need detonators, there could be other dangerous things as well.

Hopefully there could be incriminating papers in the limo and if so, they would be needed toward the mass of evidence that was stacking up against Casini — the more they found the better. He'd leave that to Steve to sort out; it seemed now that after years of frustration in chasing down this gang, they were on the verge of bringing it all together and he was feeling a sense of relief, marred only by the fact that Amos was still missing. He glanced at his watch again, although there was nothing there now to indicate that Amos was alive.

Damn! Where was Moody? Perhaps he'd changed his mind about working for the Cassini's and had decided to slip away down the hill to the village while the opportunity was there. Looking down the hill in the direction of the village he could see nothing but then Moody had been gone for some minutes according to the monks. If he was not with the monks, where was he? He didn't seem too keen about being here, obviously Victor had not enlightened him much about what to expect.

An odd little man, Jack thought but from what he knew of him, was very shrewd and clever. A master craftsman in the art of engraving, particularly banknotes, it would have been the prime reason he had been recruited into the group. He leaned against the side of one of the trucks and waited, hoping his inner senses were right that Amos and Isabella had indeed escaped.

Presently a sound came to his ears, the faint rhythmic thump of helicopter rotor blades. Jack shielded his eyes from the afternoon sun and looked toward the mountain top beyond the Abbey. Engrossed as he was in waiting for the chopper, he did not see the small brown man creeping silently up behind him, a long thin knife clutched in the skinny brown hand, but Marilla did …

She had decided to go back to her vantage point with the gargoyle. Besides wanting time to be alone, she also needed to think, to weigh up the situation that she and Bella had found themselves in. She was worried about the fate of her sister. Was Jack only saying that she and Amos were alive just to ease her worry? Somehow, she knew in her own mind that he was right.

She too heard the sound of the rotor blades cutting through the air and was about to turn her head to look in that direction, when a movement near the back of one of the trucks caught her eye. Someone was coming slowly from around the back of it.

She recognised the figure as the little brown man that she had first seen following Vinnie and the others down to the cellars.

He was creeping stealthily toward Jack who seemed unaware of his presence as he stood gazing into the distance at the approaching helicopter. Something glinted in the afternoon sunlight and she realised with a thrill of alarm that the little man was clutching a knife. She caught a glimpse of the blade as he raised his arm to strike.

With one swift movement she was on her broomstick, her green eyes flashing. She came at him, low and fast. Moody heard the rush of wind and the flapping of cloth he looked around for what was only a brief instant and in that terrible moment was embraced by his worst nightmare.

The huge 'bat' as he imagined it to be, caught his meagre body in the middle, an arm was flung over his back, strong fingers clutching him tightly and he felt himself being swept up in the air with lightning speed. His scream was lost in the thin air as he watched the ground drop away beneath him, the dramatic headlong rush that bore him upward to hover terrifyingly over the deep gorge took away any breath left in his fear-stricken body. Shaking with the sheer terror of it, he could see and hear the roar of the raging torrent crashing and fuming its way over sharp black rocks that thrust upward through the seething turbulence like the waiting teeth of some monstrous predator. He closed his eyes and waited for the worst.

Marilla was very tempted to drop him there and then into the raging waters of the mountain stream but with her initial anger subsiding she changed her mind. Instead she turned her broomstick around to follow the stream down to where it gathered into a deep wide pool below the falls. Marilla hesitated, allowing the hapless little man to glimpse what lay below him. Then to his utter horror, she began to circle the deep forbidding pool; climbing higher and higher Then without warning she released her hold, allowing him to fall. Marilla watched the little man tumble as he screamed shrilly on his descent into cold deep water.

Chapter 19

The Noose Tightens

Jack, standing beside the trucks had felt and heard the rapid intervention of Marilla and then the sudden scream of Moody as he was whisked high above, Jack followed the ascent of them both as Marilla's cloak flapped around the terrified little man with just his legs showing beneath the cloth. Jack tried to call out to her but his voice was swept away and he could only watch helplessly as she hovered briefly over the chasm, then turn and move swiftly downstream.

He had not seen Moody come up behind him from somewhere But Marilla did. His senses should have alerted him to the danger but had failed. Moody must have been hiding under one of the trucks right behind him. Jack looked down and saw the knife lying where the little man had dropped it and picked it up. If it had not been for Marilla's sharp eyes and quick action; he tried not to think about that now.

He wondered what she was going to do with Moody — not too much he hoped as he needed the little craftsman as much as the others in the group.

He watched her progress until she was just a small figure in the distant sky and noticed too that she was now circling ever higher in the one spot. Suddenly, a tiny figure, its arms and legs flailing like some disjointed doll fell from beneath the cloak it tumbled to earth or was it water, he guessed it was, as the mountain stream eddied out into deep pools near there. Not for one moment could he imagine that Marilla was callous enough to deliberately drop her captive onto hard earth or rocks. True, she had a temper but not bad enough to kill … yet.

The helicopter now in full sight, Jack turned his attention to it, tapping the thin bladed knife anxiously against his thumbnail as he watched it hover and turn as the pilot edged it fully into the vacant courtyard. Billowing clouds of dust and gravel spewed up from the whirling rotor blades as the machine settled onto the hallowed grounds of the Abbey. A door slid back and a hunched figure sprang from it, bending low to avoid the still running rotor blades as he ran to where Jack waited.

Dressed in battle fatigues a ruddy complexion highlighted by a shock of red-blonde hair, Lieutenant Steve Grayson hurried forward to grasp Jack's hand in a firm grip. 'Good to see you, Jack, we were getting a bit worried something might have gone wrong with the plan.'

'It has and it hasn't,' replied Jack 'We'll have to move quickly as we might still have a fight on our hands. Four of them, plus the two engineers are at the moment down in the crypt, somehow I don't think it will take them long to break out of there. If we move fast, we may be able to get them first. I've blocked the door but brute strength and ignorance just might get them out.'

'Okay.' Grayson had already signalled to the remaining three Special Forces officers, dressed similarly in fatigues, who had scrambled out of the aircraft and followed, guns at the ready.

'Are the monks safe?' asked Grayson.

'In the chapel at the moment and probably watching closely I would imagine, they don't like having their peace disturbed, all this is something that doesn't come along every day.'

'Where's Amos then?' Grayson asked, looking about carefully as the group hurried in the direction Jack led them.

'That I'm not too sure about,' said Jack tight lipped as they approached the entrance to the scullery and the top of the stone stairway. His voice dropped to a whisper, 'He could still be down there too, alive, I hope.'

'Careful here, quietly, I think I hear voices,' whispered Jack. 'They must have broken out of the crypt, probably found the present we left for them blocking the doorway and a nicely gift-wrapped Bruno.'

The tight group of men moved silently down the winding stairway keeping close to the curve of the wall and following Jack's signals.

Victor's angry and agitated voice came drifting up from the landing below, it was now obvious that the door had just been forced open and it was to be hoped that all were in the one spot; Jack didn't want to have to flush them out from the vastness of the catacombs below. His voice came clearly to them where they were just out of sight of the final curve of the wall. 'Where's Grimsby and how the *hell* did you get all that wine over you?'

'I don't know, Vic. I don't know! It just came out of nowhere, there was nobody else here — I don't know how it happened!' Bruno was shaking his wine-soaked head as he sat on the floor. 'I had Grimsby tied up and—'

'Why can't I trust you idiots to do *anything*!' broke in the almost hysterical voice of Victor.

'Because that's what they are.' Jack stepped down onto the landing closely followed by Grayson and his men. The surprise in Victor's eyes lasted only a second. With one quick movement he had darted to the close-by explosives box and now stood defiantly in front of them holding a grenade in his hand.

His eyes flashed dangerously as they flickered from one to the other of the group standing at the foot of the steps. They rested now on Jack. 'I don't know how you did this, Grimsby, but I'll die here before I allow you to put me in prison; you can die with me, you've plagued me long enough.'

Vinnie opened his mouth to say something but the rage in his brother's face stopped him. Victor now addressed Vinnie and Bruno without taking his eyes off Jack. 'This would have been our best enterprise yet, one we could have retired on, wealthy beyond our wildest dreams, but you three, you three *morons* have stuffed it up completely! I couldn't trust you now with anything. You've failed me, Vinnie,' Victor was shaking in anger now, 'so if *I* go, *you* go too!'

'But—Vic!' Vinnie stammered, 'we—we weren't to know—'

'*Shut up*, Vinnie, it's too late for excuses!'

'Don't be a complete fool, Casini.' Lieutenant Grayson said quietly and began to walk toward him.

'I *warned you!*' Victor's voice was hard and cold as he held up his hand holding the grenade. 'Remember, I've got nothing to lose if I pull this pin now and what's left in this box should bring the whole place down on all of us. Is that what you want, Grimsby?'

There was a tense moment of silence and all present, particularly the engineers, who had been listening to this tirade of madness, waited anxiously, barely daring to breathe. Right now, the engineers were wishing they were somewhere else other than there in a dank cellar listening to a madman threatening to blow them up, still wondering why they had agreed to come here in the first place. Steve Grayson stopped his advancement toward Victor and glanced uneasily at Jack. What was to be their next move? This was a stalemate they had not expected.

Jack's mind however had been busy and he sensed rather than saw the rat that Marilla had levitated. It was, he reasoned, close by and probably behind the box on the floor, the box that Bruno was still leaning against as he sat there feeling the lump on his head. With his eyes closed, for a second, Jack transferred his thoughts to another medium.

A moment later there was a terrified scream from Bruno. He was grasping his leg and shaking it violently. 'Aargh!' he shot to his feet and began to jump up and down shaking his leg and screeched, 'It's up my *leg–get it out–get it out!*'

Bruno, in his frantic move to get to his feet lurched heavily against Victor knocking him off balance. Jack seized his chance and threw himself against Victor and he was able to grab the raised arm holding the grenade, knocking it out of Victor's grasp to send it spinning harmlessly across the floor. Taken by surprise Victor went sprawling on the floor with Jack on top of him. Steve threw his weight in and together they soon had Victor securely handcuffed. At the same time one of the other officers made a grab for Bruno, who, while still hopping around on one leg was making whimpering noises as he tried to unbuckle his belt and drop his pants. As he did so, a rat shot out from the trouser leg and scurried away. '*Aargh*! Rats! Ugh, I can't *stand* rats!' With his pants around his ankles, he now showed little resistance to arrest.

All resistance too had gone out of Vinnie, he just stared with disgust at his scowling big brother who had now been hauled to his feet. So much for brotherhood, he thought wearily. The engineers loudly now protesting their innocence in the entire affair were grabbed by the other officers and were also handcuffed; that would be sorted out later they were told.

'Where's the other one, the thin one, he isn't here?' Grayson looked around. 'Where's cousin Leo, Leo Stefani, where is he?'

'He's—he's dead,' stuttered Vinnie. 'D—down there,' as he nodded his head toward the crypt.

'And Amos McAllister?' asked Jack through clenched teeth as he wrestled a still hostile and struggling Victor over to where the others had been ordered to sit down with their backs against a wall.

Victor looked at Jack with a flicker of triumph in his otherwise vengeful dark eyes and said in a soft mocking voice. 'Perhaps he *is* dead. As Leo said, a grenade doesn't leave much behind to sift through, does it? What a shame, such a good friend too, eh Grimsby?' He smiled, showing the expensive dentistry of gold capped teeth but the dark eyes were unsmiling and glittering with malice.

Jack said nothing and stared at the man who had eluded him for so long, inside his head he was angry; angry enough to strangle this man with his bare hands. Angry at himself too for asking Amos to come down here in the first place. The image of a body bound hand and foot with a bullet hole in the forehead came up before him, so too that of the short thick-set man with greying hair to whom he had owed his life many times over and loved as a brother. He stared back at the man before him with a feeling of hatred he had not felt before but got little satisfaction to see that Victor dropped his eyes and could no longer look at Jack.

Was losing Amos the price he had to pay for the capture and imprisonment of Casini? In his heart he hoped not. He remembered the tiny red dot that had shown on his wristwatch. That tiny red dot had told him Amos was alive but where? And there had been no red dot now for some time.

The strained voice of Vinnie broke his thoughts. 'Then—then

who killed Leo if McAllister is dead?' Vinnie was becoming hysterical as he glared at his brother. 'Who or what snapped his neck and left him like that—with that—that thing on him, and those eyes! You saw them Vic—you saw them!'

'*Shut up*, Vinnie!' growled Victor.

Jack's heart gave a quick leap. Leo with a broken neck? That surely sounded like Amos' work. He rounded on Vinnie. 'What sort of eyes?'

'Big yellow eyes that just stared,' stammered Vinnie. I fired at them, then they disappeared and there are other things down there, bodies—bones—ghosts. I could hear them whispering. There were dark things moving all around me. I want to get out of here,' he almost sobbed. 'I've never wanted to be here; this was a *crazy* idea coming to this creepy place.'

Steve Grayson gave a short triumphant laugh. 'Well, Vinnie you are about to get your wish and a nice helicopter ride in the bargain. You'll enjoy the view as we leave, make the most of it because it will be your last glimpse of the outside world. Remember what it looks like because you won't be seeing anything but prison walls for the rest of your life.'

Victor was also hauled to his feet by the affable lieutenant. 'Same goes for you too Mr Casini. It's too bad your passion for instant wealth has become your downfall. Now I believe there might be a few things in the pockets of the excellent suit you are wearing that we might need, isn't that right, Jack?'

'The keys to those trucks and that nifty little revolver you are so fond of,' said Jack dryly. 'I rather suspect that it was the nasty little piece you used to execute Daniel Montaigne with. You know Steve, I don't think Vic will look anywhere near as dapper when he swaps his Armani suit for prison clobber, though I would rather see him hanging from the end of a rope.'

Victor's face screwed up and he scowled at Jack, his face livid with fury while his clothes were searched. 'You haven't heard the last of me, *Jack Grimsby!*' he spat. 'There'll be a way of reaching you and prison bars won't stop me, just keep looking over your shoulder because one day I'll be there.'

'I doubt it,' said Jack, 'not with the charges you are facing, it's me that you should be watching out for. In the meantime, I have a message from Daniel!' Before anyone could stop him, Jack had thrown one solid punch that landed square in the middle of Victor's face and he smiled to himself in satisfaction as he felt the bone of Victor's nose give under his fist.

'*Dammit Jack!* That's not in the rule book!' said Grayson as Victor collapsed into the arms of the officer who was holding him, trying to avoid the spurt of fresh blood issuing from Victor's broken nose which was now running freely down the front of the expensively cut suit and dripping onto the expensive shoes. 'Why must you be so impulsive Jack?' Then in a quieter voice as the other prisoners were being led up the stairway he said, 'I don't want to have to explain how he got an injury, dear boy, it makes for all that extra paperwork, though I have to admit he earned every bit of it but all this is going to make a hell of a mess in our nice clean helicopter.'

The burly officer holding up the unconscious Victor spoke as he tried to avoid the bloodstained suit. 'I've worked with Dan a couple of times, he was a decent and fair man, and I don't blame you at all for the hit, Jack. He didn't deserve to die at the hands of this rabble. Now, if Mr Casini fell on his face in a scuffle while going up those steps as we were trying to control him, well, they're not exactly smooth, are they? In any case there's a roll of plastic in the back of the chopper, he can bleed all over that.'

'Well, yes, you're right,' said Grayson running a hand through his red hair. 'Daniel was a decent man and a good agent even if he was a bit unorthodox in his investigations.' He sighed and cast a glance at Jack who was rubbing his knuckles. 'This is a dirty game sometimes and you have to give as good as you get, I felt like taking a poke at him myself I'll admit.'

He clapped a hand on the officer's shoulder, 'Move him out of here and you are right, those steps are dangerous aren't they, especially with such poor lighting?' He stooped and grabbed Vinnie by the collar, hardly noticing the smug little smile that played around Vinnie's mouth … but Jack did, he guessed that Vinnie just might have agreed with them.

The message Jack was picking up from Vinnie's thought waves told him exactly that, he couldn't help but think that justice had been served in several terms.

Steve grunted as he began propelling Vinnie up the steps saying, 'Come on then, let's get this lot out of here, we've still got some cleaning up to do. Now, mind how you go, Vinnie, we wouldn't want you to fall now would we?'

As the captives were marched out and across the courtyard, Jack and Steve saw several of the monks watching anxiously from the near steps of the chapel. The elder monk who had spoken to Jack before, now hurried forward. 'Are you taking them away now; they won't come back, will they?'

'No, they definitely won't come back. The only place they are going now is prison. A trial will come later, you will be informed of that at a later date. In the meantime, you are free to go about your own business without fear. However, we do request that none of you leave the Abbey at this time until our investigations are finished.'

As he spoke, Jack was aware that a hooded figure was watching silently from the top of the steps. He had noticed him before and unlike the others this one kept his cowl well over his head, he seemed a little apart from the others. Jack had no time to dwell on this, as there was still much to do and the afternoon was swiftly drawing to a close.

'Yes, yes, thank you,' said the elder, 'the brothers are all weary and would like to retire to their rooms after we have had a meal. We have been living in a stressful situation for much too long.'

'Well, you can rest easy now, but there are matters here that still need to be cleared up,' replied Jack 'so that means there will be officers of the law here for a few days still.'

'We understand that of course,' the monk said, nodding his head, 'but, the A–Abbot, we have to know!' He clutched Jack's arm and said in an anxious voice. 'We fear he is not coming back. Is that so? The woman who was with you, is she really a–a witch?'

The elderly monk held Jack's arm tightly and whispered, his eyes wide as he spoke. 'She said that he had broken his neck. Did she …' his voice trailed off.

'No,' of course not!' Jack laughed lightly. 'Look, I will admit she is a witch, you might as well know that now and so is her sister, broomsticks and all but really, two nicer ladies you could ever want to meet.' He smiled again at the monk's startled expression. 'I know it's hard to believe that witches do still exist but these two are quite harmless and really, I have to tell you that they are much more nervous of the brotherhood here than you might think. As for Brother Peter,' Jack's voice became serious again, 'Marilla was actually trying to save him and in his hurried flight, he fell before she could reach him. I'm afraid it was his own folly that led to his death. I think he was running from himself as well as those who wanted to protect him.'

The older man relaxed his grip on Jack's arm and said softly,

'You are right of course, he was a victim of his own inordinate desires and we allowed that to happen instead of a higher court of reprimand. We are just as guilty as he.' He sighed deeply, releasing his hold on Jack's arm to place a hand on his shoulder. 'Thank you for our salvation, but alas we have such a penance now to serve and a troubled mind to pray for.'

Jack in turn laid a hand on the old man's shoulder and said quietly. 'Rest easy, Brother, we know that temptation is our greatest antagonist, not all of us are strong enough to resist. We all are only human with normal human frailties. In light of what has happened Peter would not have wanted to live under such persecution; it was, perhaps, for the best.'

The aged one nodded understandingly and began to move away toward the chapel. Jack looked up, but the hooded figure had gone from atop the steps. Behind him he could hear the engine of the helicopter starting up and the heavy thrust of the rotor blades as they began to cut through the air. He watched it for a moment as it rose slowly from the courtyard, he caught a glimpse of Vinnie's face through the window wearing an expression that was difficult to comprehend. Jack also was reminded that there was another one still unaccounted for — Moody.

In a moment Steve Grayson was by his side. 'Well, Jack my boy, lead me to this box or two of tricks that the Casini's have left for us, then we can begin to close this case once and for all.'

The two engineers, still somewhat bewildered by the turn of events had been locked safely away in one of the cells and two of the other officers left to sift through and note the contents of the trucks. The helicopter would return in the morning to collect the engineers as they were not considered to be an immediate danger to anyone but were nevertheless important witnesses.

'I have to find Amos,' Jack said as he and Grayson began to walk back in the direction of the underground rooms.' I'm pretty sure he's alive as I received a signal from him which was *after* Leo threw that grenade, how else would Leo finish up with a broken neck; that has to have Amos's thumbprint on it. It was a promise Amos made to him.'

Steve grunted, 'Yes, but what if he hasn't been able to get out from down there? Weren't the Casini's trapped down there for a while as well? Who knows what could have happened during that time, Jack?'

'Well, I'm going to find out, one way or the other,' replied Jack grimly. 'We'll need torches, it will be dark down there.' He had stopped at the door of the scullery and began taking down powerful lanterns stored on a shelf just inside the door.

Steve was silent for a moment as they began to tread carefully down the flight of steps, then said, 'Umm, Jack … I am aware as you know, that you do have some acquaintances and talents that are … shall we say, different. Of course, it's not common knowledge among the ranks,' he said quickly, 'it's just that the pilot was a tad anxious as we were coming in this afternoon; apparently, as we were coming in over the top of the Abbey, there was something ahead of us, almost hovering over the gorge. He thought it was a large bird that had caught something, an eagle perhaps, he said, he couldn't watch it as he was concentrating on getting our bird down safely. I took a very wild guess as I was able to see it better from where I was. There was a confusion, so I thought, of arms and legs before it moved off downstream. I might have been wrong as I've never seen one before — in the flesh that is, but I figured you'd have more of an idea. Any explanations?'

'There could be,' said Jack hiding a wry smile, 'but I won't know until my … colleague returns, hopefully with Mr Mahoud Brahman in a recognisable form.'

'Oh, I see,' replied Steve, 'Yes—oh and er—clever thinking with that rat too.'

After briefly examining the boxes of printing equipment and satisfying himself that, as Jack had stated, there would be plenty of clear evidence to convict the Casinis many times over, they turned their attention to the crypt.

It didn't take Steve and Jack long to work out what had happened in the crypt, the explosion impact from the grenade was not where they, or the Casinis had expected it to be, so it had obviously been redirected before it went off. The untidy heaps of black dirt and the many skeletal remains were a clear indication that an ancient burial catacomb had been destroyed, with the remains of its long-term residents scattered. Some of the ledges in the ossuary were still intact and it was in one of these that they found the body of Leo Stefani.

Steve gave a start when he saw the white skeletal hand lying on the chest of the deceased but Jack was elated. A quick examination showed that Leo's neck had indeed been broken, but it was the piece of cloth and the positioning of the ghostly hand that held it that had raised Jack's hopes.

'This is Amos and Isabella's work, I know they are alive, I can sense it but where are they?' exclaimed Jack.

'Isabella, who's Isabella?'

'The sister of my … colleague.'

'There's two of them?'

'Sisters,' replied Jack matter-of-factly.

'Oh and er—er, are they, umm—' stumbled Steve.

'If you are trying to say, are they witches? The answer is yes,' replied Jack. 'They arrived very unexpectedly during that stormy night we had just recently, I was as surprised as you to see them arrive. Here of all places and at this time but I can tell you they have both been very helpful. In fact, if it were not for Marilla's intervention, I would probably be dead. So, when you do see them, I must ask you to treat them with respect.'

'Of course, Jack, you know I will … it's just that, well, I haven't really thought about folk like that still being … around.'

'These two are quite rare and haven't quite found their way around the world, as we know it, Steve, so they are a little bit naïve about some things, so tread carefully.'

'Whatever you say, Jack.'

'There's recent signs of activity here,' exclaimed Jack, dropping to his knees beside the tomb stone that stood but a stone's or a grenade throw away from the broad step at the crypt entrance. He was examining the soft soil deposit carefully and the stone itself. 'Amos and Isabella must have been hiding behind this, there's a lot of disturbance and some prints, not to mention a few new pieces broken off the top here, Vinnie's careless aim I expect. He smiled to himself as he examined small footprints, animal footprints leading away and toward the back of the crypt.

'This way, Steve,' he said shining his torch into the darkness beyond the massive columns that stretched infinitely away into the blackness.

'Who would have thought there was so much space under here,' said Steve as his torch raked over the huge arched ceilings. 'One would wonder what they would do with so much space, other than to inter their dead.'

'Casini was going to find a use for it, nobody would ever have thought of using this space for what he had in mind. He could have remained hidden here for years churning out fake bank notes, with nobody any the wiser of where they were coming from.'

'Do you smell that?' queried Steve as they were nearing the end of the crypt and the last of the columns, here the great roof was narrower, it had given way to rough stone, not far over their heads. 'It's only faint but it's familiar.' He sniffed again and said, 'That's cordite; I would say that dynamite has been used here very recently. The closeness of the walls and the ceiling has trapped the smell.'

'You're right there,' replied Jack who was sweeping his torch light over what appeared to be a great tumble of rocks ahead of them. He directed the powerful beam upward to where the cavern roof and the walls met, then he was rewarded by a glimmer of light through what appeared to be a crack between the wall of rock and the ceiling. 'There must be a way up there, I can see no other way out from here. Let's have a closer look at this rock pile.'

Investigating further, they were surprised to find ancient steps that lay partly concealed behind the pile of rocks that appeared to have been cut into the back wall of the cavern and followed the face of the rock upward. The steps were rough, widely spaced in some parts and narrower in others. A fall of rock had partially obstructed the steps, this had been cleared away leaving a mass of rubble. The steepness of the steps and the closeness of the overhanging bulk of the rock forced them to clamber at times on all fours, but the chink of light was stronger now, then after rounding a huge slab of rock they were able to claw their way up the last steep pitch to find themselves above the Abbey and close to the northern stream that ran down the mountain above the village.

'Well,' said Steve as he stood, hands on hips gazing at the

view from this vantage point, 'it would appear that Amos would have come out this way but which way would he go from here?'

The late afternoon sun was throwing its last golden rays over the distant mountains, highlighting the snow-clad peaks across the valley. A distant bank of heavy blue-black clouds sat threateningly in the Northern sky, a promise of more stormy conditions perhaps but for the moment they savoured the pale warmth of the setting sun. Below them they could see most of the Abbey buildings, the ancient stone of its walls and dark grey slate roofing that gave the appearance that it and the mountain it sat on had been carved as one by nature's hand.

'Amos knows his way pretty well around the woods here and he definitely came out this way, don't you agree, Lucifer?'

Steve Grayson's heart gave an extra thump as he turned from the vista he had been admiring to see that Jack was talking to a pair of yellow eyes gleaming from a small cavity in the jumble of rocks behind them. Eyes on a level with their own, the owner of them was growling, a deep rumble that echoed in the rock cavity, making Steve's hair stand on end. He relaxed somewhat when Jack's torchlight revealed a large black cat lying there, its paws resting neatly on the front edge of its retreat in the rock.

'A cat!' he said, relief sounding in his voice.

'Ah yes, but no ordinary cat, are you, Lucifer?' Jack reached out and rubbed the cat's head. There was no friendly bite on the wrist this time, just the deep rumbling purr. Lucifer stood upright and began to rub his head over Jack's arm, looking at him, blinking those large yellow eyes. 'So, Lucifer, they left a message for me, did they?' The cat moved its paw and a flash of colour caught Jack's eye. He reached into the cavity and extracted a small piece of coloured cloth, the same as that which had been slipped between the fingers of the skeletal hand on Leo's chest.

Steve looked on in amazement. 'That's the same as the bit of fabric we saw …'

'Yes, I know,' said Jack, 'that's what's telling me, they *both* came out this way and are no doubt heading back to the Abbey.' Jack looked at the thick mass of underbrush beneath the pine forest and said, 'Well, I don't fancy pushing through that lot. Amos might know his way through it but if it's alright with you, we'll go back the way we came. Who knows, he might already be back there by now.'

'Agreed,' said Steve, 'though it's hard to say which would be worse — fighting your way through that lot or negotiating those perpendicular steps down there. However Jack, I'll let you go first, you're younger than I am.'

<DTO Pls Insert Cat sitting on ground with grass illustration>

Chapter 20

When A Bat Is Not A Bat

Marilla hovered above the deep pool and wondered whether she had done the right thing or not. That little brown man was going to stab Jack with a knife. Now she had probably drowned him. She shrugged her shoulders and decided that it was more important now to look for her sister but that would mean going down into that place under those cellar rooms. She shivered slightly, one part of her did not want to venture there ... afraid of what she would find and yet, she had to know for certain if her sister was still alive.

She looked up toward the Abbey, she had heard the sound of the helicopter approaching as she had moved downstream with Moody dangling over her broomstick. The thumping rhythm of its rotor blades came clearly to her, as the pilot manoeuvred the heavy craft into the main courtyard, now she could no longer see it below the great bulk of the Abbey buildings.

Marilla sighed, she did not want to go back to the Abbey, not yet. There would be too many people there who would look at her strangely and ask questions. Jack was there, he could deal with that. She thought for one brief moment she had heard her sister call her name, but the sound of the whirling rotor blades on the helicopter had covered anything she may have heard.

She had now floated down to where the great cairn of rocks marked the bend in the path that led up the steep hill to the Abbey. Sitting on one of the smaller groups of moss- covered rocks, she allowed a tear to escape from her green eyes; in fact several, as she sat miserably on the cold rock and tried to contemplate what life would be like without her sister. What would the future hold for her if Isabella were not there with her impassive but sensible influence?

Her thoughts turned toward her grandmother. How she wished she were here now to tell her what to do, which way she should go, she sighed again and wished she had paid more attention to some of the things grandmother Hilda had told her when she was growing up.

'Marilla! We're here!'

This time she did hear her name called; Marilla jumped off the rock and stood waiting, wondering. She could hear rustling noises somewhere behind the pillar of rocks and voices too. It wasn't long before two figures emerged from behind the great jumble of enormous stones, and Isabella, ragged and dusty ran toward her, followed by an equally dishevelled Amos.

The two sisters embraced each other while Amos leant up against the nearest rock in stunned silence. He wasn't sure he had seen what was happening only a few minutes before, but he reasoned, a lot of things had been happening that he couldn't explain, this was just another one. He felt like he was living in some fairy tale and the Seven Dwarfs would come striding up the path any moment. However, his practical mind surfaced, he cleared his throat and said thickly. 'Marilla, you, er ... dropped something in the water a few minutes ago, what was it? We could see you from the top of that rocky tor up there, we wondered ...?'

Marilla barely heard his question but spoke quickly to

Isabella. 'That ugly little man, Leo, said you would be dead after he threw that — whatever it was at you. How did you get out, Jack and I were so worried about you but he assured me that you would find a way out and—'

'It's a long story,' broke in Amos, 'but first, Marilla, what or should I say *who* did you drop in the river?'

'Oh,' she said frowning, 'that horrible little brown man that came with that Victor person. He was creeping up on Jack while his back was turned, with a knife in his hand. I was really angry after what Leo did, so I just swept him up and got rid of him.'

Amos nodded his head. 'Moody; that would have been Moody,' he looked carefully at Marilla and said quietly, 'Marilla, this is important, do you think you could find him, alive perhaps?'

'What for?' she countered crossly. 'I didn't like him anyway, he looked creepy.'

'Creepy!' Amos opened his mouth to say something else, then thought better of it. 'No, Marilla, you don't understand, we would prefer to have him alive, if possible. He is part of this gang of forgers and criminals who are wanted by the International Police. I really would like to find him and put him away with the others.'

Marilla shook her head impatiently. 'Well, I hope he can swim, because I dropped him into that deep pool down there,' and she pointed to a spot not far distant from where they stood.

'Okay, perhaps we'll go down there and see if he did survive your ah ... method of disposal, otherwise we'll just have to wait until his body washes up later.'

'But you're hurt!' she exclaimed seeming to notice his bandaged head for the first time.

'Let's worry about that later,' retorted Amos, 'I'm more concerned about locating Moody.'

Together the three of them began to follow the river back to where the deep pool swirled and bubbled below the last of the natural waterfalls created by the stricture of rock barricades to the rapid flow of the cold mountain stream. The undergrowth close to the river was thick in parts, and difficult to see through.

'Do you think he drowned?' asked Isabella.

'Don't know, he's a wily old bird and can be a slippery customer. He seems to have a charmed life and always manages to turn up again somewhere, so I don't trust that he's probably drowned.'

They had reached the pool at the base of the falls and began to tread more warily. The ferns and bracken mingling with reeds and watergrasses grew quite thickly right down to the water's edge, making progress slow and difficult.

Isabella slipped around a large clump of bracken fern to where she thought the marshy ground would be firmer underfoot. As she did so, she suddenly felt her ankle seized in a vice- like grip, looking down she saw a hand. Thin brown fingers clenched tightly around her ankle, then a face appeared from behind the thick fronds. Brown and wrinkled like very old and badly stained parchment, it gazed up at her with startlingly bright eyes.

'Oh,' said Isabella, but before she could utter another word, the little man had sprung from his hiding place like a waiting predator and wrapped a bony brown arm across her throat stifling off any further cries.

Amos and Marilla hearing Isabella's gasp and the scuffle amongst the fronds turned around to see Isabella, her eyes wide, a thin arm across her throat and peering behind her shoulder, the puckered little face of Mahoud Brahman. Amos reached for the gun he had taken from Leo in the crypt and pushing Marilla to one side confronted him.

'Let her go, Moody.'

'Oh, no, no,' said the little man in his husky whisper of a voice, 'I not. Please to put gun down there,' and he indicated with a nod of his head to a spot some five feet in front of where he stood with the captive Isabella. 'You be putting gun there and move away. I still have knife and very sharp too — would you like I use it?'

Amos could see Moody's eyes flickering every now and then to Marilla as he spoke, and he detected fear in them. He had to play for time now and catch Moody off guard ... but he could not be sure that Moody actually did have a knife or was he just bluffing.

Amos also knew that Mahoud Brahman would have no qualms of killing anyone who got in his way, even a woman. It didn't matter who it was, as an assassin, he was a master, skilful and quick and a knife was always his chosen weapon.

'Come on now, Moody, she's done you no harm, let her go. You will have heard the chopper up there at the Abbey; that means the law has arrived and your services won't be needed by Victor Casini now, so don't add an unnecessary murder to your record.'

A tense silence ensued, then Amos became suddenly aware of a long indrawn breath from Marilla, with what he could only describe later as a distant rushing sound that seemed to come from nowhere in particular. It grew louder and louder even Moody seemed transfixed, as all attention centred on Marilla, who stood tall and still as if in a trance. The rushing sound was all about her, where all else was still. Whirling clouds of green and blue vapours pulled at her hair and whipped her clothing about her body. As she turned to face them, the unusual green of her eyes shone with an almost phosphorescent glow, as the others watched, mesmerised, she slowly lifted her hand and pointed a finger at Moody, whose facial expression was now rigid with terror.

A brilliant flash of the blue green vapour left her body and channelled itself from the tip of her outstretched finger and struck the hapless little man as he tried to hide behind Isabella's plump form.

There was a sharp crackling noise and all was suddenly still again. The vaporous mists had vanished and Marilla stood as before. Her face was grim, the green eyes, now back to normal, were fixed on Isabella and what was still behind her.

Moody's arm no longer around her neck, Isabella moved hesitantly forward, revealing what was behind her back.

Fluttering frantically amid the coarse fronds of the clump of bracken was a largish brown bat, baring its sharp pointed teeth in a wrinkled, leathery face. It was heavily entangled in the thick mesh of a spider's web, the original owner of which had scuttled away and was now visible only by the tips of its legs showing from beneath a broad leaf nearby. The bat was struggling to free itself from the sticky strands, which seemed to have extra tenacity in the strong filaments holding it fast by its thumb claws. The bright little eyes glittered in the puckered leathery face as the others surveyed the struggling creature.

Isabella stooped and peered down in amazement. 'I didn't know you could do that Marilla!' she exclaimed; her voice full of wonder. 'That was a wonderful piece of magic, I've never seen you do anything like that before, what spell did you use?'

Marilla's voice sounded far away when she spoke. 'It was not my magic.'

'Not yours, Marilla but how? We saw it happen.'

Marilla looked carefully into her sister's face. 'There are other forces here, Bella, we have both felt it. There are forces here not known to us, an aura of power that you nor I could ever hope to achieve.' Marilla's hands were trembling as she grasped her sister by her shoulders and looked deeply into her eyes. 'Bella, I could feel it coursing through me and I had no control. There is something here that is calling us ... I know it now. Jack was right when he said that our path was directed to this place on purpose but for what — surely not just for this,' as she indicated to the bat still hopelessly enmeshed in the spiders web. 'There must be another reason for us to be here at this time. We must speak to Jack again, surely he knows more than he's willing to tell us.'

'Ye Gods!' Amos had sunk down onto one of the rocks that bordered the edge of the falls. 'I can't believe what I'm seeing.' He put both his hands to his head and shook himself. 'How am I going to explain all this to the Division Commander? They'll put me in a padded cell for sure, nobody is going to believe this!'

'Don't be too concerned, Amos.' Marilla was suddenly regaining some of her old self. 'Those sorts of spells, if I remember correctly, are temporary. It will wear off quickly and completely in a few hours then he'll be back to his normal self, though I rather think it suits him just as he is.'

'I hope it doesn't wear off too quickly then,' said Amos, still struggling to comprehend what he had just witnessed. 'It will be dark very shortly and we don't want him or whatever he is now taking off somewhere. I just want to get him back to the Abbey and locked up.'

Isabella was clutching her sister's arm. 'Oh, Marilla you have no idea what Amos and I have been through, I have so much to tell you, you know, it was Lucifer who found us, or we would never have known how to get out from that awful place under the cellars.'

'I understand, Bella, I have to admit I was so sure that ... well, never mind, you're here now and safe. It hasn't exactly been a picnic for Jack and me either, so I've got a lot to tell you too but it will have to wait. Right now, we have to do something about this creature, look, the spell is just beginning to wear off.'

The slight sound of popping noises came to their ears and as they watched, a small flurry of blue green stars were whirling around the struggling form of the entangled bat. When all became still again, the small, bewildered form of Mahoud Brahman was staring stupidly from amid the fern where he was crouched. Strands of sticky spiders' web were still clinging to his hands and face, like a child given too much fairy floss.

In a moment Amos had pounced on the frightened little man, ordering him to his feet. 'Come on, Moody, we've got a bit of a walk ahead of us, up that hill to join your friends. Any not so smart moves right now and I just might let these nice ladies play with you some more.'

Moody gave one terrified yelp and began the trek up the path ahead of his captors, fearfully looking over his shoulder every now and then as if the hounds of hell were after him and he would be swallowed by demons at any moment. Every so often he would flap his skinny arms as if he felt the urge to fly, but his feet only stumbled over the rough path that led him and his attendant escort up to the Abbey looming above them.

In the meantime, Jack and Lieutenant Grayson had made the tortuous descent down from the broken stairway and back through the depths of the crypt. They paused on the broad step below the massive oaken door and looked back into the eerie darkness of the vast chamber that stretched away into inky blackness. Steve Grayson cleared his throat with an almost nervous cough and whispered, 'You know, Jack, I think er, I think I can almost understand Vinnie's apprehension about being down here, particularly if you were on your own. Mind you,' he said, his voice becoming bolder and more resonant, 'they really built things to last in those days didn't they and it was obviously built for a purpose, even if it was just to bury their dead. Makes you wonder how old this place is?'

'Most certainly a tad older than you are,' answered Jack 'around fourteenth or fifteenth century I should think, I'm sure the resident ghosts down here could give you a more accurate time frame, if you ask them nicely.'

'Aah, never mind,' said Steve quickly, 'let's get back shall we, a hot mug of coffee would be welcome right now don't you think, Jack?'

'Whatever you say,' grinned Jack broadly.

'I'll get in touch with the army wallahs first thing in the morning,' said Steve as they began to make their way back to the staircase. 'I won't feel comfortable till that box of explosives is out of here but we'll start transporting the printing press and other evidence straight away. We don't want to lose anything now with that dodgy stuff lying about.'

Dusk was closing in when they regained the courtyard and began to make their way to the kitchen, where it was hoped the fire under the huge water kettle had not gone out and a hot drink could soon be available. They had almost reached the great vaulted doorway when a distant shout from the outer perimeter of the great courtyard alerted them.

'It's Amos and the girls!' cried Jack. 'Not sure, but it looks like they might have Moody with them. Steve, could you go and stir that fire up in there please, I'm sure they are going to want a hot drink more than we do. I'm going to meet them.'

'Hmm, not sure that I'm quite ready to meet "the girls" as you call them, Jack,' said Steve, 'but it could make an interesting end to a successful day.'

Steve Grayson entered the kitchen still shaking his head in some disbelief. He had known Jack Grimsby a long time but this was the first time he had been a direct witness to the strange powers the man possessed. That rat, he mused, how did he know it was there behind the box or did he conjure it up for the purpose? It was no accident that it came around the box and ran directly up Bruno's trouser leg when it could easily have escaped into the gloom beyond, taking a path of a least inconspicuous exit. Even though Steve had known Jack for some years now, very little was known about his personal life; Amos knew him better than anyone else. They had worked together for a long time now and understood each other perfectly. Amos was also known for his tight lip; if he knew anymore about Jack Grimsby than anyone else, then he had never talked about it — it was nobody else's business.

Entering the huge old kitchen Grayson was surprised to find two of the elderly monks still there. The fire in the enormous grate was blazing merrily away and he could see mugs and plates set out on the long table and a simple meal laid ready. Apologising for the intrusion he turned to leave but was stopped by one of the monks who had stepped forward.

'No,' he said haltingly, 'please don't go, this has been prepared for you and your companions. It's not much, but the best we can offer to our saviours and later perhaps we can talk for we must know what is to become of us now.'

'But what of your own needs?' said Grayson, 'we can have supplies airlifted in here in the morning and—'

'No, no,' insisted the monk, laying a hand on the officer's arm. 'This is not for us, we have already eaten and will retire to our rooms. We have concerns for our brother Amos, even though we do know now and understand that he was not truly one of our own but for the time he was with us, we considered him one of our order, for he carried out his duties admirably and he shall indeed be missed.'

'I see, well, we are grateful for your hospitality,' replied the other.

'Amos and his friend Jack have risked much to bring Mr Casini to the custody of the law, for that we are grateful but … are we to be arrested too? The brothers are extremely anxious.'

'For the moment I don't see that there is any need for concern from the brotherhood,' said Grayson gently. 'Of course, there will eventually be an inquiry into Casini's affairs and even then you would only be called as witnesses. You were being held against your will, weren't you?'

'In a manner of speaking, yes, we were,' answered the monk slowly, 'but we were only doing as instructed by the Abbot, though we were unsure of … of his intentions.' A frown crossed the lined face of the elderly monk. 'Brother Peter — the Abbot — when can we retrieve him from where he has fallen?'

'If we can locate him tonight, we will attempt a retrieval, otherwise I'm afraid it will have to be at first light tomorrow,' answered Lieutenant Grayson.

The sound of voices and the heavy door being swung open interrupted any further conversation, they looked around as Jack and his companions entered.

'Hail the conquering heroes,' said Grayson in a somewhat relieved tone as five figures entered the room. 'God, you look a mess, Amos, what happened to you?'

Amos grunted as he came into the room propelling a hesitant wide-eyed Moody in front of him. 'A slight altercation with an explosive thrown by a now deceased Leo Stefani.'

'What's with the bandana? Nice and colourful I must say,'

grinned Steve masking the look of concern on his face. 'Hope there's not too much damage done?'

'Nothing a couple of stitches can't fix,' said Jack ushering in an equally bedraggled and dirty Isabella, with Marilla close behind.

'Oh, my goodness, I'll get a pan of hot water and some towels,' said the elderly monk, who had introduced himself as Brother Ethan. 'You all look quite exhausted; Brother Elias will make you some tea while I gather some things together.'

'No need to trouble yourself any further, Brother Ethan, you look exhausted yourself, you have done enough. I'm sure Brother Elias and I can attend to the situation now. Why don't you retire to your rooms? I feel certain the rest of our brethren are most anxious to hear from you that all is well here.'

The speaker was another monk who had entered the room from the pantry, his cowl still partly covering his head. Jack looked up as the man spoke and felt that he had seen him before. Wasn't he the one he had seen standing partly in the shadows at the top of the steps when he had spoken to Ethan earlier in the courtyard? At the moment he could not be sure, and yet …

'Yes, yes, of course, Joseph. I am a little weary I must confess, I do admit that you are in a better position to help, under the present circumstances.' He turned to Lieutenant Grayson and Jack saying, 'I must introduce you to Brother Joseph. He is in charge of the Infirmary and treats all of our ills; his herbs and potions have kept us in good health, we owe much to his healing hands.'

'And if you are not careful, good Brother Ethan, I shall find you abed with a severe chill if you do not find your way to the comfort of your quarters, you have done enough here thank you,' replied the cowled monk as he placed a bundle of cutlery onto the long table.

'Indeed yes,' said Ethan but his progress from the room was delayed as he became aware of the little brown man who was sitting hunched on the floor almost at Amos's feet. He stopped to stare at him but at a nod from Joseph, the elderly monk slipped through the door and was gone.

Moody, who had not said a word since his remarkable metamorphosis was staring fixedly at the lofty ceiling. Every now and then his tongue would lick around his lips and he attempted to make flapping motions with his arms.

Steve had been watching him while he helped Elias hand out steaming mugs of tea. As he handed one to Amos who had sat himself wearily down on the end of the long bench, he whispered quietly, 'Amos, perhaps I shouldn't ask, but, what's wrong with Moody?'

Amos took a mouthful of the hot tea before replying nonchalantly, 'He thinks he's a bat.'

'A bat!'

'I wouldn't pursue it any further at the moment Steve, it's all too hard to explain.'

'Oh, I see.'

Only Marilla and Isabella were aware of the broad grin on Jack's face as he shepherded the two sisters to a place close to the fire, but far enough away from the others so as not to embarrass them, then went into the huge pantry room to fetch the little medical kit from its hiding place.

The Lieutenant turned his attention to the two women sitting warily a little distance away and acknowledged their presence with a nod of his head, 'Now you would be the two ladies Jack was telling me about, friends of his I believe. My name's Steve — Steve Grayson.'

'Yes, they are,' Jack had returned from the pantry carrying

the medical kit. 'Steve, I'd like you to meet Marilla and Isabella, two very dear friends of mine and who, I might add, have played a major role in rounding up this Casini lot, wouldn't you say so, Amos?'

'Well, if it hadn't been for Isabella tossing that live hand grenade out of the way, neither of us would be here now,' growled Amos untying the makeshift bandage wound around his head.

'Hand grenade — you mean, she threw a hand grenade — and after the pin was pulled! That would have taken some nerve!' Steve was shaking his head in disbelief. 'There's only seconds before—'

'To tell the truth, I don't really think she knew what it was, am I right, Isabella?' said Amos quickly, trying to turn his head to look at her, but drawing a response from Jack who, with help from Joseph, was trying to clean the cut on Amos' head before inserting a couple of stitches.

'Keep still damn it,' exclaimed Jack, 'or you'll finish up with stitches in your eye as well!'

'Grenades,' said Steve thoughtfully, 'sticks of dynamite as well I should think. I would hazard a good guess and say that box of old explosives was the one stolen from the Army Base over at Willaston about five months ago. It disappeared from the arms depot right under the noses of the brass, nobody knew it was missing till they held an inventory on stuff that was considered unstable and it was due to be detonated under controlled conditions.

They haven't used dynamite for years now. It was initially brought in for blasting when they carved away some of the cliffs near the Army Base. Anything left in the way of other explosives considered suspect finished up in that box too I believe. Interesting to know how the Casini's got away with it.'

He rubbed his chin thoughtfully and glanced again at Isabella. 'I have to say, I'm surprised none of it went off while it was being handled by that mob of morons. Had it done so, it could have blown this entire Abbey off the face of the cliff.'

'I'm glad I didn't think too much about that before,' grunted Amos, 'Isabella was carrying a half stick of it in her pocket all the time we were down in that crypt. We used it to blast our way out of the back door.'

'She *what?*'

'That was what we could smell at the back of the crypt, Steve,' said Jack, busy with his stitches, ignoring the strained look on Amos' face.

'Well, I'll be!' muttered Steve, looking at the two sisters who still sat silently at the end of the table. He shook his head and picked up his mug of tea draining the rest with one gulp. Placing the empty mug back on the table he thrust one hand in his pants pocket, the other rubbing at his red hair as he walked about muttering, 'I can't believe what I'm hearing, how the hell am I going to put all this in a report.'

Elias, a stocky, ruddy faced monk with the hands more befitting of a workman placed a bowl of hot water, soap and towels in front of Isabella and said quietly, 'There is a private bathroom in the Abbots quarters, although I thought you might like to clean the worst off your hands and face now, if you wish.'

'Thank you,' murmured Isabella, 'oh, and for the tea as well.'

Elias nodded and went back to where Steve was standing watching Jack's skill with needles and sutures, his mind still trying to comprehend the danger they could all still be in if those explosives were not moved.

'What about him?' Elias asked in a half whisper, indicating

Moody who was now crouched down in a corner, his arms folded to either side of his face.

'I don't think he'll be any more trouble tonight,' said Jack tying off his last suture. 'Put him in a quiet room by himself, he can leave with the others tomorrow. Now let's have a look at those ribs, Amos.'

After some careful prodding and poking by Jack and Amos it was decided that the vicious kick from Leo had resulted in some severe bruising, even if the rib was cracked, there was little to be done except to strap it firmly. This was done properly now with the expert assistance of Joseph who was surprisingly adept at first aid. Jack looked at him keenly, thinking the face somehow looked familiar but he couldn't quite place it. It reminded him of someone, someone he had seen recently and yet … He was certainly skilled in medical procedures Jack sensed and was about to ask a question on his practicability, when the question was answered for him unprompted.

Joseph explained as they worked, that he had done several years of medical schooling before taking on pharmacy previous to his entering the monastery. Because of his experience, he had been appointed as the healing hands of the order and was, apart from his other duties in charge of the infirmary.

'It might interest you to know, Brother Joseph, that Jack here was Dr Jack Grimsby before he gave up medicine to chase criminals all over the globe,' said Steve casually.

'That, Steve,' retorted Jack rather briskly, 'was a very long time ago, I don't think Joseph is the least bit interested in my past life!'

'Oh, but I am,' said Joseph in his carefully modulated but slightly nervous soft voice. 'You would be surprised at the men who give up careers in ordinary life to join a fraternity such as ours.'

'Anyway, that's history now,' said Jack quickly, let's get on with the present. Isabella, now that you've washed the dirt off, perhaps you'll let me check you for any damage. Cuts and scratches can infect very easily after contact with that dirt that was down there.'

'I'm alright really,' said Isabella, 'just this one scratch on my arm, I was lucky I guess.'

'Oh, if you will allow me,' said Joseph quickly, bustling forward, 'if Mr Grimsby has no objection, it does appear to be a simple scratch and I would like to apply a herbal balm with which we have had great success here dealing with cuts and bruises. It heals quickly, it is also an antiseptic and leaves no scarring. I'm sure Amos would find it useful too. It is produced here from certain herbs that are peculiar to this area, we have proven its worth, would you care to try it, Miss Isabella?'

Jack looked at Amos and got a confirmation nod of the head in return. Isabella, in return was quite flattered at Joseph's old-world courtesy. 'Why yes,' she said, 'I'm very interested in anything to do with herbs and herbal remedies.'

'Excellent!' beamed Joseph, 'We always keep several pots handy here in case of burns,' and he hurried off to the pantry where he kept a small supply.

Jack, passing close to Marilla on his way to return the medical kit to its place, bent down and whispered something in her ear and squeezed her shoulder in a comforting way. He was rewarded by a wan smile, before her composed features returned, even though she sat as immobile as ever, she was obviously a bit more relaxed.

'Now, Amos,' said Jack as he sat down and reached for the mug of hot tea that Elias had placed in front of him. 'After we've had something to eat, you might tell us what did happen down there. We found the staircase at the back of the crypt. Did you know it was there, or did you find it by accident?'

'Lucifer rescued us, he seemed to know the way out. We just followed him.'

'Lucifer!' said Steve, who had been engrossed in watching Moody's behaviour. 'Do you mean that cat we saw, that big black one sitting where the steps came out on top?'

'Yes, Lucifer,' said Amos, 'he distracted Vinnie when he started taking pot shots at us, then showed us a way out. We just followed him, he seemed to know where he was going and he led us to the back of the crypt, after a few minor problems, we found our way out from there.'

Amos was about to continue, when one of the officers entered to tell Grayson that they had found an extremely nervous monk locked up in one of the side rooms off the colonnade and that they were returning him to the monks' private quarters.

'Ah,' said Amos, 'that would be Carlos no doubt, a troublemaker. We would have had the Cassini's all nicely packaged up for you, Steve, if Carlos had behaved himself and stayed where he was. He has caused us quite a lot of unnecessary trouble, I'd like to give him a belt over the ear. There's something not quite right about him but I can't put a finger on it.'

'What do you suggest then?' grunted the Lieutenant.

'Put him in a room by himself and make sure he's locked in,' answered Jack. 'We can sort out his problems later. On second thought, you can take Moody with you and put him in with Carlos. Perhaps they can share their grievances, it might give Carlos something to think about. What do you say, Amos?'

'It could probably give Carlos a bit of a shake up as you say, I can't see Moody being a danger to anyone for a while but keep an eye on them just the same.'

Joseph had looked up from where he had been dressing Isabella's scratched arm as Moody was being half carried by the guards out of the kitchen. 'Will the little man be alright?' he asked, looking not at Jack, but directly at Marilla.

Marilla, who had remained silent until now, fixed her green eyes on Joseph, murmured carefully, 'Most ... conditions like that usually wear off in about eight hours or so, then he'll probably think it was all just a bad dream.'

'I see,' said Joseph almost nervously as he finished bandaging Isabella's arm, then moved so he was sitting opposite Marilla. 'Mr Grimsby,' he looked about him, then lowered his voice almost to a whisper. 'Mr Grimsby — Jack, told me that the Abbot fell, you were trying to save him. Can you tell me how it happened and where he has fallen?'

'I tried to stop him as Jack asked me to,' said Marilla quietly after some moment's hesitation. 'He wouldn't stop running, even when I caught up with him. Then he vanished behind some thick bushes and when I went to look for him, I could see that he had fallen down a very steep part of the bank of a stream just north of here. There are a lot of big mossy boulders at the bottom of the cliff, when I got down to see if I could help him, I found he was dead. There was nothing I could do.'

'Yes, yes, I know the area you mean, it is very steep there, the worst place he could have blundered over,' said the monk sadly looking down at the small jar he had been turning over and over in his hands. He looked up, and Marilla saw a deep sadness in his eyes.

'Thank you for telling me.' Joseph placed the small jar on the table between them. 'This,' he said, indicating the jar, addressing both sisters, 'is the real treasure to be found here. It has taken years to perfect it with the correct mix of herbs and oils, but

Peter — the Abbot, could not see its potential as a means of bringing much-needed funds into the Abbey. He only saw the more material kind to adorn the walls and shelves of the library ... and other places. He was, unfortunately, a misguided soul, tempted beyond reason. The brotherhood's decision to appoint him as surrogate leader was indeed a bitter mistake but we have had to live and abide by that ruling.' He stood up, 'Ah, now that we are all here, I think it's time to eat, there will be time for talk later when we are replenished.'

Chapter 21

A Light in the Darkness

The simple but adequate meal the monks had prepared was gratefully dispatched, complemented by several bottles of the rich red wine produced from the small vineyard adjacent to the orchard. Lucifer, whom Steve had warily avoided, had greedily demolished that which had been put on his plate by Amos and was now curled up on the hearth seemingly asleep but the twitch of an ear or the slow opening to a mere slit of those yellow eyes showed an awareness to all that was going on about him.

The remaining two officers had re-joined the group in the warmth and comfort of the big kitchen for a short while, then left to check on their charges before retiring for the night in their allocated quarters. The possibility of retrieving the body of the unfortunate Abbot was discussed but would have to be delayed until the morning. To push through the dense thickets to find the exact spot at night was just too risky in an area not known to them. Not even those in residence here ventured out beyond the walls at night.

Marilla and Isabella, still a little nervous and tense among this mixed group of strangers, did, in spite of Jack's reassurances, consent only to move down from their end of the bench a short distance, remaining aloof and mostly silent as the inscrutable monks of the Abbey of St. Dominica.

Lieutenant Grayson studied the two sisters carefully over the rim of his wineglass. So, these two most unalike sisters were witches! They really didn't look like one's childhood visions of the traditional witches — no great hooked noses, ugly warts, or high pointed caps and wicked cackles of laughter. They were fine looking young women, even though the rest of it was there, the broomstick, the black cat ... well, black, except for the white tip on the end of the tail that twitched slightly every now and then, as he lay curled up by the warmth of the fire.

Marilla reminded him of someone, yes ... a maiden aunt of his. His mind drew comparisons. Lofty, impenetrable and certainly not one to trifle with but smooth away that resolute layer of grit and modestly hiding beneath, was a kind and compassionate nature. He wondered what secrets lay behind those serpentine green eyes, perhaps things he really did not want to know ...

Isabella, on the other hand, with her soft liquid brown eyes and round pleasantly chubby face atop an ample figure, could have been the tea lady at the base canteen. Always cheerful and ready to please but he suspected those innocent puppy-dog eyes also harboured a superior intelligence few would know about.

'So, Amos,' said Jack, his humour returned now that his friend was safe and relatively in one piece. 'Now that we are fortified satisfactorily, perhaps you can tell us what happened in that underground dungeon and how Lucifer came to be your rescuer. Incidentally,' he went on, a wry smile lighting up his fine features, 'we noticed your piece of whimsy on Leo's chest.'

'That was Isabella's "piece de resistance" answered Amos, 'and whatever, it had the desired effect, particularly on Vinnie, he was never happy about setting up business in a monastery. He was more superstitious and vulnerable in that way than Victor cared to notice, it was eventually going to be a wedge between him and his brother. Victor could only see what *he,* himself wanted.'

He then went on to relate how Lucifer had found them in the rubble and stayed with them while Isabella did her first aid bit. 'I got the feeling he was keeping watch,' said Amos. 'Which brings me to say how thankful I am that Isabella had the presence of mind to redirect that grenade as quickly as she did, otherwise neither of us would be here. Pity about that burial chamber, Joseph but it was going to be them or us, they wouldn't have felt the blast as much as we would have.'

Joseph nodded understandingly. 'Unfortunately, they have been largely forgotten over the centuries, I don't believe anyone would remember just who they were in this day and age.'

Amos continued his narrative of events after they had disposed of Leo in one of the intact burial ledges. 'We had decided to quietly make our way to the other side of the crypt where there was perhaps a better chance of catching Vinnie off guard and escaping that way. To our surprise, Lucifer jumped up onto the tombstone we had hidden behind earlier and created a nice diversion, allowing us to cross the intervening space unseen. I had to rule out the attempt to get past Vinnie, he was trigger happy enough as it was, one small handgun was not going to be much use against a rapid fire, so the odds were not good. The situation was looking pretty hopeless when Lucifer appeared beside us again and seemed to indicate that he wanted us to follow him. We could just see the tip of his white tail ahead of us as he led us right to the back of the crypt. He must have come in that way, so perhaps there was a way out for us too. I activated my transmitter after Vinnie let fire at where Lucifer was in the hope that the signal would be picked up by Jack and he would know we were at least still alive.'

'Yes,' said Jack. 'I did get that faintly but there was nothing more after that.'

Amos nodded and his story continued thus. 'Do you think they will follow?' Isabella had asked nervously as they crept as silently as we could through the last of the great columns.' They had crept to where the rough stone walls seemed to close in and they realised that they were standing in a great cavern hewn from the bedrock of the mountain itself. Gone was the great arched roof the columns had supported, now there was just the rough stone of the cavern roof not far above their heads. Directly in front of them was a wall of solid rock, with large boulders littering the floor in front of it. Worse still, Lucifer had disappeared.

'I don't think so,' Amos had answered, 'I rather think they may have lost their nerve to come this far in and are just content to leave us here.'

Bewildered and exhausted Isabella sat on the nearest rock and hid her face in her hands. 'We're never going to get out of here Amos and now we've lost Lucifer, though I can't understand why he should leave us now.'

'I don't believe he has,' said Amos. 'He's come in this way from an entrance somewhere — we just have to find it.' Amos felt he could now risk using the torch, even though there was the faintest hint of natural light still in the cavern. He began examining the rock wall with what little light was left in the torch. Nowhere could he see a crack or gap where Lucifer could have come from. He shone the torch upward and swept it across the top of the rock face. Something glinted faintly at a point where most of the rubble and fallen boulders were piled up. He swept the torch back to where he had seen it, a tiny chink of light and next to it the yellow eyes of Lucifer shining like tiny beacons in the light of the torch.

'There, up there Isabella, it's Lucifer; that could be an entrance hole, that's where he must have come in but how did he get up there?'

The eyes had disappeared. They could hear a scrambling noise and after a moment Lucifer was again, rubbing against their ankles and growling that now familiar growl.

Isabella was happy to see him and hugged him, scolding him for leaving them. Amos rubbed the cat's ears and whispered, 'I don't know how you got up there but if we were cats like you old fellow we'd be up there in a flash. As it is I can't see how we can get up there to get out, if there *is* a way out.'

Amos turned the torch off to conserve the battery and sat beside Isabella in the semi darkness of the cave to think. Lucifer still rubbed around Isabella's ankles and several times he grabbed her hand in his mouth. Suddenly she jumped up and said, 'Lucifer *can* show us a way out, it's just that we're not listening to what he's trying to tell us!'

Next moment, she had moved to a large boulder near where they had been sitting. Lucifer had already leapt to the top of it. Isabella hoisted up what was left of her skirts and with some effort scrambled up on to the top of the rock and disappeared down the other side. After a brief moment she called to Amos to bring the torch. 'I can feel a step here — and another — Amos, I think there are steps going up but I can't see how far!' Excited by her discovery she called out to Amos to climb over the rock and see, then she remembered, 'Oh, I'm sorry, Amos I forgot about your sore chest. Wait a minute though, pass the torch over if you can, there seems to be a gap here closer to the wall that I think you could squeeze through.'

Amos pushed his thick body between the jumble of rocks and soon found the spot where he could just squeeze through, a tight fit for a man his size but he managed it, though it punished his ribs terribly. Once through he found as Isabella had indicated, a bit more space and what appeared to be steps cut into the face of the rock wall. Much of the overhang of rock had been cut away to allow a little amount of head room. 'You're right, there are steps here and they've been deliberately cut into the rock, so this must be another exit. This is where Lucifer got in!'

He swung the torch upward and found that the steps were indeed spiralling upward to where the chink of light had been, but the way was blocked a few feet above them by a large boulder that almost filled the space. It was too big to push past or clamber over, the only space between it and the wall was only large enough for a small animal, like a cat, to squeeze through. Their hopes of finding their way out were suddenly dashed. Their spirits deflated, they sat on the bottom step to think what else to do. For Amos there seemed no other way but to go back to the where the door to the crypt was and take their chances there. Perhaps the Casinis had left, thinking he and Isabella were dead or was there any other way out — they had not explored any other part of the crypt as yet.

To Isabella's mind, it was different. Lucifer was a smart cat; he wouldn't lead them all the way back here if he didn't have a reason, what was he trying to tell her? Was there some sort of magic she could use to shift that boulder? She didn't think so, her powers of moving things were not that good, she could think of no other form of magic to spirit them out of their predicament.

'Well, that's it,' said Amos standing up. 'I guess we had better go back the other way and hope the rescue troops have given up waiting for a signal and have decided to come looking for us.'

'But would anyone think to come looking down here?' said Isabella quietly. 'Jack and Marilla know we are down here, but what if …' she didn't finish the sentence, deflated.

Amos put an arm around her shoulders. 'I know what you're thinking my girl, but we'll just have to go back and find out, one way or the other.' He shone the fading light of the torch back up to where the big rock was blocking the stairway and muttered half to himself, 'Makes me almost wish I'd grabbed one of those sticks of dynamite from that box. One of those in the right place just might shift that rock or bring the whole roof down on us.

Anyway, it's too late to think of things like that now, come on, Bella let's try and find another way out. Who knows there may be more than one entrance to this rabbit hole?'

Isabella had stood still, not following, as Amos began to push through the crack again. 'Is this the stuff you mean?'

Amos stopped, alarmed at the sound of her voice, it was a quiet determined tone. He stopped and turned to look at her. It didn't sound like Isabella when she had first spoken but she stood there, unmoved, holding something in her hands, something he couldn't quite see at first.

She stood, a totally dishevelled figure, her normally bushy head of hair wilder than ever framing a dirt and tear-stained face. Her skirts hung at odd angles where she had torn bits off but it was what she held in her hand that startled him.

'I had it in my pocket,' she explained looking fearfully now at the shocked expression on his equally grimy face.

Amos was staring at her, his blue eyes wide with amazement, 'You mean to say, you– you've had that in your pocket, all the time?'

She just nodded but the brown eyes were beginning to fill with tears again as she watched the range of expressions passing over his face in the dimming glow of the torchlight. 'I know you told me not to touch them,' she stammered, 'but I thought–I thought they would be useful things.'

'Oh, Isabella,' he said finally, 'you are the most amazing woman, I don't think you have any idea what it is you are holding.' He came over to her and took it gently from her hand. A small stick of the dynamite, one of those he had removed from the box earlier and placed on the floor. He began to examine it carefully under the torchlight.

The coarse waxy paper covering was greasy and beginning to fret away in several places, it looked very old and dangerous. If only she had known–if only *he* had known but it was not going to help being angry with her. He just looked at Isabella and said rather humbly, 'I think I should be very careful what I wish for in future when you're around.'

Amos weighed the small stick of explosive material in his hand, then examined the fuse. It was short, too short, otherwise it might have worked.

The explosive piece was not too large and more than enough he figured to blast away one rock — or more. He looked up at the obstructing rock and realised with sinking heart, that even if it was placed where he figured, it would blast the rock away from the back wall of the steps, there would not be time to get clear before it exploded, *if* it exploded — the fuse was way too short. There was something else too, he had nothing to light it with anyway.

'Isn't it going to be any good?' Isabella asked cautiously.

'Well, yes, it just might work, but ...' He explained as carefully as he could about the fuse, the possible risk of having the entire roof of the cave collapse on them, then finished up by saying, 'and we don't have anything to light it with anyway, plus the fact that the dynamite stick is very old and may not detonate at all.'

'Oh, umm, Amos … I have a light. I can show you if you like.' 'And what else have you got in those mysterious pockets of yours?' he grinned at her. 'It's not in my pocket, it's umm … here,'

and she lifted her finger and as he watched, a flicker of blue flame issued from her fingertip.

Amos opened his mouth to say something but no words came. He was speechless. Recovering his composure, Amos had to remind himself that this was no ordinary person standing in front of him, though, in truth, she couldn't have looked any more home spun than a typical 'next door neighbour'. His practical mind however was beginning to accept these strange happenings as if they were everyday occurrences, now he was really thinking rationally. 'Bella, how close do you have to be to—to light anything? I don't much like the look of this stuff but if I can get it up behind that rock, could you, er—could you light it from a safe distance, or doesn't it work like that?' He was shaking his head. 'I wouldn't have believed I would be saying something like this in a million years!' But Isabella was ahead of him.

She went as far as the crack between the rocks Amos had squeezed through and putting her head on one side she took in the distance. 'I think I could light it from here, I've never projected a flame quite so far before but I think I could do it, I would have to really concentrate on it.'

'Are you prepared to give it a try?'

She nodded, Amos gave her shoulder a quick squeeze, before clambering up the few steps to where the huge rock sat squarely on the steps and began to feel for any gaps beneath it.

Amos tried to ignore the pressure on his injured ribs as he lay on the rough stone steps probing the underside of the rock as far as his groping fingers could reach. He did not want to place the dynamite too close to the wall itself, as it could blow away any remaining steps that were there. A small hollow appeared under his fingers close to the edge but was still fairly well under the centre of the rock. Satisfied about the position, he carefully pushed the greasy stick in the hollow and trailed what little there was of the fuse over the rest of the bulk of the rock and away from the steps.

'Can you see it, Bella?' he called anxiously.

Isabella directed the fading light beam of the torch at the rock, 'Yes, just, we'll have to move quickly now, the battery in the torch is almost gone.'

'Okay.' Amos scrambled back to stand beside her, 'Bella, come on girl, do your thing, as soon as it's lit we have to move away fast, we can shelter against that wall behind this rock — where's Lucifer?'

'He's right behind me,' she answered.

Amos scooped the cat up in his arms, and said, 'Now we'll do it just as we planned. If you can hit the fuse from here, we'll have this rock plus a few yards of distance to get clear of the blast — ready, Isabella?'

He watched in fascinated awe as Isabella extended her arm and a pale blue light began to issue from her fingertip. It grew in intensity for a moment, then to his dismay began to decrease. He groped for her other hand and found it shaking. 'Come on girl, you can do it, you've proved yourself that you are someone very special before this; I wish I could help you.' He squeezed her hand firmly and found to his surprise that she had suddenly become calm as her trembles ceased.

He could hear her whispering strange words that he did not understand, it seemed as if she was possessed of a new power as the outstretched finger once again produced its light, but brighter and stronger than before. They could just discern the frayed end of the fuse as it dangled down from the rock, after a few breathless moments, Amos thought he detected a faint wisp of smoke from the end of it. Then suddenly there was a splutter and a crackle and the fuse was alight!

Clutching Isabella's arm now with his free hand he pushed himself through the crack and dragged her with him. Together they stumbled back as far as they could and partially behind the great wall of rock, and pulling her to the ground, he threw his body across hers and Lucifers'.

A split second later a blinding flash lit up the cave as the dynamite exploded sending a blast of hot air and debris flying in all directions. The low roof of the cavern kept the explosion contained, the thick acrid smoke filling the cave, blinding them, choking their throats and nostrils with the fumes. They could hear stones rattling to the floor around them, one or two finding their mark as they felt themselves struck by several. Then just as suddenly, all was quiet.

Amos rolled himself aside and struggled for breath with his arms wrapped around his chest, trying to stifle the cough as the burning smoke filled his lungs. Isabella was sitting up with her back to the rock, knees drawn up and her face buried in her skirt, her shoulders shaking as she also struggled for breath.

'Is—is it all over yet, Amos?' whispered Isabella, wiping her eyes again with the hem of her skirt, and reaching for Lucifer who had emerged from some hidden spot and was now happy to stay close to her.

'Are you alright, Isabella; you're not hurt, are you?' he asked between gasps for breath. 'You stay here with Lucifer,' he said, as he painfully got to his feet. 'I'll see what damage we've done.' He located the torch and switched it on. At first there was nothing, but he shook it and it responded with a faint yellow beam. The floor of the cavern was littered with broken pieces of rock and stone but there was also a new and stronger source of light issuing into the cavern.

Cautiously edging around the great rock that had partly sheltered them, he noticed that the gap between it and the wall was also a little wider now, it had rolled slightly and fortunately not in their direction. Casting the dull yellow beam upward, he was able to see that the boulder blocking the steps had gone, but so had a good half of the ancient steps. Further up and close to where ceiling and wall met, he could see a small gap, a pale stream of light issuing from it like a guiding beacon. He turned around to call to Isabella, but she was already standing close behind him and Lucifer had not waited to be called either he was already part way up the steps.

Together they began to clamber up the steep and irregular set of steps, the overhang of the roof so low in some places that they were forced to move on hands and knees. Reaching the spot where the boulder had been, they could see that it had taken a good part of the step it had been resting on and the remainder was cracked and broken. However, they managed to find just enough space to get through safely. Isabella had peered over the edge and was surprised to realise just how high up they were. Amos was also aware that the light coming from the top did not appear to get brighter, perhaps the opening at the top would be too small to get through. This thought had been running through his mind but as they crept around a curve in the rock face, they could see the truth.

There was a hole there and it would be big enough to get through from what he could see of it but the rays of the sun were being reflected off the smooth surface of yet another great rock that appeared to be wedged in just below the exit. Though certainly not as large as the first one, this great stone was almost square in shape, it was still blocking the exit to some degree. The torch was now almost useless, but with the light coming from outside, it seemed to him that the stone was almost balanced there, as if on a hinge.

With what little was left in the torch Amos moved to the outer edge a little to see how much rubble was behind it. In doing so, his foot slipped on the loose broken stone and gravel, only his quick reaction in throwing himself backward saved him from falling over the edge to follow the torch, which was now bouncing its way over the broken escarpment of rock.

He heard it crash at the bottom and breathed a sigh of relief. Isabella had instinctively grabbed at his shirt and was now attempting to haul him back to the comparative safety of the steps close to the wall.

'Oh, Amos, that was close,' she breathed.

'Yes, it was a bit,' he answered breathlessly, 'but I'm positive that with a bit of push and shove from up a bit further we can dislodge this one enough to give us more room to get through. It's sitting almost on the edge, there's not much behind it from the glimpse I got.'

'Let's try then shall we? We've come too far to have to go back now,' replied Isabella.

Reaching the rock, they discovered that the space between it and the wall was barely wide enough to allow either of them to get through but there was a little more space in the undercut of the rock face. Isabella, being a bit smaller than Amos and not physically handicapped by bruised ribs, managed to wriggle her way in behind the boulder, then lay her body almost flat in the narrow crevasse. From this most uncomfortable and claustrophobic position she could exert pressure with her legs on the boulder. Amos meanwhile was able to exert pressure the same way with his back hard up against the rock face as close in behind the boulder as he could.

'Are you ready?' he called. 'When I say push, give it all you've got, with some luck we'll have this thing off the step.'

Uniting their strength, they pushed and were rewarded with a movement of the rock as it moved from its original position. *'Again!'* yelled Amos and with a last mighty effort from both of them they felt the rock move, almost imperceptibly, until its rolling momentum carried it over the edge and rumbling its way down onto the cave floor. Exhausted by their efforts, they lay on the steps now bathed in late afternoon sunshine that streamed into a now open space, gratefully accepting the meagre warmth.

Amos and Isabella sat on the steps for some moments regaining their strength, relishing the fresh cool air and the overhead view of clouds scudding across a sky they had feared they might not ever see again. 'I don't know whether you saw it or not, Amos,' said Isabella after a few moments, 'but that stone had some markings carved into it. I could see them from where I was under the rock face, it was sort of smooth, not like any of the others,' she paused for a moment more, then said, 'I'm thinking that the stone we pushed down there was deliberately placed against this hole to hide it. It was a sort of door, the markings on it were to indicate to whoever needed to know that this was a secret way in …'

'Or out,' finished Amos, who had sprung to his feet and was standing shading his eyes from the low hanging sun. The heavy whumping sound of helicopter rotor blades had reached his ears and he noted with a grunt of satisfaction that the cavalry was indeed on its' way.

'Come on, Isabella,' he said as he helped her to her feet with a grin on his face, 'let's see just where we are and find our way back to the Abbey.'

They both stood and looked about them, they could hear

water rushing somewhere near and to their right, catching a glimpse of water every now and then. 'We must be near the North stream, that's the one that passes a little distance above the village. Hope you don't mind a walk in the woods at this hour but there should be a trail near here that will lead us back, at least to the path below the Abbey.'

'Amos, look!' cried Isabella, pointing a finger at a small figure in the distance hovering over the steep gorge that bounded the Abbey on one side. 'It's Marilla!'

'Where?' said Amos, startled by her sudden outcry.

'There — over the river, see, now she's going further down, what *is* she carrying?'

Amos shaded his eyes and stared at the tiny figure flapping like some strange bird, then realising it was a cloak flapping and whatever it was, 'it' was on a broomstick, with legs, tiny legs like a doll's, hanging limply beneath but kicking every now and then.

'If it is Marilla as you say, then it's a matter of not *what* she is carrying, but *whom!*'

He grabbed her hand and they started to descend, the path was rough and littered with great rocks of all sizes and sometimes there was just no path at all, they just slid down the steep slopes. Amos looked up again at the figure of Marilla before they left the high jumble of monoliths behind them. They could see her as she appeared to be soaring over where the water from the mountain stream ended its last frenetic passage to rush in a waterfall from towering black rock and plunge into a deep pool below, before wending its majestic way to the vast lake and beyond.

Isabella called out to Marilla but her voice could not carry far enough. She stumbled on the rough ground but was saved from falling by Amos' strong hand. 'She won't hear you above all this other noise, there's a path here now and I know just where it will lead us.'

The thickets of brambles and bush were closing in on them now but Amos knew where he was going and in a few moments, they had pushed their way through to where huge stones stood upright like frozen giants. A narrow passage between them brought them out to the edge of the river and the path to the Abbey and the tear-stained face of a very surprised Marilla.

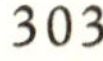

Chapter 22

Two Burials in One Day

Amos finished his narrative of events and the meeting with Marilla at the falls but of the strange affair with Moody, he said nothing. He would tell Jack about it later. The string of events had so far been enough for the monks to contend with, they didn't need to have a lot of other supernatural things heaped on them as well. The presence of two witches in an Abbey of monks was strange enough but to subject them fully to the powers these two most unlikely looking women possessed might be a tad too much to expect them to appreciate. In his narrative of events, he had also disguised the fact that Isabella had used her finger to light the fuse on the stick of dynamite but a quick look at Jack's face told him that Jack knew better and Steve didn't need to know that either.

However, Amos also harboured a sneaking suspicion that Brother Joseph and Brother Elias were more aware of witchcraft and wizardry than they cared to show. For now though there was another question he wanted an answer to.

He turned to Joseph who had been sitting quietly with eyes half closed but listening intently. 'Brother Joseph, were you aware that there was another exit from the crypt and are there any other secret places down there?'

Joseph clasped his hands in front of him and it was a long moment before he answered. 'I was aware of a rough staircase that existed but as to its exact location, I had never myself investigated but wherever it was, a severe rock fall blocked the exit, so it was reported. Steps were hewn out of the mountain rock face sometime during the 16th Century, and was, so I believe, an escape route when the Abbey fell into troubled times during that period. There is a history of the Abbey in the library, if you would care to read it.'

'And no other exits?'

Amos and Jack both caught the very brief look that was exchanged between the two monks but pretended not to notice.

'There are other places under the Abbey,' replied Joseph, 'and there are the dungeons of course but they all date back to those troubled times as well, nobody from here has any need or desire to visit them, so they too would remain untouched, frozen in time, one might say.' He paused and said, 'I do believe there may be other exits, but no other to that crypt.'

'So, now we know,' said Steve as he listened to Amos' carefully worded story, 'you both had a lucky escape, I can't see myself making a full written report on that,' he yawned.

'I don't think there's anything more we can do now until the morning,' he said as he stood up to leave. I'll get the lads to recover the Abbot first thing in the morning, as there's nothing else we can do, I'm heading off to join the troops, see you all tomorrow.' He gave a brief wave and was gone.

Jack moved down the bench closer to where the sisters sat, while Amos and the monks cleared the table. 'Marilla,' he said softly as he gazed into her green eyes. 'I know what you did this afternoon, with Moody. I should have realised he was there, but for once my sense of danger failed me. I have you to thank for saving me, however,' and the mischievous grin crept over his face again, 'you've created a minor problem for one of Steve's pilots. He caught a glimpse of you carrying Moody and he's quite convinced there are either very large eagles in this area, or we have some sort of pterodactyl-type predatory flying creatures inhabiting these distant mountains. I think Steve has convinced him that he's had too many flying hours and needs a short break.' Jack was pleased to see a wry smile creep over Marilla's face.

She looked sheepishly at him. 'Perhaps it is time I traded in my old broom, as you so caustically remarked and fly a helicopter thing instead, it might not draw as much attention, and I wouldn't get caught in a rainstorm, would I and be in the wrong place at the wrong time.'

Jack grinned again and gave Marilla a light kiss on the cheek, 'I see you've not lost your caustic sense of humour, love it!' He turned then to Isabella, with a much more serious tone to his voice. 'Bella, are you alright now, you've had a pretty torrid time down in that crypt, I don't think I will ever forgive myself for sending you and Amos down there in the first place. I'm supposed to be looking after you two, then I go and put your life in peril. It's enough that we have had to lose Dan, I couldn't bear it if—'

Isabella cut in. 'You were not to know that those men were going to do what they did, Jack, you had no way of knowing they were there, it seems they caught us all by surprise but it's over now, isn't it?'

'Yes,' said Jack with a sigh, 'that's all over now but Amos and I have a few things to tidy up here yet. However, we would like to once again offer you the use of the Hospice; Steve's lads are using the Infirmary otherwise I'd offer you that.'

'No thank you,' both sisters almost spoke together, we—we

would prefer to go back to our own corner, for now at least,' added Marilla, not unkindly. She suddenly turned to face him. 'So, you are not leaving when the others do?'

'No, I'm not,' said Jack, 'well, we do have to leave some time shortly, there's still the matter with the Casinis to finish up and all the official paperwork.'

'I see,' said Marilla slowly. 'Jack, we need to talk to you–about being here–there's something–something strange here. There's someone else, someone we can't see, but seems to have control — more control than we have.'

Jack did not say anything for a while, then said, 'I know what you mean, Marilla, but I'm not entirely sure I understand it all either, except that I have to be here, I have to be here– to meet someone–and for something, that seems important somehow– and not just to me but, to my family.'

'Your family!'

'Yes.'

'Family, you mean your grandmother, Edwina?'

'Not just Edwina, for my, mother.'

'Your mother, but Edwina said—'

'Marilla, I don't want to talk about it now, I'm still not sure myself what it's all about,' Jack said rather impatiently. Well, I sort of do–and yet–there's someone I need to see first.'

'Then why are we here?' asked Marilla dryly.

'That I'm not sure about either, but I *am* sure Edwina must have something to do with it.'

The conversation came to a halt, as Amos who had been helping Elias clean up the dinner plates and things in the scullery now joined them. He was following Elias who was carrying a tray of steaming hot mugs of coffee, which he set down before the group at the table. Amos thanked Elias and spoke to him briefly before taking a seat opposite. 'Elias and Joseph are heading back to their own quarters, Jack. Joseph said he would meet us in the morning about … what we have to do tomorrow.' He sighed and clasped his big hands together on the table and shook his head. 'Always an unpleasant business.' He looked up and found Isabella watching him, concern in her eyes.

'All right now, Isabella?' He smiled at her, his blue eyes matching his smile. He reached across the table and placed one of those big hands on top of her smaller one and squeezed it tenderly. 'I have you to thank for saving my life down there and that reminds me, I think I owe you a new wardrobe too, you made a hell of a mess of that pretty skirt.'

Isabella smiled back at him and said rather shyly, 'I think we have to thank Lucifer, if it hadn't been for him, we may never have got out. I told you he was smarter than the average cat.'

'Makes one wonder whether he is *just* a cat,' Jack said under his breath. 'Marilla, now we are alone here, perhaps you will tell us what *did* happen down near the waterfall with Moody.'

*　　*　　*

The next few days passed in a blur of activity and noise such as the monks in this distant refuge had ever seen. They confined themselves to their workroom and library. However, it did not stop them from watching with great interest through the windows as squads of officers swarmed through the Abbey collecting evidence.

A slight pang of guilty conscience wafted over several of the lay brothers, who had momentarily glimpsed a different life beyond the cloistered walls of this ancient edifice of tradition. But the sight of so many efficient uniformed figures tramping the sacred soil of the courtyard was immediately instrumental in bringing about a complete absolution and a total exoneration of such thoughts, consummated only by a short period of self-imposed imprisonment. Time indeed in their own private cells to consider what might have been, if fate had not intervened.

A party of men, led by Joseph had gone very early to the spot where the Abbot had fallen and with some difficulty, were able to get his body up the cliff top and back to the Abbey where he was lain ceremoniously in the chapel while the elders made arrangements about his funeral.

The unfortunate Leo was removed from his quiet little resting place in the crypt and bundled up in a body bag and put to one side, until they could transport him back in the chopper. However, Dan was to stay where he was for the moment. Steve had walked around with Jack to the tiny cells where he lay, Steve who was visibly shaken at what he saw, was vehemently wishing he had thrown a punch or two at Victor himself while the opportunity was there.

At about the same time a heavily armoured vehicle arrived from the nearby Army Base with a group of military men in attendance. The box in the cellar was very carefully removed and was to be transported back to the Armoury, where it would be marked for immediate destruction but not before photographic evidence and reports were efficiently filed by a small group wandering about with cameras and clip boards.

The two engineer's trucks yielded boring and drilling equipment, pumps, electrical gear and great coils of cables, along with a couple of large generators, plus a considerable quantity of plastic explosive and detonators. These had all been taken from the trucks, photographed and marked for evidence as well.

Lieutenant Grayson and Jack were leaning against the side

of one of the trucks watching the removal of the contents and talking over the events to date. 'The Casinis might know a lot about art treasures' said Grayson as he had looked over to where the Army group were carefully loading the dynamite box into the back of the vehicle, 'but they sure didn't know what a bundle of dodgy dynamite would do if it went off under the Abbey. 'You know even Amos took a hell of a chance letting some of that stuff off where he did.'

'That's what Vinnie was intimating that first night I questioned him,' said Jack. 'Apparently Leo had picked up the wrong stuff, according to him, the dynamite was old and dangerous, the engineers were bringing what was really needed. I gathered Leo had a lot to do with acquiring that box, from the muffled protests we were hearing behind the gag and the dirty looks given him from Vinnie. How Leo contrived to get that box out of the Army Base undetected is beyond me, he was not the brightest banana in the bunch, but I got the impression he was trying to do something clever for his boss and once again failed to meet "requirements".'

'Sometimes, it isn't so much about being clever,' said Steve, 'sometimes it's just pure cunning on their part. From what I'm seeing here the Casinis just might have pulled this whole enterprise off if they hadn't had Leo tagging along making mistakes.'

'Well, he can't make any more,' said Jack, 'He's being personally escorted out with those crates containing the printing press. Amos said he needed something to rest his feet on. He was with that first consignment that lifted out this morning.'

'So that's where Amos disappeared to. So apart from missing his morose sense of humour, I guess we'll see him back here later tonight.'

'I don't think so,' said Jack slowly smothering a grin, 'I think he's got some shopping planned and it might take some time.'

'Shopping?'

'Shopping,' said Jack after a short pause, and Steve was quick to notice the half smile that played around Jack's mouth.

'Amos hates shopping — told me so himself. What's he up to, Jack?'

Jack folded his arms across his chest and answered, 'After he's overseen the transportation of the presses to the authorities and not forgetting those are our prime pieces of evidence, I believe he was just going shopping, you know, just shopping.'

'Anything in particular?'

'Can't really say, you know Amos, he never says any more than he has to.'

A big grin was beginning to spread over Jack's face as he tried to picture Amos in an environment he would probably not feel altogether comfortable in. 'Alright, if you *must* know, he's picking up a few things for the girls, particularly Isabella.'

Steve Grayson chuckled and ran a hand through his mane of red-blonde hair. 'Those women, aren't they something? I never ever imagined I would meet a real modern-day witch, even more and one who still rides a broomstick!'

Jack turned to face him. 'Careful how you approach them, Steve,' he said seriously, 'particularly Marilla, she can be a bit feisty at times and she has a short fuse. I guess you noticed the state Moody was in when Amos brought him back; even so, I'm not sure that was all Marilla's doing.' He finished half under his breath as he turned away again to check one of the boxes of equipment that was still being catalogued by one of the personnel.

'Yes,' said Steve thoughtfully, 'that was really weird, the

way he was acting. Amos said he had thought he was a bat. I shouldn't ask I suppose but I'm just assuming he's had a sort of out-of-body experience. Would he get over it, or is it, um … permanent?'

'He'll get over it,' said Jack briskly, 'probably have a few bad nights for a while, but it will wear off.'

As they continued to re-check the equipment from the catalogued files, Steve's curiosity was still pondering at the back of his mind. 'How long have you known these, ah, girls, Jack,' he asked cautiously, 'are they really sisters, because they look nothing alike?'

There was a long pause before Jack spoke. 'We grew up together, it seems so long ago now but seeing them again, it could have been yesterday. They haven't changed and I guess, to them, neither have I. They *are* sisters, it's just that they have inherited different aspects from their parents. Their grandmother raised them from a very young age, as did mine.'

He sighed heavily and sat on one of the boxes and faced his friend. 'Look, Steve, I've already told you more than I should. You know how I feel about the value of privacy in a person's life and I appreciate the fact that you have shielded mine — to a certain extent. These girls have lived very secluded lives and they would like it to stay that way. Any sort of public notice would be the very last thing they would want, they are, for the record, just visitors who happened to be here at this time. So, I would sincerely ask that you keep what you have experienced here to yourself, if there are any questions asked, then refer the inquisitor to me, okay?'

'You're right, Jack, I guess I was asking too many questions but you have to admit; it's not something you come across every day. You have my word that I'll keep it to myself.' The sound of the helicopter returning stilled any further conversation, they watched in silence as it settled itself and the rotors had ceased turning. A short grey bearded man stepped down from the craft and Jack and Steve walked to meet him.

'Glad you could come at such short notice, Doctor Edwards,' said Steve shaking the newcomer's hand. 'You've met Mr Grimsby before, haven't you?'

'Yes, yes, of course I have,' he said in a gruff voice as he took Jack's extended hand. 'How are you, Jack, still traipsing around the globe chasing criminals I expect?' He picked up a bag from the ground where he had placed it and said impatiently, 'Well, Steve, what you have got for me?'

It was Jack who spoke. 'Another piece of evidence, George and one I wish I didn't have to present,' he sighed.

Together the three made their way to the small cell where the remains of their friend Daniel lay on the rusting iron bed.

'Nasty piece of business,' said the Forensic Officer as he surveyed the bullet hole in the forehead, 'poor devil didn't stand a chance by the look of it and it would appear he was still tied up when he was shot.'

'Yes,' said Jack grimly, 'I expect when we turn him over, we'll find the slug at the back of his skull.' He took a plastic-wrapped object from his pocket. It was a small revolver, set with ivory inserts around the butt. 'You'd better take this too, George, it should match up nicely with the bullet and yield some incriminating fingerprints as well.'

The formalities of evidence gathering continued throughout the day, statements taken from the monks themselves were recorded individually, they all had much the same story to tell. Carlos still clung doggedly to the story about becoming steadily discontented with life at the monastery and had foolishly sought a way out by freeing the Casinis, in the hope that they would let him escape its further constricting confines, in exchange for their own freedom. Jack and Steve seriously considered charging him with aiding and abetting, for if it had not been for his rashness in freeing the three captives when he did, then Amos, Isabella and Jack himself would not have been in the danger it imposed. Jack looked now at the miserable dumpy figure seated nervously on the edge of the chair opposite to where he sat with Steve taking the statements.

The pale eyes were watery and a little red in the rather bloated plumpish face as he stammered his excuses in a high-pitched quavering voice, all the while twisting the sleeves of his robes with shaking hands. He did indeed look a thoroughly miserable creature, Jack did feel pity for him, even though he had critically endangered their lives. 'We should be placing you under arrest, Carlos, you know that don't you?' said Jack, not unkindly.

'I know—I know,' he stammered but I didn't think of the consequences at the time. I just wanted—I just wanted to leave this place, it was like—like, being in a—in a—'

'In a jail?' answered Jack, raising his eyebrow.

'Yes, I suppose so,' he answered slowly, the sleeves of his robes now thoroughly twisted and damp from sweat. He suddenly clasped his pudgy hands together in an attitude of prayer in front of him and surveyed them both through his wet eyes. 'Please let me stay here— I know I wanted to leave—but—I see now that my place is here. I don't think I could survive in the outside world. There is still much for me to do here, in the Abbey—and I would really like to continue my work here.'

For a few fleeting seconds Jack felt something else behind those small watery eyes, a presence almost of foreboding, that there was more to this miserable creature that showed on the outside but he was tired now, for the moment he could not see that the extra paperwork and putting Carlos behind bars was going to be of any benefit. Amos, he knew had a mistrust of Carlos but if the man had received a big enough fright over what his actions had caused, then perhaps it was better to leave him where he was, at least for the moment anyway. He dismissed the gut feelings that had momentarily taken over his mind and scribbled something on a pad and pushed it toward Steve, who read it and nodded. Jack turned his attention back now to Carlos. 'You are free to go for the moment, Carlos, we will let you know if there are any further questions.'

*   *   *

The next day brought the return of Amos, and with him came two huge suitcases, which he carefully deposited in a corner of the kitchen. When asked what was in them, he grunted that it was nobody's business and seemed more concerned at what progress had been made in the more important investigations at the Abbey. When it came to the decision of Carlos's affair in the matter, Amos frowned. Regardless of his seemingly remorseful attitude, Amos declared that he still did not trust him but agreed that if charges were to be laid at a later date, then at least he would be easy to find–if he was still going to be holed up in a monastery.

Meanwhile the monks had been occupied with funeral arrangements for their departed Abbot and with Amos and Jack's approval, a decent burial for Daniel. A decision had been made amongst the elders that the Abbot should be laid to rest in the Abbey grounds. There was a quiet corner close to the outer wall behind the church that already contained several burial plots and here the remains of Paul Gleeson would be interred. Jack and Amos watched as the coffin was lowered carefully into the plot which Elias and one or two others had dug the day before in readiness.

'Pity,' murmured Jack quietly to Amos, as they stood a little apart from the others. 'I'd hoped to get a bit more information out of Paul Gleeson, I believe there's a lot he hasn't told me.' He paused, then added, 'However I rather feel Joseph and Elias might be persuaded to open up under the right circumstances. There are questions here that need to be answered.'

As Daniel Montaigne had no other family, at least none that they knew of, it was decided that he would have his own private place on the side of the mountain. A small grove surrounded by pine trees that overlooked the Abbey and the wide sweeping lake with the valley beyond was the choice. Little was said as they went about their grim task, each with his own thoughts. The ground was hard in that spot but many hands in a show of reverence accomplished the task. A great cairn of stones was carefully placed over the spot and the simple cross that Elias had fashioned placed at its head. There would be a more permanent headstone placed there later, Jack promised as they stood in the quiet shade of the pines. The Brothers of the Order had come to the little patch on the mountain side to pay their respects to a man they had considered one of their own. It was a sad day for them to bless, make their final farewells and prayers, not only to their pseudo-Abbot, temporary head of the Order, but to a man who had lain without a blessing on his soul for so long.

Jack, Amos and Steve stood for a while longer after the other personnel in attendance had left. The three stood, quietly reflecting on past events and the role Daniel had played in former enterprises. Even though he had worked as a lone agent, his observations and doggedness in tracing a source, his skill with languages, which had been invaluable to the French Surete, they still considered him one of theirs, he would be hard to replace.

It was while they stood in silent repose that they were suddenly startled by a great black bird, a raven, which swooped down from seemingly nowhere and perched on the rough headstone. It put its head on one side and looked at them gravely for a brief moment before ruffling its feathers, two white ones down the front in stark contrast to the jet black of the rest of the bird. It cawed loudly before spreading its wings and departing as swiftly as it had come.

'I guess there's not much more we can do here now,' said Steve breaking the silence that had fallen once again. He placed a hand on Amos' shoulder. 'That scowl on your face, Amos tells me that perhaps its fortunate for Victor that he's not within arm's reach at this time. He'll get all that's coming to him, I'll be seeing to that personally.'

Amos muttered something under his breath and turned away to make his silent walk back down to the Abbey. Steve turned with him but looked back to where Jack still stood, silent and alone. He hesitated for a moment, then shaking his head sadly, he followed Amos, leaving Jack not quite alone in that quiet little grove. A raven with two white feathers down its front was making wide slow circles high above.

Chapter 23

Joseph Reveals a Secret

A relative calm had begun to settle on the Abbey of St. Dominica but still an uneasy calm for some within. The last few weeks of autumn were upon them and the tumbling, shapeless drifts of grey-white clouds that scurried overhead held a portent of a cold and early winter. Colder winds had now begun to sift their way through the stiff pines on the mountain top and exhale their petulant breath down upon the Abbey. It swirled and sighed around the rooftops, pulling and tugging at the loose robes of the monks as they went to and fro across the open courtyards intent on their business.

They were leaving the Abbey. Franciscan Monks would probably never dwell here again. The tranquillity of its isolation and peace had been violated, it could never be the same.

The noisy confusion of the comings and goings of the helicopters had long ceased, and the sounds of the forest had slowly returned to its unruffled harmony. The wreckage of the front wall and the ruined refectory building the only reminder of the havoc that had reigned within those hallowed grounds so recently, the scars that only time would perhaps obliterate.

A Priory at St. Helena, some hundred and twenty miles to the east had offered a permanent place of refuge within their walls and as the Dominican Franciscans were so few in numbers, with the talents of the Artisans among them immeasurable, they would be a most welcome addition to the Priory. Approaching years and creaking joints of a few of the elders had also painfully reminded them that another Winter in such a vast rambling fortress where many steps and corridors traversed day in and day out was an added discomfort to older bones. Nimble and steady hands were required for restorative work and the numbing cold of winter necessitated the constant warming of chilled fingers. Not only that, there were also so few of the younger lay brothers who were content to stay for too long in such isolated surroundings to become apprenticed to the tasks involved.

So indeed, it would seem that if apprentices would not go to the mountain retreat, then the masters of the mountain would go to St. Helena, once there, teach and pass on the skills of an almost forgotten and consummate craft, which would otherwise be forgotten, or lost in the annals of time.

It was after much persuasion, Marilla and Isabella accepted the offer of receiving the Hospice as their own. Marilla was still somewhat reluctant; the presence of so many robed figures of an ecclesiastical Order unnerved her slightly, even though their speech and mannerisms were kindness itself. Isabella seemed more at home with them and was quick to point out to her sister that with winter fast approaching, it would be much more sensible to take up residence in the Hospice. Joseph, who had now assumed a leadership role, added his voice to the suggestion, insisting that it was the very least the grateful monks could offer them, they would be failing in their ministerial duties if the utmost care to visitors was not provided.

As the Hospice and its immediate surrounds stood a little apart from the monastery and was fully self-contained, there need be no interaction. Joseph also pointed out, rather ruefully, that the Abbey would indeed soon be abandoned in any case as the Brothers were leaving. Until he himself were relieved of the present role that he had undertaken as administrator and guidance counsellor for the Franciscans, it would be difficult for him to return, for some time yet. So it was with deep regret that he would have to abandon his small herb garden and laboratory set up at the back of the Infirmary, from where he had produced the healing balm, as well as many other herbal remedies. He had spent many years in this solitary haven, much of it in his small laboratory, cultivating the many herbs and aromatic plants that he so lovingly grew and collected.

'Why—why don't you stay?' Isabella heard herself saying. 'Surely there must be someone else who could go with the monks and help them, then you could finish your work here. It seems a shame you know…' her voice faltering as he looked at her with interest in his eyes, 'and see?' she said, pulling up her sleeve to show him her arm, 'it's all healed and you can hardly see where the scratch was.'

Joseph looked at her arm and surveyed her solemn brown eyes. 'I would stay, if I could, as there is more involved here than one would think, there are tasks to be completed.' He hesitated a moment more, then went on quickly, 'The herbs for instance, they must be tended to closely and gathered at the right time, fortunately those for this year have been gathered. Then there is the processing and the still to be maintained. However now that Peter … is gone.' He paused again, then drew himself up straight and seemed to be looking at a spot above her head. 'I have a duty to the brethren; they will look to me for guidance. They have lived within these walls for many years and so too those before them. I cannot send them to a new home without leadership, I must go with them to help in their transition, they will need me, but, perhaps, one day I shall return here, yes, I shall return—' he broke off and looked at Isabella. She was not sure whether it was a trick of the light, but she thought she saw a tear glistening in the corner of his eye.

He had suddenly turned to face her now and executed a curious half bow as he spoke earnestly. 'Miss Isabella, would it trouble you too much to see my workplace? You say you are interested in herb lore, I have discovered plants here that are found in no other place and their properties are still to be analysed. These plants are unique and I might also draw your attention to what herbs are important to preserve here.'

'Why yes, I would,' said Isabella delightedly. 'Now?'

'If you like,' answered Joseph. 'I do have time at the moment but I shall be otherwise occupied later in the afternoon.' He cast a meaningful glance at Jack and Amos before leaving the room with Isabella following closely behind.

Jack and Amos, who had been helping the sisters move their meagre possessions into the Hospice looked at each other and grinned. Amos was grunting half under his breath. 'Sounds like the old line, "come up to my place sometime and see my etchings". There could be more in this than meets the eye.'

Marilla, who had also been listening, dropped another of their books rather sharply on the nearby bookshelf and remarked tartly, 'Nonsense, I'm sure you're quite wrong, Isabella's always been potty about plants and weeds.'

There was no answer, just a quick glance between the two men.

The only item not moved to the new living quarters was the old cauldron. It looked more comfortable where it had first been placed in the corner of the shelter of the overhanging roof. It would have looked completely out of place at the Hospice at this time. Later, perhaps they would move it to the new quarters, when the monks were gone.

Amos had somewhat sheepishly handed over the huge bulging suitcases, amid many cries of protest. However, for all their protests the sisters found a treasure trove of garments that actually fitted! Pretty blouses and skirts but more importantly, warmer garments for the approaching Winter, including thick fur-lined coats A large outer pocket on the outside of the cases revealed scarves, woollen hats and gloves, warm socks and an assortment of hair combs and strings of bright coloured beads right at the bottom. For Isabella there was another package, this one containing a brightly coloured cotton skirt, with two deep pockets on either side.

Lucifer had not been forgotten either. Apart from a huge cache of assorted packets and tins of cat food stowed into the pantry, there was a thick woollen rug that found a place on the hearth in front of the old kitchen stove Amos certainly had been shopping!

It was later that afternoon when Joseph knocked on the door of the private quarters that Jack and Amos had taken. It was the same suite of rooms that had been occupied by Henri Du Pont. Amos opened the door and ushered him inside. Stepping into the room Joseph accepted the glass of wine with a polite nod that Jack handed him from the small table set in front of the fireplace. A warming fire crackled noisily in the grate and threw flickering shadows over the faces of the men standing there.

'Thank you for coming,' said Jack.

'Not at all.' Joseph seated himself in the armchair directed to by Amos. 'You know, I have always liked this room,' he remarked casually. 'Peter found it oppressive and dingy; I think were his words but to me it is full of character and, shall we say, mystery, particularly so when Henri was here.'

'Then you know him well?' asked Jack.

'Yes,' said the monk now pushing back the cowl, that usually covered his head, 'and it is perhaps regretful that he has been obliged to move on, for the time being.' He paused and took a sip of the wine before setting the glass down on the table.

Jack had seated himself on the sofa opposite and quietly studied the man in front of him. Amos had been able to tell a little about Joseph, but the man had usually kept very much to himself and spent most of his time pottering about the herb garden or shut away in the Infirmary.

There was something vaguely familiar about the features, the shape of the face, angular, with high cheekbones and an aquiline nose supporting rimless glasses, through which hazel brown eyes looked inquisitively at Jack. His now uncovered head showed a greying head of short hair above a prominent brow and where he had seemed of a nervous and tense disposition when Jack had first spoken to him in the kitchen, there appeared to be no sign of that now. The voice, when he spoke, was strong and well-modulated, with no trace of the nervousness detected before. It was as if a different Joseph had emerged as does a butterfly from a chrysalis. He was looking at Jack now over the rim of his glasses.

'I am aware that there are many questions left unanswered in your mind,' he said in his slow even voice.

'Yes, there are,' said Jack watching the other curiously. 'I was only sorry I could not have further conversation with the Abbot, Peter. I felt there was a lot more he could have told me.'

'Indeed, there was,' Joseph had picked up his glass, put it to his lips and almost drained the contents before he spoke again, 'and no doubt that is the purpose of this meeting — you wish to know more about him.'

'As a matter of fact, it is, among other things.'

Joseph lowered his eyes and swirled the remainder of the wine around the bottom of the glass and spoke quietly, almost to himself. 'Peter was a very clever man; he was also a very clever thief.'

'Yes, well, I'm not sure we'll use the word thief at the moment,' said Jack, 'but we do know that he falsely kept certain artefacts that he knew did not belong to him.'

There was a long moment of silence, then Joseph suddenly got to his feet and began pacing the room. It was some moments more before he spoke, and when he did his voice had taken on a hard and bitter edge.

'There are many reasons why a man will forgo the, shall we say "normal" paths of human existence. People choose what they want to do with their life and for the majority of us, it is a matter of their own choosing. Some may tread upon the path of righteousness with all good intentions and keep to that path, however there are those whose good intentions are flawed, they inevitably fall victim to the passion of greed and covetousness of someone else's treasures.' He turned to face them, his eyes moving from one to the other in the room. 'You no doubt have knowledge,' began Joseph in his carefully modulated voice, 'of the disappearance from the Museum in Cairo of one of the Dead Sea Scrolls. Also, the vanishing of several ancient manuscripts from the Museum of Fine Arts in Rome, plus the brazen theft of rare Icons from the Monastery of St. Catherine, not to mention the Durham Book of St. Cuthbert's Gospel, plus other precious objects of antiquity from the treasure houses of Europe.' His voice had become louder and angrier. Joseph began to pace the room. He stopped and drained the wine glass.

'Yes, we do,' it was Amos who spoke, 'they were investigated, it was believed the thefts were the work of those involved with Victor Casini.'

'Not entirely,' said Joseph dryly as he stepped to the table and filled his wine glass again from the decanter that stood there. 'Victor Casini more than met his match with Peter Gleeson, though he did not know it. Peter was the Master, Casini was but an apprentice in all of this. The subservient face he showed to Casini and others about him was just a sham, a clever mask hiding the true professional within, it would have pleased his ego immensely even more to know that someone else was taking the blame.'

'How do you know all this?' asked Amos with suspicion and some surprise.

Joseph looked at him steadily with tired eyes. 'Because, Amos, those precious objects are here, secreted in a special place in this Abbey. I know because I have seen them and I have seen the perpetrator lovingly gloating over these ill-gotten gains, it repulsed me.'

He walked over to the window and stood there silently gazing out with unseeing eyes at the vista of snow topped mountains rising majestically over the green swathe of pines be- ribboned beneath them. The vast lake below the falls, mirror like in its stillness, reflecting that which sheltered under it in perfect likeness. Nor did his eyes take in the fragile beauty of the almost leafless poplars and elms on the near side, raising their almost bare arms to the sky as if in sorrow of the fierce stripping of their autumn dress.

A chevron of wild geese marked a pattern against the lowering sky, the perfect arrowhead formation hurrying swiftly toward a warmer and more hospitable climate, their cries unheard, as the winds blew them swiftly away but Joseph's eyes barely saw these things.

Jack, who had remained somewhat silent until now, looked at the tall thin figure of the monk as he stood as a sentinel staring out of the window, then said softly, 'Why are you telling us this now? Is it because there was more to your relationship with Peter than was generally known?'

Joseph did not turn around to answer Jack immediately, but then spoke quietly, a tremor in his voice that he could not disguise. 'Peter was … my brother … my blood brother.' Joseph sighed heavily and turned away from the window to seat himself in the chair again and set the wine glass down upon the table. He paused, lacing his fingers together as if trying to find the right words, then spoke. His voice was quiet but steady, the pent-up words flowing now like a stream let loose after long being held in check.

'As you already know, in my former life I was a pharmacist and a good one but I steadily grew dissatisfied with the business. Too many unsafe drugs, too many dangerous chemical preparations poisoning people, not enough research — there had to be other alternatives. I turned more and more to natural remedies and in my own research found that certain herbs that grew only in this area of the mountains were useful to me. Tired of the rat race entirely and a bitter end to a love affair, I found myself inexplicably drawn to this place. I joined the Order of St. Francis here and began a happy contented life, kept busy continuing my experiments and ministering to the brothers when the need arose.

Peter had visited me a couple of times and spoke much of a theatrical career, to which, even as a child, he seemed well suited for. To my surprise then, he suddenly became interested in throwing all that talent away to join the Order here a little over a year after my own arrival.'

At first, he was content to follow the laws of the Order to the letter and marked himself as a true and devoted member and won much approval from the Brethren. However, it became apparent to me as time went on that he showed more than a professional interest in the rare books and manuscripts that came into the Abbey for repairs. He coveted them.'

He was almost fanatical in his knowledge of the antiquities, particularly in the ancient parchments. Having had considerable training in the Arts when younger he was in a perfect position to recognise the value and rarity of an art object, he was able to detect fake from genuine. Busy with my own interests, I was, at first, completely unaware that his obsession with these sacred objects should divert his love of restoration to that of privileged possession ... and his inevitable downfall.

'He was younger than you then,' said Jack.

Joseph paused in his narrative to take up his glass again and give Amos a grateful nod as it was topped up again.

'Yes,' said Joseph wearily, as he took another sip from his glass. 'A bare two years younger, but much more at one with the world than I was.' He stared at the ceiling and sighed heavily.

'Please continue with your story,' murmured Jack.

'We had both been left a reasonable inheritance when our parents died. Much of mine was eventually used to equip my own laboratory here, furnish the Infirmary and assist in the installation of the generator. Peter, however preferred to travel widely, even after he joined the Order, he made frequent trips to major and minor museums, places of worship around Europe, objectively to further his knowledge and gain more insight into the diminishing methods of illumination from the Florentine and Sienese schools that had flourished during the Renaissance. He was also able to procure the foils and rare inks necessary to make the restoration work that is carried out here the best in the country, if not the world. This also cemented his position here as an invaluable one, he became a popular figure, as he recounted his many journeys to other countries. As a very young student of the Arts before his decision to come to this monastery, he was able to go to many places with the assistance of the money left to him,' continued Joseph, 'and so it was his love of travel that took him one time to Venice, while there he was witness to the aftermath of the great flood when the river Arno broke its banks in 1966, where it almost destroyed an incomparable treasure house of irreplaceable art. There were many students there at that time, so I believe; they came from everywhere in the days after that terrible flood to help drag books, manuscripts and paintings out of the mud and attempt to restore them.'

I believe it was while he was there, that he saw fully what rare treasures there were in the world, it was there too that he succumbed to temptation and the ease in which some items of value could be procured without suspicion. I have seen several small ivories and bronze pieces in his "collection" that still bear the faint traces of oily ooze that could only have come from that flood. However,' he went on, 'in his later travels while he was a resident of the Order, he would redeem his conscience by bringing back a small work of art, an atonement gift for the Abbey library, a painting to adorn the walls, or a religious artefact of some value, but nothing compared to what he brought back for his own pleasure; that none knew about.'

Joseph moved uncomfortably in his seat, 'I am of the opinion now, that Peter intended to leave the Abbey soon and take his treasures with him, however, the temporary appointment by

Henri of the pseudo-Abbot thwarted that move for the time being, he dare not make a move until Henri returned.'

There was silence for a short while, before Amos spoke, 'But most of the thefts that were reported were thoroughly investigated by our department, though we could never quite find enough evidence, it was all attributed to Casini. He was the unseen mastermind in a profitable but dangerous business, it had to be his work, he was so well known in the trade. We knew his methods — blend in with the crowd, install a couple of "stand ins", a bit of bribery and blackmail, then dispose of the extras. Anyone in his employ didn't last long enough to enjoy the money they would have earned.'

'Too well known perhaps,' smiled Joseph ruefully. 'It's easy to hide the sheepdog among the sheep and it not be noticed by the marauding wolf, not forgetting, Amos, that anyone is deemed trustworthy under the mantle of a monk's habit, is that not so?' He glanced up at Amos with that half smile still on his face.

Amos had the grace to allow a slow blush to creep over his face, Jack to stifle the grin that enveloped his own. 'Changing one's appearance and personality are one of Amos' finer attributes to the cause, Joseph and I think he did it very well, don't you?'

'Indeed, he did,' agreed the other as he raised his glass again and gestured a salute to Amos, before giving a short bitter laugh. 'Would you believe me if I told you our parents were theatrical folk?' He put his head to one side and the grim line of his mouth turned up slightly at the corners as he looked from one to the other. 'No? Well, they were. Father was a magician and an expert in his craft. In fact, I often wondered if he was more wizard than magician. Mother was part of his stage act, both were highly skilled in the art of deception. Is it any wonder then that Peter also became so adept in disguise and deception? Would he not put that inherent skill to use — of course he would. Often as a young boy he would dress in all manner of concealments, with clever use of make-up, wigs, and other tools of the trade, he could completely fool me. I, his own brother could not detect the real person. Any wonder then that anyone would approach a religious defender of the faith so attired in robe and cowl, and question his fidelity in his handling of sacred objects or deny him admittance to treasure houses of irreplaceable works of art, in order to just admire them? I think not! To Peter, it was the thrill of the chase and to get away with it was the ultimate goal.'

Joseph stopped and shook his head sadly. 'So much a pity that such rich talents were wasted. Even as a child Peter threw himself completely and utterly into any project that took his interest. He would live and breathe nothing else till he had exhausted his enthusiasm. Had he not joined the Order of St Francis I declare he would have made a fair name for himself in the theatre. However, I was also of the opinion that joining the Order at the time that he did was to escape from someone, or something. He never spoke of his true reasons, I did not question him closely of his fear and in any case, I doubt I would have been told the truth.'

'Tell me, how then he became appointed as Abbot in Henri's place?' asked Jack. 'Was Henri aware that Peter had a past history and one that was dishonest?'

Joseph gave a bitter laugh again and said, 'You might be surprised to find all manner of the world's flotsam residing in a place such as this. Some, or most redeem themselves and become righteous members of society, as long as they prove themselves useful and not offend the Clerical Hierarchy or bring disrepute to the Abbey or the Order itself, then you are free to go about your duties and pastimes, as long as you live by the rules as stated. It can be a unique experience for those who have the spirit to conform and forgo some of the trappings of outside elements and portentous possessions, in other words, you give only of yourself and how you can help your fellow man.' He paused and shook his head sadly.

'When Henri left us on the mission that had called him, we had hoped that Ethan or one of the other elders would be appointed as Head of the Abbey pending Henri's return. He had hoped to return within the year. To my complete surprise he appointed Peter to take his place, I must admit I questioned his decision rather heatedly. To me it was a dangerous and unwise move — it was a bit like putting the cat in the same cage as the canary. However, he stilled my protest by saying that he had good reason for the motion and was aware that

Peter's downward spiral had begun, the hand of fate would fall either way for him and he could change the course of his future if he wanted to. I was instructed not to interfere but to keep a close watch. My own course was set but he still believed that Peter would set his feet on the right path given the opportunity and put his past behind him. When his past turned up so soon in the form of Casini and company, Peter found himself at a point of no return; for him there would be no right path.'

'I believe he made an attempt to kill himself by trying to hang himself in the bell tower,' said Jack after a prolonged pause.

'A futile and half-hearted attempt, I'm surprised he got as far as he did. He had an aversion to taking life, even his own.' Joseph put his head in his hands and leaned back in the armchair. 'If only he had listened to me,' he muttered behind his hands, 'I had warned him for so long that his past would eventually catch up with him.'

'Did anyone else know that you were actually brothers?' asked Amos, 'I never heard any whispers that you may have been family connected.'

Joseph stood up and began to pace around the room again. 'Apart from Henri, Elias was the only other person here who knew we were siblings. He had heard me arguing with Peter when I had thought we were quite alone at one time, I was compelled to take him into my confidence and he has never spoken of it to anyone. Elias is a man of honour and integrity, worthy to be a brother to me and the Abbey, he understood my dilemma completely.'

'One thing puzzles me,' said Jack. 'Why *did* Henri Du Pont leave when he did, I almost expected to find him here, to explain something to me.'

Joseph stopped pacing and looked closely at Jack. 'Before I answer that question,' he said slowly and deliberately, 'let me ask one of you.' He stepped over to the huge desk and taking up paper and pen, he drew a symbol on it and handed it to Jack saying, 'does this mark mean anything to you?'

Jack took the paper and looked at it. Instinctively, his hand went to his right shoulder, a look of surprise on his face. The mark on the paper was a stylised zed with two stars either side — the same mark that had been tattooed on his right shoulder as a boy.

'How did you know that?' asked Jack in astonishment.

Joseph stood in front of Jack and held his surprised gaze with his own. 'Then you do not deny that you are Jacques Vladimir Von Zaharoff, of the house of Baron Ernst Von Zaharoff?'

"then you do not deny that you are Jaqves Vladimir Von Zaharoff?

Chapter 24

A Vision From Mysterious Depths

There was silence in the room for a long time with no sound apart from the crackling of the fire in the grate. Amos sank down into the sofa and stared incredulously at Jack. He had known that Jack was different from any other agent he had worked with and had accepted the fact that there was a strange touch of the supernatural about him and that he had mixed easily with others of his kind, as was evident with Marilla and Isabella. He was also aware that he lived in the shadow of some sort of danger. He had been constantly shadowed by unknown persons now for some years, though neither of them knew just who they were, Amos had always remained alert, vigilant as a bodyguard. Jack had recognised in Amos a core vein of courage and sincerity of faith and a bond of brotherhood had sprung up between them. Jack had revealed something of his life to Amos, his closeness to his grandmother and of the quest that had been haunting him. A mission, a promise he had made to his grandmother to reclaim a precious heirloom that had belonged to his family, he also knew this Abbey was to hold the key to Jack's search but he had never revealed he was connected to the realm of a Baron … and that same Baron had already been to this place in search of a missing treasure!

Amos was now beginning to make some wild guesses and hoped he was wrong, but for the moment his full attention was on the man Joseph — how could he possibly know Jack's true identity, when Amos himself had not really known? For the moment Joseph had ceased to be just a monk, who was he? The grey robed figure in front of them was a stranger whom he now did not know! What was his true purpose in being here if he was aware of Jack's identity?

'How did you know about the mark?' Jack asked the question quietly, still with that puzzled look on his face. 'I cannot look into your mind, it is closed to me — who are you, and how do you know me?'

'I am an emissary of Henri Du Pont,' came the clear answer.

'Then he has taught you well but now you must answer my question. Why did Henri leave the Abbey and where is he now?'

'He had urgent business to attend to elsewhere and it kept him many months longer than he thought,' said Joseph. 'When he attempted to return, the Casinis were unfortunately here and he considered it most unwise to show himself openly. Events that had been put into place would unfold in due time. He knew Zaharoff had searched the Abbey, he also knew that the thing that he was seeking was quite safe. However, the one person he was now not sure about was Peter. He guessed that Peter was aware that something of value had been brought into the Abbey and possibly hidden here but then neither could Peter be sure that the Abbot had not taken it with him. The element of distrust had crept in, Henri felt that Peter just might succumb to temptation again and risk his new appointment to seek out the prize. He had shadowed Henri, to no avail I might add, as he walked about the grounds and the church, particularly at night as Henri considered all the possibilities of his plans, while I did my best to keep Peter off the track. Henri, of course knew Peter was curious but also that Peter did not know enough about what had been hidden, nor its whereabouts, it kept Peter occupied. It was only when the Casinis arrived that all chances of Peter hunting down that which intrigued him ceased.'

Joseph paused a while before he continued. 'I might add that Peter considered Henri Du Pont not a fit person to run his own Abbey and in a vain effort to get rid of him, he had vowed to put a case to the Ecclesiastical Councils to have him removed from the post. It was only on my intervention that he did not do so. However, Henri had to leave on his errand and the matter was dropped by Peter, particularly so when he was reminded of his appointment as acting Head in Henri's absence, with certain other facts that could emerge to undermine that coveted position.'

He laughed grimly, and picking up his wine glass, took a mouthful and studied the colour of the wine against the light from the window, then said slowly and carefully, 'However before my dear brother could now revel in his new and illustrious position, his shady past caught up with him in the form of some old acquaintances in the form of Victor Casini and company. Peter suddenly found he had no choice but to bow to a new master and be subservient to their wishes. No wonder he aged so quickly in such a short time.' He shook his grey head sadly.

Jack had sat quietly his fingertips together in front of his chin as Joseph revealed this information but now spoke. 'I see his dilemma, no wonder he struck me as a deeply troubled man. Had you considered, Joseph, that Henri, in appointing Peter as pseudo-Abbot was making a deliberate move to evaluate him? Henri would know what the condition of his mind was and what the future would hold for him, if he did not rise above his personal torment?'

Joseph continued to stare at the wine glass and murmured, 'I believe that was what he had in mind but I could not interfere, he had not observed that fate was to take a hand and it was not his.'

Setting the glass down now upon the table, Joseph stood up. He turned to the two men and looked at them thoughtfully. 'As for the second part of your question, I have to remind you that Henri Du Pont is very aged now, though you may not realise that when you see him. You may have felt his presence here, though perhaps not been fully aware of it — he has his own way of keeping watch over his domain.' He looked at Jack keenly. 'Now that your identity has been established, you shall see for yourself. As for you, Amos, you have proven yourself to be worthy of standing by Jack's side and Henri would want to acknowledge your loyalty to his nephew.'

'*Nephew?*' the word was frozen on Amos' lips, as he stared at Jack.

There was no time for question or answer for Amos, as Joseph strode quickly to the end of the room where it was darkest. They had barely noticed the great tapestry that hung there, a medieval hunting scene in rich dark colours. He drew aside the heavy tapestry to reveal a door of the same dark wood as the wall panelling, which at first glance could easily be mistaken for part of the wall itself. Reaching into the neck of his vestment, he produced a long silver key and pushing aside a small section of the panelling, he inserted the key into the lock that was suddenly revealed to them. With a quiet click it opened, he passed through, lighting some lamps as he did so, then stood in the flickering light of the lamps and bade them enter.

They found themselves in a smallish circular room hung about with heavy drapes. In the centre of the room stood an intricately carved tripod table, which was supporting what looked like a shallow basin filled almost to the brim with some dark liquid. Its mirror-like surface was smooth and unruffled, reflecting the flickering light from the wall sconces.

Joseph walked around to the other side of the tripod and stood motionless; his hands deep in the sleeves of his robe as he regarded them. 'You are aware,' he said quietly as he looked at Jack, 'what this is?'

Jack turned to Amos who had hung back a little as they entered the room and spoke to him. 'It's a scrying glass, a crystal ball to put it another way. It will, under certain circumstances, show you what you want to see, or don't want to see. That was how Isabella was able to see the cottage in the forest you may remember, though I think there's was a mirror. It will work just the same, it's only how you use it.'

'Oh,' said Amos, a trifle nervously as he stepped into the room and approached the tripod. He glanced cautiously at the liquid in the basin, 'so this is the thing that Peter saw standing in the room that Henri didn't really want him to see.'

'I would imagine it was, it would be somewhat difficult to explain it to anyone,' said Jack.

'Yes,' replied Joseph. 'To him, the curious things in Henri's room were tools of devilry and had no place here and I suppose one could be forgiven for thinking that, considering where we are. However, the common thought that anything to do with witchcraft is an evil practice is often a misaligned factor. The tools of wizardry are more often used for producing truth and honesty, sadly a thing my misguided brother did not patronise, though there is the odd exception in some wizards unfortunately,' Joseph added quickly, 'but they are quickly weeded out of course.'

Joseph stepped forward to the basin and looked deeply into it for a moment, then slowly passed his hand across its dark surface, just above and without touching the liquid. As he did so, he murmured soft words neither Jack nor Amos could hear. He then stepped back and waited.

A slow ripple began to disturb the tranquil surface and as they watched, the water began to bubble a little in the centre, then stopped. It seemed as if that was all it was going to do, the liquid lay as still as before, then suddenly it began again, and the bubbling became a boil as the water seethed in the basin. A light seemed to be glowing under the surface and as the water began to gather itself to rise in its centre, so the strange light began to get brighter, changing colour from a deep blue to an iridescent green as the water rose higher and higher in the basin. As the bubbling fountain of liquid rose higher still above the basin, it began to spin itself into a vortex of shimmering colour as bright stars of blue and green filaments whirled rapidly around the tower of liquid. The faces of the three men were lit by this shimmering spiral of light emanating before them, Amos, who had stepped back a pace, watched open mouthed in astonishment. It was a magic he felt sure he had seen before with Marilla at the foot of the falls.

They had been aware of a soft whispering that seemed to echo in the small chamber, it now became a swift rushing sound. The glittering blue and green stars blended themselves together in a blindinzg flash and were gone, in their place there now stood the figure of a man.

It was an old man, stooped with age and wrapped in a white gown, the girdle of which he was still attempting to fasten around his middle with fumbling fingers. He poised over the basin as if hanging in mid-air, his snow-white hair untidily standing up on end and his long white beard tied in the middle by a blue ribbon. About four foot tall and surrounded by a greenish glow, he hung there peering around him with a surprised look on his face.

'Just about to take a bath,' he grumbled in a surprisingly deep voice. 'I heard you call, Joseph, ah, yes.' He glanced at the three figures standing expectantly in front of him, before reaching into the pocket of his gown and producing a small pair of *pince*

nez glasses, which he perched precariously on the end of his long nose. 'Jacques!' he boomed, the deep voice sounding extremely odd coming from such a diminutive figure. 'Jacques, so at last we meet. Oh, don't be concerned about the size you see me, I'm usually much taller, is that not so, Joseph?'

'Indeed yes, Henri,' said Joseph, then, turning to Jack he began to explain about the properties of the scrying mirror and the necessary reduction in size for convenience.

'You don't need to explain,' broke in Jack, 'I know what happens with a scrying mirror, it is enough to see my mother's brother no matter what size he shows himself.'

'Ah, Jacques my dear boy, or is it Jack that you call yourself — I assume Joseph has made you aware of some of the matters that have occurred and no doubt passed his scrutinous eye over you as to your identity, but I see myself that you have many of the qualities of your mother.'

'I have little to remember her by,' said Jack, 'nor yet my grandmother, Anna.'

'Dear Edwina has kept their memories alive for you, has she not?'

Jack nodded, the old man drew himself a little more upright and tightened the girdle about his waist. 'You do know then that the Baron is attempting to find the precious icon that is yours by birthright. You do remember it don't you?'

'I remember it very well, she showed it to me a long time ago and explained its significance and its history.'

'Excellent!' the old man beamed and laced his long fingers together in front of his beard. 'Well now, we must let him find it.'

'No!' said Jack, 'No, it must not fall in to his hands, Edwina said I was to prevent …' his voice trailed away as Henri held up both hands to stop Jack's protests.

When Henri spoke again, his voice was hard and ominous. 'It is our wish, Jack — Edwina's and mine — that this villain should die by his own hand, that you *do not* prevent it, but only bear witness to it and so avenge the deaths of your mother and grandmother!' He put his head on one side and continued, 'I know what you are thinking, that we could have made a move to destroy the Baron earlier but he was still too strong and his powers over others too great. While you still lived, he would not harm you because he knew that sooner or later you would lead him to the prize. You yourself needed to be stronger and wiser but it is neither right nor moral that you should strike the fatal blow to one so close in kinship.'

The old man's voice boomed and echoed in the small room as he raised one clenched fist in the air and shook it as he spoke angrily, '*You will not stain your hands with his blood!*' Regaining his composure, he went on, 'The Baron believes in his own cleverness and desires this particular treasure above anything else, if only to appease his lust for ultimate power over what has now passed into a sad and violent history.' The voice became softer now and his hands laced the long fingers together as before. 'However, he is not as clever as Edwina or had you forgotten the secret the treasure conceals for those who act in haste, hmm?' He peered closely at Jack over the rims of his *pince nez*.

'No, I had not forgotten, I saw every detail of Edwina's work. I am aware of the danger, even though it was so long ago now.'

'Good, good,' Henri rubbed his gnarled old hands together, 'The trap is set, though I was getting a trifle concerned when Peter was getting a little too close but thanks to Joseph's vigilance, he never found it. The Baron has been given a clue, that which he found in the Russian bible and you, Jack no doubt, have the same message delivered by Daniel, ah, Daniel … how I wish I could have prevented his death.' The old man hung his head and sighed, a long slow sigh and softly said, 'He had been cruelly dealt with by that mob of gangsters before anyone knew of it. If only I had stayed close by but sadly I was not here and completely unaware of his mortal danger. It's still very difficult to be in two places at once.'

Joseph, who had been standing to one side of the scrying dish now spoke, 'The arrival of the Casinis was something we had not quite expected, though it did have the desired effect in keeping Peter otherwise occupied.' Then he too added sadly, 'I was also unaware at the time that they were known to each other. Victor recognised him from various other affairs that had occurred but particularly from the affair in Venice, during which I was led to believe Casini also obtained treasures by deceit. He was actually more conscious of Peter's indiscretions than anyone supposed and had eventually tracked him here, Casini saw his opportunity to use him and the Brethren of this Abbey to his advantage.'

'Ahem,' the gravelly voice of Amos cut in. 'So it was a little bit of coercion on Victor's part that kept Peter from alerting the authorities and then, if he did, he would also be incriminating himself. He *was* in a nasty bind, wasn't he?'

'Yes, you could say that,' said Joseph thickly. 'He was very afraid of the Casinis, he knew their reputation for swift retribution. So rather than admit to his own part in thefts or submit to more pressure from them in what they were doing to the Abbey and its reputation, he tried, unsuccessfully to commit suicide. It would seem now that his fall from the cliff was, in effect, a successful way of ending a life of transgression.' He sighed heavily and stood silent with his head bowed.

The silence was broken by the old wizard, who, still poised above the basin, was running a gnarled hand through his sparse crop of hair in an effort at smoothing it down. 'I had warned Peter that his life could take a disastrous turn, it was up to him to right the wrong. He could still deliver himself from the pit he had fallen into … and I believe he may have made such an attempt to do so in thinking of the reputation and the innocence of his fellow brothers. However now caught in a web of deceit in which they were given no choice, it was a little too late to redeem himself. He remained caught in a situation where a move either way was fatal, as Amos has so carefully described.'

'Then what of Daniel?' said Jack impatiently, 'He knew I was interested in locating the Icon, he had sent me a garbled message but it was many months before I received it. I could do nothing about it at the time and for months more, before Amos and I found that there was a parallel purpose in finding this particular Abbey. Not only did our trail with the Casinis lead us here but I have known that Edwina has been channelling my thoughts in this direction for some time.'

'And mine too,' said Henri. 'You were being led here regardless of Daniel's message. The fact that the Casinis were using the Abbey and the brethren here to their advantage, then with your intense search for them, it brought it all together in the one place, so it seemed the right time to put our plan into action.'

'Couldn't there have been an easier way to handle this, without all the secrecy of hidden messages?' said Jack, spreading his hands in an impatient gesture.

'Just hear me out please, Jack, my boy and perhaps you will understand more, though sometimes even plans made by wizards, can, I admit, go a little … umm, astray …' He pushed the *pince nez* down a little firmer on the long nose and looked down at Jack as if regarding a schoolboy for whom he had to assess for a punishment.

'Peter was the most immediate problem. His curiosity was getting the better of him, I couldn't have him poking around too much. He could not understand the Russian language but he knew that Daniel could, so he, casually, asked if Daniel could translate it. He firmly believed it had something to do with what was hidden in the book, not forgetting of course that Peter had probably used that same technique in transporting his own small treasures. Daniel had told him that it was little more than a family heritage notation and nothing whatsoever to do with anything that might have been hidden there. He did make a copy of the words and said he would try to translate it but it was very old Russian and difficult to put it into understandable modern Russian and might take some time. Peter seemed satisfied with that for the time and it was a suitable excuse to put it out of his reach each time he asked about it.

'Then Von Zaharoff appeared. Edwina and I had been consciously aware that he had finally discovered that I was Camille's brother and that letters had been sent to me not long before her death. He naturally assumed then that it was not Edwina who now had the icon, but me, although he kept a furtive watch over our movements, he was afraid to approach outright. Though we were never far away, we did not want to be here at the Abbey when he arrived. Edwina and I with help from Daniel had hatched our plan some time previously.

Daniel placed a cryptic message we had devised concerning the location of the icon in the book, which was meant to make the Baron search for it. He also made the copy you were to have, he kept that, intending to hand it to you. I believe he sent you a message to confirm that.'

'Yes, he did, so then you decided to turn the whole thing into a treasure hunt, is that it?' said Jack, 'Then it just happened to coincide with our mission to capture the Casinis here in this Abbey.'

'Ah … well, yes,' the old man replied, as he fumbled with the ribbon tying his beard together. 'Von Zaharoff arrived here and was most annoyed to find me gone, he presumed at first that I had taken the icon with me and began questioning the brothers here quite closely. Of course, they knew nothing about it … even Peter, whose curiosity was now further aroused.'

'Von Zaharoff was very angry when he arrived here,' said Joseph pointedly. 'He asked all sorts of questions about Henri — whether he had received any visitors and if he had, he demanded to know who they were. Nobody, of course, could tell him anything, I just simply said that the Abbot had been called away to a convention, the monks knew nothing about his personal affairs. Peter was terrified of him and stayed firmly in the background, though admittedly still very curious. Zaharoff took it upon himself to search the Abbey and found the Russian bible with the cryptic message hidden inside. He seemed very excited about what he found and decided to stay here for a few days. In that time, he and his associates prowled over every part of the Abbey, even down to the crypt and through the chapel. He asked a lot of questions about calendar dates, times of sun rises, sun sets, and of moon phases. Henri's private quarters were searched thoroughly rather to my indignation, and I remained in the room while he went through everything, he kept hinting darkly that if his sister was a witch, then he too must have some connection with the "dark side". He was a thoroughly unpleasant and to my mind, a dangerous man. He also stated, as he glared at me, while clutching the piece of parchment that he would return again when it was at the right time to claim what was his, then, thankfully, he left.'

'Yes,' said Henri, 'now sadly a cunning and dangerous man but I knew he would do no harm to the monks here. His violence, I knew, would not extend that far toward men of the cloth. However, due to Joseph's vigilance, he never discovered the whereabouts of this chamber, otherwise he just may have had reason to justify his suspicions. Is that not so, Joseph?' The old man chuckled quietly to himself and tightened his girdle, which had slipped a little.

There was a cough and a grunt from Amos who now spoke. 'I guess the Casini mob arrived soon after that, because that was the last time we heard from Dan, am I right?'

'Indeed, they did,' replied Joseph sadly, 'that's when Peter's problems really started … Daniel's too I'm afraid. It was only a day or two after their arrival that the man Bruno placed Daniel as an officer of the law and "blew his cover" as you would say. Victor was very angry when he found Daniel was an agent and was a danger to the business enterprise he intended to set up using the brothers expertise here, so he had to get rid of him.' Joseph closed his eyes for a moment, then said huskily, 'To further terrorise Peter into doing exactly what he wanted, he made him watch Daniel's "execution" … it was very traumatic for him, I think that may have been what finally tipped him over the edge. Leaving that poor man to lie undisturbed in that room was meant to show the rest of us that he meant to have total control.'

'Couldn't *you* have done something to stop him?' said Amos, looking inquiringly at the diminutive figure still poised above the dark basin, 'after all you are a–a—'

'Wizard, yes,' replied Henri turning his attention to Amos,

'but the workings of the law are an area I don't like to meddle in. I considered it, at one time, yes, in order to help, but it would mean showing my hand and frankly the less people who know what my true vocation is, the better. There are still those who do not understand us but I would have intervened if any of the monks were in mortal danger. I knew the Baron was not far away he would be watching and waiting. I also had other very important matters to attend to that would take me away from the Abbey for a short while. Joseph kept in constant contact and would summon me immediately if I was needed. The monks were in no danger as long as they kept on doing what they were supposed to do. As it was, I came back in time to assist in some small matters that were occurring here, which had unfortunately got out of control through no fault of either you or Jack. Amos, your bravery and your loyalty to my nephew are beyond reproach, we are most grateful to you … you are indeed a man among men. However, I really could not interfere with the task you both had in bringing the perpetrators of these crimes and many others to justice, as I knew you would, but,' here the dark eyes began to twinkle and an eyebrow was raised, 'I must confess to a certain, er–helping hand with Marilla; down by the waterfall.'

'I had already suspected that,' said Jack, 'Marilla does have her limitations.'

'Ah,' said Henri, wagging one of his long fingers at Jack. 'I have not taken credit for all their actions. These are courageous young ladies who just need a helping hand in finding themselves and some confidence in the art in which they have been born into, from what I can see so far they have been most helpful, wouldn't you agree?'

'Could that be why their paths crossed mine — *that* was certainly not a coincidence, wouldn't *you* agree?' said Jack a little coldly. 'You do realise that they could have been in serious danger as well as putting Amos' and my mission in peril as well. Two extra people to worry about, especially women and an inexperienced pair as they are, could have jeopardised this whole exercise, an extensive long-standing operation involving a lot of others as well, at an international level! This was not a game, these men were extremely dangerous and the girls should not have been involved. What if they had been killed ... what then?'

Henri pursed his lips and stared at the ceiling for a moment before replying. 'Hmm, you could say it was a little more than coincidence perhaps but then one doesn't think of the repercussions unfortunately when one's mind is so distant from the reality of the action. I admit I had not thought about what or who else would be involved in bringing the thugs to justice and for that, my dear Jacques, I do humbly apologise, but –' here he waggled his finger again with a gleam in his eye, 'you must admit they were wonderful, wonderful; Hilda would have been most proud.' he clasped his hands together in front of his beard, his eyes twinkling with pleasure.

'So, whose idea was this in dropping them here at this particular time — yours or Edwina's?'

'A little of both I have to say. We considered you might need a little help in your quest, once you had finally captured the perpetrators of justice, who were, I might say holding up our own measure of justice, you would then be free to pursue the matter of the hidden icon. You must admit Isabella showed great courage in the crypts, Lucifer; well, what more can we say about such a remarkable cat, he's almost human.'

'So, you had a hand it that too I presume?' grunted Amos.

'No, not entirely, it is rather difficult to be in two places at once, even for a wizard, Lucifer knew his way in by that back entrance and acted accordingly. As for what happened beforehand, I could not prevent that, it was indeed Isabella's quick reaction that saved you both. I had only just arrived on the scene and was in time to assist a little at the waterfall but had to rely on Lucifer to guide you out of the crypt. It has been almost centuries since that exit has been used, you no doubt had some difficulty in gaining your freedom Amos but gain it you did with Isabella's assistance. So, you see I have kept my finger on the pulse, as it is said,' and he smiled benignly.

A thought suddenly struck Amos, he looked keenly at the figure of the old man. 'How come we haven't seen you, yet you claim to have been at the waterfall with Marilla and knew what was happening in the crypt?'

'Ah, my dear, Amos,' said Henri, lacing his long fingers together again over his beard. 'You wouldn't really expect a wizard to divulge his secrets, nor yet how he employs his tools would you?'

'I think you'll find, Amos,' muttered Jack half under his breath, 'that Uncle Henri and Lucifer are on equal speaking terms, if you get my drift.'

Henri was raising one bushy eyebrow at Amos and Jack. 'All the same,' he sighed, 'I must admit things were happening rather more rapidly than I had expected. Must be feeling my age I expect, not as quick off the mark as I used to be.'

'Well, that brings us back to what to do about the icon,' said Jack. 'I am to presume, by the riddle we both now have, that it is hidden somewhere here in the Abbey and it's a race between us to find the icon. Why not just tell us where it is and we'll take it from there?'

'You still don't understand do you, Jacques? The Baron does not expect you to just hand it over to him without a fight. He has spent many years waiting for the chance. His fear of witchcraft has kept him at a distance from us so far but he knows it will eventually come to you, he wants to pit his wits against yours, he wants to prove to you that he is still the master,' replied Henri. 'He believes he can outwit you and find the treasure himself but will take it from you by force only if absolutely necessary, his obsession for it has long outweighed his concept of fair play.'

The old wizard chuckled quietly almost to himself. 'Yes, it is as you say, a treasure hunt, although you will find it before he does, I'm sure you will, you have the same clues to follow, two very helpful young ladies to assist you and of course the indomitable Amos. I'm sure the four of you can outsmart Von Zaharoff, and of course, time is still on your side, you have the advantage, the Abbey is yours to search at will and I do so love treasure hunts,' he remarked gleefully, ' so too the Baron, as we have perceived a sense of adventure for all.'

Joseph, who had been standing silently to one side, now spoke, 'We will both be absent from the Abbey for a short while, there are other matters to be attended to but rest assured that you will not be entirely alone — a watch will be kept to see that you come to no serious harm.'

'Indeed yes,' said Henri, 'however, I must warn you of Von Zaharoff's treachery, you can expect no quarter from him, Jack. Once he is aware of your presence here, your life will be in danger, he has sworn before this to kill you; but one must now wonder whether he would carry out that threat after so long a time. He may have softened his heart a little although I still have some doubts. This, my dear Jacques, is the end of all those years of wondering and waiting for the final blow to fall, you must be there to witness it. There is only so much I can do to protect you, so be on your guard at all times and remember too, he will not be alone!'

'This has all been very well planned, hasn't it?' said Jack angrily, 'right down to the last detail. Even diverting Marilla and Isabella to fit into your two-fold little plot, so that they can improve their witchcraft skills at the expense of endangering our lives! Why couldn't they have just gone on their way and found their own place like they started to do and wanted to do. This is a dangerous situation you've dropped them into, are you going to be here if something *does* go wrong? I don't like the idea of them being in any sort of danger over something they know nothing about, all for just learning to hone their skills!'

'I will be here, in one form or another,' replied Henri firmly. 'What you can't see my dear, Jacques, is that there is no future for Marilla and Isabella in the direction they *were* heading, their future is here — in this Abbey, though they do not know it yet. The skills that they possess are already becoming more powerful, they themselves are aware of it, they just needed a, shall we say … stimulant. This has been prophesised, so too of the task ahead that must and will, be brought to an end, as Edwina has foretold, justice done … for your dear mother's sake.' They heard the soft whispering sounds, the swirl of blue/green stars begin to envelop the figure as he raised a hand in farewell saying, 'Jack, don't forget the curse!'

'Well, at least we have some warning of what to expect I suppose,' said Amos, shifting his feet uncomfortably, 'where are we supposed to start looking?'

'That's what the clues are for, Amos,' replied Henri as his figure began to fade away, until all that was left was a cloudy greenish mist. There was a faint sighing noise and the mist gathered itself together then disappeared as a column of spray into the basin with a loud plop.

Amos leaned forward and watched with amazement as the ripples spread across the surface and the water became still and dark once more.

'Phew!' he said softly, 'never a dull moment working with you, Jack, never a dull moment!'

Chapter 25

The Exit Of The Monks

The days passed swiftly, with little for the sisters to do but watch from afar at the busy comings and goings of the monks of St Dominica as they made their preparations to leave the Abbey that had been home to them for so long. The tools of their trade were packed carefully into boxes for the long trip east to the priory of St. Helena. Many of the books were stripped from the library shelves and also packed into cartons unearthed from somewhere in the cellars for the purpose. A considerable number of books were left remaining upon their shelves, as, according to Joseph, St. Helena boasted a very considerable library of its own and any more would be superfluous to requirement. Besides, said Joseph, what point is there in having a library still here without books, there were many volumes that had not had their pages turned in a decade?

He pointed out one particular shelf containing an array of books. 'I have left these here for you to read Miss Isabella,' he intoned quietly, 'you may find them useful.'

Isabella inclined her head to read the spines and perceived that they were mostly dealing with the properties of herbs and herb lore in general. She had also noticed in glancing over the remaining stacks of volumes and indeed on a small number that the monks were packing, that they still had thick layers of dust and festoons of cobwebs clinging to them. However, those indicated by Joseph were clean and dust free.

'But, but—these are yours,' she said gently, 'why aren't you taking them with you?'

He hesitated a bit before replying, 'I have no room for them now and I may come back for them sometime later. Now then,' he added briskly, 'let me show you the work room, just through here.'

Passing through another doorway midway along the length of the library, she found herself in a long lofty room partially lit by the narrow windows set into the imposing facade of the ancient monastery walls. Long trestle-like tables were arranged on either side of the room, here and there stood several architectural type desks and lecterns. Much of the natural light came from large glass panels set in the vaulted ceiling but small individual lamps scattered about the room afforded more necessary light for the fine work involved in the repair and finishing of some of the illuminated manuscripts. A mustiness hung in the air here, a smell of old parchments, inks and chemicals. Here and there on the ink-stained flag stoned floor lay some pieces of old carpet or animal skin, no doubt to keep the feet warm of the artisans who spent so many hours at their craft. Isabella noticed too, that there were two fireplaces set into either end of the long room, one of which still sheltered some red coals beneath a blackened log. This then was the working area for these dedicated men.

'This,' said Joseph, waving his arm around, 'is what we call the scriptorium, at this time of the year and on into winter, it can unfortunately be rather cold, so the monks are grateful of a little warmth. When we have fine weather, they can take some of their work outside and work in the cloisters but, mostly the work is done here. Even so, we find that the inks will freeze overnight in winter, also the delicate parchments almost too frail to work on.' He sighed and went on, 'In a way I'm almost sorry to be leaving here as many of the older brethren are. Apart from the winter's chill and the whole place in need of such repair, it has been home for a good many years, it has now outlived its usefulness.'

'Can't it be fixed up?' said Isabella as she looked about her, noticing perhaps for the first time, that the walls were cracked in places and a few of the heavy wooden doors were difficult to close properly.

'Possibly,' said Joseph, 'but it would take a great deal of money to effect repairs, there has never been enough funds to do so. This entire part of the Abbey is in a bad state of disrepair I'm afraid.' He too surveyed the time-damaged walls and clicked his tongue impatiently.

Joseph turned around to gaze ruefully at the room in which they stood. 'So, in truth, I guess our move to St. Helena is a timely one regardless of the havoc Mr Casini has caused us. It will be a new beginning. We have received many invitations from St. Helena over the years to join their fraternity, until now we have preferred to press on here, hoping perhaps for a benefactor to emerge from the mists with a sizable wallet that is not earmarked for any particular use. Such a pity, such a pity,' he mused and for a moment he seemed to forget that Isabella was there. His fingers stroking the cover of a book lying upon a lectern. 'But if it is to be found ... if it is there ... then who knows?' The voice had descended to little more than a whisper as if his mind was turned inward to somewhere else.

'And such a pity Mr Casini could not see the potential to put his wealth to better purpose here, isn't that right, Joseph?' A voice behind them made them turn around to see Elias coming toward them from the library with Marilla close behind him. His ruddy face was etched in a deep frown as he came closer. 'Ethan wants a word with you when you are free Joseph but said there's no great hurry. I've brought Miss Marilla with me; she would like to be with her sister.'

'Well, let's move on then, shall we?' said Joseph drawing himself up and regaining his serenely austere manner. 'Perhaps we can show you both something that may be more useful to you than what you see here.'

They moved out of the scriptorium and passing down a wide corridor, found themselves entering into another courtyard, this one completely different from those they had passed through previously. Banked by the high outer wall on one side and the long wall of the scriptorium and library on the other, this haven was filled with light and colour. Pumpkin vines trailed at random over beds of onions and other leafy vegetables, a trellis of green beans vied for space with the last of a late crop of tomatoes. Further back the fluffy green of carrot tops looked like strips of lush carpet bordered by the rounded heads of cabbages set in orderly rows. Waving plumes of yellowing corn stalks marched evenly down another, while a little beyond was glimpsed the last of the seasons mulberries sheltering beneath the leaves of a large old tree gracing one corner.

This Garden of Eden followed the contour of the great wall as the small party moved onward. They saw more fruit trees — apple, lemon, orange and a small grove of olive trees tucked away by themselves, in between stretched rows of grape vines with clusters of the rich red fruit still evident amidst the already yellowing leaves.

'This is amazing!' gasped Isabella delightedly. 'We had no idea this existed. We thought the old gardens beds around the other side—where we, er … dropped in were all that there were here.'

'They used to be,' said Elias, as he stooped to cut off a small cluster of grapes, 'by that old broken wall but there was not enough protection there from forest animals, we'd lose more than would be gained. As you can see here, this garden is surrounded by high walls, the foundations are quite deep, so it's difficult even for the rabbits to dig through from outside.' He handed a small bunch of grapes to the two sisters. 'These make an excellent wine and are just as palatable taken straight from the vine too. We have a small plant in the cellars, the wine is all pressed and bottled by hand in the time-honoured tradition. It's a busy time then, we all help out with the crushing and pressing, the same goes for the olives when they are ripe too. There is always plenty of work here to keep us occupied.'

'However, do you find time to attend to all this and still do the work required in the Abbey?'

'The garden and the produce that comes from it are just as important as restoration work, we all take our turn in the field of horticulture but I think it is going to be Elias that is going to miss this more so than any of us, is that not so, Elias?'

Elias sighed, a deep and sorrowful sigh, 'I'm afraid it is, yes. I don't want to leave all this, in fact it's been my life's work but with nobody here, well … it will just run wild. I suppose I could stay on by myself, there's too much to attend to here for just one person to manage, so a lot of it will have to go.'

'Why am I hearing chickens?' said Marilla suddenly.

'Perhaps it's because there are,' said Joseph.

They had reached the end of the walk through the garden and were approaching a rough stone wall in which was set a tall wooden gate. Opened by a simple latch, they found themselves in a walkway bounded by the Abbey walls on one side and an extensive chicken coop on the other. A number of fat white and brown hens were scratching busily among the debris of food scraps and wheat that one of the lay brothers had just put down for them. Just beyond the chicken coop they could see a great open area studded with piles of rocks and dotted here and there with large shade trees. Presently the sound of other animals came to their ears; the sound of goats calling and the braying of donkeys.

Isabella clapped her hands joyously, 'Why, it's just like a real farm.'

'Yes,' said Elias ruefully, 'unfortunately they have not had the attention they should have had while the Casinis were here, now we will have to try and sell them off to the folk in the village, as there is nowhere else for them to go, unless ...' He stopped and stared at the ground; his ruddy face looked even more ruddy as he began to walk quickly away in the direction of one of the barns nearby.

'What Elias is trying to say,' said Joseph stopping and turning toward the sisters, is — this place, though old admittedly, is in need of someone who–who–do you have any plans for your immediate future?' he asked, suddenly changing the course of the conversation. 'I am led to believe, from what Jack has told me, that you were looking for a place to stay a while. I have already assumed that this is so, am I correct?'

'I–we–' stammered Marilla, 'well, yes, I guess we are, but this isn't what we had in mind, we were—'

'Oh, but it is!' broke in Isabella, 'it's perfect, there's everything here that we need and we wouldn't have to go back to Harewood!' Isabella's brown eyes were sparkling as she looked about her. 'There's so much we can do here, Marilla and the little donkeys are just, beautiful–I'm going to ask Elias if I can pat them.' She threw one last beseeching look at her sister and hurried after Elias who was now busy at one of the feed stalls.

Marilla watched her sister for a few moments as she wrestled with an answer. She could feel Joseph's eyes on her and she turned to face him. He looked into Marilla's face and held her gaze. 'Do we make you feel nervous, Miss Marilla, because we are monks of a holy order' he said gently, 'and the fact that this is a monastery … does all this bother you?'

Marilla drew herself up and some of her old haughtiness returned. 'Of course not, what you do is your business but you have to admit we're not exactly—not—well, you know what I mean,' and she kicked at a stone in her path.

'I see,' said Joseph slowly and smiled at her. 'Well, I have to say that you are not exactly what we would have thought compatible either but Marilla, we all have the same needs, were we to discard our robes for everyday work clothes, would you still have the same depiction of us … would you still see us as Franciscans?'

It was a moment before Marilla replied. 'No, I guess not but you must admit it has been pretty daunting for us to be thrust into the middle of all this and not know why. I'm going to have to have another word to say to Jack Grimsby about it.'

'Perhaps you should,' murmured Joseph.

'Anyway, we're not at all sure we really want to stay here, if that is what you are asking us to do. There are plenty of other places we can go to.'

'Are there?' said Joseph quizzically, 'hasn't your curiosity been aroused as to *why* you are here? There's more to this Abbey than you think and I believe you were both meant to be here. It would appear that it was a most fortuitous wind that brought you here at this time.'

'How could you *possibly* know that!' said Marilla sharply.

'Perhaps you should really have that talk with Mr Grimsby,' replied Joseph with finality, 'come, let us catch up with your sister, she seems to have made up her mind anyhow.'

They began to walk toward the stables where Elias and Isabella were fussing over one of the donkeys.

Marilla was thinking hard. Everything that had happened so far seemed to indicate that someone was trying to keep them here. Why? How much did Joseph know about them, perhaps Jack had discussed their arrival with him … yet, he had repeated Jack's very words, 'I believe you were both meant to be here.' She was beginning to think that Joseph was not a monk at all, was he part of the other reason Jack was here? Why all this secrecy? Jack had not told them the other reason he was staying on here after the capture of the Casini gang. Another thought entered her mind and she suddenly stopped and said very firmly, 'Doesn't it bother you that we are … witches?'

Joseph turned to face her again and said in his carefully modulated voice, 'Indeed not, why should it? I've met some very nice wizards and witches … including Jack's grandmother.'

A startled gasp came from Marilla's open mouth, and she stared at Joseph and the enigmatic smile that was creeping over his face, 'You've met Edwina! How, when–here?' She sank down onto one of the large rocks that littered the yard, her mind in a whirl. Why would Edwina come here … to a monastery! What business could she have had with a Holy Order?

So many thoughts were running through her mind now. The storm that night intensifying the way it did to blow them off course, then to meet up with a childhood companion after so many years. The strange feeling that someone else was in control that afternoon down at the waterfall when the little brown man turned into a bat. Everything had all happened so quickly that she hadn't had time to reason why. Somehow it all seemed to come back to Edwina … she *had* to be behind it but *why*, what possible reason could she have had in directing them here — Jack's affairs were nothing to do with them.

Joseph sat down beside her and laid a hand on her arm. 'Marilla, Jack will explain all I am sure when you talk with him. In the meantime, let us be candid and consider the situation. You need a place to stay, we have need of a resident caretaker. If you wish to stay, then so will Elias. It grieves him to even think of selling the animals he has so patiently cared for and of course the garden. There is no point in him staying on if there is no one to keep it all for. Here you will find everything you need to survive; it is, as we have made it, a self-sufficient colony, it just needs to be kept that way. There is still work for me to finish here and I will return,' and he smiled at her, 'though perhaps not as you see me now.'

He put his hand into a small pocket in his robe and pulled out a large handsome silver watch on a chain and looked at it. 'Ah, I see that it is getting on, I must go and no doubt this is Amos coming to tell me that I am needed.'

They had heard the click of the latch on the gate and turned to see the stocky figure of Amos ambling across the yard to where they sat.

'Sorry to bother you now, Joseph, but Ethan has a few concerns about the packing and requires your help,' said Amos as he came closer.

'Yes, I know, Amos, I am coming now.' He stood up and helped Marilla to her feet retaining her hand in his for a moment as he looked steadily into her bewildered green eyes. 'Don't be too long in giving it some thought, Miss Marilla, we must know soon as we leave in a few days.'

He stood, still holding her hand and said quietly, 'Ask any questions you wish of Elias or Amos about the running of things in general, they will have the answers to most of them.'

Upon releasing her hand and his gaze, he executed a slight bow in a quaint old- fashioned manner, nodded to Amos, then sweeping his robes about him against the sudden breeze that had sprung up, Joseph strode away leaving Marilla to stare after him.

'Quite a character, isn't he?' said Amos watching the retreating figure of Joseph pass through the latch gate. 'You know, in the time that I was here, Joseph was the one person I never got close to. He spent most of his time in his laboratory and fussing among his plants, he hardly ever spoke. Who would have thought that Peter Gleeson was his brother?'

'His *brother!*'

'Yes, the man you were trying to catch up with back there in the woods before he fell over that cliff was Joseph's brother. I don't think anyone here knew that they were brothers. Now where's—'

'Amos—Amos, where is Jack? I want to talk to him.'

'Well now, isn't that a coincidence, because he sent me to find you.'

At that moment Isabella appeared at Marilla's elbow. She nodded to Amos and said excitedly. 'Marilla, Elias and one of the others are going to harness the donkeys up to go down to the village. They're running short of stock feed and … and Elias is going to look around for a buyer.' Her brown eyes filled with tears, 'he really doesn't want to sell them, it's a shame they can't stay here don't you think?'

Before Marilla could find an answer, Isabella gushed on, 'I'm going to go with them Marilla, Elias says I can … if I want to … you don't mind, do you?'

Marilla looked at her younger sister, perhaps really seeing something about her for the first time, Marilla herself was feeling a force, a sense of purpose that she had not felt before. Perhaps, just perhaps, there was truth in what Joseph had said — they were meant to be here … but why, why here?'

'No, of course I don't mind, you do what you want, Isabella. I have to talk to Jack, where is he, Amos?'

'In the kitchen, I'll just have a quick word with Elias and meet you there.'

Marilla found Jack alone in the warmth of the great kitchen. A fire flickered comfortably in the huge grate, he was sitting with his back to it, a mug of coffee at his elbow and a large book open in front of him. He looked up as she entered and gave her a quick smile. 'I'll get you something hot to drink.' He busied himself at the stove for a minute and soon she had a steaming mug in front of her as she took a seat opposite him. She thanked him with a nod and wrapped her chill fingers around the mug for its warmth, then said slowly and deliberately, 'I think it's about time we laid all our cards on the table, Jack. I don't know what's going on here, this is a very strange place. I'm not even sure that this is actually a monastery at all. Why is Joseph telling us now that Isabella and I are "meant to be here", for what and why? Most importantly, Jack Grimsby….' she said leaning further over the table and fixing him with her challenging green eyes. 'What connection has Edwina with this place, and why with a monk?'

'So, you have been speaking with Joseph?'

'Yes, he tells me he has met and spoken with her, was it here, if so, why?'

'I believe it might have been here, but some time ago now,' replied Jack. He pushed the book he had been reading to one side, leaning his forearms on the table said, 'I am aware now of why we are being drawn to this place and yes, it is being used as a monastery but it doesn't mean to say that it is inhabited only by monks. In fact, this whole place belongs to my uncle, my mother's only brother.'

'Your *uncle*! Who?'

'His name is Henri Du Pont, he has owned this pile of decaying splendour for many years.'

'Well, where is he — is he here?'

Jack hesitated. 'Sort of … in a way he is, perhaps more than we are aware of. He's a wizard, Marilla and a very powerful one I fancy.'

He then proceeded to carefully relate just a little of his meeting with his disembodied uncle in the small circular room with the scrying glass but was careful not to reveal too much about the icon itself. Nor indeed did he tell her that she and her sister were brought down here on purpose and it *had* definitely been Edwina's doing.

Marilla listened in mute amazement and was at last beginning to understand why she had felt another presence about her. Something or someone she herself had no control over but could obviously control her. It was an uncomfortable feeling, she wasn't happy about not being able to have domination over her own thoughts. She sat silent for a few moments while she absorbed this information, then, 'Jack, you had said earlier that you had other business to attend to here, I presume it is this "treasure hunt" as you call it that you have to conduct. Has this been planned to include Isabella and myself, why? We don't even know what this treasure is!' She pushed a strand of hair from her face and sat back, watching him closely. 'Joseph has as much hinted, in fact he was almost insistent that we should stay, as caretakers of some kind. He seems to think we need a place to stay but what happens if we don't — are we going to be permitted to leave? Who or what is going to hold us here?'

'Your conscience perhaps, or your curiosity and the fact that I'm asking for your help,' replied Jack, his grey eyes fixed steadily on her defiant green ones. He wasn't going to tell her all that Henri had said about their future being tied up in the Abbey itself. They wouldn't understand that any more than he could at the moment.

'Then from what you have said, this is all about finding this missing heirloom belonging to your mother.'

'Yes; but there's more to it than just finding it, Marilla, you see, I'm not the only person looking for it.'

Marilla gave an exasperated shake of her head. 'If your uncle is the wizard that you say he is, why can't he tell you where it is, or find it for you?'

'Because he was the one who hid it.'

'Oh,' Marilla buried her head in her hands, 'this is all too hard, Jack and I don't understand any of this at all, why hide it, then expect you to find it?'

Jack grimaced and gave a short bitter laugh. 'My very odd uncle also has a strange sense of humour and he has turned this whole thing into a "treasure hunt" — us against the enemy, a race to see who gets to it first.'

Marilla lifted her head and looked at him questioningly, 'And just who is this enemy we are talking about?'

Jack sat back and folded his arms across his chest. 'Well, for a start, he holds the inherent title of a Baron. His full title is Baron Ernst Stefan Vladmir Von Zaharoff — you wouldn't know him. However, Marilla,' Jack leant his forearms back onto the table again. 'I will explain to you as much as you need to know if you will just listen and try to understand,' he said softly.

'I know it does sound strange that my uncle should hide the heirloom here and yet not tell me exactly where it is. This … other person who is looking for it has been here before to try and find it but it was the wrong time. He will come again … and soon. The treasured piece is hidden in a place that apparently can only be revealed at a certain time of the year. I have to say, Marilla that this other person is a very dangerous man, he was responsible for my mother's death and this man will not hesitate to kill anyone who gets in his way. It is Edwina and Henri who want to see justice done, this is their way of arranging it, odd as it may seem.'

Marilla sat in silence for a long time while she finished her coffee, letting its warmth seep into her. Jack in turn said nothing also. He could see that she was having some difficulty in getting her head around all that he had told her. Finally, she put the mug down on the table and said in a calm even voice, 'What do *you* want us to do, Jack?'

'Stay here for a while, you really don't have anywhere else to go, we both know that. There's everything you need here and best of all it's private.'

'And in return, we help you hunt for your family heirloom, is that right?'

'Yes, it would appear that whatever force brought you here was a planned event, we don't have any choice but to follow it through, or as far as we dare. I do not want to put you and your sister in any danger, though you both certainly proved that you could handle a dangerous situation where the Casinis were concerned but this could be different, if you would rather not be here, then I would willingly put you out of harm's way, perhaps back in Harewood for the time.' He reached out and placed his hand over hers. 'I would never have thought that I would meet you both again after I left Harewood. I really don't want any harm to come to either of you, I have always regarded you both as family, just remember this was *not* my idea!'

'I realise that, I think you should also realise that we are not about to turn our back on a friend, or family, whatever the danger.'

Jack gave her hand a light squeeze and stood up to begin pacing the floor. 'I would have preferred that no one else be involved with—with the Baron. I feel it is my responsibility alone but my uncle has made this complicated, the stage is set unfortunately. However, I do trust my uncle, strange as his ideas may seem, plus Edwina would have all our interests at heart and not expose us to danger if she did not have faith in us … do you see what I mean, Marilla?'

'So, it would seem, I guess,' she said, 'but it still does not explain why you need us here, unless this was the purpose in us being tossed down here to help you look for it. It's *your* family heirloom, you know what it looks like, why can't you solve this riddle and find it yourself?'

'You forget, we are policemen, there is still unfinished business with the Casinis that Amos and I have to attend to but should not take us away any longer than three or four weeks at the most to get the necessary paperwork out of the way. The monks will be ready to leave in a day or so now, so Joseph tells me but Elias has decided to remain for a while. If it is agreed that you will stay, Elias will be here to fetch and carry for you, firewood and provisions, anything you need, as you are still not familiar with the place. Elias has been here for a long time, you will need someone with intimate knowledge of the monastery to guide you, even though you will be free to wander where you will.'

He came and sat down again resting his intertwined fists on the table. 'So, what's your answer; are you prepared to venture into the unknown again and help me find this treasure?'

Marilla looked into the grey eyes and saw the concern there of a troubled mind. 'Well, I don't see why not now. Isabella certainly has made up her mind about it. She seems to have found this place to her liking. She's absolutely potty about animals and growing things, always has her pockets full of odd things she finds, she would be happy to be here.'

'And you?'

She looked down at her fingers for a moment, before glancing up catching his gaze again, and hesitated briefly before she spoke, 'Somehow … I think I just might find a niche here … at least for a while. I have to admit that this pile of decaying splendour as you call it has an air of mystery and intrigue about it, except for one thing.'

'What is that?'

'Your uncle,' said Marilla flatly, 'knowing that he is a wizard and that he is here somewhere, is just a little bit unnerving!'

'Why should that bother you? I would have thought he could be helpful, in any case he won't be here. He's off somewhere for the next few weeks, you won't see him.'

'I just don't like the thought of being controlled … by someone else,' she said testily.

'There's no control over you,' said Jack, 'that incident at the falls when Isabella was in danger from Moody was only to show you what you can be capable of, his capture was largely due to you.'

'But it was his magic, not mine!'

'Not entirely, Marilla, you do have strong magical powers but you're still so unsure of yourself. It's all there within you,

you have to bring those powers into being and hone those skills without losing confidence in your unique abilities. Remember also, there are great things to be achieved with or without magic, it depends on how and when you use it … or not at all. It's up to you whether you rely on magic or your own natural resources.'

'You're beginning to sound like Grandma Hackett,' she retorted.

There was silence again for a short while, with no comment from Jack. Then Marilla continued. 'Do you remember when we were kids at Harewood, do you remember the games we used to play by the stream?'

'Yes, I do,' he replied, 'I used to tease you mercilessly then, I had hoped you would have been able to eventually push outside influences aside and not let your concentration stray. Complete concentration is all part of it, without that you can have little or no control over your magic. However, I have to say that you certainly did get it all together when we were down in the cellars, you dropped that bottle of wine on Bruno's head. That was a sight I will never forget.'

'Why didn't you stay at Harewood, Jack?' Marilla asked suddenly, 'Why did you leave?'

Jack hesitated before answering. 'Several reasons I suppose. I could never see myself in the role of a warlock or wizard. I couldn't see any future in it. I would probably finish up like your mother, eking out a living telling fortunes in a circus tent. I wanted to help people and I suppose I had great ideas when I took up medicine fairly early in my life but I soon learned that magic and medicine don't mix in the present day. It might be alright for some Shaman in the jungle but it's a dangerous liaison and only leads to more confusion that can only do more harm than good. Magic has its place I suppose but it's only a very small place, unless you can merge those talents with something that's really useful, so I couldn't see any point in it. You can't change the world with a few incantations and a couple of mystic spells, sometimes it takes a bit more than that to find the right answer to make a credible conclusion to a problem.'

He looked keenly at her from across the table. 'Where you and Isabella have had rather a sheltered life, I guess I've seen more of the world and the different people in it than either of you have, I've learnt to find my way around problems without having to over exercise those inborn gifts — if you could call them that — unnecessarily but then, I'm only half warlock,' and he grinned at her, she couldn't help but smile back but her thoughts were elsewhere, there was something about him and where he had come from that still eluded her.

She was just about to ask the question she had pondered on in those early years ... his parents, when the door opened, and Amos strode in heading straight over to the fire to warm his hands. 'Hey, you two, you're not keeping an eye on this fire here, how about a bit of wood on it!'

As he opened the grate and began re-fuelling the glowing coals, he announced in his deep resonant voice that Elias and one of the lay brothers had been making an estimate of what feed stocks were left in the barns for the coming winter and that when he had left, three grey robed figures were already making their way down to the village in the donkey carts, and one of them was Isabella.

'Isabella wearing monk's robes!' exclaimed Marilla incredulously.

'Better to conceal herself under all that grey cloth than have the whole village gawking and gossiping if she went like she was,' said Amos as he slammed the grate shut. 'Anyway, we don't want to tarnish the reputation of the monastery now do we, even if the lads are leaving?' He had turned around to face them and was rubbing his backside in the ensuing warmth.

'The villagers accept the monk's grey habit and show respect for them,' he said seriously, 'and they don't look too hard to see just who is under the cowl, we've proved that right enough. I don't know whether you are aware of it, Miss Marilla but the female equivalent of the Franciscan Friars are the "Poor Clare Nuns" and the habits are identical, well mostly. Isabella was quite enjoying herself dressing up when I left them and looking forward to the adventure of going down to the village with Elias. It makes a good disguise and an easy transition wouldn't you say?' He winked at Jack as he turned back to the kettle which was now beginning to come to a boil again and was issuing a strong head of steam.

'I don't know about you lot,' he said, 'but a large hot drink would go down well right now.'

Part Two

Chapter 26

The Search Begins

Isabella was sitting thoughtfully on the long window seat that occupied a niche in the far corner of the library. Her knees were drawn up around her chin and her hands wrapped around them. She had been staring almost unseeing out of one of the small panes of glass set in the vaulted Gothic window beside her, her thoughts alternating between what she had been reading and what she could see.

It had been snowing now since the previous evening, a thick blanket of white covered all that she could see of the courtyard below. The roofs of the adjacent buildings were also wearing a mantle of white, where soft flurries of fresh snow had recently added another layer. Even the gargoyles that adorned the top of nearby buildings were hung with stiff beards of frost giving the appearance of small dwarfs crouching there. As she watched, a pale winter sun gradually emerged from behind the now retreating clouds, its' watery glow strengthening, as the veils of rolling mists diminished.

'I'm tired of looking at all these books. Jack certainly left us with a difficult problem to solve,' her sister's voice interrupted her train of thought. 'I'll be glad when he gets back, and he can solve this puzzle himself.'

Marilla leaned back in the simple wooden chair and rubbed the back of her neck as she continued, 'I don't see why we couldn't have just asked Jack's uncle where he's put it and save us the trouble. The only problem with that is, I'm not sure *I really would* want to ask him ... if he's still around. I keep having this feeling that someone is watching us all the time, do you?' She turned to face her sister.

'No, not really, anyway; that's not the point, is it?' said Isabella patiently. 'We have to do as Jack has asked us to. That was the way Edwina had planned it and you know she must have had her reasons for doing it this way. Edwina never did anything without good reason. She must have more knowledge of what this Baron person is like and what he will do to get this heirloom thing of Jack's.'

'Well, all I can say is, it must be pretty important and valuable to be fighting over it, although seems to be a long-winded way to go about finding it.'

'Oh, I don't know.' Isabella unclasped her knees and ran a hand through her mop of bushy hair. 'It is helping to pass the time, we can't do much exploring outside while it's still snowing and you must admit, Marilla that the snow makes everything look so ... so, ethereal. Yes, that's the word ... like we're living in another world and the clouds have come down to meet us. It's lovely don't you think?'

'No, I don't, all I know is my feet are cold, even though I've got my thickest socks on. I wish Elias would hurry up and load that wood box up again; we've only got a couple of big pieces left and they won't take long to burn up.' She looked toward the fires burning steadily in the old fireplaces and began estimating how long it would take before she had to re-fuel them.

Isabella tore her eyes away from the stark white beauty that had so entranced her, swung her feet to the floor and picked up the book she had been reading. 'Well, we certainly know a lot more about the monastery now; there are some wonderful books here. I'm glad the monks didn't take them all. There's an amazing amount of history about this place, it's almost too much to believe that it was built so many centuries ago. It almost feels like we're walking back into time, though I don't know that I'd really like to have lived back then, they must have been very stressful times,' she mused, raising her arms above her head and stretching up.

She got up from the window seat and walked over to where her sister was seated at one of the reading tables, a large heavy book open on the lectern in front of her.

'Which one are you reading?' she said as she leaned over her sister's shoulder. 'Oh, I've only partially looked through that one so far, I found it very interesting; see here it shows some old pictures of the abbey including when the church was built but what's more, it gives a complete floor plan of the church; but of course that was built at a much later date.' She stabbed at the page with her finger. 'I've got the feeling that that's where we should be looking, not in the abbey itself. Didn't Jack say that his uncle took to wandering around the church as well at night?'

*   *   *

It had been several weeks since the monks had left the abbey, followed by Jack and Amos a short time later, using the expensive limousine Victor Casini had left behind. It would be needed as evidence anyway but for the moment it would be comfortable transport for the Special Forces agents as they left to finalise documentation of the mountain of incriminating evidence that would put the Casinis well out of the public eye for a considerable amount of time. There was also the Coroner's inquiry they would need to attend in the cases of their colleague, Daniel Montaigne and the accidental death of the unfortunate acting Abbot — Peter Gleeson.

In the meantime, the sisters had not been left entirely on their own. Elias could barely contain his delight at the prospect of staying on at the abbey and ministering to the needs of the sisters. He extended his gratitude towards them, particularly Isabella, whom he regarded as a kindred spirit and with the help of both girls he was always ready to help in the running of the farm part of the monastery. Little matter that Elias was now gardener, woodcutter and general handyman to the two witches. As Jack and Amos rightly guessed it did not take too much persuasion to encourage Marilla to stay, particularly when a riddle was produced as a guide to the treasure they were to help find, she and Isabella loved solving riddles.

Jack had spoken earnestly to them when they had met to discuss their task in the warmth and comfort of Henri's private quarters. The great oak panelled room's Gothic obscurity giving an aura of medieval mystery to the complicated problem he was to set before them.

He had now produced the carefully folded piece of paper they had seen him take that first day from within the lining of the boot that had still clung to the body on the bed in that dreadful room. It now lay as a yellowing scrap carefully opened upon the huge oaken desk together with a calendar and some writing paper.

'This I expect,' said Jack indicating the aged piece of parchment, 'is Edwina's work, she would have had the imagination to construct this. I would like you both now to read it carefully and then each make a note of it, word for word for yourselves.' Marilla leaned forward and carefully picked up the paper, still slightly crumpled from its many folded creases. Badly stained by time and dampness, the yellowed parchment was barely decipherable but she could still read it. She held it prudently between her fingers and read the words aloud.

'Take heed the angel borne on high
That rides aloft the rainbowed sky
For a golden shaft shall light the way
At the dawning of mid-winters day
Thirteen across and nine as deep
Would'st wake the cherub from his sleep
For he that will with patience bide
The tree of Life would'st be thy guide
Cursed be he who moves with haste
For life therein is doomed to waste
Beware ye then the wrath of Ka
Who's sword would'st slay thee as thou are.'

Isabella carefully took the paper from Marilla and read it herself, before placing it back on the desk. 'That seems very positive doesn't it? I guess from what I can understand of that, is we are looking for an angel, or perhaps a cherub ... is it a picture or a figure we are looking for? Can you tell us any more Jack?'

'Yes, Bella I can,' said Jack. 'It's a small figurine of a cherub but it's not the cherub itself that matters so much at this point ... it's what it's in.'

'How do you mean, "What it's in"?' said Marilla.

Jack pulled the writing paper toward him, he quickly drew a rectangular shape. 'It's an ivory box, about that size,' he explained. 'It's roughly about seven inches by about four and a half inches to make dimensions easier to understand. A very intricately carved and beautifully crafted box from what I can remember, a magnificent piece of work in itself. I was still quite young when Edwina showed it to me but I do remember it ... more importantly, I remember what she did with it and that is what I have to make very clear to you both now. If you do manage to locate the box and figurine before I get back, I would ask that you leave it in its hiding place. You must on no account be tempted to open it. This is extremely important.'

His grey eyes darkened as he spoke next and his voice had taken a more sinister note. 'If you pick it up and attempt to open it, it would be fatal to you — witches or no. No amount of magic will bring you back from death. Now, if you will I must ask you to give me your word on this. You are witches yourselves and you must know what consequences can occur in the realm of high witchcraft.'

The sisters nodded and gave their oath. Edwina was not one to be taken lightly in the world of witchcraft. They then copied out the words carefully from the parchment on the paper provided, so each had a copy. The original was carefully folded again; Jack would keep that ... it would give him something to think about in the quieter moments.

Those chilling words Jack had spoken remained uppermost in the minds of the sisters as they began delving into the task of understanding the meaning of the puzzle set before them.

*   *   *

Marilla pushed back her chair, stood up and yawned. 'All the same,' she added wistfully, 'I wish Jack and Amos were still here. I don't like the sound of this Baron person, he sounds positively evil. The fact that he was responsible, as Jack claims, for his mother's death was reason enough for personal revenge.'

She stood for a moment idly leafing through the pages of the book on the lectern, then turned to her sister. 'You know there's something still very mysterious about Jack Grimsby ... if that is his real name.'

'What do you mean — "if that's his real name"?'

'Bella,' said Marilla patiently, 'you had more to do with him than me when we were kids. Did he ever say anything about his parents to you at any time?'

'No, never, he rarely ever said anything at all, why?'

'Because ... I'm not sure Edwina ever had any children of her own. Let alone a grandson.'

'Why would you think that?' asked Isabella, her curiosity aroused.

'I'm not really sure,' mused Marilla. 'I'm just wondering if there is a connection with a Baron. You must admit there's a lot we don't know about Jack Grimsby, even after all these years and I feel certain that even though Edwina adopted him, he's no relation at all!'

'Even if she did adopt him, she can still call him her grandson, can't she?'

'Yes, but it's his real parents I'm curious about,' replied Marilla. 'And he claims he's half warlock!' She sat down again in the chair becoming engrossed in her own thoughts for a few more minutes before she spoke again. 'Isabella, you know ... we're not sure just what we are getting ourselves into here. Where does the Wiccan heritage come from with Jack?'

Both sisters looked at each other in mute uncertainty.

Marilla sat broodingly for a few more moments, then said quietly, 'I didn't understand it at first; but I once chanced to overhear a conversation between Edwina and Grandma Hackett. Edwina had just come back from one of those long trips away that she used to make when we were growing up. As a matter of fact, it was not long before we left Harewood ourselves. They were talking about Jack and Edwina was referring to someone I'm sure was Jack's mother ... something he had to find for his mother's sake and not let him have it.' She paused and looked at her sister who was listening in wonderment. 'It's all fitting together now, that evil person Edwina was alluding to must have been this Baron person ... Zaharoff that was the name Jack said. Edwina said he would kill anyone who got in his way, that's exactly what Jack has told us!' She turned back to the desk and picked up the piece of paper she had placed there. 'Edwina also said something about a code, it would lure him there and the hand of fate, which had been a long time coming now, would play the rest.'

'Lure who — Jack or this Baron?'

'Both, I think,' murmured Marilla softly. 'It sounds like something that can only be sorted out between two people, Jack Grimsby and the Baron and it's going to be played out here, in this old abbey.'

'You've never mentioned any of this before.'

'Because I've only just remembered it, Bella,' said Marilla almost crossly. 'As I said it was just before we left Harewood ourselves, there were a lot of other things to think about at that time. Plus there has been so much going on here since the night we dropped in, that it just didn't register!'

'So if this Baron what's-his-name killed or had a hand in Jack's mother's death, where is his father? Which one was Wiccan? Where does this Baron fit into the family, if he ever was part of the family?' said Isabella half to herself.

'He may be an uncle or something, who knows. Anyway, one thing is for sure,' said Marilla as she carefully slipped the piece of paper with the riddle on it into the book she had been reading, 'there's a lot more to this than Jack has been willing to tell us, he has even admitted that.' She shivered slightly as she stood up, pushing her chair back. 'I've got an itchy feeling up my spine Isabella that this could be a lot more sinister than anything the Casinis could ever dream up.'

'Then perhaps we had better take Jack's warning a lot more seriously.' replied Isabella. 'I wonder ... I wonder if we shouldn't try to talk to this Uncle Henri through that scrying glass of his.'

'I think you'll find Jack has already anticipated that thought so I don't think we can access that room.'

'Why not?'

'Because Joseph is apparently the keeper of the key to that room and he's not here, is he?' Marilla replied bluntly. 'Besides which, Joseph is his emissary and as far as we know he is the only one who can reach Henri, so more than likely there is a spell on that door to stop anyone else from getting in. In any case,' she added seriously, 'I'm not sure that I'm really ready to meet this wizard just yet.'

Isabella was just about to ask another question when there was a soft knock at the door, it opened to reveal Elias standing there. 'Sorry to bother you ladies but I've got a load of wood to bring in. Should have had it in here for you earlier but I've been checking supplies, I've discovered there's a couple of things I need to get from the village.

'It has stopped snowing and it should be quite nice out. I was wondering, er, well, I was wondering if you'd care to join me. It would get you out for a bit.'

'You go, Bella, I'll stay here.'

'No, I want you to come too, Marilla, it's a charming little place. You do have to see it sometime you know, so why not now

... and we do need some fresh air, we seem to have been cooped up for days. The donkey carts are really quite comfortable and we shall see so much more of the scenery than we can from our windows, who knows when we'll get another fine afternoon.'

Marilla hesitated, 'Would I have to wear one of those grey robe things?'

'I'm afraid so,' said Elias. 'You see, they do disguise you very well, you would be most conspicuous as you are,' he said with a smile, his eyes quickly travelling over the bright multitude of clothing the sisters were fond of wearing. 'The cloaks are voluminous and will cover your other clothing adequately and ...' he hesitated before continuing, 'it would appear that a rumour exists in the village that a group of "Poor Clare Nuns", who incidentally wear the same habit are to become residents of the Abbey of St Dominica for an indeterminate period. Of course, it doesn't mean anything much to the locals,' he hurried on to say as he watched the expression on Marilla's face changing, 'they are so used to seeing the cowled habit, they never look to see the person beneath.'

Marilla was looking at Elias with a stunned look on her face; then to his surprise, she laughed, albeit a little grimly and said, 'Now, I wonder who put a rumour like that around?'

The air was still crisp and cool but it had indeed stopped snowing, even though the falls had been light; now bright sunlight flooded the courtyard as the feet of three grey- hooded figures crunched their way over the thin layer of snow to the stables. Two donkeys were already patiently waiting, harnessed into the sturdy little wooden carts they were so accustomed to pulling up and down the mountainside. Even though part of the stables held a motor vehicle that had been bought by Peter Gleeson some time ago, Elias still preferred to use his patient four-legged form of transport. Elias had no trust in cars, maintaining they were too troublesome to handle, he would only drive it if he had no other choice.

Elias helped Isabella into one of the little carts, then turned his attention to Marilla. 'Isabella can handle Faith quite well on her own, you and I will take Flora. Don't worry they are very sure-footed on the slope, even with the snow. I would rather trust them than that four wheeled contraption in the back of the shed.'

So it was with that, they trod their slow and careful way

down the mountain slope toward the village, nestled far below them amongst the snow-clad pines, the little donkeys placing their feet carefully on the path they knew so well. From her perch on the wooden seat next to Elias, Marilla gazed about her. This was certainly a new form of travel, seeing things from a different angle and as they began to wind their way around the mountainside road, the view down the long valley opened up, she could see the lake and the encompassing pine forest bordering its' edges. The high peaks of the distant mountains rose above them, their tops lost in the snowy swirl of white clouds, remaining there as a permanent veil of white mistiness. The dark green of pines standing to attention, straight and tall, dusted with an icing of snow, looked like defenders on guard below the majestic mountains. As Marilla gazed at the vista spreading out before her, she was reminded of the picture postcards one sees in tourist brochures, an almost unreal representation of alpine wilderness, the image doubled in the still icy waters of the lake, presenting a double delight.

Marilla's mind shifted, she was recalling their last place of lodging, she was also remembered the lingering smell of cooking, mingled with stale tobacco smoke and alcohol that hung thickly over everything. The constant sound of shuffling feet, the wheezing and coughing of too many people in one small place jostling for survival in a different sort of wilderness. Marilla quickly shut that picture from her mind and breathed in the fresh pure air.

The road widened a little as they came down onto the lake road, Marilla recognised the waterfall and the craggy rocks at the edge of the lake. She remembered with a jolt the strange feeling of power that had enveloped her that day when Isabella's life was threatened by the odd little brown man they called Moody ... and she ... or something else had turned him into a bat. She closed her eyes, trying to remember again how it felt; but it was vague now. However; it had given her a sense of the positives that she could achieve. All it needed was confidence and that was growing.

How different it all looked now with just the tips of the reeds and the water grasses protruding from their covering of snow. Even the elms and poplars stretching their bare branches upward were garlanded with wreaths of the crisp whiteness, there was more snow piled deeply in the hollows and roots of these stately sentinels. Exempt from the sun's rays of light and warmth, they would remain as deep drifts throughout the winter.

Glancing back, she could see Isabella, seated like a little Buddha with her grey cloak wrapped tightly around her, following closely behind and noted how easily she held the reins of the sturdy little donkey that trotted along so obediently under her control. Marilla had also noted how easily her younger sister had adapted to life in the old abbey, which, since the monks had gone did not seem like an abbey at all now, just a big old and rambling empty house. Isabella was changing, she thought — she was happier, more contented with life and perhaps, just perhaps, she herself should look through her sister's eyes. Marilla had always considered her sister too immature to make major decisions but somehow, now, that seemed a contestable point. Isabella had shown maturity and courage in a dangerous situation when trapped in the crypt with Amos, she had seemed completely unfazed by it all, quite contrary to Marilla's own anxieties.

Perhaps too, when this 'treasure hunt' of Jack's was over and they were free to make their own choices, what would that choice be for her? Marilla had a feeling that she knew already ... if that were possible.

She turned back to watch the road ahead and sighed. Elias

who had said very little during the trek down the mountain track now turned to speak to her. 'You've been very quiet, Miss Marilla, what are you thinking, or are they private thoughts?'

'I don't know, Elias,' she said softly. 'I think I'm beginning to see why you were reluctant to leave this place. It's really quite beautiful, even now in the winter.'

Elias laughed, a good-humoured throaty laugh. 'Well, I've had a good few years to let this place take over me, I wouldn't want to be anywhere else. The abbey is home to me and always will be, despite its draughty corridors.'

Marilla smiled but then grew suddenly quite serious again. 'Elias, you do know that we are witches and capable of all sorts of witchcraft? Isn't it going to ... worry you, being alone all the way up here ... alone with us?'

'I can't see why it should,' replied Elias carefully. 'I have seen and heard enough to know that there are distinctions between what could be called black magic and white magic. One is used for evil destructiveness and the other, white magic, which can be used to ward off such attacks of evil, as well as to perhaps prevent or lessen such calamities. In itself, one can say magic is not good, or evil, it is the intention in the mind of the witch that makes the difference.'

Marilla opened her mouth to say something but quickly shut it again before taking a sidelong glance at her companion. His square-jawed, homely farmer's face gave nothing away as he directed the donkey's path across a small wooden bridge that marked the entrance to the little village. Before she could say anything, Elias answered for her. 'We do more than just repair books, manuscripts and things, Miss Marilla; we read them and so much other information as well. Reading and learning all manner of things is an occupation other than gardening in a place like the abbey. Now, keep your cowl down more over your face and stay silent for a little, while I get through this bit of business.'

Marilla did as instructed but looked furtively about her from under the folds of the hood. It did indeed look as Isabella had described to her, almost a storybook village with its neat rows of timber houses and white picket fences facing a tree-lined main street.

Across the road a different building caught her eye; a double storey building, one of very few in the town. Its' steep grey slate roof overhung whitewashed walls and its' deep bay windows facing the street set with mullioned windows were prettily edged with a frosting of snow, as was the roof similarly encrusted. Dark timbers patterned the high-pitched gables in stark contrast, so too the tenacious ivy that etched its tortuous path across the face of the Inn. Its' front court was dominated by a huge elm sheltering several small weather-worn tables and benches beneath the spreading branches, bare now all carrying their mantle of snow.

They were soon past it, and Marilla looked with interest at the little shops crowded near what must be the village square, a bright patch of what would normally be a swathe of green, but now dotted thickly with the winters' snow. Several tall spreading elms would offer summertime shade, which now, stood naked, except for their sparse clothing of fresh snow. Beyond the village square she could see the single spire of what would be the village church, standing tall amongst the surrounding roofs of the houses.

Marilla caught glimpses here and there of colourful goods displayed in the shop windows, but Elias did not pause in his progress through the village. His major destination was the flour mill set on the other side of this hamlet bordering the green fields that seemed to stretch on forever. Nearby, an all-purpose hardware establishment provided another essential, then on to the grain store, where Isabella enthusiastically assisted Elias in loading up the second cart with feed grain. His shopping list completed; Elias asked the sisters if they needed anything for themselves before they began the return journey.

'No,' they replied, Amos had been thoughtful enough to provide all that was needed for the moment from the bulging suitcases of goods he had presented to them, though how he had managed to obtain everything in the correct sizes and needs for two women he had only just met was still a mystery to them. In any case Isabella had remarked, there was no reason why they shouldn't come down by themselves later, should there be a need.

Very few people were about, even though the early afternoon was still full of sunshine and those that were, gave the small group little more than a passing glance. Their passage back past the Inn however, drew much more interest from the man seated at one of the bay windows. He had closely watched their passage across the rustic bridge and on through the village from his vantage point in the corner of the far window. He was still there, a half empty glass in front of him when the little cavalcade passed by again to take the lake road and out of the village. His swarthy body was made even more gorilla-like in a fur coat, a head hugging cap of the same pulled down low over his face. Dark eyes under heavy lids, glittered as he watched the grey-cloaked procession pass by. His thick fingers closed around the glass and he picked it up and drained the contents. Then easing his great body out from behind the table, he rose from his seat and climbed the wooden staircase that led to the upper floors of the Inn and knocked softly at the door of one of the rooms.

Chapter 27

A Watchful Eye

In the days that followed the return of Jack and Amos to their police duties, Marilla and Isabella, somewhat tentatively at first began exploring the abbey. Empty of monks and their simple belongings, the deathly silence that now settled on the empty halls and corridors was almost unnerving. Even the sound of their own footsteps echoing in the vast emptiness of the cloistered walls aroused an eerie presentment and they more than once found themselves looking furtively over their shoulders.

The sisters had now become settled in their new home, which had been renamed, 'The Lodge' at Jack's suggestion. The change of name had made the transition complete and the sisters found that it was indeed much more spacious than anything they had called home previously. Though both sisters had also declared that they could look after themselves quite adequately in their own way and had done so since leaving Harewood, it was still very comforting to have Elias around.

He was a quiet man who kept mostly to himself, his daily chores revolved around his basic responsibilities. There was always a good supply of wood needed to feed the huge kitchen stove and the few other fireplaces that would be in use. There were livestock to feed and care for and of course the garden to keep in order, though at this time of year, most of it lay dormant. Isabella had taken great delight in helping Elias with the chores and took it upon herself to feed the hens and collect the eggs from the straw nesting boxes. He had watched her with a grin on his rugged face as she walked through the hen house chattering to the hens as if they were children and scattering the grain for them while they clucked and scratched beneath her feet.

Isabella had once asked Elias how long he had been at the abbey. 'All my life pretty well, at least as much as I can remember clearly,' he said as he removed his old cap and scratched lazily behind one ear. 'My parents were dead and a maiden aunt, my only relative; couldn't really care for me, as she was getting on in years; so she brought me here thinking the monks could find work for me in exchange for my keep. As it turned out they needed someone to fetch and carry for them, then when I showed a natural aptitude for gardening, that became the major part of my duties. A place, isolated as much as this is, has to be self- sufficient for everything and I have to say it's pretty well set up the way I like it. That's why I just couldn't walk away from it. Can you see that now, Miss Isabella?'

Isabella had nodded her head in agreement, remembering with delight the fusion of colour and productivity in the garden when they had walked through that first day.

Elias had already shown them much of the working parts of the complex. They had also ventured below again to the cellars, the scene of their dramatic encounters with the Casinis. This time however, it was to show them where the storage rooms were with the big freezer and refrigerators. Even though he had turned lights on, the darkened corners and the eerie silence, broken only by the distant hum of the generator, still made their skin prickle. The only sign of the recent struggle was a dark wine stain on the floor of one of the rooms, where the wine bottle had smashed down onto Bruno's head. Marilla had glanced at the room opposite and noticed the pile of crates she had hidden behind still there.

Isabella's eyes were drawn to the short flight of steps that led down to the heavy door she could just see in the light of the single bulb from the ceiling. Even though the thick oaken door was shut, she thought she could still smell that musty, earthy smell again, the dust of centuries and long dead bodies. She shivered as she recalled how close she and Amos had come to dying down there. The danger had washed over her then but the thought now filled her with a delayed sense of shock.

It was with a sense of relief that they finally emerged from the cellars and Isabella was able to breathe the pure, if somewhat chilly air, appreciating how good it felt. Elias then left them, to go about his duties so the sisters made their way back to the complex.

They had roamed over most of the abbey in the weeks that followed, marvelling at its high timbered ceilings, ornate mouldings and the half-hidden niches sheltering dusty works of art. In a contrast to this ambience, there was a suit of medieval armour gracing the huge front hall.

Though this ecclesiastical and ancient monastery breathed pure Gothic in its outer form, the impressive façade now bore the signs of deep decay in its age-old walls. The massive buttresses still stood firm but there were places where cracks in the vaulted arches and ornate stonework had widened slowly over the passage of years, as water seeped in, discolouring the stone. Weathering and the stains of centuries pockmarked the thick stone walls, while atop them the carved figures of leering gargoyles adorning the frayed battlements crouched in defiant postures of demonic scorn at the minions below. Though it still stood, an imposing and formidable structure, it would still take some time and of course money, to repair it, if it ever was going to be repaired.

The interior was, of course, kept in a reasonable state of repair, retaining much of its original identity. The lofty rooms with the dark beamed ceilings and the walls were still hung with time enamelled tapestries and paintings; these had been left as they were. Small, exquisite statues and bronze pieces in the niches around the walls lent their air of mystery to this medieval monastery with its chequered history. It was still, after all, a private residence and owned by a wizard.

The adjacent chapel built at a much later date, standing a little apart from the abbey itself, stood, a spiritual haven poised on the brink of infinity, so to speak; its outer walls almost as one with the soaring cliffs of the deep gorge, like the eyrie of some great bird. Even with its recent damage and the shattered panes of stained glass leaving a gaping hole where they had once been, the chapel still retained an air of dignity and solace. Though abandoned by the monks, it still left a reverential aura and the sisters approached it now with slight feelings of trepidation. This seemed the most obvious place to search ... where else to find an angel but in a church ... a place they had been somewhat reluctant to conduct a thorough search of ... until this moment.

Marilla was in fact stating as much, their boots crunching over the covering of crisp snow, as they walked toward the church. 'To me, it seems the most obvious place,' she said as she pulled her thick woollen scarf close about her neck. 'Where else then are we supposed to look for an angel if not in a church?'

'Didn't I tell you that days ago?' said Isabella pointedly. 'We haven't found anything remotely resembling an angel or a cherub in any of the other places in the abbey itself, let alone a rainbow in any of the pictures or tapestries and it has to be a window or opening of some sort anyway, so it's got to be in here somewhere.'

'I know,' grumbled Marilla, 'but it was just as well to have a good look through the abbey first. You don't know until you look.'

'I feel sure there will be something in one of those coloured glass windows,' said Isabella enthusiastically. 'Don't you remember how the sun was shining through them that day we came here? It was throwing coloured patterns on the floor, just like a rainbow.'

'I really didn't take much notice at the time I must admit. I was more concerned about finding out where we were, so I suppose now we'll just have to look at them more closely to see if we can find an angel in one of them,' replied Marilla, as they mounted the steps that led into the back of the nave. 'You know, I would have thought Elias might have been a bit more informative about where this icon thing is.'

'I don't think he was ever given any information about that riddle,' replied Isabella after some thought. 'It did appear to be something just between Jack and this uncle of his.'

'Did you ever think to ask him?' ventured Marilla. 'You seem to be spending a lot of your time in his company.'

Isabella felt the colour rise to her face and she was glad of the dimness of the shadows around the short passage that led into the nave. She hesitated a moment before replying. 'As a matter of fact, I did ... sort of.'

'What do you mean, "sort of", you either asked him or you didn't!'

Isabella stammered hesitantly, then said, 'Um, er, well, you remember when we were going down to the village that day to get feed for the animals, I asked him if he knew what was going on in the abbey ... you know, about Jack and Amos staying on and all that after the Casinis had been taken away. I asked him if he knew why we were, sort of ... being pressured to stay on here after the monks had gone and I just thought he might know the reason why.'

'And?'

'He said that whatever the reason, it was Jack Grimsby's business and he was not going to say anything, whether he knew or not. It was nothing to do with him and that fate had to take its course. So I didn't say anything more about it and we just talked about other things.'

'Well, that was not a lot of help.'

They had entered the interior of the chapel and stood silently in the nave. The omnipresent air of dignity seemed to seep from its very walls, they found themselves almost talking in whispers as their eyes roved this reverential place of worship so beloved of the monks who had lived there.

The remnants of the broken windows had been swept to one side and left as a jumbled mass of glassy colour, like a jigsaw cast aside. Marilla gazed intently at the stained-glass windows that were left and at the vacant spaces on the walls, glaringly bare, like empty eye sockets from whence colour and light had once shone. She walked up and down looking intently at the remaining windows, her forehead creased in a deep frown.

'I can't see anything here that resembles an angel, aren't they supposed to have big white feathered wings?'

'I'm not sure that they're all pictured like that,' said Isabella, tilting her head to one side as she admired a particularly beautiful shade of blue in the bottom corner of one window.

'Some of those in the old paintings from the books we were looking at were more like cherubs with little wings and halos around their heads, like that one up there.' She pointed to a saintly figure garbed in white, hands held in an attitude of prayer with a shining corona encircled above its head.

'Hmm, I wonder if it was in one of those that are broken. It would be a nightmare to try to piece that lot together,' said Marilla, indicating the pile of broken glass with a wave of her hand. 'Jack will be back in a few days' time and we're still no closer to finding this treasure of his.' Her frown deepened further, as she muttered half to herself. 'It's also getting closer to the winter solstice ... mid-winters day, when a golden shaft shall light the way,' she chanted loudly as she turned on the spot, arms held wide, 'but through what and where?' She threw her arms high in frustration. 'Who knows how this crazy wizard's mind was working when he hid the thing.' Her voice echoed in the hollow vastness of the great hall, but no one answered, just her own voice coming back to her.

Isabella was not listening to her sister's impatient ramblings; she was staring up at the huge central dome. 'I wonder if there are windows up there?' she said to no one in particular. Craning her neck, she revolved slowly on the spot slowly scanning the vast dome for any sign of colour; but there was nothing, just the carved wooden beams that met in frescoed panels that ran in sequence to the very top of the dome. Some of the panels were just clear glass to let in some light but there was nothing there that would resemble an angel and it was the same with the smaller dome further back in the inner sanctum.

It would seem they were not going to find an angel anywhere here, even though it appeared to be the most obvious place.

'I don't know where else we can look,' sighed Marilla as she walked to the first of the steps that ran up and into the inner sanctum, she sat there with her elbows resting on her knees. 'We'll just have to wait until Jack gets here and see if he's got any ideas about where else to look. Why did Jack's uncle have to make it all so complicated?'

'I'm sure there must have been a good reason,' replied Isabella as she came to sit beside her sister. 'If he's the wizard Jack says he is and if Edwina had a hand in all this, then you know as well as I do that there must have been a purpose behind all this secrecy, Jack did say the Baron was a dangerous man. We have no reason to think otherwise and apparently, this Baron likes the challenge of a treasure hunt. Plus it is something to keep us occupied too when you think about it.'

'Yes, I suppose so,' sighed Marilla. 'It just seems a mysterious way to go about it.'

As the two women sat in the oppressive silence on the step, Marilla had begun to think. The half-hearted attempts she had been making were gone now and the logical part of her mind was taking over. At last she spoke, 'Bella, it's pretty obvious that there's something about the ivory box that is more important than the treasure itself. You remember Jack told us we were not to attempt to open it if we found it. They *want* the Baron himself to find it because there's something about the box and what is in it, or on it that is apparently fatal to anyone who picks it up. I believe they want the Baron to be the first to handle it, so I suppose they've got their reasons. We have to think like Edwina — now where would I put something like that?' She paused and lifted her head then looked carefully about her as if seeing it all for the first time, she pursed her lips as she thought aloud. 'The first light of the sun, where does the sun-shine through at dawn in here, because this is where it has to be, I'm sure of it now.'

She pointed at the tiled floor in front of where they sat. 'I've been looking at these floor tiles and even though the rest of the floor is paved with all plain ones, there are these coloured ones that run all the way up the centre.' She turned her head to one side. 'Those mosaic ones with pictures in them almost run in a zigzag pattern all the way. It's like a crazy pathway, Bella, but we need that shaft of light to show us if that's the path and just where that path might lead.'

Isabella nodded in agreement, saying, 'We've been looking at the wrong windows too.' she gestured to where pale patterns on the tiled floor were cast from the remaining stained-glass windows. 'That's the wrong direction for the sun at that time of day; because according to what we've been reading, the mid-winter solstice, being the shortest day of the year, the sun should be coming up more to the south at that time.' She stood up and said excitedly, 'There's something else too. I remember reading somewhere in one of the books on the Abbey's history that the sun's rays strike at a very oblique angle at that particular time, so we should be looking for a window on the southern wall, only there are no windows there. The ones we can see, are the big ones we've been looking at and they're in the wrong place to where the sun will be travelling at that time of day. Seems that there's got to be a window of some sort, somewhere in the front but so far all I can see are the tops of those sort of arch things in that front wall. It's a bit dark down there and hard to see anything clearly, there are no more windows anywhere else that we can see.'

Isabella sat down again and stared at the end wall, which was some distance in front of them. She could see a set of heavy doors set in the stone of the church and surmounted by a cluster of ornate columns. She presumed that it could only be the original front doors that looked as if they had not been opened for decades. Her eyes travelled to an area above them scanning the wall area and then she elbowed her sister in the ribs as she said excitedly, 'Look, look, up there Marilla; see where that little balcony overhang thing is, well, look above that. There's an outline, where that arch shape is, see … and it's a little bit lighter than the other parts. It's very dull down that end so it's hard to see and with no direct light coming through, it's very hard to make it out. Can you see it? What do you think — could that be the window we're looking for?'

Marilla stood up and walked back up the steps a short distance in order to get a better look. Being taller than her sister, she was able to see that Isabella was right. There did appear to be a section in the middle of the wall where the faintest of light was visible. A wide ledge supported at intervals by a series of great carved corbels ran across the wall at a height and formed a sort of gallery, surmounted by a narrow balustrade. It did not seem to serve any useful purpose that she could see as there were no steps leading up to it, possibly it was accessed from another direction but what was visible through the gloom behind it was, as Isabella had surmised, the top of a round window. At least it looked like a window and the more she stared at the dimmed outline, the more she was convinced that it held something in coloured glass.

'Perhaps we might be able to see it better from the outside, because that's the front of the building,' suggested Isabella.

'Let's take a look then,' said her sister and together they moved back down the great hall adorned with its splendid columns to where the short flight of steps led them to the front of the church and the ruined gate, through which they had crept in what now seemed another age. They had not bothered to take too much notice of the building they were entering then but now it was different.

What they did notice was the large antechamber or vestibule that they had given little thought to before but now it took their attention. Attached to the front of the church it must have served as the main entrance and no doubt led into the nave through those heavy oaken doors, which were now firmly shut. 'I know what that is,' said Isabella in a hushed whisper, 'there are tombs in there; burial places of benefactors of the old abbey in years gone by, well

... according to that book I read on the history of this place. Apparently, the monks of latter days had no need to use the front entrance, so they closed it up and just use those side steps. I suppose it saves disturbing the ghosts of the old ancestors.' She gave a nervous giggle at her own joke.

Marilla gave her younger sister a withering look but did not comment. They had now reached a point almost out on the stretch of road that served as an entrance to the gates and turned back to get an overall view of the church.

What they saw was a possible answer to their search. High above the sloping roof of the vestibule, the southern wall was deeply etched with a vaulted recess that ran almost its entire width. It was set with four slender columns, supporting three stone arches, two were set at one level and the centre one a little higher. Fret-worked stone ran between them and around them in an intricate network of patterns. Above and just below the curve of each arch were round window-like apertures. Two sat side by side with the centre one a little higher in the middle arch. The outer two were filled with stone filigree, like the spokes on a wheel but the centre one was filled with a delicate pattern of coloured glass.

'This has to be what we are looking for,' said Marilla shading her eyes from rays of the afternoon sun that had dared to escape the confines of scattered cloud cover. 'I can't quite see what's in it but whatever it is, it's pale in colour.'

'Yes and it would be in the right position too, I feel sure!' exclaimed Isabella excitedly. She turned and looked across the valley to the range of mountains and studied them for a moment. Marilla turned too and followed her sister's gaze. 'See those two peaks over there, almost side by side and about the same height as each other?' said Isabella.

'You mean those ones over to the left?' 'Yes, those.'

'Well, what about them?'

'If my guess is correct,' said Isabella, 'that's where the sun will rise on the morning of the solstice ... right between those two peaks.'

'What makes you so sure of that?'

'I've been noticing these past few weeks when we do have sunny mornings that the sun is almost rising between those two mountain tops. I get up earlier than you, Marilla, so I've had the chance to observe it.'

'Hmm, well, I must admit I'm not such an early bird as you are and I probably wouldn't have noticed anyway, but are you sure?'

'Positive, since I've been helping Elias with the chores I've been up and about a lot earlier as you know.'

'I see,' said Marilla thoughtfully, as she gazed at the peaks and then back at the afternoon sun, mentally tracing its line of ascent. 'If you are right, Bella, this then, could very well have some significance as to where the sun's rays will fall at dawn on the solstice. My guess is that this wizard has taken a bit more into consideration than just the timing of the shortest day of the year.'

She pulled her cloak about her as a gust of wind suddenly sprang up. 'Anyway, now that we seem to have solved part of this problem, at least I hope we have, I need to get indoors out of the cold, the temperature is dropping and my feet are freezing. It's getting colder by the minute standing around out here are you coming, Bella?'

Isabella, who had been gazing at the two distant peaks, turned to follow her sister. 'Yes, you're right, it is colder now but it's so nice when the sun is shining, it makes everything sparkle, I rather like the winter here, it looks like a fairyland when the snowflakes fall and cover everything. It's different, isn't it, even if it is cold?'

'Don't know that I'll ever get used to it,' muttered Marilla, 'however, I have to admit that it's a lot better than the last place we were in, at least the air is fresher, sometimes a little too fresh. By the way, Bella, did you tell Elias that our wood box is getting low?'

Marilla became suddenly aware that the sound of Isabella's footfalls in the crisp snow behind her had ceased. She turned around to see her sister standing quite still and staring fixedly at the mountain face high above the abbey.

'Did you see that?'

'See what?'

'Up there, on the side of the mountain.'

'Where?' said Marilla irritably. 'What am I supposed to see?'

Isabella was still staring upward. 'There it is again, look, see where that group of pines are by that big outcrop of rock?'

'Yes, I think so, why, what's up there?'

'There was a flash of light there, like the sun reflecting off something shiny ... there it is again, did you see it?'

Marilla had shielded her eyes and was looking at the spot Isabella had indicated and caught the briefest glimpse of something that glinted in the afternoon sun, just above the outcrop of rock Isabella had pointed out. It was visible for only a few seconds then it vanished.

'There's somebody up there,' murmured Marilla softly. 'I think we are being watched. Why and by whom I wonder?' she added thoughtfully.

'Could it be someone from the village, curious about the abbey now that the monks have gone?'

'I hardly think so,' answered Marilla. 'From what we've been told the village folk don't come near the abbey at all, they think it's haunted. Just keep walking, Bella, I think we may have to keep our wits about us from now on. This Baron person won't be entirely on his own we were told and we can't be sure how many others he's got with him. We really don't know who or what we are up against, it's scary. I'll be glad when Jack and Amos get back.'

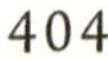

Chapter 28

Mirror, Mirror On The Wall ...

The morning dawned cold and chilly. Even at this early hour it was still dark enough to have to keep a lamp burning. Snowfalls during the night had deposited a thick drift over the landscape and the still falling snowflakes all but blotted out the surrounding mountain peaks.

Isabella yawned as she tried to peer through the darkness of the window from the warmth and comfort of the Lodge and sighed, 'We won't be tracing the sun's path today, Marilla, it will barely come through as a blur in the sky.' She yawned again and stretched, then moved to examine a calendar pinned to the wall beside her. 'According to this, we've got barely a week now until mid-winters day and if the weather stays like this, we're never going to see the sun shine through any window.' She tumbled out of her bed, gathered up some warm clothing and began to dress as she continued to chatter. 'At least we are nice and comfortable here. Having Elias around to help with firewood and everything is really good too and ...' She stopped herself from saying more on the subject of Elias but added quickly, 'I expect Jack and Amos will be back some time tomorrow or at least the day after, well soon anyway.'

Stifling another yawn, she reached down to the foot of the

bed and snatched up a thick jumper, narrowly avoiding a swipe from Lucifer's claws. He growled his displeasure at having his warm pillow removed so abruptly and glared disdainfully, watching from slitted eyes as Isabella pulled it over her head. However, it also meant that breakfast was not far off, so he sat up and began to meticulously groom himself, ever watchful from the corners of his yellow eyes as Isabella began to bustle about the kitchen.

'I'm making breakfast, Marilla,' Isabella called out to her sister. 'Are you up?'

Receiving no reply after a few minutes, she poked her head around the bedroom door to see Marilla sitting on the side of the bed in a half dressed state and staring dreamily into space.

'Breakfast, Marilla, do you want me to make your toast now?'

'Yes, yes, I'm coming,' answered Marilla in a vaguely impatient voice.

Isabella busied herself in the kitchen, humming as she placed the breakfast things on the table in readiness. Lucifer sat on a chair hungrily watching every move, until Isabella put a large spoonful of canned fish into his metal plate. He leapt down and greedily began to demolish it, all the while rumbling his deep growl as his rough tongue scraped the sides of his bowl cleaning up the last few pieces clinging there. His tongue licked around his mouth briefly before he sprang back up onto the chair and eyed the pieces of toast hopefully, just as Marilla stepped through into the kitchen dragging her fingers through her tangled hair, which she had not as yet pinned up into her usual severe bun.

'Come on, Lucifer, get off, you've had yours,' she said sharply as she gave him a push so she could sit down before he reclaimed the chair. Lucifer stomped away to sit close by Isabella's chair in the hope something might eventually fall his way. Isabella put two steaming mugs of tea down beside the plate of toast and sat down. Placing toast on her plate, she reached for the pot of jam at her elbow and began her usual chatter about anything and everything that came into her head first thing in the morning; talking and eating very efficiently at the same time.

It wasn't until they were almost finished that she noticed her older sister had said very little, in fact she was unusually quiet and seemed otherwise preoccupied with other thoughts as she went through the vague motions of consuming her breakfast.

'You've got something on your mind this morning, Marilla, you've been very quiet and that usually means you are up to something. What is it?'

Marilla buttered her last piece of toast with a little more vigour before replying briskly, 'I'm thinking that we need to see who this "enemy" is, so we know what to expect and there's only one way to do that.'

Isabella had been about to drop a small piece of toast down to where Lucifer sat waiting and paused to stare at her sister, her brown eyes wide in expectation. 'That means using Grandmother's scrying glass … are you sure? Ouch!' She withdrew her hand hurriedly and rubbed the tooth imprint on her finger where Lucifer had grabbed impatiently at the waiting piece of toast so temptingly within his reach.

'Yes I am,' replied Marilla firmly. 'You do know, Isabella, that we should both be aware of the risks.'

'I know, I do remember what Grandma Hackett warned us about all the time when we were kids,' said Isabella patiently, 'we might see things we don't want to, things that might come to pass that we shouldn't know about but, Marilla, really, I honestly only saw the cottage that time, nothing else!'

'That's because it was the only thought on your mind at the time.'

Marilla nibbled around the edges of her last piece of toast before saying thoughtfully, almost to herself, 'Then again, Grandma could have just been making that up to keep us from touching the mirror, but we can't be sure. In any case,' she said as she shoved the remainder of the toast into her mouth and talked thickly through it, 'I'm going to try it!' She licked a bit of jam from her forefinger and thumb before continuing. 'I've been reading through some of her old books while you've been up at the yard playing "farmer's wife" — feeding the chooks and whatever else you do with them, so I feel pretty sure I can do it. It's no good dragging all of her books around with us if we're not going to use them, is it?'

'Marilla, I can show y—'

'Perhaps you may have done it once, Isabella but it doesn't mean to say you could be successful a second time,' Marilla broke in forcefully.

'Well, I don't see why not!' said Isabella peevishly.

Marilla was about to make another remark, but stopped and looked pensively at her younger sister and the hurt expression on her face pricked at her conscience. She had to remind herself that Isabella had actually been able to decipher Grandma Hackett's strange way of writing the incantations necessary to make the mirror reveal its secrets, where she herself had failed. Not only that, her younger sister was showing a sense of maturity that she had not cared to notice before, but could see now. Since their unexpected entry into the Monastery, Isabella had begun to change; a subtle change that did not require the presence and authority of her older sibling to monitor. She had begun thinking and acting for herself and indeed, her brave performance in saving herself and Amos from an almost fatal demise deep within the bowels of the old crypt, was certainly proof enough in itself.

Perhaps, in her own mind Marilla knew that Isabella might have a greater hold on the powers of magic than she had cause to give her credit for, perhaps more than her own. She would have to concede that fact now, but privately of course.

'Alright, Bella,' she said brightly, 'I'll tell you what, we'll do it together, right after we clean these things up.'

*   *   *

The precious mirror was retrieved from its resting place under Marilla's bed, unwrapped from the blanket keeping it secure, and carried into the kitchen where it was carefully propped up on the table against a pile of books. The smooth surface of the mirror itself was dull and uninteresting, but the perfect circle of its frame was burnished a dull gold with the most delicately carved and moulded figures intertwined among branches and twigs in tortuous confusion. It was like looking into a forest, full of living, moving creatures.

When looked at closely, the tiny figures were elves and sprites, peering from behind or hanging from the thick tangles of forestation. It didn't matter how often you looked at it, it always looked different as if the figures were changing places and moving about, their tiny faces showing a variety of expressions. Just to look at the frame itself was a fascinating pastime.

Several volumes of ancient and somewhat tattered books lay in profusion about the room. Marilla had certainly done some heavy reading but hating to admit, even to herself, that she was no closer to bringing the mirror to life.

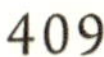

'Let's see now,' she said, staring intently into the mirror, but seeing her own reflection mockingly looking back — an image, curious and out of proportion and focus.

Marilla looked at her vague reflection for a long moment, turning her head this way and that, but the image in the mirror did not move, it remained fixed as when she had first looked into it. The green eyes stared back at her and the wisp of hair that had fallen over her face that she had now brushed back only seconds before was still there exactly as it had been when she had looked upon it. Isabella's face now appeared over her shoulder and as if they were depicted in a family photograph, neither face showing expression changes, their images remained frozen, caught in that moment of time.

'It does that all the time, when you first look in it,' murmured Isabella in a reverential whisper.

'I know it does, it's weird,' replied Marilla. She tore her eyes away from the reflections and turned back to the book open on the table, once more studying the strange cipher. 'It's these strange symbols scattered among the letters that are confusing. I've been trying to figure out what they mean, I've tried some incantations from some of the books, but nothing happens in the mirror.'

'Actually, they are letters,' said Isabella, 'but written in a different way.'

'How do you mean, written in a different way? They're either letters or they're not!'

Isabella leaned over her sister's shoulder and pointed to one of the symbols. 'Grandma used different symbols to represent some of the letters. See, that one that looks like a paw print is an 'm', and those that look like an arrow head are 'i', the star is an 's' and so on. It just takes time to figure them all out, then, to make it a bit more confusing, she changes some of the symbols to something else, you just have to use your imagination.'

'Oh, well, that explains a lot, so now it shouldn't be too difficult to follow,' said Marilla confidently, even if she didn't feel confident.

'Yes, I suppose so, once you know and understand the code then recognise the changes when they occur,' agreed Isabella, 'but there's more to it than that.'

'How do you mean more?'

'It's written back to front.'

'Back to front!' exclaimed Marilla. 'Why would it be written back to front?' She turned and looked squarely at her sister. 'How could you have worked that out?'

Isabella sat down and folded her hands in her lap. 'Well,' she answered slowly, I did spend a lot of time by myself when we were young and I use to imagine I was someone … like Grandma and I would pretend that I wanted to send messages to someone, or write spells and conceal them in hidden writings. I thought about it a lot, particularly when I was walking by myself in the forest at Harewood. So I made up a cipher using drawings of certain wildflowers, leaves of herbs and insects to represent some of the letters, even the imprints in the mud of the creek of bird's feet. I knew it wouldn't take a smart person long to work out the letter substitutes, providing there were enough of the same letters, there had to be a further catch to a code, so I reversed it to make it further confusing. Then I found out that it was just the same as Grandma did with hers. I know it sounds weird, but it's true!'

Marilla was looking at Isabella with a mixture of amazement, mild annoyance and grudging admiration. After a long pause, while she gathered her thoughts, Marilla managed to say, 'You must have spent a lot of time then looking through these books, Isabella.'

Isabella looked somewhat abashed at her sister. 'You know how I love books, Marilla and as you have just said yourself, why carry all these books around if we don't read them? Plus, I like solving riddles. It was a challenge; I had nothing else to do a lot of times so I just played games using the cipher.' Isabella looked up at her sister's face regarding her closely and continued. 'It was hard to figure out at first but once I got started, I just seemed to know what was in Grandma Hackett's mind, I could see it all so clearly!'

'I see,' said Marilla, momentarily lost for words. She sat back in her chair and regarded her younger sibling with renewed interest. 'I was not aware that you had opened any of Grandma's books, I suppose I should have known your curiosity would get the better of you. So, perhaps under these circumstances then, *you* should let the mirror tell us what we want to know.'

'I can do it, Marilla, I know I can.'

'I hope so, Bella, because my instincts tell me that we are going to have to be prepared for anything, whether Jack and Amos are here or not and I'd like to see what this Baron looks like before he sees us!'

'Alright then,' replied Isabella and she moved up closer to the dark face of the mirror and gazed fixedly at the images of herself and Marilla. Passing her open hand slowly across the glass she murmured in a soft voice, 'We seek in truth to see in the clouds. By your wisdom and insight, show from within the source that is evil.'

For a long tense moment nothing happened, just their two stony faces peering back at them from the surface of the mirror. Marilla was just about to remark on the failure of the experiment, when she noticed a faint misting creep around the edge of the glass. The tiny figures around the frame had begun to move about a little more rapidly, some peering furtively from behind twisted trunks of trees, others appearing and disappearing quickly among the leaves and shadows that were constantly changing in shape.

Isabella was holding both sides of the mirror now and had closed her eyes. She opened one hand and passed it closely over the surface again, this time she was uttering different words in a low hushed whisper that issued from her lips like a sigh, '*Revela adintra meovoto estum malora* … reveal!'

To Marilla's astonishment the mirror began to cloud over and tumbling masses of vapour filled its surface. For several moments neither sister could see anything beyond the swirling clouds but gradually a scene emerged from the haze, but it was not what they expected to see. The vision revealed to them was of Harewood; Harewood as they remembered it from their childhood. There were children playing by the stream and even as they looked, Isabella could see herself, sitting with her knees drawn up under her chin as she usually did, while she watched the other children play.

Someone else was there too, a small dark haired boy sitting alongside her on the big old tree trunk. He was watching Marilla who was all gangly and tousle haired, her face flushed with exasperation, as she wrestled mentally with a large toad which refused to bend to her will and kept hopping away from her clutches, she would chase after it and begin again.

The scene changed, two middle-aged women could be seen sitting close together and deep in conversation; they recognised their Grandmother and Edwina. Edwina was holding something in her hand and as she opened it and laid it on the table they could see that it was a small box that appeared to be heavily carved and was a deep ivory in colour. Edwina was showing it to the second woman but someone else was there too, a slim figure of a man.

Then just as suddenly as they had appeared, the visions faded and the swirling clouds of vapour once more filled the surface of the glass. Marilla broke the silence, 'I thought the mirror was going to show us who this enemy of Jack's is?'

'Wait!' cautioned Isabella. 'The mirror is clearing again.'

Sure enough the clouds of vapour had rolled away and they were now looking at the little bridge that led into the village below the Abbey. Two small carts drawn by sturdy little brown donkeys and occupied by three grey robed figures were making their way across the bridge and into the village itself.

'Why … that's us with Elias!' exclaimed Isabella. 'I wonder why the mirror is just showing images of ourselves?'

'I don't know but perhaps the visions are leading up to something, this happened not that long ago, there must be something else here we are supposed to see.' Marilla was peering closely at the glass. 'Yes, look, look, Bella — there's someone watching through the window of the Inn, you can see his outline through the glass, there, in that corner window — see?'

Even as she spoke the scene shifted and it was as if they were standing directly outside the window looking in. A great hulk of a man was seated there in the alcove staring out. His heavy lidded black eyes in a large florid face were glittering as they watched the progress of the grey clad figures pass by. They saw him pick up the glass of ale from in front of him with thick gnarled fingers and drain the contents in one gulp. As they watched, he clambered to his feet with a grunt and ambled over to the staircase that led to the upper rooms.

Now the vision changed and they were inside the Inn and watching as he climbed the stairs, his bulk filling the staircase and as he knocked softly at a door at the end of a corridor. It was opened immediately by a similarly built man, an ugly man, his face made even more hideous by a jagged scar that began at the corner of one eye and ran across his face to the base of his chin, giving a puckered grotesque mask to the otherwise flat features. The two men spoke quickly in a foreign tongue and the first man entered, closing the door behind him.

Once again the mirror began to cloud over, in a moment the vaporous mists had cleared, the mirror was going to show them more. This time they found themselves standing in a room as invisible entities — a large comfortably appointed room, warmed by blazing logs flickering in the grate of an ample fireplace. Furniture and the trappings of ambience along with luxury one would not have expected in a simple country Inn, filled the room including a table heavily laden with food dishes standing to one side, the fire glistening on crystal goblets standing amidst the fine china.

Their attention however, was riveted on the man who sat in a deep armchair drawn up to the fire, who was listening intently to what the florid-faced man was saying and again in that foreign tongue. The listener's head was thrust forward, thin aquiline features heightened by piercing dark grey eyes under carefully arched eyebrows. A short, perfectly trimmed van- dyke beard and close cropped grey hair gave the man an air of nobility, which was further enhanced by an immaculately tailored jacket emblazoned with a coat of arms on the breast pocket, a wide red rib-band hung with an ornate insignia lay about his neck. As he raised a hand to dismiss the messenger, the sisters caught a glimpse of heavy gold rings and the flash of diamonds on the long elegant fingers.

'This must be the Baron person Jack has told us about,' whispered Isabella.

'I don't like the look of him,' added Marilla. 'He looks like the sort of gentry who gets what he wants, no matter what.'

The man who had delivered the message executed a stiff half bow from the waist and moved away, but the mirror was not finished yet …

*   *   *

Baron Von Zaharoff was smiling, his thin lips drawn into a twisted sneer as he gazed in deep satisfaction into the blazing fire. His plans were going well, there was little he did not know now about what was happening at the Abbey of St. Dominica. He tapped his fingers on the arm of the chair in an impatient gesture. It would not be long now before the one thing he desired above all else would be in his hand. The long fingers clenched over the arm of the chair; how dare they rob him of what was rightfully his — that treasure which *had* lain within the walls of his own house! Whatever was in the house of Zaharoff at any time, whether it be on the walls or hidden amongst other family treasures, it was rightfully the property of the Master of the House. Of even more significance to him was the unrivalled and secretive history that surrounded such a treasure within itself — it was a priceless heirloom, with a legend that would shake long-dead bones in regal circles.

However, there were some problems still to be overcome before he could at last see what he had desired for so long. His thin lips tightened even more as his thoughts strayed to the one man who stood between him and what he sought, his conscience pricked him smartly as he remembered a small, frightened boy cowering behind the skirts of these women — the women Baron Von Zaharoff chose to blame for his fall from grace.

*   *   *

He shook his head as if to erase the memory and the watching sisters saw him lift a hand and the fingers snap in command. The action immediately brought another person whom they had not seen as yet into focus in the mirror's image. A hand reached out from the cloaked figure who had stepped forward to pick up a silver cigarette case from a nearby table and hold it open for the occupant of the armchair. The Baron accepted a light from the manservant, leaned back and exhaled a thin stream of smoke at the ceiling, his lips still twisting in a sardonic smile.

The sisters, however were staring aghast and open mouthed at the fourth occupant of the room.

'Bella!' cried Marilla. 'He's a monk — a monk, in service to the Baron!'

Indeed it was, but who? They could not see his face as the cowl covered it completely. Only the hand that had emerged from the long trailing sleeves had been glimpsed. A hand, somewhat fleshy and white … and then, it was withdrawn as the figure moved away from their line of vision.

Then, they could see no more, the vaporous clouds were rapidly covering the surface of the mirror and in a few moments, all they could see were their own immobile reflections staring back.

Chapter 29

An Informative Discussion

'I wonder how Elias is coping with those two women on his own since we've been gone.' Amos mused as he skilfully manoeuvred the four-wheel drive vehicle around a heavy snow drift partially blocking the road.

'I doubt he would have had any problems with Isabella,' answered Jack with a yawn, 'but Marilla may have caused him a headache or two. She can be a feisty piece when she wants to but she's also very smart. Ambitious too, although clever enough to know her limitations without making it too obvious to anyone else around her. Perhaps, in a way that's a good thing — she does not like to be seen as a failure. She's very proud and arrogant with it but deep down she's really got a great heart. She just doesn't show it easily, there's a lot of insecurity there.'

Amos dodged another snowdrift, changing gears at the same time. 'I thought you said you last saw them both when you were kids at that commune, what was it — Harewood?'

'I did but Edwina always kept in close contact with their grandmother, in that way, I also kept up with what was happening with the girls. They very rarely saw their mother, she was a bit of a scatterbrain, on the whole a nice person; but she only drifted in occasionally. So the responsibility to rear them was left to their grandmother, Hilda Hackett. It was a bit tough on them all but there was always someone else to help. They all looked after each other there.'

'Where was their mother?'

'Telling fortunes in a circus tent,' explained Jack, almost bitterly. 'Got herself tangled up with a dodgy salesman when she was young and when he left, she found herself a job in a travelling circus; had the talent for it, because nobody knew she was Wiccan. The girls apparently got too much for her and Hilda was not happy about them being dragged all over the country with no chance of education, so she took them in and brought them up herself. The only drawback to that was that they saw very little of the world outside the commune, so they were very naïve.'

'Sounds like both grandmothers had a lot of responsibilities they never expected to have,' replied Amos.

'Well, it was a bit like one big family, though I never had a lot to do with the girls, except for Isabella, I did regard them as close family, perhaps the only family I knew,' he added almost wistfully. 'I did try to keep track of them through Edwina after I left, it was sometimes many months before I'd hear anything of them. When they lost Hilda, their whole world fell in; it was left to Edwina and those in the commune to look after their welfare but of course they were young women by then.'

'Was that when they took off on their own?'

'One could say it was pretty obvious they weren't going to stay at Harewood forever, at least not for Marilla. She had too many ambitious ideas for that and Bella would do whatever her sister suggested. Given a choice though, I think Isabella would have been quite happy to remain in the commune and get lost in her own little world of fantasy.'

Amos grunted. 'From what I've seen so far, I'd say Isabella is making a few decisions of her own. I can't see her hiding too much behind Marilla's skirts at all now.' he added dryly.

Jack stifled another yawn and stretched his arms. 'You're right there, Amos, it does seem as if she could be suddenly finding her own personality and can think for herself. There's quite a brain behind those big brown eyes of hers; I think she's quite capable of handling situations more than she's been given credit for ... even by her own sister.'

'Yet, to look at them, it's hard to believe that they are sisters,' said Amos shaking his head. 'They're so unalike in looks and personality, I guess it all comes down to parentage — you get a little of both whether you like it or not.'

Amos suddenly became serious as he recalled Isabella's uncanny skills and presence of mind when they had both been entombed in the ancient crypt under the abbey. 'You know, Jack, I've been in some tight situations before but I can tell you now, that little episode in the crypt really had me worried. If it hadn't been for her quick thinking, whether she knew what she was doing or not—' He broke off awkwardly.

'I guess I could say the same for Marilla, just the way she handled the nasty little bit that Casini brought along with him. If it hadn't been for her, I probably wouldn't be here either. My fault of course, I should have realised Moody wouldn't have been far away and I dropped my guard; should have remembered that apart from his skill in forgery, he's an efficient assassin.'

Jack laughed then as he recalled his astonishment at seeing Moody hanging precariously off Marilla's broomstick. 'I don't think I'll ever forget the brief glimpse I got of Moody's face when she swept him up like that. That old broomstick of hers might be ancient, but she can certainly move fast on it.'

'Beats me how they stay on those things,' muttered Amos.

'All part of witchcraft, old boy,' laughed Jack, 'way too hard for mere mortals to understand. Don't ask me to explain any more than that.'

'Do you know what they've been doing since they left this Harewood place? I got the impression they've been a tad out of their depth in getting around,' said Amos as he dodged yet another snowdrift.

'That's just the trouble,' sighed Jack. 'It *was* a big worry when they left with little or no knowledge of the way of the world outside the confines of the sheltered life they had been living. They could have stayed there if they wished; but they had itchy feet, well, Marilla mainly did. They couldn't follow their mother, as half the time one didn't know where she was and I don't think they really cared too much about her anyway. She would have been much of a stranger to them.'

He paused before he continued. 'I gathered from Edwina the last time I saw her, which incidentally, has been a while now; that the girls have been wandering around like gypsies, not really fitting in anywhere, even though Edwina has been able to keep track of them without them knowing of course. I believe they caused quite a bit of mischief and mayhem in a couple of places, just escaping prosecution by a whisker, or a quick flit on their broomsticks each time. It has taught them to live by their wits; which is something I guess.'

'Well, now, perhaps I'm not much up with this Wiccan business,' Amos remarked candidly, 'but I do get the idea that their escapades could have been enough reason why they were deliberately led to such an out of the way place as this. In fact your uncle intimated that.'

'You've hit the nail on the head,' answered Jack with a trace of annoyance in his voice. 'This little *affaire-de-honneur* obviously has a two-fold purpose. A little scheme dreamt up by my uncle and Edwina, I did have a sneaking suspicion that there was more behind this move than was immediately obvious. I don't think either of them have fully realised how dangerous their little plan is and all the things that can go wrong with it. Henri's lost touch with reality!' He gazed out the window of the vehicle at the white blankets of snow-covered fields. 'To tell the truth, Amos, I would rather not have the girls involved in this exercise, even though I know the main purpose behind it is to give them a sense of direction and purpose in life, to test their mettle, but why here — and now! This isn't a family reunion picnic! It's between me and the Baron.'

Jack half turned to Amos and touched his shoulder. 'Amos, I'm sorry I didn't tell you who he was before; or who I am or what I am supposed to be. It's not something I'm proud of, it's a name I have never used and never will. It means nothing to me, it disgusts me to even hear it and I think only of *him* now as the enemy.'

'You don't have to apologise for anything, Jack,' said Amos, his voice, a little gruffer than usual. 'I admit it was a shock at first when you verified your birth identity to me that day when we were leaving the abbey to tidy up the paperwork on the Casinis; but I had realised by then that everything about this venture here made sense and somehow, I think I kind of knew but just had to have it spelled out for me. Any name you have inherited makes no difference to me whatsoever; it's you I feel for, I can't fight your battle or your conscience over what you have to do. I can only be there when you want a hefty shoulder, okay?'

Jack did not answer but squeezed his friend's shoulder; a loyal and understanding friend who didn't ask awkward questions, who always knew the answers would come eventually.

'As far as Marilla and Isabella are concerned Jack; I feel the same as you do — keep them out of it, it just makes another responsibility.' emphasised Amos, 'But to be fair, when the situation with the Casinis got out of control, it could have been fatal for both of us if they hadn't been there and you know, I get the feeling that the old bloke, your uncle, seems to know what he's doing somehow. If he's the wizard you say he is, I don't think he would deliberately put their lives or ours in any great danger just to prove a point. It wouldn't make any sense it would defeat the whole purpose of his plan!'

'True, I suppose but even wizards can get it wrong, Amos, so I'm not expecting too much in the way of spiritual intervention, though I could understand his reluctance to interfere with the Casini situation. It wouldn't do to show who he really was at that time. I blame myself for the screw up with that mob. I should have called Steve and his crew here earlier, to stake out the place before it got out of hand but Carlos was the unexpected fly in the ointment I didn't count on; I should have trusted your instincts my friend.'

Jack gave another long sigh and stretched himself. 'I'm getting too old for this game, Amos, I'm losing touch, making mistakes; that's something you can't do in this sort of job. Maybe it's time I retired and did something a little less traumatic.'

'Perhaps you're right but with other things on your mind it doesn't make the job any easier. You'd soon miss the thrill of the chase and die of boredom. If anyone is getting old and slower, it's me,' chuckled Amos. 'I'm not seeing the punches quickly enough now to dodge them!'

They were now entering the outskirts of the Lake Village when Amos spoke again. 'Is there anything you want in the town before we climb the hill?'

'Yes. The Post Office if you wouldn't mind, Amos, I want to have another word with the local "oracle". She's probably dying to know what's happening up at the abbey, we may as well scotch the rumours and set the record straight before it grows out of all proportion. Besides which, she just might have some useful information to impart about who's who that could be of interest to us — she's a mine of information.'

'Well, if you don't mind, I'll wait in the car,' said Amos gruffly, 'I don't have the patience right now to listen to someone raving on with local gossip, my ears are too sensitive today.'

He was drawing the vehicle to a halt at the kerb outside the old red brick building. 'Hmm, while you're in there dispensing your diplomatic dogma, Jack my boy, I just might nip over to the bakery and look at a few goodies. It smells just too good to pass by.'

Jack inclined his head to look at Amos through the window of the car as he alighted and drew his face into a disapproving frown. 'The trouble with you, Amos McAllister, is that your stomach has absolutely no memory whatsoever.'

'Careful what you say, Jack Grimsby or I may decline to shout you a little edible luxury.' Amos levered his body out from behind the wheel. 'I don't need you to preach to me about the intake of calories; my body is perfectly happy the way it is. It doesn't need your professional opinion.'

Jack grinned as he turned and ran up the few steps to the Post Office, he was about to push against the door when it opened and an old man carrying an armful of papers emerged, the two of them almost colliding. The old man stumbled and dropped one of his papers. Jack put out a hand to steady him and in doing so the hood of the man's heavy winter coat slipped down a fraction, Jack caught a brief glimpse of his face before the aged one pulled the hood back up again and mumbled, 'I'm alright, young man, I can still keep my feet.'

Jack uttered an apology as he bent down to pick up the paper that had been dropped, as he straightened up his eyes caught those of the old man. He couldn't be sure, but there seemed to be something familiar about the face ... and the voice, deeply intoned. Dark eyes had flashed briefly at him before lowering under heavy brows, the long fingers held the coat buttoned to the neck, but not before Jack glimpsed scraps of a white beard floating free from the confines of the coat.

Wavering slightly, the old man began to make his way down the few steps, withdrawing gloves from his pocket as he went and was now pulling one on.

Jack stood for a moment on the step, one hand on the door watching, as the ancient one stooped to untie the lead of a small dog that had been tethered to an iron railing around a street tree. Shifting his papers to under one arm, he turned his head while pulling the other glove on to cast a very brief look at Jack. Nothing could be seen now of the face under the hood but Jack had felt sure in that momentary glimpse, that he had seen that face before. As the elderly one shuffled slowly down the street, the little dog following obediently behind, Jack shook his head; maybe it was just coincidental, but in that split second of eye contact, he had felt recognition.

Shrugging his shoulders, he entered the Post Office and approached the counter, the little bell above the door ringing shrilly as he did so. Edna was busy looking for something under the counter, he could hear her muttering to herself. She popped her head up on hearing the bell and peered at him over the top of her glasses.

'Oh, it's you, the writer fellow, I wondered where you'd got to.' She raised a forefinger and said, 'Are you aware that—' she began to say in her emphatically admonishing tone before Jack interrupted her.

'Edna, who is that old man who was in here just a moment ago?'

Edna looked at him in surprise, 'Which old man?'

'The man who was in here just now, he was wearing a thick brown coat with a hood, he just came out of here, I saw him go down the street with a little dog; who is he?'

'Oh,' she exclaimed, 'you must mean Mr Pinnay. Yes, he comes in for his weeklies. You see we keep some newspapers and magazines and sometimes I do have to hold them for him when he's away; as he often is, but—'

'Does he live here?' Jack interrupted her again.

'Of course he does, been here for years, on and off. Lives in a little cottage up the other end of High street, opposite the Lake Inn. Keeps very much to himself, when he's home, one hardly knows he's there half the time. Originally French I think, though it's hard to say with some people, why do you ask?'

'I, er—just thought I knew him that's all.'

'Oh,' was all Edna could say, having other more pressing things on her mind. She pointed the offending forefinger at him. 'When you first came through here, you said you were going up the mountain to have a look at the abbey, maybe do a story on it or something. Well, let me tell you there have been all sorts of strange things going on up there, people and cars coming and going, it's been quite disturbing. The locals are quite unnerved, then some army people came through with a big truck, the army, of *all* people! What ever would they be doing coming here, what's been going on up there?'

'Edna—' Jack started to say, but her shrill voice drowned him out as she went on.

'Some of the young lads have said they've seen and heard those helicopters they use these days flying around up there and now we hear that all the monks have left. In the paper today, it said that—'

'*Edna!*' Jack managed to get the word in as she drew breath.

'Edna,' he said again as he held his identification card up in front of her face, 'just listen to me for a minute and I'll explain it all to you.'

The Post Mistress adjusted her glasses on her nose and peered closely at the identification card. 'Aha, so you are a policeman and not a writer!' she exclaimed, looking at him again over the top of her glasses, but the expression that showed on her face was decidedly indecisive as to his real identity.

Jack had a vague impression that she was slightly disappointed at him not being a writer. He also had the feeling she might have been looking forward to seeing her name in print as the informative historian in a forthcoming publication on the charming little Lake Village. She would have seen herself as one of the more important residents, from whom much valuable history had been obtained along with the part she and her ancestors had played in its quaint history, being of particular interest to the readers. That bubble effectively burst, her enthusiasm for his new character got the better of her curiosity and she now insisted on knowing all the details.

She pursed her lips and frowned as Jack gave a brief outline of events and only the merest details of the Casini takeover of the abbey. After all, an account of the drama had reached the daily papers; Jack was quick to tone down the incident. As he said ruefully, the press always like to dramatise events, particularly anything unusual in a small country town; it sold more papers. Careful then not to elaborate too much on the actual criminal activities, he concentrated more on the forced confinement of the monks within their own walls invoking a thread of sympathy for those unfortunate residents.

Every time Edna opened her mouth to ask a question, Jack overrode it with another fact and was emphatic in his assurances that the village had at *no* time been in any danger from the Casinis. All of the gang had been detained and would face charges with the full force of the law, hence the presence of the helicopters in rounding them up. Peace had been restored and life could return to normal. In any case, he told her, the departure of the monks from the abbey had been planned for some time and though the arrival of the Casinis had inconvenienced them considerably, they were now free to move to their new home and workplease several miles distant.

'*Humph!*' she snorted derisively when Jack had finished. 'If my father — he was the Mayor here for eight years, eight years mind you — if he was here, he would have run these criminals out of town quick smart!' She drew herself up with a very important air and added, 'I just *knew* there was something wrong. They weren't like the old monks when my father was around, no, this lot were a bit, well, shifty, yes shifty I would say. I always thought there was something wrong with them, all dressed up in monk's clothes, but they didn't do business the same as the monks of years ago. If only my father had been here, he would have seen straight through them!'

'Even if your father had been here, you realise he would have had no say in what happens at the abbey,' said Jack firmly.

'And why not?'

'Because the Abbey of St Dominica does not come under

Council jurisdiction; it is a separate identity and is outside the realm of Village Council bylaws. What happens there is the concern of the abbey itself and perhaps the governing Ecclesiastical Order, what has occurred there recently has been a matter of International Police business only.'

Edna opened her mouth to protest this statement but Jack cancelled her protest as he looked at her steadily, meeting her indignant gaze. 'I am only telling you this now, Edna to put the record straight, for the peace of mind of the villagers and your customers. The resident monks who were there, being held under duress, were to move to another Priory, but their departure was delayed due to the circumstances I have just described. They are now settled elsewhere and are quite happy in their new home, there is nothing in Council or village laws that says this should not be so. Your rules do not apply to the Franciscan Order of Friars and never has.'

The Post Mistress still looked at Jack with a stony expression on her face. 'So, we can assume that the abbey has now been abandoned and will just become a crumbling ruin?'

'I really must point out to you, Edna, that the abbey is *not* abandoned, it is in fact private property and has been so for some considerable time; even when the monks *were* there. In fact,' he said, thinking rapidly while ignoring the look on Edna's face, 'the abbey will still be in use as a monastic teaching establishment, for the time being anyway, as there are still some members in residence there. As a matter of interest,' he said quickly, now that he had Edna's full attention, 'there are two ladies already in residence — students you understand. A study group who are special guests of the estate. Unfortunately, they ah—they got caught up in the trouble that occurred and are staying on for a while, to recuperate from the drama, you understand.'

Jack shook his head and tutted in a sympathetic tone. 'They have been quite shaken up by the affair and being, ah—genteel ladies, naturally it was rather a shock to them as you can imagine.'

Edna's facial expression had softened a little and she nodded her head in agreement as she digested this; for a few serious moments said nothing, then, 'Of course, yes, it must have been quite a trial for them but ... two women, what on earth would they be studying in a monastery? I thought it was only the domain of men?'

Jack's mind was racing now, but the path was set. 'Ah, well, I believe they are studying Medieval History and umm, Apostolic Histrionics, a new curriculum you understand.'

The frown deepened on Edna's face and she seemed, for the moment, lost for words as Jack continued. He was beginning to savour this moment and was going to make the most of it, getting these thoughts into Edna's mind and hoping the girls would follow through on the path he was laying out for them.

'As I am trying to explain to you, Edna, the abbey is not just a monastery, it is a private estate and women are to be accepted into some of the new teaching programs that are being put into place. There could be a lot of changes going on up there in the future.'

'I see,' said Edna thoughtfully. 'I guess it just goes to show that one can never be certain of anything, even when it happens right under your nose.' She looked up at him inquiringly. 'I suppose there will be more women coming if these changes are taking place?'

'Depends how the pilot program goes I expect.' He leaned over the counter and his voice became softer and complaisant. 'Now it may be possible you understand that these ladies would have need to come down to the village from time to time in the near future, so I do hope the people of the village will show them the courtesy of privacy and not harass them with questions. They are very private persons and do keep very much to themselves. Now, you being the mature intelligent woman that you are, can understand this I am sure.'

Edna almost blushed and seemed a little taken aback at this remark but inwardly relished his honeyed tones in reference to herself, so wholeheartedly agreed that they would be treated kindly. 'Yes, yes, of course.'

Jack began to move toward the door then stopped. 'By the way, Edna, is there anyone else in town at the moment who normally isn't here, any visitors for instance?'

Shaken out of her momentary trance Edna replied, 'No. I don't think so, no one that I can think of, only that titled chappie down at the Inn but he comes and goes all the time, so he's not really a stranger. I have to admit they are a queer lot though but it does add an extra something to the prestige of the village having someone like that here occasionally. Apparently, he comes here for his health I believe — needs the clean air and we've got plenty of *that.*'

'A queer lot you say, how do you mean — queer — and when did this person come here?'

'Several days now I think, at least that's what Mary said. I was talking to her only yesterday and she said he'd come back again.'

'Who is Mary?'

'Mary Gilford, you know; she does the rooms for Mr Bartlett, the publican who owns the Inn. She said that the thin rather elderly gent who has half the top floor at his disposal always looks like a grand duke or something. Very toffy, like Royalty, she says, with such expensive looking clothes. Mind you, she doesn't "do" his rooms, his valet or whatever does everything for him. He doesn't leave his rooms much except for short walks in the evenings so I believe.'

She gave a toss of her head as she said impressively. 'We don't often get people of that calibre in town and of course, not that we need it; but it does give the village a bit more class, don't you think?'

'Of course,' said Jack rather dryly. 'Does this ... gentleman have any companions with him?' he asked in an offhand manner.

'Oh, yes!' Edna pulled a grim face, 'dreadful looking men; they are rather huge and ugly men too. Shouldn't say it I suppose, but they remind me of pictures you see of the big gorillas in places like Africa. They can't help their looks I suppose and after all, they are supposed to be bodyguards. These important people all have bodyguards, so I'm told.' A perplexed frown creased her forehead for a moment. 'Don't really know why he should have chosen our village to spend time in when there are all those big fancy resorts down on the coast. Still perhaps he does like the peace and quiet of a small village and of course the clean air.'

'Yes, I'm sure he does,' answered Jack quietly, his hand on the door. 'Edna, I have to go, it's been nice talking with you again, but I have someone waiting for me, I'm sure they are getting quite impatient.'

'Oh, well, if you must, but you will call in again some time, won't you?' she called out, as he gave a wave and disappeared out of the door.

Running down the steps Jack reached the vehicle and scrambled in beside Amos, who was licking the remains of a cream bun off his fingers. 'Well?' he said as he licked the last bit of cream off his thumb.'

Reaching for the seat belt, Jack replied grimly, 'The enemy is at the gates! Drive on, my friend, methinks the battle is about to begin.'

He cast a cursory glance at the Inn as they drove past it, but nothing in its external features could give even a glimpse of the infamous guests within. As the car began its long climb up to the abbey, Jack related to Amos all of his conversation with that worthy stalwart of village community and keeper of information.

'I'm glad I didn't go in there with you,' said Amos grinning. 'I just might not have been able to keep a straight face; Apostolic Histrionics, I wonder if the girls can handle that one effectively.'

'Well, the Histrionics part shouldn't be too difficult, they've been acting their way out of trouble for years,' replied Jack.

*   *   *

'Are you sure you don't want me to help you with this?' asked Isabella as Marilla sorted clothes for washing in the laundry.

'No, thanks, there's not much here, I have to do something to keep myself occupied,' replied Marilla. 'You go up and help Elias with the chores, he's got more than enough to attend to, I'm sure he needs more help than I do.'

'Alright then,' said Isabella cheerfully, 'Elias wants to rake out the hen house and I want to be there to collect any eggs. Elias is hoping for some extra eggs this morning. The hens have been a bit slow these past few weeks, but he's hoping they'll pick up as soon as the weather changes. Jack and Amos should be back today too.' she chattered as she went out the door.

Marilla shook her head at her younger sister as she watched her make her way up the snow-covered path that led to the rear of the abbey grounds. She was also glad that Amos and Jack would be back today. Mid-winters' day was close, even though they had discovered the possible source of the ray of light required; there was still the exact location of where the beam of light would fall to be considered, providing the morning was clear of cloud cover. This morning had dawned clear and though there was some cloud, the sun continued to shine intermittently, she was intending to make another visit to the chapel before midday to try to narrow the search area. Marilla had worked out the approximate path the shaft of light would take but at what point it would touch was the question still to be answered. She sighed as she bent to her task, she would be glad when Jack's treasure was found. Marilla had not liked what she had seen in the mirror and a deep sense of foreboding began to settle on her. Who was the person dressed as a monk? Was it someone they should know and who was the watcher on the mountain? Her skin tingled and she had the strange feeling that whatever was going to happen, would happen soon ... very soon.

'Been waiting for you,' grunted Elias as Isabella swung through the latch gate, 'thought you wanted to collect the eggs? Better hurry yourself so I can rake out the yard, can't have you slacking on the job.' A grin covering Elias's face; with dark overalls over his clothes tucked into high rubber boots, his old woollen hat pulled down over his head and granite face ruddy with the morning chill, he looked every inch the farmer. He continued to grin at her as she took up the egg basket. 'Nice of you to come and help, now if you could take that bag of feed with you as you go and keep the birds busy up that end while I rake out here, I'd be much obliged. There's still only a few eggs this morning, but we'll get by.'

Isabella did as she was asked and then with her basket over her arm began to collect eggs from the nests of soft straw, delighting in the still-warm feel to some of them.

'There's still quite a few here Elias,' she called out, 'and with Jack and Amos coming back they—' she stopped, someone was watching her, she could feel eyes staring at her.

Isabella looked up and met the hidden gaze of a man standing at the gate of the hen house. Startled she almost dropped an egg and though she could not see his face, she knew he had been watching her. Elias had seen him too and was walking down to the gate. He seemed to recognise the man and called out as he strode down.

'Carlos,' he said as he approached the man, 'what are you doing here? I thought you had gone to St. Helena with the others.'

The figure at the gate shuffled forward in answer to Elias but did not speak immediately. He was making a soft guttural noise as if clearing his throat before answering.

'Yes, I did go there,' the man's voice was soft and hesitant, almost a stutter, he appeared nervous. 'I'm still not sure whether it's right for me, Elias, I don't feel comfortable there; it's not the same you know.'

Elias looked at the man curiously. 'How did you get back here?'

'Took a coach that was coming this way to the village and …' he looked about him, 'do you mind if I sit down? I've walked up from the village, one doesn't realise just how far it is. I looked in at the kitchen as I came through, there was no one there so I thought you would be up here,' he said, as he sat down on a nearby upturned crate.

Isabella, still standing inside the hen house, studied the man. Shortish in stature and inclined to plumpness, made even more so by the long black coat he wore buttoned high to the neck. A thick scarf was draped about his neck which partly covered his lower face. A close fitting felt hat with the brim turned down made his face even more shadowed, his hands were thrust deep into his coat pockets and he had shifted uneasily from foot to foot, before seating himself upon the crate.

'But you did go to St. Helena's?' asked Elias. 'I would have thought you'd have been happy there, more to do and more people to interact with.'

'No,' answered Carlos, 'too many people; so many coming and going all the time. I was beginning to miss the peacefulness of the abbey. I didn't realise how much I would miss it and I also remembered I'd left a couple of things here, so it seemed right to come back, if only just to collect them.' He peered at Elias thoughtfully from under the brim of his hat. 'You're looking well, Elias, I suppose you're glad you stayed on here, though it must be lonely for you with everybody gone.'

'Not at all!' replied Elias good-heartedly. 'I've had these two fine ladies for company, and I expect Jack and Amos back at any time now. I'm just glad I was able to keep things going here.'

'That's nice,' said Carlos slowly as he gave Isabella another quick glance. He shrugged his shoulders and shivered slightly. 'Elias, do you think I could stay here tonight — use my old room? I have a couple of things to collect from it anyhow and there's a book I left in the library I'd like to pick up. If–if Amos and Mr Grimsby do not want me here–I know I caused them some trouble, if they object, then I can leave straight away.'

'I don't see any reason why you shouldn't and if you insist on leaving, I could take you down in the donkey cart. As you can see there's plenty of work here to keep a man busy if you really want to stay on here, we can always do with an extra pair of hands.'

Carlos was suddenly wracked with a harsh cough as he stuttered, 'Oh no — I really didn't want to put you to any trouble, I'm not here to stay permanently, I just wanted the things I left behind.'

'You know you didn't have to come all the way back here to collect some forgotten items. We could have posted them on to you?'

'I know you could have,' said Carlos shifting uneasily on the crate, 'but I was coming to the village anyway. You see I'm—er—negotiating for a position with the village newspaper office. I have the experience you know and it's not just the abbey, I really wanted to come back here because it's so much more peaceful than the big towns or cities. I'm not cut out to be a Friar, Elias, at least not to spend the rest of my life as one. It has been an experience, but I want to move on now you know.'

'Well, it's not for everyone, it's a way of life not suited to all who take it up, it does teach you to appreciate the simple things in life.'

'Yes, yes, you're right as usual, Elias,' said Carlos quickly, 'the village life here is simple and uncomplicated. I know I could settle down here once I get this job.' He gave another harsh cough and said apologetically, 'Oh, dear, I hope I've not caught a chill, one does not realise how cold it gets up here.'

'You shouldn't have walked all the way up here,' answered Elias, concern showing on his ruddy face. 'The middle of winter and all, you'll catch your death of cold, wouldn't be in the least bit surprised if you haven't done so already.'

Carlos looked pensively at Elias before replying, 'No, perhaps I shouldn't have but then we all do some things on impulse, don't we?'

Isabella could feel the man's eyes on her as she stood with the egg basket over her arm. He was peering curiously at her from under the brim of his hat. He turned his face then to Elias and said in his half-whispered voice, 'I would have thought that the ladies would have left after that dreadful business with the Casinis — are they going to stay?' he said addressing his question solely to Elias, as if Isabella were just part of the background.

'For a while, as long as they like,' said Elias. 'They've been extremely helpful and are excellent company. I'm hoping we can persuade them to stay on permanently,' he answered brightly.

Isabella suddenly came to life and stammered, 'If you like, Elias, I'll take these down to the kitchen now.'

Clutching the basket tightly, she hurried from the hen house, passing close to the man as she did so. She looked down at him as she went by and encountered a pair of watery eyes staring back at her. For a brief moment she sensed both fear and malice in those eyes, an icy chill ran through her, there was something about those eyes that made her flesh creep. As she closed the latch gate behind her, she thought that perhaps she had misread that look, perhaps he was, after all a lost soul, not sure of his path in life. However, the niggling feeling at the back of her mind that the man known as Carlos was not all he appeared to be on the surface troubled her deeply.

Isabella didn't like to think bad of anyone, but her recent experience with the Casinis had made her a bit more cautious and to trust her inner senses more.

She hurried on through the garden, down to the kitchen and as she crossed the open courtyard, all those thoughts were driven from her mind as a big four-wheel drive came lumbering through the gates. Jack and Amos were back!

Chapter 30

Trouble Brewing

'You used the mirror?'

'Yes, we did, and we saw him!'

'How did you know it was the Baron?'

'It couldn't have been anyone else, could it?'

'No, I think you saw what the mirror wanted you to see.' Jack was seated on one of the long benches in the kitchen with Amos and listening to accounts of the sister's experiment with the scrying mirror. Amos himself was quietly marvelling that such things existed outside his world of ideology but he had seen so many strange things of late that nothing now surprised him.

'And you say he had two men with him ... big men,' he found himself asking as if this were an everyday happening, that one could just glance in a mirror and see what was occurring somewhere else.

'Yes,' said Marilla, 'one had a big, horrible scar that ran right across his face but it was the other person in the room with them, Jack, it was a monk!'

'Either that, or someone disguising himself as one,' chimed in Isabella 'It's easy enough to cover yourself with one of those robes.'

'Yes it is,' said Jack thoughtfully. He looked at his watch. 'Let's not dwell on that just now. I think it might be a good time to do a survey of the church ladies, after you, if you please and we'll go over your calculations, Marilla.'

As the three of them made their way across the courtyard, Isabella pointed out the two significant mountain peaks across the valley and the possibility of them coinciding with the sun's path across the sky on the morning of mid-winters day. Jack had looked at the two snow-covered peaks, then up at the small circular window from the outside of the chapel. 'You just might have something there Isabella, it certainly looks to be in the right quarter for the sun as it rises. Let's see if we can track it inside.'

Entering the church Marilla began to outline her theory on the angle of the sun's passage through the high set window and the area she had calculated the sun would light up. 'The only trouble is,' she said her face creasing in a frown, 'the sun's rays are widespread and to be accurate, according to that poetic little piece of parchment you have, they should focus on a particular point. It's too big an area to search in the few short minutes the sun is in position ... if it is shining at all, so there has to be one area that stands out as a possible search arena. What do you think, Jack?'

'I know what you're getting at Marilla,' replied Jack, 'but I rather think dear old Uncle Henri just might have another little card up his sleeve. However, I do agree that we have to narrow the search area within this radius and refer further to what he says in the code.'

'Yes, but does the "thirteen across and five as deep" refer to tiles on the floor, or parts of the wall ... or even those panels up there. See those decorated panels on that overhang thing above the altar? It could be there,' said Isabella.

'I don't think so,' said Jack shaking his head. 'I rather think it's more at floor level, or just about.'

He then spent some little while traversing the area of the nave in silent thought, even getting down on his knees to peer intently at the floor tiles. Finally, he joined the girls who by now had given up and were seated thoughtfully on the lower steps of the raised area that led to the inner sanctum. Jack's attention was fixed now on the pattern of tiles in front of him, and once or twice he stood up and gazed intently at the raised altar at the end of the sanctum, then turned to what could be seen of the little window above the gallery.

Jack stood up and said excitedly, 'I think I may have found the answer,' but before he could explain his thoughts, there came the sound of footfalls from behind them.

'Sorry to have to break up the search party Jack, but I think we have another small problem.' Amos had come in through the side door with a worried frown creasing his normally benign face, 'We've got a visitor, and it's someone you won't be pleased to see.'

'Who?' Jack asked.

'Carlos,' said Amos with a disgruntled look. 'I've just been talking with Elias, and apparently, he just walked in this morning. Came up from the village, walked up, so he said and wanted to collect a few things he had left here.'

Jack cursed under his breath. 'Where is he now?'

'I knew you'd be pleased to hear that bit of information, the one person we don't want right now,' remarked Amos cynically. 'He's in his old room. Elias seems to think he's caught a chill. He's been coughing badly and shaking quite a bit. Elias has told him to stay in his room and not move from it.'

Jack was already walking briskly out of the chapel closely

followed by the others. muttering, 'why has he come back now *and* been stupid enough to have walked up in the middle of winter? What's so important about these belongings that he had to come back personally to get them? In any case I thought he was settled at St. Helena?'

'Apparently, he's left St. Helena and the Order all together. He's told Elias that he's going into the local newspaper business here, at the village ... however I'm not inclined to believe anything he says,' grumbled Amos.

'He was the cause of all our troubles with the Casinis, putting all our lives in peril with his stupidity ... or a very clever front. I wonder what he's up to now?'

'I didn't trust him then Jack and I don't trust him now. Something doesn't feel right about him turning up at this particular time.'

'I think you're right Amos but I can't see any connection with Von Zaharoff, it could be just coincidental that he's here now, other than the fact that he's a nuisance factor and a troublemaker.'

Marilla and Isabella were hurrying to keep up with Jack's long strides. 'What about the person we saw in the mirror wearing monk's robes?' said Marilla breathlessly. 'Could that have been him?'

'Well, if it was, he wasn't wearing them when he came to see Elias, when we were cleaning out the hen house,' said Isabella, puffing a little as she tried to keep up.

'Yes and if it was him, he could have been the one up on the mountain watching us, plus we really don't know how long he's been in the village, do we?' panted Marilla.

'That thought hasn't been entirely lost on me,' said Jack, 'but we're all jumping to conclusions here a bit — he may be nothing to do with Von Zaharoff. Carlos doesn't fit the pattern of the Baron's entourage but, *if* he is, then my friends, we may be harbouring a spy!'

*   *   *

Amos had been collecting and stacking wood for the fires he had deposited a great bundle of logs into the kitchen wood box, when Elias, busy cutting up vegetables, had informed him of the arrival of Carlos. Amos had grunted disapprovingly but felt the presence of Carlos important enough to convey the news to Jack as soon as possible. This was a visitor they did not welcome, but the code of conduct for the "wayside traveller" was still a fundamental principle according to the rules laid down by the Order and as the visitor appeared to have taken ill, then all the more reason to care for him; he could not be immediately turned away. This was still an Abbey of St Francis, for the moment and Amos was certain Jack would not be pleased about the arrival of Carlos.

He had pondered this as he walked to the chapel to convey the latest development. Now that the monks had, in effect, left the abbey, the code of conduct was now an unresolved point. He could see no reason why they shouldn't bundle him into the car, with his forgotten possessions and take him down to the village Inn out of the way or was there an alternative reason for him to turn up just at this time? This was the question that hovered over the group as they stood around the fire letting its warmth thaw out their chilled bodies.

*   *   *

'You say he's not well?' Jack cocked an eyebrow at Elias who was stirring a large pot of chicken soup that had been simmering on the hob.

'Carlos seemed quite exhausted from the walk up from the village,' replied Elias. 'He was shivering a lot and had rather a harsh cough and said he felt he had caught a chill. Then he asked if he could spend the night in his old room and that he would leave in the morning. I saw no reason why we shouldn't let him do so, under the circumstances.'

'And did he go there?'

'Yes, I gave him a bottle of cough syrup from Joseph's store and a couple of hot water bags, plus an extra blanket, so I guess he's tucked himself up in his bed.'

'Hmm, perhaps we might pay him a clinical visit hey, Amos,' said Jack. 'You lead the way old chap, you're more conversant with those quarters.'

Carlos was indeed tucked up in bed in the small but adequate room the fraternity were allocated. After a gentle knock at the door Jack and Amos admitted themselves where they found the occupant, a blanket clutched in plump pink hands pulled up under his chin. He surveyed them with bleary watery eyes as they stepped into the room, almost as if he had been expecting visitors. A smell of camphor and eucalypt hung thickly in the air and the bedside table was crowded with bottles of cough syrup, aspirin, boxed tissues and a carafe of water.

'Perhaps you had better let me take your temperature and make an assessment Carlos,' said Jack, as he approached the bed, 'we wouldn't want this to develop into pneumonia.'

'Oh, no ... it's not necessary,' half whispered Carlos, pulling his blanket up a little higher. 'It's really only a slight chill, I just need to sleep for a while, I'm sure I'll be fine.' He gave a short cough and stuttered, 'I shouldn't have attempted to come up in this weather … but the day looked so fine, I—'

'Why did you come up?' The question came suddenly from Amos who had taken up a position at the foot of the bed and was surveying the occupant with a critical eye. 'You know we could easily have sent anything left behind on to you without you having to go to all this trouble.'

'I–I know that,' stammered Carlos, his eyelids drooping over pale eyes, 'but as I told Elias, this place has always been so peaceful, I had a desire to see it again and to pick up the rest of my belongings while I was in the vicinity.' He gave another harsh cough and half buried his head under the blanket.

'Elias tells us you have left the Order and that you are looking for work in the village, is that correct?' queried Jack.

'Yes,' the voice was now a husky whisper. 'I really am very tired and so would like to sleep, I'm sure I'll feel much better in the morning, then I shall leave here and not be of any more trouble to you.'

'Well, what do you think?' said Amos when they had closed the door to Carlos' room behind them and began making their way back along the corridor of the dormitory. 'Is he faking this chill or not, to be honest Jack, I don't trust him, I still reckon he's up to no good.'

'It's hard to say,' mused Jack thoughtfully. 'He wasn't going to let me touch him; that makes me a bit suspicious but then you and Elias know him a bit better than I do. Perhaps it's just the nature of the man.'

'I still don't trust him, I don't buy his story about walking all the way up here from the village just because he likes the place. That was not the impression I got when I first met him, he never did any more than he absolutely had to,' said Amos scornfully.

'I have to admit it does seem to be an unlikely story, considering his obvious state of fitness,' said Jack, 'which brings me back to my first query ... is he anything to do with Zaharoff, because if he is, he seems a most improbable choice of confederate. Then again Amos my old friend, we could be forgetting one of the most important factors in this business. Never underestimate the small cog in the works of big machinery, it could very well be the dominant factor in a larger failure.'

Amos grunted. 'Sounds like we had better keep a tight hold on the situation here from now on, I'll get Elias to keep a very close eye on Carlos from this point on too. I want to know just where he is, even if we have to lock him in that room until all this is over,' he growled, as their steps led them past the door at one end of the library and on down a short staircase.

'That reminds me,' said Jack glancing back at the door to the library. 'I found something interesting in that book Marilla had been reading. The coloured tiles on the floor in the chapel and those leading up to the altar form an interesting and significant pattern, if Marilla's assumptions are correct, then they are going to lead us to where the spot of light will fall.'

'All I can say is, if you have a notion as to where that point is, you'll have to get a move on,' said Amos, 'you've got less than two days to find it, I don't think Von Zaharoff and his band of apes will be too far away.'

'I realise that,' replied Jack, 'that's why we'll have to be on full alert and keep watch on that entrance road ... that's if he comes that way, I can't see him coming in by any other means. In the meantime, while there's still plenty of light, I'm going to have another look at that chapel and those floor tiles.' He glanced up at the sky and frowned, 'I very much doubt that we are going to see much sunlight anyway by the look of those clouds. Keep an eye on those ladies too Amos, it's quite possible they'll get wind of our uninvited visitors before we do, they can sense trouble sometimes before it happens.'

Amos watched Jack disappear in the direction of the church, then with a sigh he cast a look at the cloud covered sky before pulling his woollen beanie down further over his ears and made his way back to the warmth of the big old kitchen.

Elias was ladling some of the rich chicken soup into a wide mouthed thermos when Jack returned to the kitchen, stamping his feet and rubbing his hands together as he stood close to the fire in the big old stove. He stood for a moment in thought as he warmed himself, then turned to Elias who was now preparing a tray and asked, 'So, what's the situation with Carlos now, have you spoken to him again?'

Elias looked up from where he was cutting thick slices of bread from a loaf and adding them to items laid out on a covered tray. 'I'm taking some supper over to him now, and then on to the stables to bed the animals down for the night. He might want to talk a bit more but I doubt it, he's rather a strange sort of fellow ... never did seem to quite fit in. You might like to help yourself to some of that soup, there's plenty there.'

Amos was seated on a stool pulling thick socks over his already clad feet before stepping into heavy boots which had been warming on the hearth as Jack came in. 'If you don't mind Elias, said Amos 'I'll take some of that in a thermos too. It'll be a trifle cool up in that tower. I'm taking first watch up there, Jack, it gives a good view of the top end of the lake road and we'd like to have some warning, unless this Baron is already close by and laying low.'

'That's alright with me Amos, I'll relieve you in three hours, we won't make the shifts any longer than that, otherwise it'll take us too long to thaw out each time. Look for my signal so you'll know I'm coming.' Jack gave a sidelong look at Marilla sitting up at the other end of the table. 'Of course we could always put our "spy in the sky" up on the roof on her broomstick.'

Marilla snorted derisively, giving him a scornful look, 'I wouldn't count on that, Jack Grimsby. That air is much too cold for my liking, I'm staying where it's warm thank you.'

'By the way,' said Jack, 'where's Isabella?'

Marilla, who had been leafing through the book Jack had been reading earlier answered, 'She went over to the library; she wanted to get that book she had been reading a little while ago. She was going to bring it back here, apparently there was something in it that she thought might interest you.'

Amos finished pulling on his heavy boots and jacket and jammed his beanie down over his ears. 'Not exactly a warm summer's night out there yet,' he said ruefully. Then after checking his pockets to make sure he had everything, he picked up his thermos and a packet of sandwiches and crossed the flagstone entrance calling out over his shoulder as he did so, 'See you in three hours ... and don't be late, I don't want to freeze any longer than I have to.'

Elias was also donning his outdoor gear having finished preparing the supper tray and with the thermos under one arm, picked up the covered tray, saying, 'I'll drop these in to Carlos, then I'll be over at the stables for a while. I've still got plenty to do, I'll come back here when I've finished.'

'Just make sure he stays where he is Elias,' said Jack, 'though if he's as unwell as he says he is, I can't imagine he'll want to poke his nose outside on a cold night like this.'

Elias gave an answering nod and was gone, leaving Jack and Marilla in the warmth and comfort of the big, homely kitchen.

*   *   *

'Come in,' the voice sounded feeble and strained. 'Oh, it's you Elias.' The figure under the covers of the bed stirred and attempted to sit up as Elias entered the room.

'Brought you some chicken soup,' rumbled Elias, 'that should help get you back on your feet.' He cleared a space on the crowded side table and set the tray and thermos down.

'Oh, er ... yes, thank you,' whispered Carlos. 'I really didn't mean to be any trouble to anyone,' he began to mumble apologetically.

'Don't worry about it now,' said Elias, eyeing the man carefully. 'We'd just like you to stay where you are for now, please don't consider moving too far from your room, only where you have to. It's very cold outside and it's best if you stay warm, in the morning, if you are well enough, Amos will take you back down to the village.'

'That's very kind of him,' replied Carlos.

'Well, Amos and Mr Grimsby have your best interests at heart, you seem to have taken rather a risk coming all the way back here now, under the circumstances they would

prefer that you did not go wandering about, but stay in this room, so I'll say good night to you, as I have other chores to attend to.' Elias had turned as was about to leave when Carlos spoke hurriedly.

'Wait, wait a moment ... I'd like to talk to you for a bit, if you've got time.'

Elias faltered and turned back to stand near the foot of the bed. 'I do have to bed the animals down but I guess I can spare a few minutes.'

Carlos fixed his pale bleary eyes on Elias and said, 'Those

... ladies, are they going to stay here, where do they come from? Are they nuns, because they don't look like nuns. Who are they and why are they here?'

'Sort of, in a way they are,' replied Elias carefully, 'they're here on a mission, as guests, why do you ask?'

'Oh, no special reason,' said Carlos quickly, 'just curious really. As you know we rarely saw women come to the abbey and these two are ... a little different to what one would expect.' He stopped to give a short cough, then went on in his soft dreamy voice. 'That one that was helping you in the chicken coop today, she seemed like an intelligent person ... do they like being here?'

'I believe so,' said Elias. 'Miss Isabella, the one you saw today is very knowledgeable, she reads a lot, loves books and knows a lot about plants and animals. When she's not helping me, she's usually buried somewhere in the library, there's still plenty there for her to look through. As a matter of fact, I believe she's still there hunting up a book she was going to show Jack ... Mr Grimsby. She found something of interest there yesterday and was anxious to show it to him, she's very keen when it comes to books.'

'Really,' murmured Carlos. 'Well, there's always something to learn in a library isn't there?'

'Yes there is,' answered Elias, 'but I must get moving or it will be dark before I get done with my chores. Now, you will stay put won't you, Carlos?'

'Of course, yes, I mustn't keep you any longer, it was nice of you to call, and thank you for the supper.'

Elias nodded and went out of the room closing the door behind him. He wondered for a moment whether he should lock the main door to the corridor that led into the wing that comprised the general quarters of the inmates as Amos had been suggesting. However, that seemed a rather drastic action to take. Yes, Carlos had caused trouble with the Casinis, making their capture much more hazardous for the authorities, but that could have been just blind panic on the part of Carlos too. He was a strange man admittedly, thought Elias shaking his head as he made his way down the corridor, didn't seem to really fit in with the other inmates, rather like a square peg in a round hole. Always seemed to be just wandering around the place, asking questions about the abbey in that soft faltering voice and mostly pottering about in the library carrying books from one place to another. Whatever reasons he may have had for joining the Order were never very clear in anyone's mind.

He shrugged his shoulders as he reached the steps that led through the cloisters and the latch gate beyond the garden. The cold air hit him like a knife, he pulled his jacket tighter around his body and the woollen cap further down over his head. For a brief moment he almost envied Carlos tucked up in a warm bed but the farm animals were his responsibility and they needed to be tended to first. In any case he doubted that a man with a feverish chill all snug in a warm bed was about to create any trouble; indeed the man didn't look capable of hurting anybody. Best to leave Carlos alone, let him sleep, Amos could sort him out in the morning. Elias slipped the latch gate and went quickly about his business of getting the evening chores done.

*   *   *

The heavy door to the kitchen slammed shut as Elias had gone through leaving Jack and Marilla to soak up the warmth alone ... except for Lucifer of course. He had licked his food bowl clean and was now busy washing his paws and staring dreamily into the fire.

Silence had reigned heavily for some minutes, while they ate their supper but Jack's mind was busy, something nagged at him. Somehow, it seemed far too quiet, he had half expected the Baron to make a move before this ... or perhaps he was waiting for Jack to retrieve the treasure from its hiding place before he pounced. That would more likely be the case, let Jack do the searching then he would step in and just expect to have it handed over. Whatever reason, it was proving to be a nervous wait for Jack.

Dealing with the Casinis was something he was trained for ... but this was different, this was personal, a confrontation he would prefer to avoid at all cost.

Was he now afraid to come face to face with the man who had so ruthlessly murdered his mother? That was a question he had asked himself many times but could find no answer. He should feel anger, implacable hatred, a desire for revenge and at times these feelings overwhelmed him, but there were moments, fleeting moments when he had felt tenderness and pride, a time when all was well in his world. Then suddenly it would all changed, there was some confusion and violence, raised voices, accusations that he did not understand. His child's mind was confused and he asked the question, why? But was given no answer. Jack closed his eyes and searched his memory for that night of terror that had haunted him throughout his life. It was so long ago, but he could still remember. He remembered the screaming, the sound of men's rough voices yelling, the whinnying of terrified horses, he could even smell their fear as they plunged and pulled at the reins. A voice, his mother's voice calling anxiously from a distance, urging Edwina to flee

— the last time he was to hear her voice. Then there was the carriage swaying dangerously, the wheels rumbling over rough broken ground, speeding onward, through flashes of strange light as he lay sprawled in a terrified heap on its heaving floor. Jack recalled the vision of Edwina, seated above him, her cloak flapping wildly about her body, shouting, urging the horses to go faster as she shook the reins, uttering words that seemed to have no meaning and then…. silence. In the long misty months and into the years that followed it was Edwina who was always there for him, but of his mother … there was nothing, only vague memories.

Perhaps Edwina and Henri were right, the demons that had haunted him for so many years had to be removed from his mind and what they had foretold would come to pass, then he himself would be at peace, his mother's death avenged.

Marilla's voice broke into his thoughts. 'Jack, did you notice that the pattern on the tiles in the centre of the church floor have that small, repeated pattern at intervals, in those that run up to that altar thing in the sanctum. We noticed it earlier and there's something else there too, a small dot of a gold colour on every second one in the top corner that doesn't seem part of the original pattern. I don't know whether that means anything or not, does it?' She looked up at him and was quick to notice the troubled look on his face. Closing the book, she got up and moved to sit beside him. Laying a hand on his arm she said softly, 'You don't really want to face this Baron person, do you, Jack?'

For a long moment he said nothing, then gave a sort of soft half laugh, half sigh, and said, 'Your perceptiveness is working overtime, old girl.'

'Perhaps it is,' she said, 'but there's something about this whole business you haven't told us. This isn't just about a man who was responsible for your mother's death, it goes deeper than that. Who is he Jack, and what connection is he to you and Edwina?'

That question was never answered. Neither had noticed that Lucifer had assumed a rigid listening stance, his ears pricked forward and the fur bristling on his back. At about the same time Marilla's skin began to tingle and a feeling of alarm began to sweep through her. A low growl and a hiss from Lucifer was further warning. 'Jack, they're here,' said Marilla in a hoarse whisper.

Jack's hand flew to his shoulder holster, his gaze riveted on the door of the kitchen as he half rose from his seat, only the attack was not to come from the door, but from behind them. Lucifer's eyes had been fixed on the passage that led out into the scullery and the cellars beyond, but Jack and Marilla seated as they were, with their backs to the scullery did not see this. Too late they became aware of the plan of attack and the room seemed suddenly full of heavy bodies and of dark sacks being pulled over their heads, the sweet sickly smell of a powerful anaesthetising substance they were impregnated with choking in their throats. The feeling of helplessness as they were hoisted effortlessly onto broad backs and carried off, their minds slowly numbing as the effects of the narcotic took place.

<DTO Pls Insert Cat sitting on ground with grass illustration>

Chapter 31

The Priests' Hole

The library held a fascination for Isabella. As soon as she would put one book down another would catch her interest. Even though many of the books had been removed when the monks had gone, there were still enough left to satisfy her curiosity and now that curiosity was focused on a small alcove in the far end of the library she had not had time to explore thoroughly before. Now it drew her like a magnet, she made her way to the alcove. Here the walls narrowed in to form a small nook, a square mullioned window that almost filled the end wall of the nook providing the only light source. The shelves on both sides and the wide windowsill was thick with dust and cobwebs, the tiny area gave the impression that it had been little used, perhaps useful only for those books not always needed at hand.

Old books that had obviously sat undisturbed for years, time-worn covers pockmarked by the relentless ravages of moths and silverfish that had dined on them for an indeterminate time frame, stood in their neat rows, like sleeping sentinels of knowledge, daring one to open them and awaken the stilled words within. Isabella stepped up the one broad step separating the nook from the rest of the library and entered the tiny area, she looked about her. She ran her fingers over the tattered spines of the old volumes on a lower shelf disturbing the dust and an anxious spider whose web had suddenly been torn asunder.

Isabella's attention was drawn to a large volume at the far end of the shelf, almost under the windowsill. It looked a bit cleaner than the others as if it had been recently taken up, even though it was still covered with a layer of dust. With an effort she pulled the book out from where it had been jammed in-between two other thick volumes, it plopped down into her lap when she sat on the floor in order to peruse the ancient tomes more easily. Blowing the dust from it, Isabella examined the outer cover. Originally perhaps of a deep red Morocco leather, it had once been a handsome book. The corners were bound in filigree silver, now dull with age, there were two bands of the same ornately traced silver that held it firmly top and bottom on both sides. Two small solid silver hasps hung from them over the front of the book, each one fastened with a slender pin hanging from silver chains. Isabella wondered why such a valuable looking book had been left behind but even so, it was here, and her curiosity begged her to open it.

Carefully she slipped the pins out of the hasps and with a breath of excitement opened the ancient tome. Its heavy cover fell back with an ominous creak and the smell of old parchment seared her nostrils. With trembling fingers, she turned the first few stained pages and stared at the strange writings. Even though it had been written in a much earlier century, she could still read most of it; but it was the drawings, neat and concise that held her interest. It appeared to be the original history of the building of the abbey and contained detailed floor plans of the imposing structure, not only that above ground, but of what also lay beneath, enclosed in its very foundations. Turning another yellowed page, she found herself looking at something familiar — the underground crypt where she and Amos had barely escaped with their lives, but there was more.

The crypt was only part of a vast underground maze of tunnels and rooms that seemed to stretch almost further than the area the abbey itself sat on. 'My goodness,' she whispered to herself, 'who would have thought that there would be so much hidden under this place?'

So engrossed was she in examining the book that she was startled when a slight sound drew her attention, she became suddenly aware that she was not alone in the room, someone was watching her. Closing the book, she scrambled to her feet and clutching the book tightly to her bosom stepped from the alcove to see a hooded figure observing her from a short distance away.

Time stood still for a brief moment as they stared at one another, then the cloaked figure threw back the hood and she recognised the man who had taken them by surprise in the chicken coop that morning. Carlos, Elias had called him, he had been one of the monks in the abbey. Apparently, he had left some of his belongings behind and had walked up from the village to collect them. Then she remembered also that this was the man Amos and Jack said had caused so much trouble in the capture of the Casinis. Looking at the plump pale faced figure standing in front of her Isabella found it hard to believe that he could have caused so much mischief, he didn't look at all a dangerous person but there was something about him that felt wrong. She could see it in those pale watery eyes that were now fixed on her, when he spoke the voice was soft and faltering.

'Oh, dear, I'm sorry if I startled you, I didn't think there was anyone else here. I came to get a book; I thought it might help pass the time you know.' He looked at her carefully, and said in a philosophical whisper, 'I see you like reading too, books are wonderful things aren't they? One can learn so much that is useful.' He had moved a little closer to her and she instinctively took a step back.

'Oh, don't be afraid,' he said quickly, 'I see you have been looking at some of the very old volumes that contain so much history about this wonderful place, did you know,' he said raising a plump pink finger, 'there are some books at the top there on the other side of the alcove that have the most marvellous pictures in them? I have looked at them many times and never cease to be amazed by them. There are some original drawings in one of them of all the plant life that is in this area, meticulously drawn by one of the old monks many years ago ... are you interested in plants at all?' he asked, putting his head on one side and smiling benignly at her.

'Why, yes ... yes I am actually,' said Isabella haltingly. She was beginning to feel a little less anxious as he spoke of the many interesting old books he had found that no one else seemed to care too much about. 'I get so much pleasure from reading, there's so much to learn about in a place like this,' he went on in his dreamy voice. 'I am really quite tired though ... I'm not well at the moment you see, I only came in here to get a book then go back to my room but if you like I'll show you which book has those drawings in it ... that's if you're interested in seeing it of course,' he said and gave a harsh little cough grasping the edge of a table for support as he did so. 'Oh, are you alright?' she said a little more anxiously than intended.

'I'm fine,' he said grimacing a little, 'just this nasty cough that seems reluctant to leave me but if you'll just step into the alcove, I'll show you which book it is.'

He moved silently past her and into the alcove and began to

scan the topmost shelves. 'Come dear girl, see if you can see it ...
it has a green cover, there's so much dust up there and my poor
eyes are not that good. I know it's here, I just can't see it ...' he
seemed to be talking almost to himself. 'Oh, dear, looking up
like that does make my poor head spin.'

Isabella still clutching her book stepped into the alcove and
stood at his side also looking up at the shelf of books. 'Did you
say it had a green cover?' she said as she craned her neck to scan
the row of books.

'Yes, yes, I do believe it's still there, see if you can reach it, my
dear, it's right at the top, the third from the left, see ... however
I do believe the colour has faded a little more since I last took it
down but I'm sure you can reach it,' he said chattering amiably.

Isabella was obliged to stand on tiptoe to reach the top shelf,
Carlos stepping to one side to give her room. As she leaned
against the shelves, she suddenly found herself falling forward as
the entire wall of books moved away from her and she tumbled
into complete darkness.

Somewhere she could hear the whir of cogs or wheels and
realised that the wall was closing behind her, the faint slit of
dim light that had been there was diminishing quickly, as the
gap closed and the sound of someone laughing, but now there
was only complete and enveloping darkness.

Elias had been working steadily, the lowering clouds
promising a quick nightfall, but his practised mode of efficiency
made short work of the evening chores. After leading the goats
into their night enclosure and filling his pail with the rich fresh
milk, he left them comfortably in their byre while he moved
on to stable the donkeys. Bundling their feed into the racks
in their enclosures he talked to them, calling them by name
and fondling the long ears, man and beast seeming to have

that special understanding that comes from a long and close association. Their soft braying's and rumblings, the twitching of ears and swishing of tails told him that they were content, if they were content, then so was he.

However, all at once something changed, they appeared nervous, tossing their heads and stamping their feet. Sensing that which was alarming them was somewhere behind him, Elias turned and in that moment received a vicious blow to his head. A blinding flash, in that split second before the blow fell and he lost consciousness, he glimpsed a grey-robed figure, a hand aloft, a heavy piece of wood in the hands, with pale watery eyes gleaming viciously at him. He fancied he heard a harsh voice saying triumphantly, 'That's two down now' before darkness closed over him.

*   *   *

Isabella was crouching in the darkness suppressing the urge to panic, swift memories returning of a similar situation not that long ago. This darkness had a different feel and smell to it though, woody and dank like a cupboard that had not been opened in years. Where was she ... and why had she been locked up in this place? That man Carlos must have been responsible, he had done something to make the wall open up, but why? How was she going to get out and if she screamed, would anyone hear her? She could feel a wooden floor beneath her, the edges of a rug or piece of carpet close by. As she began to accustom her eyes to the darkness around her, she realised that there was light, faint light that seemed to be emanating from somewhere above her.

Isabella rose shakily to her feet and snapped her fingers. The pale blue light that issued from an outstretched finger only made shadows dance eerily in front of her, there was a wall and she followed it with an outstretched hand feeling for any extrusions or cavities. Pushing and pressing at different parts of the wall had no effect, there were no secret exit buttons or levers, just solid wall. She had found nothing for the second time around her small prison, when her hand encountered a wall sconce set high with a candle or firebrand fixed into it. She flicked her finger again and applied it to the ends of the firebrand and was rewarded with a burst of flame and the smell of oil breaking the darkness around her, setting flickering shadows dancing on the walls of her prison room.

Taking the flaming torch from its bracket, Isabella held it aloft and surveyed her prison. It was little more than a very large cupboard, no windows, no doors, with just a square of carpet in the middle of the floor. Resisting the rising tide of panic that was beginning to sweep over her, she sank to the floor and tried to think logically. Marilla knew she had come to the library but would she come to look for her and could she be heard if she screamed out. Somehow, she didn't think so.

Something clicked into place in her memory as to what this space was ... a priest's hole! She had read about such hiding places where those of a high order could disappear when an enemy threatened. Taking a step across the square of carpet she felt the boards give a faint creak beneath her feet. Grasping a corner of the rug, she threw it back to reveal a trapdoor in the floor space with a recessed iron ring set into one end of it. Of course! There had to be a way out, a route of escape.

The silver-bound book still lay where she had dropped it. Placing the torch back into the sconce, she sat with her back to the wall beneath the flickering light and began to search through the yellowed pages for a clue as to where she was. There had to be an exit from this tiny room! She was trying hard not to let tears cloud her eyes as they searched the pages.

It was difficult at first to follow the lines and symbols depicted in the ancient volume, but her experience in deciphering Grandma Hackett's obscure writings made defining the ancient script that much easier and eventually she began to make sense of the drawings.

Finding and identifying the long room, now the library was fairly easy; but to equate its location in relation to the underground passageways was a little more daunting. She put the book down in frustration and put her head in her hands; it was all too hard to figure out. Closing her eyes she leaned back against the wall. Why didn't she trust her instincts when Carlos led her into that little nook? She had read evil in those eyes when she had first seen him, she should have kept her distance and not trusted him. He had known this room was there and how to get in but did he know how to get out? Why had she been thrust in here anyway? Slowly the swirling thoughts in her mind began to channel themselves into some sort of analytical order. This man Carlos was a monk ... or had been ... or still was. When she and Marilla had looked in the scrying glass, they had seen someone dressed in a monk's habit attending the needs of the Baron, a fleshy white hand that had lit a cigarette ... was it the same pale fleshed hand that had pointed out a fictitious book on that high shelf? Isabella was sure it was, she had been drawn into a trap. Carlos was in the employ of this Baron Von whatever, and if she had been targeted, then what of Marilla and the others — they would be in danger too! Perhaps they were already captive or ... Isabella turned her attention back to the book.

Banging on the walls and screaming out she figured was only going to exhaust her energies and it was doubtful now that there would be anyone to hear her. Turning the yellowed pages, she again found the diagram of what she believed was now the library and fixed its position firmly in her mind, noting as she looked more carefully at the stained pages that the room she perceived to be the library had a tiny square at the top of it and barely visible was a tiny cross marked on it. Surely this then must be the Priest's hole! As carefully as she could in her mounting excitement, she turned pages until she found the drawings of the underground passages. She noted that they all seemed to begin at a central hub, an almost circular placement that would have been just off to one side of the area she had marked as the library, but where did her trapdoor lead, if anywhere at all?

There were several passages that linked with the central hub, some culminating in rooms and others obscured by other writings or where a page was so badly stained it was impossible to see where they went. There were even one or two of the passages that did not lead anywhere; they were 'dead ends'. She also noted that the huge area that was the crypt was connected by a passageway as well but a grid had been drawn part way across it as if it was not intended to have access from that direction.

There was one very short passage that entered the central hub and she ran her finger slowly along it examining the lines carefully and saw very faintly, a tiny cross, so faint she could easily have missed it. To her, it coincided exactly with the cross, marked on the surface diagram! But where did it go from there? Turning her attention back to the underground plan again she studied the short passageway and noted that there was one close by it that turned almost back on itself and ran a short distance before terminating under a cluster of buildings. She looked carefully at the cluster of buildings and realised that it could only be the stables and general outhouses to the back of the abbey. That was it, of course! Anyone who wanted to escape the abbey would take that route and escape quietly in the night by means of a horse, as it would take them swiftly on a roundabout route that could easily hide them from watchers at the gates. Now she was beginning to make sense of it all! After all what was the sense in having a hiding place like the Priest's Hole, if you couldn't escape from it? Isabella put the book down and looked at the trap door. She did not really want to go down under the abbey again, once had been enough. Perhaps she would try banging on the walls and screaming out. After a few futile minutes of that, she sank down to the floor again exhausted. It had to be the trap door.

Isabella grasped the rusting iron ring and pulled hard at it but it did not move. She tried again and heard a grating noise as it moved slightly, she managed to lift it a fraction before having to let it fall. It was heavy and almost beyond her strength to lift it at all. She could tell by the way it grated, that the hinges holding it closed were rusty and were not going to move easily.

She sat on the floor again close to tears now. How was she going to get out! No magic she could produce here was going to lift that weight. It had obviously been many years since that door had been moved. She looked up at the flickering torch and realised it was not going to burn forever, she had to lift that door. Then through her mists of tears she saw the book still lying on the floor where she had dropped it. A thought was beginning to take shape in her mind.

The book was heavy, bound with metal and was perhaps four or five inches thick ... a prop! She wiped the tears away from her face with the hem of her skirt and fetched the book from where it lay and put it close to the edge of the trap door. Now, she not only had to lift the timbers up far enough but also had to edge the book into the opening with her foot. If she could just get it up high enough to insert an arm or a leg through, then she could use her body weight to thrust it upward.

This proved a lot harder than Isabella had first thought and her first few attempts only succeeded in pushing the book away as the trap door came down again. Sobbing with frustration, she exerted all her remaining strength and heaved at the iron ring again, this time she pushed the book hard forward with her foot, however, the kick was almost too hard and it looked as if the precious book was going to slide completely down into the hole. She hastily dropped the lid and it jammed on the book; at last there was a gap she could work on.

Exhausted again by her efforts, she sat on the floor and gazed at the small opening she had created ... if only she could get it a little higher. There was nothing else in the room that she could use! She sat staring at the book wedged in the gap visible between her feet as she sat on the floor.

Her boots! The heavy lace up boots she always wore just might give a few more inches. She took them off and lay them side by side on the top of the end of the book visible from the hole, then thrusting her arm as far as it would go in the gap and bracing her elbow she pushed as hard as she could, at the same time wriggling the boots forward until she had gained those few extra inches. The rusted hinges were now beginning to give way to easier movement, although the timbers were still heavy enough to be a problem to lift. By slow degrees Isabella was able to squeeze enough of her shoulder into the cavity to work the book to an upright position, this gave enough space now to see what she was about to drop into.

Producing that small blue flame again from her fingertip, she cautiously thrust her whole arm through the gap. Her nose wrinkled at the musty earthy odour that arose from the depths and her flicker of light revealed a short flight of steps, the top one some three feet away from the top of the hole. Hoping her prop would not give way Isabella slowly squeezed as much of herself as she could into the space until her feet found that top step, then with the door of the trap on her shoulders she heaved upward and with a grunt of satisfaction she felt the whole door drop away behind her ... the way was open! After lacing her boots on again, Isabella removed the still flaring torch from its bracket and taking up the book prepared to enter the cavernous realm that now lay open beneath her feet. Reaching the bottom of the small flight of steps she found herself in the short passageway she had noted on the map and she did not have to progress far along it to suddenly emerge into a large area, where the roof of this large cavern soared above her head. Holding her torch high she could see it was just as the book had shown, an almost circular space, the yawning mouths of other tunnels, like hosts of dark empty eye sockets stretching out in different directions. She shivered, it was eerie, and she had visions of all sorts of things issuing from those dark caverns.

Looking about her, Isabella could see brackets and wall sconces with firebrand torches in them at intervals around the cavern. She lit one from her own and the smell of burning oil filled the air as the torch sputtered to life, she lit another and another, until the whole area was filled with light and dancing gyrating shadows. She didn't mind the flickering shadows ... at least it was light. For a brief moment a thought crossed her mind ... why were the sconces oil saturated ... had someone been keeping them fuelled? She wouldn't have thought the monks would have come down here very often ... but someone had.

However, the point now was to find her way out, she began

to search for the tunnel that should lead her to the stables. She looked apprehensively at the dark entrances about her, shadowy and foreboding. Who knew what lay beyond their subterranean portals; but it was the one behind where she stood at the foot of the steps that beckoned her. Fearfully, she raised her torch and surveyed its cobwebbed strung gloom. Was this dark orifice going to lead her to freedom ... or to another trap? Hopefully, if she had read the book correctly it would lead her out of this underground vault and into the familiar surroundings of the stables and freedom.

'Well, I won't know if I don't try,' said Isabella to herself resignedly. Her heart was thumping against her ribs and every nerve seemed to be standing on end, she took a deep breath then brushing aside the thick cobwebs that veiled the entrance, passed into the unknown darkness, holding her flaming torch high.

Thought came back slowly to Elias. His first thought was pain, his head throbbed. The next was restriction, his wrists and ankles were securely tied, he was also very cold, even though he was lying on a half bale of straw. He could see the flicker of a fire through half closed eyelids and then these scattered thoughts gathered themselves together as he tried to remember where he was and why he was in this situation. These thoughts had now manifested themselves into stark reality. He was a prisoner!

Carlos! He had been deceived into believing the man was tucked up in his warm bed. Carlos, who had looked too ill and frail to do anything harmful; had followed him to the stables and attacked him, why? Elias moved his head painfully and looked to see where the fire was.

A small brazier on the floor some fifteen feet or so away from he lay was being fed slivers of wood by plump pink hands. The robed and hooded figure was also wrapped in a blanket which he had pulled close about him. Elias could hear him muttering to himself as he drew the blanket closer and crouched over the fire.

Struggling against his bonds only made Elias aware of how really cold he was, his fingers were stiff and he could barely move them. He called out to the robed figure, 'Carlos, is that you?'

The figure by the brazier stirred and looked to where Elias was struggling against the ropes that held him. 'What do you want?'

'Why, Carlos. Why are you doing this?'

There was a pause before Carlos answered, 'Because I have to,' came the reply in a very different voice. Gone was the hesitant whisper, the voice that answered him was hard and cold and it made Elias's flesh creep as he began to realise the trap that they had probably all fallen into.

'Then you really are a spy and no doubt working for this Baron person, am I right?'

'What if I am? I'm being paid good money just to keep a couple of you out of the way and pass on valuable information to the Baron. I've been very helpful to him; he likes the way I work.' Carlos got up from his place by the brazier and walked over to the darkened corner where Elias lay and looked down at him. 'This has been a long time coming to me, Elias. I will have earned my money and it's not been easy. I've got nothing against you or the others that were here but I've got a job to do that I'm being well paid for, so don't try anything funny, or you won't get off so lightly next time.'

He laughed mockingly. 'You all thought you had me worked out didn't you, thought I wouldn't be capable of causing any trouble with my simpering ways. Well, I fooled you all!' He laughed again. 'Been working for the Baron for a long time, he finds me very useful, sussing this place out with one thing and another but I'll be glad to move on to where it's a bit warmer, this is like living in a freezer.' He started to walk back to his fire, 'Anyway this place is getting creepier by the minute.'

'What do you mean, creepy? You've never presumed that before. According to what you've told me, you have always liked being here in the abbey, you like this place ... peaceful I believe you said it was.'

Carlos turned and went back to where Elias lay and dropped down on his haunches, so that Elias was staring straight into those pale eyes. 'Yair, creepy and you know it too Brother Elias ... ever since those two women turned up, don't say you haven't noticed it ... and Jack Grimsby 'ain't all that he seems to be too. There's something about all three of them that just 'ain't natural. Weird things have been happening since they've been here.'

'But they are old friends of Jack's, they just happened to arrive at an awkward time and were not aware that this was a special mission drawing to a close. As you are now know Carlos, Jack and Amos are Special Agents sent to round that Casini lot up, which they did, there's certainly nothing sinister about that,' said Elias attempting to sit upright but gave up and lay still again.

'Not from a few things I heard,' muttered Carlos. 'So, they just happened to drop by, nobody saw them coming did they? What did they do, just fall out of the sky?' Carlos snorted his disbelief and pulled his blanket closer and stood up. He laughed coarsely, 'You know what I find funny; Amos McAllister comes here posing as a monk to get inside information on the Casini mob and then there's me, also posing as a monk to find out how the land lies for the Baron, how to get in and out of this place easily and neither one of us aware of what the other was really up to. In any case, Jack Grimsby wasn't just here to get the Casinis, oh no ... he was here for something else, something that doesn't belong to him and those two women are staying here to help him find it ... but they won't get it!' he spat defiantly.

Elias was still trying to get his head around this turn of events but had to know just how much Carlos knew about the quest that had brought Jack here. 'What makes you so sure he won't?' asked Elias quietly as Carlos made to move back to his fire again.

Carlos turned to look at him disdainfully, 'Because the Baron's "boys" can make mincemeat out of Grimsby and McAllister, as well as that other woman that was here any time they like.' He gave another short harsh laugh. 'Probably got 'em locked up already in one of those underground dungeons until the Boss finds his treasure, then he'll get rid of them.' He turned his pale face closer to where Elias lay and leered at him and said in gloating tones, 'Then I'll get the rest of my money and be out of here like a flash.'

'Why do you say ... the *other* woman? Aren't they both together?'

'Nope, I saved the Baron the trouble and got rid of one of them.'

'Which one and how?'

'The short fat one, the one that was helping you in the chicken coop this morning. She was in the library like you said she would be, so I showed her the Priest's hole ... very interested in it she was too!' he said with a mocking smile on his face, 'You know Brother Elias, once you're in there, there's no easy way out!'

Elias struggled to regain control over his feelings. 'I knew I should have locked you in,' he said angrily.

Carlos shrugged his plump shoulders as he made his way

back to his fire. 'Wouldn't have made any difference, Elias, I still had a key to get out.'

'You could at least find something to keep me warm!' Elias called after him.

Carlos paused, there was a rack on the wall nearby hung with several of the old robes. He picked one up and went back to Elias and obligingly laid it over him. 'Might as well be comfortable,' he grunted. 'We'll be here for a few hours.'

Elias was angry, he cursed himself for telling Carlos about Isabella going to the library. Why couldn't he have trusted his own instinct and seen through Carlos in the beginning when he had first arrived at the abbey but he had to admit, the man was a dammed good actor. He had fooled everybody, his persona had been good, too good; but too late now ... and what of Isabella?

Elias knew about the Priest's hole and he knew what lay under the piece of carpet.

No, Isabella wouldn't know how to get out that way and even if she did, there were too many tunnels and not all of them were safe ... he shuddered and closed his eyes at the thought. No one would ever find her if she did go through there ... and take the wrong path ... they wouldn't know where to look. If she was still in that tiny room, she was at least safe, for the time being anyway.

A slight noise behind him silenced his thoughts, there it was again! Probably just a rat getting at the grain sacks again, he'd have to set more traps. Odd that he should be thinking of setting traps for rats when he was like a rat in a trap himself. His body stiffened and he held his breath, it didn't sound like a rat foraging amongst the grain sacks ... something was moving slowly toward him from the deep shadows behind where he lay. He could hear heavy breathing and the spasmodic dragging of a heavy body.

There was no way to turn himself to see what it was, but whatever it was, he could hear it getting closer to him. He glanced over to where his captor sat and wondered if he could hear it too.

Suddenly something touched his shoulder and he felt hair brushing against his face, then the heavy breathing manifested itself into a voice that whispered hoarsely close to his ear, 'Don't say anything, just stay very quiet, it's me — Bella.'

Chapter 32

A Contestable Discussion

Jack, by degrees, was becoming aware that the heaviness against his ribs was due to a boot nudging him. He forced his eyes open and tried to clear his fogged brain. He could see the boots, large, very large boots and thick legs that seemed to go up forever, like tree trunks. A fat, florid and somewhat featureless face peered down at him from atop a huge barrel chest. For one strange moment he felt he was living a fairy tale — he was Jack and this was the giant. He didn't have long to ponder the situation however, as the giant reached down and with one hand grasping a handful of his clothing, Jack was hauled upright to stand shakily on his feet.

'Master wants to see you,' grunted the giant, bringing Jacks' face closer to his own, peering intently at him, 'and don't try anything stupid,' he muttered heavily, still clutching the front of Jacks' jacket.

Not having the strength or interest in doing anything stupid, Jack was pushed forward, his slowly returning faculties trying to ascertain just where he was and what had happened to Marilla. He turned his head to see where he was imprisoned and saw that it appeared to be a cell or cage of some sort with steel bars all around it. It was also somewhere underground, the walls and ceilings surrounding the cage were rock and the air smelled damp and musty. The only light came from burning firebrands set high on the opposite wall of what appeared to be a large cavern, the cage set to one side of it. Marilla, where was Marilla?

A low groan came from something lying in one corner. 'Marilla!' Jack broke away from the giant's grasp and moved quickly to where Marilla lay huddled. He grasped her shoulder and turned her towards him and was relieved to see the green eyes open. He looked earnestly into her face. 'Marilla, I hope you're not hurt, are you?' He received a shake of her head in reply. 'Listen to me. Don't do anything, not just yet — sit tight and wait, understand?' he managed to whisper before the none-too-gentle giant hauled him to his feet again and marched him out of the cell door with a primal grunt.

'We don't keep the master waiting, *move!*'

*   *   *

'Such a long time is it not, Jacques?'

The speaker was seated in the warmth of the kitchen at one end of the long table, a bottle of wine in front of him and two glasses. 'Sit down, Jacques, I'm sure you would appreciate a glass of wine, though I have tasted better.' He picked up his glass and held it to the light. 'It's rough but it is palatable.'

Jack remained standing, looking intently at the man seated before him. He saw a thin, sallow pinched face with high cheekbones sheltering deep-set and sinister dark eyes that seemed to burn in the sallow complexion. A short neatly trimmed grey beard made the aristocratic face look even longer and thin nervous lips twitched imperceptibly as a smile was forced from them.

'I see you have inherited much of … your mother's looks.' The voice was dry and harsh as the dark grey eyes tentatively probed his own, before he continued, 'one must wonder how much more you have inherited.'

Baron von Zaharoff put his lean head on one side as he too looked Jack over. 'I hope that Sergei was not too rough with you. He does forget his strength sometimes but I can see that you are still intact.'

Jack said nothing but continued his appraisal of the man who had remained faceless but predominant throughout his dreams and waking moments. It was not a face that he had held vaguely in his memory; this face and figure was old, tired and haggard. He had to remind himself that he should feel fear and loathing but at this point, those early memories were dulled by time and he could feel nothing but an emptiness that almost bordered on pity.

Confronting him now was the decaying shell of a once powerful and feared authority. Jack noticed the nervous twitch to the mouth, the slight tremor of the hand holding the wine glass, the short grey hair thinning on the top but the eyes were still bright, perhaps a little too bright, still deep and penetrating. He noted too, the expensively tailored jacket that was fraying slightly at the cuff ends and which was shiny from too much brushing. He had recognised the insignia on the pocket, the colours faded and slightly the worse for wear but there was still a regal imperious air about the man that time would not decay. The proud arrogance was still evident in his speech and mannerisms, one could sense there was power there still. Power and a fierce desire to succeed in a burning ambition that time would not quell.

There were a few more moments of silence as each surveyed the other, then Von Zaharoff spoke again. 'I see you are at a loss for words, Jacques. Please do me the honour of being seated and let us enjoy the fruits of the good monk's labours while we discuss this ... delicate situation.'

A heavy hand on Jack's shoulder made him aware that the messenger was still standing behind him. Reluctantly he sat and Von Zaharoff nodded to the giant and waved him away with a long, elegant hand. 'You may leave us for the moment, Sergei but do not stray far.'

With a deep grunt of obeisance, the big man melted into the shadows.

The second glass was taken up by the bejewelled fingers and filled from the bottle, the precious stones glinting in the light from the fire and once again Jack detected the slight tremor, though the Baron tried hard to conceal it. The filled glass was carefully placed in front of Jack, but he chose at this point to ignore it. Von Zaharoff picked up his own and taking it halfway to his lips, stopped and looking at Jack over the top of it, met Jack's eyes, he asked, 'Just who are these two women that you burden yourself with, Jacques? Where do they come from and why are they here?'

Jack had now found his voice and said steadily, 'They are old friends of mine and have nothing to do with what you seek.'

'Ah, then you do know about it; how can I be sure these women are not of the same bewitchment?' His eyes narrowed and the voice became hard and cold. 'That wretched woman has filled your head with her lies and so too that mad uncle of yours and you—you have believed them!'

'What would it matter if they are? Why should I doubt Edwina's words and my own childhood memories,' answered Jack firmly. 'I do have some memories and not all of them happy ones.'

'Ah, a child's mind is like a sponge, it will absorb anything that is poured into it!' answered Von Zaharoff contemptuously. 'The memories you have are only those instilled there by the devious minds of those who would destroy me and rob me of the last treasure from my father's house!'

'As I recall,' answered Jack evenly, meeting the others' gaze with his own, 'the icon belonged to my grandmother and has always remained in her possession. It was never yours and never will be.'

'Indeed!' a flash of anger crossed the Baron's face and his eyes glittered dangerously even though they were held in Jack's relentless gaze. With an effort he broke away and rose to his feet, dashing the wine glass to the floor. 'Damn you, damn you, *damn you* — you are bewitched like your mother!'

After a few moments of rapidly pacing the floor and muttering to himself, Baron Von Zaharoff regained his composure and sat down again intertwining his long, elegant fingers together. This time he avoided Jack's direct gaze and spoke in a menacing voice. 'I should make you aware that you can expect no help from your companions. They are being … detained. So, it would be in theirs and your best interests to cooperate. Do I make myself clear?'

Jack felt a shock run through him but he did not let it show on his face, instead he answered in a crisply controlled voice, 'Perfectly.'

Well, he knew where Marilla was at the moment, provided she did as he had asked and stayed where she was. Isabella had gone to get a book from the library but something in the way the Baron spoke told him that this was no longer the case … and what of Amos, where was he? A quick glance at his watch showed him that at least two hours had elapsed since he and

Marilla had been taken unawares. Was Amos still up in the tower, or had he too been taken by surprise and captured, or worse. Amos was a strong man but if Sergei was an indication of the Baron's personal army ... Jack didn't want to think about that. He shook those thoughts from his head and spoke carefully now; perhaps he could persuade a little information from the Baron's surreptitious advantage. His dealings with the criminal element often produced a surprising amount of material that otherwise would not be forthcoming unless you prodded the egotism of the antagonist.

'I don't believe I heard you knock at the door; is there some reason we did not hear you?' Von Zaharoff's thin lips stretched into a lazy mocking smile. 'Having inside information is always an advantage, is it not? One can always find a willing servant open to earning a little extra on the side and Carlos has been more than helpful, you must agree.'

Carlos! Amos was right, thought Jack. He should have realised earlier that the man was a fraud. The simpering hesitant manner, the weak character had all been an act, he was just as cunning and dangerous as those who employed him. He cursed himself under his breath, he had not trusted his inner feelings again.

'Ah, then you didn't come through the front door; that was a clever idea, I should have thought of that,' said Jack calmly, knowing it was better to bow to the Baron's accomplishments and his vanity if he was to get any idea of the fate of the others and just how he had been able to get into the grounds unseen.

'Not my preferred mode of admittance to enter by a back door but a necessary precaution,' stated the Baron as he poured himself some more of wine into a new glass. 'A rather tortuous and dirty, not to mention dangerous entry via a long-lost passageway shown me by the inscrutable Carlos, who has spent much of his time here not, as one would think, labouring in abortive clerical duties but in an acute study of what lies beneath this unimposing edifice.' He picked up the glass and took a delicate mouthful before continuing, 'Unless you yourself my dear, Jacques have ventured under this ruinous pile, you have no idea of what lies beneath — a veritable maze of passageways and rooms to delight the explorer. Distasteful to me of course with its dank mustiness admittedly, but it has served my purpose. We have arrived, unannounced and triumphant!' He leaned forward slightly, placing the glass down in front of him. 'Now, I will ask you, Jacques, have you found it?'

A heavy silence prevailed with just the crackling of the fire in the old wood stove still burning brightly, breaking the ominous hush that hung in the air.

'No, I have not,' replied Jack truthfully. 'I have not as yet had the time to "explore this unimposing edifice" as you put it. I have been detained with other matters.'

'Ah, the disreputable Casini group no doubt,' replied the Baron. 'You have been shadowing them for some time now, they have made both our lives difficult you must admit. Their presence here made it extremely hard for Carlos to have a free hand in his explorations. However, they are no longer in command here now and I shall assume sovereignty in their place.'

Reaching into a fob pocket in his jacket, he withdrew a gold watch and studied it momentarily. Snapping the lid shut, he slid it back into his pocket and lifted a long thin finger to point it at Jack, he spoke in a voice that now became now became harsh and menacing.

'There are still a few hours until dawn. You will be returned to imprisonment with your unsavoury companion for the time being, then at the appointed hour, I'm sure you will have the same desire as I to seek out the hiding place of the property that is rightfully mine ... regardless of the foolish untruths you have had impregnated into your mind.' He raised his hand and clicked the long fingers and Jack heard a shuffling movement behind him.

The heavy hand of Sergei fell on Jack's shoulder but he ignored it. Instead, he leaned across the table to fix his eyes firmly on those dark malevolent orbs that confronted him.

'Where are my companions, what have you done with them, you can at least tell me that?'

'They have not been harmed — as yet,' answered Von Zaharoff slowly. 'Carlos has your gardener fellow under control and so too, I believe the other woman. As for your other confederate, Alexis is keeping watch on him, what you might call, a close surveillance but no doubt he will be joining you in your cell, unless Alexis has other ideas. Your man is a strong one but not as strong as my Alexis, it would be a foolish move to test the strength of one so formidable just now. At another time, perhaps for sport ... it might be an interesting combat.'

The Baron stood up and signalled Sergei to escort Jack back to the underground cell, with a parting remark. 'For your own sake, Jacques, it will be easier to work with me than against me, do understand that?'

Jack made no answer but rose and walked out of the room with the big man following closely behind.

It was with some relief that Jack found Marilla still sitting in the corner of the prison cage when he was roughly escorted back underground by the sullen Sergei. He had been a bit concerned that she might attempt to escape on her own, using magic of some sort but then he reminded himself that Marilla's magic would be hard pressed to get out of iron bars.

Sergei opened the cell door, a great old-fashioned padlock hanging from it. From over his thick wrist, he took an iron hoop and suspended from it, the cumbersome key with which to lock the door again.

'Sergei,' Jack spoke the man's name softly.

The black eyes in the round fleshy face peered at him through the bars.

'Sergei,' Jack repeated the name, his voice growing more authoritative. 'Be very careful with the key, you wouldn't want it to fall off your wrist now would you. If you lost it in these dark passages, the master would be very angry with you and you know what he's like when he's angry.'

The black eyes blinked at him as the big man stood motionless, staring at Jack, who continued talking in a soft steady voice. 'It would be much safer to hang the key up somewhere where you could find it easily when the master calls for us.'

The black eyes blinked again as the significance of Jack's suggestion was pondered and absorbed. Marilla, curious as to what he was saying had come from her corner to stand beside Jack and was about to say something when a touch of his hand silenced her.

Sergei stared at Jack a few seconds longer, then shook his great head and grunted something to himself as he began to walk away slipping the iron hoop over his wrist again.

'Jack!' Marilla had grasped his arm tightly. 'Jack, he's the one we saw in the window of the Inn when we looked in the scrying glass! What did you say to him?'

'Just watch,' Jack whispered back.

Sergei had walked a short distance down the darkened

passageway, then faltered in his steps, turned and walked back to where the firebrand burned brightly in its sconce on the near wall. Taking the iron hoop off his wrist he carefully hung it on a hook projecting from the wall there, then turned and lumbered back up the passageway.

Marilla watched the giant form disappear out of sight in the darkness. 'What was that all about? Just where are we and where did you go?' Her questions came thick and fast as she tugged at Jack's sleeve. 'What's happened to the others, are they alright?'

'I don't know, old girl,' said Jack leaning up against the bars of the cell, 'but it appears there is a lot more to this place than first thought, for instance you wouldn't believe just where the entrance to this part of the complex is. As for where we are, I would say we're in an old part of the underground system and this was a political prison of some sort. From what I've been told and from what I have observed, there is a veritable rabbit warren of passageways and rooms down here; you and Amos were right about Carlos too. He has been working for the Baron and apparently spent his time playing the role of explorer rather than the expected theological tasks he was here for.'

Jack slid down the bars and sat on the floor, Marilla followed suit, peering earnestly into his face. 'But what about Bella, Amos and Elias, have they been captured too?'

'That I'm not sure about and I don't think he is either.'

'He! So that's where that Neanderthal type took you, to see this Baron person. What's he like, what did he say?'

Jack remained silent for a moment or two, much to Marilla's impatience but she had sensed that this was a difficult time for Jack. At last, he broke his silence, 'Well, the Baron is not much to look at now, any grandeur that he may have had has long since gone and I would classify him as a psychotic megalomaniac.' He shook his head slowly. 'He's definitely paranoid; however, for all that, together with his "heavies" he keeps close to him, he's still a very dangerous man.'

Jack sighed and said heavily, 'At least with the Casinis, for all their murderous ways, they had a code of conduct an investigator could work on. A paranoid killer is like dealing with a hand grenade with a loose pin, it's difficult to follow their line of thinking.'

He turned his head to look at her and made a grimacing face, 'Oh and by the way, he considers you an unsavoury companion.'

Marilla's eyebrows shot up and the green eyes flashed. 'Is that so? Well, I'd like to tell him what I think of him!'

'Not until we get out of here you won't, unless you're angry enough to encourage that key hanging up where the Neanderthal so carefully put it to make its way over here.' He gestured to where Sergei had hung the key on a large nail beside the wall sconce.

'So that's what you were trying to impregnate into that gorilla's tiny brain, good thinking, Jack!'

A Change of Plan

Chapter 32

In the deep gloom of the stables Elias had been holding his breath as he lay with his hands trussed-up behind his back, the rope cutting painfully into his flesh. His whole being had also been concentrating on the shuffling noises and heavy breathing coming from somewhere behind him. With his feet tied also, it was almost impossible to turn himself to see what it was. Now however, he let that breath out in a sigh of relief as Isabella's voice whispered close to his ear.

He whispered back, 'Miss Bella, how did you get out ... no, no time to talk now. Can you undo these ropes?'

'I think so.'

Carlos, who had been bending over his fire looked over to where Elias lay and Isabella shrank back into the darkness and held perfectly still.

'Were you saying something?' he called out.

'No, no,' said Elias quickly, 'I was talking to myself. I ... I was wondering how you managed to get away with this deception for so long without anyone questioning your integrity.'

There was a surly grumble from Carlos as he poked at his fire.

'Apart from being dead boring at times, I suppose it wasn't that hard to keep up appearances.' He paused, as if he was glad to talk to somebody. 'That Casini mob turning up when they did didn't help and then Jack Grimsby hot on their heels. Of course, I was prevented from getting out to keep the Baron ahead of events. He wasn't too pleased about all the attention the place was getting, you know it was mucking up his plans to take over.'

Elias could feel Isabella's fingers fumbling at the ropes, aware of how close Carlos actually was to them, so he decided it would be better to keep him talking to hide the activity. But because of the darkness of the corner where he lay and the brightness of the fire between them, he hoped Isabella would not be noticed as she struggled to untie the knots. Also, he got the impression Carlos wanted to talk.

'How did you get tangled up with someone like Von Zaharoff anyway? Doesn't seem like the sort of person you'd meet every day.'

'Ah, it's a long story and a long time ago,' said Carlos, 'not one I'm going to tell you now but I've been useful to him in many ways. This is not the first abbey we've infiltrated you know. He's been looking for his family's heirloom for some time.'

'Must be an important heirloom to go to all this trouble for,' said Elias, as he felt the ropes that were binding his wrists giving way under Isabella's strong fingers.

'Yes, it is!' replied Carlos and stood up. For a moment Elias was afraid he would walk over to the straw bales but he merely stooped down to drag his bundle of firewood closer before sitting down again and continuing. 'And I can tell you that Grimsby 'ain't staying on here just to look at the view. He wants to get his hands on it, he has no right to it. It belongs to the Baron. It's apparently an important part of his family history and he needs to reclaim it.'

'Is that what he has told you?'

'Yes, he did and I don't doubt his word. He's almost royalty you know, not many people like me can have the privilege of being "right-hand man" to a person of such high status.' Carlos's voice had taken on an important air. 'Once the master has found what belongs to him, I've been promised a big reward for my services and he knows I deserve it. I've got plans I have and life will be sweet.' He laughed softly to himself as he threw another stick on his fire.

Elias could now feel the last of the ropes taken off his wrists and Bella was rubbing them gently as she bent and whispered in his ear. 'We've got to catch him off-guard when I undo your feet. I've got a plan in mind ... just keep him occupied. I've got a little conjuring trick to do; I hope it works, Elias, so just go along with what I'm suggesting. I just hope he falls for it.'

Bella's mouth bent close to Elias's ear. 'I'm going to untie your feet but these ropes are tight. Tell him–tell him that the abbey is haunted and particularly around the stables.

Make it convincing, Elias. I'll do the rest, just repeat what I say.' 'What?' said Elias in a whisper.

'Please, Elias, we'll make something up, now listen.'

Elias listened for a moment to the whispered instructions from Isabella, then spoke. 'Ah, Carlos, what about the ghost? I'm surprised you decided to stay here in the stables after dark,' he said cautiously.

Carlos looked up from tending his fire. 'What ghost?'

'Didn't you know about the resident ghost that we have here? I would have thought that with all the books you said you read in the library; you must have come across one that made mention of it. I thought everybody knew about the runaway ghost that haunts the stables and there are the ones who haunt the crypts of course.'

'I've seen nothing about a ghost,' replied Carlos a little tensely, 'just some early history of the place being used as a political prison at some stage.' He laughed grimly. 'That'd be a fate worse than death that would — locked up in one of those prisons down there and risking being eaten alive by rats, while you were waiting to die, *ugh*!'

There was another whisper from Isabella and Elias went on, feeling his cramped ankles now free of the bindings. 'Well, it's a wonder you've never seen him or heard of him in the time you've been here. He was beheaded right here in the stables. He was a monk of the Order, you see and was apparently held responsible for a valuable prisoner escaping.

Turned out he was a traitor anyway and was in the pay of the opposition, so they decided to make an example of him to any others who might betray them.'

'So ... what did they do?' The question was asked hesitantly.

'Caught him as he was trying to escape in the middle of the night, sneaking away on one of the donkeys, so they brought him back here and beheaded him — executed him on the spot — not far from where you are now.'

Carlos looked around him briefly and shrugged his shoulders defiantly. 'I don't believe that. You're making this up just to try and scare me. Well, it won't work!'

'Shall I tell you when it happened?' continued Elias, ignoring Carlos' remark. 'It was right on mid-winter's eve and that's when he comes around again, looking for his head because he can't really escape properly without it.'

'That's a load of rubbish! Now you just shut your trap and lay nice and quiet or I may have to tie a gag around your mouth until—'

Any more words froze on his lips as his gaze became riveted on something moving slowly toward him from the shadows at the back of the stables, a dark shadow that seemed to be floating in mid-air. He sprang up as it moved toward him and he fancied he heard a low swishing sound with a faint groan. The flickering flames of the small brazier revealed a shapeless grey mass that slowly moulded itself to become the cowled cloak of a Franciscan monk. Floating eerily above Carlos, its folds billowed slightly in the cold breeze that it invoked in its passing through the semi-darkness of the stables. Another low moan and what sounded like a sob seemed to issue from the apparition.

Carlos opened his mouth to scream but no sound came. Instead, he stood transfixed in fear, except for his pudgy pink fists opening and closing. Suddenly he came to life, terrified, he turned to run but in his blind haste he tripped over his bundle of firewood and landed heavily on his back. Carlos' last vivid memory before he fainted was the grey cloak dropping onto him, enveloping his face and body.

Isabella was the first to act, Elias a little slower as he tried to get movement into his stiff limbs as he stood up. He himself had been astounded by this turn of events — of Isabella lifting the cloak off his shoulders, of strange words issuing from her lips and the gestures whereupon the cloak had become airborne. He too had watched, fascinated, as the cloak seemed to take on form as it floated in the dim light. He managed to rouse himself from his trance-like state and gathered up the ropes that had bound him. With Isabella's help, he soon had Carlos tied into a neat bundle and dumped unceremoniously onto the straw bales. As an afterthought, Elias picked up the cloak and covered the still-swooning Carlos with it.

'Wouldn't want him to catch cold, would we?' he said, as he tucked the cloak around the trembling corpulent body. He turned to Isabella then in the dim light of the brazier he regarded her keenly. 'I don't understand what you did or how you did it, I've never seen anything like that before in my life but I'm grateful to you, Miss Isabella, you—you're an amazing woman!'

Isabella herself was feeling quite stunned. Had there been a little more light, Elias might have seen Isabella blushing. 'I don't really know either. I've never done it quite like that before. I've seen Marilla do it dozens of times but I've never attempted it myself until now. Even the moans and groans seemed authentic, I have to admit.'

Elias crouched over the small fire and rubbed his wrists as he warmed his cold hands. 'Tell me how you got out of the Priest's hole?' he looked up at her.

'How did you know I was in there?' asked a surprised Isabella.

'Carlos offered the information. He was the one who pushed you in there. Seemed quite pleased with himself for having tricked you. Said you'd never get out.' He stood up and looked at her enquiringly. 'How *did* you get out?'

'Through the trap door, but it was so hard to shift. I don't think that door has been moved for years.'

'It hasn't,' said Elias with surprise and wonder in his voice. 'Nobody has been through there in all the years I've been here, at least not that I know of. I don't know how you did it!'

'Well, it wasn't with any magic, I can tell you. It was just plain hard work and frustration, not to mention it was scary being locked up in a small place like that,' she answered with a tremble now in her voice.

Elias put an arm around her shaking shoulders and said quietly, 'You were extremely brave to even try to get out that way. There are a lot of passageways down there and not all of them would lead you to freedom. How did you know which one to follow?'

'Oh,' said Isabella, 'wait, I'll get it. It's a book I found in the library. I left it under the trapdoor. The passage I followed led me here.'

She moved back into the deep shadows behind the straw bales, followed by Elias, he watched as she reached down into the cavity of the underground passageway and drew out a heavy silver-studded book from a ledge where she had placed it.

'Yes, I know that book!' he said. 'Though, I must admit I've not seen it for years. It is very old, I found it somewhat difficult to read.'

'Yes, it did take a little bit to work out and it's useful too,' replied Isabella. 'That's how I found the right passage through to the stables!'

'Isabella,' said Elias anxiously, 'we have to find the others. I rather think we have all been taken by surprise and it might be that our friends are being held in the old dungeons down below the abbey.'

'Oh,' said Isabella, a worried frown creased her round, homely face. 'Oh, my goodness, then this Baron person is here ... now!'

'I believe so, otherwise Carlos wouldn't have been instructed by this man to keep us out of the way, so he can concentrate on Jack and obtain access to the icon.'

'Then you *do* know about it?'

'Yes, I do,' answered Elias, 'but I meant what I said that day. It is something Jack has to take care of himself; we can only be there to help if he wants us to.'

'Well, I think he may need help now.'

'I agree but first, we have to find out for sure just where they are.'

Isabella looked down at the book she held in her hands.

'Would one of those passages down there lead us to the dungeons then?'

'Yes, as I said, some are quite dangerous and lead to open wells. The monks of yesteryear used to draw water from the underground streams that run beneath the abbey.' Elias hesitated, then said, 'I have never really ventured too far down there. I'm not very good with being in enclosed spaces like that. I prefer to be above ground.'

'Well, someone must have been down there fairly recently I think,' said Isabella thoughtfully, 'because there are oil-soaked firebrands on the walls; I lit some of them.'

'You did?'

'Yes, right where that circular bit runs away to all those tunnels. One of them, you would think, would lead to the dungeons, wouldn't it?'

'There is an entrance from the top,' said Elias thoughtfully, 'but it could be dangerous trying to get in from there and we would have to cross a lot of open ground first; we don't know just where the Baron's guards will be. As much as I dislike the thought, we may have to use the tunnel you came through, though whether I can remember where they all go is another thing.'

'We do have the book to guide us, Elias,' said Isabella, 'I can understand the writing, and you know the layout of the abbey better than I do, so ... what do you think?'

Elias was silent for a few moments, then said, 'The main entrance to that set of underground rooms is just off the scullery. The door to it is hidden behind a cupboard there. The one that goes to the dungeons, I think, leads at right angles off that. There is another passageway that it crosses some short distance in, I think that is probably the one that we would come in on.'

'Do you want to try it then?'

'It seems to be the only way at this time,' said Elias. 'When I left the kitchen to come over here, Amos was getting ready to stand a watch from the bell tower. I don't know that he's still there,' he murmured slowly. 'If Carlos was telling the truth and I rather think he was, then Amos may have been caught unawares too. We have had no warning signal of an approach, which leads me to believe they have somehow found the old, abandoned tunnel from the waterfall and came up through that; that's the only other way they could have entered the abbey unseen.'

'What tunnel?'

Elias wearily sat down on a nearby upturned crate and sighed. 'I'd forgotten about its existence until now and I wouldn't have thought it would be trafficable after all this time.' He looked up into Isabella's inquiring brown eyes and explained. 'It's a long, twisted and rather dangerous tunnel that use to make its way down the hill, as far as those big moss-covered rocks at the turn of the path that goes down to the village. There used to be an exit ... or entry cavity between that largest elm and the surrounding rock but on the orders of the old Marquis Du Pont during the latter part of the eighteenth century, other heavy boulders were rolled in front of the cavity to stop fugitives getting in or out. Apparently, there were some heavy rock falls part way along the tunnel itself at some time, which would have added to the danger of using it.'

He looked anxiously at Isabella, with a heavy frown creasing his pleasant farmer's face. 'However, if these men are as big and powerful as we believe they are, they may have been able to move those stones and make a safe enough passage to get through. Even though there are iron bars at this end, they'd be rusted with age. So, they could have been able to bend them apart enough to allow them access to the underground passage system or Carlos may have been clever enough to already weaken them by sawing through them. It's a slim chance, but one that, that sort of people could be expected to take. Any other approach with us on our guard would be heard or noticed. You can't hide big bodies like that amongst a few trees and not expect them to be noticed as they crash through the brambles and hedges. My bet is that is the way they have come in.'

'That also means they could have taken Marilla and Jack completely by surprise, if this end of it leads up to passages as far as the scullery!'

'Probably,' said Elias ruefully, 'they were sitting in the kitchen when I left them to come and do my chores. They certainly would not have expected to be ambushed from that direction.' He looked over to where Carlos lay trussed-up in the far corner of the barn. 'This fraudster has done his homework very well, very well indeed. No wonder he spent such a lot of his time delving into the ancient history of this place.'

He stood up and taking Isabella's arm, he walked her to where the open trap door beckoned. 'You are a very courageous young woman, Miss Isabella but now that courage will have to be tested even further ... and mine also. We'll just have to try and outsmart these

intruders and do a little ambushing of our own. It won't be of any use to go to the bell tower, as I doubt that Amos would still be there. We have to go underground. If you think you can find your way down there, I'm willing to follow.'

*   *   *

Amos had been glancing at the dial of his luminous watch. Almost nine thirty! Jack should have been here by now to relieve him of his surveillance watch from the top of the bell tower. Jack was always punctual. Besides, he had received no red flash on the bottom of the dial to warn of his approach. A growing uneasiness that something was wrong took hold. He picked up the powerful night vision binoculars and swept them over the outer perimeter and into the abbey grounds again. Von Zaharoff and his henchmen would have to come that way. He could not imagine anyone pushing through the dense thickets of bush and brambles to reach the abbey via the rear walls, unless they knew the area intimately. Then again, he thought, they may not make their move into the abbey until the very early hours, but that still did not explain Jack's lateness.

From this elevated position there was a good overall view of the approach road and the surrounding outer walls or what there was left of them, the binoculars were powerful and especially suited to pick up the smallest movement and magnify it.

Something had moved now. A slight movement, a shadow, close to the old refectory wall caught his eye and he quickly turned the binoculars in that direction. A small black shadow was creeping slowly past the rubble. Lucifer! Amos could just see the lighter end of the tail. He smiled to himself as he watched the slow deliberate steps of the cat, which was obviously stalking something ahead of him. Amos swung the binoculars beyond the cat to see what had caught his interest.

A flitting shadow, a shadow of something large, was disappearing into the blackness of the surrounding colonnades. A trespassing forest animal was his first thought but that momentary glimpse bothered him. He could not recall forest animals wandering through the abbey grounds at night and that shadow was too large! Now he knew something was wrong! Could they have been taken completely by surprise after all? That would explain Jack's non- appearance at the appointed hour. But how had they managed to get past the gate without being seen?

He must leave his post now and investigate. Swiftly checking his revolver and grasping the small powerful torch in the other hand, Amos began to cautiously make his way down the narrow winding staircase of the tower. Staying close to the wall, he carefully felt his way down the spiralling walls, feeling for the steps, not daring to turn the torch on just yet.

He reached the bottom where the steps widened out to a squarish room, set with a series of deep alcoves at intervals around its walls. These recesses were furnished with wall sconces and had originally contained the firebrands necessary to illuminate the area but were now empty. As he faltered there, listening, he heard the faint crunch of a boot on gravel just outside the door of the tower room. Moving quickly, he squeezed his body into the last recess at the bottom of the steps, which fortunately faced slightly inward toward its neighbour, giving him enough cover so as not to be seen by the person entering, even if they had a torch.

Presently, the sound of heavy breathing filled the small room, a deeper heavier shadow darkened the space even more. As Amos listened, his stiffened body motionless and pressed hard up against the rear wall of the niche, he heard a soft deep grunt that echoed slightly in the close confines, then the snap of a torch switch. A small pool of light appeared at the feet of the invader. Huge, booted feet began to make a slow ponderous ascent of the steps, the small pool of light preceding them. Surprisingly, they made little sound, despite their size.

Amos let out his breath. He would have to move quickly now. If this was one of Zaharoff's 'heavies' there was probably little chance now that Marilla and Jack would still be where he had left them. He would skirt round the courtyard and make his way to the scullery end. If there was anyone in the kitchen, he would be able to see from there. As quickly and as quietly as he could, he crossed the courtyard and reached the step of the scullery without incident. He was about to creep through when he noticed one of the high wooden cupboards that lined the wall there had been pushed aside and now a dark cavity beckoned. A secret entrance! Who would have known that was there? It was supposedly just another cupboard. He had walked past it many times never knowing it's secret, but now it was open and the faintest glimmer of light was emanating from somewhere beyond the immediate blackness.

Stepping into the scullery, Amos listened for movement or voices from anyone in the kitchen itself but could hear nothing. The dark cavity of the cupboard still beckoned. Had Jack and Marilla been captured and spirited away down those dark passages? He knew there were the old dungeons down there, left over from days when the abbey was used not only as a refuge but a stronghold against invaders. Many conflicts had been fought within the ancient walls. Prisoners had been held there indefinitely, many for political bargaining. Others never saw the light of day again. His instincts told him now that it would be there that he would find his friends.

Amos wondered for a moment why Joseph and Elias had not been entirely truthful when they were asked if there were any more entries or exits under the abbey that should be known about and both had replied that, to their knowledge, there were not. Did they know about this one, or were they being deliberately deceptive? He had felt at the time that both knew a little more about what secrets lay beneath this ancient monastery but perhaps did not see reason to expand on them at that time.

However, now was not the time to wonder about that. It was time to see for himself. He listened carefully before stepping into the semi-darkness of the tunnel, noting that it was very different from the crypt. Here the walls and floor were rough stone, hewn from the surrounding rock and earth, whereas the crypt was covered with flagstone and pillared with high arches of sculptured stone.

Creeping along the darkened tunnel toward the faint source of light and intent on what lay ahead, Amos failed to hear the step behind him until it was almost too late. The crunch of a boot on stone alerted him to danger and he spun around, bringing his flashlight up to full beam as he did so.

What he saw briefly, before a heavy fist sent the torch spinning from his hand, were two coal-black eyes glittering in a round flat face, made hideous by a livid scar that ran from eyebrow to chin across the otherwise featureless countenance. A crushing blow from his assailant's shoulder sent Amos heavily to his knees. His gun was snatched from his other hand before he could squeeze the trigger and he was sent sprawling onto the floor of the tunnel. Still stunned, Amos was dragged to his feet, his arms pinioned firmly behind his back, and marched forward down the narrow passageway.

In most instances Amos was well able to take care of himself against an attacker, but he had been caught completely off-guard and any thought of fighting back at this point would be like hand-to-hand combat with a cave troll and all in a confined space!

His captor's heavy breathing was close to his ear and Amos heard him mutter, 'You leave good binoculars in tower ... ha! Easy to see where you go. Alexis, he follow, he find you.' The giant's guttural laugh echoed off the narrow walls as he propelled Amos along, his gorilla-like arms holding him in a vice-like grip. 'Master says keep you out of way, Alexis know good place keep you!' He laughed again, making Amos' skin crawl.

The troll-like giant pushed Amos ahead of him, the path leading him deeper into the subterranean depths. Amos glimpsed several other tunnels running off at angles but it was to one where a faint light was glowing that he was directed, he soon found himself shoved into a large cavern. Light was coming from a couple of flaming torches set high on an end wall. The flickering light from them showed little in the cavern but an old forge standing to one side and many old iron implements lying about. On a portion of the wall behind were hung several more and Amos could only guess at their use. The rest of the cave was in relative darkness but seemed ominously large and there seemed to be a cool breeze emanating from somewhere beyond in the blackness.

It was time to fight back. Amos made a sudden move to twist out of the big man's grip and almost succeeded but a great fist smashed into the side of his head, he reeled back, struggling to keep his feet. He was able to trade a few blows with the big man but strong as he was, he was no match and Amos had the feeling the assailant was just playing with him — as a cat does a mouse before the 'coup de grace' is inflicted. Eventually, apparently tiring of the sparring, the giant slowly dragged Amos to the back of the cave to where the flickering light from the torches played sparingly on something that seemed suspended. As he was pushed closer Amos could see that it was a small rope-woven cage, into which he was unceremoniously shoved. The huge man laughed softly to himself as he tied the door firmly with more rope. He then moved to a side wall of the cavern and flicked a match at an oil- soaked firebrand in a sconce nearby and unhooked a rope from a large hook protruding from the rough-hewn rock wall.

In the sudden flare of light Amos was beginning to see and hear just where he was. The cage was being moved out and over an abyss, where it stopped and swayed uncertainly. Amos could hear water rushing below and cool air drifting upward to where he dangled in mid-air high above. He dropped to his knees and peered through the slats at the bottom of the cage and saw to his horror that he was being dangled over a wide, deep well, where a swift underground stream issued from a large gap in the surrounding rock wall below him. The water swirled and bounced off large rocks that jutted out into the widening stream. But he was also able to glimpse small stretches of open ground where the water did not reach, a little further downstream on the near side, before he became aware that the cage was being pulled back a little.

Amos had been in some sticky situations before but never like this! He could see the giant standing at the edge of this pit, his ravaged face set in a vicious grin. He had now picked up a long pole with a hook at the end and had caught the rope of the cage and sent it swinging and spinning with only a time-worn hook above holding it — but for how long?

Standing at the edge of the well, the laughing man sneered at him as he reached out again with his pole to catch the bottom of the cage. The disfigured face made even more hideous split to an evil grin showing blackened and broken teeth, heightened Amos' nightmare. Desperately Amos looked around for a way of escape but there was none. The woven structure of rope was old, the spaces between the knots nowhere near large enough to push his body through. What was worse, as he looked upward to where the rope was suspended, he could see that it would not take long for the rope to rub through on the great hook that it was slung through. The friction being generated by swinging the cage to-and-fro was adding to the disintegration of the rope.

He sank to his knees in despair and closed his eyes as he saw a vision of himself plunging through that hole to certain death, either by the fall or to drown in the stream below, trapped in the cage.

Alexis was delighted and was gleefully pulling and pushing with the pole. He too had looked up and said in his rough voice, 'The rope, she old, maybe she hold few more minutes ... maybe no, then ... swoosh!' He pointed his thumb down and laughed even louder.

Amos cursed loudly. Where were the others? More so, where was this damn wizard who had gotten them all into this? Wasn't he supposed to be watching out for them? He was going to die here and no one would know. He could see there was no point in trying to reason with this maniac anthropoid who was intent on killing him just for the enjoyment of it. Then something caught his eye.

Something was moving against the far wall of the cavern, something small and as it got closer into the edge of the pools of light thrown by the burning torches, Amos recognised what it was. Lucifer! He was slowly creeping up on Alexis, never taking those yellow eyes off him as he stalked him. The beast-man was still taunting Amos as he pulled and poked at him in the cage with the long pole, enjoying mastery over his victim; while Amos was desperately wondering what a small creature like a cat could do to about two hundred and fifty pounds of a man.

He didn't have much time to think about what was going to happen, for in the next instant the animal had taken a mighty spring and landed squarely on Alexis' back, right between his shoulder blades, claws embedded deeply. Dropping his pole, Alexis screamed, twisting and turning his body to try and see what had attacked him. He tried to slash at Lucifer with his hands but the big cat just dug in harder and sank his teeth into the flesh of the man's neck. Twisting and flailing with his arms did nothing to dislodge Lucifer. Then in his mad attempts to reach the cat, Alexis took a step too far and suddenly found nothing beneath his feet. He tried to make a grab for the edge of the well, but fell, screaming into its depths.

Amos looked on in horror from his high perch as he saw Alexis fall but it appeared his fall had taken Lucifer with him. He sank back in despair in the bottom of the cage. Lucifer had saved him for the moment but there was still no escape and now he was really alone ... and Lucifer was gone too. Lucifer ... he had grown to love and respect that cantankerous cat.

He put his head in his hands and would have wept but for the low growl that seemed to be issuing from somewhere beneath him. He peered down through the ropes and two baleful yellow eyes glared back. Lucifer was clinging tenaciously to the lower ropes of the cage by his front claws, the rest of his body hanging in space.

Lucifer! Quickly Amos stretched his arms through the network of ropes to grab a large handful of neck scruff, then after he'd pulled him up, he hugged him close and rubbed his ears. Lucifer ran a rough tongue over Amos' chin before settling down to a rumbling purr.

'Thanks, Lucifer, you've solved one problem, I don't mind telling you that gorilla was scaring the life out of me but I'm glad he's gone to the bottom of that well and not me. However, my friend, there's still the problem of how to get out of this. If that rope breaks, then I'll be joining him down there and frankly that's not the way I intended to leave this life.'

Amos looked up to where the rope still clung to the hook. He could see loose threads drifting in the breezes that wafted up through the canyon below and wondered just how much was left holding his rope prison. Amos still had his knife beneath his boot but even if he cut his way out of the cage, he was still a short distance away from the safety of the cavern floor and the rope that 'gorilla' had been holding now trailed uselessly below.

He sat carefully on the cage floor, trying to make as little movement as possible while he considered his options. Stroking the cat's head, Amos spoke to him. 'You know, Lucifer, if I were a cat like you, I'd climb through the top up there where the ropes have left that hole, and tiptoe very carefully along the holding rope then jump that gap to the cave floor ... but, I'm not a cat.'

He looked warily at the top where the rope went over the hook and felt it shudder as he shifted his weight slightly. 'I don't think that rope is going to hold for much longer, Lucifer my friend, there's no sense in both of us going to the bottom, so go for it now Lucifer, save yourself. The girls will miss you more than me.'

Lucifer rumbled his deep purr, he wasn't looking at the rope; he was sitting upright and expectant; his eyes fixed firmly on the entrance to the cavern, where the faintest glow of another source of light seemed to be creeping closer.

<DTO Pls Insert Cat sitting on ground with grass illustration>

Chapter 33

A Timely Deliverance

Two figures were making their slow and cautious way back through the gloomy and cobweb-laced tunnel that led away from the stables and on past the place where Isabella had emerged from the close confinement of the priest's hole after her imprisonment by Carlos. They arrived at the circular floor where Isabella had lit several of the torches that surrounded the perimeter of this underground citadel and found them still burning. She pointed back up the short passage almost immediately behind them. 'That's where I came from, Elias. We could go back that way; except you'd have to know how to open that wall again. I pressed everything I could find, but nothing happened.'

'I believe it's the wall sconce, you just turn it and—shh—what's that?'

A sound had come faintly to their ears, a sound that seemed to come from deep within the labyrinth of tunnels that faced them. 'It sounds like someone laughing,' said Isabella, 'and it seems to be coming from down that one.' She pointed to one just to the right of where they stood.

'I believe that's one of those that connects back to the scullery. If my guess is correct it would lead to one of the wells where the old monks drew water from and there's one here that leads to the old dungeons and cells but I'm not sure now which way they run,' said Elias a little uncertainly. 'It's been a while since I've been down here,' he added, almost to himself.

Isabella had already taken one of the firebrands down and begun to enter the passage from whence the faint sound had issued. They were only part way along it when the laugh sounded again, this time louder and after a short interval of other confusing guttural sounds, the silence was broken by a long and drawn-out scream that chilled them to the core.

'Oh *dear!*' gasped Isabella, 'I do hope that was not—not, oh dear—*quickly*, Elias, we have to see where that's coming from!'

The passage they found was only a short one and ended, as Elias had described, in the tunnel that eventually wound its way back to the scullery. 'It's on further, that way,' whispered Elias and pointed to where the other end of the tunnel stretched away. As they paused to look and listen, they fancied they could see a faint light that was emanating from deep down and glancing off a bend in the rock wall to send flickering shadows dancing on the rough surface.

'Down there,' whispered Elias. 'There's someone down there. Perhaps we should move closer with less light ... we don't know who or what it is, there's not much point in advertising our presence.'

'You're right,' Isabella whispered back. 'We'll leave the torch against the wall here and creep down without it. It's not far. There's enough reflected light to see where we're going anyway.'

As silently as they could, they crept down the rest of the rough-hewn tunnel until they could see the opening of a large cavern. They stopped just outside and listened intently. All they could hear now was a soft murmuring voice, no screams or laughing.

Peering around the edge of the cavern wall, Elias and Isabella could see that it was empty, or appeared to be, other than an old forge in one corner and bits of old iron lying about, while on the solid stone wall behind were set iron rings and chains. Its medieval ambience invoked a vague feeling of terror in Isabella but it was the stocky figure sitting in a rope-woven cage suspended above the floor that left her astounded.

'Amos, Amos!' she cried out and started to hurry to where the cage hung, slowly turning as the weight of the man inside shifted, an ominous creaking sound accompanying his slight movement. To her surprise, he yelled at her to stop where she was—*now!*

'Don't come any closer,' Amos said, his voice shaking a little. 'There's a deep well right underneath me, it's already claimed one victim. If this rope goes, I'll be the next one.'

Isabella paused and then went forward slowly to peer down the hole. She shuddered. 'How did you get up there?'

'It's a long story, Bella,' said Amos, 'just get me out of here. Elias, there should be a long pole with a hook on it lying there somewhere, the guiding rope for this thing has fallen underneath. See if you can grab it with the hook and at least get me back onto solid ground. Please be careful and don't let it move any more than you can help, as I think the rope at the top is about to give way.'

Elias looked up at where the rope passed over a pulley block and then the hook holding the cage. The rope was old and he was surprised it had still held as it looked as if that device had not been in use for many years. It did indeed look ready to disintegrate. In fact, he was not even sure the rope would be able to be wound back on the old pulley block without jamming, because of all the loose threads of frayed rope fibres. However, he had to try. So, seizing the pole that had fortunately been dropped on the cave floor, he carefully reached out for the trailing rope. After several tries, Elias managed to hook up the rope and get it back onto the spindle that normally held it against the wall of the cave and began to carefully pull the cage back to above solid ground, while Isabella guided its progress with the hooked pole through the mesh of the cage. Amos was already slashing with his knife through the piece of rope holding the door closed, as they pulled him to safety and in another moment Amos tumbled out. However, to Isabella's complete astonishment the other occupant of the cage stepped daintily out with a flick of his white-tipped tail and sat regarding them with sombre yellow eyes.

'Lucifer! How did you get in there? Amos, what happened; how did you and Lucifer get caught up in that?'

'That's another part of the long story, Bella and I have to thank you two for arriving when you did. I don't think that old rope would have held my weight for much longer,' said Amos as he stretched his cramped limbs. He jerked his thumb at the well, now safely behind him. 'One of Zaharoff's trained gorillas went over the edge thanks to our four-footed friend here. That is one very smart and very brave cat!' he said to Isabella, 'You're very lucky to still have him. He very nearly followed him to the bottom.'

'Oh, yes,' said Isabella scooping the cat up into her arms, 'he seems to be making a habit out of rescuing us but it still doesn't explain how you came to be up there and who was it that we heard scream ... was it ... whoever fell over there?' She pointed to the open well.

Amos nodded. 'All I can say is I'm glad Lucifer turned up when he did. If it hadn't been for him taking on an animal many times his own size, I'd be at the bottom of that right now dropped there by that nasty piece of goods.' He cast another glance toward the well and said hurriedly, 'Let's get out of here. Do you know where Jack and Marilla are, Elias?'

'At the moment, no; but then I guess you are aware that Von Zaharoff has infiltrated into the abbey and caught us all off-guard,' said Elias. Then he added bitterly, 'and we have Carlos to thank for that — he has apparently been working for Zaharoff all this time and we never suspected.'

Elias proceeded to give Amos a quick run-down on events to date. Amos swore heavily under his breath, 'I knew we should have locked him up before this; but if you've got him tucked up nicely in the barn, at least that's one out of the way. Now Elias, where do you think Jack and Marilla might be? If they have been caught, then they must be somewhere where the Baron would keep them until he's ready to make his move.'

'I'm not sure, but I do suspect that these men have been down here on and off for some time. Otherwise, how did they know all this was here? They may also be using the old prison cells that are down here as well,' said Elias.

'Mmm, I'd imagine that the Baron would want to keep them securely under lock and key until sunrise, then use Jack to get what he wants,' Amos said thinking aloud; then, more directly, 'Elias do you have any idea as to where these cells are, if that's where he's holding them?'

'Somewhere back along this corridor there are other passages that lead off. It would be one of those and I think I know which one. There are certain marks on the walls to look for. A couple of the other passages just lead to dead ends; some of the others to open wells, so you do have to be very careful. Whoever designed all this centuries ago did not intend to lose too many prisoners once they got down here,' Elias said ruefully.

'Let's go then,' said Amos, squaring his shoulders. 'You lead the way, Elias. You probably know this area under here better than we do.'

Elias gave him a sharp look, but then his face resumed his stolid countenance, as he began to lead the small party out of the cavern that had probably seen more suffering than any of them could ever imagine.

With Elias leading the way, the small party made their way back along the tunnels until they once more stood in the circular area that had been their starting point. Listening carefully for any signs of approach, Elias hesitated.

'I'm not sure now which one it is that leads to the dungeons,' he said, as he quickly examined the right-hand side of the yawning mouths of the tunnels. 'But as I said, there should be a mark on the wall there to signify where it leads to; yes there's a symbol scratched here, sort of crossed lines. This would have to be it.' He pointed to one directly in front of them.

Isabella went to where she had left her book on a rough outcrop of rock and with one hand firmly holding Lucifer, she turned the pages with the other until she found the system of underground passages. Tracing a finger along the faint lines, she said, 'I think you're right, there's a square there at the end of it; and—' Before she could say anything more, Lucifer, who had been squirming in her grasp, broke free and began to scamper up the tunnel and vanished into the gloom.

'I think he knows where to go,' said Amos, quickly grasping one of the torches and striding after the disappearing white tail tip. This tunnel seemed wider than the one they had just left and from signs on the dirt and rock-strewn floor, it had seen a bit of traffic moving along it. It was not long before they found what they were looking for.

Rounding a bend in the tunnel, a gleam of light led them to an open cavern similar to the one they had just left. In the middle of this cavern was a large steel-barred cage, its door locked but nobody inside. Behind it, hard up against the rock wall, they noticed several more cells, smaller in size and also empty. Two torches were still burning on the opposite wall, and their light was bright enough for the details of the cavern to be seen clearly.

Lucifer had squeezed himself through the bars of the large cage and was sniffing at a spot in one corner and walking around its perimeter, examining the floor with interest and stopping to sniff the bars now and then. Isabella too had stopped and sniffed the air and stood very still, as if listening to something. 'They *were* here,' she said quietly, 'Lucifer knows it too.'

Amos looked at his watch. 'It's now a little more than four hours until dawn. The question is then, are they on their way to the chapel on their own or are they still in the hands of Zaharoff … and just waiting for dawn?' Amos studied the tiny dial at the bottom of the watch face. He had noticed just a flicker of the red pinpoint of light, then nothing. Jack was somewhere, but where? He and Marilla could be anywhere within the abbey itself — hiding, waiting — or being held prisoner there.'

Elias was examining the lock on the door and explained, 'This is a very old lock, the original and the big keys to open it use to be carried on an iron hoop that hung from the jailer's wrist or they were fastened to a broad belt around the waist. It's impossible to break the door open; the key would have had to be used.'

'Would it be like that one up there?' Isabella was pointing to the nearby wall sconce. A large hook protruded from the wall beside it. Hanging from the hook was an iron hoop and suspended beneath it, a big old-fashioned long-shanked key.

'Why, yes. I guess it would be,' said Elias. 'It certainly does look like that could be the key.'

Isabella walked over to where the key hung. Reaching out a hand, she furtively touched it then quickly drew her hand back as a spark flashed from it.

'Marilla has used that key,' she exclaimed excitedly. 'Her magic is still on it!' She looked at the others, her brown eyes gleaming. 'The after-magic only lasts for a short while, so they must have escaped from here only recently.'

Isabella stood for a while in thought, then said, 'I don't believe they are in any real danger at the moment; there are no bad feelings coming from here. I think ... I think they are playing a waiting game somewhere. Wouldn't you agree, Amos?'

'You're probably right, Isabella so it's no good hanging around here. We could very well find ourselves behind those bars, come on, let's get out of here while we can.'

They quickly found their way back to the central circle and stood in the short corridor that led back to the Priest's hole.

Amos had turned to Elias and said in a firm but friendly voice, 'Now Elias, my friend, perhaps you can redeem yourself of a statement in which you told Jack and myself that you did not recall any other entries or exits from under this abbey. Obviously, there are, otherwise how has Von Zaharoff and his men managed to get in and out without our knowing and why all the secrecy about what is under here?'

'I'm sorry, Amos, I should have told you but at the time I never thought that passage could be used and yes, there was perhaps another reason,' stammered Elias, 'but it concerns Joseph more so than I and has nothing whatsoever to do with the present situation. The fact that you and Miss Isabella were able to escape from the crypt ... well, any other information regarding cavities and other passageways under the abbey seemed irrelevant at the time. Besides which, it is dangerous wandering around down here — the open wells you see ...'

'Somebody, named Carlos, seemed able to know their way around here, otherwise where else could the Baron have got in and *what* passage are we talking about? Is there something we should know that *is* relevant?' broke in a perplexed Amos. 'Von Zaharoff obviously didn't come through the front door.'

Elias's ruddy complexion was becoming even redder as he repeated to Amos what he had told Isabella about the long-abandoned tunnel that terminated at the bend in the path that led to the village. 'The stones that were rolled in front of the narrow opening were huge. It would have taken some strength and several men to move them.'

Amos grunted. 'If these "several" men were the size of the one that went for a dive in that well, then they would have had no problem — we're talking bulldozers on legs!'

'Do you think it's possible then that Marilla and Jack have found that passage and been able to get out that way?' said Isabella.

'We can only hope so,' replied Amos, as he put a friendly hand on Elias' shoulder 'and yes, Elias, I can understand your reluctance to say anything about what else was under the abbey at the time. It probably did seem irrelevant considering we were all safe and well above ground.'

'They would have to know just where to look,' said Elias, 'though I'm not really sure where the entrance this end is, I do know it was said that there were steel bars across the entrance. Though if these men are as big and powerful as you say Amos, then they may also have had the strength to bend those bars enough to get through. Plus, they may have rusted away a bit by now. They were put there a long time ago.'

*   *   *

'Are you sure this is going to get us out of here?' Marilla was wiping her dusty face with the hem of her skirt as she leaned against the rock wall of the dark sloping tunnel.

'If they came in this way, Marilla, then we can get out. There's enough evidence of activity here to tell us exactly that, though just where it comes out, I'm not sure, but I'm beginning to get a fair idea.'

*   *   *

'We seem to be moving further away from the abbey.'

'Yes it does, but I don't think we've got far to go now,' replied Jack. 'I can see a faint glimmer of light ahead, we will still have to go carefully. There's certainly some evidence of rock falls here at different times. Ah, look, you can still see where some of those rocks have been moved aside. I can see the imprints of their size seventeen boots in the dust.' He shone the flaming torch lower to the floor, where the impressions could be clearly seen.

After their escape from the cage that had held them prisoner, they had crept furtively out into what appeared to be the main passageway. Jack remembered he had been taken this way when Sergei had hustled him on to see the Baron. Their plan had been to creep quietly along this same rough corridor until they found the opening that led back into the scullery. After that Jack was not sure, but he had hopes of being able to slip out of the scullery area, unseen.

Hurrying down the darkened corridors with just the

occasional flash of light from Jack's small torch, Marilla's toe had struck a small rock and she had fallen headfirst. In trying to save herself she had clutched at a projecting stone that stood a couple of feet off the floor. She felt it give under her hand and then suddenly a whole portion of the rough stone wall had given way and she was tumbling into a cavity that had opened up. Her momentum as she rolled, brought her up against bent and twisted old iron bars a few feet inside. Pulling herself upright, she was amazed, as was Jack, who had followed closely behind to where they found themselves. The cavity itself was small; but it was what lay beyond it that grabbed their attention — a long, dark and most uninviting tunnel. Jack shone his torch at the iron bars. It was obvious that they had recently been pulled apart, wide enough to allow entry to their captors.

'So, this must be how they were able to creep up on us unannounced,' mused Jack, as he shone his powerful little torch down the mouth of the tunnel. 'I wonder where it comes out.'

Marilla had peered through the gloom of the dark orifice and muttered, 'Surely you're not thinking of going that way.'

'Why not? Look, see the marks on the ground? Footprints ... big ones. They certainly came in this way and they obviously had very useful inside information. Carlos the informer presumably.'

Jack was about to plunge into the darkness of the tunnel when he noticed a firebrand in a sconce just inside the entrance. He grasped it, noting by the smell that it was oil saturated and had recently been burned. He held it out to her.

'Come on, Marilla, my girl, a little of your magical fire here would be much appreciated. I don't want to run the battery down in my torch. We may have a long walk ahead of us and the firebrand will throw more light.'

Marilla gave him a long look but obliged with a pointed

finger and the torch soon flamed into sputtering light. She took a deep breath and said, 'I just hope you know where you're going.'

He grinned at her in the half darkness. Grasping her hand, he pulled her along behind him, as together they entered the long dark tunnel and began to follow its twisting, winding course around old rock falls and some newer ones, there were places where the stones had been pushed aside. The path led ever downward. Marilla could only follow; but her thoughts were of Isabella ... where was she ... and Amos? Was Elias with them? Perhaps her sister had taken refuge in the library after all and might still be hiding there.

'Wait, Jack. This tunnel seems to be going on forever. What if there's more of them coming the other way?'

He brought the torch light up a little to show her face as she leaned against the wall. 'It's alright, Marilla,' he said kindly, 'don't worry. I don't think we'll run into any more of those gorilla types. From what I've been able to gather there were only two and I think they are both at the abbey.'

'But what about Amos? I hope he hasn't been caught by them. They are a lot bigger than he is. That one that came to get you was so huge. Amos wouldn't stand a chance against him and I'm worried about Bella.'

'I'm sure she's alright. Your sister has a way of looking after herself, if she's with Amos or Elias, then I'm sure she is fine.'

'I don't know, I'm just getting that feeling that ... oh, look, are we near the end? I can see starlight ... I think,' said Marilla as she stumbled forward again.

'You're right, old girl and guess where we are?'

Pushing past the last big boulders, Jack and Marilla staggered out into the fresh cool air. After the closeness of the tunnel, the freshness of the air made them gasp. Jack wedged the burning firebrand into a crevice in the inside wall of the tunnel and produced his own torch again.

'Didn't need it while we had that other source of light and I have to conserve what's left in the battery,' he explained as he began to examine the ground around where they stood and then at the huge boulders that guarded the entrance to the tunnel.

'Who would have thought there was an entrance here? See, Marilla, where the layer of snow has been pushed away?And there's been a lot of activity here that's turned it all to slush and we know by whom now.'

'Would they have had the strength to move them? Those stones are awfully big ... they must weigh tonnes!'

'Undoubtedly, but I rather think the Baron's henchmen are ex-weightlifters or wrestlers. They are exceptionally strong men.' Jack was shining his torch around their immediate surroundings. 'Do you know where we are then, Marilla?'

Marilla listened. 'Well, we are somewhere near water. I can hear it gushing. Are we near the waterfall?'

'You're right, we are. These are the rocks that mark the turn in the path, this is where I met up with Amos that first day I got here. I wouldn't like to try the path that he took me through somewhere behind those rocks at night. He might know the path through the bush, but I think we'll make our way quietly up the road; we'll keep to the edge in the shadows. It's a bit of a walk but at least this way there's a chance of getting into the chapel without too much risk of being seen. Not forgetting the Baron would still be under the impression we are locked away in that cell.'

'Dammit!' expostulated Marilla, 'We've just come all the way down from the abbey. Now we've got a long steep climb to get back up!'

'Ah, come on, the exercise will do you good, we've got a couple of hours to kill anyway.'

Marilla groaned. 'How did I ever get myself talked into all this cloak and dagger stuff in the first place?'

'Look at it this way,' said Jack patiently, 'at least it's not raining or snowing and there's a few breaks in the clouds for starlight to shine through, so it's a nice night for a walk. But if you like we can rest here for a couple more minutes.'

'I'm cold!'

'Then the walking will soon warm you up.'

Jack leaned back against the rock and put his arm around Marilla's shoulders. 'You know, Marilla, I never wanted you or Isabella involved in this in the first place,' he said seriously. 'This was never my idea, you know that; but I have to follow it through now. If it was not for you and Bella, neither Amos nor I would be here now. We owe our lives to you both.' He sighed and continued, 'I would never have thought in a million years that our paths would cross again, not this way at least; but I can say here and now that I can only feel grateful that you have been here at my side through all this. I've been in some tough situations before and there has always been back-up not far away; this time though back up was too far away and you and Bella were right there when both Amos and I needed help.'

'I'm sure you would have managed with or without us. Isn't that what being a policeman is all about?'

'In an isolated place like this, it has been different and a lot more dangerous than we expected. Things could have turned really nasty several times; but neither you nor Bella were daunted by the Casini mob or this madman and his heavies we now have to contend with. I have admired your courage. I know we have had different opinions of each other when we were kids but, in reality, there is very little difference between you and me. We think the same.'

'Really?' She raised her eyebrows. 'I wouldn't have thought so.'

Jack laughed and squeezed her shoulders. 'Yes and I think you'd make a great secret agent too. Those green eyes and tigerish temperament would scare the hell out of any criminal.'

'Humph!' was the only answer he got.

Jack turned now to face her. The soft starlight falling full on her face made the green eyes shine from within her dust-smeared face. Even with her hair escaping wildly from its untidy bun, she still looked quite beautiful — something he had tried not to notice, until now. He suddenly felt afraid for her. He was leading her into something that could spiral out of control and he doubted whether his uncle would be nearby as he said he would be, if things did begin to go wrong. After all, they had seen nothing of him or any sign that he was even close to them so far ... and that was a worry. He spoke earnestly now, the serious note back in his voice. 'Marilla, what I'm trying now to say is ... when we get to the abbey, I want you to go back to the lodge. I feel sure that if Amos and Bella are safe, then that's where she will be. Amos would see to that.'

Marilla opened her mouth to say something, but Jack overrode her protest. 'Marilla, these men are very dangerous and killing someone, with or without Von Zaharoff's orders, is second nature to them, particularly as the Baron has assured himself that you are witches and that gives him all the more reason to dispose of you, whether by his hand or that of one of his henchmen. It's far too dangerous for you to be anywhere near them. This is a personal vendetta against me and the one thing that remains an issue between us. I would rather face Von Zaharoff alone.'

Marilla noted the earnestness in his voice and the sadness

in his eyes. He was right about one thing she decided; perhaps they did think the same. Her tigerish temperament was fully roused and the green eyes flashed. 'If you think I've come all this way, through all this drama and dirt to be sent to my room, just when things begin to get heated; you've got another thing coming, Jack Grimsby!'

She pushed herself from the rock and stepped away from him onto the path. 'You don't get rid of me that easily.' She stood defiantly facing him, hands on hips. 'One way or another, Jack we'll *all* see this through — *together*! The way we started off! *You* might want to face von Zaharoff alone, but *he* won't be alone. You're still going to need help and I don't see your dear Uncle Henri hovering anywhere to keep those gorillas off your back. I might not be able to do too much, but I can damn well try. Besides which,' she remarked over her shoulder as she began the climb to the abbey, 'I also think I know just where to look for this icon thing. So let's get moving!'

Jack grimaced. He knew it would do no good to argue with her; she was going into the chapel with him whether he liked it or not. Perhaps her small methods of magic might be of some use, but he would keep her out of the way as much as he could, even if he had to resort to drastic measures.

Amos. Where was Amos? He looked at his watch again and there was still no tiny red light that would indicate he was somewhere nearby. Marilla was right, Amos wouldn't stand much of a chance if it came to hand-to-hand combat with the Baron's minders. Once they were back at the abbey he would try to communicate again; in the meantime, he could just hope that the others were together and safe somewhere.

*   *   *

Isabella, meanwhile, was sitting disconsolately on a bale of straw, slowly stroking Lucifer's back as he sat beside her. She had grudgingly allowed herself to be talked into returning to the stables to guard Carlos and await the return of Amos and Elias. They had remained in the underground system of tunnels to continue a brief search for traces that could ensure that Jack and Marilla were not there. Perhaps they had found the secret tunnel and escaped that way. Then again, they might still be prisoners of the Baron and held elsewhere. Whatever the outcome of their brief search, they had intended to return to where Isabella waited with Lucifer, then, together they would go on to the chapel at the break of dawn. They could be sure that Von Zaharoff would also be there, with or without Jack, clearly, in the Baron's eyes, as his prisoner and hostage.

Isabella sighed, she didn't like being left here to watch this silly little man as he occasionally struggled against his bonds and muttering things at her, words she didn't want to hear. Her mind was elsewhere. She had come this far in this escapade of Jack's and was beginning to feel that she shouldn't be left out now. Besides, she was worried about her sister. Her instincts had told her that she was still alive somewhere ... but where?

She looked down at her captive who had changed his tone and begun to plead with her now, in the quavering persona he had adopted when they first met him, to untie his bonds, or at least loosen them a little more. He had meant no harm to anybody but had been forced to comply with the Baron's orders in fear of his life, he had whined. She had already loosened the ties upon his wrists a fraction when she had been left on guard, as he had complained bitterly about the rope cutting into his flesh. She had almost begun to feel sorry for him in his pitiable state as he lay there.

Now she just remained silent and unsympathetic to his pleas, lost as she was in her own intense and troubled thoughts. His voice had suddenly changed now from the simpering pleading to a harsher grating tone.

'I wouldn't bother waiting for your friends to come back for you. They won't, you know. They just don't realise who they're dealing with,' he sneered. 'Haven't you seen the Baron's "boys"? They'll just tear 'em to bits — make mincemeat out of 'em!'

He was derisively taunting her now as he gazed up at her with his pale fish-like eyes. A mocking smile spread across his plump pink face. 'Why do you think they left you here eh?' he sneered at her again. 'I may be a trifle overweight myself, but a big fat tart like *you* would be as much use to them as a leaky boat. I'm surprised you could even get through those tunnels down there. I can just imagine you getting stuck halfway and blocking the exits up. Then how would they get out? Ha ha.' He began to laugh at his own joke, his fat jowls quivering as he chortled to himself.

Isabella said nothing, but her solemn brown eyes darkened as she gazed back at the insipid, detestable features of the man lying at her feet. This was the person who had pushed her into the bewildering darkness of the priest's hole without a thought as to whether she would ever be found or even a thought to her discomfort, alone in the darkness. She looked at him now in disgust and something moved in her mind.

Her usually pleasant and amicable character hardened as he continued to smile mockingly at her. She felt a new and dangerous power rising within her, something she had never felt before, a new resolve of authority that declared she would bow to no one. If justice was to be administered here and now to one who deserved it, then it would be done, without permission. She did not need her sister to think for her, nor anyone else for that matter. She was herself and she felt a rising tide of strength and confidence coursing through her.

She sat quietly for the moment, one hand in her lap, the other still fondling the big cat's ears. At last, she spoke, ignoring a fresh tirade of perverse insults and demands to untie the ropes that still bound him.

'There's a lot of rats in this barn isn't there, have you noticed?' she said in a quiet thoughtful voice, as if they had just been discussing the weather. 'Elias is always setting traps to catch them but it's as if they know what's there and how to avoid them. Such a nuisance too as they keep breaking into the grain sacks and then it spills everywhere when you move them, such a mess to clean up.'

'Rats! Who cares about rats?' Carlos grumbled. 'If you've got any sense in that ugly head of yours, you'd untie these ropes before the Baron's boys catch up with you and there won't be anything of you left for even a rat to eat. Now, untie me!'

'Oh, there's one right now by that feed box,' went on Isabella, as if he had not spoken at all. 'Shall I show you a different way to catch them? I'll bring one over here to show you. They're actually quite intelligent creatures, did you know that?'

Raising her hand from her lap, she pointed her finger in the direction of the feed box and at the same time uttered some words that Carlos could neither hear properly nor understand. But lying flat on his back as he was, he was soon to be aware of what she meant.

A large brown rat was suddenly hovering above him. He let out a yell as the loathsome creature dangled as if held by an invisible string only about a foot off his chest.

'They're such big ones too,' she said quite casually, looking it over carefully before allowing the bewildered animal to drop gently onto his heaving chest.

'*Get it off—get it off!*' shrieked Carlos, '*I don't like rats—get it off!*'

Isabella's brown eyes were gleaming. Her voice was calm and casual but mysteriously omniscient. 'Why, what do you want me to do with it?'

'Take it off me—*kill it, kill it!*' Carlos was still shrieking and bubbling with terror, as its sharp claws scratched his skin.

'Well, it does seem a shame to do that. It's probably a very nice rat and hungry too. Did you know that rats will eat just about anything, and have huge appetites?'

The pale eyes were rolling around now in sheer terror as the impact of her words hit home, and he began sobbing in fear as he pleaded with her.

Isabella hesitated an agonising moment or two more. 'Alright then; if you insist.' She clicked her tongue. 'Such a shame, he's probably got a family to feed too.'

She pointed a finger at the rat, which immediately became enshrouded in a pale blue mist that swirled about it. The rat squeaked and began twitching as it scrabbled on Carlos' chest, while the watery eyes of the stricken man grew wider in sheer terror of the creature so close to his face. He could see its mouth opening and closing, revealing needle-sharp teeth, and its whiskers quivering as it writhed in the power that held it. Suddenly its struggles ceased and it lay quite still on his chest, less than six inches from his horrified face.

Lucifer, who had been watching with interest, jumped up onto Carlos and grasped the rat by the back of its neck and began shaking it, growling his deep ominous growl.

Carlos swallowed hard and said haltingly, 'Is he–is he going to eat it–there?' He was whimpering now, his face fully drained of colour and sweating, his body shaking in fear.

A soft hooting noise seemed to emanate from somewhere above Isabella's head, she briefly looked up to see a great tawny owl staring at her from its perch in the rafters of the old barn, its great luminous eyes blinking now and then. It was ruffling its feathers as it gave another soft hoot. Before returning her gaze to the trembling wreck of the man at her feet, Isabella was surprised to see the owl put its head on one side and blink just one eye, nodding its head at the same time. There were often owls roosting in the barn and she thought no more about it. An owl was an owl. Her attention was elsewhere, she was still angry and determined to see justice — her justice — done.

Isabella stood up and smoothed down her skirt before replying. 'No,' she said in a quiet, even voice, 'I don't think so, not now. Its' dead you see and that takes all the thrill of the chase out of it. He prefers to tackle something much larger than a rat ... and alive. He has unusual tastes, very definite ... not quite what one would expect; he's such a messy eater and always takes the choicest bits first, if you know what I mean.'

Carlos was crying now and struggling to shake the dead rat off his chest. He looked up at her and the pale eyes fixed on her intense brown ones. 'Then it's true. What they were saying,' he stuttered shakily, 'you ... you really are a witch. I didn't believe them!'

Isabella drew herself up and glared down at the man. 'Yes, I am a witch and so is my sister and I can assure you that were she here now she would have transformed you into a fat pink pig to probably end up on a platter with an apple stuffed in your rude mouth. I'm going to leave Lucifer to guard you while we deal with your precious Baron, so I suggest you behave yourself while I'm gone.' She turned to leave, then said, 'Oh, and don't underestimate Lucifer's capabilities. He's smarter than you think he is and can be quite savage if roused.'

With that, Isabella swished her skirts about her and walked out of the stables and toward the latch gate that led into the garden and the abbey buildings beyond, Carlos' pleading cries for her not to leave him still echoing faintly.

She really didn't have a clue as to her next move and stood for a while on the other side of the latch gate, breathing deeply and trying not to think about the man lying in the stables, trying also to absorb what she had just done. A situation had arisen and she had taken charge of it. She had not allowed herself to be intimidated. Where had all that confidence come from? Lucifer, she knew, would not harm him, apart from a nip or two, but his presence would be enough to keep Carlos quiet for a bit longer. What was important now was to find Marilla and Jack. As for the Baron ... well, she would wait and see. She didn't want to have to face him if she could avoid it. She didn't feel quite that brave, though she had pretended to be.

Chapter 35

A Potion For A Potentate

Isabella's footsteps were leading her toward the familiarity and warmth of the kitchen. She was thinking hard. What if Marilla and Jack *had* found that secret tunnel that Elias had spoken of and if they had, then from what Elias knew, it would bring them out somewhere near the waterfall on the road from the village. She remembered the huge pile of boulders there at the turn of the path, right next to where the water tumbled over its massive barrier of rocks. It was also the place where she had seen Marilla dump the odd little brown man, then turn him into a bat. Inwardly she knew her sister was in no immediate danger that feeling had come to her when she had touched the ancient key that unlocked the cell that she and Jack had been imprisoned in. Even when apart the sisters knew inclusively if the other was in trouble, so close was that invisible bond between them and right now she had no real cause for concern.

She wondered too about Elias and Amos. After some discussion, Amos had decided to go back the way they had come after sending Isabella back to the stables, supposedly for her safety. He was not altogether convinced about this 'secret tunnel' Elias had spoken of and was concerned that Jack might still be trapped somewhere down there and if not then he could be anywhere within the abbey itself. They would conduct a short search below first.

There were still a few hours until dawn and if Jack *had* managed to negotiate the tunnel, then he would make for the chapel anyway, with or without the Baron at his heels; but he needed to be sure. Elias himself had seemed edgy and unsure of its location, which only made Amos all the more certain he had to find it. Elias would have to go with him, as he did at least know where some of the tunnels went and Amos didn't fancy falling down any unexpected wells.

*   *   *

Isabella stopped at the corner of the library building and looked out across the still dark and deserted courtyard. The whole abbey seemed empty of life, but she knew it wasn't so. A prickling sensation around the back of her neck told her that danger was close and she would have to move carefully.

Suddenly she stiffened and pressed her body closer to the old stone wall. Footsteps on gravel, heavy stomping footsteps were coming, but from where? Pressing closer to the wall in the shadows she held her breath and waited. They were coming closer, until out of the gloom, the burly figure of a huge man suddenly appeared around the near corner of the great building that housed the library and work rooms. He passed within a few feet of her as she huddled under her dark cloak, his heavy breathing punctuating the air together with the solid crunch of his boots on the layer of snow covering the cobbled courtyard. The heavy oaken door of the kitchen was only a short distance away and it was to there that the man had directed his footsteps.

Isabella watched as the door was opened and the big man stepped into the circle of light from the kitchen lobby, then the door was shut again.

All was still and quiet once more save for an owl hooting in the nearby forest. Isabella let out her breath slowly and it gathered as a cold mist about her face.

Well, at least somebody was in the kitchen, but who? Perhaps the Baron ... she would find out, go through the scullery. If she could just sneak in quietly enough there may be a chance to get a glimpse of this Baron person. She should feel afraid she told herself but somehow fear seemed to have left her, curiosity had taken its place and she would rather be doing something other than standing guard over that dreadful man in the stables.

So, clutching her cloak tighter about her, she crept furtively, like a small dark shadow down the outside wall of the kitchen complex, until she reached the broad step that led into the scullery.

She found the door partly open and after listening carefully, she crossed the step that led into the scullery itself. The mutter of voices reached her ears, voices that sounded foreign to her. As she crept closer to the other door that led into the pantry, the voices became clearer, a coldly eloquent, but commanding voice answered by a deeper guttural grunt that was almost inaudible.

Curious now, she slipped into the pantry itself and positioned herself in a corner between a serving bench and a large cupboard. From this vantage point she could see the lower end of the long table that dominated the room. Most of her view was blocked by the back of the man she had seen crossing the courtyard, one huge fist holding a wine glass, which he lifted to his mouth.

It was the man on the other side of the table that held her interest. Tall and thin, with short cropped grey hair and a small, neat beard of the same grey, he gave the appearance of nervousness or impatience as he tapped long elegant fingers on the age-old stained wood. Then picking up a wine glass from in front of him, he took a sip of its contents. Gold rings and the flash of diamonds on the tapered fingers gleamed in the glow of the firelight.

Isabella drew in her breath; this was the same man she and Marilla had seen in the mirror! This then, was Baron Von Zaharoff, and the other, one of his 'minders'. Were there more than just the two? She quickly looked over her shoulder but saw only the familiar shelves and cupboards of the pantry.

Her senses now on full alert, she watched the Baron thrust his long fingers into his elaborate waistcoat and withdraw a gold watch. He looked at it briefly and snapped it shut. He turned to face the other man and said in his clipped heavily accented voice, 'Alexis should have them all under control now and there is no one as you say in the tower or the church and of course, the one that matters is safely locked away.' He gave a deep sigh and continued. 'We must be patient, Sergei, patient, the time will come when we can collect that which we have desired for so long, but the waiting is *interminable*! How I *curse* that fool Henri Du Pont. Fortunately he will be no trouble to us for a while, eh, Sergei?' He laughed, a hard mirthless laugh that made a chill run down Isabella's spine, even more so when she heard what followed.

'You are a suspicious man, Sergei,' said the Baron looking fondly toward his swarthy companion. 'Fortunately, your suspicions have served us well. Who would have thought that the old man with the beard ... this accursed wizard, would be hiding under the mantle of a simple villager! Right under our noses too. Did he not think to conceal his whereabouts better, than to choose a cottage across the road from the Inn?' He laughed again and was joined by the soft deep chuckling from the man seated opposite, an ominously sardonic sound. Von Zaharoff picked up his glass again and took another draught of wine. 'It is easy enough to gain information once you know how, is that not right, Sergei? It will take him some time to free himself, if he ever does, from his own cellar; by then we shall have retrieved what we came for and I shall hold the treasure in my own hand at last; may all the witches and wizards go to *hell!*' He raised a clenched fist in the air and shook it in triumph. 'Just a few more hours.'

Von Zaharoff then lapsed into silence twisting the stem of the glass idly in his fingers as he gazed at its contents, his thoughts obviously far away.

Isabella slowly made her move to leave her hiding place; this was something quite unexpected, she would have to warn the others not to expect help from the wizard ... Jack's uncle was himself a prisoner. Jack could no longer rely on him to be there when he would be needed!

Wait, she thought, Sergei was muttering something to the Baron and had half risen from his seat. It was almost unintelligible to Isabella's ears, as his back was toward her, but it sounded like — 'Check on stables and monk.' Her heart leapt at the thought, the escape of Elias would be discovered!

The Baron was speaking again as he held up his hand to still Sergei's move. The carefully modulated voice was unctuous in its delivery, 'In a few more moments my friend, enjoy the warmth a little more first and we have yet another bottle of this barely acceptable wine to finish. There is no immediate need at the moment and I have trust in Carlos doing what has been requested of him, he has not failed me, as yet. After all, how hard is it to keep a simple farmer out of the way, let alone a stupid woman? As for Alexis, he is, no doubt keeping the companion of Jacques fully occupied.'

His smile became icily whimsical, the thin lips stretched over small white even teeth. 'Ah, but sadly we cannot be there to be amused at his sport ... pity, the waiting game is so tiresome, Sergei, we must remain here. You may stoke the fire again as I have no wish to *attendre le finalement* in the cold mid-winter's air, so we may as well be comfortable here, where there is at least a *little* warmth. Though the furnishings leave much to be desired and comfort to be only a stark necessity but obviously so desirable of servitude in this place. For why, I fail to understand. A man's comfort and needs should be considered paramount!'

The big man half turned to look into the pantry, as Isabella shrank back into the corner and out of sight. 'Would you like me to get it for you now?' he rumbled in his deep guttural voice.

'No, no, later will do, we still have a half bottle here,' answered the other, waving his long fingers in the air languidly. 'Just see to the fire, there is no rush for the last draught, it can wait, as we must do.'

Isabella had noticed the opened wine bottle on the serving bench and suddenly a mad, half formed thought sprang impulsively into her head. She had to try and keep them there for as long as was possible. How?

As Sergei moved to open the fire grate door and put more wood on, Isabella seized the moment while his broad back concealed her movement, to seize the bottle and slip out the door. An idea, a spontaneous divergent was forming in her mind; but would there be time? She thought anxiously. Holding the wine bottle tightly, she ran quickly down the colonnaded walkway that would take her to the infirmary and Joseph's little laboratory behind it. She was remembering what he had shown her that afternoon not long after the affair with the Casinis. Joseph had found Isabella's interest in his experiments most profound and was himself quite amazed at her own knowledge of the various properties of the plants.

Isabella moved quickly through the infirmary and entered the cluttered little workroom. A long, badly stained bench ran down the middle of the room and was still crowded with old glass bottles, retorts and beakers, still retaining grim-looking residual smudges of former experiments. A small distillation plant stood in one corner, while against the back wall were a large number of glass-fronted shelves. Under these were several sinks amid more bench space, while below that again were a multitude of drawers, each containing individual compartments for the storage of dried herbs.

However, it was the small bottles of liquids and powders that sat in the glass-fronted shelves that were her prime interest. She quickly cast her eyes over the tiny phials scanning the labels. Valerian, no that would not be enough, and possibly take too long ... and yet, considering the time required, it might do, and in the right amount. A small box caught her attention, and she took it down, *Amanita Phalloides* it read on the label — poisonous mushroom. That would be far too slow, fatal of course and it could be a few days before bodily organs shut down completely. She did not want to *kill* the Baron or his bodyguard, though she suspected it would probably take more than a poisoned mushroom to fell that giant, she just wanted to slow their reaction time down a bit.

It was obvious from what had been said that Jack and Von Zaharoff should meet, otherwise why go through all this elaborate treasure hunt business? The ivory box and whatever it contained was a destiny for both of them, so Jack should at least have a fighting chance against these enemies.

Isabella figured that a man like the Baron could have some dirty tricks up his well- tailored sleeve and Sergei would take some getting past. She didn't fancy Jack's chances if it came to a one-on-one with the huge man, he could kill with a single blow from those huge fists.

She scanned the bottles again. *Hemlock* and *water hemlock*, hmm ... no, too potent. Her eye caught one marked *Monkshood* — that would be aconite ... fatal. *Deadly Nightshade*, no perhaps not, he might have a weak heart, but the *Monkshood* was rather apt she thought, considering where they were. *Jimson Weed* that had much of the properties of *Deadly Nightshade*, but ... wait a minute. She took down another bottle marked *Scopolamine*. Another next to it was labelled *Mandragora* — *Mandrake Root*. She hesitated, remembering what Joseph had said about these poisons and of course, what she knew of them herself. *Scopolamine* was extracted from plants such as *Deadly Nightshade* and *Jimson Weed* and in its distilled form was a narcotic, which produced a sort of 'twilight sleep'. She wondered briefly if it had much taste. No time to think about taste now. She took the phial down and the bottle of Valerian; after pouring some of the wine down the sink, emptied both containers into what remained of the wine, shook it and watched as the added contents swirled around. Then on an impulse she shook a few drops of *Mandrake Root* into the bottle as well and gave it another shake. She clutched the bottle to her chest and hurried out of the laboratory and back down the colonnaded walkway to the kitchen.

Now she began to worry, what if they had discovered the bottle of wine missing? What if she suddenly ran into Sergei in the darkened corridor? What if—Isabella stifled a scream and almost dropped the bottle as something soft, furry, but with leathery taloned wings fell on to her shoulder, a bat! She stopped, breathless and sank back against the wall, her heart thumping dangerously in her chest. After a few seconds she realised it wasn't going to fly away, then another thought struck her. Isabella had an affinity with creatures of all kinds and bats were no exception. She liked them, but not when they scare the wits out of one like that, she admonished in a half whisper. 'Come with me,' she whispered, 'I may need your help.' So clutching the bottle tightly in one hand and grasping the bat with the other, she raced back to the scullery door.

Listening carefully, Isabella crept silently back into the scullery and was about to slip across into the pantry when she heard Sergei's gruff voice saying rather loudly, 'It right here? I, Sergei, put it! Open, ready, I—' Suddenly he found himself ducking and weaving as a bat flew past his ear and brushed its taloned wings against his face before soaring right into the room. The bat swooped around the lofty room for a few more minutes with Sergei feebly attempting to swat it, before it finally reached the top rafters and hung there well out of reach and sight of the infuriated big man.

The Baron had silently watched this pantomime being played out until Sergei dropped back onto the bench seat. Speaking in a cold admonishing voice, he said, 'Isn't that the bottle of wine you could not find?' Pointing to the part of the bench he could see in the pantry.

Sergei looked around and sure enough there was the bottle just where he had left it. Isabella though, was nowhere to be seen ...

*   *   *

'Why were all these passages put in here in the first place?' Amos was relighting another torch in readiness to enter one of the tunnels from the central hub.

'This abbey has a very long and often violent history,' replied Elias after some moments of silence before answering. 'It has been a citadel, a refuge, a place of power ... and despair. Most of the tunnels were constructed for a purpose, others merely to confuse and misdirect the unwary, should an escape be attempted. The abbey has seen some dark days in its time and there's many a life been lost down here.'

'And you say you have never explored them all?'

Elias hesitated. 'Yes, and no, I mean, I did venture down here out of curiosity when I was a lad and I don't feel comfortable in these enclosed spaces but coming down here with Joseph, I did learn a little more about navigating through the various passages and of course, there is a lot of historical accounts of the abbey to be found in the library.'

'What reason would Joseph have for coming down here?' queried Amos casting Elias a questioning look. Even in the half light of the burning torch Amos could see the nervous twitch that played over the impassive features of the ruddy farmer's face and his colour deepen a little more. 'Never mind now,' he went on hurriedly, 'let's just see if we can quickly find this particular passage that Jack and Marilla may have found.' If Joseph and Elias were harbouring some secret that involved anything within these dank dark subterranean tunnels, then it was something that could wait. He felt sure it had nothing to do with the present situation.

'Perhaps this way I think,' said Elias and started off down one of the dark openings.

The twisting turning path, rough and stony underfoot, led

them onward, the walls of the passageway seeming to narrow as they progressed. Then without warning, as they rounded a slight bend, a wall of solid rock confronted them.

Elias sighed. 'Ah, one of the many traps, a false escape tunnel, we shall have to go back.' Amos swore under his breath as they hurried back along the darkened length of the tunnel and reaching the hub again, he angrily threw the flaming torch at the entrance where it left a black scorch mark on the facing stone. 'At least we won't make that mistake again.' He turned to Elias. 'Now think man, you must remember *something* about where these go.'

'I–I'm sorry, Amos, I only followed where Joseph took me and ... and I'm really not very good in enclosed spaces like these, I get claustrophobic, and I ... oh, it was so long ago now!'

'That's okay,' Amos said soothingly, 'do you want to go back and keep Isabella company?'

'No, no,' the voice was firm in defiance, 'I just have to think for a minute, I wish I had remembered to get that old book that Miss Isabella had, there were maps in it that would have helped, however ...' He sat on a nearby rock and looked slowly about him at the dark ominous openings, his hands clenched tightly in his lap. Suddenly he sprang to his feet and pointed at one of the forbidding shadowy portals. 'That one, I'm sure it's that one.' He grasped one of the flaming torches and held it high. 'See — there's a different coloured stone there at the top left-hand side of the entrance, that should bring us back to the main passageway and we can find our way from there. There's a loose rock part way along, so I believe, with the entrance is hidden behind it.'

So torches held high, Amos and Elias made their way through the dark aperture, very soon finding themselves in the cross tunnel. 'I think we go to the left here,' whispered Elias as they cautiously crept down the tunnel examining the walls for any sign of another opening.

They had not gone far when Amos became aware of a flickering light behind them. He quickly touched Elias on the shoulder and whispered, 'Elias, there's someone coming behind us, I can see another light!' Shielding their own torches somewhat they stared back down the tunnel to where a faint light could be seen occasionally flashing on the rough stone wall. They were being followed, but by whom?

They had left Isabella to keep a watch on Carlos. Surely she hadn't decided to follow them after all? Amos thought. The shadow looming up on the wall as the light got closer did not look as if it belonged to Isabella. Amos grabbed Elias by the arm and propelled him roughly down the narrow corridor, their feet stumbling on the rough surface. Elias glanced quickly over his shoulder and was alarmed to see the shadow take on immense proportions as it rounded a bend. A grotesque shape, huge and menacing, like some medieval monster, it was bearing down on them and there was no place to go but forward. Extinguishing their torches, they stumbled forward in the darkness looking for somewhere to hide, when they almost fell into the yawning mouth of a cavern. Pressing their bodies up against the inner walls of the cavern, they waited.

The cavern, Amos realised, was in itself dimly lit; there was something about it that was familiar. With a jolting feeling in the pit of his stomach, he suddenly became aware that this was the same chamber where he had been imprisoned by Alexis! The firebrands still burned bleakly in the sconces, but still with enough light to illuminate the dreadful instruments of torture arranged along the back wall. The sound of ponderous footsteps and harsh heavy breathing were upon them now, then in another moment the rough-hewn doorway was filled with a huge figure.

It was Alexis! Alexis ... alive, but how? Amos had seen him tumble into that well, it couldn't be, but it was!

A gasp of horror escaped from Elias's lips and the big man turned at the sound and leered at them. His face, with its livid and terrible scar, now made even worse with blood running freely down it through a deep gash on his head, filled them with fear and mortal dread.

Amos stood transfixed for a second, then acted. He dived at the big man's legs in a tumble turn that would bring him up behind his adversary. At the same time, he loosened a small knife from a holster strapped to his leg and stood at bay. Before he could do anything, Alexis let out a bellowing roar and swung his massive arm out catching Elias and sent him flying to crash heavily into the wall where he lay in a crumpled heap. The roar ended in a snarl as he turned to face Amos. The distorted blood-soaked face a hideous mask of blazing hatred with the coal-black eyes fixed firmly on Amos.

'Ha, think you kill Alexis, Alexis *tough*, he look for you, now throw you down hole!' The voice was cold and merciless and he grinned, his mouth a fiendish black toothed gash that was as lopsided as the scar that split his face.

Amos' heart sank, what chance did he have now of evading this monster that was intent on destroying him. This time, at least he was free to move and not helplessly enclosed in a cage. He could move quicker perhaps than this mountain of a man and slip past him, out of the cave ... but he could not leave Elias in the not-so-gentle hands of this monster. If ever he needed help, divine or otherwise, it was now. Where was Jack's uncle? This was not supposed to happen like this, he had said that they would come to no harm! Well, if this wasn't harm, he'd like to know what he considered was!

'How did you get out?' said Amos. He parried now, looking desperately for a way of attack, while keeping clear of those huge hands. He knew, once in their embrace, he would stand little chance of survival. Though with strength enough of his own, he was only too well aware that here was a challenge it might be impossible to overcome.

Alexis was clenching and unclenching his huge fists, his shoulders hunched over, his black eyes glittering. 'Alexis found ladder, it strong, bring to top. Alexis very angry at demon attack, now *your* turn go down well!'

He lunged forward and Amos quickly sidestepped, lashing out with his knife as he did so. The move only served to inflict a small scratch on his opponent's arm. Wheeling around, his face glowering with rage, Alexis advanced again, completely ignoring the fresh attack and the thin red line of blood dripping from the scratch.

'Not hurt Alexis; Alexis hurt you!'

Before Amos was aware it was coming, a great fist had punched into his chest and he collapsed into a heap on the stone floor, his breath completely knocked out of him. The knife fell from his nerveless fingers and clattered onto the stone floor, where it was promptly kicked out of reach. Lying on his back gasping for air, Amos looked up and saw the giant form towering above him; he would not have believed that a man his size could move so fast.

He tried to roll away but a massive, booted foot held him firmly where he was and began to exert pressure on his already winded body.

'Alexis crush like beetle, throw down hole, what think *eh*!'

Amos had no breath to answer, his head was whirling, and he felt as if his life was being slowly crushed from him. With his senses reeling and his brain beginning to fog as he struggled for breath, Amos was somewhat surprised to be aware that his nostrils were detecting the smell of burning rags or hair. Perhaps it was the brain's way of reminiscence of some memory, however vague and insignificant, he thought, but he was also aware that the pressure on his chest was lessening slightly.

A heavy grunt and a sniffing noise emanated from the giant form towering above him and the strange smell seemed to get stronger. Finding some hidden strength, Amos grasped the huge, booted foot in both hands and wrenched it sideways, at the same time rolling his body out from beneath its crushing pressure. Struggling to his feet and clutching his chest, Amos turned to see Alexis slapping furiously at his head and turning his great body around in an effort to see who or what was attacking him. The burning smell seemed to be coming from his hair, it was on fire!

As Alexis turned around, Amos could see a line of blue flame running from his great backside up to what was left of his thatch of black hair. He was roaring and bellowing with rage but also cowering before something advancing toward him. Following his line of vision Amos was also startled to see a dark hooded apparition emerging from the gloom of the cavern entrance. It appeared to easily float a few feet off the ground, with an outstretched arm pointing directly at Alexis and a finger protruding from the draperies emitting a brilliant glow of blue flame from its tip.

In spite of the hurt in his chest, Amos chuckled to himself. Even in the gathering gloom cast by the fallen torch, he could just make out the dumpy figure astride the elongated shape of the broomstick. Not so Alexis, all he could see was a ghost, a ghoul, a shrouded demon advancing toward him, hurling fire at him, the heat of his burning clothes and hair intensifying as it came closer. With a terrified yell, he turned and ran wildly Alexis had only gone a few yards before his headlong rush found him with nothing beneath his feet. He was plunging into the same abyss he had meant for Amos.

The apparition paused and pushed back its hood to reveal a mass of untidy brown hair and turned large fearful eyes on Amos. 'Are you alright? I was dreadfully afraid I'd be too late.'

Amos came forward, and without saying a word, hugged Isabella. After a few moments he released her, looking into her tearful brown eyes and laughed. 'I don't know what brought you down here but you know, this is beginning to be a habit ... in more ways than one,' and he hugged her again, tears of relief pricking his own eyelids.

'What did bring you down here again anyway? I thought we had left you up at the stables?' he said as he held her at arm's length and wiped a tear from her cheek with his finger.

Isabella quickly explained what she had seen and heard in the kitchen finishing with the worry that the Baron had somehow managed to imprison Henri in a cottage in the village. 'He won't be able to help Jack, if he's locked up somewhere, will he?'

'Well, we'll just have to do the best we can without him,' sighed Amos. 'We've still got two willing witches to help, haven't we?'

A low groan from behind them reminded Amos of Elias. He had been thrown aside by the great man's arm and dashed against the wall.

'I'm alright ... I think,' he mumbled as Amos and Isabella rushed to where he had pulled himself to a sitting position against the wall. 'Just a bit dazed I guess.' He was rubbing at his shoulder ruefully. 'Not exactly the sort of person you'd want to have a grudge against, is he?'

'That's a fair assumption my friend,' agreed Amos, 'however—' he broke off and looked to where the dark edge of the chasm yawned in the fading light. 'Isabella, see if you can get some more light out of those torches. I'm going down that well just to make sure our ogre doesn't make another reappearance.'

Isabella clutched at his arm. 'Oh, Amos, do be careful.'

He grinned at her, 'Just keep that broomstick handy, Bella, if I yell you might have to use it again.'

Amos retrieved his knife from where it had fallen and fishing in his pockets, he produced a small, but powerful torch. Isabella and Elias watched as the torch light flashed here and there about the rim of the well, then finally begin to vanish from view below the edge. Amos had obviously found the ladder. Meanwhile Isabella re-ignited the firebrands in the wall sconces, then came back to sit beside Elias who seemed nervous and strained. Isabella patted his hand and began to tell him all that had occurred since they had left her supposedly guarding Carlos, however, Elias was barely listening.

After what seemed to be an eternity, they saw the torch light and Amos' nuggetty shape emerging from the depths of the well and walking slowly toward them.

'Well?' said Isabella, her brown eyes wide and questioning.

'He's gone,' said Amos quietly. 'He must have hit the rocks where the stream rushes up against them. There's a fair amount of blood there and I think the current has pulled his body off the rocks and away downstream. I shone the torch down and got a glimpse of something big being carried along and being bumped against other rocks, so we can only assume it was Alexis and the fall did kill him this time.' He paused and looked hard at Elias who was still sitting with his back against the rock wall and clutching his left arm. 'That's not the only thing that's down there ... one drama ends and another mystery begins, but this is not the time to discuss it.'

He dropped to one knee and looked at Elias, who was by now looking rather pale and was beginning to shake. Amos touched his arm gently just below the shoulder and Elias bit his lip as the pain hit home.

'It looks like you've got a bit more damage that you thought. I'd venture to say you might have a dislocation, or a break in the bone there. Let's see if we can make some support for your arm until we can get it seen to.' Grasping the long sleeve of the monk's robe, Amos drew the arm gently up as if in a sling, then stripping down part of the girdle he used a length of the cord to tie the end of the sleeve together and fastened the free ends around Elias' neck. With the injury supported now Elias was helped to his feet where he swayed groggily for a moment but was insistent on walking unaided.

Amos was looking at his watch. 'It's getting close to sunrise, we'll have to move, there'll be no time to search for that passage now, Isabella, which way did you come?'

Isabella quickly explained how she had noticed the dark opening in the wall of the scullery after she had returned the bottle of doped wine to the pantry. Intending to pick up her broomstick from the scullery where it had been left and go down the river path to find Marilla, she had hesitated. The faintest flicker of light was coming from that dark tunnel, this intrigued her enough to want to follow it; was it Amos and Elias down there? She had to know, so instinctively grabbing her broomstick she had begun to follow the flare of the torch. After stepping carefully down into the darkness, she perceived another source of light flickering against the walls of what appeared to be a cross tunnel a little way ahead of her. She had remained quite still as this other source revealed itself to be something or someone rather large that almost filled the passageway. She watched, heard it give a soft grunt, then begin to move troll-like down the tunnel, the heavy body moving with surprising speed and quietness, obviously with intent to catch up with whoever was in front of it. With a stab of fear she realised that the distant torches must be in the hands of Amos and Elias and this creature was almost on top of them. She had followed at a small distance and had arrived in time to see the swift attack on Amos. The rest of her actions had been pure instinct, but it had the desired effect.

'Then, if we go back the way you came in, it should bring us back to the scullery,' said Amos.

'I believe you came by the main tunnel, but I'm still not certain about those that run off it,' Elias said quietly. 'I wouldn't like to lead you into any more danger, I can't remember just where they all go.'

'We could take a chance and go back through the scullery, maybe the Baron isn't there now, even so, if we are quiet, we can slip out from there without being seen from the kitchen,' said Isabella.

'It sounds a bit risky, but at least we could try,' answered Amos.

They crept as quietly and quickly as they could along the passageway, but there was no opening to the scullery to slip out of ... the door had now been closed from the other side, and they could see no way of opening it without creating a lot of noise.

'We'll have to go back,' said Elias. 'The tunnel to the stables, we'll get out that way.'

They had little trouble finding the right passage and stumbled onward, eventually finding themselves back at the odd circular hub, where Elias thankfully lowered himself onto one of the large stones that littered the area. Isabella felt concern for Elias, his arm and shoulder must have been causing a lot of pain, his usually ruddy face was now pale and his step unsteady.

'I'm alright, Miss,' he said as she looked at him with a frown creasing her usually smooth forehead. 'I just need to rest a moment before we tackle that tunnel, at least we know where we're going now.'

An easy exit from the labyrinth was to be denied them here as well, as they soon found when they made their toilsome way to the small flight of steps that led to the trapdoor in the stables from which Isabella had appeared some hours previously. Where before, the trapdoor had opened easily to her touch, now there was no way it could be shifted. Amos put his broad shoulder to it, and felt it give a little but not nearly enough to allow them to escape that way. A very heavy object had been pushed over the trapdoor trapping them in those subterranean depths.

'Damn!' muttered Amos in exasperation. 'My guess is that Carlos must have escaped and is trying to make sure we stay down here.'

'Well, I think when I was hiding in the pantry, I heard that big man say that he was going to check on Carlos, perhaps he has and released him, he might have pushed something over the trapdoor,' she finished lamely.

'There's got to be another exit, we've got to get out of here,' said Amos.

'The only other way would be through the 'Priest's hole', I'm not sure that Carlos knows the trick of opening the book wall from the inside,' suggested Elias. 'We could try that?'

'Can you open it then?' asked Isabella.

'I can show you how it works, even if I can't do it myself,' he answered.

The trap door was as Isabella had left it, so it wasn't long before all three of them were standing huddled together in the almost total darkness of the tiny room; Isabella's thoughts went swiftly back to those few moments she had found herself closeted in the dank darkness. She had been frightened then but with Amos and Elias beside her, there was no fear, just relief and the knowledge that she had, at least, had a measure of revenge in dealing with Carlos.

'The wall bracket that holds the torch,' Elias said painfully, 'twist it around to the left until you hear it click, and the wall should open up.'

'Got it,' said Amos as his groping fingers found the bracket; he gave it an almost full turn to the left as instructed. A grinding whirring noise issued from somewhere within the walls, as hidden machinery was put into action. They watched spellbound as a portion of one wall in the semi-darkness of the small room slid out of sight, revealing the alcove where Isabella had sat engrossed in the ancient dusty books. As they stepped gratefully into known territory, Isabella clicked her tongue and remarked almost petulantly, 'If only I'd known that was all I had to do, it would have saved me a lot of trouble.'

'If you *had* known, then I doubt that I for one, would be here now!' growled Amos. He gave her a quick hug and continued, 'Not forgetting Elias would still be trussed-up like a Christmas turkey, so we can both be thankful that you took the long way round. Now, let's get down to business, we've got one belligerent Baron and one overly large thug to deal with. Not forgetting one traitorous monk,' finished Elias, his usually ruddy complexion now pale and stressed as he nursed his injured arm.

Suddenly they became aware that the faint light that had greeted them from the stifling half dark of the Priest's hole was growing infinitely stronger. Shadows that had been menacingly dark and mysterious were melting away to recognisable structures, vague forms and features were becoming distinct familiar shapes as the light grew in intensity.

'Oh, it's happening!' Isabella had run to the other side of the room and peered through the dusty mullioned glass. 'Look!' she cried agitatedly, 'look there, the sun is rising and it's coming up just where I thought it would, see ... between those two peaks we can see across the lake!' She turned to face Amos, her brown eyes were wide with excitement. 'We have to get to the chapel quickly, because the sun's rays will show us just where this treasure of Jack's is hidden. If he is not there already, then ... then, we'll have to find it ourselves.' She clutched at his sleeve, her face turned up to him, the brown eyes dancing with a mixture of trepidation and awe. 'Amos, it's where the rays of the sun come through the angel window high up in the front wall and follow a pattern across the floor. That is the key ... Marilla and I worked it out!'

Amos was already looking at his watch and saw with some relief that the pinpoint of light that glowed there was pulsing slowly. Jack was indeed close by. Perhaps he was, as Isabella said, already in the chapel; but if so, was the Baron there too? From what Isabella had told them about doping the bottle of wine, he still felt unsure that it would have had much effect on the Baron and even less on the bodyguard but she was right about one thing, they would have to move and move quickly. Even so the sickening feeling in the pit of his stomach reminded him that if the Baron were there, he would not be alone. The thought of having to face another of the size and strength of Alexis was something he really didn't want to think about yet. Though very much aware that Jack had to face his nemesis in the end, he felt afraid for his friend, now more than ever.

Together the three of them hurried as quickly and as silently as they could through the library, listening for any sound that signified danger. Approaching the staircase that led down to the cloistered walkway, the only sound that came to their ears was the hooting of an owl. Amos had quickly reached the top step and was about to run down it, when he stopped in complete surprise. A large tawny owl was sitting calmly in the middle of the bottom step, ruffling its feathers and peering up at them with luminous round eyes. The owl gave another loud hoot and to their amazement as it ruffled its feathers once more, a strange aura of light engulfed the creature; it began to spin into a tight spiral of golden flashing light. Then, as suddenly as it had started, the light was gone and so too the owl, but in its place stood the figure of a woman, clothed in a long flowing garment of tawny browns interwoven with golden threads that shimmered in the pale glow of the approaching day, as she raised her hand in greeting. The hood of the cloak was thrown back to reveal a still youngish looking face despite the advancing years. Tawny flecked brown eyes regarded them through large round spectacles that only served to make the diminutive figure standing there more owlish than the alter ego she portrayed.

Isabella gazed at the figure in dawning comprehension. 'Ed–Edwina?' she stammered haltingly, peering out from behind Amos' broad back where she had run into him, when he stopped suddenly to stare at this new phantasmal vision that had appeared in front of him.

'Edwina?' Isabella repeated cautiously, stepping out from behind Amos and hurrying down the steps, 'Edwina ... it is you, isn't it?'

The vision spoke, the voice strangely matching the figure, a firm authoritative tone. 'Hush girl, we have a small problem to deal with here, we must act quickly and decisively.'

She turned her attention to Amos still standing at the top of the steps. 'Amos, Jack is in the chapel as you may have guessed, he has Marilla with him and the accursed Baron is almost at the steps. Fortunately, his appearance has been hampered by this young lady's pharmaceutical skills with a bottle of wine but he will quickly regain his full senses. Jack will want you by his side, now more than ever. You have been his closest companion through many years my dear Amos and he would have you beside him in his hour of need ... but remember,' she raised a finger in a rustle of brown and gold as she moved, 'on no account are you to interfere with the inevitable — as you have no doubt been made aware of by Henri — no matter what happens.'

Amos, who by now was getting used to these strange ethereal materialisations, found his voice. 'Where *is* Henri Du Pont, Jack's uncle? He was supposed to prevent any harm coming to us and as yet there has been no sign of him ... we almost met our deaths down there!' and he pointed angrily back in the general direction of the underground passages. 'This childish game of hide and seek has gone too far!'

For a moment the tawny eyes flashed dangerously but softened as she spoke, 'I know, I know, but soon you too will understand the reasons behind this game of "hide and seek" as you call it, one thing we did not count on was the sheer cunning of the Baron which has not diminished with age. We also did not count on Henri being made a prisoner in his own home, but there is no time to explain more now, except to assure you that Henri is once more as free as a bird and *will* be here. I ask you to go quickly now and take Isabella with you, her sister will need her and she should be there at the end of things, as we all must be. There will be time for explanations later.'

'What about Elias?' said Amos, the anger still in his voice as he looked to where Elias had now sat wearily down on the top step. 'He's hurt and needs medical attention; he needs someone with him!'

'Joseph is also on his way,' said Edwina soothingly. 'Though perhaps by slower means. If Elias can make his way to the infirmary, Joseph will join him there shortly and tend to his injury. I will see him there safely myself, now go, time is short!' and she pointed one long finger in the direction of the church, her gold and brown garments glinting in the rosy flush of the new dawn.

Amos flashed a look at Elias and receiving an affirmative nod of his tired head, wasted no more time. Grasping Isabella's hand, he began to move swiftly toward the chapel dragging her behind him.

An Execution Of Redemption

In the cool light of an opalescent dawn, two figures could be seen making their way furtively across the open roadway leading to the ruined gate of the old monastery and the safety of the chapel or what they hoped to be the safety of that sacred place. For all they knew they could be walking into a trap, but it was a chance they had to take.

Jack had cast a glance across the valley to the two distant peaks Marilla had drawn his attention to, their snow-capped tops already bathed in a rosy glow. He observed with a mark of admiration the sisters' correct assumption that the rising sun would indeed emerge directly between them on this, the dawning of the mid-winter's solstice. He glanced up at the sky still faintly sprinkled with stars and wondered too, after all the weeks of leaden snow-filled skies if his uncle hadn't somehow had a hand in the prediction of a clear snow free night but even for a first-class wizard, that would be a bit beyond the boundaries of probability.

They had reached the front of the chapel and Marilla was directing Jack's gaze to the top of the ornate round windows that could just be seen from where they were. 'Up there, Jack,' she whispered, 'you can't see it properly now, the middle one that stands a bit higher than the other two has the angel figure in it and that's where those first rays will fall. We need to be inside when they do because if our guess is correct, they will fall on a path set into those tiles.'

'I'd already noticed the pattern in the tiles led to something of interest, old girl,' Jack whispered back, 'and had connected the window was part of it, no time to expand the theory; but I do have two very helpful ladies to thank for doing the leg work for me.'

'That's okay,' she said softly, 'now let's get inside.'

'Wait,' he said quickly, taking her by the shoulders and holding her back. 'Marilla, please consider what I said and go back to the lodge and wait there.' He looked earnestly into her eyes, holding her gaze. 'The Baron does not have you in his sights, it's just me he wants ... and something that belongs to me.'

She looked into his grey eyes for a long moment, then said dryly, 'Don't try that trick on me, Jack, it won't work, we both know that and I'm *not* going. I told you I intend to see this through' With an effort she tore her eyes away from his saying, 'and what's more important, we don't have time to stand here arguing about it, we need to be in the right place if and when that ray of light comes through that window.'

Jack smiled as he shook his head. Maybe he didn't have Amos with his comforting strength and sense of humour when the going began to get tough but Marilla was something else again. Stubborn and resolute when her pride and intellect was questioned and fiercely defensive, those flashing green eyes and tigerish temperament belied any female frailty that might have hovered there ... for the moment anyway. He sighed and took a quick look about the old open courtyard before following close behind Marilla who was still muttering to herself. 'It's a good thing the sky is clear for a change,' then added a touch sarcastically, 'I wonder if Uncle Henri had a mystical finger in the weather pattern.'

She clutched his sleeve, 'Do you think we were seen coming across the road?'

'I don't know, in any case the Baron will soon be aware that we are here, once he knows we're not where his gorilla left us.'

Quickly they ran up the steps and reached the nave where they halted, listening carefully. Hearing nothing, they ventured out from behind the great columns to examine the tiles that ran the length of the building. Many were broken or cracked, some were plain simple colours, others fine works of art.

Mosaics depicting religious themes, faces and figures, while others were of fish, birds, and flowers common to the area; but Jack and Marilla were searching for something else among the blues, reds and soft russet tones. Here and there among the richly coloured tiny tiles was one colour of a different hue, a tiny square of deep gold, whether on the bottom of a tile or nearer the top of the picture made little difference, only the fact that it was there. It was to these tiles that their attentions were directed.

Jack slowly walked the length of tiled flooring stepping up to the top step and on into the area between the rows of seats that led to the inner sanctum and the high altar draped in its cloth of white linen. He spoke quietly, 'If our guess is correct Marilla, these gold dots should all line up and—'

'Jack!' Marilla had been staring up at what could be seen of the round window and pointed at it excitedly. 'Jack, the sun, it's coming up, it's about to light up the window; quickly stand here and see if we are right about its path!'

They stood and watched in silence as a golden glow began

to spread over the entire window above where they waited expectantly, completely oblivious to anything else about them.

Where before there had only been the vague outline of a figure, now the growing light from the rapidly rising sun began to fully reveal that image to them. It was indeed that of an angel, its cherubic face and hands lifted upward. Clad in diaphanous misty blues and pale gold, the feathered wings gracefully folded, it gleamed in the rosy brilliance of the morning sunlight.

As the sun rose higher still to completely engulf the tiny window, a narrow piercing shaft of light suddenly speared down from it to strike the floor at their feet. They watched spellbound as the narrow shaft burned brightly on each tiny golden tile as the beam crept slowly upward from where they stood. Up the steps it crept following the line of the tiles that marked its passage between the rows of seats upon the raised dais. Onward it crept until the shaft of pure light hit the altar stone and to the astonishment of the silent watchers, it exploded into a starburst of blue and gold sparks. Then, just as quickly, it was over, the whole chapel was filled with the morning sunlight. They looked back at the trail of tiles that had glowed so brightly in the sun's ray, they were now barely visible in the mosaic design, appearing to have no significance whatsoever.

'It's in the altar stones!' cried Marilla and she darted forward to lift the embroidered white linen cloth. The high altar was long, long enough to take up almost all the space at the end of the short passage to the sanctum. Built of small blocks of white marble, it was unadorned except for a simple cross, carved in bas relief in a centre panel.

'*Wait!*' said Jack sharply. He was looking about him and listening carefully. 'I'm surprised we haven't seen anything of the Baron yet, he's missed the extravaganza, although I'm sure he'll close in for the kill. Marilla, we have to work quickly now, one of us will have to keep watch.'

'I'll keep a watch,' said Marilla firmly, 'you just look for the right stone, Jack.'

Speaking of watches, Jack thought to himself, where was Amos? He really needed him now, but what if Amos was in trouble of his own. He pressed the tiny button at the bottom edge of his watch again and hoped that this time he would get an answering flash. To his surprise and relief, the pinpoint of red pulsed briefly, then remained steady. Amos was alive, but where? No time to dwell on it now, he had to find the stone that would deliver the precious icon and its sinister secret.

He had counted the stones, was it left to right, or right to left. The puzzling words had not indicated which direction. Without thinking too much about it he began counting right to left. Thirteen across and nine as deep — that was what the riddle had said he recalled. Could this be the one? His fingers touched the small square of cold marble, and he began to examine it carefully for signs that it had been removed, but he could see none.

Cursing silently, he quickly counted from the other end, and once again could detect no sign of interference. It had to be from the right, didn't his probing fingers detect a slightly rough patch at the extreme edge of the stone, or was it a natural fault in the marble?

Taking his small knife from the inside heel of his boot, he began to probe a minute crack between the close fitted stones. As he worked his senses fully alert for any sound that would herald the arrival of the enemy, he wondered just where Amos was and for that matter, Uncle Henri? Jack worried too about Marilla, he seriously doubted that, for all her powers, she could conjure up something in a hurry to stop Von Zaharoff ... unless Uncle Henri's wizardry was looking over her shoulder again. He was really beginning to wonder about his uncle's state of mind as well. They had seen no sign of his presence anywhere. He and Edwina seemed to be taking a great risk with their lives in order to bring a prophetic conclusion to a bitter end ... or what they hoped would be an end. The annihilation of one whom they saw as an enemy and so automatically, his own antagonist as well, was the fulfilment of a destiny planned so long ago. If this had to be so, why couldn't he have faced it alone and not put his friend's lives at risk as well!

He stabbed angrily now at the join between the stones and felt the knife blade slide through easily. It was only a matter of moments then before he lifted the entire block out. Shining his powerful little torch into the cavity, it lit upon something that gleamed pearly white in its glow. The ivory box!

Jack removed it very carefully from its resting place and laid it on the palm of his hand. He had only seen it once before and that was when he was quite young. He had marvelled then at its exquisite beauty when Edwina had shown it to him. The finely sculptured figures that adorned the box were just as he remembered them, when he had traced his fingers lovingly over them as he had turned the box this way and that, trying to capture all the details in his mind's eye. Now, however, he reminded himself, was not the time to admire it.

Before he had even regained his feet from his kneeling position, Jack knew there was someone standing behind him. He turned his head and saw the tall lean figure of Baron Von Zaharoff.

The Baron was standing at the first row of seats leaning on the high back of one, leaning a little too heavily was Jack's first thought, but their eyes became level as Jack eased himself upright and stood facing him. The dark eyes were flashing above the hooked nose and the neatly trimmed grey goatee beard. They were also eagerly observing the ivory box cradled in Jack's hand.

'So sorry I was delayed,' he said in his mockingly smooth voice. 'It seems we overslept slightly, either too much wine ... or, perhaps an additive we were not aware of. However, I see we have arrived just in time and you have saved me the trouble of having to probe for it myself.'

The Baron's eyes kept flickering to the ivory box, the dark eyes glittered, perhaps a little too brightly. Jack noticed that the pupils were little more than pinpoints and his body was swaying ever so slightly. He immediately dismissed this diagnostic element as he caught sight of Marilla held firmly in the massive arms of Sergei. One huge hand was over her mouth and the other held her arms firmly behind her back Jack started forward, but the cold gleam of a revolver pointed at him ensured he would get no further. Marilla's eyes were flashing dangerously as she struggled against her captor.

'The more she resists, the greater the possibility of her demise,' said the Baron dryly.

Marilla caught the glance from Jack as he slowly shook his head and he could only watch helplessly as Sergei tied her to one of the smaller supporting columns a short distance from the steps. Before she had a chance to mutter anything, the big man had a gag tightly around her mouth. He was quick and efficient in his handling of her, Jack could now see why the Baron had chosen these men to do his dirty work for him. Marilla had noticed the danger too late behind her and yet she would have sensed it ... she had been overpowered too quickly. These men were professionals in stealth as well as strength.

'Where are the others?' said Jack stiffly. 'What have you done with them?'

'Why, nothing!' was the silky-smooth reply. 'To my knowledge they are being cared for by Alexis and the venerable Carlos, otherwise they would be here with you, wouldn't they?'

Jack felt his mouth go dry, he had felt Amos was close, the signal on his watch had told him so ... perhaps Zaharoff was lying ... he would have liked to think so, there was still some hope. Hope that his uncle and Edwina could have foreseen such a situation and would take appropriate action then come riding in like the cavalry. Whether it was on broomsticks or horses he didn't care, as long as they were close by. He had faced men with guns before, this shouldn't be any different, but it was.

He was unarmed, except for his small knife, apart from the Baron himself, how was he going to get past Sergei to even make an attempt at rescuing Marilla?

'Now it is my turn to ask a question before we get down to business.' The Baron waved the gun briefly in the direction of the box still held firmly in Jack's hand. He had moved slightly, placing one foot behind him on the next step as if to steady himself, and rested his gun hand lightly upon his knee, the barrel still pointing directly at Jack.

'Tell me,' he said in his smooth, heavily accented voice, 'how did you manage to get out of that locked cell? Sergei tells me the key was exactly where he left it and the cell door was still locked. Just curiosity I might add, but then, perhaps you have added another odious aspect to your accursed ways that seem to inflict those of your kind?'

Jack smiled and began to walk slowly down the aisle of the dais and then carefully down the steps. Von Zaharoff straightened up and moved to one side, the hand holding the gun following his move as he let him pass. Jack was quick to notice that although he did not hinder the movement, the hand holding the gun was now steadier. Whatever the cause of his semi-drugged state, it was rapidly wearing off.

Jack, who now stood on a lower level than the Baron, looked up at him and smiled a little as he said lightly, 'Don't know whether you noticed it at all, but there are a lot of bats around here. It can be most difficult to tell them apart, they look so much the same.' He thought he detected a faint flush of fear on the other's face and the thin lips tighten a fraction. Von Zaharoff came quickly down the steps and began to circle where Jack was standing, unobtrusively searching the immediate area for any sign that might indicate that help was at hand but could see nothing.

There was anger now, with only a trace of fear as the Baron spoke, his voice hard and cold. 'Your friends, so I believe are still alive, I have not given authority to kill them ... yet, but although Alexis is unpredictable and can be irrational at times, he is extremely loyal and will not hesitate to destroy them at any signal from me ... I have only to pass on the order, but we can always begin with this one first,' waving the pistol in Marilla's direction. He took a step toward Jack, the morning sun flooding the chapel gleaming on the barrel of the weapon in his hand. 'You will give me that which was unlawfully stolen from my house *now!*'

There was complete and total silence for an electrifying moment as Jack considered the order. He had wanted to play for time in the hope that Amos was not imprisoned, he knew he would come if he could. He glanced at Marilla now helplessly bound and gagged and he felt angry with himself for allowing her to be trapped so easily. He should have protected her.

He did not care about himself, the last thing he had wanted was for his friends to be hurt in all of this, but it had been an inevitability right from the start with this crazed plan.

His own anger rising within him, Jack stood his ground defiantly. 'It was never yours and well you know it. Nor is it solely mine to give ... nor yours to just take at your whim. It was my mother's, and meant a great deal to her, so too my grandmother, it rightly belonged to her.'

'*Indeed!*' spat the Baron with a snarl, taking another step forward. 'Can I remind you of the immortal words of a mighty Emperor — "to the victor belong the spoils" — come, give it to me now, willingly and we may yet share the fruits of my searching. Or I can take it from you by force and though I am loathe to do so, your blood may be spilled as was your mother's and you may yet join her in her eternal hell!'

Marilla saw the muscles in Jack's jaw tighten at the mention of his mother and she saw his grey eyes become darker still, the hand clenched so tightly on the box, his knuckles shone white. She tried hard to struggle from her bonds to help him, her mind racing for a suitable spell to disarm the Baron and ward off Sergei, but with the gag tight in her mouth, she could not utter a word. Von Zaharoff, aware of her movement, took a side-step to the column where she was bound and pressed the barrel of the gun to her forehead.

Marilla felt the pressure of the cold steel, but instead of fear, she felt only cold determination. Something stirred strongly inside her and the green eyes flashed a poisonous look at the hard grim face poised just above hers. Von Zaharoff was slowly lifting a lock of her hair that had fallen across her face with the gun barrel before pressing it back onto her forehead. Momentarily mesmerised by her eyes, he said almost dreamily,

'Why you must keep the company of such unworldly trash is beyond my comprehension Jacques ... or is it that the ties of your mother's breed are hard to break? The world would be well rid of yet another shrew to cast her witchery over the unsuspecting among us. I think we might deal with this sorceress first, then my dear, Jacques ... we might discuss our bargaining without her ... foul presence.' His voice trailed off as he continued to stare for a moment longer into those green eyes as if fascinated by their colour.

Jack's voice, cold and bitter broke into his reverie. 'Haven't you forgotten something? Why should I bargain with the devil's advocate for something that is *my* birthright ... and with one who destroyed an innocent life just to appease his own insatiable greed, a remorseless lust for power and domination? I despise you and resist you.' His voice now changed to become as venomous as the man who stood before him. 'I may also be of your blood but I can now be grateful to dear Edwina for saving my life that fateful day so that I may confront you and see you for what you are ... a cold-blooded *murderer*!'

Von Zaharoff spun around to face him, his face livid with anger, his dark eyes glittering dangerously. 'Do not remind me of it! Had it not been for that evil sorceress, that cunning viper that took her shelter within my walls, had it not been for her spiriting you away once the hideous truth was known to me, I would not have to parry with you now!'

The lean figure of the Baron was trembling with rage and his voice was hard and menacing as he pointed a quivering finger at Jack. 'You may bear the mark of the House of Zaharoff, but you are not worthy of it! I will *not* have you defile my name!' he shouted. 'The time for talk is over, hand me the box or I will shoot you now regardless of what blood flows through your veins!'

He had moved away from Marilla and taken a step closer to where Jack stood. An ominous silence reigned for a few moments, broken only by the soft hooting of several small owls that had flown in silently and taken up positions among the tall timbered arches. No one had noticed the little barn owls as they fluttered about amongst the ornately carved timbers ... except Jack.

He stood there, holding the ivory box in both hands and turning it over, seemingly reluctant to part with the treasure and seeking to only admire it for one last time. 'Wait!' he said abruptly, 'the box has been tampered with and it could be empty. How are we to know if the icon is still inside?'

A frown had replaced the look of rage on the Baron's face as he watched Jack turn the box over in his hands again. 'What do you mean, empty? You are trying to trick me, give it to me *now*!'

'You saw me remove the box from its hiding place, I have had no chance to open it and you can see for yourself that the seal is broken.'

'If that is so, then one of those here with you have taken it previously and left an empty box to fool me,' barked the angry voice of the still enraged Baron. 'I will have the icon now no matter who has it!' he said as he levelled his dark eyes onto Jack's steady grey ones.

Jack continued to meet his gaze and said quietly, 'If I or any of my friends had done so, would not the curse that the thing carries have struck them down before this?'

The other's face darkened and for a moment time stood still as this fact deepened into a possible reality. Could it have remained hidden and untouched all this time, could its hiding place been discovered, the contents removed and just the empty casket left as a decoy. Would anyone really believe those strange mystic words supposed to thwart those who dared to take the icon from its resting place?

Baron Von Zaharoff shook his head impatiently, he had heard and seen enough of so- called witchcraft and the grasping thieving gypsies, who made up these tales to prey on the fanciful and vulnerable minds of the guileless masses. There was no curse, just a clever foil to frighten those who would possess it. Right now this priceless treasure was within his grasp and it had come from his house and was, as with all the other treasures left within its walls that he had not squandered, rightfully his.

He pointed his pistol at Jack's heart and said in a voice that was low and more menacing than before. 'Hand it over to me now or would you like Sergei to cut her throat, quickly or slowly, however it pleases him,' he gestured toward Marilla, still staring transfixed at the drama being played out in this place of sanctuary.

Surprisingly then, without further words, Jack obliged and held out the box in his open hand. There was a fleeting moment of hesitation, as if the move was unexpected but the Baron snatched it eagerly from the outstretched hand and stepped away from Jack. Before pocketing his pistol, he motioned to Sergei still standing close to Marilla to watch Jack closely while he examined the object of his obsession, at last, finally in his own hands. Hands that trembled as he held the coveted prize, his eyes glittered in triumph as he turned the ivory box over, fingering the intricate carving lovingly before examining the seal. A waxen seal stamped with a fleur-de-lis, but clearly cut right through cleanly, as if with a sharp instrument.

'Yes,' he said with alarm, 'the seal is broken, the box *has* been tampered with but I will know if it is inside, I will open it and—' There was a sharp intake of breath that seemed to hang in the air for an eternity as the man stood stock-still staring down at his hands.

The precious ivory box had fallen from his fingers, but not before he had taken an object from it, which he held firmly in his left hand. The object was momentarily forgotten as he slowly held up his right thumb where two pin pricks were oozing the bright red blood that began to drip onto the icon clutched firmly to his chest.

He slowly opened his left hand and looked down on the golden cherub, representing an image of the Christ child that had nestled in the velvet lining of its ivory casket, its emerald eyes glinting in the glare of the morning sunlight as it stared back at him. Its exquisitely carved hands were holding the edges of a large magnificent perfect ruby, its rich red colour was now being further enhanced by the drops of blood falling upon it.

Jack had not moved from where he stood, his expressionless face fixed on the tall man in front of him. Marilla was watching spellbound, even Sergei looked on with a mixture of alarm for his master and a fascination at this turn of events. Nobody noticed the great tawny owl that had taken her place among the smaller of her kind.

A range of expressions were passing over Von Zaharoff's thin features as his tortured mind tried to come to grips with what had occurred. His euphoria at finally holding in his now blood-soaked hand that which he had desired for so long was mingled with surprise and terror. His lean body began to twitch and shake in spasms but he had eyes only for the glittering ruby, wet with his own blood. With a trembling hand, he slowly held it up to the spectrum of light from the huge arched windows, to flood the precious gem with an inner fire that almost hurt the eyes to look upon it.

'Beautiful, so beautiful, so ... precious ... so ... so perfect ...' Then as another spasm shook him, he wavered and slowly dropped to his knees and tearing his eyes away from the image clutched in his hand he looked up at Jack, fear now clearly etched over the thin, still elegant features.

'This ... this curse ... it was a trick ... to make me open the box ... and you knew it!' He looked again at his thumb, the tiny punctures still dribbling blood. 'I did not believe it ... this is devilry ... accursed devilry.' His body shuddered as another violent spasm convulsed him and he fell forward onto the cold hard floor of that sacred citadel. The icon was still

clutched firmly in the quivering fingers, the precious ruby uppermost and alive, glowing in its own brilliance, the emerald eyes reflecting those of the great tawny owl that stared down from immediately above the drama that had unfolded below.

Jack had remained motionless, his face devoid of any emotion but now he stepped forward, knelt beside the dying man and gently turned him on his back, the laboured breathing rasping in the stillness of the great hall. Ernst Von Zaharoff grasped at Jack's sleeve, his lips moving, his eyes staring fixedly into Jack's, but no sound came. Slowly the grip loosened and the hand fell away, sightless eyes now fixed vacantly up at the huge beams that arched overhead. Marilla watched as Jack, his own hand trembling, reached out and almost tenderly she thought, lay his hand on the Baron's face and closed those staring eyes.

A long moment of silence followed, then, as Jack stretched his hand forward to remove the cherub from the dead fingers, he heard the cold calculating voice of Sergei right behind him.

'I take that!'

For that brief dramatic moment, Jack had forgotten the

presence of the Baron's bodyguard, who had crept up behind him and as Jack turned his head slightly, he could see the sun glinting on the muzzle of a revolver held in the giant fist.

565

When A Wizard Is Not A Wizard

Jack's mind was racing. He knew Sergei would not hesitate to shoot, so sensing how close Sergei was to him, he made as if to rise and hand the icon over. Instead, he threw himself suddenly backward, knocking the big man off balance, sending the pistol shot wide to ricochet off the stone wall behind them. In that moment, Jack sprang and the two men grappled for possession of the gun. Sergei was a man of great strength and Jack knew he would be powerless against him, particularly if he got too close to those huge arms that would crush the breath from his body. He quickly dodged a wildly aimed punch from Sergei, then ducked in close and rammed his knee hard into Sergei's groin. The blow hit home and the big man began to double up, giving Jack the chance he needed to knock the gun from the great ham fist and send it spinning across the tiled floor to land at Marilla's feet.

Still securely bound, Marilla could do nothing ... or could she? Quickly taking careful aim with her foot, she kicked the gun as hard as she could, sending the weapon sliding across the floor to bounce off the next column and spin further away.

Sergei gave a surprised yell of pain and anger as the gun shot out of reach of either of them. But with surprising speed for such a large man, he produced a knife from somewhere under his clothing and lunged at Jack, slashing furiously at him. Surprised by the counterattack, Jack had thrown himself sideways, but still received a deep cut to the top of his left arm. However, the sideways movement and his attempt to avoid another slashing stroke caused him to crash heavily into the wall behind him and he stumbled to his knees as he tried to regain his balance.

Sergei was advancing closer now and despair began to fill Jack's heart. Where was Amos and more importantly, Henri? This was not how it was to end. If ever he needed a dose of magic, it was *now*!

The face of the big man was twisted in anger. The small heavy-lidded eyes glittered like black beetles as he raised the blood-stained knife to strike the final blow. Above him, he could hear the owls hooting and the whirring of wings as the tawny owl flew ever closer to Sergei's head, as if to distract him, but he would not be distracted from his murderous purpose.

Reaching behind for the broken window to steady himself as he rose to his feet, Jack's fingers closed over some shards of the coloured glass still embedded in the edges of the window frame. Wrenching a piece from its setting, he held it out before him and was immediately aware that even if he couldn't use it as an effective weapon, the morning sun glancing off the glass of the angel window high above just might blind him enough to slip out of Sergei's reach. The Baron's inert body was lying just a few yards away and with a quick glance Jack could see the gun half protruding from a pocket. If he could be quick enough ... Holding the glass up, he let it flash and a brilliant shaft of colour hit Sergei full in the face. But that was not the only thing that struck the big man.

There came a sudden loud screech and a flash of black

feathers as a great black raven shot through the broken window behind him and raked its talons over Sergei's face. Screaming in pain, Sergei dropped the knife to put his hands up to his torn and bleeding face, while the raven, cawing loudly, circled the nave, together with the tawny owl. Marilla watching closely, saw that it was the same one they had seen on the steps that day — there were two distinct white feathers on the bird's breast.

A strangled bellow came from Sergei at this unexpected attack but he was still quick enough to place one large foot on the fallen knife. Now he lunged forward, expecting to pin Jack against the wall with one arm while retrieving the knife with the other hand.

Another flash of black feathers and the raven was on top of the big man's head, stabbing furiously at the almost bald head with its sharp, pointed beak.

Enraged, Sergei flung his arms upward, the knife slashing at the air above him while the raven swooped this way and that, the blade missing it by mere inches.

Then suddenly out of nowhere a large hairy arm wrapped itself around his throat and the hand holding the knife was held in a vice-like grip. Another strangled cry came from Sergei at this further attack, Jack was still in his range and too close to the struggling titans to make an escape. Sergei threw himself and his attacker forward and crushed Jack against the wall, bringing his elbow up as he did so to deliver a crushing blow to Jack's chest.

Fighting for breath, Jack slid down the wall to collapse in a crumpled heap. A loud hooting brought him almost immediately to his senses. The tawny owl was fluttering just above him, its wings beating only a few inches from his face, bringing a rush of air to his lungs. Amos and Sergei were locked in a fierce struggle only a few feet away, but the Baron's body and the pistol were still a little distance beyond. If Amos could hold Sergei off long enough, just long enough to get to where the Baron lay and retrieve that gun, then ... but other things had been happening!

A figure had appeared beside Marilla. It was Isabella, who had tugged at the gag in Marilla's mouth, and was now attempting to untie the rope that bound her to the pillar.

'Burn the ropes!' gasped Marilla as soon as she could speak. '*Hurry*, Bella!'

Realising quickly that there was no other way to release Marilla from the tight knots that bound her, Isabella summoned all the power she could and directed it at the ropes through her outstretched finger. There was a bright flash and wisps of smoke arose, but the knots still held fast. Fearfully Isabella had glanced to where the two heavyweights were fighting and could see Jack slump to the floor and the knife wrenched from Sergei's hand and flung through the window. Pointing her finger again, she summoned her power once more. Suddenly, a powerful image of Grandma Hackett appeared in her mind, as a blinding flash occurred this time and the rope was seared through as if struck by lightning.

Marilla shrugged off her bonds muttering, 'Our magic is not going to save us here, but back me up, Bella, whatever I do.' To Isabella's surprise, she darted quickly to where the body of the Baron lay just a few feet away and was fumbling at something in the pocket of the jacket. When she stood up, Isabella could see she was holding the gun in her right hand.

Holding the unfamiliar weapon out in front of her with both hands, Marilla began to circle the two combatants while keeping close to the wall. She could hear Jack yelling something at her, but it was lost in the sudden triumphant shout from Sergei, who had his back to Marilla and had just smashed a vicious blow to Amos' head, which sent him sprawling backward to fall heavily on the floor. With his great fists clenched, Sergei was moving in for the kill over the stunned and almost helpless Amos.

'You not beat Sergei in fight little man. It give much pleasure tear you with bare hands. You weak now, I strong. Strongest man in world. *No one* beat Sergei.'

'Perhaps that's because you're all brawn and no brain,' said a cold voice behind him.

Sergei stopped and half turned his great body to see who had spoken and was confronted by a thin wisp of a woman pointing the business end of a pistol wavering it at him. Marilla, if she had not felt confident before, began to feel that surge of power she had felt at another time. She knew Jack was watching her and this time his mind was perfectly in tune with hers. She could feel his strength enveloping her. She stood her ground, defiantly facing Sergei and the gun barrel was no longer wavering but being held by a steady hand.

He stared at her in surprise but only momentarily, before he spoke.

'So,' he said mockingly, a curious half smile indenting his flat, normally expressionless face, 'big bad witch going *shoot* me. Oh, Sergei *so* scared!' He held his arms out in sham fear and began to advance toward her.

Jack had risen to his feet, clutching his arm to stem the bleeding. Amos was beginning to come to his senses and Isabella was standing stock-still a little behind Marilla, her mouth open as she watched in horror at the scenario being played out in front of her. She did not even attempt to raise a finger, so entranced was she at the sight of her sister standing up to this giant of a man.

Marilla, however, knew exactly what she was doing as she

raised the pistol and pointed it directly at him. 'You're damn right she is!' she muttered and squeezed the trigger.

The loud bang, when it came, and the recoil of the weapon sent Marilla staggering back to fall into the arms of her sister, the gun still clenched in her hand and hanging limply at her side.

The grin on the round flaccid face of the man standing before them was slowly fading, to be replaced with one of complete surprise. His step faltered. A large red stain was blossoming over his massive chest, he slowly looked down at it, touched it with a thick forefinger and stared at the blood oozing through the hole. Then still with a look of total disbelief on his face, he shook his massive head at the two women standing before him before toppling over and crashing down heavily at their feet.

'Nice shooting, Marilla.' Jack was standing beside her and unclenching her frozen fingers carefully from the gun. 'It's a good thing the safety catch wasn't on.'

'Safety catch? *What* safety catch?' Marilla was too confused by what she had just done to fully understand what Jack was referring to.

'Never mind, it's all over now,' said Jack soothingly, then turned to where Amos was sitting up on the floor rubbing his head. 'Are you alright, Amos?'

'Bloody great gorilla caught me with one I didn't expect.' He was inspecting his bruised and battered knuckles as Isabella went to help him to his feet. He got up and they walked to where Marilla and Jack were standing over the body of Sergei.

'Thanks, Marilla,' Amos growled, 'but I sure would have liked to finish him off myself. What you did just now took a pretty cool head though.'

Marilla was too shaken to answer, her vivid green eyes the only splash of colour in the paleness of her face.

'Oh, Jack! You're hurt!' said Isabella. 'Your arm, it's bleeding badly. That cut looks awfully deep!'

'Yeah,' said Jack grimacing, 'but it's more the ribs that are giving me hell.'

Amos cast a quick appraising look over Jack's arm. 'Come on, let's get out of here. What we need is a nice hot cup of tea and a few stitches.'

'Wait.' said Jack, 'there's something I have to get first.' He went over to where the motionless body of Baron Von Zaharoff lay and kneeling down beside it, he began to prise the golden cherub from the dead fingers. He held it in his hand briefly before wiping the blood away from it with the silken handkerchief that he extracted carefully from the top pocket of the ornately emblazoned jacket. He replaced the handkerchief in the pocket. Somewhere above his head he heard the rustle of wings as two birds took flight and flew out of the chapel into the morning sunlight.

As he rose to his feet to join the others, Jack saw Isabella walk to where the ivory casket lay, until then unnoticed on the floor, and stooped to pick it up.

'No! *Bella no! Don't touch it!*' Jack was yelling. '*Don't touch the box ... leave it!*'

Before she could open her mouth to answer, Jack was there and gingerly picked up the box, holding it carefully at its base. 'Alright,' he said grimly, 'now let's get out of here.'

Casting another look at the huge, now lifeless, body of the big man lying in an expanding pool of blood, Marilla shuddered. She followed under the protective arm of Amos, who ushered her with the others to the doorway that led to the set of white stone steps and the openness of the vast courtyard.

As they emerged into the pale warmth of the winter sunlight, they were surprised to see the raven sitting on the same pedestal, just as where Marilla and Isabella had first seen it the day they had arrived at the abbey. The great bird looked at them with its beady black eyes and ruffled its feathers, puffing out its chest, the two white feathers stark against the glossy black plumage.

'Oh, by the way,' said Jack, stopping at the top of the steps, 'Marilla, Isabella, I'd like to introduce you to my Uncle Henri.' He then addressed the bird, who sat with its head on one side, regarding him. 'Thanks to your hair-brained scheme we almost got ourselves killed in there. You left your arrival a bit late. I could have been carved up into mincemeat.' He clutched his injured arm. 'We could have done with your help a little earlier — or was that part of your plan too — keep us on our toes? Marilla should never have had to go through what she did.'

Marilla looked at Isabella in astonishment, then back to Jack. Whatever was Jack doing, talking to a bird? Isabella said nothing. It was as if she were waiting for something to happen and it did. A vortex of blue and green stars began to suddenly whirl about the raven, and a whispering noise, as if many tongues were talking softly together at once, filled the air around them. Suddenly the raven was gone and in its place stood a very tall thin man with a long white beard that extended past the girdle around the waist of the shimmering black robe he wore. He inclined his body in a deep bow that threatened to topple the rimless glasses he wore perched at the end of his long aquiline nose. The voice, when it came, was deep and rich with just a touch of tentativeness.

'I do apologise ladies and particularly to you, my dear Marilla, but you were marvellous!' His eyes gleamed as he clasped his hands together in front of him. 'You showed great courage and initiative. Hilda would be so proud of you both.'

Isabella nudged Marilla and without taking her eyes off the old man, said quietly, 'The two white feathers, see? I told you, Marilla, black birds don't have white feathers. It's the beard.'

Henri continued in response to Jack's outburst. 'I'm sorry if there were any delays in my actions. Even though magic is a powerful tool it doesn't stop the ageing process or the intervention of other wickedness. I will explain more later but as I remarked before, I'm not as quick as I used to be and I realise now that it is a condition I should have taken into account more. But one does not always connect the quickness of the brain to the degeneration of the body.' He shook his old head sadly and the glasses teetered dangerously.

'Unfortunately, things did get a trifle out of hand, as you might say. But then, all's well and Marilla would have come to no harm, I assure you. She acted on her own impulse and did it very well!'

Marilla looked at the old man carefully before she spoke. 'Why all this secrecy and the "treasure hunt" business? You knew where the box was, why go to all this bother when you could have taken the Baron out of the equation when he first came looking for it?'

Henri paused for a long moment before he replied, as he turned his dark eyes on her. 'Perhaps there were other reasons behind all this, of which you are unaware, my dear. But it will all be made clearer to you shortly. Yes, I could have destroyed the Baron many times but that was not the way Edwina, nor I and my dear sister Camille, would have wanted. No! That was too easy. He had to die by his own wicked hand and with the one he so cruelly abandoned as witness to his destruction ... and now it is done!' His dark eyes twinkled as he clasped his hands together. 'Now Amos, dear boy, I think you mentioned a cup of tea ... but, I forgot ... Jack you do need some attention to your wounds, do you not? How remiss of me. Perhaps when that is attended to, we can all sit down and talk. You'll find Joseph is already attending to Elias, with Edwina's help, in the infirmary.'

Jack shook his head impatiently at his uncle. 'You and Edwina have had your wish and were witnesses as much as I in bringing about your devious brand of justice but right now I need Amos' help with some needlework, so let's cut the chatter and get on with it.'

A Confession Of Wizards

As they approached the infirmary, Edwina, her tawny brown eyes looking even larger and spilling over with tears, came running out.

'Jack, oh my dear Jack, I was so worried for you. That man was so strong and with Henri delayed ... I was on the point of transforming and firing off a blast but wasn't sure that it would hit the right one. I knew it was going to turn out alright but for a moment there I really wasn't too sure. We thought we had taken everything into consideration, then ... oh, Jack.' She went to put her arms around him, but Jack held her off.

'The ribs, Edwina, careful, they're a bit tender at the moment but it's good to see you again.' He gave her a light kiss on the cheek. He looked down at her and said in an admonishing voice, 'Plans do have a habit of going astray, even those of wizards. It just takes one mishap to stuff it all up and that's when it gets dangerous. One, or all of us could have been killed in this venture of yours, fortunately we have all survived, even if we are battle- scarred and in need of attention.' He walked quickly onward to enter the infirmary, with Amos and the girls trailing at his heels and Edwina fluttering along behind.

On entering the infirmary, they found Joseph adjusting a

sling around Elias' neck to support his injured shoulder. Elias, it seemed, had suffered a partial dislocation of his shoulder, Joseph had been successful in relocating the joint and a much more comfortable Elias had now regained much of his normal ruddy complexion. Joseph insisted on attending to Jack's wounds himself and although the ribs were just bruised, he generously applied his special healing salve, then a light strapping.

Amos submitted then to having his scrapes and bruises attended to while having to recount his tale of the two close escapes from Alexis, his saviours in the form of Lucifer and Isabella with the demise of Alexis into the fast-flowing underground river.

Then the question arose — Carlos! On investigation it was found he was no longer in the stables. Had he escaped by himself and was it he who had blocked the trap door to the stables?

Joseph had an answer to that. He told them how he had been hurrying through the secret tunnel at the waterfall entrance and had encountered the bulky shape of Carlos coming toward him. His pink chubby face was wet with sweat, his lank hair plastered to his forehead and his shrewd pale eyes screwed up against the light of Joseph's lantern. He had been surprised at seeing anyone else in the passageway and going back the way he had come was not an option under the circumstances. Joseph had pinned him to the wall of the dank tunnel and asked him some searching questions. Joseph let him go, realising that even after further spying and his fear of witches, Carlos' actions would not be favourable to him.

Carlos, however, had turned back to him and made a remark that worried Joseph a bit; but for the moment he had put it behind him. Carlos had smiled a sickly smile in the half- light that the lantern threw and said in his soft whispery voice, 'Don't think I don't know why you're spending a lot of time down in the tunnels ... doing a little digging, eh?' He gave another soft giggle and disappeared out of the opening into the pale morning light. Joseph, however, kept that part of his narrative to himself.

So, Carlos was gone and they hoped, for good. Elias couldn't help but smile a little to himself. Carlos was certainly not going to reap the rich reward he had been promised by Baron Von Zaharoff and live happily ever after. Rather, he would slink back into the murky shadows from whence he came until another opportunity came along.

'What did you mean, Uncle Henri, when you spoke about intervention of other wickedness? Is that the thing that kept you?' asked Jack, as he slid off the examination bench where he had been sitting as Joseph finished the ministrations to his wounds.

The old man had sat perched on one of the high laboratory stools in one corner, his hands folded under his voluminous sleeves, watching the procedures. Now he sighed and said after a moment's interval, 'Unfortunately I was set upon by the Baron's bodyguards — caught me completely unawares, which is a rare occurrence for a wizard, I might add.' He sighed heavily again and pushed his glasses back up his long nose with a forefinger.

'It's a wonder we found him at all,' broke in Edwina, 'trussed-up like a bag of potatoes and left to die in his own cellar!' She snorted and adjusted her own large round glasses on her nose. 'It was Joseph who found him and still with that dreadful smelling bag over his head.'

'Chloroform,' muttered Jack and cast a glance at Marilla, who was sitting on the end of one of the beds. 'We know about that; but how did they get you in the first place?'

Henri examined the tip of one of his long fingers as he spoke.

'I knew they would be watching *me* as much as I was observing *their* movements. My little cottage is just across the road from the Inn, you see. I was returning home with my little dog that I have as a companion, and—'

'So it *was* you I saw come out of the Post Office that day!' interjected Jack.

'Yes, it was but I had hoped you would not recognise me, because I was, as you might put it in your terminology, "working undercover". But, as I said, I was walking home and even though it was dusk, my sense of awareness is usually acute, however, I did not anticipate the reaction of Theodore when he suddenly bounded away from me and tore the lead from my hand. I tried to hurry after him as quickly as these old legs could carry me but had only gone a couple of steps when I was grabbed from behind and this evil smelling bag was pulled over my head.' The old wizard spread his hands helplessly. 'There was no magic I could produce as my mind was totally clouded by whatever was on the bag. I remember very little until Joseph released me from that dreadful prison, which incidentally was my own cellar.' He shook his old head and cursed silently. 'I should not have underestimated the Baron's cunning mind. I should have realised it would not have been diminished with age.'

Joseph took up the story, 'I was actually on my way back to the abbey when I received garbled mesmeric thoughts about Henri — he was calling me, only I found it difficult to fully comprehend what he was requesting. So, I hurried to his house and found Theodore whining and scratching at the door to the cellar and that's when I found him as Edwina has described.'

'Yes but that wasn't all that plagued me,' said Henri, scratching his head and adjusting the glasses that threatened to topple off his nose again. 'I knew Edwina was keeping watch at the abbey and I knew I had to get there quickly at all costs so I metamorphed into my alter ego and took off for the abbey.' He stood up and began pacing in small circles, wringing his lean hands as he continued. 'I did not count on being totally harassed by a pair of vicious eagles that have taken up residence in one of those pines on the lower slopes. By the time I had convinced them I meant no harm to their territory, I was way off course and had to rest awhile on the top of the mountain above here but where I could also just see the great windows of the chapel. The rest you know.' He stopped pacing and looked at Amos, forcing a half smile to his tired and lined face. 'Now, Amos, how about that cup of tea?'

They sat once more in the comfort of the great old kitchen. Amos and Joseph had coaxed the old reliable stove into life again and warmth flooded the room, easing the aches and pains of the old as well as soothing the hurts of the injured. Marilla and Isabella were handing around mugs of hot tea, while Joseph busied himself cutting slabs of bread and laying out butter and jam. It had been a while since they had last eaten. Jack noticed how tired and drawn Henri looked. He had been badly shaken by the brutal actions of the Baron's heavies. His face was still pale and his eyes had lost a little of their lustre. Both he and Edwina looked as if they had come to the end of a long, exhausting journey. Nevertheless, Henri insisted on knowing all the details of events that had occurred, shaking his head occasionally as he listened.

There was still something that had to be done and though Jack hated to broach the subject, it had to be said. 'Uncle Henri, we can't leave him there ... both of them. I don't know how I'm going to make a report of this. It will mean dragging it all out in the open, and—'

'There will be *no report!*' said Henri, some of the authoritative tone back in his voice, 'because there will be nothing there to report about. Edwina and I will take care of the details. There will be nothing to show he was even here — and no one will miss him. He has gone to his own private hell, one that he made long ago for himself.'

Henri let his tired head droop and Edwina put her arm around the thin body. 'It is done now, Henri and your dear sister can rest in peace. I too can feel the burden lift from my own shoulders knowing that I have done as my dear Camille had requested, though it has taken many long years. Justice was served, even though it all nearly went very wrong,' she said, half to herself.

There was a meditative silence for a while and it was Marilla who eventually spoke. 'Edwina, I have to ask, why did it take so long for all this to come about? I still don't understand what the significance of the icon is and why the Baron had been trying to get it. Who does it really belong to and if it was, as he said, stolen so long ago, why wait all this time to extract justice?'

'Yes, I know it must seem strange to both of you and hard to understand why we waited so long for this day; but you would have to have known Baron Von Zaharoff to understand the nature of the man.' Edwina sighed and said, 'Jack will fill in all the other details for you but you have to understand that Von Zaharoff was a very powerful and influential man, he came from a highly connected and proud family heritage. We kept the icon out of his reach until he had, through his own follies in gambling and bad investments, reduced his family possessions to almost the bare bones. The icon had always been the one thing he desired above anything else, even though he knew it was not rightly his to take. His powerful urge to find it and possess it became an obsession. To him, it *was* a treasure hunt. He *wanted* to match his wits against Jack to prove that he was superior and could crush him, but he also liked the thrill of the chase, being the predator of the hunt, keeping his quarry in sight but not capturing until he was sure.'

'Did he know who had the icon?' asked Marilla quietly.

'No, he was never *entirely* sure,' answered Edwina. 'For many years I kept it with me, while Jack was growing up in Harewood, but the Baron made no attempt to reach for him there. He was secretly very afraid of the sisterhood of witches, though he would never admit to that. It was only when Jack left Harewood that he came under the Barons' notice again, but the Baron was also dealing with his own financial problems and could spend little time on the hunt. Then he became aware that it was still not in Jack's possession. He had his many spies and contacts everywhere but was afraid to come direct to me, though the Baron had tried several times to catch me off-guard. Then he found out that Camille had a brother — Henri Du Pont — and turned his attentions there. He found Henri after some searching, and by this time of course the Baron had gone through almost all his own fortune and was becoming increasingly obsessed with finding the treasure for himself. Jack had grown to manhood and had settled on a career where he drew strength and resolve in his work but he still suffered terribly from the nightmares that had plagued him from his early childhood.'

'There had to be an end to it,' Henri spoke up in his deep voice. 'I had received several letters much earlier from my sister regarding the dangerous situation that existed and the need to preserve the icon — the only link Jack would have with his mother and more importantly the history surrounding his grandmother. Edwina and I began to put a plan together long before Jack reached full maturity, knowing that the Baron's strength would begin to weaken while Jack's would only increase. We moved the icon from place to place to confuse and lead false trails for the Baron to follow. Then we constructed our cryptic conundrum, to draw him here for Jack to hear the truth from his own lips and so meet his nemesis and here put an end to it all.'

'Is that why you decided to turn it all into a treasure hunt then, to lure the Baron here?' Marilla queried.

'We knew he couldn't resist the last chance he would have of defeating Jack. He still believed he had enough power over him to force him to just hand the cherub over. Although we couldn't be sure there was still enough hatred there to kill Jack outright, we also knew his greed would make him less cautious,' said Henri, the tiredness now fully evident in his voice. 'However,' he said, as he stood upright and the gleam began to come back into his old eyes, 'Edwina and I have one last task to complete and we will need your help, Joseph. Then I'm going back to my cottage to sleep.' He turned to Jack and said very quietly, 'unless you would like to see—'

'No!' Jack shook his head. 'I heard and saw enough. I have no wish to create further memories. My mind will find its peace in time now. I only want happier moments to remember and move on.'

'You are right, of course,' said Henri. 'It would not do now to dwell on the past; it is but another page in the annals of history.'

'We shall return,' said Edwina, 'when Henri has rested, in a day or two. Meanwhile Jack will answer any questions you may have and I'm sure there are many.' She leaned over to Jack and kissed his cheek saying, 'Now you will do something about the casket won't you, my dear? We don't want any unforeseen accidents to occur right now.'

Joseph went to help the old man to his feet. Edwina rose from her seat as well and turned to face the sisters. 'I know you have both questioned the reason for your being here during this time and all will be explained to you, but now is not the time. We shall talk later.'

Jack sat silently for some moments then reached into his pocket and withdrew the golden cherub. He held it in his hands for a few moments then placed it reverently on the table in front of him. It lay there, the perfectly crafted body of a plump cherub, wrought of solid gold. Its dimpled baby arms were held slightly away from its body and outstretched, the exquisitely formed chubby fingers were holding the edges of a magnificent ruby. The rosebud mouth was smiling slightly as it peeped from behind the precious stone and the emerald eyes glittered from beneath a head of glorious curls that framed its chubby face.

Then slowly from his other pocket, Jack withdrew the ivory box. He sat for a while just holding the box and staring at it. His thoughts were far distant and he barely heard the question put to him, or the surprised murmurings from the sisters as they gazed with awe at the rosy cherub as it lay on the rough-hewn table, a stark contrast to the humble surroundings.

'Where did the figure come from in the first place?' asked Isabella. 'Did it belong to your family?'

'It was my grandmother's,' Jack said dully, his head lowered in silence. Then suddenly he lifted his head and spoke, his face now grim and set. 'Amos, that small pair of forceps in the medical kit, would you get them for me please?'

Amos hurried to do so and Jack set the ivory box down close to him on the old worn table and looked at the girls. 'This is the reason I did not want you to touch it, Bella.' Then holding the casket carefully in both hands, he appeared to caress the lid. To their surprise the lid slowly opened, revealing the pale-coloured velvet lining and the deep impression where the small figurine had nestled. Jack took the forceps from Amos and proceeded to attack the lining just under the lid where the catch was on the side of the casket. He probed carefully, pushing aside the threads of velvet until the inner side of the lid was exposed; then grasping at what looked like only a thread of hair, the instrument dislodged two very tiny brown pieces of tissue-like material. He held them up, and as he moved them around in the light the sisters could see that there were identical needle-like projections hanging from the bottom of each one — so tiny, they were barely visible.

Jack pulled toward him one of the empty plates that littered the table and carefully lay the strange object on it. Then, with the end of the forceps he gently pressed down on the pieces of tissue.

'See there, at the tip of those points,' he exclaimed. The sisters bent forward over the table in order to see as Jack pushed the plate closer to them. 'Look but don't touch!' Amos and Elias also crowded around to get a glimpse of what Jack was showing them, they were surprised to detect the tiniest drop of a pale, almost straw-coloured liquid appear at the two sharp points. 'Curare poison!' said Jack grimly. 'Obviously its potency hasn't diminished with age.'

'Oh dear,' said Isabella, 'that's deadly. No wonder he ...' She stopped herself from saying more as Marilla broke in hurriedly.

'The little bags — they look like tiny bat's wings.'

'They are,' said Jack. 'Edwina fashioned the bladders from the tough membrane of bat wings and attached the hollow fangs of a cobra to the bottom of the bladders. There is a strong but tiny coil spring that attaches to that little bar across where the bladders fit into the crevice of the lid. When a thumb pressure is applied to the edge to open the box, the spring releases the fangs with force, and ...'

'And that's what killed the Baron ... your father. Am I right, Jack?' Marilla ventured softly.

Chapter 39

The Icon Gives Up Its Secrets

There was silence in the old kitchen for a very long moment. Marilla's green eyes were fixed on Jack's grey ones. It was a look of understanding, not one of pity but an earnest kindred gaze that said more in that one look than a thousand words.

'You are the son of Baron Ernst Von Zaharoff aren't you, Jack?' she continued in a voice so soft, it was barely heard.

He nodded slowly and put his hands to his face. When he took them away, he was smiling at her, though she could see the smile was forced, the emotions were still raw. 'Bravo, Marilla,' he said lightly. 'Your perceptiveness is working overtime again and you even remembered the name though you only heard it from me once. Edwina was right again, both of you have changed more than one would have thought possible ... I think you've really grown up, what do you think, Amos old friend?'

Amos had walked around behind Jack and his strong hand had rested on Jack's shoulder, in a gesture that didn't need explaining, then put his other hand up to his own face. 'Damn, got a bit of soot from that stove in my eye, won't take a minute to get it out.' He disappeared in the direction of the scullery. It was hard to be convinced about a microscopic fragment of soot in his eye, when the unmistakable sound of a nose being blown came to their ears.

Isabella had been quietly studying Jack as he sat making attempts at light conversation with Marilla and Elias, about watching Edwina work on the box when he was still a young lad. She herself was seeing a small dark-haired boy again, sitting on a log by a stream swinging his legs in time with hers, not talking much to each other, but knowing they shared a similar childhood loss in a bond that only those who lose either one or both of their parents can feel. That sense of vulnerability, of being held in a suspended chain of events chosen for you and overall, an emptiness that could not be explained. Jack looked up, caught her eye and gave her a wink; he understood her train of thought, but then, he always did.

'Anyway,' Jack said in a controlled voice, 'I don't think we have any further use for this,' as he stood up, Jack picked up the plate, he went across to the stove, opened the grate and threw the contents into the fire.

A clattering in the direction of the pantry announced the return of Amos. He had a couple of bottles of wine under his arms and was trying to balance a tray full of glasses. 'Thought a drop or two of wine, for medicinal purposes of course, would be appropriate,' he announced. He looked at Isabella and grinned. 'I hope this isn't one you put a drop or two of something extra into.'

She shook her head. 'No, Amos there wasn't time to open any more bottles, it was enough to handle just the one that was already opened on the servery top.'

While Amos was busy pouring wine, Isabella looked curiously at Jack. 'You opened the box a different way,' Isabella said suddenly, 'so there was an alternative way to open it. May I touch it now?'

'Of course,' said Jack handing her the casket. 'It's completely safe now that it has been disarmed, but I'll put the icon back in it if you've finished looking at it.'

Isabella took the ivory box from his hand and began to examine it. In itself the box that held the precious icon was indeed an exquisite work of art. The colour of the ivory had deepened over the years but its mellowness still gave it a rich subtlety that glowed with an inner fire. She turned it over and over in her hands examining all the tiny details. Marilla joined her and together they studied the intricate carvings, marvelling at the finely sculpted figures that filled the entire surfaces of the beautifully crafted piece of work.

Its central feature was a tree, old and gnarled whose branches forked near to the top of the box and then spilled over and down the other side, spreading its leaves and smaller branches to almost cover the reverse side and edges. Even the tiny leaves on the tree were finely detailed but no more so than the tiny birds sitting among them. At the base of the tree itself, were several small animals, including a unicorn, its head up as if looking into the tree. Half hidden at the very bottom, where the roots of the tree trailed above the ground, Isabella's sharp eyes could just discern the coils of a snake and the tip of its tail. Turning the box over again she followed the body of the snake, expertly concealed among tall grasses until its head became visible, looking much like the fallen branch it rested on, but it was there, mouth open and poised to strike.

'Ugh!' said Marilla grimly. 'If this is following the rhyme that Edwina thought up, then that must represent "ka", and his fangs represent the sword.'

'That's correct,' said Jack as he took up the glass of wine Amos had set before him. 'The carvings are also a representation of the words in that cryptic message we were given to solve. However, I was the only one who knew what the last part of the rhyme meant. I knew about the poison, because I had watched Edwina make the little pouches and attach the springs and the fangs — it was a delicate task and one she was adept at.'

'So, there must be a special place then to open it without touching the sides,' said Isabella excitedly. Jack said nothing but waited while Isabella's sharp eyes and sensitive fingers once more travelled over the magnificent carvings. 'There, there, I think I see it now, the tree of life the verse said, there's a slightly thicker spot, here, just where the tree branches out and if I press just there …' They both watched spellbound as the lid slowly opened and the golden cherub was revealed to them again, its emerald eyes gleaming.

'Curare,' mused Isabella, as she accepted the glass offered to her by Amos. 'That's from South America so I've read. How did Edwina get curare poison?'

'It's a long story, Bella and all part of my grandmother's history. Edwina never kept anything from me, she made sure I knew everything about my family, so there could be no mistaking my … heritage and what I was up against.'

'Do you want to tell us about it? Where did the cherub come from and why it means so much to you?' said Marilla, quietly watching Jack closely. 'You don't have to if you don't want to but I hate a mystery that doesn't have an end.'

Jack sighed. 'Alright, but as I said it's a long story and begins with a history lesson, so I hope you're prepared for this, plus some parts will not be easy for me to relate. I have memories of my own but most of what I will tell you has come from my mother and grandmother and verified by Edwina; to whom I owe my life and apart from my Uncle Henri are the only living links I have left. You probably wondered, when we were young and living in Harewood why Edwina never spoke of my parents.'

'We did for a while but then we forgot about it,' said Marilla. 'It didn't seem important at the time, but now, after what has happened, how can we not be curious as to who your parents were?'

Jack picked up his glass of wine and studied the contents for a moment before taking a mouthful. 'As I said, I would need to relate some things that might seem irrelevant but you would have to know the full circumstances of how the icon came into being and how it finished up where it did.

'To begin at the beginning is to go back to about the mid-fourth century. I did some research some time back to verify the authenticity of the icon and it would appear that it was crafted by the Greek sculptor Phidias. He was under the patronage of the Greek statesman, Pericles and in his time under that patronage, executed such pieces of sculptor as the huge statue of Zeus at Olympia and oversaw much of what is now referred to as the Elgin marbles.

'They were sculptured friezes that once adorned the Parthenon and included the statue of Athena that dominated the interior of the Parthenon. However, he was also commissioned to produce small pieces because he worked so well with gold, ivory and bronze. These smaller works of art were often used as gifts of atonement or trading of good will between other countries or as a thank you for not slaughtering our children during the last conflict sort of thing. Though most of the markings on the back of the figure are indecipherable, it is generally believed to have been one of his finest miniatures and in fact a parchment discovered later near his workshops in

Greece described the figure down to the last detail, including the precise setting of the jewels.'

'But how did it come into your family if it was made that long ago?' Isabella asked.

'I'm coming to that,' said Jack. 'This particular piece was chosen from the Grecian treasury to be presented to the then Tsar of Russia as a diplomatic gesture, somewhere around the late eighteenth or early nineteenth century. It was taken to Russia by an emissary and was to be presented at a special ceremony to Alexandra, wife of Nicholas the second, Tsar of Russia. It became known as the Icon of Phidias, presumably to foster good relations between the Baltic States and those on the Mediterranean, of which Greece was considered the most active.'

'The Tsar of Russia,' mused Isabella. 'Didn't they have another name ... Romany, no Romanov or something like that? I'm sure I read something about it somewhere and their only son had something wrong with his blood that was supposed to be hereditary.'

'Yes, he did. It was Haemophilia — a condition caused by a deficiency in the coagulation factor of the blood cells. Nothing much was known about those things in those days and in the event of a serious accident a person could bleed to death very quickly. So, he was cosseted and watched very closely all his young life.' Jack paused, then said, 'Have you ever heard of the mad monk known as Rasputin?'

'I did read something in this same book about a monk, yes, they did call him the mad monk as I remember, tall and dark with very dark eyes that seemed to hypnotise people, well, so it said in the book.'

'That was about right,' said Jack and gave Isabella a curious look, as he went on with his story. 'Rasputin was born of Siberian peasants but all his life he believed that a particle of the supreme being was incarnated in him and the doctrine that governed his life was, "that one had to sin in order to obtain forgiveness".'

'That's a strange way to go about life, doing wrong things so that you can be forgiven, but what has he to do with the icon?' said Marilla impatiently.

'I'm coming to that also,' said Jack patiently. 'In spite of his radical views, he believed he could heal people and had special powers because of his oneness with the Supreme Being so before long he found himself in the Royal Court of Nicholas and Alexandra. He believed he could cure the young Royal of his affliction and he, in fact, did make an improvement in his young life but the disease was always there. It would never be cured. Because of the partial success with the boy's health, he became a favourite at the palace and had an almost hypnotic effect on all the members of the Royal Family he became so much a part of the Tsar and Tsarina's lives that they began to consult him before making important governmental decisions. Rasputin was virtually ruling Russia through his dominance of the Romanovs. It did eventually invoke the wrath of certain aristocratic members of the country and in their eyes, he had to go. So, their leader, a Prince Yussopov and the rest of the conspirators set about to kill him but found he was almost indestructible. Poison, potassium cyanide in wine, a bullet in the chest.'

Jack looked up in time to catch the amused look on the face of Amos as he watched Isabella and Marilla flinch at these words but he carried on. 'They beat him, then tied him up, shot him twice again and threw him in the Neva River. Even then, he was still alive, but drowned because they weighted him down, so he would sink to the bottom of the river. This was discovered when his body was recovered and water was found in the lungs, which meant he was still breathing when he was thrown in and had struggled against the ropes around his wrists. This all happened in about 1916.'

There was another period of silence from the listeners as they pondered the fate of this strange man. Elias, sitting close by the fire and listening intently shuddered and remarked, 'They certainly meant to make sure he was dead and here am I worrying about a slightly dislocated shoulder.'

'If the Tsarina had the icon, what did all this have to do with Rasputin, how does he come into it?' asked Marilla.

'Because Alexandra gave the cherub to Rasputin after the supposed death of their love child as a keepsake and memento of their loss.'

'*Love* child!'

'Yes, as I said, Alexandra in particular, was fascinated by Rasputin; she was completely under the spell of his charismatic persuasion in everything. Nicholas had to leave occasionally to command the troops, leaving the palace to be run by, well, mainly I suppose, Rasputin. Alexandra became pregnant and all assumed it was Nicholas' child, but Rasputin was the father. She had a somewhat difficult pregnancy and only Rasputin and a nursemaid attended her. Rasputin prescribed drugs and kept her in a somewhat hypnotic state during the birth and when she woke, he informed her that sadly the child was stillborn, he himself was devastated. In truth, the child was alive and well, a terrible scandal would have ensued were the truth be known, the Romanovs were already losing favour with the people, so he had the nurse, who had recently lost her own child and with whom he had complete and total trust in, spirit the baby girl away, to bring up as her own, with Rasputin as her benefactor and guardian.

'Then came the revolution early in 1917. The Bolshevik government announced in Moscow that the Tsar and all his family had been executed for what they determined were crimes against the people. Of course, it was officially stated that they had been removed from their sumptuous palace surroundings to a secret place. However, the story was changed several times so historians have never been exactly sure what did happen, but the blood- stained walls and floor of a cellar in a place called Ekaterinburg in the Urals, which was a Bolshevik stronghold, was reputed to have been where the Royal family were murdered.'

'Ugh, how horrible — the whole family murdered,' said Isabella and shook her head sadly.

'Well, supposedly murdered but there were servants and their family doctor with them, who left their own bloodstains in the cellar and it's possible the Romanovs were just hidden away in exile; but, what I'm coming to, is that almost the entire fortune of the Romanovs, which was an immense amount of money and treasures, was missing. It was all smuggled out of Russia before the Revolution and some deposited in Western and Swiss banks. Rasputin himself knew that the Romanovs were in danger of being overthrown by the Revolutionary uprisings and was probably very instrumental in stashing the cash as it were, so even if the Tsar himself was killed, at least the rest of the family would have money; if they were able to flee Russia, as they had many relatives in Germany and England. There were also several valuable estates in Germany owned by the Romanovs, but we don't know what became of them. Later, the counter Revolutionary Army took their revenge on the Bolshevik group and regained control, all too late to save the Royal family.

'Rasputin made sure his child was well taken care of financially. He and the nursemaid companion, who was completely devoted to Rasputin and the child, together sewed precious gems into the baby's clothing and also into her own and had much more hidden away. The icon, which Rasputin treasured more than anything else, was to be become the sole property of his daughter, among other small treasures that they managed to confiscate.

'He had blessed it and it was sacrosanct to the holder, to protect and bring good fortune to her, to ensure she be kept safe and no harm befall her as she grew to adulthood. Apparently, her name is scratched on the back of it somewhere, as well as his. Rasputin's instructions were that should anything happen to him and he feared that it would, given the fierce nature of the uprisings, that his and Alexandra's daughter should be made aware of her birthright ... the daughter of the Tsarina and no truth kept from her.'

'Couldn't this woman have decided to take the icon for herself if it was already in her keeping?' asked Marilla.

'She had no need to, she had riches enough for herself and beside which Rasputin was a very powerful person, he had far reaching contacts and would have discovered a deceit very quickly even if he did survive the Revolution. The woman, whose name incidentally was Olga, devoted the rest of her life in caring and rearing that child, whose name was Anna and she was my grandmother.'

'Your *grandmother*!' they all chorused together.

'Yes, my grandmother.' Jack ignored the surprised looks on the faces of his listeners. 'Now I suppose you're wondering where Edwina and I come into all this lesson in ancient history?'

'Of course we are,' they said almost in one voice. 'You can't stop now.'

Jack continued his narrative of these past events to his

enraptured audience. 'When Rasputin was murdered, Olga, who was a very smart and capable woman, took Anna and the wealth they had gathered and fled the country, per Rasputin's instructions should anything happen to him. They travelled extensively to such places as the North of Africa, South America and many of the smaller island colonies, keeping well away from Northern Europe. To keep the icon safer, Olga embedded the ivory box in a Russian Orthodox Bible, the pages of which had been hollowed out in order to conceal it. The Bible also had metal clasps on it, which were kept locked and it remained safe with them for many years while Anna grew up.

'Anna eventually returned to the Baltic States when she was in her early twenties and began life again as a vibrant exotic young woman of the world. Well-travelled and educated she became readily accepted into society circles, she soon captured the attention of Count Vladimir Von Zaharoff, a wealthy and eligible aristocrat himself of some notoriety and fame. They married in 1939 and two years later, their only child was born. A boy, whom they named Ernst and who later took the title of Baron Von Zaharoff some fourteen years later, after his father died in a hunting accident.'

'So, your grandmother married a Count?' exclaimed Isabella, her brown eyes wide. 'Well, she moved in all the right circles and it pleased Olga because it meant her charge had made a marriage her father would have approved of. She had not forgotten her promise to Rasputin and Anna was kept very much aware of her own identity and in fact kept a diary, in which she recorded everything Olga had told her of her parentage.'

Jack continued his tale just as Marilla was about to interrupt him again with a question he didn't want to answer yet. 'From what we understand from Anna's diary, which she kept up faithfully following her marriage, Ernst became a very strange young man after he lost his father. He became very possessive and dogmatic in his beliefs. In fact, he could very well have been likened to his grandfather.'

'Who would have been the strange monk, Rasputin,' finished Isabella.

'Yes, one could say that,' agreed Jack. 'He believed himself invincible and without his father's influence, Ernst grew up to be both proud and arrogant, according to Anna's diary, he would use his inherent power and influence of his heritage to take what he wanted from life. From what Anna wrote, he quickly became bored with the aristocracy-raised debutantes. Their shallow simperings and parading for his wealthy attentions irritated him. Although he could have his choice of many women in his exclusive circle, he could just as quickly cast them aside. He yearned for something different and exciting to enter his life.

'He began to show a deep fascination for the Bohemian lifestyle and would frequent the bazaars and haunts of the less ignoble classes. It became his playground, his escape from the social prestige he was obliged to carry. It was here he saw the woman he was later to marry.

'He had seen her several times as he wandered through the bazaars, moving around amongst the tinkers and rug sellers, the hawkers' cries renting the air above the constant murmur of a drifting throng of people. He had first caught sight of her as she stood fingering a fine cashmere shawl. There was something about her that made him stop to watch her and then a throng of noisy children barred his path momentarily, when he looked up again, she was gone. A curious fascination had gripped him about who she was, where she came from and as he later told his mother in his enthusiasm, she seemed different from those around her. There was something regal about her, he had said, as if she didn't really belong there either, but like himself, had only come to that place to be amused.

'Anna described her in her diary as Ernst did in great detail. Tall and willowy with long dark hair framing a creamy complexion and once when he passed close to her, she had looked at him briefly through clear grey-blue eyes. She walked with a grace and carriage curiously alien to those about her, he had said, yet she seemed to fall easily into the Bohemian quality of life. Ernst found himself frequenting these haunts more often in order to see her, he was quick to notice she was never alone, a woman, slightly older perhaps, was always close beside her, a smaller shadow that never left her side.

'He had asked questions about her among the many stall holders, but they shook their heads. They knew nothing, but here and there he gained a little knowledge, yes, they had said, she came from a high-born family who lived quite handsomely in the French region of the chateau-studded "Val de Loire" — the country of Counts and Kings originally — but would look with sidelong glances at each other and say awkwardly, that she was ... a little different, and would say no more.'

'You are describing your mother, aren't you, Jack?' exclaimed Marilla enthusiastically. 'Who was she?'

Jack drained his glass and rose from his seat. Thrusting his hands deep into his pockets he walked around for a few minutes before replying. 'Her name was Camille Du Pont and yes she was French born and the lady who accompanied her was her friend and guardian, known only as Edwina.'

There was a gasp of astonishment from Isabella, 'Edwina?'

'Yes, dear Edwina, always so close but not even she could ...' he bit his lip before going on. 'Ernst eventually was able to arrange an introduction to Camille and they met, but still under the watchful eye of Edwina, who incidentally was not in favour of her charge being courted by the young Baron. Anna later stated in her diary that Edwina had confessed to her that she did her best to dissuade Camille from a romantic entanglement and for a time Camille resisted, perhaps because she herself could see dark shadows in her future. However, she fell for his persuasiveness, hoping maybe that those shadows would fade. In due course they married and Camille, with Edwina, became part of the Baron's household.

'Anna, who was well aware of her son's eccentricities and contrary to what one would have believed, welcomed this strange and beautiful woman and her companion into the stately House of Zaharoff. She herself was now in failing health and was concerned that her son should settle down with a wife before she died. She wrote that Camille reminded her so much of herself at the same age and she declared too, that there was indeed an air of aristocracy about her. There was something else there as well ... something Ernst *hadn't* seen.

'The only relevant portion of Camille's ancestry that mattered to the Baron at the time, was that his wife was of French nobility and intriguingly coloured with a Bohemian candour that bewitched him entirely. Plus, of course, she was a beautiful adornment to his house — much like a prized painting,' said Jack, a bitter note creeping into his voice.

Amos had also risen from his seat, but it was to refill Jack's glass and hand it to him silently, before reseating himself.

Jack thanked Amos with a nod and resumed his narrative. 'The following year Camille gave birth to her son. He was named Jaques Vladimir Von Zaharoff then Ernst had the family crest tattooed on the boy's right shoulder on his fifth birthday, as he himself was so marked at the same age. Everything was fine, even though I was often lonely and there were few of my own age to share time with, I would sit in the garden with my grandmother for hours and listen to her tales of travel. It was a happy, close family group and there were … were many remarkable events to remember. Holidays in Paris and Venice, skiing in the Alpine resorts. There were receptions and big house parties held at the Manor, people, some very important people coming and going and then, quite suddenly, they stopped coming.

'Even though he was wealthy in his own right, Ernst had begun to change from a contented family man to a beleaguered captive of his own inordinate desires. He had begun to immerse himself heavily into matters of political and monetary gain … and gaining very little in the monetary side of his investments. He made enemies and from unsound advice, he began to lose heavily on the stock market; too proud to admit defeat, he drew more and more on the family fortune. It became as Anna had been afraid would happen and the earlier prediction that Edwina had foretold, Ernst's eccentric nature intensified, he would hurl abuse at the servants, the villagers … his own family and anyone else who dared cross his path.

Where there had once been love and contentment there was now only fear.'

Jack paused and drank deeply from the glass clutched in his hand before resuming. 'Then the reasons for the possible causes of his misfortunes began to take root in his mind. Those whom he had turned on in his rage, particularly those in the Manor village, now began to speak openly of what had been kept secret for so long, even though they held no grudge against the mistress of the Manor. "Look into your own house" they would say slyly, "Look to your wife, what do you really know about her? She may be of noble birth, but we hear whispers from the folk who know ... that she is a witch and so is her companion".'

'So, he had never realised that during all that time,' said Marilla with some astonishment.

'No, Camille never spoke of it, anything to do with witchcraft was never used or referred to during all the years of their marriage. Anna knew, she had guessed the truth not long after she had met Camille and Edwina, but to her it made no difference. They became very close to each other despite who and what they were. Anna found Edwina's companionship a great comfort and the two of them shared their innermost secrets.' He paused again as if the memories were painful but went on. 'Of course in the Baron's now twisted mind, he began to read dark thoughts. Small things that had occurred over the time of their marriage began to surface, things that were innocent in the happening, he was sure these same events had evil meanings. He became convinced that his failure to succeed was due to witchcraft. He was also aware that Edwina had opposed his marriage to Camille, he had never trusted her, believing she had too much hold on Camille. Even his mother seemed against him, taking him to task overusing family assets to further his ailing stock investments.'

'Were you old enough to know what was happening?' asked Marilla quietly.

'Yes, I was,' said Jack, as he sat down again. 'I suppose I would have been about ten years old when all this was happening. I remember feeling sad yet angry that my father had begun to turn against my gentle loving grandmother whom I adored and would reduce her to tears with his ravings and abuse. I remember creeping down the staircase when my father came home late. There was a certain spot there where you could see into my grandmother's sitting room and yet not be noticed by anyone in the room. I would hear him arguing with her over money and the selling of various family items of value. She would beg him not to take any more of their precious possessions. She tried to make him understand that there were things there from the estate that should pass on to his son, that he had no right to squander them just for his own errors of judgement; he had to take some responsibility for his actions.

'I remember him getting very angry and he was screaming at her that it did not matter what his mother thought now, the Von Zaharoff estate and all that went with it were his, by birthright and he would take what he wanted of it. His voice was loud and frightening, I recall creeping quickly back up the stairs but not before I heard my grandmother crying and I was angry with him for making her cry.'

'That must have been terrible times for your grandmother,' Isabella murmured.

'It was, it was bad for my mother too, she could make no sense of the change that had taken over him, she more than once tried to reason with him, all to no avail. Then when the whispering started from those he had trodden on in his ambitious but flawed trail of financial ruin, he turned on his family with a savage and brooding vengeance.'

'Do you want to tell us what happened when your father found out that your mother and Edwina were Wiccan? You don't have to, if you feel uncomfortable about it,' Marilla added quickly.

'No, no, it's alright, I've gone this far with this hapless story of my life, I might as well continue. I can only repeat now the events that unfolded as Edwina related them to me ... part of which I had seen and heard for myself ... and it terrified me.

There were lots of places for a small boy to hide in those old draughty castles and not be seen; I had explored them all.

'Edwina never kept any secrets from me, she felt it was her duty that I should know the truth in all things and be well prepared for any events that could cross my path where my father was concerned. She had seen things no one else could and was afraid for me. I didn't fully understand at first why I should be concerned about my father but after that terrible night when the world and the family that I knew disintegrated ... I knew and understood.'

Chapter 40

Escape In The Night

Ernst Von Zaharoff's suspicions and anger had increased, someone was to blame for his misfortunes, even his own mother suggesting that he had accepted bad advice on his investments, was too much. What would she know about money or how to capitalise on it? Besides which, wasn't it his own father's money — *his* inheritance? He had every right to use it however he wanted, hadn't he always got what he wanted? What he had wanted...

'What he wanted and what he married was another question that burned in his brain. The rumours from those who would know had to be true. He had never trusted those sly gypsies who lurked on the outskirts of the town and slunk around like hungry dogs waiting for someone to drop something tasty in their path. His informant in the bazaar had directed his feet in the direction of the gypsy camp, silver had changed hands and gold on this one he reflected as he made his way back to his carriage from the shady riverbank that housed the colourful gypsy caravans. He was aware of their dark eyes boring into his back as he left them, aware of the shrieks of their low-caste brats as they raced each other along the banks, their bare feet barely touching the grass as they ran.

'What he had learned from the elder in the camp still festered in his brain driving all other thoughts away. Camille had never talked openly about her family, except that they came from the Loire Valley in France, but none of her family had attended their wedding, only a dowager aunt and of course her constant companion — the woman known as Edwina. He spat the bitter taste out of his mouth. How could he have not seen through them? The fact that she came from a titled family was true enough, the dowager aunt was proof enough of that and the family name known amongst his exclusive circle but what of her life before he had met her wandering through the bazaar, like a lost and beautiful princess waiting for her prince to rescue her?

'He had seen and taken what pleased him and his princess had fitted easily into the role he had made for her, a beautiful and elegant centre piece in a dynasty that had its roots in Tsarist history. He had not looked behind the beautiful grey-blue eyes and had known he was binding himself to a witch.'

'So it was that in a blind explosive rage, he confronted the women in his house, as they sat with their needlework, their afternoon tea things spread out on the elegant side table, and their conversation hanging in the air at this unexpected intrusion. Jack took a deep breath and spoke slowly.

*   *   *

'Pierre Michelet! No doubt that name means something to you, Camille!'

All three women looked at the grim figure standing in the doorway of the little drawing room, his tall figure with his hands on his hips filling the space. 'Pierre Michelet!' He spat the name out again as he advanced into the bright little room, into which there now crept a cold chill. 'One of your ex-lovers; gypsy ex-lovers! I've just had an interesting conversation with him at that wretched filthy camp down by the river. So, it would seem that all the rumours are true; you *are* a witch!'

When his tirade of accusations against her was exhausted, there was only a tense electrifying silence. Camille rose slowly to her feet and despite her mothers-in-law's touch of repression on her arm, stood tall and erect in front of her husband. 'Yes,' she said, looking directly into his eyes. 'I am Wiccan by birthright, it is in my blood and nothing that I am ashamed of, despite what you have heard. I do know, Pierre Michelet, to add to your information, he too is Wiccan but he would not have told you that. He has long held a grudge against me. He had asked me to pledge to a marriage, but I refused him. I was but seventeen at the time and not ready to marry so young.'

'So, you waited for something better to come along — money and a title, which was your goal wasn't it!' His voice was raised in anger as he glared at her.

A cold deadly silence filled the otherwise pleasant little room.

Nobody noticed that the noise had attracted the attention of a small boy playing in the garden just outside the windows of his grandmother's drawing room. Clutching the ball, he had been playing with, he crept close to the window and hid himself amongst the dense shrubbery. He had hardly dared to breathe as he listened to his father's outrageous outburst, a deep sense of fear slowly filling his consciousness. Though he could not understand his father's growing indifference to his family, the coldness that had crept into his relationship with his father had deepened and his confusion grew as he tried to understand why.

He also knew that a time would come when he would have to leave the home he had known and put his whole faith in

Edwina's hands. She had taken him aside one day and explained to him why it was certain things were happening that he was thinking hard about, they would suddenly seem to occur and then to realise that he was part of a family that had powers one could only read about in books. She had told him many things, which had to be kept secret, because his father would never understand and it could lead to a lot of trouble for all of them. He could hear his mother's voice now also raised in defence as she answered his accusations.

'I did not consider that part of my heritage would have caused you such anguish and might I remind you that I gave many refusals to you before finally consenting, title or money had *no* part in my acceptance of your proposal. Edwina, my dear friend and companion can also lay claim, as you have spoken, to be of the same kind, however, neither she nor I have practised our craft since entering these walls and have *never* done anything to bring hardship upon you; any blame for misfortune must lie at your own feet.' Her eyes met his in a steady look and the clearness of those grey-blue eyes unnerved him.

He tore his gaze away and fixed his torment on his mother. 'And you—you have known it, you have sheltered this vile secret and never spoken of it to me—you have encouraged them. You have all conspired against me, to ruin me with your whisperings and your witchcraft!'

'No, Ernst, *no!*' gasped his mother, clasping her hands together in distress. 'Our concern has only been for your wellbeing, there has been no witchcraft done here. You must understand, Ernst, no form of witchcraft can change the path you take one way or the other. You have yourself chosen a path of disaster and ruin despite my words of warning. Your father's inheritance to us is rapidly being depleted; soon there will be nothing left of value to identify the House of Zaharoff and we will be left destitute. Already there is much of what your father and I treasured missing from this house, there is little left that is precious to us. Surely you must see that it is your folly alone that has brought this about.'

'What I choose to do with my father's inheritance is my affair,' he said curtly. His eyes darkened as he took a step closer to his mother and spoke in a low and ominous tone, 'I will also have that one treasure you keep hidden from me. I shall find it and claim it as is my right—you know I will. I *will* have it, one way or another!'

The Baron turned from his mother to where Camille still stood, meeting the steady blue grey eyes that seemed to be boring into his soul. 'What concerns me more now, is the shame and disgrace that has befallen the House of Zaharoff since these shrews have been under my roof! I see now that I have been caught in a web of sorcery since the very beginning—you bewitched me into marrying you. You have deceived me and I blame you both for my present misfortune.'

His face now a mask of fury, he turned to Edwina, who had remained seated, her needlework lying untouched on her lap. '*You!*' He hissed, pointing an accusing finger, '*You're* the one who has unleashed the demons of witchery into this house. From the beginning it was *you*. You have always despised me and this is your vengeance, but that will soon change,' he added in a deeply menacing voice.

Edwina sat motionless and said nothing but heard and recognised the faintest trace of fear in his voice and noticed the slight tremble in the outstretched finger.

Baron von Zaharoff gave them all a scathing contemptuous look as he moved toward the door, but stood for a moment, his long lean hands clenching and unclenching in his anger, then spoke. 'It grieves me deeply now to know that I have placed the mark of my father's house on a half-bred spawn, however ...' and his voice took on a more malevolent tone, 'I shall deal with that also in due time.'

When he had left the room, it seemed as if time had stood still, an eerie silence had descended to enshroud the once cheerful and airy chamber with a darkening cloud of despair and foreboding. The three women were silent for some moments, Camille had remained standing, her face still turned toward the door, the Baron's words leaving no doubt in her mind as to her fate. Finally, she turned to where Anna sat, a lace handkerchief pressed to her tear-stained face and knelt down in front of her, taking her hands in her own. 'Edwina and I will leave here, Anna, we will leave and take little Jacques with us, though I fear for your safety too, will you come with us?'

Anna shook her head and clasped her hands tightly together in her lap. 'No, Camille, no—my illness has made me too frail now to flee. Once, I was compelled to, now I have a choice, I am not afraid of Ernst, I doubt he would ever carry out a threat to my life. I will spend the rest of what time I have here regardless of his threats. This is my home and I will remain here, though it will grieve me greatly to lose my beloved grandson and my dear friends.'

Edwina stood and went to Anna, folding her arms around her and kissed her forehead. 'If I had the power to change things, I would my dear, Anna, but to dabble with the human mind is a most dangerous undertaking; we can only do what we can to protect ourselves from the danger that overshadows us.'

'He wants the cherub—he wants it, I cannot give it up, Edwina—I *must* not let him take it!' she sobbed, clutching Edwina's sleeve. 'It is the only thing now I can give to Jacques that is part of me and his maternal heritage, I know he would cherish it as I have done. I must ask you to take it, it is now your burden to bear, I can think of none better to entrust it to.'

'Ernst will not have it!' said Edwina firmly. 'Anna, do you remember me telling you that I would see to that when the time came?' She pulled a chair closer to where Anna sat twisting her handkerchief between her fingers. 'You knew what Camille and I were when we first came here, you embraced us and accepted us. The fact that we are witches was never odious to you, but I knew Ernst would never accept it, that is why we kept our own heritage a secret, known only amongst ourselves. Even young Jacques has been blessed with powers he knows little about yet but will learn to control as he grows older.'

'Jacques knows something of our craft, Anna, he is fully aware of our skills, but was sworn to silence,' said Camille. 'Edwina has spent some time with the ivory box the cherub rests in, young Jacques has watched her preparing its secret, a deadly enigma that will bring instant death to anyone not handling it correctly. She has placed her own curse upon it and only one who knows its danger can open the box safely. We have been quietly preparing for this for some time and are ready to leave, even Jacques knows that, although it grieves him greatly to see the change that has devoured his father's senses and destroyed his own family.'

To Anna and her then faithful nurse companion and protector of years ago, the Icon of Phidias had become the keeper of their fate, they had survived many turbulent years with it in their keeping but survive they did.

Anna had shown it to Ernst shortly after his father had died, but the interest he had shown in the precious object was only of monetary value to him even then. He had asked what it would be worth if and when, it could be sold, as he admired the treasure in his hands.

So, Anna hid the icon, vowing she would never reveal its hiding place to him; it would not leave her keeping. As he grew to manhood, he often asked about the icon, but she never revealed it to him again. Even at that age and now the head of the house following his father's unfortunate death, he had become increasingly conscious of his power and influence and in this Anna had sensed danger, only too aware that his power over others he considered lesser than himself, could spiral out of all control. When he had married Camille, she had hoped that the responsibility of having to share his life and his world would have a calming influence on his extravagant and somewhat selfish ways.

For a time it did, so entranced was he by Camille's steady influence, but now, she sighed, it was all too late. It would seem now that not only had she lost her own son but was very shortly to lose her other greatest treasure — her grandson. Her thoughts turned to her own childhood and Olga. How she had been loved and protected by this stalwart homely woman and knowing that Olga could not only care for her with gentle loving hands but could just as easily kill with those same hands and had done so, when her charge was duly threatened while in their worldly travels, they had found themselves in mortal danger more than once by overzealous miscreants who thought them an easy target. Her father had been very wise in his choice of a guardian for his daughter. Anna thought about it now and the terrible thought that crossed her mind appalled her. Wouldn't it be easier for Ernst to just disappear? His path of self-destruction was set and no amount of talk or pleading for a sense of sanity would prevail.

Although it would solve the problem, she shook her head to

rid her mind of such thoughts, he was still her only son. It was now, more than ever that she missed Vladimir, they had such a happy life together, he would have kept their son in check, and Vladimir would have groomed him to take his place in the Zaharoff dynasty to rule with dignity and fairness, as well as pride. She sighed again, he had lost his father and she, her only love far too soon.

Camille and Edwina had helped fill that gap of loneliness and little Jacques, so close to her in spirit and character. For many hours he would sit at her feet in the garden and listen to her stories of travel and adventure in the faraway places she and Olga had visited, answering his questions and painting mental pictures for him of exotic scenes in strange lands.

'You warned me this could happen,' she said finally, 'both of you, but I found it hard to believe it then all those years ago, but now—' she broke off in a shudder of sobs. 'Now, I feel afraid for my grandson. I know already that he will not grow to be like his father, you have foretold this to me Edwina and like so much before, it has come true.' Anna reached out and took Edwina's hand and that of Camille, she held them tight. 'The only thing I ask of you now is to keep Jacques safe and Camille—Camille, you *must* get away from here as quickly as you can now. Ernst I feel will not hesitate long before he acts, this–this obsession that he has brought upon himself is destroying his mind and who knows what he is capable of? I fear he will hunt you down, his compulsion to erase any stigma that he considers dishonourable to the Zaharoff line will lead to violence — you must get away quickly and safely and take my little Jacques with you both!'

The covert plans that had been gradually put in place sometime before had been completed, but with household duties still carried out as if nothing was amiss, just a cold quietness that had descended amid the residents of the house, with nothing said or done to provoke unwanted interest among the servants. In any case, all of the domestic servants were sympathetic to the plight of the women of the house, they feared the feisty young Baron and kept their respectful distance. It did not do to rouse the Baron's ire; many a servant had been sent packing for daring to make even the smallest mistake in his presence.

Anna meanwhile, quietly went about making sure there were precious gems and other small items of value that she had long kept hidden, secreted in hems of clothing and small leather pouches to be worn next to the skin, much as had been done by Olga when she had fled all those years ago. Edwina and Camille protested that they would have none of it, but Anna insisted that it was necessary.

Jacques would need an education, she argued, she could not let him leave his grandmother's house with nothing, her time was ending and money would be wanting to see to their needs. She herself had known the wisdom of this when Olga had taken her up and fled her homeland, with the babe kept safe in her arms and left to wander the world in exile. In the end they had to agree, accepting the treasures bestowed upon them ... and the ivory casket.

However, as much as those well laid plans were meant to hide the exodus, such was the cunning of Baron Von Zaharoff, already suspicious of flight, that he had bought the confidence of an eager stable hand. The hand had no such qualms about the fate of the mistress, as long as he was well paid, as were several others he had recruited for whom the lure of riches was too good to turn down. The Baron was duly informed that a carriage had been made ready for flight but he was not certain when that would transpire. So, an unobtrusive watch was kept.

Edwina was concerned, as was Camille, that it would be no easy escape, it had to be quick. Camille herself sheltered a personal fear but had faith in Edwina to get her son to safety. So it was, not long after that dreadful day in Anna's drawing room when the world as they knew it had come crashing down on them, that the weather changed, heavy storm clouds gathered, bringing a night of heavy blinding rain. Thunder rent the air and the brilliant flashes of lightning momentarily revealed a fleeting vision of three shrouded figures moving quickly across the cobbled yard to the stables, where the carriage awaited, the horses stamping their feet and blowing the warm air from their nostrils. The old man holding their heads had waited patiently for Anna's pre-arranged signal from an upper room overlooking the stables. Old Josh had been in the Count's employ since a lad and had no liking for the brash young Baron, and anything he could do for his Mistress, he would do, whatever the consequences...

Camille had hurriedly bundled the boy into the carriage, telling him to stay on the floor, then turned to help Edwina in beside him but their flight to freedom was to be short lived. A great outcry was heard along with the raised voices of men as some tried to restrain the horses and a hoarse cry from old Josh as he was knocked heavily to the ground. A hand reached out to grasp Camille's wrist and drag her bodily away from the carriage. Edwina heard the strident tones of the Baron's voice as Camille was dragged further into the darkness of the stables. Jacques was clutching the door of the carriage and peering out in fear, calling for his mother as she struggled in the grasp of his angry father. He heard her scream to

Edwina to flee, to leave her and save herself and Jacques, then he heard her voice no more, it was lost in the noise and confusion.

The terrified horses were plunging in their harnesses as the servants of the Baron fought to control them. Jacques could feel rough groping hands endeavouring to grasp at his ankles and pull him out of the carriage, but he kicked and fought and screamed at them and then, utter confusion reigned as a thick enshrouding mist appeared from nowhere and enveloped the scene.

Voices were raised, as vision was lost to the stable hands and villains as they tried to obey the Baron's orders. Then suddenly the horses were away, the groping hands of the men torn away from the harnesses as they reared upward and sped forward. The enraged Baron had a final glimpse amongst the swirling fog of a cloaked figure sitting above the horses, a shrill voice uttering strange words and the horses responding with high-pitched whinnying, the whites of their eyes rolling as they galloped away.

'*The gate! Stop them at the gate!*' Ernst was shouting, '*Keep it shut!*'

The horses were gathering speed down the long winding concourse that separated the large manor house from the main village thoroughfare; nothing would stop them now.

Too late, for those standing there to obey the Baron's orders. Blinding flashes of light, cold blue light that did not come from the raging stormy sky lit up the gates and they were flung wide open as if by invisible hands, the horses sped through and vanished into the night, still enveloped in the swirling mist. The clatter of the wheels and the pounding of the horse's hooves on the rough ground beyond the realm of the high walls of the manor fading into the distance punctuated the night.

To a small and terrified boy, his eyes stinging with tears and clinging tightly to the seat supports as he lay sprawled on the shuddering floor of the carriage, it was a nightmare that would live in his brain forever.

Some short while later, a statement was issued by an apparently distraught Baron Von Zaharoff that a bold kidnap attempt had resulted in the unfortunate death of his wife, The Baroness Zaharoff. She had been accidentally shot while trying to protect the child Jacques from the intruders, who had made off with their quarry. The Baron claimed that the companion woman to his wife, whom he had always suspected of thefts from his house over many years, had obviously been part of the conspiracy as she had also disappeared with the boy. A roughly written ransom note was delivered to the Manor several days later, so he claimed, but any attempts to find the missing pair were to no avail.

The heartbroken Baron had lost both his wife and child, so it was stated and to add to his grief, his dear mother died within a few months of these events. Soon after, Baron Von Zaharoff closed his estate and he announced his intention to spend the next few years travelling.

To the people in the village, who knew better, it was a crime he would never be forgiven for, but they held their tongues and only spoke of it among themselves, until the passage of time eventually stilled their tongues to the merest occasional and overt whisper, but it was never forgotten by those who knew the truth. Even then they were still afraid to speak out, lest the Baron hear of it and life had been difficult enough with the new lord of the manor. His father, the Count had been a fair man, an honest man, if perhaps a trifle unconventional sometimes but never a violent man. Not so his one and only son, who had himself defiled his own name.

Unbeknown to Baron Von Zaharoff however, several letters from the Baroness Camille Von Zaharoff had found their way into the hands of a Franciscan monk in a retreat high on a mountain top, surrounded by pine forests and snowy mountain peaks and bounded by a swiftly flowing stream.

Chapter 41

The End of a Dynasty

A profound silence prevailed in the old abbey kitchen for quite some moments after the tale had unfolded. The fire had slowly been burning down in the enormous old stove and the tumble of a log, now reduced to a charred crumble, dropping down amongst the warm ashes awoke the small group from their enraptured reverie.

'No wonder Edwina never said anything to us, or anybody about your parents,'

remarked Marilla understandingly. 'I would never have thought it was so involved, or, so—so cruel!' she finished lamely.

'What dreadful memories you must have had during those years of growing up,' said Isabella sadly, her big brown eyes filling with tears. 'And you never told anybody about it, not even me.'

Amos grunted, as he got up from his seat to see to the fire. 'You always were a mystery, Jack and having Rasputin for a great grandfather will make me doubly cautious of you in future, I'll never know what you might come up with.'

'Well, I would very much prefer it wasn't made public anyway, that goes for all of you. I've told my story as I know it and I've got that damn mark on my arm to prove that I am who I am ... but I'd prefer to be just plain Jack Grimsby.'

Amos' voice took a on a more serious tone now. 'I know and I've seen the mark before, it's very faded and you'd be hard put to make anything out of it, you've grown some since you were five don't forget, Jack and tattoos done then don't last as long as those they do today.' He slammed the stove door shut and said decisively, 'Soon as I get this old girl up to scratch again, I think a mug of hot coffee would go down well, then I'll rustle up some more grub.'

Elias, who had sat quietly listening but not saying a word now spoke. 'I would never have thought that I would ever hear a story as strange and sad as the one you have just related, Jack. I know I lost my parents when I was very young but there was nothing as traumatic as that. I never really had a family I could relate to either, so there was no bonding

... but you did and I think that is the saddest part — to have that all torn away from you and at such a vulnerable age.' He shook his head sadly. 'What sort of man would turn on his own wife and child like that?'

'I don't really know, Elias,' said Jack thoughtfully, 'but there are those who fear what they don't understand and don't want to understand. Blend that with delusions of grandeur, a little too much wealth and power, so it's not too hard to see how a man can go off the rails, particularly when his reputation and social predominance amongst his peers comes under close scrutiny, such as being wed to a witch and not knowing it.'

'Isn't it odd,' said Marilla curiously, 'that as soon as someone mentions the word "witch", it seems to strike an ominous chord in some people? What a pity they don't take the time to understand that we are not really much different to anyone else, well, in some ways I suppose we are,' she added quickly.

'It seems odd too, that all of us here have lost our parents in one way or another doesn't it?' observed Isabella after a moment's thought. 'I've almost forgotten what our mother looks like now, it's been so long since we've seen her and I don't believe she really cares,' she added almost wistfully, 'but you wouldn't think she's ever really forgotten us even if she didn't care much for us, has she, Marilla?'

'Well, we've managed to survive without her and we owe that to Grandma Hackett,' retorted Marilla. 'I guess we should be thankful that Grandma was there for us when our mother wasn't. She was too busy making a life for herself in the circus, you're probably right, Bella; I don't think she did really care for us at all, when you stop and think about it. Maybe she considered we were too much trouble to look after anyway and figured Grandma could do a better job of it than she could, but that's all in the past now, Bella, we've got to think about where we're going from here.'

Marilla turned to face Jack. 'Oh, I'm sorry, Jack, we shouldn't even be talking about our own mother ... under the circumstances but I'm sure you can understand. Where you lost your mother in a tragic and bitter situation, ours was not like that. Ours was pure neglect and selfishness, unless in mother's befuddled mind, we didn't really exist. Not having your own flesh and blood parents beside you as you grow up can be pretty hard, particularly when you know you're not really an orphan.' Marilla sighed and laid her hand on Jack's. 'I've got a knack of saying the wrong things at the wrong time, haven't I?'

'No you haven't, Marilla.' Jack squeezed her hand comfortingly. 'I think that's the first time either of you have ever spoken openly about how you feel about your mother leaving you when she did. Perhaps it is time you spoke your thoughts on that.' Marilla and Isabella glanced at each other and exchanged a comforting look.

'However,' said Marilla, her businesslike manner swiftly returning, 'apart from all this, Jack, I'm curious about that ivory box,' she said thoughtfully. 'When you took it out of the cavity in that altar thing, you said that the seal on the edge of it was broken. How could it have been broken if supposedly no one had touched it?'

'Yes,' broke in Isabella, 'and where did Edwina get the curare from?'

Jack grinned at them and the grey eyes sparkled for the first time in days. 'Remember I told you that Anna and Olga had travelled extensively after escaping Russia? Well, it was while they were in South America that they visited a native camp, the head man was captivated by Anna and particularly Olga; he considered her a warrior, because of her build and strength. When they were leaving, he presented them with a small quiver of the little darts that the natives use to bring down game. They use them in blow pipes and are extremely accurate with their kill. The tips of these darts are dipped in a virulent poison the natives obtain from a certain type of frog that has these little poison glands down its back and some poisons are also obtained from the woody sap of some of the local trees. They accepted the gift graciously and put it amongst the other treasures they had gathered in their travels and thought no more about it.

'When Anna was showing some of these curiosities to Edwina, she decided to examine the quiver a little more closely and found a tiny earthen pot at the very bottom of it. It was still almost full of the poison and heavily concentrated. She tested it and found that it was still very potent, so that's when she decided to sabotage the ivory box. Edwina allowed me to watch what she did with the little pouches she made of bat's wings and fix the snake fangs into each. She wanted me to be sure I understood the danger the box carried. They all knew that Ernst was determined to find the icon, as he considered it rightfully his. He had already searched places in the house for it and was becoming obsessed with finding it and had taken to threatening his mother to reveal its hiding place.

'As for the broken seal — it was simple, it was never really sealed in the first place. The sealing wax was left with a clean-cut edge and deliberately left to look as if it had been cut, it was a decoy, so it would look as if the box had been tampered with. If one had looked closely, it might have been seen but the Baron, in his anxiety to make sure he was not being cheated wouldn't have thought about that. As the verse stated, "Cursed be he that moves with haste, for life therein is doomed to waste".' His eyes darkened again briefly and he suddenly got up and walked around to the old stove and stood there with his back to the group for only a few moments. Then noisily taking the lid off the heavy old kettle, he said in a slightly strained voice, 'The water is almost on the boil, Amos, I'll go and get the mugs from the pantry and you can do the honours.'

The afternoon was drawing to a close and the effects of the morning were beginning to tell. Elias did not look well at all; his normally ruddy complexion had taken on a greyish tone and his eyelids were beginning to droop. He had risen from the table and declared that he was going to do his chores before it got much later, as he intended to have an early night. His announcement brought an ardent outburst from the company, and particularly Isabella.

'Oh, no, you don't,' she said laying a restraining hand on his arm, 'Marilla and I will see to that, you can come along and supervise ... if you like.'

Elias grinned, his homely face an expression of delight. 'My my, who would have thought I would have two lovely ladies as assistants ... or is it still only the one?' He glanced sideways at Marilla. 'Unless you would just like to feed the chooks and collect any eggs, while Isabella gives me a hand getting the other animals bedded down.'

'Of course I will, Elias,' said Marilla standing up. 'I should have to earn my keep sometime, I can handle the chooks but I'm not too sure about the donkeys.'

'Well, I guess that leaves me in the kitchen again,' said Amos with a yawn, 'but at least I'll have Jack here to peel the spuds for me, he has to earn his keep too. Can't have any slackers around this place, plenty of work here for everybody.'

Jack watched the two girls and Elias scrabbling for their warm jackets and scarves from the pegs in the large foyer and listened to their bantering as they carefully shepherded Elias out of the door, his arm still warmly encased in a sling, and he smiled to himself.

*   *   *

A week or so had gone by and though it was still cold, the weather had begun to change a little. The girls had noticed the buds beginning to show on some of the fruit trees and new soft leaves, though still only tiny shoots, appearing here and there on the vines as they walked through the garden to attend to their chores. Marilla had not talked so much about moving on now as she had done before and showed a willingness to help in all manner of things to do with the running of the household. Jack and Amos however, had made it clear that they were still employed and were required to have to report back to their department very soon.

It was while they were walking back from the garden one day, that Joseph suddenly appeared on the steps of the scriptorium. This time he was not dressed as they had last seen him in his grey Franciscan robes, indeed he now looked quite different. He stood before them dressed in tones of brown, twill trousers and a plaid jacket with leather patches on the sleeves. A warm scarf in a mixture of soft greens was thrown about his neck and a woollen cap of the same tones pulled low over his head.

'Joseph!' Marilla exclaimed, 'you, well, you look so … different!'

'Do I?' he answered, in his softly modulated voice. 'So what do you see me as now, still a monk of a holy order?' He inclined his head and gave a rare smile. 'It is said that "clothes maketh the man", and even though I may be dressed differently, there is still the same person underneath, I myself have not changed. Do I still worry you, Marilla?'

'No, um—no—I guess not,' she stammered. 'It's just that we did not expect to see you again for a while, and … well, you did say you had work here to finish.'

'And so I have, important work that has kept me away for too long. However, that is beside the point at this particular time. It would seem your presence, both of you, is required in Henri's rooms, there are important issues at hand. If you would like to accompany me, I shall escort you there.'

Marilla and Isabella followed the tall, now casually dressed figure to the suite of rooms that had once been occupied by the former abbot. Joseph said little during the walk, remarking only that the weather was showing promise of an early spring and a good growing season. They were ushered into the oak panelled room, where it seemed not so long ago that Jack had produced the strange riddle that had set them on the trail of discovery and the ultimate death of a tyrant.

They were not alone however, Jack and Amos were engaged in a quiet conversation with Henri around the huge desk and Edwina, sitting with one leg tucked beneath her, was seated on the big sofa. A warming fire blazed in the grate; but it was the object next to Edwina on the sofa that left them with totally surprised looks on their faces.

At their approach, two large yellow eyes surveyed them critically for a second or two, then closed, as the large black cat stretched his forepaws and rolled on his back purring contentedly as Edwina continued her gentle stroking of the rich black fur on his fat tummy.

Isabella was about to say something regarding Lucifer's brashness, when Henri looked up and seeing them there, greeted them cordially. 'Come in come in, my dears, take a seat by the fire, I'm sure Lucifer will share, Elias will join us shortly to complete our ensemble.'

'Can I get you something to drink ladies?' Joseph was at their elbow and holding a tray upon which glasses and a bottle were placed.

'Oh, er, yes, thank you,' stammered Marilla, and Isabella almost in the one voice.

Isabella walked over to the sofa where Edwina looked up at her, a smile creasing the corners of her eyes behind the enormous glasses. 'He always did like a tummy rub, they all do, don't they? He has been rather spoilt, haven't you, you great lump,' she crooned as she spoke to Lucifer. 'Now, off you go and sit by the fire so your mistresses can sit down.'

Lucifer rolled over again and obediently jumped down from his coveted place beside Edwina and dutifully went to sit on the hearth and began to groom himself, occasionally looking up at Marilla and Isabella with eyes that plainly said, 'So, you caught me out enjoying normal things cats do with someone else, so what!'

'He never lets anyone else scratch his tummy like that, only us and not very often either, unless you want to lose a lot of skin,' said Isabella cautiously.

'I think you'll find that he just wants you to know your place in the hierarchy of your household and will accept his tummy rubs when *he* chooses. There's a lot more to Lucifer than one would think, he's a remarkable cat and very loyal to you, he just likes to show who's boss.'

Edwina turned her attention to them now completely. 'My, my, how much you have both changed since I last saw you at Harewood. Mind you though,' she continued with a wink of one tawny brown eye, 'I have never been far away from you in all of your ramblings since you left the commune, though you have not been aware of it. I made a solemn promise to Hilda to keep an eye or two on you both, it has been rather difficult I must say. What with having to attend conventions and sort out other problems, as well as trying to keep you both out of trouble — and you have found yourself in some trouble at times too I must say.' A frown creased the finely lined face as she said this but the smile returned as she said warmly, 'however, I rather feel you may have both shown that you are capable of thinking and acting independently of each other and using the courage and integrity you were blessed with.'

A soft knock at the door interrupted her and Elias' homespun ruddy face looked cautiously around the door.

'Come in, Elias, do come in,' said Henri waving a hand. 'We are waiting for you, I do hope your shoulder has given you no more trouble.'

'No, not at all now,' he answered quickly, 'It's fine, I'm just careful that I don't push things too far, don't want it to pop out again.'

'Good, excellent!' exclaimed Henri,' his beard waggling approvingly. 'Now let's get down to the business at hand. As you can see, I am not getting any younger, wizards unfortunately don't live forever, which is more the pity,' he said shaking his head and almost dislodging his *pinc nez* again. 'There's not too many young ones that are aware of their potential, or even that they are wizards, or witches at all!' He sighed and pulled at his beard.

'However, that's not really what I want to talk about. What you have to decide, amongst us all here, is what you want to do with the abbey and what you can envisage it would be most useful for. I know Joseph has a few ideas but it really comes down to a joint decision.'

'What do you mean — what to do with the abbey? We understood that this place belongs to you and it was for Franciscan monks.'

'Yes, yes, I does,' said the old man looking at Marilla over the top of his glasses, 'but you see, I no longer need it, or want it. The monks have gone and I see no point in it deteriorating any further, so I am asking you, what do *you* want to do with it?'

Marilla and Isabella sat silently trying to understand what he meant, the abbey was nothing to do with them; if Henri wanted some advice on what to do with his own abandoned abbey, he was speaking to the wrong people.

Jack, who had been watching the expressions of confusion flitting across the sister's faces, now got to his feet and approached them. 'What my confused and lamentably aged uncle is trying to say is that he wants to give the abbey and all its surroundings to the group you see here, which includes yourselves, to do whatsoever we want with, within good reason of course.'

'Yes, that's it, Jack, my boy, that's what I want to do, isn't that right, Edwina?'

Edwina turned to face the girls and explained further, 'Henri is getting on in years and finds it very difficult to get around this old place. He has his comfortable little cottage in the village and with Theodore to keep him company, he is perfectly happy to stay where he is. So you see it was his thought that you might want to remain here and make this your home.

There is plenty of potential here for you to expand your skills and—'

Marilla broke in, 'But, Edwina, we only stayed on because Jack asked us to help him find this icon thing and now that he has it, we can really see no point in staying. We were going to go ...' her voice trailed off.

'Go where!' said Edwina firmly, shifting stiffly in her seat. 'There was absolutely no future whatsoever where you were supposedly heading and I would have had to haul you both out of trouble again, if it was possible. As a matter of fact, had we not stopped you, you may both very well have been either dead or in very deep trouble with the law, you know very well, Marilla, that I see things you don't!'

Marilla opened her mouth and shut it again. Grandma Hackett might not be here anymore, to guide them, but there was no arguing with Edwina either.

'Then ... then, you really mean what you are saying,' said Isabella haltingly, 'that we are to belong here, that this is to be our home!'

'Yes,' said Jack. 'I'm sure you haven't grasped it properly yet, Marilla and Isabella, but you have become part owners of an abbey. We, as a group will take over ownership. Joseph still has his research to get back to, Elias has his garden and the animals that he won't part with and now won't have to. Amos and I have to get back to work, so we won't be here, only coming back occasionally to make sure that everything is still in one piece ... and you haven't set fire to it.' He winked at Marilla as he said the last remark. 'So you see, you both have the right to say what you would like to see the abbey used for in the interests of all.'

'One thing we must make clear to you all is that, though you all have equal rights to the abbey, Jack is the main beneficiary and has the last word in what happens to it in due course.' Edwina got up from the sofa and walked over to Henri's enormous desk. 'Though Henri has not said so formally, Jack was to be the sole heir to the property but he does not want that to be so, he feels it would be more useful to be left to the residents that are still here to continue on. There is much that can be done here, we just need to sort out the finances.'

'Yes, yes, that is so,' said Henri in his deep resonant voice. 'I might also point out that I have been rather busy these past few years. In between my other duties as head of the Wizards Council, I have also been investigating the legalities of the estate of the Du Ponts in the Loire Valley in France. My dear sister Camille and I were the only beneficiaries of that estate. There are no other kith and kin to be considered, so I have signed all that estate and its grounds over to Jack. Quite a magnificent residence too I might add; that has been lovingly cared for by a resident caretaker and his wife now for some years. I, myself have been back there many times over the years and always found it a most pleasant and restful experience. However,' he sighed, 'travel to me these days is very trying but I will go back to my old home eventually when my old bones are ready.' He closed his eyes and it seemed to all those gathered that he had drifted off to sleep, suddenly, he roused himself and continued on.

'There is a small rose garden there and a bower, close to the river. My ancestor is buried there.' He opened his eyes and nodded his head. 'He was a wizard too you know, a very good one. He also had the reputation of being a very powerful individual and was one of the last remaining leading members of the Order of the Knights Templar, though shrouded in great secrecy I might add, as many of them did not survive.'

Edwina said quietly, 'Jack already knows that Henri and I have ensured his mother has been lain to rest in the family crypt there, under her full name of Camille Francesca Louise Du Pont. There is no reference to the Zaharoff name.'

The two sisters seemed to have been momentarily struck dumb as they listened to Henri. They were both having trouble getting their heads around the legacy that had just been dropped in their laps, until finally Isabella spoke. 'Shouldn't—well—um— shouldn't Jack now also become heir to the Zaharoff title?' she asked cautiously.

'No,' said Jack firmly. 'I reject that part of my heritage. The Zaharoff castle and its properties will be sold. I believe that there has been a lot of interest in turning much of the land over to a private housing estate and the manor itself an object of curiosity, perhaps a museum of some sort. My grandmother's remains will be taken from the crypt there and placed next to my mother before any changes take place on the estate. I no longer will have any reference to it, though I believe there are distant relatives who will carry the name on.'

He sighed deeply and said almost to himself, 'But for the

selfishness and ignorant attitude of one man, a whole dynasty is destroyed and a family torn apart for nothing.'

There was silence among the group for some moments.

'So, you have no intention of going back there then?' questioned Marilla.

There was a pause from Jack before he replied. 'Yes, I will go back there, but only to collect what is left of what my mother and grandmother left there. Anything that belongs to Ernst will stay and become part of their museum and curiosity shop.'

Amos, who, like Elias had said nothing until now, was heard to mutter under his breath, 'What one might call a "little shop of horrors".' He glanced at Jack and said sheepishly, 'Sorry, Jack, couldn't help that, it just slipped out.'

'That's okay, Amos, probably that description does sum it all up anyway.'

Henri had been quietly tapping his long fingers on his desk with one hand and stroking his long beard absently with the other while Jack had been speaking. Now he coughed slightly to get the attention of the company. 'There is of course the question of money to keep the abbey going and to pay for any improvements that will be necessary. Jack has promised to put most of the money from the sale of the Zaharoff estate into much-needed repairs here; but I do believe Joseph may also have a ready answer to that as well.' His eyes focused on Joseph and a slow smile spread across his face, 'Is this not so, Joseph ... have you found it yet?'

There was a discreet silence as all eyes were turned to where Joseph stood by the door. There was an ever so slight colouring to his face but his answer was direct and to the point. 'I do believe I may have discovered the burial chamber but there has been so much confusion these past few months ... and with the brethren leaving, I have had little chance to pursue the matter further.' He gave a slight cough. 'I had rather thought Henri that you had become aware of my clandestine operations by now, I know the treasure there and it would do so much to rebuild this place. There is so much potential here and history, Henri — it must be retained!' he said with an intensity in his voice they had not heard before.

'Perhaps I should explain,' said Joseph coming forward to stand near Henri's desk. He looked around the room and his eyes alighted on Amos and lingered for a few seconds. Clearing his throat then, he spoke. 'I have long known that a hoard of gold and silver coins was secreted here many years ago. I came across an ancient paper that had been slipped in between the covers of an old book that indicated this was so. The treasure, which consists mostly of European Ducats was apparently given in exchange for an important political figure who had been imprisoned here. Some precious stones and other items of great value were later added to the treasure trove and carefully hidden away by the third Marquis. His position here was at the best of times a precarious one and should he have needed to take flight from his enemies, then he would have the means to survive. I might add that in those days, life and labour was cheap and anyone else who might have aided the Marquis in the burial of this treasure hoard were, shall we say conveniently disposed of, or well paid for their silence. The parchment that I found was hidden in the bindings of a book that indicated where all the underground tunnels were as well as the original history of the abbey. A large silver bound book that, to my knowledge, had remained undisturbed for many years in the library alcove. Elias was the only other person who knew, but understandably reluctant to assist. He does not feel comfortable in such enclosed places, so I did most of the work down there and was, I felt, almost to the point of recovering the treasure, when "all hell broke loose" to use a phrase and we were engulfed in the business of the Casinis. I was, I might add, rather nervous that they would discover the diggings and had sworn Elias to secrecy, even to you, Jack.'

'Oh, dear,' said Isabella quickly. 'Did the book have silver bands across it and little silver pins holding it together from chains ... and was it bound in reddish leather?'

'Indeed it was, you know of it?'

'Well, yes I do,' she said haltingly, 'it was the book I was looking through when that man Carlos pushed me into the Priest's hole.'

Joseph nodded. 'Ah, I see, and did you understand anything in it, as it was not an easy volume to read?'

'Oh, yes I did ... after a fashion. That was how Elias and I found our way to the dungeons when we rescued Amos from that dreadful little cage he was trapped in.'

Amos who had said little until now looked from Joseph to Elias, who was beginning to look a trifle uncomfortable.

'It seems I may have stumbled on your activities by chance, Joseph. That deep hole in the ground on one side of the torture chamber seems to have another level before it falls away to the underground river. I noticed signs of activity there and evidence of digging tools near an entrance cut into the underside of the cliff.' He rubbed a hand over the stubble on his chin as he gazed directly at Joseph. 'I hope I haven't given too much away.'

Joseph gave a short cough as if clearing his throat. 'No, Amos, no more than Henri has clearly been aware of, so we should at least now make it public knowledge, at least known only to those in this room, though I fear that Carlos was also somehow aware.' Joseph recounted his chance meeting with Carlos in the long secret tunnel and of his last remark as he made his escape to freedom.

'So that's where he went,' snarled Amos, 'well, let's just hope he comes to a sticky end somewhere, although his kind seem to have charmed lives.'

'I don't think he would want to come back here though, not after what I did to him.' Isabella said thoughtfully. Carefully Isabella described what had happened in the stables when she had been left to guard the hapless Carlos. 'Lucifer really wouldn't have hurt him,' she said casting a glance at the cat now blissfully sleeping curled up close to the fire. 'He must have grown tired of guarding him and wandered off, perhaps I am to blame for him escaping, as I had loosened the ropes around his wrists a couple of times because he complained that it was hurting him.'

It didn't matter that there were amused smiles on the faces of all the company as they perceived a mental picture of Carlos' fat pink face contorted in horror at the sight of a recently dead rat under his nose and Lucifer's yellow eyes staring hungrily down as he sat on his chest.

Edwina had the widest smile of all. 'She's right you know, I was up in the rafters at the time and I saw it all. He was sweating like a pig, absolutely sure that Lucifer was going to bite into him as well after what Isabella had said to him. She had him absolutely in her power, and showed him no mercy, I was really proud of her.'

It was Isabella's turn to be surprised. 'So it was you up there! I heard an owl hooting several times and never thought any more about it. Edwina, how do you do it, turn into an owl I mean? I've read a bit about it in Grandma's books, but it sounds awfully complicated, and Uncle Henri ... into a raven? I thought ravens were despised by wizards as harbingers of ill omen.'

Henri waggled a long finger at her. 'You are right, my dear, though only in one sense, here, who would notice one more. In any case,' he said blithely, 'I always did have a bit of rebel in me and am rather inclined to–to throw caution to the wind, to also coin a phrase.' He adjusted his glasses awkwardly as they showed signs of slipping off his nose again as he shook his head. 'I do believe though that I may almost have taken my rashness too far; it could have so easily turned out rather nastily, as Jack here has reminded me and for putting you all through a lot of unnecessary danger I must here and now humbly apologise.'

Another moment of silence befell the group in the room as they quietly reminisced on what had befallen them and indeed how close they had all come to not being there at all, if it had not been for each other.

Henri suddenly raised his head and looked at Isabella raising one eyebrow questioningly. 'How did you know I was a raven?'

Isabella's brown eyes twinkled as she said with a laugh. 'I don't think anyone has ever seen a raven with two white feathers down its front ... you forgot about the beard.'

'So I did!' said the old wizard. He looked across at Edwina and said in as serious a tone he could manage as he chuckled softly to himself, 'You know, Edwina old girl, I rather think these young ladies have at last got it all together.'

A New Beginning

'So, what do you think, Marilla?' said Edwina, there were three of them sitting quietly in the small sitting room of the lodge, Edwina was balancing one of Grandma Hackett's books on her knee, juggling a cup of tea as well. 'It would be a perfect place, there are no religious orders now to consider and I don't feel that it would interfere with the abbey itself; it sits quite apart from it.'

'What does Henri think about it, or should we consult Jack first, after all he is the head of the company?' asked Marilla.

'I've already approached Jack before he left, he says that it's alright by him as long as it doesn't interfere with anything else and we would be responsible for keeping the meetings in order,' replied Edwina. 'After all I am a Grand Witch of the Order, so I don't see that as a problem.'

'I think it's a good idea,' chimed in Isabella. 'Joseph has been awfully busy in his laboratory and has some interesting experiments in hand that would make fascinating subjects for discussion. He's had me busy helping to make up more of his special healing balm.

Grandma's cauldron has come in very handy for making up the quantities, so we would have a ready market for that as well.'

'Yes, I do believe he's on a winner with that one.'

'I've lent him some of Grandma's books and he's been very interested in them too. Did you know that he found out that his father was actually a wizard and not just a magician? It really didn't come as such a surprise to him though, he said that he sort of expected that it was so, I think that underneath he was quite pleased about it.'

'Henri knew,' said Edwina candidly, as she passed her empty cup over to Isabella's waiting hand. 'He had met Joseph's father many years ago, when they were younger but he had refused to accept that he was Wiccan and preferred to work on the stage as a magician. As he said to Henri, "I can make more money as just a plain magician to support and educate my sons than to let the world know the true heritage — it turns people off, so I'll just stick to stage work". He also made Henri promise never to tell his sons of their heritage, as he feared they would take too much advantage of it and he wanted them to grow up well educated in the normal way and do something useful with their lives.'

'It would appear that Joseph's brother, Peter, must have realised a bit of his potential to become the master criminal that he was,' remarked Marilla, as she gathered up the remaining tea things and carried them to the sink. 'In fact, I think he was quite confused by it. I got the impression he was torn between the power of being able to take what he wanted and the teachings of the religion he chose to hide behind.'

'I do believe you could be right, Marilla — his mind was certainly torn between what was good and what was evil, ah well, some of us do go off the rails a bit as they say.' Edwina got to her feet, yawned, and stretched her back. 'Like Henri, I'm not getting any younger either, my bones are beginning to feel old. Anyway, give the old chapel a bit of thought girls, I know I'm not part of your ownership committee, but it does have Jack's approval, it would make a much better venue that what we have been using. I have had a word about it to Joseph, after all he is your deputy chairman and he seemed quite interested.' Her brown eyes twinkled behind the large glasses. 'Now that the shadows have been lifted from Joseph's own life, perhaps, as you surmised, Bella, he will be more than happy to present the end products at a full assembly. He has such a lot to offer in the way of herbal preparations.'

She turned to go but stopped in the doorway and looked at both sisters for a long moment. Her eyes looked more enormous than usual behind the large glasses and for a mere moment, there appeared to be a glistening as if a tear were forming, but the eyes blinked a couple of times, and the illusion was gone.

Edwina spoke and her voice was firm, though the sisters detected a slight quaver. 'When I first saw you both as scruffy little girls with hardly a brain between you that day when Hilda brought you back to Harewood, I must admit, there were a few times when I had my doubts but overall, I knew my predictions were right. Henri and I *were* taking a chance in bringing you here when we did. It was a challenge, even though I know you, in particular, didn't agree, Marilla; you being the more headstrong one. Even wizards and witches can't foresee everything that happens and you both proved yourselves as ready and capable to help when danger threatened and things began to happen that we could not interfere with. We could only safeguard your lives as much as we dared.'

She smoothed a non-existent crumb from the front of her robe and regarded the sisters again, this time the glasses were a trifle misty. 'I have watched over Jack from the time he lost his mother in those dreadful circumstances in his young life but my thoughts can't be everywhere at once and I have you both to thank for preserving that life; that could so easily have been lost.

Marilla cleared her throat with an embarrassed cough. 'Jack was so much a part of our lives too when we were in Harewood, so of course we wouldn't turn away from him when he needed help. We just had no idea his life was such a complicated one ... or who he really was.'

Edwina quickly agreed. 'I know, but it had to be kept secret for his own safety, until he was mature enough, mentally and physically to ... do what he had to do.'

'We are all aware, Edwina, how traumatic it has been for Jack and the decision he's had to make, it was a little frightening I must admit but when he left here with Amos to go back to his police work, you must admit he was a lot more relaxed,' said Marilla.

Isabella was giggling quietly. 'I can't say he looked terribly relaxed when you suggested that Marilla should join him as a special agent on the side, Edwina, did you see the look on Amos' face? I thought his eyebrows were never going to stop going up, he looked positively horrified at the thought.'

'Oh, I don't know, it might be sort of interesting being an agent ... except for the paperwork,' mused Marilla. 'Jack had already suggested that I should but of course he was joking, as usual. If only they didn't have to provide written reports on everything they do. I guess we could get away with it, from what Jack was telling me. He told me they had to fudge quite a few things on the report on the Casini case. Even his friend Steve had to delete some details from his account of the capture because nobody would have believed him.'

'Who would have thought, when that storm dropped us down here that we would have been mixed up in bringing international criminals to justice, let alone meeting up with Jack, but I'm glad we did ... meet up with him I mean. We're going to miss them not being around, all the time.' Isabella sighed wistfully. 'I already miss Amos' cooking.'

Marilla not unkindly shot her sister a look. 'Well, your waistline isn't and that's not a bad thing for you, you have to admit, Bella that the exercise you get from helping Elias is doing you good.' Marilla pushed her stray lock of hair away from her face before adding, 'I hate to admit it; but I'm missing them too, it's good that we're going to meet them again when we get to France. I don't mind doing a bit of cooking, even if it isn't quite the same as Amos prepares. His rabbit stew was exceptional.'

Edwina stood there smiling as she listened to the chatter between the girls. She had a vision of Hilda in her mind and felt sure that were she here now, she would have approved of the way the sisters had grown and blossomed into separate identities but with a single purpose.

'I have to go, girls. Henri is leaving to visit the chateau tomorrow and I want to be with him to help him with the arrangements. As you know we are to arrange a special reliquary that is being chosen to be attached to Anna's tombstone. We will see you both when you join us later in the month when Jack and Amos and indeed all the company will witness the placing of the icon into its final resting place and with its rightful owner, I'm sure the time away from here will do you both good; it's been a trying time for us all, a change of scenery is always an acceptable tonic.'

'Are you sure it will be safe there?' queried Isabella with a worried frown.

Edwina looked at her with a half-smile on her lined face. 'Safe? Of course, it will be safe, as safe my dear girl as it has ever been.' The tawny eye winked knowingly from behind the huge spectacles. In another moment she had gone, leaving the sisters to stare after her in bewilderment.

'I wonder what she meant by that?' Marilla mused.

'I don't dare to think what she really means but we're just as anxious that the icon be returned to Jack's grandmother ... his real grandmother that is,' replied Isabella gaily. 'Just think, Marilla, we're going to France!' She danced around the small kitchen waving the tea towel.

However, her sister was barely listening, her mind was elsewhere as she filled the sink in preparation for washing the cups and saucers.

'You know, Bella, I do think I'm really getting to like this place after all, I'm not just thinking of France and the visit to the Du Pont Chateau. I'm also thinking of the plans that have begun to take place here as regards the abbey and the ideas that have been put forward by Joseph.' Marilla gazed out of the kitchen window. 'You know Jack was right when he said that great things can be achieved with or without magic. Depending on how you use it ... or not at all; just use your own natural abilities to achieve the ultimate end.'

Isabella eyed her sister and a grin slowly spread across her face. 'That sounds like something Grandma Hilda would say.' Isabella picked up a cup and dried it.

'Now, I know you're not smiling about Grandma Hilda; just what are you smirking about?'

Continuing to dry another cup, Isabella sighed and found a spot on the cup that needed extra attention. 'I think you know what I mean, Marilla. Jack this; Jack that — you have a soft spot for him and always have.' Realising that she had likely gone a little too far, she sighed and put the cup down.

Indignant, Marilla blushed profusely and stuttered lamely, her cheeks giving her away. '*What?* What rubbish–I–I, that's not true! Besides don't think I don't know about *your* thing with the gardener! *Anyone* with eyes can see you like him and he you!'

Startled, Isabella was about to protest, when the look on each other's face spoke volumes. As if by mutual and unspoken consent, the two now had a better understanding and decided to change the subject, now that the truth of the matter was understood.

Softening, Marilla acknowledged in her mind what she had not been prepared to do until now. 'I'm also thinking of something else ...'

'Like what?'

Marilla didn't answer for a moment. Her green eyes swept over the part of the valley that could be seen from their cosy little home tucked away in its private corner of the abbey Estate. Spring was definitely in the air as a soft breeze riffled the pale green leaves thrusting forth from the poplars and elms that lined the road beside the river. The last of the winter snows had rapidly disappeared from beneath their shadowed hollows. This was now home, and it felt good.

'I'm thinking of Grizelda Fenwick.'

'Grizelda Fenwick?'

Marilla turned away from the window to face her younger sister and said in as serious a voice as she could muster, 'Yes, Grizelda, who said we would *never* amount to anything. I wonder how she will react when she gets an invitation to the next convention and be one of the privileged house guests at the newly restored Grimsby House. A place of refuge and healing of body and spirit, while catering also for retired witches and wizards and others in the know, then to attend the functions arranged for their pleasure in the Great Hall, once a place of worship and now an open arena for anything we want it to be,' she finished in an airy tone.

Isabella giggled and pulled a face. Marilla looked at her younger sister and laughed, a sound that had been missing for a long time. She had found her place now, a niche where she could make a name for herself, she didn't have to prove anything to anybody ... and even less to herself.

Marilla had already shown that she possessed a natural instinct in running the financial side of 'Grimsby House' and a pride in ensuring that it ran efficiently. Isabella, on the other hand, apart from helping Elias manage the farm and the produce from the garden that serviced the needs of the household, had proven to be a very valuable assistant to Joseph in his work in the preparation of the many herbal products used and sold within the House itself.

Destiny for the two sisters had been duly fulfilled.

So it was, that the old abbey had gradually taken on a new look as the hidden treasure was recovered from exactly where Joseph said it would be and money poured in from the estates of the late Baron von Zaharoff.

Repairs were made and the abbey restored to almost its full glory. The monk's quarters were updated and enlarged to provide comfortable accommodation for those inmates who sought the peace and solace their minds and bodies craved. A new wing was built where the old refectory had once stood and the visiting clientele could enjoy the luxury of warm spa baths and massages with the healing lotions and potions made on the premises, at their disposal. Large pavilions, glassed in for comfort provided a modern concept away from the chill air, where the snowy mountains and the lake provided a view to soothe the troubled mind. The chapel was renovated to become a convention centre and theatre. Though all this was not widely advertised, it became a focus of attention to those who knew.

There was only one stipulation — the solemn grey cloaks that had been worn by the monks were standard issue and were to be worn without fail should any of the inmates wish to enter the village. After all, there was still the rumour that the abbey was remaining a school of Monastic teachings, even though it was privately owned and run, that was the way the inhabitants wanted it. There had been many changes made, if the number of trucks carrying building materials and such were to be believed, but the Postmistress, who after all knew pretty well everything that went on in the village, would shake her head and say, 'It's private property and what the people do up there is nobody else's business but theirs.'

It all was, in essence, just the thing Victor Casini, who now languished in a tiny cell he would never be released from, could only dream about ... after all, it *was* his idea, wasn't it?

*　　*　　*

For prisoner number 362, who mostly sat thinking dark thoughts while grinding gold capped teeth and staring vacantly at bare walls amidst the noisy clamour of fellow inmates, it was a painful memory. The thought of what might have been, was now just a haunting dream that occupied his waking moments. Indeed, it had been just the place that Victor Casini had in mind and to spend the rest of his life in while raking in the money from wealthy clientele as master of a coveted lifestyle in a safe mountain retreat. An exclusive enterprise designed to conceal, as well as separate his fellow confederates from their wealth for the purpose, privilege and the guarantee of their safe concealment. It was a grandiose plan and would have given him the lifestyle he so desired and the power he could exert over his fellow opponents in the field of larceny, but it often was accompanied by the extra cost of concealment for murder.

The ancient abbey in its isolated cliff top had been the perfect hideaway but he had not counted on the presence of the strange women there who did not appear to be what he would have expected women to be, they were — well, different and if he didn't know any better, he would have imagined them to be witches, but everyone knows that witches only exist in children's fairy tales ... don't they?